The Broadview Anthology of
SHORT FICTION

THE BROADVIEW ANTHOLOGY OF SHORT FICTION

third edition

EDITED BY
SARA LEVINE,
DON LEPAN,
and
MARJORIE MATHER

broadview press

Library and Archives Canada Cataloguing in Publication
The Broadview anthology of short fiction / edited by Sara Levine, Don LePan and Marjorie Mather. — 3rd ed.

ISBN 978-1-55481-141-0

1. Short stories, American. 2. Short stories, English. I. Levine, Sara II. LePan, Don, 1954- III. Mather, Marjorie.

PS648.S5B763 2013 813'.0108 C2013-900369-X

Broadview Press is an independent, international publishing house, incorporated in 1985.

We welcome comments and suggestions regarding any aspect of our publications—please feel free to contact us at the addresses below or at broadview@broadviewpress.com.

North America	PO Box 1243, Peterborough, Ontario, Canada K9J 7H5 2215 Kenmore Ave., Buffalo, New York, USA 14207 Tel: (705) 743-8990; Fax: (705) 743-8353 email: customerservice@broadviewpress.com
UK, Europe, Central Asia, Middle East, Africa, India, and Southeast Asia	Eurospan Group, 3 Henrietta St., London WC2E 8LU, United Kingdom Tel: 44 (0) 1767 604972; Fax: 44 (0) 1767 601640 email: eurospan@turpin-distribution.com
Australia and New Zealand	NewSouth Books c/o TL Distribution, 15-23 Helles Ave., Moorebank, NSW, Australia 2170 Tel: (02) 8778 9999; Fax: (02) 8778 9944 email: orders@tldistribution.com.au

www.broadviewpress.com

Broadview Press acknowledges the financial support of the Government of Canada through the Canada Book Fund for our publishing activities.

Canada

PRINTED IN CANADA

CONTENTS

For website selections, please visit
<http://sites.broadviewpress.com/shortfictionstudent3e>.

PREFACE

And the less said about that, the better.

This tends to be my motto in life. I like short things. Compression, intensity, swiftness. Essays the size of handkerchiefs, novels the length of nosebleeds, conclusions detached from tedious arguments, tall tales, but only in bare feet. You know those toy capsules children drop in a glass of water and watch unfurl into spongy dinosaurs or sea horses? I like them *before* they expand—when they're hard masses of potential in the palm of my hand. Give me a good pill; I can *dream* the animal.

In my experience, readers of fiction may be divided into two camps: those who read novels and stories, and those who read only novels. These latter types—deficient in Vitamin D? not loved enough, perhaps, as children?—not only stick to novels, but righteously *refuse* short stories. "They're so short! You can't get *into* them! Just when you get introduced to a character, his story is over; then you turn the page and you're in a *new* story."

I can't deny it. Short stories are short.

You can read a short story in one sitting, Edgar Allan Poe famously said—and probably you should. Maybe that's why some people shirk them; they demand that you light a steady fire of concentration. Reading a novel—though it's sacrilege to say it—the flame may flicker now and then, with no deleterious effect.

Brief as they are, short stories offer curiously prolonged effects. I read "Bartleby the Scrivener" in high school and now, 25 years later, still find him in the office corner, saying with deathly calm: "I prefer not to." I read novels then too—ardently—but can't remember a scene from any of them, whereas Bartleby, is lodged forever in my imagination, placidly eating ginger nuts behind his green screen. Who knows why this is so? You would think a novel, if only because it takes longer to read, would burn deeper in the memory. But short story writers know their space is limited, so they home in on the essential. Consider Thomas Hardy's "The Son's Veto"—a story that covers more than 20 years of Sophy Twycott's life and might easily have been expanded into a novel. Instead Sophy's husband dies and the funeral rites are over before the narrator's finished a sentence: "Mr. Twycott had never rallied, and now lay in a well-packed cemetery." This omission—of the illness, the funeral, the mourning—allows Hardy to throw a tighter focus on Sophy's romantic fate.

Short stories abound with such startling instances of narrative economy—events that might have grown thick as orchards become bonsai in ceramic pots. In Grace Paley's "Wants," two exes meet on the library stairs, and their back-story is accomplished with one astonishing simile: "He had had a habit throughout the twenty-seven years of making a narrow remark which, like a plumber's snake, could work its way through the ear down the throat, half-way to my heart. He would then disappear, leaving me choking with equipment."

More could be said, but why bother? You understand why they didn't stay married, right?

When a person says *I want to tell you a story*, you grasp the rules of the game. What follows should not be a mathematical formula, or a series of images, or an argument against capital punishment, though a story may contain all those things. "Story" means something will happen to somebody. In fiction these expectations can be messed with—extended, transformed, or joyfully ignored—but always they're there. An anthology of stories whose publication spans the nineteenth to the twenty-first centuries invites you to think about how a story's procedures may be related to its origins in a specific historical place and time. Read Hawthorne and Poe, and then pick up Chekhov; you will feel a change. The author's attitude toward the characters is different, as is the idea of where a story should begin and end. Leap ahead to Barthelme, and you will sense that the writer cares about something different. The narrator of "The Palace at 4 A.M." is mixed, being—rather inexplicably—part-man, part-donkey. But the language is also a crazy mingle. Trained to expect magic in stories about kings and queens, we easily can accept the presence of a "bogle," but what a shock to learn the bogle is charged with a "tax evasion case"! And since when does a prince in an "ermine robe" carry a "Walther .22"? The verbal planes keep shifting, and the reader, alongside the lovelorn king, is left "in a condition of doubt."

"There is but one art, to omit! O if I knew how to omit, I would ask no other knowledge. A man who knew how to omit would make an *Iliad* of a daily paper. He learns it in the crystallization of daydreams." Thus wrote Robert Louis Stevenson in a letter to his cousin; regrettably, we didn't include any of Stevenson's daydreams in this anthology. But it is impossible to include every writer I love and still make a book you can carry without self-injury. Here, then, are the chosen ones, 45 in all. Some are realistic; some are fantastic, some are of conventional length and one is less than a page long. I love these stories for what they do as well as what they refuse to do. They are all paragons in the art of omission.

—Sara Levine

NATHANIEL HAWTHORNE

Among Nathaniel Hawthorne's paternal ancestors was one of the judges who participated in the 1692 Salem witch trials; on his mother's side, rumors of incest and public shaming that occurred generations before circulated in the family. Thomas E. Connolly has suggested that a "deep family guilt settled upon [Hawthorne], and this guilt undoubtedly prompted him to critical attacks in his literary works on the rigours of Puritanism." Whether or not it was Hawthorne's "family guilt" that drove him to write what he did, a number of his works are concerned with exposing the hypocrisy of Puritan culture—among them, the short stories "Young Goodman Brown" and "The Minister's Black Veil," and his best-known novel, *The Scarlet Letter* (1850).

Hawthorne was born in 1804 in Salem, Massachusetts. His sea captain father died of yellow fever while in Suriname when Hawthorne was only four years old. His mother then moved him and his two sisters to her family home, where he was raised among his eight unmarried aunts and uncles, and where he had a large library at his disposal. At the age of nine, an injury to his foot required him to stop attending school; he spent much of the three years it took him to recuperate reading his favorite authors—among them Edmund Spenser and William Shakespeare. From 1821 to 1825, Hawthorne attended Bowdoin College, where he counted Franklin Pierce and Henry Wadsworth Longfellow among his colleagues. He was not a brilliant student—he came in eighteenth in a class of thirty-eight and was once fined for playing cards.

Hawthorne returned home to Salem after graduation to live with his mother and devote himself to his writing. During this time he wrote work that was often rejected (he burned the manuscript for one short story collection in frustration). In 1828 he privately published anonymously and at his own expense *Fanshawe*, a work he would later refuse to acknowledge or reprint. He published stories anonymously in various periodicals, and in 1837 his friend Horatio Bridge secretly gave a publisher $250 to publish Hawthorne's *Twice-Told Tales*, a collection of short stories. This collection was not widely noticed, though it received favorable reviews from Longfellow and from Edgar Allan Poe.

Hawthorne married Sophia Peabody in 1842, and they moved to a house once inhabited by the famous American writer Ralph Waldo Emerson in Concord called the Old Manse. It was here that he published a volume of short pieces entitled *Mosses from an Old Manse* in 1846. When Sophia gave birth to their two children in rapid succession, the Hawthornes struggled to meet the financial demands of their new family. During this time of financial hardship, Hawthorne concentrated his efforts on writing *The Scarlet Letter*, the book that would make his literary reputation. His novel *The House of Seven Gables* followed in 1851. He died in 1864 and was buried at Sleepy Hollow Cemetery in Concord, Massachusetts.

A story from *Twice-Told Tales*, "The Minister's Black Veil" takes place in a town in Puritan New England. When the town Reverend appears one day wearing a black veil, a darkness sets in on the congregation as those within it are forced to grapple with the guilt, hypocrisy, and questions of morality that hover behind their own unseen veils.

The Minister's Black Veil
A Parable

NATHANIEL HAWTHORNE

THE SEXTON[1] stood in the porch of Milford meeting-house, pulling busily at the bell-rope. The old people of the village came stooping along the street. Children, with bright faces, tripped merrily beside their parents, or mimicked a graver gait, in the conscious dignity of their Sunday clothes. Spruce bachelors looked sidelong at the pretty maidens, and fancied that the Sabbath sunshine made them prettier than on week days. When the throng had mostly streamed into the porch, the sexton began to toll the bell, keeping his eye on the Reverend Mr. Hooper's door. The first glimpse of the clergyman's figure was the signal for the bell to cease its summons.

"But what has good Parson Hooper got upon his face?" cried the sexton in astonishment.

All within hearing immediately turned about, and beheld the semblance of Mr. Hooper, pacing slowly his meditative way towards the meeting-house. With

1 An officer responsible for maintaining a church.

one accord they started, expressing more wonder than if some strange minister were coming to dust the cushions of Mr. Hooper's pulpit.

"Are you sure it is our parson?" inquired Goodman Gray of the sexton.

"Of a certainty it is good Mr. Hooper," replied the sexton. "He was to have exchanged pulpits with Parson Shute, of Westbury; but Parson Shute sent to excuse himself yesterday, being to preach a funeral sermon."

The cause of so much amazement may appear sufficiently slight. Mr. Hooper, a gentlemanly person, of about thirty, though still a bachelor, was dressed with due clerical neatness, as if a careful wife had starched his band, and brushed the weekly dust from his Sunday's garb. There was but one thing remarkable in his appearance. Swathed about his forehead, and hanging down over his face, so low as to be shaken by his breath, Mr. Hooper had on a black veil. On a nearer view it seemed to consist of two folds of crape, which entirely concealed his features, except the mouth and chin, but probably did not intercept his sight, further than to give a darkened aspect to all living and inanimate things. With this gloomy shade before him, good Mr. Hooper walked onward, at a slow and quiet pace, stooping somewhat, and looking on the ground, as is customary with abstracted men, yet nodding kindly to those of his parishioners who still waited on the meeting-house steps. But so wonder-struck were they that his greeting hardly met with a return.

"I can't really feel as if good Mr. Hooper's face was behind that piece of crape," said the sexton.

"I don't like it," muttered an old woman, as she hobbled into the meeting-house. "He has changed himself into something awful, only by hiding his face."

"Our parson has gone mad!" cried Goodman Gray, following him across the threshold.

A rumor of some unaccountable phenomenon had preceded Mr. Hooper into the meeting-house, and set all the congregation astir. Few could refrain from twisting their heads towards the door; many stood upright, and turned directly about; while several little boys clambered upon the seats, and came down again with a terrible racket. There was a general bustle, a rustling of the women's gowns and shuffling of the men's feet, greatly at variance with that hushed repose which should attend the entrance of the minister. But Mr. Hooper appeared not to notice the perturbation of his people. He entered with an almost noiseless step, bent his head mildly to the pews on each side, and bowed as he passed his oldest parishioner, a white-haired great-grandsire, who occupied an arm-chair in the center of the aisle. It was strange to observe how slowly this venerable man became conscious of something singular in the appearance of his pastor. He seemed not fully to partake of the prevailing wonder, till Mr. Hooper had ascended the stairs, and showed himself in the pulpit, face to face with his congregation, except for the black veil. That mysterious emblem was never once withdrawn. It shook with his measured breath, as he gave out the psalm; it threw its obscurity between him and the holy page, as he read the Scriptures; and while he prayed, the veil lay heavily on his uplifted countenance. Did he seek to hide it from the dread Being whom he was addressing?

Such was the effect of this simple piece of crape, that more than one woman of delicate nerves was forced to leave the meeting-house. Yet perhaps the pale-faced congregation was almost as fearful a sight to the minister, as his black veil to them.

Mr. Hooper had the reputation of a good preacher, but not an energetic one: he strove to win his people heavenward by mild, persuasive influences, rather than to drive them thither by the thunders of the Word. The sermon which he now delivered was marked by the same characteristics of style and manner as the general series of his pulpit oratory. But there was something, either in the sentiment of the discourse itself, or in the imagination of the auditors, which made it greatly the most powerful effort that they had ever heard from their pastor's lips. It was tinged, rather more darkly than usual, with the gentle gloom of Mr. Hooper's temperament. The subject had reference to secret sin, and those sad mysteries which we hide from our nearest and dearest, and would fain conceal from our own consciousness, even forgetting that the Omniscient can detect them. A subtle power was breathed into his words. Each member of the congregation, the most innocent girl, and the man of hardened breast, felt as if the preacher had crept upon them, behind his awful veil, and discovered their hoarded iniquity of deed or thought. Many spread their clasped hands on their bosoms. There was nothing terrible in what Mr. Hooper said, at least, no violence; and yet, with every tremor of his melancholy voice, the hearers quaked. An unsought pathos came hand in hand with awe. So sensible were the audience of some unwonted attribute in their minister, that they longed for a breath of wind to blow aside the veil, almost believing that a stranger's visage would be discovered, though the form, gesture, and voice were those of Mr. Hooper.

At the close of the services, the people hurried out with indecorous confusion, eager to communicate their pent-up amazement, and conscious of lighter spirits the moment they lost sight of the black veil. Some gathered in little circles, huddled closely together, with their mouths all whispering in the center; some went homeward alone, wrapt in silent meditation; some talked loudly, and profaned the Sabbath day with ostentatious laughter. A few shook their sagacious heads, intimating that they could penetrate the mystery; while one or two affirmed that there was no mystery at all, but only that Mr. Hooper's eyes were so weakened by the midnight lamp, as to require a shade. After a brief interval, forth came good Mr. Hooper also, in the rear of his flock. Turning his veiled face from one group to another, he paid due reverence to the hoary heads, saluted the middle aged with kind dignity as their friend and spiritual guide, greeted the young with mingled authority and love, and laid his hands on the little children's heads to bless them. Such was always his custom on the Sabbath day. Strange and bewildered looks repaid him for his courtesy. None, as on former occasions, aspired to the honor of walking by their pastor's side. Old Squire Saunders, doubtless by an accidental lapse of memory, neglected to invite Mr. Hooper to his table, where the good clergyman had been wont to bless the food, almost every Sunday since his settlement. He returned, therefore, to the parsonage, and, at the moment of closing the door, was observed to look back upon the people, all of whom had their eyes fixed upon the minister. A sad smile gleamed faintly from beneath the black veil, and flickered about his mouth, glimmering as he disappeared.

"How strange," said a lady, "that a simple black veil, such as any woman might wear on her bonnet, should become such a terrible thing on Mr. Hooper's face!"

"Something must surely be amiss with Mr. Hooper's intellects," observed her husband, the physician of the village. "But the strangest part of the affair is the effect of this vagary, even on a sober-minded man like myself. The black veil, though it covers only our pastor's face, throws its influence over his whole person, and makes him ghostlike from head to foot. Do you not feel it so?"

"Truly do I," replied the lady; "and I would not be alone with him for the world. I wonder he is not afraid to be alone with himself!"

"Men sometimes are so," said her husband.

The afternoon service was attended with similar circumstances. At its conclusion, the bell tolled for the funeral of a young lady. The relatives and friends were assembled in the house, and the more distant acquaintances stood about the door, speaking of the good qualities of the deceased, when their talk was interrupted by the appearance of Mr. Hooper, still covered with his black veil. It was now an appropriate emblem. The clergyman stepped into the room where the corpse was laid, and bent over the coffin, to take a last farewell of his deceased parishioner. As he stooped, the veil hung straight down from his forehead, so that, if her eyelids had not been closed forever, the dead maiden might have seen his face. Could Mr. Hooper be fearful of her glance, that he so hastily caught back the black veil? A person who watched the interview between the dead and living, scrupled not to affirm, that, at the instant when the clergyman's features were disclosed, the corpse had slightly shuddered, rustling the shroud and muslin cap, though the countenance retained the composure of death. A superstitious old woman was the only witness of this prodigy. From the coffin Mr. Hooper passed into the chamber of the mourners, and thence to the head of the staircase, to make the funeral prayer. It was a tender and heart-dissolving prayer, full of sorrow, yet so imbued with celestial hopes, that the music of a heavenly harp, swept by the fingers of the dead, seemed faintly to be heard among the saddest accents of the minister. The people trembled, though they but darkly understood him when he prayed that they, and himself, and all of mortal race, might be ready, as he trusted this young maiden had been, for the dreadful hour that should snatch the veil from their faces. The bearers went heavily forth, and the mourners followed, saddening all the street, with the dead before them, and Mr. Hooper in his black veil behind.

"Why do you look back?" said one in the procession to his partner.

"I had a fancy," replied she, "that the minister and the maiden's spirit were walking hand in hand."

"And so had I, at the same moment," said the other.

That night, the handsomest couple in Milford village were to be joined in wedlock. Though reckoned a melancholy man, Mr. Hooper had a placid cheerfulness for such occasions, which often excited a sympathetic smile where livelier merriment would have been thrown away. There was no quality of his disposition which made him more beloved than this. The company at the wedding awaited his arrival with impatience, trusting that the strange awe, which had gathered over him throughout the day, would now be dispelled. But such was not the result. When Mr. Hooper came, the first thing that their eyes rested on was the same horrible black veil, which had added deeper gloom to the funeral, and could portend nothing but evil to the wedding. Such was its immediate effect on the guests that a cloud seemed to have rolled duskily from beneath the black crape, and dimmed the light of the candles. The bridal pair stood up before the minister. But the bride's cold fingers quivered in the tremulous hand of the bridegroom, and her deathlike paleness caused a whisper that the maiden who had been buried a few hours before was come from her grave to be married. If ever another wedding were so dismal, it was that famous one where they tolled the wedding knell. After performing the ceremony, Mr. Hooper raised a glass of wine to his lips, wishing happiness to the new-married couple in a strain of mild pleasantry that ought to have brightened the features of the guests, like a cheerful gleam from the hearth. At that instant, catching a glimpse of his figure in the looking-glass, the black veil involved his own spirit in the horror with which it overwhelmed all others. His frame shuddered, his lips grew white, he spilt the untasted wine upon the carpet, and rushed forth into the darkness. For the Earth, too, had on her Black Veil.

The next day, the whole village of Milford talked of little else than Parson Hooper's black veil. That, and the mystery concealed behind it, supplied a topic for discussion between acquaintances meeting in the street, and good women gossiping at their open windows. It was the first item of news that the tavern-keeper told to his guests. The children babbled of it on their way to school. One imitative little imp covered his face with an old black handkerchief, thereby so affrighting his playmates that the panic seized himself, and he well-nigh lost his wits by his own waggery.

It was remarkable that of all the busybodies and impertinent people in the parish, not one ventured to put the plain question to Mr. Hooper, wherefore he did this thing. Hitherto, whenever there appeared the slightest call for such interference, he had never lacked advisers, nor shown himself averse to be guided by their judgment. If he erred at all, it was by so painful a degree of self-distrust, that even the mildest censure would lead him to consider an indifferent action as a crime. Yet, though so well acquainted with this amiable weakness, no individual among his parishioners chose to make the black veil a subject of friendly remonstrance. There was a feeling of dread, neither plainly confessed nor carefully concealed, which caused each to shift the responsibility upon another, till at length it was found expedient to send a deputation to the church, in order to deal with Mr. Hooper about the mystery, before it should grow into a scandal. Never did an embassy so ill discharge its duties. The minister received them with friendly courtesy, but became silent, after they were seated, leaving to his visitors, the whole burden of introducing their important business. The topic, it might be supposed, was obvious enough. There was the black veil swathed round Mr. Hooper's forehead, and concealing every feature above his placid mouth, on which, at times, they could perceive the glimmering of a melancholy smile. But that piece of crape, to their imagination, seemed to hang down before his heart, the symbol of a fearful secret between him and them. Were the veil but cast aside, they might speak freely of it, but not till then. Thus they sat a considerable time, speechless, confused, and shrinking uneasily from Mr. Hooper's eye, which they felt to be fixed upon them with an invisible glance. Finally, the deputies returned abashed to their constituents, pronouncing the matter too weighty to be handled, except by a council of the churches, if, indeed, it might not require a general synod.

But there was one person in the village unappalled by the awe with which the black veil had impressed all beside herself. When the deputies returned without an explanation, or even venturing to demand one, she, with the calm energy of her character, determined to chase away the strange cloud that appeared to be settling round Mr. Hooper, every moment more darkly than before. As his plighted wife, it should be her privilege to know what the black veil concealed. At the minister's first visit, therefore, she entered upon the subject with a direct simplicity, which made the task easier both for him and her. After he had seated himself, she fixed her eyes steadfastly upon the veil, but could discern nothing of the dreadful gloom that had so overawed the multitude: it was but a double fold of crape, hanging down from his forehead to his mouth, and slightly stirring with his breath.

"No," she said aloud, and smiling, "there is nothing terrible in this piece of crape, except that it hides a face which I am always glad to look upon. Come, good sir, let the sun shine from behind the cloud. First lay aside your black veil: then tell me why you put it on."

Mr. Hooper's smile glimmered faintly.

"There is an hour to come," said he, "when all of us shall cast aside our veils. Take it not amiss, beloved friend, if I wear this piece of crape till then."

"Your words are a mystery, too," returned the young lady. "Take away the veil from them, at least."

"Elizabeth, I will," said he, "so far as my vow may suffer me. Know, then, this veil is a type and a symbol, and I am bound to wear it ever, both in light and darkness, in solitude and before the gaze of multitudes, and as with strangers, so with my familiar friends. No mortal eye will see it withdrawn. This dismal shade must separate me from the world: even you, Elizabeth, can never come behind it!"

"What grievous affliction hath befallen you," she earnestly inquired, "that you should thus darken your eyes forever?"

"If it be a sign of mourning," replied Mr. Hooper, "I, perhaps, like most other mortals, have sorrows dark enough to be typified by a black veil."

"But what if the world will not believe that it is the type of an innocent sorrow?" urged Elizabeth. "Beloved and respected as you are, there may be whispers that you hide your face under the consciousness of secret sin. For the sake of your holy office, do away this scandal!"

The color rose into her cheeks as she intimated the nature of the rumors that were already abroad in the village. But Mr. Hooper's mildness did not forsake him. He even smiled again—that same sad smile, which always appeared like a faint glimmering of light, proceeding from the obscurity beneath the veil.

"If I hide my face for sorrow, there is cause enough," he merely replied; "and if I cover it for secret sin, what mortal might not do the same?"

And with this gentle, but unconquerable obstinacy did he resist all her entreaties. At length Elizabeth sat silent. For a few moments she appeared lost in thought, considering, probably, what new methods might be tried to withdraw her lover from so dark a fantasy, which, if it had no other meaning, was perhaps a symptom of mental disease. Though of a firmer character than his own, the tears rolled down her cheeks. But, in an instant, as it were, a new feeling took the place of sorrow: her eyes were fixed insensibly on the black veil, when, like a sudden twilight in the air, its terrors fell around her. She arose, and stood trembling before him.

"And do you feel it then, at last?" said he mournfully.

She made no reply, but covered her eyes with her hand, and turned to leave the room. He rushed forward and caught her arm.

"Have patience with me, Elizabeth!" cried he, passionately. "Do not desert me, though this veil must be between us here on earth. Be mine, and hereafter there shall be no veil over my face, no darkness between our souls! It is but a mortal veil—it is not for eternity! O! you know not how lonely I am, and how frightened, to be alone behind my black veil. Do not leave me in this miserable obscurity forever!"

"Lift the veil but once, and look me in the face," said she.

"Never! It cannot be!" replied Mr. Hooper.

"Then farewell!" said Elizabeth.

She withdrew her arm from his grasp, and slowly departed, pausing at the door, to give one long shuddering gaze, that seemed almost to penetrate the mystery of the black veil. But, even amid his grief, Mr. Hooper smiled to think that only a material emblem had separated him from happiness, though the horrors, which it shadowed forth, must be drawn darkly between the fondest of lovers.

From that time no attempts were made to remove Mr. Hooper's black veil, or, by a direct appeal, to discover the secret which it was supposed to hide. By persons who claimed a superiority to popular prejudice, it was reckoned merely an eccentric whim, such as often mingles with the sober actions of men otherwise rational, and tinges them all with its own semblance of insanity. But with the multitude, good Mr. Hooper was irreparably a bugbear.[2] He could not walk the street with any peace of mind, so conscious was he that the gentle and timid would turn aside to avoid him, and that others would make it a point of hardihood to throw themselves in his way. The impertinence of the latter class compelled him to give up his customary walk at sunset to the burial ground; for when he leaned pensively over the gate, there would always be faces behind the gravestones, peeping at his black veil. A fable went the rounds that the stare of the dead people drove him thence. It grieved him, to the very depth of his kind heart, to observe how the children fled from his approach, breaking up their merriest sports, while his melancholy figure was yet afar off. Their instinctive dread caused him to feel more strongly than aught else, that a preternatural horror was interwoven with the threads of the black crape. In truth, his own antipathy to the veil was known to be so great, that he never willingly passed before a mirror, nor stooped to drink at a still fountain, lest, in its peaceful bosom, he should be affrighted by himself. This was what gave plausibility to the whispers,

2 A creature that causes great fear or anxiety.

that Mr. Hooper's conscience tortured him for some great crime too horrible to be entirely concealed, or otherwise than so obscurely intimated. Thus, from beneath the black veil, there rolled a cloud into the sunshine, an ambiguity of sin or sorrow, which enveloped the poor minister, so that love or sympathy could never reach him. It was said that ghost and fiend consorted with him there. With self-shudderings and outward terrors, he walked continually in its shadow, groping darkly within his own soul, or gazing through a medium that saddened the whole world. Even the lawless wind, it was believed, respected his dreadful secret, and never blew aside the veil. But still good Mr. Hooper sadly smiled at the pale visages of the worldly throng as he passed by.

Among all its bad influences, the black veil had one desirable effect, of making its wearer a very efficient clergyman. By the aid of his mysterious emblem—for there was no other apparent cause—he became a man of awful power over souls that were in agony for sin. His converts always regarded him with a dread peculiar to themselves, affirming, though but figuratively, that, before he brought them to celestial light, they had been with him behind the black veil. Its gloom, indeed, enabled him to sympathize with all dark affections. Dying sinners cried aloud for Mr. Hooper, and would not yield their breath till he appeared; though ever, as he stooped to whisper consolation, they shuddered at the veiled face so near their own. Such were the terrors of the black veil, even when Death had bared his visage! Strangers came long distances to attend service at his church, with the mere idle purpose of gazing at his figure, because it was forbidden them to behold his face. But many were made to quake ere they departed! Once, during Governor Belcher's administration,[3] Mr. Hooper was appointed to preach the election sermon. Covered with his black veil, he stood before the chief magistrate, the council, and the representatives, and wrought so deep an impression, that the legislative measures of that year were characterized by all the gloom and piety of our earliest ancestral sway.

In this manner Mr. Hooper spent a long life, irreproachable in outward act, yet shrouded in dismal suspicions; kind and loving, though unloved, and dimly feared; a man apart from men, shunned in their health and joy, but ever summoned to their aid in mortal anguish. As years wore on, shedding their snows above his sable veil, he acquired a name throughout the New England churches, and they called him Father Hooper. Nearly all his parishioners, who were of mature age when he was settled, had been borne away by many a funeral: he had one congregation in the church, and a more crowded one in the churchyard; and

3 Jonathan Belcher was governor of the British colonies of Massachusetts, New Hampshire, and New Jersey from 1730 to 1741.

having wrought so late into the evening, and done his work so well, it was now good Father Hooper's turn to rest.

Several persons were visible by the shaded candle-light, in the death chamber of the old clergyman. Natural connections he had none. But there was the decorously grave, though unmoved physician, seeking only to mitigate the last pangs of the patient whom he could not save. There were the deacons, and other eminently pious members of his church. There, also, was the Reverend Mr. Clark, of Westbury, a young and zealous divine, who had ridden in haste to pray by the bedside of the expiring minister. There was the nurse, no hired handmaiden of death, but one whose calm affection had endured thus long in secrecy, in solitude, amid the chill of age, and would not perish, even at the dying hour. Who, but Elizabeth! And there lay the hoary head of good Father Hooper upon the death pillow, with the black veil still swathed about his brow, and reaching down over his face, so that each more difficult gasp of his faint breath caused it to stir. All through life that piece of crape had hung between him and the world: it had separated him from cheerful brotherhood and woman's love, and kept him in that saddest of all prisons, his own heart; and still it lay upon his face, as if to deepen the gloom of his darksome chamber, and shade him from the sunshine of eternity.

For some time previous, his mind had been confused, wavering doubtfully between the past and the present, and hovering forward, as it were, at intervals, into the indistinctness of the world to come. There had been feverish turns, which tossed him from side to side, and wore away what little strength he had. But in his most convulsive struggles, and in the wildest vagaries of his intellect, when no other thought retained its sober influence, he still showed an awful solicitude lest the black veil should slip aside. Even if his bewildered soul could have forgotten, there was a faithful woman at his pillow, who, with averted eyes, would have covered that aged face, which she had last beheld in the comeliness of manhood. At length the death-stricken old man lay quietly in the torpor of mental and bodily exhaustion, with an imperceptible pulse, and breath that grew fainter and fainter, except when a long, deep, and irregular inspiration seemed to prelude the flight of his spirit.

The minister of Westbury approached the bedside.

"Venerable Father Hooper," said he, "the moment of your release is at hand. Are you ready for the lifting of the veil that shuts in time from eternity?"

Father Hooper at first replied merely by a feeble motion of his head; then, apprehensive, perhaps, that his meaning might be doubtful, he exerted himself to speak.

"Yea," said he, in faint accents, "my soul hath a patient weariness until that veil be lifted."

"And is it fitting," resumed the Reverend Mr. Clark, "that a man so given to prayer, of such a blameless example, holy in deed and thought, so far as mortal judgment may pronounce; is it fitting that a father in the church should leave a shadow on his memory, that may seem to blacken a life so pure? I pray you, my venerable brother, let not this thing be! Suffer us to be gladdened by your triumphant aspect as you go to your reward. Before the veil of eternity be lifted, let me cast aside this black veil from your face!"

And thus speaking, the Reverend Mr. Clark bent forward to reveal the mystery of so many years. But, exerting a sudden energy, that made all the beholders stand aghast, Father Hooper snatched both his hands from beneath the bed-clothes, and pressed them strongly on the black veil, resolute to struggle, if the minister of Westbury would contend with a dying man.

"Never!" cried the veiled clergyman. "On earth, never!"

"Dark old man!" exclaimed the affrighted minister, "with what horrible crime upon your soul are you now passing to the judgment?"

Father Hooper's breath heaved; it rattled in his throat; but, with a mighty effort, grasping forward with his hands, he caught hold of life, and held it back till he should speak. He even raised himself in bed; and there he sat, shivering with the arms of death around him, while the black veil hung down, awful, at that last moment, in the gathered terrors of a lifetime. And yet the faint, sad smile, so often there, now seemed to glimmer from its obscurity, and linger on Father Hooper's lips.

"Why do you tremble at me alone?" cried he, turning his veiled face round the circle of pale spectators. "Tremble also at each other! Have men avoided me, and women shown no pity, and children screamed and fled, only for my black veil? What, but the mystery which it obscurely typifies, has made this piece of crape so awful? When the friend shows his inmost heart to his friend; the lover to his best beloved; when man does not vainly shrink from the eye of his Creator, loathsomely treasuring up the secret of his sin; then deem me a monster for the symbol beneath which I have lived, and die! I look around me, and lo! on every visage a Black Veil!"

While his auditors shrank from one another, in mutual affright, Father Hooper fell back upon his pillow, a veiled corpse, with a faint smile lingering on his lips. Still veiled, they laid him in his coffin, and a veiled corpse they bore him to the grave. The grass of many years has sprung up and withered on that grave; the burial stone is moss-grown, and good Mr. Hooper's face is dust; but awful is still the thought that it moldered beneath the Black Veil!

—1836

EDGAR ALLAN POE

Edgar Allan Poe was born in 1809 in Boston, Massachusetts, the son of itinerant stage actors David Poe and Elizabeth Arnold Poe. David Poe disappeared when Poe was two, and his mother, although a popular performer, struggled with poverty as she tried to raise her three young children. She died of tuberculosis when Poe was only four years old, and he and his brother and sister were split up and sent to live with three different families. By all accounts Poe was a happy child, but in adolescence he began having conflicts with his foster father, a well-to-do tobacco and dry goods merchant. His university education at the University of Virginia was terminated after he incurred huge gambling debts, at which point he ran away to Boston and published his first collection of poems, *Tamerlane and Other Poems* (1827), under the pseudonym "a Bostonian." Poe enlisted in the army in 1827 using a false name to hide himself from his creditors. He managed to publish a second collection of poems, entitled *Al Aaraaf, Tamerlane, and Minor Poems*, in 1829. In 1830 he was accepted into the US Military Academy at West Point, but he was expelled for carousing and irresponsible behavior.

Having been cast out by his foster family, Poe continued to struggle financially, often taking on substandard writing jobs in order to pay the bills. He achieved some level of comfort by taking on editorial work for various publications, but his drinking and subsequent unreliability made him unable to maintain a job for long. Throughout this time, he wrote numerous short stories and poems that were published in periodicals and that occasionally appeared collected in book form, including *Tales of the Grotesque and Arabesque* (1840) and *The Raven and Other Poems* (1845).

In 1836, Poe married his cousin, Virginia Clemm. In spite of recurring bouts of grinding poverty, the marriage was reported to be a happy one. In 1845, Virginia died of tuberculosis. In 1849 Poe became engaged to Sarah Elmira Royster, a widow who had been a childhood love. In October 1849, Poe was returning to his home in New York from Richmond, Virginia, when he was found delirious on the street in Baltimore, Maryland, and taken to a charity hospital, where he later died. There has been much speculation about the cause of Poe's death, but no medical records survive, and his death remains a mystery.

During his lifetime, Poe was well known, but his work did not sell widely. With the exception of one novel written at the urging of a publisher, *The Narrative of Arthur Gordon Pym of Nantucket* (1838), his works were all oriented toward periodical publication. He mastered the form of the short story, and, in the words of Alberto Manguel, "set out the laws that govern a tale of horror." Published in 1843 and 1846 respectively, "The Black Cat" and the "The Cask of Amontillado" are perfect examples of Poe's brilliance as a skilled practitioner of horror fiction.

The Black Cat

EDGAR ALLAN POE

FOR THE most wild, yet most homely narrative which I am about to pen, I neither expect nor solicit belief. Mad indeed would I be to expect it, in a case where my very senses reject their own evidence. Yet, mad am I not—and very surely do I not dream. But to-morrow I die, and to-day I would unburthen my soul. My immediate purpose is to place before the world, plainly, succinctly, and without comment, a series of mere household events. In their consequences, these events have terrified—have tortured—have destroyed me. Yet I will not attempt to expound them. To me, they have presented little but Horror—to many they will seem less terrible than *barroques.*[1] Hereafter, perhaps, some intellect may be found which will reduce my phantasm[2] to the common-place—some intellect more calm, more logical, and far less excitable than my own, which will perceive, in the circumstances I detail with awe, nothing more than an ordinary succession of very natural causes and effects.

From my infancy I was noted for the docility and humanity of my disposition. My tenderness of heart was even so conspicuous as to make me the jest of my companions. I was especially fond of animals, and was indulged by my parents with a great variety of pets. With these I spent most of my time, and never was so happy as when feeding and caressing them. This peculiarity of character grew with my growth, and in my manhood, I derived from it one of my principal sources of pleasure. To those who have cherished an affection for

1 Grotesque or strangely irregular.

2 Delusion or imagined reality.

a faithful and sagacious dog, I need hardly be at the trouble of explaining the nature or the intensity of the gratification thus derivable. There is something in the unselfish and self-sacrificing love of a brute, which goes directly to the heart of him who has had frequent occasion to test the paltry friendship and gossamer fidelity of mere *Man*.

I married early, and was happy to find in my wife a disposition not uncongenial with my own. Observing my partiality for domestic pets, she lost no opportunity of procuring those of the most agreeable kind. We had birds, gold-fish, a fine dog, rabbits, a small monkey, and *a cat*.

This latter was a remarkably large and beautiful animal, entirely black, and sagacious to an astonishing degree. In speaking of his intelligence, my wife, who at heart was not a little tinctured with superstition, made frequent allusion to the ancient popular notion, which regarded all black cats as witches in disguise. Not that she was ever *serious* upon this point—and I mention the matter at all for no better reason than that it happens, just now, to be remembered.

Pluto—this was the cat's name—was my favorite pet and playmate. I alone fed him, and he attended me wherever I went about the house. It was even with difficulty that I could prevent him from following me through the streets.

Our friendship lasted, in this manner, for several years, during which my general temperament and character—through the instrumentality of the Fiend Intemperance[3]—had (I blush to confess it) experienced a radical alteration for the worse. I grew, day by day, more moody, more irritable, more regardless of the feelings of others. I suffered myself to use intemperate language to my wife. At length, I even offered her personal violence. My pets, of course, were made to feel the change in my disposition. I not only neglected, but ill-used them. For Pluto, however, I still retained sufficient regard to restrain me from maltreating him, as I made no scruple of maltreating the rabbits, the monkey, or even the dog, when by accident, or through affection, they came in my way. But my disease grew upon me—for what disease is like Alcohol!—and at length even Pluto, who was now becoming old, and consequently somewhat peevish—even Pluto began to experience the effects of my ill temper.

One night, returning home, much intoxicated, from one of my haunts about town, I fancied that the cat avoided my presence. I seized him; when, in his fright at my violence, he inflicted a slight wound upon my hand with his teeth. The fury of a demon instantly possessed me. I knew myself no longer. My original soul seemed, at once, to take its flight from my body and a more than fiendish malevolence, gin-nurtured, thrilled every fiber of my frame. I took from my waistcoat-pocket a pen-knife, opened it, grasped the poor beast by the throat,

3 Excessive consumption of alcohol.

and deliberately cut one of its eyes from the socket! I blush, I burn, I shudder, while I pen the damnable atrocity.

When reason returned with the morning—when I had slept off the fumes of the night's debauch—I experienced a sentiment half of horror, half of remorse, for the crime of which I had been guilty; but it was, at best, a feeble and equivocal feeling, and the soul remained untouched. I again plunged into excess, and soon drowned in wine all memory of the deed.

In the meantime the cat slowly recovered. The socket of the lost eye presented, it is true, a frightful appearance, but he no longer appeared to suffer any pain. He went about the house as usual, but, as might be expected, fled in extreme terror at my approach. I had so much of my old heart left, as to be at first grieved by this evident dislike on the part of a creature which had once so loved me. But this feeling soon gave place to irritation. And then came, as if to my final and irrevocable overthrow, the spirit of PERVERSENESS. Of this spirit philosophy takes no account. Yet I am not more sure that my soul lives, than I am that perverseness is one of the primitive impulses of the human heart—one of the indivisible primary faculties, or sentiments, which give direction to the character of Man. Who has not, a hundred times, found himself committing a vile or a silly action, for no other reason than because he knows he should not? Have we not a perpetual inclination, in the teeth of our best judgment, to violate that which is *Law*, merely because we understand it to be such? This spirit of perverseness, I say, came to my final overthrow. It was this unfathomable longing of the soul *to vex itself*—to offer violence to its own nature—to do wrong for the wrong's sake only—that urged me to continue and finally to consummate the injury I had inflicted upon the unoffending brute. One morning, in cool blood, I slipped a noose about its neck and hung it to the limb of a tree;—hung it with the tears streaming from my eyes, and with the bitterest remorse at my heart;—hung it *because* I knew that it had loved me, and *because* I felt it had given me no reason of offence;—hung it *because* I knew that in so doing I was committing a sin—a deadly sin that would so jeopardize my immortal soul as to place it—if such a thing were possible—even beyond the reach of the infinite mercy of the Most Merciful and Most Terrible God.

On the night of the day on which this cruel deed was done, I was aroused from sleep by the cry of fire. The curtains of my bed were in flames. The whole house was blazing. It was with great difficulty that my wife, a servant, and myself, made our escape from the conflagration.[4] The destruction was complete. My entire worldly wealth was swallowed up, and I resigned myself thenceforward to despair.

---

4 Destructive fire.

I am above the weakness of seeking to establish a sequence of cause and effect, between the disaster and the atrocity. But I am detailing a chain of facts—and wish not to leave even a possible link imperfect. On the day succeeding the fire, I visited the ruins. The walls, with one exception, had fallen in. This exception was found in a compartment wall, not very thick, which stood about the middle of the house, and against which had rested the head of my bed. The plastering had here, in great measure, resisted the action of the fire—a fact which I attributed to its having been recently spread. About this wall a dense crowd were collected, and many persons seemed to be examining a particular portion of it with very minute and eager attention. The words "strange!" "singular!" and other similar expressions, excited my curiosity. I approached and saw, as if graven in *bas relief*[5] upon the white surface, the figure of a gigantic *cat*. The impression was given with an accuracy truly marvellous. There was a rope about the animal's neck.

When I first beheld this apparition—for I could scarcely regard it as less—my wonder and my terror were extreme. But at length reflection came to my aid. The cat, I remembered, had been hung in a garden adjacent to the house. Upon the alarm of fire, this garden had been immediately filled by the crowd—by some one of whom the animal must have been cut from the tree and thrown, through an open window, into my chamber. This had probably been done with the view of arousing me from sleep. The falling of other walls had compressed the victim of my cruelty into the substance of the freshly-spread plaster; the lime of which, with the flames, and the *ammonia* from the carcass, had then accomplished the portraiture as I saw it.

Although I thus readily accounted to my reason, if not altogether to my conscience, for the startling fact just detailed, it did not the less fail to make a deep impression upon my fancy. For months I could not rid myself of the phantasm of the cat; and, during this period, there came back into my spirit a half-sentiment that seemed, but was not, remorse. I went so far as to regret the loss of the animal, and to look about me, among the vile haunts which I now habitually frequented, for another pet of the same species, and of somewhat similar appearance, with which to supply its place.

One night as I sat, half stupified, in a den of more than infamy, my attention was suddenly drawn to some black object, reposing upon the head of one of the immense hogsheads[6] of Gin, or of Rum, which constituted the chief furniture of the apartment. I had been looking steadily at the top of this hogshead for some minutes, and what now caused me surprise was the fact that I had not sooner

5 Relief sculpture characterized by slightly raised features that project from the background.

6 Large flask.

perceived the object thereupon. I approached it, and touched it with my hand. It was a black cat—a very large one—fully as large as Pluto, and closely resembling him in every respect but one. Pluto had not a white hair upon any portion of his body; but this cat had a large, although indefinite splotch of white, covering nearly the whole region of the breast. Upon my touching him, he immediately arose, purred loudly, rubbed against my hand, and appeared delighted with my notice. This, then, was the very creature of which I was in search. I at once offered to purchase it of the landlord; but this person made no claim to it—knew nothing of it—had never seen it before.

I continued my caresses, and, when I prepared to go home, the animal evinced a disposition to accompany me. I permitted it to do so; occasionally stooping and patting it as I proceeded. When it reached the house it domesticated itself at once, and became immediately a great favorite with my wife.

For my own part, I soon found a dislike to it arising within me. This was just the reverse of what I had anticipated; but—I know not how or why it was—its evident fondness for myself rather disgusted and annoyed. By slow degrees, these feelings of disgust and annoyance rose into the bitterness of hatred. I avoided the creature; a certain sense of shame, and the remembrance of my former deed of cruelty, preventing me from physically abusing it. I did not, for some weeks, strike, or otherwise violently ill use it; but gradually—very gradually—I came to look upon it with unutterable loathing, and to flee silently from its odious presence, as from the breath of a pestilence.

What added, no doubt, to my hatred of the beast, was the discovery, on the morning after I brought it home, that, like Pluto, it also had been deprived of one of its eyes. This circumstance, however, only endeared it to my wife, who, as I have already said, possessed, in a high degree, that humanity of feeling which had once been my distinguishing trait, and the source of many of my simplest and purest pleasures.

With my aversion to this cat, however, its partiality for myself seemed to increase. It followed my footsteps with a pertinacity which it would be difficult to make the reader comprehend. Whenever I sat, it would crouch beneath my chair, or spring upon my knees, covering me with its loathsome caresses. If I arose to walk it would get between my feet and thus nearly throw me down, or, fastening its long and sharp claws in my dress, clamber, in this manner, to my breast. At such times, although I longed to destroy it with a blow, I was yet withheld from so doing, partly by a memory of my former crime, but chiefly—let me confess it at once—by absolute dread of the beast.

This dread was not exactly a dread of physical evil—and yet I should be at a loss how otherwise to define it. I am almost ashamed to own—yes, even in this felon's cell, I am almost ashamed to own—that the terror and horror with which the animal inspired me, had been heightened by one of the merest chimaeras[7] it would be possible to conceive. My wife had called my attention, more than once, to the character of the mark of white hair, of which I have spoken, and which constituted the sole visible difference between the strange beast and the one I had destroyed. The reader will remember that this mark, although large, had been originally very indefinite; but, by slow degrees—degrees nearly imperceptible, and which for a long time my Reason struggled to reject as fanciful—it had, at length, assumed a rigorous distinctness of outline. It was now the representation of an object that I shudder to name—and for this, above all, I loathed, and dreaded, and would have rid myself of the monster *had I dared*—it was now, I say, the image of a hideous—of a ghastly thing—of the GALLOWS!—oh, mournful and terrible engine of Horror and of Crime—of Agony and of Death!

And now was I indeed wretched beyond the wretchedness of mere Humanity. And a brute beast—whose fellow I had contemptuously destroyed—*a brute beast* to work out for *me*—for me a man, fashioned in the image of the High God—so much of insufferable woe! Alas! neither by day nor by night knew I the blessing of Rest any more! During the former the creature left me no moment alone; and, in the latter, I started, hourly, from dreams of unutterable fear, to find the hot breath of *the thing* upon my face, and its vast weight—an incarnate Night-Mare that I had no power to shake off—incumbent eternally upon my *heart*!

Beneath the pressure of torments such as these, the feeble remnant of the good within me succumbed. Evil thoughts became my sole intimates—the darkest and most evil of thoughts. The moodiness of my usual temper increased to hatred of all things and of all mankind; while, from the sudden, frequent, and ungovernable outbursts of a fury to which I now blindly abandoned myself, my uncomplaining wife, alas! was the most usual and the most patient of sufferers.

One day she accompanied me, upon some household errand, into the cellar of the old building which our poverty compelled us to inhabit. The cat followed me down the steep stairs, and, nearly throwing me headlong, exasperated me to madness. Uplifting an ax, and forgetting, in my wrath, the childish dread which had hitherto stayed my hand, I aimed a blow at the animal which, of course, would have proved instantly fatal had it descended as I wished. But this blow was arrested by the hand of my wife. Goaded,[8] by the interference, into a rage

---

7 A wild creation of the imagination.

8 Provoked.

more than demoniacal, I withdrew my arm from her grasp and buried the ax in her brain. She fell dead upon the spot, without a groan.

This hideous murder accomplished, I set myself forthwith, and with entire deliberation, to the task of concealing the body. I knew that I could not remove it from the house, either by day or by night, without the risk of being observed by the neighbors. Many projects entered my mind. At one period I thought of cutting the corpse into minute fragments, and destroying them by fire. At another, I resolved to dig a grave for it in the floor of the cellar. Again, I deliberated about casting it in the well in the yard—about packing it in a box, as if merchandize, with the usual arrangements, and so getting a porter to take it from the house. Finally I hit upon what I considered a far better expedient than either of these. I determined to wall it up in the cellar—as the monks of the middle ages are recorded to have walled up their victims.

For a purpose such as this the cellar was well adapted. Its walls were loosely constructed, and had lately been plastered throughout with a rough plaster, which the dampness of the atmosphere had prevented from hardening. Moreover, in one of the walls was a projection, caused by a false chimney, or fireplace, that had been filled up, and made to resemble the red of the cellar. I made no doubt that I could readily displace the bricks at this point, insert the corpse, and wall the whole up as before, so that no eye could detect any thing suspicious. And in this calculation I was not deceived. By means of a crow-bar I easily dislodged the bricks, and, having carefully deposited the body against the inner wall, I propped it in that position, while, with little trouble, I re-laid the whole structure as it originally stood. Having procured mortar, sand, and hair, with every possible precaution, I prepared a plaster which could not be distinguished from the old, and with this I very carefully went over the new brickwork. When I had finished, I felt satisfied that all was right. The wall did not present the slightest appearance of having been disturbed. The rubbish on the floor was picked up with the minutest care. I looked around triumphantly, and said to myself—"Here at least, then, my labor has not been in vain."

My next step was to look for the beast which had been the cause of so much wretchedness; for I had, at length, firmly resolved to put it to death. Had I been able to meet with it, at the moment, there could have been no doubt of its fate; but it appeared that the crafty animal had been alarmed at the violence of my previous anger, and forebore to present itself in my present mood. It is impossible to describe, or to imagine, the deep, the blissful sense of relief which the absence of the detested creature occasioned in my bosom. It did not make its appearance during the night—and thus for one night at least, since its introduction into the house, I soundly and tranquilly slept; aye, slept even with the burden of murder upon my soul!

The second and the third day passed, and still my tormentor came not. Once again I breathed as a freeman. The monster, in terror, had fled the premises forever! I should behold it no more! My happiness was supreme! The guilt of my dark deed disturbed me but little. Some few inquiries had been made, but these had been readily answered. Even a search had been instituted—but of course nothing was to be discovered. I looked upon my future felicity as secured.

Upon the fourth day of the assassination, a party of the police came, very unexpectedly, into the house, and proceeded again to make rigorous investigation of the premises. Secure, however, in the inscrutability of my place of concealment, I felt no embarrassment whatever. The officers bade me accompany them in their search. They left no nook or corner unexplored. At length, for the third or fourth time, they descended into the cellar. I quivered not in a muscle. My heart beat calmly as that of one who slumbers in innocence. I walked the cellar from end to end. I folded my arms upon my bosom, and roamed easily to and fro. The police were thoroughly satisfied and prepared to depart. The glee at my heart was too strong to be restrained. I burned to say if but one word, by way of triumph, and to render doubly sure their assurance of my guiltlessness.

"Gentlemen," I said at last, as the party ascended the steps, "I delight to have allayed your suspicions. I wish you all health, and a little more courtesy. By the bye, gentlemen, this—this is a very well constructed house." [In the rabid desire to say something easily, I scarcely knew what I uttered at all.]—"I may say an *excellently* well constructed house. These walls—are you going, gentlemen?—these walls are solidly put together;" and here, through the mere phrenzy of bravado, I rapped heavily, with a cane which I held in my hand, upon that very portion of the brick-work behind which stood the corpse of the wife of my bosom.

But may God shield and deliver me from the fangs of the Arch-Fiend! No sooner had the reverberation of my blows sunk into silence, than I was answered by a voice from within the tomb!—by a cry, at first muffled and broken, like the sobbing of a child, and then quickly swelling into one long, loud, and continuous scream, utterly anomalous and inhuman—a howl—a wailing shriek, half of horror and half of triumph, such as might have arisen only out of hell, conjointly from the throats of the damned in their agony and of the demons that exult in the damnation.

Of my own thoughts it is folly to speak. Swooning, I staggered to the opposite wall. For one instant the party upon the stairs remained motionless, through extremity of terror and of awe. In the next, a dozen stout arms were toiling at the wall. It fell bodily. The corpse, already greatly decayed and clotted with gore, stood erect before the eyes of the spectators. Upon its head, with red extended mouth and solitary eye of fire, sat the hideous beast whose craft had seduced me into murder, and whose informing voice had consigned me to the hangman. I had walled the monster up within the tomb!

—1843

The Cask of Amontillado

EDGAR ALLAN POE

THE THOUSAND injuries of Fortunato I had borne as I best could, but when he ventured upon insult I vowed revenge. You, who so well know the nature of my soul, will not suppose, however, that I gave utterance to a threat. *At length* I would be avenged; this was a point definitely settled—but the very definitiveness with which it was resolved precluded the idea of risk. I must not only punish but punish with impunity. A wrong is unredressed when retribution overtakes its redresser. It is equally unredressed when the avenger fails to make himself felt as such to him who has done the wrong.

It must be understood that neither by word nor deed had I given Fortunato cause to doubt my good will. I continued, as was my wont, to smile in his face, and he did not perceive that my smile *now* was at the thought of his immolation.

He had a weak point—this Fortunato—although in other regards he was a man to be respected and even feared. He prided himself on his connoisseurship in wine. Few Italians have the true virtuoso spirit. For the most part their enthusiasm is adopted to suit the time and opportunity, to practise imposture upon the British and Austrian millionaires. In painting and gemmary, Fortunato, like his countrymen, was a quack, but in the matter of old wines he was sincere. In this respect I did not differ from him materially;—I was skillful in the Italian vintages myself, and bought largely whenever I could.

It was about dusk, one evening during the supreme madness of the carnival season, that I encountered my friend. He accosted me with excessive warmth, for he had been drinking much. The man wore motley. He had on a tight-fitting parti-striped dress, and his head was surmounted by the conical cap and bells. I was so pleased to see him that I thought I should never have done wringing his hand.

I said to him—"My dear Fortunato, you are luckily met. How remarkably well you are looking today. But I have received a pipe of what passes for Amontillado, and I have my doubts."

"How?" said he. "Amontillado? A pipe? Impossible! And in the middle of the carnival!"

"I have my doubts," I replied; "and I was silly enough to pay the full Amontillado price without consulting you in the matter. You were not to be found, and I was fearful of losing a bargain."

"Amontillado!"

"I have my doubts."

"Amontillado!"

"And I must satisfy them."

"Amontillado!"

"As you are engaged, I am on my way to Luchresi. If any one has a critical turn it is he. He will tell me—"

"Luchresi cannot tell Amontillado from Sherry."

"And yet some fools will have it that his taste is a match for your own."

"Come, let us go."

"Whither?"

"To your vaults."

"My friend, no; I will not impose upon your good nature. I perceive you have an engagement. Luchresi—"

"I have no engagement;—come."

"My friend, no. It is not the engagement, but the severe cold with which I perceive you are afflicted. The vaults are insufferably damp. They are encrusted with nitre."

"Let us go, nevertheless. The cold is merely nothing. Amontillado! You have been imposed upon. And as for Luchresi, he cannot distinguish Sherry from Amontillado."

Thus speaking, Fortunato possessed himself of my arm; and putting on a mask of black silk and drawing a *roquelaire*[1] closely about my person, I suffered him to hurry me to my palazzo.

There were no attendants at home; they had absconded to make merry in honor of the time. I had told them that I should not return until the morning, and had given them explicit orders not to stir from the house. These orders were sufficient, I well knew, to insure their immediate disappearance, one and all, as soon as my back was turned.

I took from their sconces two flambeaux, and giving one to Fortunato, bowed him through several suites of rooms to the archway that led into the vaults. I passed down a long and winding staircase, requesting him to be cautious as he

---

1 A knee-length cloak.

followed. We came at length to the foot of the descent, and stood together upon the damp ground of the catacombs of the Montresors.

The gait of my friend was unsteady, and the bells upon his cap jingled as he strode.

"The pipe," he said.

"It is farther on," said I; "but observe the white web-work which gleams from these cavern walls."

He turned towards me, and looked into my eyes with two filmy orbs that distilled the rheum of intoxication.

"Nitre?" he asked, at length.

"Nitre," I replied. "How long have you had that cough?"

"Ugh! ugh! ugh!—ugh! ugh! ugh!—ugh! ugh! ugh!—ugh! ugh! ugh!—ugh! ugh! ugh!"

My poor friend found it impossible to reply for many minutes.

"It is nothing," he said, at last.

"Come," I said, with decision, "we will go back; your health is precious. You are rich, respected, admired, beloved; you are happy, as once I was. You are a man to be missed. For me it is no matter. We will go back; you will be ill, and I cannot be responsible. Besides, there is Luchresi—"

"Enough," he said; "the cough is a mere nothing; it will not kill me. I shall not die of a cough."

"True—true," I replied; "and, indeed, I had no intention of alarming you unnecessarily—but you should use all proper caution. A draught of this Medoc will defend us from the damps."

Here I knocked off the neck of a bottle which I drew from a long row of its fellows that lay upon the mold.

"Drink," I said, presenting him the wine.

He raised it to his lips with a leer. He paused and nodded to me familiarly, while his bells jingled.

"I drink," he said, "to the buried that repose around us."

"And I to your long life."

He again took my arm, and we proceeded.

"These vaults," he said, "are extensive."

"The Montresors," I replied, "were a great and numerous family."

"I forget your arms."

"A huge human foot d'or, in a field azure;[2] the foot crushes a serpent rampant whose fangs are imbedded in the heel."

"And the motto?"

---

2 A golden foot upon a blue background.

"*Nemo me impune lacessit.*"[3]

"Good!" he said.

The wine sparkled in his eyes and the bells jingled. My own fancy grew with the Medoc. We had passed through long walls of piled skeletons, with casks and puncheons intermingling, into the inmost recesses of the catacombs. I paused again, and this time I made bold to seize Fortunato by an arm above the elbow.

"The nitre!" I said; "see, it increases. It hangs like moss upon the vaults. We are below the river's bed. The drops of moisture trickle among the bones. Come, we will go back ere it is too late. Your cough—"

"It is nothing," he said; "let us go on. But first, another draught of the Medoc."

I broke and reached him a flagon of De Grave. He emptied it at a breath. His eyes flashed with a fierce light. He laughed and threw the bottle upwards with a gesticulation I did not understand.

I looked at him in surprise. He repeated the movement—a grotesque one.

"You do not comprehend?" he said.

"Not I," I replied.

"Then you are not of the brotherhood."

"How?"

"You are not of the masons."

"Yes, yes," I said; "yes, yes."

"You? Impossible! A mason?"

"A mason," I replied.

"A sign," he said, "a sign."

"It is this," I answered, producing from beneath the folds of my *roquelaire* a trowel.

"You jest," he exclaimed, recoiling a few paces. "But let us proceed to the Amontillado."

"Be it so," I said, replacing the tool beneath the cloak and again offering him my arm. He leaned upon it heavily. We continued our route in search of the Amontillado. We passed through a range of low arches, descended, passed on, and descending again, arrived at a deep crypt, in which the foulness of the air caused our flambeaux rather to glow than flame.

At the most remote end of the crypt there appeared another less spacious. Its walls had been lined with human remains, piled to the vault overhead, in the fashion of the great catacombs of Paris. Three sides of this interior crypt were still ornamented in this manner. From the fourth side the bones had been thrown down, and lay promiscuously upon the earth, forming at one point

3 Latin: No one may insult me without being punished.

a mound of some size. Within the wall thus exposed by the displacing of the bones, we perceived a still interior crypt or recess, in depth about four feet, in width three, in height six or seven. It seemed to have been constructed for no especial use within itself, but formed merely the interval between two of the colossal supports of the roof of the catacombs, and was backed by one of their circumscribing walls of solid granite.

It was in vain that Fortunato, uplifting his dull torch, endeavored to pry into the depth of the recess. Its termination the feeble light did not enable us to see.

"Proceed," I said; "herein is the Amontillado. As for Luchresi—"

"He is an ignoramus," interrupted my friend, as he stepped unsteadily forward, while I followed immediately at his heels. In an instant he had reached the extremity of the niche, and finding his progress arrested by the rock, stood stupidly bewildered. A moment more and I had fettered him to the granite. In its surface were two iron staples, distant from each other about two feet, horizontally. From one of these depended a short chain, from the other a padlock. Throwing the links about his waist, it was but the work of a few seconds to secure it. He was too much astounded to resist. Withdrawing the key I stepped back from the recess.

"Pass your hand," I said, "over the wall; you cannot help feeling the nitre. Indeed, it is *very* damp. Once more let me *implore* you to return. No? Then I must positively leave you. But I must first render you all the little attentions in my power."

"The Amontillado!" ejaculated my friend, not yet recovered from his astonishment.

"True," I replied; "the Amontillado."

As I said these words I busied myself among the pile of bones of which I have before spoken. Throwing them aside, I soon uncovered a quantity of building stone and mortar. With these materials and with the aid of my trowel, I began vigorously to wall up the entrance of the niche.

I had scarcely laid the first tier of the masonry when I discovered that the intoxication of Fortunato had in a great measure worn off. The earliest indication I had of this was a low moaning cry from the depth of the recess. It was *not* the cry of a drunken man. There was then a long and obstinate silence. I laid the second tier, and the third, and the fourth; and then I heard the furious vibrations of the chain. The noise lasted for several minutes, during which, that I might hearken to it with the more satisfaction, I ceased my labors and sat down upon the bones. When at last the clanking subsided, I resumed the trowel, and finished without interruption the fifth, the sixth, and the seventh tier. The wall was now nearly upon a level with my breast. I again paused, and holding the flambeaux over the mason-work, threw a few feeble rays upon the figure within.

A succession of loud and shrill screams, bursting suddenly from the throat of the chained form, seemed to thrust me violently back. For a brief moment I hesitated, I trembled. Unsheathing my rapier, I began to grope with it about the recess; but the thought of an instant reassured me. I placed my hand upon the solid fabric of the catacombs, and felt satisfied. I reapproached the wall; I replied to the yells of him who clamored. I re-echoed, I aided, I surpassed them in volume and in strength. I did this, and the clamorer grew still.

It was now midnight, and my task was drawing to a close. I had completed the eighth, the ninth and the tenth tier. I had finished a portion of the last and the eleventh; there remained but a single stone to be fitted and plastered in. I struggled with its weight; I placed it partially in its destined position. But now there came from out the niche a low laugh that erected the hairs upon my head. It was succeeded by a sad voice, which I had difficulty in recognizing as that of the noble Fortunato. The voice said—

"Ha! ha! ha!—he! he! he!—a very good joke, indeed—an excellent jest. We will have many a rich laugh about it at the palazzo—he! he! he!—over our wine—he! he! he!"

"The Amontillado!" I said.

"He! he! he!—he! he! he!—yes, the Amontillado. But is it not getting late? Will not they be awaiting us at the palazzo, the Lady Fortunato and the rest? Let us be gone."

"Yes," I said, "let us be gone."

"*For the love of God, Montresor!*"

"Yes," I said, "for the love of God!"

But to these words I hearkened in vain for a reply. I grew impatient. I called aloud—

"Fortunato!"

No answer. I called again—

"Fortunato!"

No answer still. I thrust a torch through the remaining aperture and let it fall within. There came forth in return only a jingling of the bells. My heart grew sick; it was the dampness of the catacombs that made it so. I hastened to make an end of my labor. I forced the last stone into its position; I plastered it up. Against the new masonry I re-erected the old rampart of bones. For the half of a century no mortal has disturbed them. *In pace requiescat!*[4]

—1846

4 Latin: Rest in peace!

THOMAS HARDY

Although Thomas Hardy once said that he considered poetry a more serious genre than fiction (and calculated that he spent more years writing the former than the latter), it is as the author of novels such as *Tess of the D'Urbervilles* (1891) and *Jude the Obscure* (1896) that he is best known. Hardy was born in 1840, the son of a stonemason and his wife who lived in Higher Bockhampton in Dorset, near Dorchester. From an early age he was made aware of the hierarchy of the rich and poor, and of the more subtle divisions between different strata of the working class—an awareness that would later inform his work as a writer.

As a young man, Hardy articled with John Hicks, a Dorchester architect, and for some years he worked as an architect, specializing in the restoration of old churches in his home region and in London. He worked simultaneously on his writing, and in 1868 he submitted for publication to several publishers the manuscript for his first novel, *The Poor Man and the Lady*. According to the publishers, the novel showed much promise, but was not good enough for publication. In 1870, during one of his assignments in church restoration, Hardy met his future wife, Emma Lavinia Gifford, the sister-in-law of a church rector. During the long engagement, Hardy managed to publish several works, including his first novel, *Desperate Remedies* (1871). The serializing of his fourth novel, *Far from the Madding Crowd*, in *Cornhill Magazine* (1874) and its subsequent publication in book form established Hardy as a serious writer. The couple settled in London. Hardy gave up architecture in order to write full time; he became recognized as a major figure in the literary world.

In 1885, Hardy and his wife moved to Dorchester and into a house Hardy had designed himself, called Max Gate. The Hardys traveled little, and, although solid, their marriage was disturbed by the conflict between Emma Lavinia's strong evangelical faith and Hardy's agnosticism.

The publication of *Jude the Obscure* in 1896 served as a major turning point in Hardy's literary career. Some of the reviews were vicious (one reviewer re-titled the novel, "Jude the Obscene"), and Hardy soon gave up novel writing to concentrate on his poetry. By this time, however, Hardy's reputation as one of the foremost novelists of the nineteenth century had already been well established. After his first wife's death in 1912, Hardy married Florence Emily Dugdale in 1914; interestingly, when Hardy died in 1928, his heart was buried with Emma Lavinia in Stinsford churchyard while his ashes were interred at Westminster Abbey.

"The Son's Veto" was first published in *The Illustrated London News* in 1891 and then included in the short story collection *Life's Little Ironies* (1894). This story—which Hardy said was his favorite—covers a familiar theme in Hardy's work: class-based division. In this case the conflict is not (as is often the case in Hardy's work) between lovers divided and defeated by their social stations, but between a mother and the social prejudices of her son.

The Son's Veto

THOMAS HARDY

I

TO THE EYES of a man viewing it from behind, the nut-brown hair was a wonder and a mystery. Under the black beaver hat, surmounted by its tuft of black feathers, the long locks, braided and twisted and coiled like the rushes of a basket, composed a rare, if somewhat barbaric, example of ingenious art. One could understand such weavings and coilings being wrought to last intact for a year, or even a calendar month; but that they should be all demolished regularly at bedtime, after a single day of permanence, seemed a reckless waste of successful fabrication.

And she had done it all herself, poor thing. She had no maid, and it was almost the only accomplishment she could boast of. Hence the unstinted pains.

She was a young invalid lady—not so very much of an invalid—sitting in a wheeled chair, which had been pulled up in the front part of a green enclosure, close to a band-stand, where a concert was going on, during a warm June afternoon. It had place in one of the minor parks or private gardens that are to be found in the suburbs of London, and was the effort of a local association to raise money for some charity. There are worlds within worlds in the great city, and though nobody outside the immediate district had ever heard of the charity, or the band, or the garden, the enclosure was filled with an interested audience sufficiently informed on all these.

As the strains proceeded many of the listeners observed the chaired lady, whose back hair, by reason of her prominent position, so challenged inspection.

Her face was not easily discernible, but the aforesaid cunning tress-weavings, the white ear and poll, and the curve of a cheek which was neither flaccid nor sallow, were signals that led to the expectation of good beauty in front. Such expectations are not infrequently disappointed as soon as the disclosure comes; and in the present case, when the lady, by a turn of the head, at length revealed herself, she was not so handsome as the people behind her had supposed, and even hoped—they did not know why.

For one thing (alas! the commonness of this complaint), she was less young than they had fancied her to be. Yet attractive her face unquestionably was, and not at all sickly. The revelation of its details came each time she turned to talk to a boy of twelve or thirteen who stood beside her, and the shape of whose hat and jacket implied that he belonged to a well-known public school. The immediate by-standers could hear that he called her "Mother."

When the end of the program was reached, and the audience withdrew, many chose to find their way out by passing at her elbow. Almost all turned their heads to take a full and near look at the interesting woman, who remained stationary in the chair till the way should be clear enough for her to be wheeled out without obstruction. As if she expected their glances, and did not mind gratifying their curiosity, she met the eyes of several of her observers by lifting her own, showing these to be soft, brown, and affectionate orbs, a little plaintive in their regard.

She was conducted out of the garden, and passed along the pavement till she disappeared from view, the school-boy walking beside her. To inquiries made by some persons who watched her away, the answer came that she was the second wife of the incumbent of a neighboring parish, and that she was lame. She was generally believed to be a woman with a story—an innocent one, but a story of some sort or other.

In conversing with her on their way home the boy who walked at her elbow said that he hoped his father had not missed them.

"He have been so comfortable these last few hours that I am sure he cannot have missed us," she replied.

"*Has*, dear mother—not *have*!" exclaimed the public-school boy, with an impatient fastidiousness that was almost harsh. "Surely you know that by this time!"

His mother hastily adopted the correction, and did not resent his making it, or retaliate, as she might well have done, by bidding him to wipe that crumby mouth of his, whose condition had been caused by surreptitious attempts to eat a piece of cake without taking it out of the pocket wherein it lay concealed. After this the pretty woman and the boy went onward in silence.

That question of grammar bore upon her history, and she fell into reverie, of a somewhat sad kind to all appearance. It might have been assumed that she was wondering if she had done wisely in shaping her life as she had shaped it, to bring out such a result as this.

In a remote nook in North Wessex, forty miles from London, near the thriving county-town of Aldbrickham, there stood a pretty village with its church and parsonage, which she knew well enough, but her son had never seen. It was her native village, Gaymead, and the first event bearing upon her present situation had occurred at that place when she was only a girl of nineteen.

How well she remembered it, that first act in her little tragi-comedy, the death of her reverend husband's first wife. It happened on a spring evening, and she who now and for many years had filled that first wife's place was then parlor-maid in the parson's house.

When everything had been done that could be done, and the death was announced, she had gone out in the dusk to visit her parents, who were living in the same village, to tell them the sad news. As she opened the white swing-gate and looked towards the trees which rose westward, shutting out the pale light of the evening sky, she discerned, without much surprise, the figure of a man standing in the hedge, though she roguishly exclaimed, as a matter of form, "Oh, Sam, how you frightened me!"

He was a young gardener of her acquaintance. She told him the particulars of the late event, and they stood silent, these two young people, in that elevated, calmly philosophic mind which is engendered when a tragedy has happened close at hand, and has not happened to the philosophers themselves. But it had its bearings upon their relations.

"And will you stay on now at the Vicarage, just the same?" asked he.

She had hardly thought of that. "Oh yes—I suppose," she said. "Everything will be just as usual, I imagine."

He walked beside her towards her mother's. Presently his arm stole round her waist. She gently removed it; but he placed it there again, and she yielded the point. "You see, dear Sophy, you don't know that you'll stay on; you may want a home; and I shall be ready to offer one some day, though I may not be ready just yet."

"Why, Sam, how can you be so fast? I've never even said I liked 'ee; and it is all your own doing, coming after me."

"Still, it is nonsense to say I am not to have a try at you, like the rest." He stooped to kiss her a farewell, for they had reached her mother's door.

"No, Sam; you sha'n't!" she cried, putting her hand over his mouth. "You ought to be more serious on such a night as this." And she bade him adieu without allowing him to kiss her or to come indoors.

The vicar just left a widower was at this time a man about forty years of age, of good family, and childless. He had led a secluded existence in this college living, partly because there were no resident landowners; and his loss now intensified his habit of withdrawal from outward observation. He was still less seen than heretofore, kept himself still less in time with the rhythm and racket of the movements called progress in the world without. For many months after his wife's decease the economy of his household remained as before; the cook, the house-maid, the parlor-maid, and the man out-of-doors performed their duties or left them undone, just as nature prompted them—the vicar knew not which. It was then represented to him that his servants seemed to have nothing to do in his small family of one. He was struck with the truth of this representation, and decided to cut down his establishment. But he was forestalled by Sophy, the parlor-maid, who said one evening that she wished to leave him.

"And why?" said the parson.

"Sam Hobson has asked me to marry him, sir."

"Well—do you want to marry?"

"Not much. But it would be a home for me. And we have heard that one of us will have to leave."

A day or two after she said: "I don't want to leave just yet, sir, if you don't wish it. Sam and I have quarrelled."

He looked at her. He had hardly ever observed her before, though he had been frequently conscious of her soft presence in the room. What a kitten-like, flexuous, tender creature she was! She was the only one of the servants with whom he came into immediate and continuous relation. What should he do if Sophy were gone?

Sophy did not go, but one of the others did, and things proceeded quietly again.

When Mr. Twycott, the vicar, was ill, Sophy brought up his meals to him, and she had no sooner left the room one day than he heard a noise on the stairs. She had slipped down with the tray, and so twisted her foot that she could not stand. The village surgeon was called in; the vicar got better, but Sophy was incapacitated for a long time; and she was informed that she must never again walk much or engage in any occupation which required her to stand long on her feet. As soon as she was comparatively well she spoke to him alone. Since she was forbidden to walk and bustle about, and, indeed, could not do so, it became her duty to leave. She could very well work at something sitting down, and she had an aunt a seamstress.

The parson had been very greatly moved by what she had suffered on his account, and he exclaimed, "No, Sophy; lame or not lame, I cannot let you go. You must never leave me again."

He came close to her, and, though she could never exactly tell how it happened, she became conscious of his lips upon her cheek. He then asked her to marry him. Sophy did not exactly love him, but she had a respect for him which almost amounted to veneration. Even if she had wished to get away from him she hardly dared refuse a personage so reverend and august in her eyes, and she assented forthwith to be his wife.

Thus it happened that one fine morning, when the doors of the church were naturally open for ventilation, and the singing birds fluttered in and alighted on the tie-beams of the roof, there was a marriage-service at the communion rails which hardly a soul knew of. The parson and a neighboring curate had entered at one door, and Sophy at another, followed by two necessary persons, whereupon in a short time there emerged a newly-made husband and wife.

Mr. Twycott knew perfectly well that he had committed social suicide by this step, despite Sophy's spotless character, and he had taken his measures accordingly. An exchange of livings had been arranged with an acquaintance who was incumbent of a church in the south of London, and as soon as possible the couple removed thither, abandoning their pretty country home with trees and shrubs and glebe[1] for a narrow, dusty house in a long, straight street, and their fine peal of bells for the wretchedest one-tongue clangor that ever tortured mortal ears. It was all on her account. They were, however, away from every one who had known her former position, and also under less observation from without than they would have had to put up with in any country parish.

Sophy the woman was as charming a partner as a man could possess, though Sophy the lady had her deficiencies. She showed a natural aptitude for little domestic refinements, so far as related to things and manners; but in what is called culture she was less intuitive. She had now been married more than fourteen years, and her husband had taken much trouble with her education; but she still held confused ideas on the use of "was" and "were," which did not beget a respect for her among the few acquaintances she made. Her great grief in this relation was that her only child, on whose education no expense had been or would be spared, was now old enough to perceive these deficiencies in his mother, and not only to see them but to feel irritated at their existence.

Thus she lived on in the city, and wasted hours in braiding her beautiful hair, till her once apple cheeks waned to pink of the very faintest. Her foot had never regained its natural strength after the accident, and she was mostly obliged to avoid walking altogether. Her husband had grown to like London for its freedom and its domestic privacy; but he was twenty years his Sophy's senior, and had latterly been seized with a serious illness. On this day, however, he had seemed to be well enough to justify her accompanying her son Randolph to the concert.

---

1 Land granted to a clergyman.

II

THE NEXT time we get a glimpse of her is when she appears in the mournful attire of a widow.

Mr. Twycott had never rallied, and now lay in a well-packed cemetery to the south of the great city, where, if all the dead it contained had stood erect and alive, not one would have known him or recognized his name. The boy had dutifully followed him to the grave, and was now again at school.

Throughout these changes Sophy had been treated like the child she was in nature though not in years. She was left with no control over anything that had been her husband's beyond her modest personal income. In his anxiety lest her inexperience should be overreached he had safeguarded with trustees all he possibly could. The completion of the boy's course at the public school, to be followed in due time by Oxford and ordination, had been all previsioned and arranged, and she really had nothing to occupy her in the world but to eat and drink, and make a business of indolence, and go on weaving and coiling the nut-brown hair, merely keeping a home open for the son whenever he came to her during vacations.

Foreseeing his probable decease long years before her, her husband in his lifetime had purchased for her use a semi-detached villa in the same long, straight road whereon the church and parsonage faced, which was to be hers as long as she chose to live in it. Here she now resided, looking out upon the fragment of lawn in front, and through the railings at the ever-flowing traffic; or, bending forward over the window-sill on the first floor, stretching her eyes far up and down the vista of sooty trees, hazy air, and drab house façades, along which echoed the noises common to a suburban main thoroughfare.

Somehow, her boy, with his aristocratic school-knowledge, his grammars, and his aversions, was losing those wide infantine sympathies, extending as far as to the sun and moon themselves, with which he, like other children, had been born, and which his mother, a child of nature herself, had loved in him; he was reducing their compass to a population of a few thousand wealthy and titled people, the mere veneer of a thousand million or so of others who did not interest him at all. He drifted further and further away from her. Sophy's *milieu* being a suburb of minor tradesmen and under-clerks, and her almost only companions the two servants of her own house, it was not surprising that after her husband's death she soon lost the little artificial tastes she had acquired from him, and became—in her son's eyes—a mother whose mistakes and origin it was his painful lot as a gentleman to blush for. As yet he was far from being man enough—if he ever would be—to rate these sins of hers at their true infinitesimal value beside the yearning fondness that welled up and remained penned in her heart till it should be more fully accepted by him, or by some other person or thing. If he had lived at home with her he would have had all of it; but he seemed to require so very little in present circumstances, and it remained stored.

Her life became insupportably dreary; she could not take walks, and had no interest in going for drives, or, indeed, in traveling anywhere. Nearly two years passed without an event, and still she looked on that suburban road, thinking of the village in which she had been born, and whither she would have gone back—oh, how gladly!—even to work in the fields.

Taking no exercise, she often could not sleep, and would rise in the night or early morning and look out upon the then vacant thoroughfare, where the lamps stood like sentinels waiting for some procession to go by. An approximation to such a procession was indeed made every early morning about one o'clock, when the country vehicles passed up with loads of vegetables for Covent Garden market. She often saw them creeping along at this silent and dusky hour—wagon after wagon, bearing green bastions of cabbages nodding to their fall, yet never falling; walls of baskets enclosing masses of beans and pease; pyramids of snow-white turnips, swaying howdahs[2] of mixed produce—creeping along behind aged night-horses, who seemed ever patiently wondering between their hollow coughs why they had always to work at that still hour when all other sentient creatures were privileged to rest. Wrapped in a cloak, it was soothing to watch and sympathize with them when depression and nervousness hindered sleep, and to see how the fresh green-stuff brightened to life as it came opposite the lamp, and how the sweating animals steamed and shone with their miles of travel.

They had an interest, almost a charm, for Sophy, these semi-rural people and vehicles moving in an urban atmosphere, leading a life quite distinct from that of the daytime toilers on the same road. One morning a man who accompanied a wagon-load of potatoes gazed rather hard at the house fronts as he passed, and with a curious emotion she thought his form was familiar to her. She looked out for him again. His being an old-fashioned conveyance with a yellow front, it was easily recognizable, and on the third night after she saw it a second time. The man alongside was, as she had fancied, Sam Hobson, formerly gardener at Gaymead, who would at one time have married her.

She had occasionally thought of him, and wondered if life in a cottage with him would not have been a happier lot than the life she had accepted. She had not thought of him passionately, but her now dismal situation lent an interest to his resurrection—a tender interest which it is impossible to exaggerate. She went back to bed, and began thinking. When did these market-gardeners, who traveled up to town so regularly at one or two in the morning, come back? She dimly recollected seeing their empty wagons, hardly noticeable among the ordinary day-traffic, passing down at some hour before noon.

---

2 Platforms placed on the backs of work horses.

It was only April, but that morning, after breakfast, she had the window opened, and sat looking out, the feeble sun shining full upon her. She affected to sew, but her eyes never left the street. Between ten and eleven the desired wagon, now unladen, reappeared on its return journey. But Sam was not looking round him then, and drove on in a reverie.

"Sam!" cried she.

Turning with a start, his face lighted up. He called to him a little boy to hold the horse, alighted, and came and stood under her window.

"I can't come down easily, Sam, or I would!" she said. "Did you know I lived here?"

"Well, Mrs. Twycott, I knew you lived along here somewhere. I have often looked out for 'ee."

He briefly explained his own presence on the scene. He had long since given up his gardening in the village near Aldbrickham, and was now manager at a market-gardener's on the south side of London, it being part of his duty to go up to Covent Garden with wagon-loads of produce two or three times a week. In answer to her curious inquiry, he admitted that he had come to this particular district because he had seen in the Aldbrickham paper a year or two before the announcement of the death in South London of the aforetime vicar of Gaymead, which had revived an interest in her dwelling-place that he could not extinguish, leading him to hover about the locality till his present post had been secured.

They spoke of their native village in dear old North Wessex, the spots in which they had played together as children. She tried to feel that she was a dignified personage now, that she must not be too confidential with Sam. But she could not keep it up, and the tears hanging in her eyes were indicated in her voice.

"You are not happy, Mrs. Twycott, I'm afraid," he said.

"Oh, of course not! I lost my husband only the year before last."

"Ah! I meant in another way. You'd like to be home again?"

"This is my home—for life. The house belongs to me. But I understand"—She let it out then. "Yes, Sam. I long for home—*our* home! I *should* like to be there, and never leave it, and die there." But she remembered herself. "That's only a momentary feeling. I have a son, you know, a dear boy. He's at school now."

"Somewhere handy, I suppose? I see there's lots of 'em along this road."

"Oh no! Not in one of these wretched holes! At a public school—one of the most distinguished in England."

"Chok it all! of course! I forgot, ma'am, that you've been a lady for so many years."

"No, I am not a lady," she said, sadly. "I never shall be. But he's a gentleman, and that—makes it—oh, how difficult for me!"

III

THE ACQUAINTANCE thus oddly reopened proceeded apace. She often looked out to get a few words with him, by night or by day. Her sorrow was that she could not accompany her one old friend on foot a little way, and talk more freely than she could do while he paused before the house. One night, at the beginning of June, when she was again on the watch after an absence of some days from the window, he entered the gate and said, softly, "Now, wouldn't some air do you good? I've only half a load this morning. Why not ride up to Covent Garden with me? There's a nice seat on the cabbages, where I've spread a sack. You can be home again in a cab before anybody is up."

She refused at first, and then, trembling with excitement, hastily finished her dressing, and wrapped herself up in cloak and veil, afterwards sidling downstairs by the aid of the handrail, in a way she could adopt on an emergency. When she had opened the door she found Sam on the step, and he lifted her bodily on his strong arm across the little forecourt into his vehicle. Not a soul was visible or audible in the infinite length of the straight, flat highway, with its ever-waiting lamps converging to points in each direction. The air was fresh as country air at this hour, and the stars shone, except to the north-eastward; where there was a whitish light—the dawn. Sam carefully placed her in the seat and drove on.

They talked as they had talked in old days, Sam pulling himself up now and then, when he thought himself too familiar. More than once she said with misgiving that she wondered if she ought to have indulged in the freak. "But I am so lonely in my house," she added, "and this makes me so happy!"

"You must come again, dear Mrs. Twycott. There is no time o' day for taking the air like this."

It grew lighter and lighter. The sparrows became busy in the streets, and the city waxed denser around them. When they approached the river it was day, and on the bridge they beheld the full blaze of morning sunlight in the direction of St. Paul's, the river glistening towards it, and not a craft stirring.

Near Covent Garden he put her into a cab, and they parted, looking into each other's faces like the very old friends they were. She reached home without adventure, limped to the door, and let herself in with her latch-key unseen.

The air and Sam's presence had revived her; her cheeks were quite pink—almost beautiful. She had something to live for in addition to her son. A woman of pure instincts, she knew there had been nothing really wrong in the journey, but supposed it conventionally to be very wrong indeed.

Soon, however, she gave way to the temptation of going with him again, and on this occasion their conversation was distinctly tender, and Sam said he never should forget her, notwithstanding that she had served him rather badly at one time. After much hesitation he told her of a plan it was in his power to carry out, and one he should like to take in hand, since he did not care for London work; it was to set up as a master greengrocer down at Aldbrickham, the county-town of their native place. He knew of an opening—a shop kept by aged people who wished to retire.

"And why don't you do it, then, Sam?" she asked, with a slight heart-sinking.

"Because I'm not sure if—you'd join me. I know you wouldn't—couldn't! Such a lady as ye've been so long, you couldn't be a wife to a man like me."

"I hardly suppose I could!" she assented, also frightened at the idea.

"If you could," he said, eagerly, "you'd on'y have to sit in the back parlor and look through the glass partition when I was away sometimes—just to keep an eye on things. The lameness wouldn't hinder that. I'd keep you as genteel as ever I could, dear Sophy—if I might think of it," he pleaded.

"Sam, I'll be frank," she said, putting her hand on his. "If it were only myself I would do it, and gladly, though everything I possess would be lost to me by marrying again."

"I don't mind that. It's more independent."

"That's good of you, dear, dear Sam. But there's something else. I have a son. I almost fancy when I am miserable sometimes that he is not really mine, but one I hold in trust for my late husband. He seems to belong so little to me personally, so entirely to his dead father. He is so much educated and I so little that I do not feel dignified enough to be his mother. Well, he would have to be told."

"Yes. Unquestionably." Sam saw her thought and her fear. "Still, you can do as you like, Sophy—Mrs. Twycott," he added. "It is not you who are the child, but he."

"Ah, you don't know! Sam, if I could, I would marry you, some day. But you must wait awhile, and let me think."

It was enough for him, and he was blithe at their parting. Not so she. To tell Randolph seemed impossible. She could wait till he had gone up to Oxford, when what she did would affect his life but little. But would he ever tolerate the idea? And if not, could she defy him?

She had not told him a word when the yearly cricket-match came on at Lord's between the public schools, though Sam had already gone back to Aldbrickham. Mrs. Twycott felt stronger than usual. She went to the match with Randolph, and was able to leave her chair and walk about occasionally. The bright idea occurred to her that she could casually broach the subject while moving round among the spectators, when the boy's spirits were high with interest in the game, and he would weigh domestic matters as feathers in the scale beside the day's victory. They promenaded under the lurid July sun, this pair, so wide apart, yet so near, and Sophy saw the large proportion of boys like her own, in their broad white collars and dwarf hats, and all around the rows of great coaches under which was jumbled the debris of luxurious luncheons—bones, pie-crusts, champagne-bottles, glasses, plates, napkins, and the family silver; while on the coaches sat the proud fathers and mothers; but never a poor mother like her. If Randolph had not appertained to these, had not centered all his interests in them, had not cared exclusively for the class they belonged to, how happy would things have been! A great huzza at some small performance with the bat burst from the multitude of relatives, and Randolph jumped wildly into the air to see what had happened. Sophy fetched up the sentence that had been already shaped; but she could not get it out. The occasion was, perhaps, an inopportune one. The contrast between her story and the display of fashion to which Randolph had grown to regard himself as akin would be fatal. She awaited a better time.

It was on an evening when they were alone in their plain suburban residence, where life was not blue but brown, that she ultimately broke silence, qualifying her announcement of a probable second marriage by assuring him that it would not take place for a long time to come, when he would be living quite independently of her.

The boy thought the idea a very reasonable one, and asked if she had chosen anybody. She hesitated; and he seemed to have a misgiving. He hoped his step-father would be a gentleman, he said.

"Not what you call a gentleman," she answered, timidly. "He'll be much as I was before I knew your father;" and by degrees she acquainted him with the whole. The youth's face remained fixed for a moment; then he flushed, leaned on the table, and burst into passionate tears.

His mother went up to him, kissed all of his face that she could get at, and patted his back as if he were still the baby he once had been, crying herself the while. When he had somewhat recovered from his paroxysm he went hastily to his own room and fastened the door.

Parleyings were attempted through the key-hole, outside which she waited and listened. It was long before he would reply, and when he did it was to say sternly at her from within: "I am ashamed of you! It will ruin me! A miserable boor! a churl! a clown! It will degrade me in the eyes of all the gentlemen of England!"

"Say no more—perhaps I am wrong! I will struggle against it!" she cried, miserably.

Before Randolph left her that summer a letter arrived from Sam to inform her that he had been unexpectedly fortunate in obtaining the shop. He was in possession; it was the largest in the town, combining fruit with vegetables, and he thought it would form a home worthy even of her some day. Might he not run up to town to see her?

She met him by stealth, and said he must still wait for her final answer. The autumn dragged on, and when Randolph was home at Christmas for the holidays she broached the matter again. But the young gentleman was inexorable.

It was dropped for months; renewed again; abandoned under his repugnance; again attempted, and thus the gentle creature reasoned and pleaded till four or five long years had passed. Then the faithful Sam revived his suit with some peremptoriness. Sophy's son, now an undergraduate, was down from Oxford one Easter, when she again opened the subject. As soon as he was ordained, she argued, he would have a home of his own, wherein she, with her bad grammar and her ignorance, would be an encumbrance to him. Better obliterate her as much as possible.

He showed a more manly anger now, but would not agree. She on her side was more persistent, and he had doubts whether she could be trusted in his absence. But by indignation and contempt for her taste he completely maintained his ascendency; and finally taking her before a little cross and shrine that he had erected in his bedroom for his private devotions, there bade her kneel, and swear that she would not wed Samuel Hobson without his consent. "I owe this to my father!" he said.

The poor woman swore, thinking he would soften as soon as he was ordained and in full swing of clerical work. But he did not. His education had by this time sufficiently ousted his humanity to keep him quite firm; though his mother might have led an idyllic life with her faithful fruiterer and green-grocer, and nobody have been anything the worse in the world.

Her lameness became more confirmed as time went on, and she seldom or never left the house in the long southern thoroughfare, where she seemed to be pining her heart away. "Why mayn't I say to Sam that I'll marry him? Why mayn't I?" she would murmur plaintively to herself when nobody was near.

Some four years after this date a middle-aged man was standing at the door of the largest fruiterer's shop in Aldbrickham. He was the proprietor, but to-day, instead of his usual business attire, he wore a neat suit of black; and his window was partly shuttered. From the railway station a funeral procession was seen approaching; it passed his door and went out of the town towards the village of Gaymead. The man, whose eyes were wet, held his hat in his hand as the vehicles moved by; while from the mourning coach a young smooth-shaven priest in a high waistcoat looked black as a cloud at the shopkeeper standing there.

—1891

KATE CHOPIN

Katherine Chopin was born in St. Louis, Missouri, in 1850. She was one of three children and the only child to reach adulthood in a family presided over by an Irish immigrant father and a mother who belonged to an aristocratic Creole family. Her father died in a train wreck in 1855 and Kate, with her mother, went to live with her widowed maternal grandmother and great-grandmother. She graduated in 1868 from the Catholic St. Louis Academy of the Sacred Heart, and in 1870 made her debut into St. Louis society. During a trip to New Orleans, she met Oscar Chopin, a cotton trader and plantation owner; they were married in 1871. The couple moved to Cloutierville, Louisiana, where Oscar owned several plantations. By all accounts their marriage was a happy one, and, while married to Oscar, Kate Chopin gave birth to six children. Her marriage was cut short, however, by Oscar's death from swamp fever in 1883. She ran the plantations for a time, but returned to St. Louis in 1884 after conducting a scandalous affair with a married neighbor.

From her teenage years and on, Chopin read and wrote with avid interest but it was not until after the death of her husband that she began writing in earnest. In 1889 she published her first story, and in 1890, her first novel, *At Fault*. Publishers rejected her second novel and she destroyed it. In 1894 her short stories began appearing in important periodicals such as *Vogue* and *The Atlantic Monthly*. Not long after, her first collection of short stories, *Bayou Folk* (1894) was published, followed by a second collection entitled *A Night in Acadie* (1897). Her work until this point garnered favorable reviews and was classified as part of the literary genre known as "local color," a kind of fiction popular in the United States in the late nineteenth century that was devoted to reproducing regional flavor (Mark Twain's depiction of life in the American west and Mary Wilkins Freeman's New England writings are also examples of "local color").

Chopin's third novel, *The Awakening* (1899), tells the story of a married woman in an uninspiring marriage who "wakens" to her own eroticism and sensuality through amorous relations with other men. The novel received mixed reviews and was banned from St. Louis libraries. The negative reviews affected Chopin very deeply; her ill fortune was compounded when her publisher also refused to publish her fourth novel, *A Vocation and a Voice*. She published very little thereafter, and died in 1904 of a cerebral hemorrhage. Her writing was ignored until the 1950s and 1960s, when scholars began to recognize the value of her work—and to treat *The Awakening* as a literary classic.

"The Storm" is a continuation of an earlier story by Chopin, "At the 'Cadian Ball" (1898), which features the same characters. It is characteristic of Chopin's work in its lyrical celebration of sensual pleasure, as in its daring erasure of the moral boundaries between married and adulterous love. As Chopin wrote in an 1898 essay, "I am inclined to think that love springs from animal instinct, and therefore is, in a measure, divine."

The Storm

KATE CHOPIN

I

THE LEAVES WERE so still that even Bibi thought it was going to rain. Bobinôt, who was accustomed to converse on terms of perfect equality with his little son, called the child's attention to certain somber clouds that were rolling with sinister intention from the west, accompanied by a sullen, threatening roar. They were at Friedheimer's store and decided to remain there till the storm had passed. They sat within the door on two empty kegs. Bibi was four years old and looked very wise.

"Mama'll be 'fraid, yes," he suggested with blinking eyes.

"She'll shut the house. Maybe she got Sylvie helpin' her this evenin'," Bobinôt responded reassuringly.

"No; she ent got Sylvie. Sylvie was helpin' her yistiday," piped Bibi.

Bobinôt arose and going across to the counter purchased a can of shrimps, of which Calixta was very fond. Then he returned to his perch on the keg and sat stolidly holding the can of shrimps while the storm burst. It shook the wooden store and seemed to be ripping great furrows in the distant field. Bibi laid his little hand on his father's knee and was not afraid.

II

Calixta, at home, felt no uneasiness for their safety. She sat at a side window sewing furiously on a sewing machine. She was greatly occupied and did not notice the approaching storm. But she felt very warm and often stopped to mop her face on which the perspiration gathered in beads. She unfastened her white sacque[1] at the throat. It began to grow dark, and suddenly realizing the situation she got up hurriedly and went about closing windows and doors.

Out on the small front gallery she had hung Bobinôt's Sunday clothes to air and she hastened out to gather them before the rain fell. As she stepped outside, Alcée Laballière rode in at the gate. She had not seen him very often since her marriage, and never alone. She stood there with Bobinôt's coat in her hands, and the big rain drops began to fall. Alcée rode his horse under the shelter of a side projection where the chickens had huddled and there were plows and a harrow piled up in the corner.

"May I come and wait on your gallery till the storm is over, Calixta?" he asked.

"Come 'long in, M'sieur Alcée."

His voice and her own startled her as if from a trance, and she seized Bobinôt's vest. Alcée, mounting to the porch, grabbed the trousers and snatched Bibi's braided jacket that was about to be carried away by a sudden gust of wind. He expressed an intention to remain outside, but it was soon apparent that he might as well have been out in the open: the water beat in upon the boards in driving sheets, and he went inside, closing the door after him. It was even necessary to put something beneath the door to keep the water out.

"My! what a rain! It's good two years sence it rain' like that," exclaimed Calixta as she rolled up a piece of bagging and Alcée helped her to thrust it beneath the crack.

She was a little fuller of figure than five years before when she married; but she had lost nothing of her vivacity. Her blue eyes still retained their melting quality; and her yellow hair, disheveled by the wind and rain, kinked more stubbornly than ever about her ears and temples.

The rain beat upon the low, shingled roof with a force and clatter that threatened to break an entrance and deluge them there. They were in the dining room —the sitting room—the general utility room. Adjoining was her bed room, with Bibi's couch along side her own. The door stood open, and the room with its white, monumental bed, its closed shutters, looked dim and mysterious.

1 Loose fitting gown that fastens at the neck.

Alcée flung himself into a rocker and Calixta nervously began to gather up from the floor the lengths of a cotton sheet which she had been sewing.

"If this keeps up, *Dieu sait*[2] if the levees goin' to stan it!" she exclaimed.

"What have you got to do with the levees?"

"I got enough to do! An' there's Bobinôt with Bibi out in that storm—if he only didn' left Friedheimer's!"

"Let us hope, Calixta, that Bobinôt's got sense enough to come in out of a cyclone."

She went and stood at the window with a greatly disturbed look on her face. She wiped the frame that was clouded with moisture. It was stiflingly hot. Alcée got up and joined her at the window, looking over her shoulder. The rain was coming down in sheets obscuring the view of far-off cabins and enveloping the distant wood in a gray mist. The playing of the lightning was incessant. A bolt struck a tall chinaberry tree at the edge of the field. It filled all visible space with a blinding glare and the crash seemed to invade the very boards they stood upon.

Calixta put her hands to her eyes, and with a cry, staggered backward. Alcée's arm encircled her, and for an instant he drew her close and spasmodically to him.

"*Bonté*!"[3] she cried, releasing herself from his encircling arm and retreating from the window, "the house'll go next! If I only knew w'ere Bibi was!" She would not compose herself; she would not be seated. Alcée clasped her shoulders and looked into her face. The contact of her warm, palpitating body when he had unthinkingly drawn her into his arms, had aroused all the old-time infatuation and desire for her flesh.

"Calixta," he said, "don't be frightened. Nothing can happen. The house is too low to be struck, with so many tall trees standing about. There! aren't you going to be quiet? say, aren't you?" He pushed her hair back from her face that was warm and steaming. Her lips were as red and moist as pomegranate seed. Her white neck and a glimpse of her full, firm bosom disturbed him powerfully. As she glanced up at him the fear in her liquid blue eyes had given place to a drowsy gleam that unconsciously betrayed a sensuous desire. He looked down into her eyes and there was nothing for him to do but to gather her lips in a kiss. It reminded him of Assumption.[4]

"Do you remember—in Assumption, Calixta?" he asked in a low voice broken by passion. Oh! she remembered; for in Assumption he had kissed her and

---

2 French: God knows.

3 French: goodness.

4 Parish in Louisiana with a large Cajun population that dates back to the mid eighteenth century.

kissed and kissed her; until his senses would well nigh fail, and to save her he would resort to a desperate flight. If she was not an immaculate dove in those days, she was still inviolate; a passionate creature whose very defenselessness had made her defense, against which his honor forbade him to prevail. Now—well, now—her lips seemed in a manner free to be tasted, as well as her round, white throat and her whiter breasts.

They did not heed the crashing torrents, and the roar of the elements made her laugh as she lay in his arms. She was a revelation in that dim, mysterious chamber; as white as the couch she lay upon. Her firm, elastic flesh that was knowing for the first time its birthright, was like a creamy lily that the sun invites to contribute its breath and perfume to the undying life of the world.

The generous abundance of her passion, without guile or trickery, was like a white flame which penetrated and found response in depths of his own sensuous nature that had never yet been reached.

When he touched her breasts they gave themselves up in quivering ecstasy, inviting his lips. Her mouth was a fountain of delight. And when he possessed her, they seemed to swoon together at the very borderland of life's mystery.

He stayed cushioned upon her, breathless, dazed, enervated, with his heart beating like a hammer upon her. With one hand she clasped his head, her lips lightly touching his forehead. The other hand stroked with a soothing rhythm his muscular shoulders.

The growl of the thunder was distant and passing away. The rain beat softly upon the shingles, inviting them to drowsiness and sleep. But they dared not yield.

The rain was over; and the sun was turning the glistening green world into a palace of gems. Calixta, on the gallery, watched Alcée ride away. He turned and smiled at her with a beaming face; and she lifted her pretty chin in the air and laughed aloud.

III

Bobinôt and Bibi, trudging home, stopped without at the cistern to make themselves presentable.

"My! Bibi, w'at will yo' mama say! You ought to be ashame'. You oughta' put on those good pants. Look at 'em! An' that mud on yo' collar! How you got that mud on yo' collar, Bibi? I never saw such a boy!" Bibi was the picture of pathetic resignation. Bobinôt was the embodiment of serious solicitude as he strove to remove from his own person and his son's the signs of their tramp over heavy roads and through wet fields. He scraped the mud off Bibi's bare legs and feet with a stick and carefully removed all traces from his heavy brogans.[5] Then, prepared for the worst—the meeting with an over-scrupulous housewife, they entered cautiously at the back door.

Calixta was preparing supper. She had set the table and was dripping coffee at the hearth. She sprang up as they came in.

"Oh, Bobinôt! You back! My! but I was uneasy. W'ere you been during the rain? An' Bibi? he ain't wet? he ain't hurt?" She had clasped Bibi and was kissing him effusively. Bobinôt's explanations and apologies which he had been composing all along the way, died on his lips as Calixta felt him to see if he were dry, and seemed to express nothing but satisfaction at their safe return.

"I brought you some shrimps, Calixta," offered Bobinôt, hauling the can from his ample side pocket and laying it on the table.

"Shrimps! Oh, Bobinôt! you too good fo' anything!" and she gave him a smacking kiss on the cheek that resounded. "*J'vous réponds,*[6] we'll have a feas' to-night! umph-umph!"

Bobinôt and Bibi began to relax and enjoy themselves, and when the three seated themselves at table they laughed much and so loud that anyone might have heard them as far away as Laballière's.

IV

Alcée Laballière wrote to his wife, Clarisse, that night. It was a loving letter, full of tender solicitude. He told her not to hurry back, but if she and the babies liked it at Biloxi, to stay a month longer. He was getting on nicely; and though he missed them, he was willing to bear the separation a while longer—realizing that their health and pleasure were the first things to be considered.

V

As for Clarisse, she was charmed upon receiving her husband's letter. She and the babies were doing well. The society was agreeable; many of her old friends and acquaintances were at the bay. And the first free breath since her marriage seemed to restore the pleasant liberty of her maiden days. Devoted as she was to her husband, their intimate conjugal life was something which she was more than willing to forego for a while.

So the storm passed and every one was happy.

—1969 (written 1898)

5 Heavy, ankle-high work boots.

6 French: I tell you.

ANTON CHEKHOV

Anton Chekhov was born in Taganrog, a small seaport in southern Russia. He became one of the most influential and respected writers in Western literature; his innovative techniques of narration and characterization have shaped the short story genre, and his work has also been formative in the development of modern drama. Both his stories and his plays have proved to be enduringly popular.

Chekhov was the third of six children, the son of a grocer. His father's bankruptcy in 1875 broke up the family; after watching his mother lose their house and all their possessions, he was left alone in Taganrog. He supported himself by publishing pieces in humor journals between 1880 and 1885, thus paying his way through medical school at Moscow University. He graduated in 1884 and began practicing in country hospitals. In a letter to a friend in 1888, he said: "Medicine is my lawful wife and literature is my mistress. When I get tired of one I spend the night with the other."

In 1885, Chekhov began publishing more serious stories. He outlined his approach in a letter to his brother, Aleksandr: "1. Absence of lengthy verbiage of political-social-economic nature; 2. total objectivity; 3. truthful descriptions of persons and objects; 4. extreme brevity; 5. audacity and originality: flee the stereotype; 6. compassion." He experimented extensively with narrative voice; in the typical Chekhov story the governing narrative voice is objective and aloof, but the narrative may frequently adopt the point of view of one or more of the characters. (This technique, which has come to be known as free indirect discourse, anticipates the more extended "stream of consciousness" narrative techniques adopted by Dorothy Richardson, James Joyce, and other modernist writers.) His stories eschew conventional plot structures, often concluding with one of Chekhov's "zero" endings, in which nothing is clearly resolved.

Late in 1884, Chekhov began to suffer from tuberculosis. As a doctor he must have recognized the disease, but he ignored it and continued to work. He settled on his own estate at Melikhovo, where he stayed until 1898, continuing to write and practice medicine, and often traveling for miles to visit the sick. He ran a free clinic for peasants and organized relief during cholera and famine outbreaks. He also had affairs with various women, but soon tired of each—a pattern that finally ended when he fell in love with the actress Olga Knipper in the late 1890s.

Chekhov's last years were spent in Nice and Yalta, as he sought a better climate to help his worsening illness. During this period he wrote some of his greatest short stories, among them "The Little Trilogy" (1898), "The Lady with a Dog" (1899), "In the Ravine" (1900), and "The Bishop" (1902). In 1904 Chekhov went to Badenweiler, Germany with his wife Olga, where he died on July 15. Famously, he announced he was dying, took a sip of champagne, and then promptly passed away.

"An Upheaval" (1886) tells the story of a young governess accused by the lady of the house of stealing an expensive brooch. An educated woman, the governess is insulted—but must reconcile her own guilt for hiding excess food in her room with the larger sense of injustice she feels at the false accusation.

An Upheaval[1]

ANTON CHEKHOV

MASHENKA PAVLETSKY, a young girl who had only just finished her studies at a boarding school, returning from a walk to the house of the Kushkins, with whom she was living as a governess, found the household in a terrible turmoil. Mihailo, the porter who opened the door to her, was excited and red as a crab.

Loud voices were heard from upstairs.

"Madame Kushkin is in a fit, most likely, or else she has quarreled with her husband," thought Mashenka.

In the hall and in the corridor she met maid-servants. One of them was crying. Then Mashenka saw, running out of her room, the master of the house himself, Nikolay Sergeitch, a little man with a flabby face and a bald head, though he was not old. He was red in the face and twitching all over. He passed the governess without noticing her, and throwing up his arms, exclaimed:

"Oh, how horrible it is! How tactless! How stupid! How barbarous! Abominable!"

Mashenka went into her room, and then, for the first time in her life, it was her lot to experience in all its acuteness the feeling that is so familiar to persons

1 Translated by Constance Garnett.

in dependent positions, who eat the bread of the rich and powerful, and cannot speak their minds. There was a search going on in her room. The lady of the house, Fedosya Vassilyevna, a stout, broad-shouldered, uncouth woman with thick black eyebrows, a faintly perceptible moustache, and red hands, who was exactly like a plain, illiterate cook in face and manners, was standing, without her cap on, at the table, putting back into Mashenka's workbag balls of wool, scraps of materials, and bits of paper.... Evidently the governess's arrival took her by surprise, since, on looking round and seeing the girl's pale and astonished face, she was a little taken aback, and muttered:

"*Pardon*. I ... I upset it accidentally.... My sleeve caught in it ..."

And saying something more, Madame Kushkin rustled her long skirts and went out. Mashenka looked round her room with wondering eyes, and, unable to understand it, not knowing what to think, shrugged her shoulders, and turned cold with dismay. What had Fedosya Vassilyevna been looking for in her work-bag? If she really had, as she said, caught her sleeve in it and upset everything, why had Nikolay Sergeitch dashed out of her room so excited and red in the face? Why was one drawer of the table pulled out a little way? The money-box, in which the governess put away ten kopeck pieces and old stamps, was open. They had opened it, but did not know how to shut it, though they had scratched the lock all over. The whatnot with her books on it, the things on the table, the bed—all bore fresh traces of a search. Her linen-basket, too. The linen had been carefully folded, but it was not in the same order as Mashenka had left it when she went out. So the search had been thorough, most thorough. But what was it for? Why? What had happened? Mashenka remembered the excited porter, the general turmoil which was still going on, the weeping servant-girl; had it not all some connection with the search that had just been made in her room? Was not she mixed up in something dreadful? Mashenka turned pale, and feeling cold all over, sank on to her linen-basket.

A maid-servant came into the room.

"Liza, you don't know why they have been rummaging in my room?" the governess asked her.

"Mistress has lost a brooch worth two thousand," said Liza.

"Yes, but why have they been rummaging in my room?"

"They've been searching every one, miss. They've searched all my things, too. They stripped us all naked and searched us.... God knows, miss, I never went near her toilet-table, let alone touching the brooch. I shall say the same at the police-station."

"But ... why have they been rummaging here?" the governess still wondered.

"A brooch has been stolen, I tell you. The mistress has been rummaging in everything with her own hands. She even searched Mihailo, the porter, herself.

It's a perfect disgrace! Nikolay Sergeitch simply looks on and cackles like a hen. But you've no need to tremble like that, miss. They found nothing here. You've nothing to be afraid of if you didn't take the brooch."

"But, Liza, it's vile … it's insulting," said Mashenka, breathless with indignation. "It's so mean, so low! What right had she to suspect me and to rummage in my things?"

"You are living with strangers, miss," sighed Liza. "Though you are a young lady, still you are … as it were … a servant.… It's not like living with your papa and mamma."

Mashenka threw herself on the bed and sobbed bitterly. Never in her life had she been subjected to such an outrage, never had she been so deeply insulted.… She, well-educated, refined, the daughter of a teacher, was suspected of theft; she had been searched like a street-walker! She could not imagine a greater insult. And to this feeling of resentment was added an oppressive dread of what would come next. All sorts of absurd ideas came into her mind. If they could suspect her of theft, then they might arrest her, strip her naked, and search her, then lead her through the street with an escort of soldiers, cast her into a cold, dark cell with mice and woodlice, exactly like the dungeon in which Princess Tarakanov[2] was imprisoned. Who would stand up for her? Her parents lived far away in the provinces; they had not the money to come to her. In the capital she was as solitary as in a desert, without friends or kindred. They could do what they liked with her.

"I will go to all the courts and all the lawyers," Mashenka thought, trembling. "I will explain to them, I will take an oath.… They will believe that I could not be a thief!"

Mashenka remembered that under the sheets in her basket she had some sweetmeats, which, following the habits of her schooldays, she had put in her pocket at dinner and carried off to her room. She felt hot all over, and was ashamed at the thought that her little secret was known to the lady of the house; and all this terror, shame, resentment, brought on an attack of palpitation of the heart, which set up a throbbing in her temples, in her heart, and deep down in her stomach.

"Dinner is ready," the servant summoned Mashenka.

"Shall I go, or not?"

Mashenka brushed her hair, wiped her face with a wet towel, and went into the dining-room. There they had already begun dinner. At one end of the table sat Fedosya Vassilyevna with a stupid, solemn, serious face; at the other end

2 Yelizaveta Alekseyevna (1753–75), an impostor who claimed to be a Russian princess. She was captured in 1775, and died of tuberculosis while in prison.

Nikolay Sergeitch. At the sides there were the visitors and the children. The dishes were handed by two footmen in swallowtails and white gloves. Every one knew that there was an upset in the house, that Madame Kushkin was in trouble, and every one was silent. Nothing was heard but the sound of munching and the rattle of spoons on the plates.

The lady of the house, herself, was the first to speak.

"What is the third course?" she asked the footman in a weary, injured voice.

"*Esturgeon à la russe*,"[3] answered the footman.

"I ordered that, Fenya," Nikolay Sergeitch hastened to observe. "I wanted some fish. If you don't like it, *ma chère*,[4] don't let them serve it. I just ordered it...."

Fedosya Vassilyevna did not like dishes that she had not ordered herself, and now her eyes filled with tears.

"Come, don't let us agitate ourselves," Mamikov, her household doctor, observed in a honeyed voice, just touching her arm, with a smile as honeyed. "We are nervous enough as it is. Let us forget the brooch! Health is worth more than two thousand roubles!"

"It's not the two thousand I regret," answered the lady, and a big tear rolled down her cheek. "It's the fact itself that revolts me! I cannot put up with thieves in my house. I don't regret it—I regret nothing; but to steal from me is such ingratitude! That's how they repay me for my kindness...."

They all looked into their plates, but Mashenka fancied after the lady's words that every one was looking at her. A lump rose in her throat; she began crying and put her handkerchief to her lips.

"*Pardon*," she muttered. "I can't help it. My head aches. I'll go away."

And she got up from the table, scraping her chair awkwardly, and went out quickly, still more overcome with confusion.

"It's beyond everything!" said Nikolay Sergeitch, frowning. "What need was there to search her room? How out of place it was!"

"I don't say she took the brooch," said Fedosya Vassilyevna, "but can you answer for her? To tell the truth, I haven't much confidence in these learned paupers."

"It really was unsuitable, Fenya.... Excuse me, Fenya, but you've no kind of legal right to make a search."

"I know nothing about your laws. All I know is that I've lost my brooch. And I will find the brooch!" She brought her fork down on the plate with a clatter,

---

3 A French preparation of sturgeon, a large, freshwater fish ("à la russe" translates literally as "in the Russian style").

4 French: my dear.

and her eyes flashed angrily. "And you eat your dinner, and don't interfere in what doesn't concern you!"

Nikolay Sergeitch dropped his eyes mildly and sighed. Meanwhile Mashenka, reaching her room, flung herself on her bed. She felt now neither alarm nor shame, but she felt an intense longing to go and slap the cheeks of this hard, arrogant, dull-witted, prosperous woman.

Lying on her bed she breathed into her pillow and dreamed of how nice it would be to go and buy the most expensive brooch and fling it into the face of this bullying woman. If only it were God's will that Fedosya Vassilyevna should come to ruin and wander about begging, and should taste all the horrors of poverty and dependence, and that Mashenka, whom she had insulted, might give her alms! Oh, if only she could come in for a big fortune, could buy a carriage, and could drive noisily past the windows so as to be envied by that woman!

But all these were only dreams, in reality there was only one thing left to do—to get away as quickly as possible, not to stay another hour in this place. It was true it was terrible to lose her place, to go back to her parents, who had nothing; but what could she do? Mashenka could not bear the sight of the lady of the house nor of her little room; she felt stifled and wretched here. She was so disgusted with Fedosya Vassilyevna, who was so obsessed by her illnesses and her supposed aristocratic rank, that everything in the world seemed to have become coarse and unattractive because this woman was living in it. Mashenka jumped up from the bed and began packing.

"May I come in?" asked Nikolay Sergeitch at the door; he had come up noiselessly to the door, and spoke in a soft, subdued voice. "May I?"

"Come in."

He came in and stood still near the door. His eyes looked dim and his red little nose was shiny. After dinner he used to drink beer, and the fact was perceptible in his walk, in his feeble, flabby hands.

"What's this?" he asked, pointing to the basket.

"I am packing. Forgive me, Nikolay Sergeitch, but I cannot remain in your house. I feel deeply insulted by this search!"

"I understand.... Only you are wrong to go. Why should you? They've searched your things, but you ... what does it matter to you? You will be none the worse for it."

Mashenka was silent and went on packing. Nikolay Sergeitch pinched his moustache, as though wondering what he should say next, and went on in an ingratiating voice:

"I understand, of course, but you must make allowances. You know my wife is nervous, headstrong; you mustn't judge her too harshly."

Mashenka did not speak.

"If you are so offended," Nikolay Sergeitch went on, "well, if you like, I'm ready to apologise. I ask your pardon."

Mashenka made no answer, but only bent lower over her box. This exhausted, irresolute man was of absolutely no significance in the household. He stood in the pitiful position of a dependent and hanger-on, even with the servants, and his apology meant nothing either.

"H'm! ... You say nothing! That's not enough for you. In that case, I will apologise for my wife. In my wife's name.... She behaved tactlessly, I admit it as a gentleman...."

Nikolay Sergeitch walked about the room, heaved a sigh, and went on: "Then you want me to have it rankling here, under my heart.... You want my conscience to torment me...."

"I know it's not your fault, Nikolay Sergeitch," said Mashenka, looking him full in the face with her big tear-stained eyes. "Why should you worry yourself?"

"Of course, no.... But still, don't you ... go away. I entreat you."

Mashenka shook her head. Nikolay Sergeitch stopped at the window and drummed on the pane with his finger-tips.

"Such misunderstandings are simply torture to me," he said. "Why, do you want me to go down on my knees to you, or what? Your pride is wounded, and here you've been crying and packing up to go; but I have pride, too, and you do not spare it! Or do you want me to tell you what I would not tell as Confession? Do you? Listen; you want me to tell you what I won't tell the priest on my deathbed?"

Mashenka made no answer.

"I took my wife's brooch," Nikolay Sergeitch said quickly. "Is that enough now? Are you satisfied? Yes, I ... took it.... But, of course, I count on your discretion.... For God's sake, not a word, not half a hint to any one!"

Mashenka, amazed and frightened, went on packing; she snatched her things, crumpled them up, and thrust them anyhow into the box and the basket. Now, after this candid avowal on the part of Nikolay Sergeitch, she could not remain another minute, and could not understand how she could have gone on living in the house before.

"And it's nothing to wonder at," Nikolay Sergeitch went on after a pause. "It's an everyday story! I need money, and she ... won't give it to me. It was my father's money that bought this house and everything, you know! It's all mine, and the brooch belonged to my mother, and ... it's all mine! And she took it, took possession of everything.... I can't go to law with her, you'll admit.... I beg you most earnestly, overlook it ... stay on. *Tout comprendre, tout pardonner.*[5] Will you stay?"

---

5 A French aphorism: To understand all is to forgive all.

"No!" said Mashenka resolutely, beginning to tremble. "Let me alone, I entreat you!"

"Well, God bless you!" sighed Nikolay Sergeitch, sitting down on the stool near the box. "I must own I like people who still can feel resentment, contempt, and so on. I could sit here forever and look at your indignant face.... So you won't stay, then? I understand.... It's bound to be so ... Yes, of course.... It's all right for you, but for me—wo-o-o-o! ... I can't stir a step out of this cellar. I'd go off to one of our estates, but in every one of them there are some of my wife's rascals ... stewards, experts, damn them all! They mortgage and remortgage.... You mustn't catch fish, must keep off the grass, mustn't break the trees."

"Nikolay Sergeitch!" his wife's voice called from the drawing-room. "Agnia, call your master!"

"Then you won't stay?" asked Nikolay Sergeitch, getting up quickly and going towards the door. "You might as well stay, really. In the evenings I could come and have a talk with you. Eh? Stay! If you go, there won't be a human face left in the house. It's awful!"

Nikolay Sergeitch's pale, exhausted face besought her, but Mashenka shook her head, and with a wave of his hand he went out.

Half an hour later she was on her way.

—1886

CHARLOTTE PERKINS GILMAN

Born in 1860 in Hartford, Connecticut, Charlotte Perkins grew up in poverty and domestic instability after her father abandoned the family. When she turned 18, Gilman went against her mother's wishes and enrolled in the Rhode Island School of Design to study art and painting, where she met a fellow artist, Charles Walter Stetson. Gilman married Stetson in 1884 and gave up her formerly vigorous intellectual life—a move that sparked a descent into depression. Her depression deepened when she gave birth to her daughter Katharine in 1885, and, after an ill-fated attempt at Philadelphia neurologist S. Weir Mitchell's famous "rest-cure" (a medical prescription that involved complete inactivity and little to no intellectual stimulation), she left her husband and moved with Katharine to California. She later divorced Stetson and gave him custody of their daughter, an incident that led to the charge that she was an "unnatural mother."

For the remainder of her life, Gilman lectured widely. She published seven novels (including the feminist utopian novel *Herland*), several collections of poetry, her monthly magazine *The Forerunner*, and numerous essays on topics relevant to feminism and socialism. In 1900 she married her first cousin George Houghton Gilman after an extended courtship. The marriage was regarded as a relatively happy one—this time Perkins Gilman did not give up her career plans or her sense of independence—but George Gilman died in 1934 of a cerebral hemorrhage. In 1935, three years after learning that she had breast cancer, Gilman committed suicide; her belief—as stated in her posthumously published autobiography *The Living of Charlotte Perkins Gilman*—was that it is "the simplest of human rights to choose a quick and easy death in place of a slow and horrible one."

Although during her lifetime Gilman was best known for her book *Women and Economics: A Study of the Economic Relation between Men and Women* (1898), modern interest in her work has centered on *Herland* and on the short story "The Yellow Wallpaper." First published in 1892 in *The New England Magazine*, the story draws on Gilman's experiences with the "rest-cure" that nearly drove her insane. Horace P. Scudder, the publisher she initially submitted it to, rejected the story, saying "I should never forgive myself if I made other people as miserable as reading your story has made me." The story's reception was mixed, and editor William Dean Howells believed that the story was "unpopular because ... it 'struck too deeply and effectively at traditional ways of seeing the world and woman's place in it.'" Although it was anthologized regularly in the decades after its publication, it was not until the explosion of American feminism in the 1970s that it began to be thought of as a classic. Gilman's uncanny ability to convey the narrator's descent into madness via the wallpaper in her sickroom resembles a horror story but without the characteristic, easily dismissible trappings of horror literature. The "horror" comes from the reader's witnessing of a sane woman's descent into madness through unrelenting, "rational" intervention.

The Yellow Wallpaper

CHARLOTTE PERKINS GILMAN

IT IS VERY seldom that mere ordinary people like John and myself secure ancestral halls for the summer.

A colonial mansion, a hereditary estate, I would say a haunted house and reach the height of romantic felicity—but that would be asking too much of fate!

Still I will proudly declare that there is something queer about it.

Else, why should it be let so cheaply? And why have stood so long untenanted?

John laughs at me, of course, but one expects that.

John is practical in the extreme. He has no patience with faith, an intense horror of superstition, and he scoffs openly at any talk of things not to be felt and seen and put down in figures.

John is a physician, and *perhaps*—(I would not say it to a living soul, of course, but this is dead paper and a great relief to my mind)—*perhaps* that is one reason I do not get well faster.

You see, he does not believe I am sick! And what can one do?

If a physician of high standing, and one's own husband, assures friends and relatives that there is really nothing the matter with one but temporary nervous depression—a slight hysterical tendency—what is one to do?

My brother is also a physician, and also of high standing, and he says the same thing.

So I take phosphates or phosphites—whichever it is—and tonics, and air and exercise, and journeys, and am absolutely forbidden to "work" until I am well again.

Personally, I disagree with their ideas.

Personally, I believe that congenial work, with excitement and change, would do me good.

But what is one to do?

I did write for a while in spite of them, but it *does* exhaust me a good deal—having to be so sly about it, or else meet with heavy opposition.

I sometimes fancy that in my condition, if I had less opposition and more society and stimulus—but John says the very worst thing I can do is to think about my condition, and I confess it always makes me feel bad.

So I will let it alone and talk about the house.

The most beautiful place! It is quite alone, standing well back from the road, quite three miles from the village. It makes me think of English places that you read about, for there are hedges and walls and gates that lock, and lots of separate little houses for the gardeners and people.

There is a *delicious* garden! I never saw such a garden—large and shady, full of box-bordered paths, and lined with long grape-covered arbors with seats under them.

There were greenhouses, but they are all broken now.

There was some legal trouble, I believe, something about the heirs and coheirs; anyhow, the place has been empty for years.

That spoils my ghostliness, I am afraid, but I don't care—there is something strange about the house—I can feel it.

I even said so to John one moonlight evening, but he said what I felt was a draught, and shut the window.

I get unreasonably angry with John sometimes. I'm sure I never used to be so sensitive. I think it is due to this nervous condition.

But John says if I feel so, I shall neglect proper self-control; so I take pains to control myself—before him, at least, and that makes me very tired.

I don't like our room a bit. I wanted one downstairs that opened on the piazza and had roses all over the window, and such pretty old-fashioned chintz hangings! But John would not hear of it.

He said there was only one window and not room for two beds, and no near room for him if he took another.

He is very careful and loving, and hardly lets me stir without special direction.

I have a schedule prescription for each hour in the day; he takes all care from me, and so I feel basely ungrateful not to value it more.

He said we came here solely on my account, that I was to have perfect rest and all the air I could get. "Your exercise depends on your strength, my dear," said he, "and your food somewhat on your appetite; but air you can absorb all the time." So we took the nursery at the top of the house.

It is a big, airy room, the whole floor nearly, with windows that look all ways, and air and sunshine galore. It was nursery first and then playroom and gymnasium, I should judge; for the windows are barred for little children, and there are rings and things in the walls.

The paint and paper look as if a boys' school had used it. It is stripped off—the paper—in great patches all around the head of my bed, about as far as I can reach, and in a great place on the other side of the room low down. I never saw a worse paper in my life. One of those sprawling flamboyant patterns committing every artistic sin.

It is dull enough to confuse the eye in following, pronounced enough to constantly irritate and provoke study, and when you follow the lame uncertain curves for a little distance they suddenly commit suicide—plunge off at outrageous angles, destroy themselves in unheard-of contradictions.

The color is repellent, almost revolting; a smouldering unclean yellow, strangely faded by the slow-turning sunlight. It is a dull yet lurid orange in some places, a sickly sulphur tint in others.

No wonder the children hated it! I should hate it myself if I had to live in this room long.

There comes John, and I must put this away—he hates to have me write a word.

o o o

We have been here two weeks, and I haven't felt like writing before, since that first day.

I am sitting by the window now, up in this atrocious nursery, and there is nothing to hinder my writing as much as I please, save lack of strength.

John is away all day, and even some nights when his cases are serious.

I am glad my case is not serious!

But these nervous troubles are dreadfully depressing.

John does not know how much I really suffer. He knows there is no reason to suffer, and that satisfies him.

Of course it is only nervousness. It does weigh on me so not to do my duty in any way!

I mean to be such a help to John, such a real rest and comfort, and here I am a comparative burden already!

Nobody would believe what an effort it is to do what little I am able—to dress and entertain, and order things.

It is fortunate Mary is so good with the baby. Such a dear baby!

And yet I *cannot* be with him, it makes me so nervous.

I suppose John never was nervous in his life. He laughs at me so about this wallpaper!

At first he meant to repaper the room, but afterwards he said that I was letting it get the better of me, and that nothing was worse for a nervous patient than to give way to such fancies.

He said that after the wallpaper was changed it would be the heavy bedstead, and then the barred windows, and then that gate at the head of the stairs, and so on.

"You know the place is doing you good," he said, "and really, dear, I don't care to renovate the house just for a three months' rental."

"Then do let us go downstairs," I said. "There are such pretty rooms there."

Then he took me in his arms and called me a blessed little goose, and said he would go down cellar, if I wished, and have it whitewashed into the bargain.

But he is right enough about the beds and windows and things.

It is as airy and comfortable a room as anyone need wish, and, of course, I would not be so silly as to make him uncomfortable just for a whim.

I'm really getting quite fond of the big room, all but that horrid paper.

Out of one window I can see the garden—those mysterious deep-shaded arbors, the riotous old-fashioned flowers, and bushes and gnarly trees.

Out of another I get a lovely view of the bay and a little private wharf belonging to the estate. There is a beautiful shaded lane that runs down there from the house. I always fancy I see people walking in these numerous paths and arbors, but John has cautioned me not to give way to fancy in the least. He says that with my imaginative power and habit of story-making, a nervous weakness like mine is sure to lead to all manner of excited fancies, and that I ought to use my will and good sense to check the tendency. So I try.

I think sometimes that if I were only well enough to write a little it would relieve the press of ideas and rest me.

But I find I get pretty tired when I try.

It is so discouraging not to have any advice and companionship about my work. When I get really well, John says we will ask Cousin Henry and Julia down for a long visit; but he says he would as soon put fireworks in my pillow-case as to let me have those stimulating people about now.

I wish I could get well faster.

But I must not think about that. This paper looks to me as if it *knew* what a vicious influence it had!

There is a recurrent spot where the pattern lolls like a broken neck and two bulbous eyes stare at you upside down.

I get positively angry with the impertinence of it and the everlastingness. Up and down and sideways they crawl, and those absurd unblinking eyes are everywhere. There is one place where two breadths didn't match, and the eyes go all up and down the line, one a little higher than the other.

I never saw so much expression in an inanimate thing before, and we all know how much expression they have! I used to lie awake as a child and get more entertainment and terror out of blank walls and plain furniture than most children could find in a toy-store.

I remember what a kindly wink the knobs of our big old bureau used to have, and there was one chair that always seemed like a strong friend.

I used to feel that if any of the other things looked too fierce I could always hop into that chair and be safe.

The furniture in this room is no worse than inharmonious, however, for we had to bring it all from downstairs. I suppose when this was used as a playroom they had to take the nursery things out, and no wonder! I never saw such ravages as the children have made here.

The wallpaper, as I said before, is torn off in spots, and it sticketh closer than a brother—they must have had perseverance as well as hatred.

Then the floor is scratched and gouged and splintered, the plaster itself is dug out here and there, and this great heavy bed which is all we found in the room, looks as if it had been through the wars.

But I don't mind it a bit—only the paper.

There comes John's sister. Such a dear girl as she is, and so careful of me! I must not let her find me writing.

She is a perfect and enthusiastic housekeeper, and hopes for no better profession. I verily believe she thinks it is the writing which made me sick!

But I can write when she is out, and see her a long way off from these windows.

There is one that commands the road, a lovely shaded winding road, and one that just looks off over the country. A lovely country, too, full of great elms and velvet meadows.

This wallpaper has a kind of sub-pattern in a different shade, a particularly irritating one, for you can only see it in certain lights, and not clearly then.

But in the places where it isn't faded and where the sun is just so—I can see a strange, provoking, formless sort of figure that seems to skulk about behind that silly and conspicuous front design.

There's sister on the stairs!

o o o

Well, the Fourth of July is over! The people are all gone, and I am tired out. John thought it might do me good to see a little company, so we just had Mother and Nellie and the children down for a week.

Of course I didn't do a thing. Jennie sees to everything now.

But it tired me all the same.

John says if I don't pick up faster he shall send me to Weir Mitchell in the fall.

But I don't want to go there at all. I had a friend who was in his hands once, and she says he is just like John and my brother, only more so!

Besides, it is such an undertaking to go so far.

I don't feel as if it was worthwhile to turn my hand over for anything, and I'm getting dreadfully fretful and querulous.

I cry at nothing, and cry most of the time.

Of course I don't when John is here, or anybody else, but when I am alone.

And I am alone a good deal just now. John is kept in town very often by serious cases, and Jennie is good and lets me alone when I want her to.

So I walk a little in the garden or down that lovely lane, sit on the porch under the roses, and lie down up here a good deal.

I'm getting really fond of the room in spite of the wallpaper. Perhaps because of the wallpaper.

It dwells in my mind so!

I lie here on this great immovable bed—it is nailed down, I believe—and follow that pattern about by the hour. It is as good as gymnastics, I assure you. I start, we'll say, at the bottom, down in the corner over there where it has not been touched, and I determine for the thousandth time that I *will* follow that pointless pattern to some sort of conclusion.

I know a little of the principle of design, and I know this thing was not arranged on any laws of radiation, or alternation, or repetition, or symmetry, or anything else that I ever heard of.

It is repeated, of course, by the breadths, but not otherwise.

Looked at in one way, each breadth stands alone; the bloated curves and flourishes—a kind of "debased Romanesque"[1] with delirium tremens—go waddling up and down in isolated columns of fatuity.

But, on the other hand, they connect diagonally, and the sprawling outlines run off in great slanting waves of optic horror, like a lot of wallowing sea-weeds in full chase.

The whole thing goes horizontally, too, at least it seems so, and I exhaust myself trying to distinguish the order of its going in that direction.

They have used a horizontal breadth for a frieze, and that adds wonderfully to the confusion.

There is one end of the room where it is almost intact, and there, when the crosslights fade and the low sun shines directly upon it, I can almost fancy radiation after all—the interminable grotesque seems to form around a common center and rush off in headlong plunges of equal distraction.

It makes me tired to follow it. I will take a nap, I guess.

---

1 "Romanesque" is a style of architecture originating in the eleventh and twelfth centuries.

○ ○ ○

I don't know why I should write this.

I don't want to.

I don't feel able.

And I know John would think it absurd. But I *must* say what I feel and think in some way—it is such a relief!

But the effort is getting to be greater than the relief.

Half the time now I am awfully lazy, and lie down ever so much.

John says I mustn't lose my strength, and has me take cod liver oil and lots of tonics and things, to say nothing of the ale and wine and rare meat.

Dear John! He loves me very dearly, and hates to have me sick. I tried to have a real earnest reasonable talk with him the other day, and tell him how I wish he would let me go and make a visit to Cousin Henry and Julia.

But he said I wasn't able to go, nor able to stand it after I got there; and I did not make out a very good case for myself, for I was crying before I had finished.

It is getting to be a great effort for me to think straight. Just this nervous weakness, I suppose.

And dear John gathered me up in his arms, and just carried me upstairs and laid me on the bed, and sat by me and read to me till it tired my head.

He said I was his darling and his comfort and all he had, and that I must take care of myself for his sake, and keep well.

He says no one but myself can help me out of it, that I must use my will and self-control and not let any silly fancies run away with me.

There's one comfort—the baby is well and happy, and does not have to occupy this nursery with the horrid wallpaper.

If we had not used it, that blessed child would have! What a fortunate escape! Why, I wouldn't have a child of mine, an impressionable little thing, live in such a room for worlds.

I never thought of it before, but it is lucky that John kept me here after all, I can stand it so much easier than a baby, you see.

Of course I never mention it to them any more—I am too wise—but I keep watch for it all the same.

There are things in that paper that nobody knows about but me, or ever will.

Behind that outside pattern the dim shapes get clearer every day.

It is always the same shape, only very numerous.

And it is like a woman stooping down and creeping about behind that pattern. I don't like it a bit. I wonder—I begin to think—I wish John would take me away from here!

○ ○ ○

It is so hard to talk with John about my case, because he is so wise, and because he loves me so.

But I tried it last night.

It was moonlight. The moon shines in all around just as the sun does.

I hate to see it sometimes, it creeps so slowly, and always comes in by one window or another.

John was asleep and I hated to waken him, so I kept still and watched the moonlight on that undulating wallpaper till I felt creepy.

The faint figure behind seemed to shake the pattern, just as if she wanted to get out.

I got up softly and went to feel and see if the paper *did* move, and when I came back John was awake.

"What is it, little girl?" he said. "Don't go walking about like that—you'll get cold."

I thought it was a good time to talk, so I told him that I really was not gaining here, and that I wished he would take me away.

"Why, darling!" said he. "Our lease will be up in three weeks, and I can't see how to leave before."

"The repairs are not done at home, and I cannot possibly leave town just now. Of course if you were in any danger, I could and would, but you really are better, dear, whether you can see it or not. I am a doctor, dear, and I know. You are gaining flesh and color, your appetite is better, I feel really much easier about you."

"I don't weigh a bit more," said I, "nor as much; and my appetite may be better in the evening when you are here but it is worse in the morning when you are away!"

"Bless her little heart!" said he with a big hug. "She shall be as sick as she pleases! But now let's improve the shining hours by going to sleep, and talk about it in the morning!"

"And you won't go away?" I asked gloomily.

"Why, how can I, dear? It is only three weeks more and then we will take a nice little trip of a few days while Jennie is getting the house ready. Really, dear, you are better!"

"Better in body perhaps—" I began, and stopped short, for he sat up straight and looked at me with such a stern, reproachful look that I could not say another word.

"My darling," said he, "I beg of you, for my sake and for our child's sake, as well as your own, that you will never for one instant let that idea enter your mind! There is nothing so dangerous, so fascinating, to a temperament like yours. It is a false and foolish fancy. Can you not trust me as a physician when I tell you so?"

So of course I said no more on that score, and we went to sleep before long. He thought I was asleep first, but I wasn't, and lay there for hours trying to decide whether that front pattern and the back pattern really did move together or separately.

o o o

On a pattern like this, by daylight, there is a lack of sequence, a defiance of law, that is a constant irritant to a normal mind.

The color is hideous enough, and unreliable enough, and infuriating enough, but the pattern is torturing.

You think you have mastered it, but just as you get well under way in following, it turns a back-somersault and there you are. It slaps you in the face, knocks you down, and tramples upon you. It is like a bad dream.

The outside pattern is a florid arabesque, reminding one of a fungus. If you can imagine a toadstool in joints, an interminable string of toadstools, budding and sprouting in endless convolutions—why, that is something like it.

That is, sometimes!

There is one marked peculiarity about this paper, a thing nobody seems to notice but myself, and that is that it changes as the light changes.

When the sun shoots in through the east window—I always watch for that first long, straight ray—it changes so quickly that I never can quite believe it.

That is why I watch it always.

By moonlight—the moon shines in all night when there is a moon—I wouldn't know it was the same paper.

At night in any kind of light, in twilight, candlelight, lamplight, and worst of all by moonlight, it becomes bars! The outside pattern, I mean, and the woman behind it is as plain as can be.

I didn't realize for a long time what the thing was that showed behind, that dim sub-pattern, but now I am quite sure it is a woman.

By daylight she is subdued, quiet. I fancy it is the pattern that keeps her so still. It is so puzzling. It keeps me quiet by the hour.

I lie down ever so much now. John says it is good for me, and to sleep all I can.

Indeed he started the habit by making me lie down for an hour after each meal.

It is a very bad habit I am convinced, for you see, I don't sleep.

And that cultivates deceit, for I don't tell them I'm awake—O no!

The fact is I am getting a little afraid of John.

He seems very queer sometimes, and even Jennie has an inexplicable look.

It strikes me occasionally, just as a scientific hypothesis, that perhaps it is the paper!

I have watched John when he did not know I was looking, and come into the room suddenly on the most innocent excuses, and I've caught him several times *looking at the paper*! And Jennie too. I caught Jennie with her hand on it once.

She didn't know I was in the room, and when I asked her in a quiet, a very quiet voice, with the most restrained manner possible, what she was doing with the paper—she turned around as if she had been caught stealing, and looked quite angry—asked me why I should frighten her so!

Then she said that the paper stained everything it touched, that she had found yellow smooches on all my clothes and John's, and she wished we would be more careful!

Did not that sound innocent? But I know she was studying that pattern, and I am determined that nobody shall find it out but myself!

o o o

Life is very much more exciting now than it used to be. You see I have something more to expect, to look forward to, to watch. I really do eat better, and am more quiet than I was.

John is so pleased to see me improve! He laughed a little the other day, and said I seemed to be flourishing in spite of my wallpaper.

I turned it off with a laugh. I had no intention of telling him it was *because* of the wallpaper—he would make fun of me. He might even want to take me away.

I don't want to leave now until I have found it out. There is a week more, and I think that will be enough.

o o o

I'm feeling so much better!

I don't sleep much at night, for it is so interesting to watch developments; but I sleep a good deal during the daytime.

In the daytime it is tiresome and perplexing.

There are always new shoots on the fungus, and new shades of yellow all over it. I cannot keep count of them, though I have tried conscientiously.

It is the strangest yellow, that wallpaper! It makes me think of all the yellow things I ever saw—not beautiful ones like buttercups, but old, foul, bad yellow things.

But there is something else about that paper—the smell! I noticed it the moment we came into the room, but with so much air and sun it was not bad. Now we have had a week of fog and rain, and whether the windows are open or not, the smell is here.

It creeps all over the house.

I find it hovering in the dining-room, skulking in the parlor, hiding in the hall, lying in wait for me on the stairs.

It gets into my hair.

Even when I go to ride, if I turn my head suddenly and surprise it—there is that smell!

Such a peculiar odor, too! I have spent hours in trying to analyze it, to find what it smelled like.

It is not bad—at first—and very gentle, but quite the subtlest, most enduring odor I ever met.

In this damp weather it is awful, I wake up in the night and find it hanging over me.

It used to disturb me at first. I thought seriously of burning the house—to reach the smell.

But now I am used to it. The only thing I can think of that it is like is the *color* of the paper! A yellow smell.

There is a very funny mark on this wall, low down, near the mopboard. A streak that runs round the room. It goes behind every piece of furniture, except the bed, a long, straight, even *smooch*, as if it had been rubbed over and over.

I wonder how it was done and who did it, and what they did it for. Round and round and round—round and round and round—it makes me dizzy!

° ° °

I really have discovered something at last.

Through watching so much at night, when it changes so, I have finally found out.

The front pattern *does* move—and no wonder! The woman behind shakes it!

Sometimes I think there are a great many women behind, and sometimes only one, and she crawls around fast, and her crawling shakes it all over.

Then in the very bright spots she keeps still, and in the very shady spots she just takes hold of the bars and shakes them hard.

And she is all the time trying to climb through. But nobody could climb through that pattern—it strangles so; I think that is why it has so many heads.

They get through, and then the pattern strangles them off and turns them upside down, and makes their eyes white!

If those heads were covered or taken off it would not be half so bad.

° ° °

I think that woman gets out in the daytime!

And I'll tell you why—privately—I've seen her!

I can see her out of every one of my windows!

It is the same woman, I know, for she is always creeping, and most women do not creep by daylight.

I see her in that long shaded lane, creeping up and down. I see her in those dark grape arbors, creeping all around the garden.

I see her on that long road under the trees, creeping along, and when a carriage comes she hides under the blackberry vines.

I don't blame her a bit. It must be very humiliating to be caught creeping by daylight!

I always lock the door when I creep by daylight. I can't do it at night, for I know John would suspect something at once.

And John is so queer now that I don't want to irritate him. I wish he would take another room! Besides, I don't want anybody to get that woman out at night but myself.

I often wonder if I could see her out of all the windows at once.

But, turn as fast as I can, I can only see out of one at one time.

And though I always see her, she *may* be able to creep faster than I can turn! I have watched her sometimes away off in the open country, creeping as fast as a cloud shadow in a wind.

o o o

If only that top pattern could be gotten off from the under one! I mean to try it, little by little.

I have found out another funny thing, but I shan't tell it this time! It does not do to trust people too much.

There are only two more days to get this paper off, and I believe John is beginning to notice. I don't like the look in his eyes.

And I heard him ask Jennie a lot of professional questions about me. She had a very good report to give.

She said I slept a good deal in the daytime.

John knows I don't sleep very well at night, for all I'm so quiet!

He asked me all sorts of questions, too, and pretended to be very loving and kind.

As if I couldn't see through him!

Still, I don't wonder he acts so, sleeping under this paper for three months.

It only interests me, but I feel sure John and Jennie are affected by it.

o o o

Hurrah! This is the last day, but it is enough. John is to stay in town over night, and won't be out until this evening.

Jennie wanted to sleep with me—the sly thing; but I told her I should undoubtedly rest better for a night all alone.

That was clever, for really I wasn't alone a bit! As soon as it was moonlight and that poor thing began to crawl and shake the pattern, I got up and ran to help her.

I pulled and she shook, I shook and she pulled, and before morning we had peeled off yards of that paper.

A strip about as high as my head and half around the room.

And then when the sun came and that awful pattern began to laugh at me, I declared I would finish it today!

We go away tomorrow, and they are moving all my furniture down again to leave things as they were before.

Jennie looked at the wall in amazement, but I told her merrily that I did it out of pure spite at the vicious thing.

She laughed and said she wouldn't mind doing it herself, but I must not get tired.

How she betrayed herself that time!

But I am here, and no person touches this paper but Me—not *alive*!

She tried to get me out of the room—it was too patent! But I said it was so quiet and empty and clean now that I believed I would lie down again and sleep all I could; and not to wake me even for dinner—I would call when I woke.

So now she is gone, and the servants are gone, and the things are gone, and there is nothing left but that great bedstead nailed down, with the canvas mattress we found on it.

We shall sleep downstairs tonight, and take the boat home tomorrow.

I quite enjoy the room, now it is bare again.

How those children did tear about here!

This bedstead is fairly gnawed!

But I must get to work.

I have locked the door and thrown the key down into the front path.

I don't want to go out, and I don't want to have anybody come in, till John comes.

I want to astonish him.

I've got a rope up here that even Jennie did not find. If that woman does get out, and tries to get away, I can tie her!

But I forgot I could not reach far without anything to stand on!

This bed will *not* move!

I tried to lift and push it until I was lame, and then I got so angry I bit off a little piece at one corner—but it hurt my teeth.

Then I peeled off all the paper I could reach standing on the floor. It sticks horribly and the pattern just enjoys it! All those strangled heads and bulbous eyes and waddling fungus growths just shriek with derision!

I am getting angry enough to do something desperate. To jump out of the window would be admirable exercise, but the bars are too strong even to try.

Besides I wouldn't do it. Of course not. I know well enough that a step like that is improper and might be misconstrued.

I don't like to *look* out of the windows even—there are so many of those creeping women, and they creep so fast.

I wonder if they all come out of that wallpaper as I did?

But I am securely fastened now by my well-hidden rope—you don't get me out in the road there!

I suppose I shall have to get back behind the pattern when it comes night, and that is hard!

It is so pleasant to be out in this great room and creep around as I please!

I don't want to go outside. I won't, even if Jennie asks me to.

For outside you have to creep on the ground, and everything is green instead of yellow.

But here I can creep smoothly on the floor, and my shoulder just fits in that long smooch around the wall, so I cannot lose my way.

Why there's John at the door!

It is no use, young man, you can't open it!

How he does call and pound!

Now he's crying to Jennie for an ax.

It would be a shame to break down that beautiful door!

"John dear!" said I in the gentlest voice. "The key is down by the front steps, under a plantain leaf!"

That silenced him for a few moments.

Then he said—very quietly indeed, "Open the door, my darling!"

"I can't," said I. "The key is down by the front door under a plantain leaf!"

And then I said it again, several times, very gently and slowly, and said it so often that he had to go and see, and he got it of course, and came in. He stopped short by the door.

"What is the matter?" he cried. "For God's sake, what are you doing!"

I kept on creeping just the same, but I looked at him over my shoulder.

"I've got out at last," said I, "in spite of you and Jane! And I've pulled off most of the paper, so you can't put me back!"

Now why should that man have fainted? But he did, and right across my path by the wall, so that I had to creep over him every time!

—1892

STEPHEN CRANE

Stephen Crane was the youngest of 14 children of a Methodist minister who wrote about the evils of drinking and dance, and a mother who lobbied on behalf of the New Jersey Women's Christian Temperance Union. Born in 1871 in Newark, New Jersey, Crane lived only to the age of 28, but produced a substantial body of work. Best known for the novels *Maggie: A Girl of the Streets* (1893) and *The Red Badge of Courage: An Episode of the American Civil War* (1895), he also wrote numerous other novels, books of poetry, short story collections, sketches, and articles.

Crane's father died of heart failure when Stephen was eight years old, and his mother supported the family by lecturing and writing about religious events and doing good works. Between 1888 and 1891, Crane attended four post-secondary institutions (including Syracuse University and Claverack College), but he never finished his schooling at any of them, stating at one point that he "preferred base-ball."

Crane moved to New York City to work as a freelance newspaper reporter and lived in poverty in the Lower East Side, fraternizing with prostitutes, homeless people, and struggling visual artists, experiences he drew upon both in *Maggie* and in *George's Mother* (1896). *Maggie* attracted the attention of writers Hamlin Garland and William Dean Howells when it appeared; the publication of *The Red Badge of Courage* (when Crane was only 23) made him an overnight sensation in both the United States and Britain.

Crane became a traveling correspondent and worked all over the world, including reporting on the Greco-Turkish and Spanish-American Wars. In 1898, he moved to England and lived with his lover and companion, Cora Taylor (the former madam of a Jacksonville brothel called House de Dream), while attempting to evade his creditors and unwelcome guests. During this period Crane and Taylor made friends with writers such as H.G. Wells, Joseph Conrad, and Henry James.

Crane never achieved the same level of success with his other writings that he had with *The Red Badge of Courage*. Never completely healthy, Crane contracted tuberculosis and sought treatment at a sanatorium in southern Germany, where he died on June 5, 1900.

The short story "The Open Boat" first appeared in *Scribner's Magazine* in 1897. It is based on a factual account Crane published shortly after he survived the shipwreck of a freighter named the *Commodore* off the coast of Florida. The story's apparent simplicity—four men rowing for their lives in a dinghy—belies the complexity of its investigation into the nature of interpretation and belief.

The Open Boat

STEPHEN CRANE

A Tale Intended to Be after the Fact: Being the Experience of Four Men from the Sunk Steamer COMMODORE

I

NONE OF THEM knew the color of the sky. Their eyes glanced level and were fastened upon the waves that swept toward them. These waves were of the hue of slate, save for the tops, which were of foaming white, and all of the men knew the colors of the sea. The horizon narrowed and widened, and dipped and rose, and at all times its edge was jagged with waves that seemed thrust up in points like rocks.

Many a man ought to have a bathtub larger than the boat which here rode upon the sea. These waves were most wrongfully and barbarously abrupt and tall, and each froth-top was a problem in small-boat navigation.

The cook squatted in the bottom, and looked with both eyes at the six inches of gunwale which separated him from the ocean. His sleeves were rolled over his fat forearms, and the two flaps of his unbuttoned vest dangled as he bent to bail out the boat. Often he said, "Gawd! that was a narrow clip." As he remarked it he invariably gazed eastward over the broken sea.

The oiler, steering with one of the two oars in the boat, sometimes raised himself suddenly to keep clear of water that swirled in over the stern. It was a thin little oar, and it seemed often ready to snap.

The correspondent, pulling at the other oar, watched the waves and wondered why he was there.

The injured captain, lying in the bow, was at this time buried in that profound dejection and indifference which comes, temporarily at least, to even the bravest and most enduring when, willy-nilly, the firm fails, the army loses, the ship goes down. The mind of the master of a vessel is rooted deep in the timbers of her, though he command for a day or a decade; and this captain had on him the stern impression of a scene in the grays of dawn of seven turned faces, and later a stump of a topmast with a white ball on it, that slashed to and fro at the waves, went low and lower, and down. Thereafter there was something strange in his voice. Although steady, it was deep with mourning, and of a quality beyond oration or tears.

"Keep'er a little more south, Billie," said he.

"A little more south, sir," said the oiler in the stern.

A seat in his boat was not unlike a seat upon a bucking broncho, and by the same token a broncho is not much smaller. The craft pranced and reared and plunged like an animal. As each wave came, and she rose for it, she seemed like a horse making at a fence outrageously high. The manner of her scramble over these walls of water is a mystic thing, and, moreover, at the top of them were ordinarily these problems in white water, the foam racing down from the summit of each wave requiring a new leap, and a leap from the air. Then, after scornfully bumping a crest, she would slide and race and splash down a long incline, and arrive bobbing and nodding in front of the next menace.

A singular disadvantage of the sea lies in the fact that after successfully surmounting one wave you discover that there is another behind it just as important and just as nervously anxious to do something effective in the way of swamping boats. In a ten-foot dinghy one can get an idea of the resources of the sea in the line of waves that is not probable to the average experience, which is never at sea in a dinghy. As each slaty wall of water approached, it shut all else from the view of the men in the boat, and it was not difficult to imagine that this particular wave was the final outburst of the ocean, the last effort of the grim water. There was a terrible grace in the move of the waves, and they came in silence, save for the snarling of the crests.

In the wan light the faces of the men must have been gray. Their eyes must have glinted in strange ways as they gazed steadily astern. Viewed from a balcony, the whole thing would, doubtless, have been weirdly picturesque. But the men in the boat had no time to see it, and if they had had leisure, there were other things to occupy their minds. The sun swung steadily up the sky, and they knew it was broad day because the color of the sea changed from slate to emerald-green streaked with amber lights, and the foam was like tumbling snow. The process of the breaking day was unknown to them. They were aware only of this effect upon the color of the waves that rolled toward them.

In disjointed sentences the cook and the correspondent argued as to the difference between a life-saving station and a house of refuge. The cook had said: "There's a house of refuge just north of the Mosquito Inlet Light, and as soon as they see us they'll come off in their boat and pick us up."

"As soon as who see us?" said the correspondent.

"The crew," said the cook.

"Houses of refuge don't have crews," said the correspondent. "As I understand them, they are only places where clothes and grub are stored for the benefit of shipwrecked people. They don't carry crews."

"Oh, yes, they do," said the cook.

"No, they don't," said the correspondent.

"Well, we're not there yet, anyhow," said the oiler, in the stern.

"Well," said the cook, "perhaps it's not a house of refuge that I'm thinking of as being near Mosquito Inlet Light; perhaps it's a life-saving station."

"We're not there yet," said the oiler in the stern.

II

AS THE BOAT bounced from the top of each wave the wind tore through the hair of the hatless men, and as the craft plopped her stern down again the spray slashed past them. The crest of each of these waves was a hill, from the top of which the men surveyed for a moment a broad tumultuous expanse, shining and wind-riven. It was probably splendid, it was probably glorious, this play of the free sea, wild with lights of emerald and white and amber.

"Bully good thing it's an on-shore wind," said the cook. "If not, where would we be? Wouldn't have a show."

"That's right," said the correspondent.

The busy oiler nodded his assent.

Then the captain, in the bow, chuckled in a way that expressed humor, contempt, tragedy, all in one. "Do you think we've got much of a show now, boys?" said he.

Whereupon the three were silent, save for a trifle of hemming and hawing. To express any particular optimism at this time they felt to be childish and stupid, but they all doubtless possessed this sense of the situation in their minds. A young man thinks doggedly at such times. On the other hand, the ethics of their condition was decidedly against any open suggestion of hopelessness. So they were silent.

"Oh, well," said the captain, soothing his children, "we'll get ashore all right."

But there was that in his tone which made them think; so the oiler quoth, "Yes! if this wind holds."

The cook was bailing. "Yes! if we don't catch hell in the surf."

Canton-flannel gulls flew near and far. Sometimes they sat down on the sea, near patches of brown seaweed that rolled over the waves with a movement like carpets on a line in a gale. The birds sat comfortably in groups, and they were envied by some in the dinghy, for the wrath of the sea was no more to them than it was to a covey of prairie chickens a thousand miles inland. Often they came very close and stared at the men with black bead-like eyes. At these times they were uncanny and sinister in their unblinking scrutiny, and the men hooted angrily at them, telling them to be gone. One came, and evidently decided to alight on the top of the captain's head. The bird flew parallel to the boat and did not circle, but made short sidelong jumps in the air in chicken fashion. His black eyes were wistfully fixed upon the captain's head. "Ugly brute," said the oiler to the bird. "You look as if you were made with a jackknife." The cook and the correspondent swore darkly at the creature. The captain naturally wished to knock it away with the end of the heavy painter, but he did not dare do it, because anything resembling an emphatic gesture would have capsized this freighted boat; and so, with his open hand, the captain gently and carefully waved the gull away. After it had been discouraged from the pursuit the captain breathed easier on account of his hair, and others breathed easier because the bird struck their minds at this time as being somehow gruesome and ominous.

In the meantime the oiler and the correspondent rowed; and also they rowed. They sat together in the same seat, and each rowed an oar. Then the oiler took both oars; then the correspondent took both oars, then the oiler; then the correspondent. They rowed and they rowed. The very ticklish part of the business was when the time came for the reclining one in the stern to take his turn at the oars. By the very last star of truth, it is easier to steal eggs from under a hen than it was to change seats in the dinghy. First the man in the stern slid his hand along the thwart and moved with care, as if he were of Sèvres. Then the man in the rowing-seat slid his hand along the other thwart. It was all done with the most extraordinary care. As the two sidled past each other, the whole party kept watchful eyes on the coming wave, and the captain cried: "Look out, now! Steady, there!"

The brown mats of seaweed that appeared from time to time were like islands, bits of earth. They were traveling, apparently, neither one way nor the other. They were, to all intents, stationary. They informed the men in the boat that it was making progress slowly toward the land.

The captain, rearing cautiously in the bow after the dinghy soared on a great swell, said that he had seen the lighthouse at Mosquito Inlet. Presently the cook remarked that he had seen it. The correspondent was at the oars then, and for some reason he too wished to look at the lighthouse; but his back was toward the far shore, and the waves were important, and for some time he could not seize an opportunity to turn his head. But at last there came a wave more gentle than the others, and when at the crest of it he swiftly scoured the western horizon.

"See it?" said the captain.

"No," said the correspondent, slowly; "I didn't see anything."

"Look again," said the captain. He pointed. "It's exactly in that direction."

At the top of another wave the correspondent did as he was bid, and this time his eyes chanced on a small, still thing on the edge of the swaying horizon. It was precisely like the point of a pin. It took an anxious eye to find a lighthouse so tiny.

"Think we'll make it, Captain?"

"If this wind holds and the boat don't swamp, we can't do much else," said the captain.

The little boat, lifted by each towering sea and splashed viciously by the crests, made progress that in the absence of seaweed was not apparent to those in her. She seemed just a wee thing wallowing, miraculously top up, at the mercy of five oceans. Occasionally a great spread of water, like white flames, swarmed into her.

"Bail her, cook," said the captain, serenely.

"All right, Captain," said the cheerful cook.

III

IT WOULD be difficult to describe the subtle brotherhood of men that was here established on the seas. No one said that it was so. No one mentioned it. But it dwelt in the boat, and each man felt it warm him. They were a captain, an oiler, a cook, and a correspondent, and they were friends—friends in a more curiously iron-bound degree than may be common. The hurt captain, lying against the water jar in the bow, spoke always in a low voice and calmly; but he could never command a more ready and swiftly obedient crew than the motley three of the dinghy. It was more than a mere recognition of what was best for the common safety. There was surely in it a quality that was personal and heart-felt. And after this devotion to the commander of the boat, there was this comradeship, that the correspondent, for instance, who had been taught to be cynical of men, knew even at the time was the best experience of his life. But no one said that it was so. No one mentioned it.

"I wish we had a sail," remarked the captain. "We might try my overcoat on the end of an oar, and give you two boys a chance to rest." So the cook and the correspondent held the mast and spread wide the overcoat; the oiler steered; and the little boat made good way with her new rig. Sometimes the oiler had to scull sharply to keep a sea from breaking into the boat, but otherwise sailing was a success.

Meanwhile the lighthouse had been growing slowly larger. It had now almost assumed color, and appeared like a little gray shadow on the sky. The man at the oars could not be prevented from turning his head rather often to try for a glimpse of this little gray shadow.

At last, from the top of each wave, the men in the tossing boat could see land. Even as the lighthouse was an upright shadow on the sky, this land seemed but a long black shadow on the sea. It certainly was thinner than paper. "We must be about opposite New Smyrna," said the cook, who had coasted this shore often in schooners. "Captain, by the way, I believe they abandoned that life-saving station there about a year ago."

"Did they?" said the captain.

The wind slowly died away. The cook and the correspondent were not now obliged to slave in order to hold high the oar. But the waves continued their old impetuous swooping at the dinghy, and the little craft, no longer underway, struggled woundily over them. The oiler or the correspondent took the oars again.

Shipwrecks are *apropos* of nothing. If men could only train for them and have them occur when the men had reached pink condition, there would be less drowning at sea. Of the four in the dinghy none had slept any time worth mentioning for two days and two nights previous to embarking in the dinghy, and in the excitement of clambering about the deck of a foundering ship they had also forgotten to eat heartily.

For these reasons, and for others, neither the oiler nor the correspondent was fond of rowing at this time. The correspondent wondered ingenuously how in the name of all that was sane could there be people who thought it amusing to row a boat. It was not an amusement; it was a diabolical punishment, and even a genius of mental aberrations could never conclude that it was anything but a horror to the muscles and a crime against the back. He mentioned to the boat in general how the amusement of rowing struck him, and the weary-faced oiler smiled in full sympathy. Previously to the foundering, by the way, the oiler had worked a double watch in the engine-room of the ship.

"Take her easy, now, boys," said the captain. "Don't spend yourselves. If we have to run a surf you'll need all your strength, because we'll sure have to swim for it. Take your time."

Slowly the land arose from the sea. From a black line it became a line of black and a line of white—trees and sand. Finally the captain said that he could make out a house on the shore. "That's the house of refuge, sure," said the cook. "They'll see us before long, and come out after us."

The distant lighthouse reared high. "The keeper ought to be able to make us out now, if he's looking through a glass," said the captain. "He'll notify the life-saving people."

"None of those other boats could have got ashore to give word of the wreck," said the oiler, in a low voice, "else the life-boat would be out hunting us."

Slowly and beautifully the land loomed out of the sea. The wind came again. It had veered from the northeast to the southeast. Finally a new sound struck the ears of the men in the boat. It was the low thunder of the surf on the shore. "We'll never be able to make the lighthouse now," said the captain. "Swing her head a little more north Billie."

"A little more north, sir," said the oiler.

Whereupon the little boat turned her nose once more down the wind, and all but the oarsman watched the shore grow. Under the influence of this expansion doubt and direful apprehension were leaving the minds of the men. The management of the boat was still most absorbing, but it could not prevent a quiet cheerfulness. In an hour, perhaps, they would be ashore.

Their backbones had become thoroughly used to balancing in the boat, and they now rode this wild colt of a dinghy like circus men. The correspondent thought that he had been drenched to the skin, but happening to feel in the top pocket of his coat, he found therein eight cigars. Four of them were soaked with sea-water; four were perfectly scatheless. After a search, somebody produced three dry matches; and thereupon the four waifs rode impudently in their little boat and, with an assurance of an impending rescue shining in their eyes, puffed at the big cigars, and judged well and ill of all men. Everybody took a drink of water.

IV

"COOK," remarked the captain, "there don't seem to be any signs of life about your house of refuge."

"No," replied the cook. "Funny they don't see us!"

A broad stretch of lowly coast lay before the eyes of the men. It was of low dunes topped with dark vegetation. The roar of the surf was plain, and sometimes they could see the white lip of a wave as it spun up the beach. A tiny house was blocked out black upon the sky. Southward, the slim lighthouse lifted its little gray length.

Tide, wind, and waves were swinging the dinghy northward. "Funny they don't see us," said the men.

The surf's roar was here dulled, but its tone was nevertheless thunderous and mighty. As the boat swam over the great rollers the men sat listening to this roar. "We'll swamp sure," said everybody.

It is fair to say here that there was not a life-saving station within twenty miles in either direction; but the men did not know this fact, and in consequence they made dark and opprobrious remarks concerning the eyesight of the nation's life-savers. Four scowling men sat in the dinghy and surpassed records in the invention of epithets.

"Funny they don't see us."

The light-heartedness of a former time had completely faded. To their sharpened minds it was easy to conjure pictures of all kinds of incompetency and blindness and, indeed, cowardice. There was the shore of the populous land, and it was bitter and bitter to them that from it came no sign.

"Well," said the captain, ultimately, "I suppose we'll have to make a try for ourselves. If we stay out here too long, we'll none of us have strength left to swim after the boat swamps."

And so the oiler, who was at the oars, turned the boat straight for the shore. There was a sudden tightening of muscles. There was some thinking.

"If we don't all get ashore," said the captain—"if we don't all get ashore, I suppose you fellows know where to send news of my finish?"

They then briefly exchanged some addresses and admonitions. As for the reflections of the men, there was a great deal of rage in them. Perchance they might be formulated thus: "If I am going to be drowned—if I am going to be drowned—if I am going to be drowned, why, in the name of the seven mad gods who rule the sea, was I allowed to come thus far and contemplate sand and trees? Was I brought here merely to have my nose dragged away as I was about to nibble the sacred cheese of life? It is preposterous. If this old ninny-woman, Fate, cannot do better than this, she should be deprived of the management of men's fortunes. She is an old hen who knows not her intention. If she has decided to drown me, why did she not do it in the beginning and save me all this trouble? The whole affair is absurd.... But no; she cannot mean to drown me. She dare not drown me. She cannot drown me. Not after all this work." Afterward the man might have had an impulse to shake his fist at the clouds. "Just you drown me, now, and then hear what I call you!"

The billows that came at this time were more formidable. They seemed always just about to break and roll over the little boat in a turmoil of foam. There was a preparatory and long growl in the speech of them. No mind unused to the sea would have concluded that the dinghy could ascend these sheer heights in time. The shore was still afar. The oiler was a wily surfman. "Boys," he said, swiftly, "she won't live three minutes more, and we're too far out to swim. Shall I take her to sea again, Captain?"

"Yes, go ahead!" said the captain.

This oiler, by a series of quick miracles and fast and steady oarsmanship, turned the boat in the middle of the surf and took her safely to sea again.

There was a considerable silence as the boat bumped over the furrowed sea to deeper water. Then somebody in gloom spoke: "Well, anyhow, they must have seen us from the shore by now."

The gulls went in slanting flight up the wind toward the gray, desolate east. A squall, marked by dingy clouds and clouds brick-red, like smoke from a burning building, appeared from the southeast.

"What do you think of those life-saving people? Ain't they peaches?"

"Funny they haven't seen us."

"Maybe they think we're out here for sport! Maybe they think we're fishin'. Maybe they think we're damned fools."

It was a long afternoon. A changed tide tried to force them southward, but wind and wave said northward. Far ahead, where coast-line, sea, and sky formed their mighty angle, there were little dots which seemed to indicate a city on the shore.

"St. Augustine?"

The captain shook his head. "Too near Mosquito Inlet."

And the oiler rowed, and then the correspondent rowed; then the oiler rowed. It was a weary business. The human back can become the seat of more aches and pains than are registered in books for the composite anatomy of a regiment. It is a limited area, but it can become the theater of innumerable muscular conflicts, tangles, wrenches, knots, and other comforts.

"Did you ever like to row, Billie?" asked the correspondent.

"No," said the oiler; "hang it!"

When one exchanged the rowing-seat for a place in the bottom of the boat, he suffered a bodily depression that caused him to be careless of everything save an obligation to wiggle one finger. There was cold seawater swashing to and fro in the boat, and he lay in it. His head, pillowed on a thwart, was within an inch of the swirl of a wave-crest, and sometimes a particularly obstreperous sea came inboard and drenched him once more. But these matters did not annoy him. It is almost certain that if the boat had capsized he would have tumbled comfortably out upon the ocean as if he felt sure that it was a great soft mattress.

"Look! There's a man on the shore!"

"Where?"

"There? See 'im? See 'im?"

"Yes, sure! He's walking along."

"Now he's stopped. Look! He's facing us!"

"He's waving at us!"

"So he is! By thunder!"

"Ah, now we're all right! Now we're all right! There'll be a boat out here for us in half an hour."

"He's going on. He's running. He's going up to that house there."

The remote beach seemed lower than the sea, and it required a searching glance to discern the little black figure. The captain saw a floating stick, and they rowed to it. A bath towel was by some weird chance in the boat, and, tying this on the stick, the captain waved it. The oarsman did not dare turn his head, so he was obliged to ask questions.

"What's he doing now?"

"He's standing still again. He's looking, I think.... There he goes again—toward the house.... Now he's stopped again."

"Is he waving at us?"

"No, not now; he was, though."

"Look! There comes another man!"

"He's running."

"Look at him go, would you!"

"Why, he's on a bicycle. Now he's met the other man. They're both waving at us. Look!"

"There comes something up the beach."

"What the devil is that thing?"

"Why, it looks like a boat."

"Why, certainly, it's a boat."

"No, it's on wheels."

"Yes, so it is. Well, that must be the life-boat. They drag them along shore on a wagon."

"That's the life-boat, sure."

"No, by God, it's—it's an omnibus."

"I tell you it's a life-boat."

"It is not! It's an omnibus. I can see it plain. See? One of these big hotel omnibuses."

"By thunder, you're right. It's an omnibus, sure as fate. What do you suppose they are doing with an omnibus? Maybe they are going around collecting the life-crew, hey?"

"That's it, likely. Look! There's a fellow waving a little black flag. He's standing on the steps of the omnibus. There come those other two fellows. Now they're all talking together. Look at the fellow with the flag. Maybe he ain't waving it!"

"That ain't a flag, is it? That's his coat. Why, certainly, that's his coat."

"So it is; it's his coat. He's taken it off and is waving it around his head. But would you look at him swing it!"

"Oh, say, there isn't any life-saving station there. That's just a winter-resort hotel omnibus that has brought over some of the boarders to see us drown."

"What's that idiot with the coat mean? What's he signaling, anyhow?"

"It looks as if he were trying to tell us to go north. There must be a life-saving station up there."

"No; he thinks we're fishing. Just giving us a merry hand. See? Ah, there, Willie!"

"Well, I wish I could make something out of those signals. What do you suppose he means?"

"He don't mean anything; he's just playing."

"Well, if he'd just signal us to try the surf again, or to go to sea and wait, or go north, or go south, or go to hell, there would be some reason in it. But look at him! He just stands there and keeps his coat revolving like a wheel. The ass!"

"There come more people."

"Now there's quite a mob. Look! Isn't that a boat?"

"Where? Oh, I see where you mean. No, that's no boat."

"That fellow is still waving his coat."

"He must think we like to see him do that. Why don't he quit it? It don't mean anything."

"I don't know. I think he is trying to make us go north. It must be that there's a life-saving station there somewhere."

"Say, he ain't tired yet. Look at 'im wave!"

"Wonder how long he can keep that up. He's been revolving his coat ever since he caught sight of us. He's an idiot. Why aren't they getting men to bring a boat out? A fishing boat—one of those big yawls—could come out here all right. Why don't he do something?"

"Oh, it's all right now."

"They'll have a boat out here for us in less than no time, now that they've seen us."

A faint yellow tone came into the sky over the low land. The shadows on the sea slowly deepened. The wind bore coldness with it, and the men began to shiver.

"Holy smoke!" said one, allowing his voice to express his impious mood, "if we keep on monkeying out here! If we've got to flounder out here all night!"

"Oh, we'll never have to stay here all night! Don't you worry. They've seen us now, and it won't be long before they'll come chasing out after us."

The shore grew dusky. The man waving a coat blended gradually into this gloom, and it swallowed in the same manner the omnibus and the group of people. The spray, when it dashed uproariously over the side, made the voyagers shrink and swear like men who were being branded.

"I'd like to catch the chump who waved the coat. I feel like socking him one, just for luck."

"Why? What did he do?"

"Oh, nothing, but then he seemed so damned cheerful."

In the meantime the oiler rowed, and then the correspondent rowed, and then the oiler rowed. Gray-faced and bowed forward, they mechanically, turn by turn, plied the leaden oars. The form of the lighthouse had vanished from the southern horizon, but finally a pale star appeared, just lifting from the sea. The streaked saffron in the west passed before the all-merging darkness, and the sea to the east was black. The land had vanished, and was expressed only by the low and drear thunder of the surf.

"If I am going to be drowned—if I am going to be drowned—if I am going to be drowned, why, in the name of the seven mad gods who rule the sea, was I allowed to come thus far and contemplate sand and trees? Was I brought here merely to have my nose dragged away as I was about to nibble the sacred cheese of life?"

The patient captain, drooped over the water-jar, was sometimes obliged to speak to the oarsman.

"Keep her head up! Keep her head up!"

"Keep her head up, sir." The voices were weary and low.

This was surely a quiet evening. All save the oarsman lay heavily and listlessly in the boat's bottom. As for him, his eyes were just capable of noting the tall black waves that swept forward in a most sinister silence, save for an occasional subdued growl of a crest.

The cook's head was on a thwart, and he looked without interest at the water under his nose. He was deep in other scenes. Finally he spoke. "Billie," he murmured, dreamfully, "what kind of pie do you like best?"

V

"PIE!" said the oiler and the correspondent, agitatedly. "Don't talk about those things, blast you!"

"Well," said the cook, "I was just thinking about ham sandwiches, and—"

A night on the sea in an open boat is a long night. As darkness settled finally, the shine of the light, lifting from the sea in the south, changed to full gold. On the northern horizon a new light appeared, a small bluish gleam on the edge of the waters. These two lights were the furniture of the world. Otherwise there was nothing but waves.

Two men huddled in the stern, and distances were so magnificent in the dinghy that the rower was enabled to keep his feet partly warm by thrusting them under his companions. Their legs indeed extended far under the rowing-seat until they touched the feet of the captain forward. Sometimes, despite the efforts of the tired oarsman, a wave came piling into the boat, an icy wave of the night, and the chilling water soaked them anew. They would twist their bodies for a moment and groan, and sleep the dead sleep once more, while the water in the boat gurgled about them as the craft rocked.

The plan of the oiler and the correspondent was for one to row until he lost the ability, and then arouse the other from his sea-water couch in the bottom of the boat.

The oiler plied the oars until his head drooped forward and the overpowering sleep blinded him; and he rowed yet afterward. Then he touched a man in the bottom of the boat, and called his name. "Will you spell me for a little while?" he said meekly.

"Sure, Billie," said the correspondent, awaking and dragging himself to a sitting position. They exchanged places carefully, and the oiler, cuddling down in the sea-water at the cook's side, seemed to go to sleep instantly.

The particular violence of the sea had ceased. The waves came without snarling. The obligation of the man at the oars was to keep the boat headed so that the tilt of the rollers would not capsize her, and to preserve her from filling when the crests rushed past. The black waves were silent and hard to be seen in the darkness. Often one was almost upon the boat before the oarsman was aware.

In a low voice the correspondent addressed the captain. He was not sure that the captain was awake, although this iron man seemed to be always awake. "Captain, shall I keep her making for that light north, sir?"

The same steady voice answered him. "Yes. Keep it about two points off the port bow."

The cook had tied a life-belt around himself in order to get even the warmth which this clumsy cork contrivance could donate, and he seemed almost stove-like when a rower, whose teeth invariably chattered wildly as soon as he ceased his labor, dropped down to sleep.

The correspondent, as he rowed, looked down at the two men sleeping underfoot. The cook's arm was around the oiler's shoulders, and, with their fragmentary clothing and haggard faces, they were the babes of the sea—a grotesque rendering of the old babes in the wood.

Later he must have grown stupid at his work, for suddenly there was a growling of water, and a crest came with a roar and a swash into the boat, and it was a wonder that it did not set the cook afloat in his life-belt. The cook continued to sleep, but the oiler sat up, blinking his eyes and shaking with the new cold.

"Oh, I'm awful sorry, Billie," said the correspondent, contritely.

"That's all right, old boy," said the oiler, and lay down again and was asleep.

Presently it seemed that even the captain dozed, and the correspondent thought that he was the one man afloat on all the ocean. The wind had a voice as it came over the waves, and it was sadder than the end.

There was a long, loud swishing astern of the boat, and a gleaming trail of phosphorescence, like blue flame, was furrowed on the black waters. It might have been made by a monstrous knife.

Then there came a stillness, while the correspondent breathed with open mouth and looked at the sea.

Suddenly there was another swish and another long flash of bluish light, and this time it was alongside the boat, and might almost have been reached with an oar. The correspondent saw an enormous fin speed like a shadow through the water, hurling the crystalline spray and leaving the long glowing trail.

The correspondent looked over his shoulder at the captain. His face was hidden, and he seemed to be asleep. He looked at the babes of the sea. They certainly were asleep. So, being bereft of sympathy, he leaned a little way to one side and swore softly into the sea.

But the thing did not then leave the vicinity of the boat. Ahead or astern, on one side or the other, at intervals long or short, fled the long sparkling streak, and there was to be heard the *whirroo* of the dark fin. The speed and power of the thing was greatly to be admired. It cut the water like a gigantic and keen projectile.

The presence of this biding thing did not affect the man with the same horror that it would if he had been a picnicker. He simply looked at the sea dully and swore in an undertone.

Nevertheless, it is true that he did not wish to be alone with the thing. He wished one of his companions to awake by chance and keep him company with it. But the captain hung motionless over the water-jar and the oiler and the cook in the bottom of the boat were plunged in slumber.

VI

"IF I AM going to be drowned—if I am going to be drowned—if I am going to be drowned, why, in the name of the seven mad gods who rule the sea, was I allowed to come thus far and contemplate sand and trees?"

During this dismal night, it may be remarked that a man would conclude that it was really the intention of the seven mad gods to drown him, despite the abominable injustice of it. For it was certainly an abominable injustice to drown a man who had worked so hard, so hard. The man felt it would be a crime most unnatural. Other people had drowned at sea since galleys swarmed with painted sails, but still—

When it occurs to a man that nature does not regard him as important, and that she feels she would not maim the universe by disposing of him, he at first wishes to throw bricks at the temple, and he hates deeply the fact that there are no bricks and no temples. Any visible expression of nature would surely be pelleted with his jeers.

Then, if there be no tangible thing to hoot, he feels, perhaps, the desire to confront a personification and indulge in pleas, bowed to one knee, and with hands supplicant, saying, "Yes, but I love myself."

A high cold star on a winter's night is the word he feels that she says to him. Thereafter he knows the pathos of his situation.

The men in the dinghy had not discussed these matters, but each had, no doubt, reflected upon them in silence and according to his mind. There was seldom any expression upon their faces save the general one of complete weariness. Speech was devoted to the business of the boat.

To chime the notes of his emotions, a verse mysteriously entered the correspondent's head. He had even forgotten that he had forgotten this verse, but it suddenly was in his mind.

> A soldier of the Legion lay dying in Algiers;
> There was lack of woman's nursing,
>   there was dearth of woman's tears;
> But a comrade stood beside him,
>   and he took the comrade's hand,
> And he said, "I never more shall see
>   my own, my native land."[1]

In his childhood the correspondent had been made acquainted with the fact that a soldier of the Legion lay dying in Algiers, but he had never regarded it as important. Myriads of his schoolfellows had informed him of the soldier's plight, but the dinning had naturally ended by making him perfectly indifferent. He had never considered it his affair that a soldier of the Legion lay dying in Algiers, nor had it appeared to him as a matter for sorrow. It was less to him than the breaking of a pencil's point.

Now, however, it quaintly came to him as a human, living thing. It was no longer merely a picture of a few throes in the breast of a poet, meanwhile drinking tea and warming his feet at the grate; it was an actuality—stern, mournful, and fine.

The correspondent plainly saw the soldier. He lay on the sand with his feet out straight and still. While his pale left hand was upon his chest in an attempt to thwart the going of his life, the blood came between his fingers. In the far Algerian distance, a city of low square forms was set against a sky that was faint with the last sunset hues. The correspondent, plying the oars and dreaming of the slow and slower movements of the lips of the soldier, was moved by a profound and perfectly impersonal comprehension. He was sorry for the soldier of the Legion who lay dying in Algiers.

The thing which had followed the boat and waited had evidently grown bored at the delay. There was no longer to be heard the slash of the cutwater, and there was no longer the flame of the long trail. The light in the north still glimmered, but it was apparently no nearer to the boat. Sometimes the boom of the surf rang in the correspondent's ears, and he turned the craft seaward then and rowed harder. Southward, some one had evidently built a watch-fire on the

---

1 From Caroline E.S. Norton's poem, "Bingen on the Rhine" (1883).

beach. It was too low and too far to be seen, but it made a shimmering, roseate reflection upon the bluff in back of it, and this could be discerned from the boat. The wind came stronger, and sometimes a wave suddenly raged out like a mountain-cat, and there was to be seen the sheen and sparkle of a broken crest.

The captain, in the bow, moved on his water-jar and sat erect. "Pretty long night," he observed to the correspondent. He looked at the shore. "Those life-saving people take their time."

"Did you see that shark playing around?"

"Yes, I saw him. He was a big fellow, all right."

"Wish I had known you were awake."

Later the correspondent spoke into the bottom of the boat. "Billie!" There was a slow and gradual disentanglement. "Billie, will you spell me?"

"Sure," said the oiler.

As soon as the correspondent touched the cold, comfortable seawater in the bottom of the boat and had huddled close to the cook's life-belt he was deep in sleep, despite the fact that his teeth played all the popular airs. This sleep was so good to him that it was but a moment before he heard a voice call his name in a tone that demonstrated the last stages of exhaustion. "Will you spell me?"

"Sure, Billie."

The light in the north had mysteriously vanished, but the correspondent took his course from the wide-awake captain.

Later in the night, they took the boat farther out to sea, and the captain directed the cook to take one oar at the stern and keep the boat facing the seas. He was to call out if he should hear the thunder of the surf. This plan enabled the oiler and the correspondent to get respite together. "We'll give those boys a chance to get into shape again," said the captain. They curled down and, after a few preliminary chatterings and trembles, slept once more the dead sleep. Neither knew they had bequeathed to the cook the company of another shark, or perhaps the same shark.

As the boat caroused on the waves, spray occasionally bumped over the side and gave them a fresh soaking, but this had no power to break their repose. The ominous slash of the wind and the water affected them as it would have affected mummies.

"Boys," said the cook, with the notes of every reluctance in his voice, "she's drifted in pretty close. I guess one of you had better take her to sea again." The correspondent, aroused, heard the crash of the toppled crests.

As he was rowing, the captain gave him some whiskey-and-water, and this steadied the chills out of him. "If I ever get ashore and anybody shows me even a photograph of an oar—"

At last there was a short conversation.

"Billie! ... Billie, will you spell me?"
"Sure," said the other.

VII

WHEN THE correspondent again opened his eyes, the sea and the sky were each of the gray hue of the dawning. Later, carmine and gold was painted upon the waters. The morning appeared finally, in its splendor, with a sky of pure blue, and the sunlight flamed on the tips of the waves.

On the distant dunes were set many little black cottages, and a tall white windmill reared above them. No man, nor dog, nor bicycle appeared on the beach. The cottages might have formed a deserted village.

The voyagers scanned the shore. A conference was held in the boat. "Well," said the captain, "if no help is coming, we might better try a run through the surf right away. If we stay out here much longer we will be too weak to do anything for ourselves at all." The others silently acquiesced in this reasoning. The boat was headed for the beach. The correspondent wondered if none ever ascended the tall wind-tower, and if then they never looked seaward. This tower was a giant, standing with its back to the plight of the ants. It represented in a degree, to the correspondent, the serenity of nature amid the struggles of the individual—nature in the wind, and nature in the vision of men. She did not seem cruel to him then, nor beneficent, nor treacherous, nor wise. But she was indifferent, flatly indifferent. It is, perhaps, plausible that a man in this situation, impressed with the unconcern of the universe, should see the innumerable flaws of his life, and have them taste wickedly in his mind, and wish for another chance. A distinction between right and wrong seems absurdly clear to him, then, in this new ignorance of the grave-edge, and he understands that if he were given another opportunity he would mend his conduct and his words, and be better and brighter during an introduction or at a tea.

"Now, boys," said the captain, "she is going to swamp sure. All we can do is to work her in as far as possible, and then when she swamps, pile out and scramble for the beach. Keep cool now, and don't jump until she swamps sure."

The oiler took the oars. Over his shoulder he scanned the surf. "Captain," he said, "I think I'd better bring her about and keep her head-on to the seas and back her in."

"All right, Billie," said the captain. "Back her in." The oiler swung the boat then, and, seated in the stern, the cook and the correspondent were obliged to look over their shoulders to contemplate the lonely and indifferent shore.

The monstrous inshore rollers heaved the boat high until the men were again enabled to see the white sheets of water scudding up the slanted beach. "We won't get in very close," said the captain. Each time a man could wrest his attention from the rollers, he turned his glance toward the shore, and in the expression of the eyes during this contemplation there was a singular quality. The correspondent, observing the others, knew that they were not afraid, but the full meaning of their glances was shrouded.

As for himself, he was too tired to grapple fundamentally with the fact. He tried to coerce his mind into thinking of it, but the mind was dominated at this time by the muscles, and the muscles said they did not care. It merely occurred to him that if he should drown it would be a shame.

There were no hurried words, no pallor, no plain agitation. The men simply looked at the shore. "Now, remember to get well clear of the boat when you jump," said the captain.

Seaward the crest of a roller suddenly fell with a thunderous crash, and the long white comber came roaring down upon the boat.

"Steady now," said the captain. The men were silent. They turned their eyes from the shore to the comber and waited. The boat slid up the incline, leaped at the furious top, bounced over it, and swung down the long back of the wave. Some water had been shipped, and the cook bailed it out.

But the next crest crashed also. The tumbling, boiling flood of white water caught the boat and whirled it almost perpendicular. Water swarmed in from all sides. The correspondent had his hands on the gunwale at this time, and when the water entered at that place he swiftly withdrew his fingers, as if he objected to wetting them.

The little boat, drunken with this weight of water, reeled and snuggled deeper into the sea.

"Bail her out, cook! Bail her out!" said the captain.

"All right, Captain," said the cook.

"Now, boys, the next one will do for us sure," said the oiler. "Mind to jump clear of the boat."

The third wave moved forward, huge, furious, implacable. It fairly swallowed the dinghy and almost simultaneously the men tumbled into the sea. A piece of life-belt had lain in the bottom of the boat, and as the correspondent went overboard he held this to his chest with his left hand.

The January water was icy, and he reflected immediately that it was colder than he had expected to find it off the coast of Florida. This appeared to his dazed mind as a fact important enough to be noted at the time. The coldness of the water was sad; it was tragic. This fact was somehow mixed and confused with his opinion of his own situation, so that it seemed almost a proper reason for tears. The water was cold.

When he came to the surface he was conscious of little but the noisy water. Afterward he saw his companions in the sea. The oiler was ahead in the race. He was swimming strongly and rapidly. Off to the correspondent's left, the cook's great white and corked back bulged out of the water, and in the rear the captain was hanging with his one good hand to the keel of the overturned dinghy.

There is a certain immovable quality to a shore, and the correspondent wondered at it amid the confusion of the sea.

It seemed also very attractive; but the correspondent knew that it was a long journey, and he paddled leisurely. The piece of life-preserver lay under him, and sometimes he whirled down the incline of a wave as if he were on a hand-sled.

But finally he arrived at a place in the sea where travel was beset with difficulty. He did not pause swimming to inquire what manner of current had caught him, but there his progress ceased. The shore was set before him like a bit of scenery on a stage, and he looked at it and understood with his eyes each detail of it.

As the cook passed, much farther to the left, the captain was calling to him, "Turn over on your back, cook! Turn over on your back and use the oar."

"All right, sir." The cook turned on his back, and, paddling with an oar, went ahead as if he were a canoe.

Presently the boat also passed to the left of the correspondent, with the captain clinging with one hand to the keel. He would have appeared like a man raising himself to look over a board fence if it were not for the extraordinary gymnastics of the boat. The correspondent marvelled that the captain could still hold to it.

They passed on nearer to shore—the oiler, the cook, the captain—and following them went the water-jar, bouncing gaily over the seas.

The correspondent remained in the grip of this strange new enemy, a current. The shore, with its white slope of sand and its green bluff topped with little silent cottages, was spread like a picture before him. It was very near to him then, but he was impressed as one who, in a gallery, looks at a scene from Brittany or Algiers.

He thought: "I am going to drown? Can it be possible? Can it be possible? Can it be possible?" Perhaps an individual must consider his own death to be the final phenomenon of nature.

But later a wave perhaps whirled him out of this small deadly current, for he found suddenly that he could again make progress toward the shore. Later still he was aware that the captain, clinging with one hand to the keel of the dinghy had his face turned away from the shore and toward him, and was calling his name. "Come to the boat! Come to the boat!"

In his struggle to reach the captain and the boat, he reflected that when one gets properly wearied drowning must really be a comfortable arrangement—a cessation of hostilities accompanied by a large degree of relief; and he was glad of it, for the main thing in his mind for some moments had been horror of the temporary agony; he did not wish to be hurt.

Presently he saw a man running along the shore. He was undressing with most remarkable speed. Coat, trousers, shirt, everything flew magically off him.

"Come to the boat!" called the captain.

"All right, Captain." As the correspondent paddled, he saw the captain let himself down to bottom and leave the boat. Then the correspondent performed his one little marvel of the voyage. A large wave caught him and flung him with ease and supreme speed completely over the boat and far beyond it. It struck him even then as an event in gymnastics and a true miracle of the sea. An overturned boat in the surf is not a plaything to a swimming man.

The correspondent arrived in water that reached only to his waist, but his condition did not enable him to stand for more than a moment. Each wave knocked him into a heap, and the undertow pulled at him.

Then he saw the man who had been running and undressing, and undressing and running, come bounding into the water. He dragged ashore the cook, and then waded toward the captain; but the captain waved him away and sent him to the correspondent. He was naked—naked as a tree in winter; but a halo was about his head, and he shone like a saint. He gave a strong pull, and a long drag, and a bully heave at the correspondent's hand. The correspondent, schooled in the minor formulae, said, "Thanks, old man." But suddenly the man cried, "What's that?" He pointed a swift finger. The correspondent said, "Go."

In the shallows, face downward, lay the oiler. His forehead touched sand that was periodically, between each wave, clear of the sea.

The correspondent did not know all that transpired afterward. When he achieved safe ground he fell, striking the sand with each particular part of his body. It was as if he had dropped from a roof, but the thud was grateful to him.

It seems that instantly the beach was populated with men with blankets, clothes, and flasks, and women with coffee-pots and all the remedies sacred to their minds. The welcome of the land to the men from the sea was warm and generous; but a still and dripping shape was carried slowly up the beach, and the land's welcome for it could only be the different and sinister hospitality of the grave.

When it came night, the white waves paced to and fro in the moonlight, and the wind brought the sound of the great sea's voice to the men on the shore, and they felt that they could then be interpreters.

—1897

JAMES JOYCE

James Joyce was born in a south Dublin suburb in 1882. The second of ten children, he was educated at various Jesuit-run schools in and around Dublin, where he excelled in his studies. In 1898, Joyce enrolled at University College, Dublin, and began writing reviews, a play inspired by Henrik Ibsen (he later destroyed it), and essays that marked him as a unique, if iconoclastic, talent. After a brief attempt to study medicine in Paris, he returned home to Dublin, where he met Nora Barnacle, a woman from Galway who would become his lifelong companion and the mother of his two children (they would marry in 1931). Joyce suffered from severe eye problems, including glaucoma, and endured over ten operations to treat his ailments over the course of his life.

Joyce and his family led something of a nomadic existence, their moves motivated variously by Joyce's flight from creditors, by his search for work, and by the dangers of war. Though several of his stories had been published in the periodical *Irish Homestead*, his breakthrough came in 1914. In that year his book of short stories *Dubliners* was published, and excerpts from his semi-autobiographical novel *A Portrait of the Artist as a Young Man* (1916) were serialized in Ezra Pound's periodical *The Egoist*.

Joyce suffered a major blow in 1922 when the US Post Office confiscated copies of the magazine *Little Review* that contained excerpts from his novel in progress, *Ulysses*; the publisher was charged with publishing pornography. *Ulysses* was finally published by American expatriate Sylvia Beach's bookstore press, Shakespeare and Co., in Paris; Joyce was soon hailed as a genius by writers such as T.S. Eliot and Ernest Hemingway. In the meantime, Joyce had begun work on his novel *Finnegans Wake*—his most ambitious text and one that would take him almost 17 years to write. When it was finally published in 1939, the novel's innovative form and structure provoked new controversy. Joyce died in 1941 after an operation for a perforated ulcer.

Dubliners was not published in its entirety until June 15, 1914. Joyce had submitted and resubmitted the collection to various publishers, but their squeamishness over the subject matter prevented the collection from being published for almost ten years. Even the collection's eventual publisher worried that the negative portrayal of Dublin and its inhabitants in the collection would provoke charges of libel. In a letter to his publisher, Joyce states his reason for leaving the stories as he originally wrote them:

> My intention was to write a chapter of the moral history of my country and I chose Dublin for the scene because the city seemed to me the centre of paralysis.... I have written it for the most part in a style of scrupulous meanness and with the conviction that he is a very bold man who dares to alter in the presentment, still more to deform, whatever he has seen and heard. I cannot do any more than this.

"Araby," the third story in the collection and one of the few recounted in the first person, examines a young boy's romantic fantasies and longing for adventure. The story "Eveline" also engages the idea of escape; the central character must choose between the dysfunctional yet familiar nature of her current reality and the promise of a better life.

Araby

JAMES JOYCE

NORTH Richmond Street, being blind,[1] was a quiet street except at the hour when the Christian Brothers' School set the boys free. An uninhabited house of two storeys stood at the blind end, detached from its neighbors in a square ground. The other houses of the street, conscious of decent lives within them, gazed at one another with brown imperturbable faces.

The former tenant of our house, a priest, had died in the back drawing-room. Air, musty from having been long enclosed, hung in all the rooms, and the waste room behind the kitchen was littered with old useless papers. Among these I found a few paper-covered books, the pages of which were curled and damp: *The Abbot*,[2] by Walter Scott, *The Devout Communicant*[3] and *The Memoirs of Vidocq*.[4] I liked the last best because its leaves were yellow. The wild garden behind the house contained a central apple-tree and a few straggling bushes

1 A dead-end street.

2 An 1820 historical novel by Sir Walter Scott about Mary, Queen of Scots.

3 Several nineteenth-century religious tracts have this title.

4 The popular autobiography of François Vidocq, a nineteenth-century Parisian criminal turned police detective.

under one of which I found the late tenant's rusty bicycle-pump. He had been a very charitable priest; in his will he had left all his money to institutions and the furniture of his house to his sister.

When the short days of winter came dusk fell before we had well eaten our dinners. When we met in the street the houses had grown somber. The space of sky above us was the color of ever-changing violet and towards it the lamps of the street lifted their feeble lanterns. The cold air stung us and we played till our bodies glowed. Our shouts echoed in the silent street. The career of our play brought us through the dark muddy lanes behind the houses where we ran the gantlet of the rough tribes from the cottages, to the back doors of the dark dripping gardens where odors arose from the ash-pits, to the dark odorous stables where a coachman smoothed and combed the horse or shook music from the buckled harness. When we returned to the street light from the kitchen windows had filled the areas. If my uncle was seen turning the corner we hid in the shadow until we had seen him safely housed. Or if Mangan's sister came out on the doorstep to call her brother in to his tea we watched her from our shadow peer up and down the street. We waited to see whether she would remain or go in and, if she remained, we left our shadow and walked up to Mangan's steps resignedly. She was waiting for us, her figure defined by the light from the half-opened door. Her brother always teased her before he obeyed and I stood by the railings looking at her. Her dress swung as she moved her body and the soft rope of her hair tossed from side to side.

Every morning I lay on the floor in the front parlor watching her door. The blind was pulled down to within an inch of the sash so that I could not be seen. When she came out on the doorstep my heart leaped. I ran to the hall, seized my books and followed her. I kept her brown figure always in my eye and, when we came near the point at which our ways diverged, I quickened my pace and passed her. This happened morning after morning. I had never spoken to her, except for a few casual words, and yet her name was like a summons to all my foolish blood.

Her image accompanied me even in places the most hostile to romance. On Saturday evenings when my aunt went marketing I had to go to carry some of the parcels. We walked through the flaring streets, jostled by drunken men and bargaining women, amid the curses of laborers, the shrill litanies of shop-boys who stood on guard by the barrels of pigs' cheeks, the nasal chanting of street-singers, who sang a *come-all-you* about O'Donovan Rossa,[5] or a ballad about the troubles in our native land. These noises converged in a single sensation of life for me: I imagined that I bore my chalice safely through a throng of foes.

5 Jeremiah O'Donovan Rossa (1831-1915), an activist for Irish independence.

Her name sprang to my lips at moments in strange prayers and praises which I myself did not understand. My eyes were often full of tears (I could not tell why) and at times a flood from my heart seemed to pour itself out into my bosom. I thought little of the future. I did not know whether I would ever speak to her or not or, if I spoke to her, how I could tell her of my confused adoration. But my body was like a harp and her words and gestures were like fingers running upon the wires.

One evening I went into the back drawing-room in which the priest had died. It was a dark rainy evening and there was no sound in the house. Through one of the broken panes I heard the rain impinge upon the earth, the fine incessant needles of water playing in the sodden beds. Some distant lamp or lighted window gleamed below me. I was thankful that I could see so little. All my senses seemed to desire to veil themselves and, feeling that I was about to slip from them, I pressed the palms of my hands together until they trembled, murmuring: *O love! O love!* many times.

At last she spoke to me. When she addressed the first words to me I was so confused that I did not know what to answer. She asked me was I going to *Araby*. I forget whether I answered yes or no. It would be a splendid bazaar, she said; she would love to go.

—And why can't you? I asked.

While she spoke she turned a silver bracelet round and round her wrist. She could not go, she said, because there would be a retreat that week in her convent. Her brother and two other boys were fighting for their caps and I was alone at the railings. She held one of the spikes, bowing her head towards me. The light from the lamp opposite our door caught the white curve of her neck, lit up her hair that rested there and, falling, lit up the hand upon the railing. It fell over one side of her dress and caught the white border of a petticoat, just visible as she stood at ease.

—It's well for you, she said.

—If I go, I said, I will bring you something.

What innumerable follies laid waste my waking and sleeping thoughts after that evening! I wished to annihilate the tedious intervening days. I chafed against the work of school. At night in my bedroom and by day in the classroom her image came between me and the page I strove to read. The syllables of the word *Araby* were called to me through the silence in which my soul luxuriated and cast an Eastern enchantment over me. I asked for leave to go to the bazaar on Saturday night. My aunt was surprised and hoped it was not some Freemason[6] affair. I answered few questions in class. I watched my master's face pass

6 The Freemasons are a secret society, believed by many in Ireland to be anti-Catholic.

from amiability to sternness; he hoped I was not beginning to idle. I could not call my wandering thoughts together. I had hardly any patience with the serious work of life which, now that it stood between me and my desire, seemed to me child's play, ugly monotonous child's play.

On Saturday morning I reminded my uncle that I wished to go to the bazaar in the evening. He was fussing at the hallstand, looking for the hat-brush, and answered me curtly:

—Yes, boy, I know.

As he was in the hall I could not go into the front parlor and lie at the window. I left the house in bad humor and walked slowly towards the school. The air was pitilessly raw and already my heart misgave me.

When I came home to dinner my uncle had not yet been home. Still it was early. I sat staring at the clock for some time and, when its ticking began to irritate me, I left the room. I mounted the staircase and gained the upper part of the house. The high cold empty gloomy rooms liberated me and I went from room to room singing. From the front window I saw my companions playing below in the street. Their cries reached me weakened and indistinct and, leaning my forehead against the cool glass, I looked over at the dark house where she lived. I may have stood there for an hour, seeing nothing but the brown-clad figure cast by my imagination, touched discreetly by the lamplight at the curved neck, at the hand upon the railings and at the border below the dress.

When I came downstairs again I found Mrs Mercer sitting at the fire. She was an old garrulous woman, a pawnbroker's widow, who collected used stamps for some pious purpose. I had to endure the gossip of the tea-table. The meal was prolonged beyond an hour and still my uncle did not come. Mrs Mercer stood up to go: she was sorry she couldn't wait any longer, but it was after eight o'clock and she did not like to be out late, as the night air was bad for her. When she had gone I began to walk up and down the room, clenching my fists. My aunt said:

—I'm afraid you may put off your bazaar for this night of Our Lord.

At nine o'clock I heard my uncle's latchkey in the halldoor. I heard him talking to himself and heard the hallstand rocking when it had received the weight of his overcoat. I could interpret these signs. When he was midway through his dinner I asked him to give me the money to go to the bazaar. He had forgotten.

—The people are in bed and after their first sleep now, he said.

I did not smile. My aunt said to him energetically:

—Can't you give him the money and let him go? You've kept him late enough as it is.

My uncle said he was very sorry he had forgotten. He said he believed in the old saying: *All work and no play makes Jack a dull boy.* He asked where I was going and, when I had told him a second time he asked me did I know *The Arab's*

Farewell to his Steed.[7] When I left the kitchen he was about to recite the opening lines of the piece to my aunt.

I held a florin tightly in my hand as I strode down Buckingham Street towards the station. The sight of the streets thronged with buyers and glaring with gas recalled to me the purpose of my journey. I took my seat in a third-class carriage of a deserted train. After an intolerable delay the train moved out of the station slowly. It crept onward among ruinous houses and over the twinkling river. At Westland Row Station a crowd of people pressed to the carriage doors; but the porters moved them back, saying that it was a special train for the bazaar. I remained alone in the bare carriage. In a few minutes the train drew up beside an improvised wooden platform. I passed out on to the road and saw by the lighted dial of a clock that it was ten minutes to ten. In front of me was a large building which displayed the magical name.

I could not find any sixpenny entrance and, fearing that the bazaar would be closed, I passed in quickly through a turnstile, handing a shilling to a weary-looking man. I found myself in a big hall girdled at half its height by a gallery. Nearly all the stalls were closed and the greater part of the hall was in darkness. I recognized a silence like that which pervades a church after a service. I walked into the center of the bazaar timidly. A few people were gathered about the stalls which were still open. Before a curtain, over which the words *Café Chantant* were written in colored lamps, two men were counting money on a salver. I listened to the fall of the coins.

Remembering with difficulty why I had come I went over to one of the stalls and examined porcelain vases and flowered tea-sets. At the door of the stall a young lady was talking and laughing with two young gentlemen. I remarked their English accents and listened vaguely to their conversation.

—Oh, I never said such a thing!

—O, but you did!

—O, but I didn't!

—Didn't she say that?

—Yes. I heard her.

—O, there's a … fib!

Observing me the young lady came over and asked me did I wish to buy anything. The tone of her voice was not encouraging; she seemed to have spoken to me out of a sense of duty. I looked humbly at the great jars that stood like eastern guards at either side of the dark entrance to the stall and murmured:

—No, thank you.

---

7 Popular Romantic poem by Caroline Norton (1808-77).

The young lady changed the position of one of the vases and went back to the two young men. They began to talk of the same subject. Once or twice the young lady glanced at me over her shoulder.

I lingered before her stall, though I knew my stay was useless, to make my interest in her wares seem the more real. Then I turned away slowly and walked down the middle of the bazaar. I allowed the two pennies to fall against the sixpence in my pocket. I heard a voice call from one end of the gallery that the light was out. The upper part of the hall was now completely dark.

Gazing up into the darkness I saw myself as a creature driven and derided by vanity; and my eyes burned with anguish and anger.

—1914

Eveline

JAMES JOYCE

SHE SAT at the window watching the evening invade the avenue. Her head was leaned against the window curtains and in her nostrils was the odor of dusty cretonne.[1] She was tired.

Few people passed. The man out of the last house passed on his way home; she heard his footsteps clacking along the concrete pavement and afterwards crunching on the cinder path before the new red houses. One time there used to be a field there in which they used to play every evening with other people's children. Then a man from Belfast bought the field and built houses in it—not like their little brown houses but bright brick houses with shining roofs. The children of the avenue used to play together in that field—the Devines, the Waters, the Dunns, little Keogh the cripple, she and her brothers and sisters. Ernest, however, never played: he was too grown up. Her father used often to hunt them in out of the field with his blackthorn stick; but usually little Keogh used to keep *nix* and call out when he saw her father coming. Still they seemed to have been rather happy then. Her father was not so bad then; and besides, her mother was alive. That was a long time ago; she and her brothers and sisters were all grown up; her mother was dead. Tizzie Dunn was dead, too, and the Waters had gone back to England. Everything changes. Now she was going to go away like the others, to leave her home.

Home! She looked round the room, reviewing all its familiar objects which she had dusted once a week for so many years, wondering where on earth all the

1 Cotton fabric.

dust came from. Perhaps she would never see again those familiar objects from which she had never dreamed of being divided. And yet during all those years she had never found out the name of the priest whose yellowing photograph hung on the wall above the broken harmonium[2] beside the colored print of the promises made to Blessed Margaret Mary Alacoque.[3] He had been a school friend of her father. Whenever he showed the photograph to a visitor her father used to pass it with a casual word:

—He is in Melbourne now.

She had consented to go away, to leave her home. Was that wise? She tried to weigh each side of the question. In her home anyway she had shelter and food; she had those whom she had known all her life about her. Of course she had to work hard both in the house and at business. What would they say of her in the Stores when they found out that she had run away with a fellow? Say she was a fool, perhaps; and her place would be filled up by advertisement. Miss Gavan would be glad. She had always had an edge on her, especially whenever there were people listening.

—Miss Hill, don't you see these ladies are waiting?

—Look lively, Miss Hill, please.

She would not cry many tears at leaving the Stores.

But in her new home, in a distant unknown country, it would not be like that. Then she would be married—she, Eveline. People would treat her with respect then. She would not be treated as her mother had been. Even now, though she was over nineteen, she sometimes felt herself in danger of her father's violence. She knew it was that that had given her the palpitations. When they were growing up he had never gone for her, like he used to go for Harry and Ernest, because she was a girl; but latterly he had begun to threaten her and say what he would do to her only for her dead mother's sake. And now she had nobody to protect her. Ernest was dead and Harry, who was in the church decorating business, was nearly always down somewhere in the country. Besides, the invariable squabble for money on Saturday nights had begun to weary her unspeakably. She always gave her entire wages—seven shillings—and Harry always sent up what he could but the trouble was to get any money from her father. He said she used to squander the money, that she had no head, that he wasn't going to give her his hard-earned money to throw about the streets, and much more, for he was usually fairly bad of a Saturday night. In the end he would give her the money and ask her had she any intention of buying Sunday's dinner. Then she had to rush out as quickly as she could and do her marketing, holding her black

2 A reed instrument similar to an organ.

3 Marguerite Marie Alacoque (1647-90), a French Catholic nun and religious mystic.

leather purse tightly in her hand as she elbowed her way through the crowds and returning home late under her load of provisions. She had hard work to keep the house together and to see that the two young children who had been left to her charge went to school regularly and got their meals regularly. It was hard work—a hard life—but now that she was about to leave it she did not find it a wholly undesirable life.

She was about to explore another life with Frank. Frank was very kind, manly, open-hearted. She was to go away with him by the night-boat to be his wife and to live with him in Buenos Ayres where he had a home waiting for her. How well she remembered the first time she had seen him; he was lodging in a house on the main road where she used to visit. It seemed a few weeks ago. He was standing at the gate, his peaked cap pushed back on his head and his hair tumbled forward over a face of bronze. Then they had come to know each other. He used to meet her outside the Stores every evening and see her home. He took her to see *The Bohemian Girl*[4] and she felt elated as she sat in an unaccustomed part of the theater with him. He was awfully fond of music and sang a little. People knew that they were courting and, when he sang about the lass that loves a sailor, she always felt pleasantly confused. He used to call her Poppens out of fun. First of all it had been an excitement for her to have a fellow and then she had begun to like him. He had tales of distant countries. He had started as a deck boy at a pound a month on a ship of the Allan Line[5] going out to Canada. He told her the names of the ships he had been on and the names of the different services. He had sailed through the Straits of Magellan and he told her stories of the terrible Patagonians. He had fallen on his feet in Buenos Ayres, he said, and had come over to the old country just for a holiday. Of course, her father had found out the affair and had forbidden her to have anything to say to him.

—I know these sailor chaps, he said.

One day he had quarrelled with Frank and after that she had to meet her lover secretly.

The evening deepened in the avenue. The white of two letters in her lap grew indistinct. One was to Harry; the other was to her father. Ernest had been her favorite but she liked Harry too. Her father was becoming old lately, she noticed; he would miss her. Sometimes he could be very nice. Not long before, when she had been laid up for a day, he had read her out a ghost story and made toast for her at the fire. Another day, when their mother was alive, they had all gone

4 An 1843 opera by Irish composer Michael Balfe.

5 A steamship company that made weekly sailings between Liverpool and western Canada via South America.

for a picnic to the Hill of Howth.[6] She remembered her father putting on her mother's bonnet to make the children laugh.

Her time was running out but she continued to sit by the window, leaning her head against the window curtain, inhaling the odor of dusty cretonne. Down far in the avenue she could hear a street organ playing. She knew the air. Strange that it should come that very night to remind her of the promise to her mother, her promise to keep the home together as long as she could. She remembered the last night of her mother's illness; she was again in the close dark room at the other side of the hall and outside she heard a melancholy air of Italy. The organ-player had been ordered to go away and given sixpence. She remembered her father strutting back into the sickroom saying:

—Damned Italians! coming over here!

As she mused the pitiful vision of her mother's life laid its spell on the very quick of her being—that life of commonplace sacrifices closing in final craziness. She trembled as she heard again her mother's voice saying constantly with foolish insistence:

—Derevaun Seraun! Derevaun Seraun![7]

She stood up in a sudden impulse of terror. Escape! She must escape! Frank would save her. He would give her life, perhaps love, too. But she wanted to live. Why should she be unhappy? She had a right to happiness. Frank would take her in his arms, fold her in his arms. He would save her.

She stood among the swaying crowd in the station at the North Wall. He held her hand and she knew that he was speaking to her, saying something about the passage over and over again. The station was full of soldiers with brown baggages. Through the wide doors of the sheds she caught a glimpse of the black mass of the boat, lying in beside the quay wall, with illumined portholes. She answered nothing. She felt her cheek pale and cold and, out of a maze of distress, she prayed to God to direct her, to show her what was her duty. The boat blew a long mournful whistle into the mist. If she went, to-morrow she would be on the sea with Frank, steaming towards Buenos Ayres. Their passage had been booked. Could she still draw back after all he had done for her? Her distress awoke a nausea in her body and she kept moving her lips in silent fervent prayer.

A bell clanged upon her heart. She felt him seize her hand:

—Come!

All the seas of the world tumbled about her heart. He was drawing her into them: he would drown her. She gripped with both hands at the iron railing.

---

6 A hill located northeast of Dublin.

7 The meaning of this phrase is uncertain; it may be garbled Irish or simply gibberish.

—Come!

No! No! No! It was impossible. Her hands clutched the iron in frenzy. Amid the seas she sent a cry of anguish!

—Eveline! Evvy!

He rushed beyond the barrier and called to her to follow. He was shouted at to go on but he still called to her. She set her white face to him, passive, like a helpless animal. Her eyes gave him no sign of love or farewell or recognition.

—1914

KATHERINE MANSFIELD

Katherine Mansfield was the daughter of a businessman who later became the affluent director of the Bank of New Zealand. She was born in 1888 in Wellington, New Zealand, the setting for a large part of her fiction. At 15, she traveled with her family to England, where she studied music for three years at Queen's College. There she met Ida Baker (later known as Leslie Moore or L.M.) with whom she would form a lifelong relationship.

Upon completing her education, Mansfield made London her home. Over the course of ten years, Mansfield had numerous affairs with men (one of whom she married) and continued to maintain her connection with L.M. (her mother committed her to "cold water therapy" in a small Bavarian town in order to "cure" her of her lesbian affection for L.M.). In 1911 she met John Middleton Murry, an Oxford undergraduate and literary editor of the new review, *Rhythm*, when he visited her in order to discuss a story she had sent to his review; soon afterward they became lovers, and they married in 1918, after her divorce from her first husband was completed.

Two of Mansfield's most important friendships were with the writers D.H. Lawrence and Virginia Woolf. Although she occasionally criticized Mansfield's bohemian behavior and attitudes, Woolf was a great admirer of Mansfield and once wrote that Mansfield was the only writer of whom she felt jealous. Mansfield's friendship with Lawrence was less stable, and Lawrence may have drawn on aspects of Mansfield's life and personality in his sometimes unflattering fictional portrait of Gudrun Brangwen in the novel *Women in Love* (1920). During World War I, Mansfield's only brother Leslie was killed in a training accident. Mansfield wrote *Prelude* (1918) and *At the Bay* (1921) in response to the tragedy and as a means of reconstructing the childhood she had shared with her brother.

In the final years of her life, Mansfield suffered from a number of illnesses—the most serious of which was tuberculosis—but she still managed to produce critically well-received works such as *Bliss and Other Stories* (1920) and *The Garden Party and Other Stories* (1922). Throughout this time she was faithfully attended by L.M. She died of a hemorrhage in 1923.

Murry collected her loose papers and notebooks together after her death, and published them under the titles *The Journal of Katherine Mansfield* (1927) and *The Scrapbook of Katherine Mansfield* (1939). Also published posthumously were two collections of fiction, *The Dove's Nest* (1923) and *Something Childish* (1924). Mansfield was a fervent admirer of Anton Chekhov's writing, and numerous literary scholars have noted the similarities between the two writers' works. Published in *The Garden Party and Other Stories* (1922), "The Doll's House" shows Mansfield's satirical eye turned to Wellington's "middle class and its rather smudged carbon copy of how the English do things." From the same collection, "The Garden Party" also deals with classist assumptions; both stories turn on petty divisions of a sort often found in the higher echelons of society.

The Doll's House

KATHERINE MANSFIELD

WHEN dear old Mrs. Hay went back to town after staying with the Burnells she sent the children a doll's house. It was so big that the carter and Pat carried it into the courtyard, and there it stayed, propped up on two wooden boxes beside the feed-room door. No harm could come to it; it was summer. And perhaps the smell of paint would have gone off by the time it had to be taken in. For, really, the smell of paint coming from that doll's house ('Sweet of old Mrs. Hay, of course; most sweet and generous!')—but the smell of paint was quite enough to make anyone seriously ill, in Aunt Beryl's opinion. Even before the sacking was taken off. And when it was …

There stood the Doll's house, a dark, oily, spinach green, picked out with bright yellow. Its two solid little chimneys, glued on to the roof, were painted red and white, and the door, gleaming with yellow varnish, was like a little slab of toffee. Four windows, real windows, were divided into panes by a broad streak of green. There was actually a tiny porch, too, painted yellow, with big lumps of congealed paint hanging along the edge.

But perfect, perfect little house! Who could possibly mind the smell. It was part of the joy, part of the newness.

"Open it quickly, someone!"

The hook at the side was stuck fast. Pat prized it open with his penknife, and the whole house front swung back, and—there you were, gazing at one and the same moment into the drawing-room and dining-room, the kitchen and two bedrooms. That is the way for a house to open! Why don't all houses open like that? How much more exciting than peering through the slit of a door into a mean little hall with a hat-stand and two umbrellas! That is—isn't it?—what you long to know about a house when you put your hand on the knocker. Perhaps it is the way God opens houses at the dead of night when He is taking a quiet turn with an angel …

"O-oh!" The Burnell children sounded as though they were in despair. It was too marvellous; it was too much for them. They had never seen anything like it in their lives. All the rooms were papered. There were pictures on the walls, painted on the paper, with gold frames complete. Red carpet covered all the floors except the kitchen; red plush chairs in the drawing-room, green in the dining-room; tables, beds with real bedclothes, a cradle, a stove, a dresser with tiny plates and one big jug. But what Kezia liked more than anything, what she liked frightfully, was the lamp. It stood in the middle of the dining-room table, an exquisite little amber lamp with a white globe. It was even filled all ready for lighting, though, of course, you couldn't light it. But there was something inside that looked like oil and moved when you shook it.

The father and mother dolls, who sprawled very stiff as though they had fainted in the drawing-room, and their two little children asleep upstairs, were really too big for the doll's house. They didn't look as though they belonged. But the lamp was perfect. It seemed to smile at Kezia, to say, "I live here." The lamp was real.

The Burnell children could hardly walk to school fast enough the next morning. They burned to tell everybody, to describe, to—well—to boast about their doll's house before the school-bell rang.

"I'm to tell," said Isabel, "because I'm the eldest. And you two can join in after. But I'm to tell first."

There was nothing to answer. Isabel was bossy, but she was always right, and Lottie and Kezia knew too well the powers that went with being eldest. They brushed through the thick buttercups at the road edge and said nothing.

"And I'm to choose who's to come and see it first. Mother said I might."

For it had been arranged that while the doll's house stood in the courtyard they might ask the girls at school, two at a time, to come and look. Not to stay to tea, of course, or to come traipsing through the house. But just to stand quietly in the courtyard while Isabel pointed out the beauties, and Lottie and Kezia looked pleased …

But hurry as they might, by the time they had reached the tarred palings of the boys' playground the bell had begun to jangle. They only just had time to whip off their hats and fall into line before the roll was called. Never mind. Isabel tried to make up for it by looking very important and mysterious and by whispering behind her hand to the girls near her, "Got something to tell you at playtime."

Playtime came and Isabel was surrounded. The girls of her class nearly fought to put their arms round her, to walk away with her, to beam flatteringly, to be her special friend. She held quite a court under the huge pine trees at the side of the playground. Nudging, giggling together, the little girls pressed up close. And the only two who stayed outside the ring were the two who were always outside, the little Kelveys. They knew better than to come anywhere near the Burnells.

For the fact was, the school the Burnell children went to was not at all the kind of place their parents would have chosen if there had been any choice. But there was none. It was the only school for miles. And the consequence was all the children of the neighborhood, the Judge's little girls, the doctor's daughters, the store-keeper's children, the milkman's, were forced to mix together. Not to speak of there being an equal number of rude, rough little boys as well. But the line had to be drawn somewhere. It was drawn at the Kelveys. Many of the children, including the Burnells, were not allowed even to speak to them. They walked past the Kelveys with their heads in the air, and as they set the fashion in all matters of behavior, the Kelveys were shunned by everybody. Even the teacher had a special voice for them, and a special smile for the other children when Lil Kelvey came up to her desk with a bunch of dreadfully common-looking flowers.

They were the daughters of a spry, hard-working little washerwoman, who went about from house to house by the day. This was awful enough. But where was Mr. Kelvey? Nobody knew for certain. But everybody said he was in prison. So they were the daughters of a washerwoman and a gaolbird. Very nice company for other people's children! And they looked it. Why Mrs. Kelvey made them so conspicuous was hard to understand. The truth was they were dressed in "bits" given to her by the people for whom she worked. Lil, for instance, who was a stout, plain child, with big freckles, came to school in a dress made from a green art-serge table-cloth of the Burnells', with red plush sleeves from the Logans' curtains. Her hat, perched on top of her high forehead, was a grown-up woman's hat, once the property of Miss Lecky, the postmistress. It was turned up at the back and trimmed with a large scarlet quill. What a little guy[1] she looked! It was impossible not to laugh. And her little sister, our Else, wore a long white dress, rather like a nightgown, and a pair of little boy's boots. But whatever our Else wore she would have looked strange. She was a tiny wishbone of a child, with cropped hair and enormous solemn eyes—a little white owl. Nobody had ever seen her smile; she scarcely ever spoke. She went through life holding on to Lil, with a piece of Lil's skirt screwed up in her hand. Where Lil went, our Else

---

1 British/New Zealand slang: an absurdly or grotesquely dressed person.

followed. In the playground, on the road going to and from school, there was Lil marching in front and our Else holding on behind. Only when she wanted anything, or when she was out of breath, our Else gave Lil a tug, a twitch, and Lil stopped and turned round. The Kelveys never failed to understand each other.

Now they hovered at the edge; you couldn't stop them listening. When the little girls turned round and sneered, Lil, as usual, gave her silly, shamefaced smile, but our Else only looked.

And Isabel's voice, so very proud, went on telling. The carpet made a great sensation, but so did the beds with real bedclothes, and the stove with an oven door.

When she finished Kezia broke in. "You've forgotten the lamp, Isabel."

"Oh, yes," said Isabel, "and there's a teeny little lamp, all made of yellow glass, with a white globe that stands on the dining-room table. You couldn't tell it from a real one."

"The lamp's best of all," cried Kezia. She thought Isabel wasn't making half enough of the little lamp. But nobody paid any attention. Isabel was choosing the two who were to come back with them that afternoon and see it. She chose Emmie Cole and Lena Logan. But when the others knew they were all to have a chance, they couldn't be nice enough to Isabel. One by one they put their arms round Isabel's waist and walked her off. They had something to whisper to her, a secret. "Isabel's *my* friend."

Only the little Kelveys moved away forgotten; there was nothing more for them to hear.

Days passed, and as more children saw the doll's house, the fame of it spread. It became the one subject, the rage. The one question was, "Have you seen Burnells' doll's house? Oh, ain't it lovely!" "Haven't you seen it? Oh, I say!"

Even the dinner hour was given up to talking about it. The little girls sat under the pines eating their thick mutton sandwiches and big slabs of johnny cake[2] spread with butter. While always, as near as they could get, sat the Kelveys, our Else holding on to Lil, listening too, while they chewed their jam sandwiches out of a newspaper soaked with large red blobs.

"Mother," said Kezia, "can't I ask the Kelveys just once?"

"Certainly not, Kezia."

"But why not?"

"Run away, Kezia; you know quite well why not."

At last everybody had seen it except them. On that day the subject rather flagged. It was the dinner hour. The children stood together under the pine trees, and

2 Thin, unleavened wheat bread.

suddenly, as they looked at the Kelveys eating out of their paper, always by themselves, always listening, they wanted to be horrid to them. Emmie Cole started the whisper.

"Lil Kelvey's going to be a servant when she grows up."

"O-oh, how awful!" said Isabel Burnell, and she made eyes at Emmie.

Emmie swallowed in a very meaning way and nodded to Isabel as she'd seen her mother do on those occasions.

"It's true—it's true—it's true," she said.

Then Lena Logan's little eyes snapped. "Shall I ask her?" she whispered.

"Bet you don't," said Jessie May.

"Pooh, I'm not frightened," said Lena. Suddenly she gave a little squeal and danced in front of the other girls. "Watch! Watch me! Watch me now!" said Lena. And sliding, gliding, dragging one foot, giggling behind her hand, Lena went over to the Kelveys.

Lil looked up from her dinner. She wrapped the rest quickly away. Our Else stopped chewing. What was coming now?

"Is it true you're going to be a servant when you grow up, Lil Kelvey?" shrilled Lena.

Dead silence. But instead of answering, Lil only gave her silly, shamefaced smile. She didn't seem to mind the question at all. What a sell for Lena! The girls began to titter.

Lena couldn't stand that. She put her hands on her hips; she shot forward. "Yah, yer father's in prison!" she hissed, spitefully.

This was such a marvellous thing to have said that the little girls rushed away in a body, deeply, deeply excited, wild with joy. Someone found a long rope, and they began skipping. And never did they skip so high, run in and out so fast, or do such daring things as on that morning.

In the afternoon Pat called for the Burnell children with the buggy and they drove home. There were visitors. Isabel and Lottie, who liked visitors, went upstairs to change their pinafores. But Kezia thieved out at the back. Nobody was about; she began to swing on the big white gates of the courtyard. Presently, looking along the road, she saw two little dots. They grew bigger, they were coming towards her. Now she could see that one was in front and one close behind. Now she could see that they were the Kelveys. Kezia stopped swinging. She slipped off the gate as if she was going to run away. Then she hesitated. The Kelveys came nearer, and beside them walked their shadows, very long, stretching right across the road with their heads in the buttercups. Kezia clambered back on the gate; she had made up her mind; she swung out.

"Hullo," she said to the passing Kelveys.

They were so astounded that they stopped. Lil gave her silly smile. Our Else stared.

"You can come and see our doll's house if you want to," said Kezia, and she dragged one toe on the ground. But at that Lil turned red and shook her head quickly.

"Why not?" asked Kezia.

Lil gasped, then she said, "Your ma told our ma you wasn't to speak to us."

"Oh, well," said Kezia. She didn't know what to reply. "It doesn't matter. You can come and see our doll's house all the same. Come on. Nobody's looking."

But Lil shook her head still harder.

"Don't you want to?" asked Kezia.

Suddenly there was a twitch, a tug at Lil's skirt. She turned round. Our Else was looking at her with big, imploring eyes; she was frowning; she wanted to go. For a moment Lil looked at Else very doubtfully. But then our Else twitched her skirt again. She started forward. Kezia led the way. Like two little stray cats they followed across the courtyard to where the doll's house stood.

"There it is," said Kezia.

There was a pause. Lil breathed loudly, almost snorted; our Else was still as stone.

"I'll open it for you," said Kezia kindly. She undid the hook and they looked inside.

"There's the drawing-room and the dining-room, and that's the—"

"Kezia!"

Oh, what a start they gave!

"Kezia!"

It was Aunt Beryl's voice. They turned round. At the back door stood Aunt Beryl, staring as if she couldn't believe what she saw.

"How dare you ask the little Kelveys into the courtyard?" said her cold, furious voice. "You know as well as I do, you're not allowed to talk to them. Run away, children, run away at once. And don't come back again," said Aunt Beryl. And she stepped into the yard and shooed them out as if they were chickens.

"Off you go immediately!" she called, cold and proud.

They did not need telling twice. Burning with shame, shrinking together, Lil huddling along like her mother, our Else dazed, somehow they crossed the big courtyard and squeezed through the white gate.

"Wicked, disobedient little girl!" said Aunt Beryl bitterly to Kezia, and she slammed the doll's house to.

The afternoon had been awful. A letter had come from Willie Brent, a terrifying, threatening letter, saying if she did not meet him that evening in Pulman's Bush, he'd come to the front door and ask the reason why! But now that she had frightened those little rats of Kelveys and given Kezia a good scolding, her heart felt lighter. That ghastly pressure was gone. She went back to the house humming.

When the Kelveys were well out of sight of Burnells', they sat down to rest on a big red drainpipe by the side of the road. Lil's cheeks were still burning; she took off the hat with the quill and held it on her knee. Dreamily they looked over the hay paddocks, past the creek, to the group of wattles where Logan's cows stood waiting to be milked. What were their thoughts?

Presently our Else nudged up close to her sister. But now she had forgotten the cross lady. She put out a finger and stroked her sister's quill; she smiled her rare smile.

"I seen the little lamp," she said, softly.

Then both were silent once more.

—1922

The Garden Party

KATHERINE MANSFIELD

AND AFTER all the weather was ideal. They could not have had a more perfect day for a garden party if they had ordered it. Windless, warm, the sky without a cloud. Only the blue was veiled with a haze of light gold, as it is sometimes in early summer. The gardener had been up since dawn, mowing the lawns and sweeping them, until the grass and the dark flat rosettes where the daisy plants had been seemed to shine. As for the roses, you could not help feeling they understood that roses are the only flowers that impress people at garden parties; the only flowers that everybody is certain of knowing. Hundreds, yes, literally hundreds, had come out in a single night; the green bushes bowed down as though they had been visited by archangels.

Breakfast was not yet over before the men came to put up the marquee.

"Where do you want the marquee put, mother?"

"My dear child, it's no use asking me. I'm determined to leave everything to you children this year. Forget I am your mother. Treat me as an honored guest."

But Meg could not possibly go and supervise the men. She had washed her hair before breakfast, and she sat drinking her coffee in a green turban, with a dark wet curl stamped on each cheek. Jose, the butterfly, always came down in a silk petticoat and a kimono jacket.

"You'll have to go, Laura, you're the artistic one."

Away Laura flew, still holding her piece of bread-and-butter. It's so delicious to have an excuse for eating out of doors and, besides, she loved having to arrange things; she always felt she could do it so much better than anybody else.

Four men in their shirt-sleeves stood grouped together on the garden path. They carried staves covered with rolls of canvas, and they had big tool-bags slung on their backs. They looked impressivc. Laura wished now that she was not holding that piece of bread-and-butter, but there was nowhere to put it, and she couldn't possibly throw it away. She blushed and tried to look severe and even a little bit short-sighted as she came up to them.

"Good morning," she said, copying her mother's voice. But that sounded so fearfully affected that she was ashamed, and stammered like a little girl, "Oh—er—have you come—is it about the marquee?"

"That's right, miss," said the tallest of the men, a lanky, freckled fellow, and he shifted his tool-bag, knocked back his straw hat, and smiled down at her. "That's about it."

His smile was so easy, so friendly, that Laura recovered. What nice eyes he had, small, but such a dark blue! And now she looked at the others, they were smiling too. "Cheer up, we won't bite," their smile seemed to say. How very nice workmen were! And what a beautiful morning! She mustn't mention the morning; she must be businesslike. The marquee.

"Well, what about the lily-lawn? Would that do?"

And she pointed to the lily-lawn with the hand that didn't hold the bread-and-butter. They turned, they stared in the direction. A little fat chap thrust out his underlip, and the tall fellow frowned.

"I don't fancy it," said he. "Not conspicuous enough. You see, with a thing like a marquee," and he turned to Laura in his easy way, "you want to put it somewhere where it'll give you a bang slap in the eye, if you follow me."

Laura's upbringing made her wonder for a moment whether it was quite respectful of a workman to talk to her of bangs slap in the eye. But she did quite follow him.

"A corner of the tennis court," she suggested. "But the band's going to be in one corner."

"H'm, going to have a band, are you?" said another of the workmen. He was pale. He had a haggard look as his dark eyes scanned the tennis court. What was he thinking?

"Only a very small band," said Laura gently. Perhaps he wouldn't mind so much if the band was quite small. But the tall fellow interrupted.

"Look here, miss, that's the place. Against those trees. Over there. That'll do fine."

Against the karakas. Then the karaka trees would be hidden. And they were so lovely, with their broad, gleaming leaves, and their clusters of yellow fruit. They were like trees you imagined growing up on a desert island, proud, solitary, lifting their leaves and fruits to the sun in a kind of silent splendor. Must they be hidden by a marquee?

They must. Already the men had shouldered their staves and were making for the place. Only the tall fellow was left. He bent down, pinched a sprig of lavender, put his thumb and forefinger to his nose and snuffed up the smell. When Laura saw that gesture she forgot all about the karakas in her wonder at him caring for things like that—caring for the smell of lavender. How many men that she knew would have done such a thing. *Oh, how extraordinarily nice workmen were*, she thought. Why couldn't she have workmen for friends rather than the silly boys she danced with and who came to Sunday night supper? She would get on much better with men like these.

It's all the fault, she decided, as the tall fellow drew something on the back of an envelope, something that was to be looped up or left to hang, of these absurd class distinctions. Well, for her part, she didn't feel them. Not a bit, not an atom.... And now there came the chock-chock of wooden hammers. Someone whistled, someone sang out, "Are you right there, matey?" "Matey!" The friendliness of it, the—the—Just to prove how happy she was, just to show the tall fellow how at home she felt, and how she despised stupid conventions, Laura took a big bite of her bread-and-butter as she stared at the little drawing. She felt just like a work-girl.

"Laura, Laura, where are you? Telephone, Laura!" a voice cried from the house.

"Coming!" Away she skimmed, over the lawn, up the path, up the steps, across the veranda, and into the porch. In the hall her father and Laurie were brushing their hats ready to go to the office.

"I say, Laura," said Laurie very fast, "you might just give a squiz[1] at my coat before this afternoon. See if it wants pressing."

"I will," said she. Suddenly she couldn't stop herself. She ran at Laurie and gave him a small, quick squeeze. "Oh, I do love parties, don't you?" gasped Laura.

"Ra-ther," said Laurie's warm, boyish voice, and he squeezed his sister too, and gave her a gentle push. "Dash off to the telephone, old girl."

The telephone. "Yes, yes; oh yes. Kitty? Good morning, dear. Come to lunch? Do, dear. Delighted of course. It will only be a very scratch meal—just the sandwich crusts and broken meringue-shells and what's left over. Yes, isn't it a

1 New Zealand slang for "a quick, close look."

perfect morning? Your white? Oh, I certainly should. One moment—hold the line. Mother's calling." And Laura sat back. "What, mother? Can't hear."

Mrs Sheridan's voice floated down the stairs. "Tell her to wear that sweet hat she had on last Sunday."

"Mother says you're to wear that *sweet* hat you had on last Sunday. Good. One o'clock. Bye-bye."

Laura put back the receiver, flung her arms over her head, took a deep breath, stretched, and let them fall. "Huh," she sighed, and the moment after the sigh she sat up quickly. She was still, listening. All the doors in the house seemed to be open. The house was alive with soft, quick steps and running voices. The green baize door[2] that led to the kitchen regions swung open and shut with a muffled thud. And now there came a long, chuckling absurd sound. It was the heavy piano being moved on its stiff castors. But the air! If you stopped to notice, was the air always like this? Little faint winds were playing chase in at the tops of the windows, out at the doors. And there were two tiny spots of sun, one on the inkpot, one on a silver photograph frame, playing too. Darling little spots. Especially the one on the inkpot lid. It was quite warm. A warm little silver star. She could have kissed it.

The front door bell pealed, and there sounded the rustle of Sadie's print skirt on the stairs. A man's voice murmured; Sadie answered, careless, "I'm sure I don't know. Wait. I'll ask Mrs Sheridan."

"What is it, Sadie?" Laura came into the hall.

"It's the florist, Miss Laura."

It was, indeed. There, just inside the door, stood a wide, shallow tray full of pots of pink lilies. No other kind. Nothing but lilies—canna lilies, big pink flowers, wide open, radiant, almost frighteningly alive on bright crimson stems.

"O-oh, Sadie!" said Laura, and the sound was like a little moan. She crouched down as if to warm herself at that blaze of lilies; she felt they were in her fingers, on her lips, growing in her breast.

"It's some mistake," she said faintly. "Nobody ever ordered so many. Sadie, go and find mother."

But at that moment Mrs Sheridan joined them.

"It's quite right," she said calmly. "Yes, I ordered them. Aren't they lovely?" She pressed Laura's arm. "I was passing the shop yesterday, and I saw them in the window, and I suddenly thought for once in my life I shall have enough canna lilies. The garden party will be a good excuse."

2 A swinging door that separated the servants' quarters from the rest of the house. Baize, a felt-like fabric, was often tacked to the inside of doors to insulate against noise.

"But I thought you said you didn't mean to interfere," said Laura. Sadie had gone. The florist's man was still outside at his van. She put her arm round her mother's neck and gently, very gently, she bit her mother's ear.

"My darling child, you wouldn't like a logical mother, would you? Don't do that. Here's the man."

He carried more lilies still, another whole tray.

"Bank them up, just inside the door, on both sides of the porch, please," said Mrs Sheridan. "Don't you agree, Laura?"

"Oh, I *do*, mother."

In the drawing room Meg, Jose, and good little Hans had at last succeeded in moving the piano.

"Now, if we put this chesterfield against the wall and move everything out of the room except the chairs, don't you think?"

"Quite."

"Hans, move these tables into the smoking room, and bring a sweeper to take these marks off the carpet and—one moment, Hans—" Jose loved giving orders to the servants, and they loved obeying her. She always made them feel they were taking part in some drama. "Tell Mother and Miss Laura to come here at once."

"Very good, Miss Jose."

She turned to Meg. "I want to hear what the piano sounds like, just in case I'm asked to sing this afternoon. Let's try over 'This Life is Weary.'"

Pom! Ta-ta-ta *Tee*-ta! The piano burst out so passionately that Jose's face changed. She clasped her hands. She looked mournfully and enigmatically at her mother and Laura as they came in.

This Life is *Wee*-ary,
A Tear—a Sigh.
A Love that *Chan*-ges,
 This Life is *Wee*-ary,
A Tear—a Sigh.
A Love that *Chan*-ges,
And then … Good-bye!

But at the word "Good-bye", and although the piano sounded more desperate than ever, her face broke into a brilliant, dreadfully unsympathetic smile.

"Aren't I in good voice, mummy?" she beamed.

This Life is *Wee*-ary,
Hope comes to Die,
A Dream—a *Wa*-kening.

But now Sadie interrupted them. "What is it, Sadie?"

"If you please, m'm, cook says have you got the flags for the sandwiches?"

"The flags for the sandwiches, Sadie?" echoed Mrs Sheridan dreamily. And the children knew by her face that she hadn't got them. "Let me see." And she said to Sadie firmly, "Tell cook I'll let her have them in ten minutes."

Sadie went.

"Now, Laura," said her mother quickly, "come with me into the smoking room. I've got the names somewhere on the back of an envelope. You'll have to write them out for me. Meg, go upstairs this minute and take that wet thing off your head. Jose, run and finish dressing this instant. Do you hear me, children, or shall I have to tell your father when he comes home tonight? And—and, Jose, pacify cook if you do go into the kitchen, will you? I'm terrified of her this morning."

The envelope was found at last behind the dining-room clock, though how it had got there Mrs Sheridan could not imagine.

"One of you children must have stolen it out of my bag, because I remember vividly—cream-cheese and lemon-curd. Have you done that?"

"Yes."

"Egg and—" Mrs Sheridan held the envelope away from her. "It looks like mice. It can't be mice, can it?"

"Olive, pet," said Laura, looking over her shoulder.

"Yes, of course, olive. What a horrible combination it sounds. Egg and olive."

They were finished at last, and Laura took them off to the kitchen. She found Jose there pacifying the cook, who did not look at all terrifying.

"I have never seen such exquisite sandwiches," said Jose's rapturous voice. "How many kinds did you say there were, cook? Fifteen?"

"Fifteen, Miss Jose."

"Well, cook, I congratulate you."

Cook swept up crusts with the long sandwich knife, and smiled broadly.

"Godber's has come," announced Sadie, issuing out of the pantry. She had seen the man pass the window.

That meant that cream puffs had come. Godber's were famous for their cream puffs. Nobody ever thought of making them at home.

"Bring them in and put them on the table, my girl," ordered cook.

Sadie brought them in and went back to the door. Of course Laura and Jose were far too grown-up to really care about such things. All the same, they couldn't help agreeing that the puffs looked very attractive. Very. Cook began arranging them, shaking off the extra icing sugar.

"Don't they carry one back to all one's parties?" said Laura.

"I suppose they do," said practical Jose, who never liked to be carried back. "They look beautifully light and feathery, I must say."

"Have one each, my dears," said cook in her comfortable voice. "Yer ma won't know."

Oh, impossible. Fancy cream puffs so soon after breakfast. The very idea made one shudder. All the same, two minutes later Jose and Laura were licking their fingers with that absorbed inward look that only comes from whipped cream.

"Let's go into the garden, out by the back way," suggested Laura. "I want to see how the men are getting on with the marquee. They're such awfully nice men."

But the back door was blocked by cook, Sadie, Godber's man and Hans.

Something had happened.

"Tuk-tuk-tuk," clucked cook like an agitated hen. Sadie had her hand clapped to her cheek as though she had a toothache. Hans's face was screwed up in the effort to understand. Only Godber's man seemed to be enjoying himself; it was his story.

"What's the matter? What happened?"

"There's been a horrible accident," said cook. "A man killed."

"A man killed! Where? How? When?"

But Godber's man wasn't going to have his story snatched from under his very nose.

"Know those little cottages just below here, miss?" Know them? Of course, she knew them. "Well, there's a young chap living there, name of *Scott*, a carter.[3] His horse shied at a traction-engine, corner of Hawke Street this morning, and he was thrown out on the back of his head. Killed."

"Dead!" Laura stared at Godber's man.

"Dead when they picked him up," said Godber's man with relish. "They were taking the body home as I come up here." And he said to the cook, "He's left a wife and five little ones."

"Jose, come here." Laura caught hold of her sister's sleeve and dragged her through the kitchen to the other side of the green baize door. There she paused and leaned against it. "Jose!" she said, horrified, "however are we going to stop everything?"

"Stop everything, Laura!" cried Jose in astonishment. "What do you mean?"

"Stop the garden party, of course." Why did Jose pretend?

But Jose was still more amazed. "Stop the garden party? My dear Laura, don't be so absurd. Of course we can't do anything of the kind. Nobody expects us to. Don't be so extravagant."

---

3 One who drives a horse-drawn vehicle used to transport goods or farming materials.

"But we can't possibly have a garden party with a man dead just outside the front gate."

That really was extravagant, for the little cottages were in a lane to themselves at the very bottom of a steep rise that led up to the house. A broad road ran between. True, they were far too near. They were the greatest possible eyesore and they had no right to be in that neighbourhood at all. They were little mean dwellings painted a chocolate brown. In the garden patches there was nothing but cabbage stalks, sick hens and tomato cans. The very smoke coming out of their chimneys was poverty-stricken. Little rags and shreds of smoke, so unlike the great silvery plumes that uncurled from the Sheridans' chimneys. Washerwomen lived in the lane and sweeps and a cobbler and a man whose house-front was studded all over with minute bird-cages. Children swarmed. When the Sheridans were little they were forbidden to set foot there because of the revolting language and of what they might catch. But since they were grown up, Laura and Laurie on their prowls sometimes walked through. It was disgusting and sordid. They came out with a shudder. But still one must go everywhere; one must see everything. So through they went.

"And just think of what the band would sound like to that poor woman," said Laura.

"Oh, Laura!" Jose began to be seriously annoyed. "If you're going to stop a band playing every time someone has an accident, you'll lead a very strenuous life. I'm every bit as sorry about it as you. I feel just as sympathetic." Her eyes hardened. She looked at her sister just as she used to when they were little and fighting together. "You won't bring a drunken workman back to life by being sentimental," she said softly.

"Drunk! Who said he was drunk?" Laura turned furiously on Jose. She said just as they had used to say on those occasions, "I'm going straight up to tell mother."

"Do, dear," cooed Jose.

"Mother, can I come into your room?" Laura turned the big glass doorknob.

"Of course, child. Why, what's the matter? What's given you such a color?" And Mrs Sheridan turned round from her dressing-table. She was trying on a new hat.

"Mother, a man's been killed," began Laura.

"*Not* in the garden?" interrupted her mother.

"No, no!"

"Oh, what a fright you gave me!" Mrs Sheridan sighed with relief, and took off the big hat and held it on her knees.

"But listen, mother," said Laura. Breathless, half-choking, she told the dreadful story. "Of course, we can't have our party, can we?" she pleaded. "The band and everybody arriving. They'd hear us, mother; they're nearly neighbors!"

To Laura's astonishment her mother behaved just like Jose; it was harder to bear because she seemed amused. She refused to take Laura seriously.

"But, my dear child, use your common sense. It's only by accident we've heard of it. If someone had died there normally—and I can't understand how they keep alive in those poky[4] little holes—we should still be having our party, shouldn't we?"

Laura had to say "yes" to that, but she felt it was all wrong. She sat down on her mother's sofa and pinched the cushion frill.

"Mother, isn't it really terribly heartless of us?" she asked.

"Darling!" Mrs Sheridan got up and came over to her, carrying the hat. Before Laura could stop her she had popped it on. "My child!" said her mother, "the hat is yours. It's made for you. It's much too young for me. I have never seen you look such a picture. Look at yourself!" And she held up her hand-mirror.

"But, mother," Laura began again. She couldn't look at herself; she turned aside.

This time Mrs Sheridan lost patience just as Jose had done.

"You are being very absurd, Laura," she said coldly. "People like that don't expect sacrifices from us. And it's not very sympathetic to spoil everybody's enjoyment as you're doing now."

"I don't understand," said Laura, and she walked quickly out of the room into her own bedroom. There, quite by chance, the first thing she saw was this charming girl in the mirror, in her black hat trimmed with gold daisies and a long black velvet ribbon. Never had she imagined she could look like that. Is mother right? she thought. And now she hoped her mother was right. Am I being extravagant? Perhaps it was extravagant. Just for a moment she had another glimpse of that poor woman and those little children, and the body being carried into the house. But it all seemed blurred, unreal, like a picture in the newspaper. I'll remember it again after the party's over, she decided. And somehow that seemed quite the best plan....

Lunch was over by half-past one. By half-past two they were all ready for the fray. The green-coated band had arrived and was established in a corner of the tennis court.

---

4 Small or cramped.

"My dear!" trilled Kitty Maitland, "aren't they too like frogs for words? You ought to have arranged them round the pond with the conductor in the middle on a leaf."

Laurie arrived and hailed them on his way to dress. At the sight of him Laura remembered the accident again. She wanted to tell him. If Laurie agreed with the others, then it was bound to be all right. And she followed him into the hall.

"Laurie!"

"Hallo!" He was halfway upstairs, but when he turned round and saw Laura he suddenly puffed out his cheeks and goggled his eyes at her. "My word, Laura! You do look stunning," said Laurie. "What an absolutely topping hat!"

Laura said faintly "Is it?" and smiled up at Laurie, and didn't tell him after all.

Soon after that people began coming in streams. The band struck up; the hired waiters ran from the house to the marquee. Wherever you looked there were couples strolling, bending to the flowers, greeting, moving on over the lawn. They were like bright birds that had alighted in the Sheridans' garden for this one afternoon, on their way to—where? Ah, what happiness it is to be with people who all are happy, to press hands, press cheeks, smile into eyes.

"Darling Laura, how well you look!"

"What a becoming hat, child!"

"Laura, you look quite Spanish. I've never seen you look so striking."

And Laura, glowing, answered softly, "Have you had tea? Won't you have an ice? The passion-fruit ices really are rather special." She ran to her father and begged him: "Daddy darling, can't the band have something to drink?"

And the perfect afternoon slowly ripened, slowly faded, slowly its petals closed.

"Never a more delightful garden party …" "The greatest success …" "Quite the most …"

Laura helped her mother with the good-byes. They stood side by side on the porch till it was all over.

"All over, all over, thank heaven," said Mrs Sheridan. "Round up the others, Laura. Let's go and have some fresh coffee. I'm exhausted. Yes, it's been very successful. But oh, these parties, these parties! Why will you children insist on giving parties!" And they all of them sat down in the deserted marquee.

"Have a sandwich, daddy dear. I wrote the flag."

"Thanks." Mr Sheridan took a bite and the sandwich was gone. He took another. "I suppose you didn't hear of a beastly accident that happened today?" he said.

"My dear," said Mrs Sheridan, holding up her hand, "we did. It nearly ruined the party. Laura insisted we should put it off."

"Oh, mother!" Laura didn't want to be teased about it.

"It was a horrible affair all the same," said Mr Sheridan. "The chap was married too. Lived just below in the lane, and leaves a wife and half a dozen kiddies, so they say."

An awkward little silence fell. Mrs Sheridan fidgeted with her cup. Really, it was very tactless of father....

Suddenly she looked up. There on the table were all those sandwiches, cakes, puffs, all uneaten, all going to be wasted. She had one of her brilliant ideas.

"I know," she said. "Let's make up a basket. Let's send that poor creature some of this perfectly good food. At any rate, it will be the greatest treat for the children. Don't you agree? And she's sure to have neighbors calling in and so on. What a point to have it all ready prepared. Laura!" She jumped up. "Get me the big basket out of the stairs cupboard."

"But, mother, do you really think it's a good idea?" said Laura.

Again, how curious, she seemed to be different from them all. To take scraps from their party. Would the poor woman really like that?

"Of course! What's the matter with you today? An hour or two ago you were insisting on us being sympathetic."

Oh well! Laura ran for the basket. It was filled, it was now heaped by her mother.

"Take it yourself, darling," said she. "Run down just as you are. No, wait, take the arum lilies too. People of that class are so impressed by arum lilies."

"The stems will ruin her lace frock," said practical Jose.

So they would. Just in time. "Only the basket, then. And, Laura!"—her mother followed her out of the marquee—"don't on any account—"

"What, mother?"

No, better not put such ideas into the child's head! "Nothing! Run along."

It was just growing dusky as Laura shut their garden gates. A big dog ran by like a shadow. The road gleamed white, and down below in the hollow the little cottages were in deep shade. How quiet it seemed after the afternoon. Here she was going down the hill to somewhere where a man lay dead, and she couldn't realize it. Why couldn't she? She stopped a minute. And it seemed to her that kisses, voices, tinkling spoons, laughter, the smell of crushed grass were somehow inside her. She had no room for anything else. How strange! She looked up at the pale sky, and all she thought was, "Yes, it was the most successful party."

Now the broad road was crossed. The lane began, smoky and dark. Women in shawls and men's tweed caps hurried by. Men hung over the palings; the children played in the doorways. A low hum came from the mean little cottages. In some of them there was a flicker of light, and a shadow, crab-like, moved across the window. Laura bent her head and hurried on. She wished now she had put on a coat. How her frock shone! And the big hat with the velvet streamer—if only it was another hat! Were the people looking at her? They must be. It was a mistake to have come; she knew all along it was a mistake. Should she go back even now?

No, too late. This was the house. It must be. A dark knot of people stood outside. Beside the gate an old, old woman with a crutch sat in a chair, watching. She had her feet on a newspaper. The voices stopped as Laura drew near. The group parted. It was as though she was expected, as though they had known she was coming here.

Laura was terribly nervous. Tossing the velvet ribbon over her shoulder, she said to a woman standing by, "Is this Mrs Scott's house?" and the woman, smiling queerly, said, "It is, my lass."

Oh, to be away from this! She actually said, "Help me, God," as she walked up the tiny path and knocked. To be away from those staring eyes, or to be covered up in anything, one of those women's shawls even. I'll just leave the basket and go, she decided. I shan't even wait for it to be emptied.

Then the door opened. A little woman in black showed in the gloom.

Laura said, "Are you Mrs Scott?" But to her horror the woman answered, "Walk in, please, miss," and she was shut in the passage.

"No," said Laura, "I don't want to come in. I only want to leave this basket. Mother sent—"

The little woman in the gloomy passage seemed not to have heard her. "Step this way, please, miss," she said in an oily voice, and Laura followed her.

She found herself in a wretched little low kitchen, lighted by a smoky lamp. There was a woman sitting before the fire.

"Em," said the little creature who had let her in. "Em! It's a young lady." She turned to Laura. She said meaningly, "I'm 'er sister, miss. You'll excuse 'er, won't you?"

"Oh, but of course!" said Laura. "Please, please don't disturb her. I—I only want to leave—"

But at that moment the woman at the fire turned round. Her face, puffed up, red, with swollen eyes and swollen lips, looked terrible. She seemed as though she couldn't understand why Laura was there. What did it mean? Why was this stranger standing in the kitchen with a basket? What was it all about? And the poor face puckered up again.

"All right, my dear," said the other. "I'll thenk the young lady."

And again she began, "You'll excuse her, miss, I'm sure," and her face, swollen too, tried an oily smile.

Laura only wanted to get out, to get away. She was back in the passage. The door opened. She walked straight through into the bedroom where the dead man was lying.

"You'd like a look at 'im, wouldn't you?" said Em's sister, and she brushed past Laura over to the bed. "Don't be afraid, my lass,"—and now her voice sounded fond and sly, and fondly she drew down the sheet—"'e looks a picture. There's nothing to show. Come along, my dear."

Laura came.

There lay a young man, fast asleep—sleeping so soundly, so deeply, that he was far, far away from them both. Oh, so remote, so peaceful. He was dreaming. Never wake him up again. His head was sunk in the pillows, his eyes were closed; they were blind under the closed eyelids. He was given up to his dream. What did garden parties and baskets and lace frocks matter to him? He was far from all those things. He was wonderful, beautiful. While they were laughing and while the band was playing, this marvel had come to the lane. Happy ... happy.... All is well, said that sleeping face. This is just as it should be. I am content.

But all the same you had to cry, and she couldn't go out of the room without saying something to him. Laura gave a loud childish sob.

"Forgive my hat," she said.

And this time she didn't wait for Em's sister. She found her way out of the door, down the path, past all those dark people. At the corner of the lane she met Laurie.

He stepped out of the shadow. "Is that you, Laura?"

"Yes."

"Mother was getting anxious. Was it all right?"

"Yes, quite. Oh, Laurie!" She took his arm, she pressed up against him.

"I say, you're not crying, are you?" asked her brother.

Laura shook her head. She was.

Laurie put his arm round her shoulder. "Don't cry," he said in his warm, loving voice. "Was it awful?"

"No," sobbed Laura. "It was simply marvellous. But, Laurie—" She stopped, she looked at her brother. "Isn't life," she stammered, "isn't life—" But what life was she couldn't explain. No matter. He quite understood.

"*Isn't* it, darling?" said Laurie.

—1922

KATHERINE ANNE PORTER

Katherine Anne Porter is commonly ranked alongside William Faulkner, Ernest Hemingway, and Flannery O'Connor, among America's foremost writers of short fiction. An exacting artist and consummate stylist, she wrote sparingly but finely, producing 27 stories and one novel. She won both the Pulitzer Prize and the National Book Award in 1966 for her *Collected Stories* (1965).

Porter was born Callie Russell Porter in Indian Creek, Texas, in 1890. Her mother died when Callie was not quite 2 years old; her father was unable to raise his four children and left them in the care of their grandmother, Catherine Anne Skaggs Porter. Though her family lived in poverty, Callie's years with her grandmother were relatively stable; her grandmother provided a model of resourcefulness, bravery, and self-sufficiency that left a lasting impression.

After her grandmother's death in 1901, Porter began a pattern of wandering that was to continue throughout her life, moving restlessly from place to place and from husband to husband. At age 16 she married John Henry Koontz, a railway clerk. After saving her spare change for years, Porter obtained a divorce in 1915, a rare achievement at that time in Texas. When the divorce was finalized, she legally assumed a variation of her grandmother's name, Katherine Anne. She moved to Chicago, Dallas, and Denver, taking various jobs: acting, singing, and writing articles. In Denver she nearly died in the Spanish Influenza Epidemic of 1918. When released from the hospital she was bald, and her hair, when it grew back, was stark white. This near-death experience, she said, "simply divided my life … and after that I was in some strange way altered, ready."

Porter shortly thereafter took off to New York and then Mexico, taking part in leftist politics and beginning to write her first short stories, beginning with "María Conceptíon," which appeared in *Century Magazine* in 1922. She was briefly married to an Englishman, Ernest Stock, whom she divorced in 1927. *Flowering Judas*, her first collection of stories, was published to critical acclaim in 1930. A Guggenheim fellowship followed, enabling her to travel Europe throughout the 1930s, mainly in Germany. Another fellowship was awarded in 1938; her nomadic life continued. She married her third husband, Ernest Pressly, in the early 1930s and divorced him in 1938, during which year she married her fourth husband, Albert Erskine, a graduate student 20 years her junior. They divorced in 1942.

Pale Horse, Pale Rider, a collection of three novellas, was published in 1939, further establishing Porter's reputation. She lived in an artists' colony in Saratoga Springs, New York, for two years and then turned to what she called "trouping" throughout the 1940s, taking up teaching assignments and writer-in-residence appointments at various American universities. Her unconventionality, brilliance, and beauty made her very popular with students. She published her only novel, *Ship of Fools*, in 1962; the book was a popular success, and it was made into a Hollywood film, providing Porter with financial security for the first time in her life. She died in Silver Spring, Maryland, in 1980, at the age of 90.

"The Jilting of Granny Weatherall" draws us closely into the mind of Granny Weatherall as she dies. Porter said of human life that it is "almost pure chaos," and that the role of the writer is to "take these handfuls of confusion and separate things … and put them together in a frame to give them some kind of shape and meaning."

The Jilting of Granny Weatherall

KATHERINE ANNE PORTER

SHE FLICKED her wrist neatly out of Doctor Harry's pudgy careful fingers and pulled the sheet up to her chin. The brat ought to be in knee breeches. Doctoring around the country with spectacles on his nose! "Get along now, take your schoolbooks and go. There's nothing wrong with me."

Doctor Harry spread a warm paw like a cushion on her forehead where the forked green vein danced and made her eyelids twitch. "Now, now, be a good girl, and we'll have you up in no time."

"That's no way to speak to a woman nearly eighty years old just because she's down. I'd have you respect your elders, young man."

"Well, Missy, excuse me." Doctor Harry patted her cheek. "But I've got to warn you, haven't I? You're a marvel, but you must be careful or you're going to be good and sorry."

"Don't tell me what I'm going to be. I'm on my feet now, morally speaking. It's Cornelia. I had to go to bed to get rid of her."

Her bones felt loose, and floated around in her skin, and Doctor Harry floated like a balloon around the foot of the bed. He floated and pulled down his waistcoat and swung his glasses on a cord. "Well, stay where you are, it certainly can't hurt you."

"Get along and doctor your sick," said Granny Weatherall. "Leave a well woman alone. I'll call for you when I want you.... Where were you forty years ago when I pulled through milk-leg[1] and double pneumonia? You weren't even born. Don't let Cornelia lead you on," she shouted, because Doctor Harry appeared to float up to the ceiling and out. "I pay my own bills, and I don't throw my money away on nonsense!"

She meant to wave good-by, but it was too much trouble. Her eyes closed of themselves, it was like a dark curtain drawn around the bed. The pillow rose and floated under her, pleasant as a hammock in a light wind. She listened to the leaves rustling outside the window. No, somebody was swishing newspapers: no, Cornelia and Doctor Harry were whispering together. She leaped broad awake, thinking they whispered in her ear.

"She was never like this, *never* like this!" "Well, what can we expect?" "Yes, eighty years old...."

Well, and what if she was? She still had ears. It was like Cornelia to whisper around doors. She always kept things secret in such a public way. She was always being tactful and kind. Cornelia was dutiful; that was the trouble with her. Dutiful and good: "So good and dutiful," said Granny, "that I'd like to spank her." She saw herself spanking Cornelia and making a fine job of it.

"What'd you say, Mother?"

Granny felt her face tying up in hard knots.

"Can't a body think, I'd like to know?"

"I thought you might want something."

"I do. I want a lot of things. First off, go away and don't whisper."

She lay and drowsed, hoping in her sleep that the children would keep out and let her rest a minute. It had been a long day. Not that she was tired. It was always pleasant to snatch a minute now and then. There was always so much to be done, let me see: tomorrow.

Tomorrow was far away and there was nothing to trouble about. Things were finished somehow when the time came; thank God there was always a little margin over for peace: then a person could spread out the plan of life and tuck in the edges orderly. It was good to have everything clean and folded away, with the hair brushes and tonic bottles sitting straight on the white embroidered linen: the day started without fuss and the pantry shelves laid out with rows

---

1 Swelling of the legs after childbirth, caused by deep vein thrombosis.

of jelly glasses and brown jugs and white stone-china jars with blue whirligigs and words painted on them: coffee, tea, sugar, ginger, cinnamon, allspice: and the bronze clock with the lion on top nicely dusted off. The dust that lion could collect in twenty-four hours! The box in the attic with all those letters tied up, well, she'd have to go through that tomorrow. All those letters—George's letters and John's letters and her letters to them both—lying around for the children to find afterwards made her uneasy. Yes, that would be tomorrow's business. No use to let them know how silly she had been once.

While she was rummaging around she found death in her mind and it felt clammy and unfamiliar. She had spent so much time preparing for death there was no need for bringing it up again. Let it take care of itself now. When she was sixty she had felt very old, finished, and went around making farewell trips to see her children and grandchildren, with a secret in her mind: This is the very last of your mother, children! Then she made her will and came down with a long fever. That was all just a notion like a lot of other things, but it was lucky too, for she had once for all got over the idea of dying for a long time. Now she couldn't be worried. She hoped she had better sense now. Her father had lived to be one hundred and two years old and had drunk a noggin of strong hot toddy on his last birthday. He told the reporters it was his daily habit, and he owed his long life to that. He had made quite a scandal and was very pleased about it. She believed she'd just plague Cornelia a little.

"Cornelia! Cornelia!" No footsteps, but a sudden hand on her cheek. "Bless you, where have you been?"

"Here, Mother."

"Well, Cornelia, I want a noggin of hot toddy."

"Are you cold, darling?"

"I'm chilly, Cornelia. Lying in bed stops the circulation. I must have told you that a thousand times."

Well, she could just hear Cornelia telling her husband that Mother was getting a little childish and they'd have to humor her. The thing that most annoyed her was that Cornelia thought she was deaf, dumb, and blind. Little hasty glances and tiny gestures tossed around her and over her head saying, "Don't cross her, let her have her way, she's eighty years old," and she sitting there as if she lived in a thin glass cage. Sometimes Granny almost made up her mind to pack up and move back to her own house where nobody could remind her every minute that she was old. Wait, wait, Cornelia, till your own children whisper behind your back!

In her day she had kept a better house and had got more work done. She wasn't too old yet for Lydia to be driving eighty miles for advice when one of the children jumped the track, and Jimmy still dropped in and talked things over:

"Now, Mammy, you've a good business head, I want to know what you think of this? ..." Old. Cornelia couldn't change the furniture around without asking. Little things, little things! They had been so sweet when they were little. Granny wished the old days were back again with the children young and everything to be done over. It had been a hard pull, but not too much for her. When she thought of all the food she had cooked, and all the clothes she had cut and sewed, and all the gardens she had made—well, the children showed it. There they were, made out of her, and they couldn't get away from that. Sometimes she wanted to see John again and point to them and say, Well, I didn't do so badly, did I? But that would have to wait. That was for tomorrow. She used to think of him as a man, but now all the children were older than their father, and he would be a child beside her if she saw him now. It seemed strange and there was something wrong in the idea. Why, he couldn't possibly recognize her. She had fenced in a hundred acres once, digging the post holes herself and clamping the wires with just a negro boy to help. That changed a woman. John would be looking for a young woman with the peaked Spanish comb in her hair and the painted fan. Digging post holes changed a woman. Riding country roads in the winter when women had their babies was another thing: sitting up nights with sick horses and sick negroes and sick children and hardly ever losing one. John, I hardly ever lost one of them! John would see that in a minute, that would be something he could understand, she wouldn't have to explain anything!

It made her feel like rolling up her sleeves and putting the whole place to rights again. No matter if Cornelia was determined to be everywhere at once, there were a great many things left undone on this place. She would start tomorrow and do them. It was good to be strong enough for everything, even if all you made melted and changed and slipped under your hands, so that by the time you finished you almost forgot what you were working for. What was it I set out to do? she asked herself intently, but she could not remember. A fog rose over the valley, she saw it marching across the creek swallowing the trees and moving up the hill like an army of ghosts. Soon it would be at the near edge of the orchard, and then it was time to go in and light the lamps. Come in, children, don't stay out in the night air.

Lighting the lamps had been beautiful. The children huddled up to her and breathed like little calves waiting at the bars in the twilight. Their eyes followed the match and watched the flame rise and settle in a blue curve, then they moved away from her. The lamp was lit, they didn't have to be scared and hang on to mother any more. Never, never, never more. God, for all my life I thank Thee. Without Thee, my God, I could never have done it. Hail, Mary, full of grace.

I want you to pick all the fruit this year and see that nothing is wasted. There's always someone who can use it. Don't let good things rot for want of using. You waste life when you waste good food. Don't let things get lost. It's bitter to lose things. Now, don't let me get to thinking, not when I am tired and taking a little nap before supper....

The pillow rose about her shoulders and pressed against her heart and the memory was being squeezed out of it: oh, push down the pillow, somebody: it would smother her if she tried to hold it. Such a fresh breeze blowing and such a green day with no threats in it. But he had not come, just the same. What does a woman do when she has put on the white veil and set out the white cake for a man and he doesn't come? She tried to remember. No, I swear he never harmed me but in that. He never harmed me but in that ... and what if he did? There was the day, the day, but a whirl of dark smoke rose and covered it, crept up and over into the bright field where everything was planted so carefully in orderly rows. That was hell, she knew hell when she saw it. For sixty years she had prayed against remembering him and against losing her soul in the deep pit of hell, and now the two things were mingled in one and the thought of him was a smoky cloud from hell that moved and crept in her head when she had just got rid of Doctor Harry and was trying to rest a minute. Wounded vanity, Ellen, said a sharp voice in the top of her mind. Don't let your wounded vanity get the upper hand of you. Plenty of girls get jilted. You were jilted, weren't you? Then stand up to it. Her eyelids wavered and let in streamers of blue-gray light like tissue paper over her eyes. She must get up and pull the shades down or she'd never sleep. She was in bed again and the shades were not down. How could that happen? Better turn over, hide from the light, sleeping in the light gave you nightmares. "Mother, how do you feel now?" and a stinging wetness on her forehead. But I don't like having my face washed in cold water!

Hapsy? George? Lydia? Jimmy? No, Cornelia, and her features were swollen and full of little puddles. "They're coming, darling, they'll all be here soon." Go wash your face, child, you look funny.

Instead of obeying, Cornelia knelt down and put her head on the pillow. She seemed to be talking but there was no sound. "Well, are you tongue-tied? Whose birthday is it? Are you going to give a party?"

Cornelia's mouth moved urgently in strange shapes. "Don't do that, you bother me, daughter."

"Oh, no, Mother. Oh, no...."

Nonsense. It was strange about children. They disputed your every word. "No what, Cornelia?"

"Here's Doctor Harry."

"I won't see that boy again. He just left five minutes ago."

"That was this morning, Mother. It's night now. Here's the nurse."

"This is Doctor Harry, Mrs. Weatherall. I never saw you look so young and happy!"

"Ah, I'll never be young again—but I'd be happy if they'd let me lie in peace and get rested."

She thought she spoke up loudly, but no one answered. A warm weight on her forehead, a warm bracelet on her wrist, and a breeze went on whispering, trying to tell her something. A shuffle of leaves in the everlasting hand of God, He blew on them and they danced and rattled. "Mother, don't mind, we're going to give you a little hypodermic." "Look here, daughter, how do ants get in this bed? I saw sugar ants yesterday." Did you send for Hapsy too?

It was Hapsy she really wanted. She had to go a long way back through a great many rooms to find Hapsy standing with a baby on her arm. She seemed to herself to be Hapsy also, and the baby on Hapsy's arm was Hapsy and himself and herself, all at once, and there was no surprise in the meeting. Then Hapsy melted from within and turned flimsy as gray gauze and the baby was a gauzy shadow, and Hapsy came up close and said, "I thought you'd never come," and looked at her very searchingly and said, "You haven't changed a bit!" They leaned forward to kiss, when Cornelia began whispering from a long way off, "Oh, is there anything you want to tell me? Is there anything I can do for you?"

Yes, she had changed her mind after sixty years and she would like to see George. I want you to find George. Find him and be sure to tell him I forgot him. I want him to know I had my husband just the same and my children and my house like any other woman. A good house too and a good husband that I loved and fine children out of him. Better than I hoped for even. Tell him I was given back everything he took away and more. Oh, no, oh, God, no, there was something else besides the house and the man and the children. Oh, surely they were not all? What was it? Something not given back.... Her breath crowded down under her ribs and grew into a monstrous frightening shape with cutting edges; it bored up into her head, and the agony was unbelievable: Yes, John, get the Doctor now, no more talk, my time has come.

When this one was born it should be the last. The last. It should have been born first, for it was the one she had truly wanted. Everything came in good time. Nothing left out, left over. She was strong, in three days she would be as well as ever. Better. A woman needed milk in her to have her full health.

"Mother, do you hear me?"

"I've been telling you—"

"Mother, Father Connolly's here."

"I went to Holy Communion only last week. Tell him I'm not so sinful as all that."

"Father just wants to speak to you."

He could speak as much as he pleased. It was like him to drop in and inquire about her soul as if it were a teething baby, and then stay on for a cup of tea and a round of cards and gossip. He always had a funny story of some sort, usually about an Irishman who made his little mistakes and confessed them, and the point lay in some absurd thing he would blurt out in the confessional showing his struggles between native piety and original sin. Granny felt easy about her soul. Cornelia, where are your manners? Give Father Connolly a chair. She had her secret comfortable understanding with a few favorite saints who cleared a straight road to God for her. All as surely signed and sealed as the papers for the new Forty Acres. Forever … heirs and assigns forever.[2] Since the day the wedding cake was not cut, but thrown out and wasted. The whole bottom dropped out of the world, and there she was blind and sweating with nothing under her feet and the walls falling away. His hand had caught her under the breast, she had not fallen, there was the freshly polished floor with the green rug on it, just as before. He had cursed like a sailor's parrot and said, "I'll kill him for you." Don't lay a hand on him, for my sake leave something to God. "Now, Ellen, you must believe what I tell you…."

So there was nothing, nothing to worry about any more, except sometimes in the night one of the children screamed in a nightmare, and they both hustled out shaking and hunting for the matches and calling, "There, wait a minute, here we are!" John, get the doctor now, Hapsy's time has come. But there was Hapsy standing by the bed in a white cap. "Cornelia, tell Hapsy to take off her cap. I can't see her plain."

Her eyes opened very wide and the room stood out like a picture she had seen somewhere. Dark colors with the shadows rising towards the ceiling in long angles. The tall black dresser gleamed with nothing on it but John's picture, enlarged from a little one, with John's eyes very black when they should have been blue. You never saw him, so how do you know how he looked? But the man insisted the copy was perfect, it was very rich and handsome. For a picture, yes, but it's not my husband. The table by the bed had a linen cover and a candle and a crucifix. The light was blue from Cornelia's silk lampshades. No sort of light at all, just frippery. You had to live forty years with kerosene lamps to appreciate honest electricity. She felt very strong and she saw Doctor Harry with a rosy nimbus around him.

"You look like a saint, Doctor Harry, and I vow that's as near as you'll ever come to it."

"She's saying something."

---

2 Legal term used with fee simple estates, where ownership of an estate is able to be transferred to heirs and assigns without limitation.

"I heard you, Cornelia. What's all this carrying-on?"

"Father Connolly's saying—"

Cornelia's voice staggered and bumped like a cart in a bad road. It rounded corners and turned back again and arrived nowhere. Granny stepped up in the cart very lightly and reached for the reins, but a man sat beside her and she knew him by his hands, driving the cart. She did not look in his face, for she knew without seeing, but looked instead down the road where the trees leaned over and bowed to each other and a thousand birds were singing a Mass. She felt like singing too, but she put her hand in the bosom of her dress and pulled out a rosary, and Father Connolly murmured Latin in a very solemn voice and tickled her feet. My God, will you stop that nonsense? I'm a married woman. What if he did run away and leave me to face the priest by myself? I found another a whole world better. I wouldn't have exchanged my husband for anybody except St. Michael himself, and you may tell him that for me with a thank you in the bargain.

Light flashed on her closed eyelids, and a deep roaring shook her. Cornelia, is that lightning? I hear thunder. There's going to be a storm. Close all the windows. Call the children in.... "Mother, here we are, all of us." "Is that you, Hapsy?" "Oh, no, I'm Lydia. We drove as fast as we could." Their faces drifted above her, drifted away. The rosary fell out of her hands and Lydia put it back. Jimmy tried to help, their hands fumbled together, and Granny closed two fingers around Jimmy's thumb. Beads wouldn't do, it must be something alive. She was so amazed her thoughts ran round and round. So, my dear Lord, this is my death and I wasn't even thinking about it. My children have come to see me die. But I can't, it's not time. Oh, I always hated surprises. I wanted to give Cornelia the amethyst set—Cornelia, you're to have the amethyst set, but Hapsy's to wear it when she wants, and, Doctor Harry, do shut up. Nobody sent for you. Oh, my dear Lord, do wait a minute. I meant to do something about the Forty Acres, Jimmy doesn't need it and Lydia will later on, with that worthless husband of hers. I meant to finish the altar cloth and send six bottles of wine to Sister Borgia for her dyspepsia.[3] I want to send six bottles of wine to Sister Borgia, Father Connolly, now don't let me forget.

Cornelia's voice made short turns and tilted over and crashed. "Oh, Mother, oh, Mother, oh, Mother...."

"I'm not going, Cornelia. I'm taken by surprise. I can't go."

You'll see Hapsy again. What about her? "I thought you'd never come." Granny made a long journey outward, looking for Hapsy. What if I don't find her? What then? Her heart sank down and down, there was no bottom to death,

3 Indigestion.

she couldn't come to the end of it. The blue light from Cornelia's lampshade drew into a tiny point in the center of her brain, it flickered and winked like an eye, quietly it fluttered and dwindled. Granny lay curled down within herself, amazed and watchful, staring at the point of light that was herself; her body was now only a deeper mass of shadow in an endless darkness and this darkness would curl around the light and swallow it up. God, give a sign!

For the second time there was no sign. Again no bridegroom and the priest in the house. She could not remember any other sorrow because this grief wiped them all away. Oh, no, there's nothing more cruel than this—I'll never forgive it. She stretched herself with a deep breath and blew out the light.

—1930

WILLIAM FAULKNER

William Faulkner (originally spelled "Falkner") is most famous for his novels and short stories set in the fictional Yoknapatawpha County, a county that corresponds to Lafayette County, Mississippi, where Faulkner grew up. More than ten of his novels and numerous short stories take place in Yoknapatawpha, including *The Sound and the Fury* (1929) and *Go Down Moses* (1942).

The descendant of a Confederate colonel, William Faulkner was born in 1897 in New Albany, Mississippi. Although he was a prolific reader, Faulkner did not do well in school and dropped out in the eleventh grade; he attempted to enlist for pilot training in the US Army, but was rejected. After World War I, he enrolled at the University of Mississippi for a short time and worked at the university post office, among other odd jobs.

Faulkner had written poetry since he was a child and published a collection of poetry, *The Marble Faun*, at his own expense in 1924. In 1927, he published his first novel, *Mosquitoes*. Two years later, Faulkner married Estelle Oldham—a match arranged by their families, and a marriage that would be troubled by both partners' periodic bouts of alcoholism.

Faulkner continued to write novels and short stories for literary periodicals; to supplement this income and support his family, he found work in Hollywood as a screenwriter. Faulkner collaborated with director Howard Hawks on several well-known films—among them *To Have and Have Not* (1945) and *The Big Sleep* (1946)—but he resented having to write for Hollywood. By 1944, most of his books were out of print, his marriage to Estelle had ended in divorce, and his drinking was at an unprecedented level of excess. In France, however, his fiction was being read enthusiastically by writers such as Jean-Paul Sartre and Albert Camus, whose admiration for his work would later contribute to the resurrection of his literary career.

In 1946, Faulkner's literary profile took a major turn for the better when American poet and literary critic Malcolm Cowley brought out *The Portable Faulkner* and reawakened American interest in the writer's work. Praise and critical accolades were unreserved in the period following: Faulkner was awarded the Nobel Prize for Literature in 1949; he was made a member of the French Legion of Honor; and he won two Pulitzer Prizes, among other awards, for his books *A Fable* (1954) and *The Reivers* (1962). In 1954 he was made an ambassador for the US State Department, and in 1957 was writer-in-residence at the University of Virginia. He died in 1962 of heart failure.

When asked about his writing process in a 1956 interview with *The Paris Review*, Faulkner said that for him, "a story usually begins with a single idea or memory or mental picture." One of Faulkner's most celebrated (and shortest) stories, "Dry September" is built around such vivid "pictures," capturing the essence of a town and its people in precise evocations of dust, heat, insects, and the night sky.

Dry September

WILLIAM FAULKNER

I

THROUGH THE bloody September twilight, aftermath of sixty-two rainless days, it had gone like a fire in dry grass—the rumor, the story, whatever it was. Something about Miss Minnie Cooper and a Negro. Attacked, insulted, frightened: none of them, gathered in the barber shop on that Saturday evening where the ceiling fan stirred, without freshening it, the vitiated[1] air, sending back upon them, in recurrent surges of stale pomade and lotion, their own stale breath and odors, knew exactly what had happened.

"Except it wasn't Will Mayes," a barber said. He was a man of middle age; a thin, sand-colored man with a mild face, who was shaving a client. "I know Will Mayes. He's a good nigger.[2] And I know Miss Minnie Cooper, too."

"What do you know about her?" a second barber said.

"Who is she?" the client said. "A young girl?"

"No," the barber said. "She's about forty, I reckon. She aint married. That's why I dont believe—"

"Believe, hell!" a hulking youth in a sweat-stained silk shirt said. "Wont you take a white woman's word before a nigger's?"

"I dont believe Will Mayes did it," the barber said. "I know Will Mayes."

"Maybe you know who did it, then. Maybe you already got him out of town, you damn niggerlover."

---

1 Spoiled.

2 This pejorative term remained in frequent use by many white Americans in the South until well into the 1960s.

"I dont believe anybody did anything. I dont believe anything happened. I leave it to you fellows if them ladies that get old without getting married dont have notions that a man cant—"

"Then you are a hell of a white man," the client said. He moved under the cloth. The youth had sprung to his feet.

"You dont?" he said. "Do you accuse a white woman of lying?"

The barber held the razor poised above the half-risen client. He did not look around.

"It's this durn weather," another said. "It's enough to make a man do anything. Even to her."

Nobody laughed. The barber said in his mild, stubborn tone: "I aint accusing nobody of nothing. I just know and you fellows know how a woman that never—"

"You damn niggerlover!" the youth said.

"Shut up, Butch," another said. "We'll get the facts in plenty of time to act."

"Who is? Who's getting them?" the youth said. "Facts, hell! I—"

"You're a fine white man," the client said. "Aint you?" In his frothy beard he looked like a desert rat in the moving pictures. "You tell them, Jack," he said to the youth. "If there aint any white men in this town, you can count on me, even if I aint only a drummer and a stranger."

"That's right, boys," the barber said. "Find out the truth first. I know Will Mayes."

"Well, by God!" the youth shouted. "To think that a white man in this town—"

"Shut up, Butch," the second speaker said. "We got plenty of time."

The client sat up. He looked at the speaker. "Do you claim that anything excuses a nigger attacking a white woman? Do you mean to tell me you are a white man and you'll stand for it? You better go back North where you came from. The South dont want your kind here."

"North what?" the second said. "I was born and raised in this town."

"Well, by God!" the youth said. He looked about with a strained, baffled gaze, as if he was trying to remember what it was he wanted to say or to do. He drew his sleeve across his sweating face. "Damn if I'm going to let a white woman—"

"You tell them, Jack," the drummer said. "By God, if they—"

The screen door crashed open. A man stood in the floor, his feet apart and his heavy-set body poised easily. His white shirt was open at the throat; he wore a felt hat. His hot, bold glance swept the group. His name was McLendon. He had commanded troops at the front in France and had been decorated for valor.

"Well," he said, "are you going to sit there and let a black son rape a white woman on the streets of Jefferson?"

Butch sprang up again. The silk of his shirt clung flat to his heavy shoulders. At each armpit was a dark halfmoon. "That's what I been telling them! That's what I—"

"Did it really happen?" a third said. "This aint the first man scare she ever had, like Hawkshaw says. Wasn't there something about a man on the kitchen roof, watching her undress, about a year ago?"

"What?" the client said. "What's that?" The barber had been slowly forcing him back into the chair; he arrested himself reclining, his head lifted, the barber still pressing him down.

McLendon whirled on the third speaker. "Happen? What the hell difference does it make? Are you going to let the black sons get away with it until one really does it?"

"That's what I'm telling them!" Butch shouted. He cursed, long and steady, pointless.

"Here, here," a fourth said. "Not so loud. Dont talk so loud."

"Sure," McLendon said; "no talking necessary at all. I've done my talking. Who's with me?" He poised on the balls of his feet, roving his gaze.

The barber held the drummer's face down, the razor poised. "Find out the facts first, boys. I know Willy Mayes. It wasn't him. Let's get the sheriff and do this thing right."

McLendon whirled upon him his furious, rigid face. The barber did not look away. They looked like men of different races. The other barbers had ceased also above their prone clients. "You mean to tell me," McLendon said, "that you'd take a nigger's word before a white woman's? Why, you damn niggerloving—"

The third speaker rose and grasped McLendon's arm; he too had been a soldier. "Now, now. Let's figure this thing out. Who knows anything about what really happened?"

"Figure out hell!" McLendon jerked his arm free. "All that're with me get up from there. The ones that aint—" He roved his gaze, dragging his sleeve across his face.

Three men rose. The drummer in the chair sat up. "Here," he said, jerking at the cloth about his neck; "get this rag off me. I'm with him. I dont live here, but by God, if our mothers and wives and sisters—" He smeared the cloth over his face and flung it to the floor. McLendon stood in the floor and cursed the others. Another rose and moved toward him. The remainder sat uncomfortable, not looking at one another, then one by one they rose and joined him.

The barber picked the cloth from the floor. He began to fold it neatly. "Boys, dont do that. Will Mayes never done it. I know."

"Come on," McLendon said. He whirled. From his hip pocket protruded the butt of a heavy automatic pistol. They went out. The screen door crashed behind them reverberant in the dead air.

The barber wiped the razor carefully and swiftly, and put it away, and ran to the rear, and took his hat from the wall. "I'll be back as soon as I can," he said to the other barbers. "I cant let—" He went out, running. The two other barbers followed him to the door and caught it on the rebound, leaning out and looking up the street after him. The air was flat and dead. It had a metallic taste at the base of the tongue.

"What can he do?" the first said. The second one was saying "Jees Christ, Jees Christ" under his breath. "I'd just as lief[3] be Will Mayes as Hawk, if he gets McLendon riled."

"Jees Christ, Jees Christ," the second whispered.

"You reckon he really done it to her?" the first said.

II

She was thirty-eight or thirty-nine. She lived in a small frame house with her invalid mother and a thin, sallow, unflagging aunt, where each morning between ten and eleven she would appear on the porch in a lace-trimmed boudoir cap, to sit swinging in the porch swing until noon. After dinner she lay down for a while, until the afternoon began to cool. Then, in one of the three or four new voile dresses which she had each summer, she would go downtown to spend the afternoon in the stores with the other ladies, where they would handle the goods and haggle over the prices in cold, immediate voices, without any intention of buying.

She was of comfortable people—not the best in Jefferson, but good people enough—and she was still on the slender side of ordinary looking, with a bright, faintly haggard manner and dress. When she was young she had had a slender, nervous body and a sort of hard vivacity which had enabled her for a time to ride upon the crest of the town's social life as exemplified by the high school party and church social period of her contemporaries while still children enough to be unclassconscious.

She was the last to realize that she was losing ground; that those among whom she had been a little brighter and louder flame than any other were beginning to learn the pleasure of snobbery—male—and retaliation—female. That was when her face began to wear that bright, haggard look. She still carried it to parties on shadowy porticoes and summer lawns, like a mask or a flag, with that bafflement of furious repudiation of truth in her eyes. One evening at a party she heard a boy and two girls, all schoolmates, talking. She never accepted another invitation.

She watched the girls with whom she had grown up as they married and got homes and children, but no man ever called on her steadily until the children of the other girls had been calling her "aunty" for several years, the while their

3 Gladly.

mothers told them in bright voices about how popular Aunt Minnie had been as a girl. Then the town began to see her driving on Sunday afternoons with the cashier in the bank. He was a widower of about forty—a high-colored man, smelling always faintly of the barber shop or of whisky. He owned the first automobile in town, a red runabout; Minnie had the first motoring bonnet and veil the town ever saw. Then the town began to say: "Poor Minnie." "But she is old enough to take care of herself," others said. That was when she began to ask her old schoolmates that their children call her "cousin" instead of "aunty."

It was twelve years now since she had been relegated into adultery by public opinion, and eight years since the cashier had gone to a Memphis bank, returning for one day each Christmas, which he spent at an annual bachelors' party at a hunting club on the river. From behind their curtains the neighbors would see the party pass, and during the over-the-way Christmas day visiting they would tell her about him, about how well he looked, and how they heard that he was prospering in the city, watching with bright, secret eyes her haggard, bright face. Usually by that hour there would be the scent of whisky on her breath. It was supplied her by a youth, a clerk at the soda fountain: "Sure; I buy it for the old gal. I reckon she's entitled to a little fun."

Her mother kept to her room altogether now; the gaunt aunt ran the house. Against that background Minnie's bright dresses, her idle and empty days, had a quality of furious unreality. She went out in the evenings only with women now, neighbors, to the moving pictures. Each afternoon she dressed in one of the new dresses and went downtown alone, where her young "cousins" were already strolling in the late afternoons with their delicate, silken heads and thin, awkward arms and conscious hips, clinging to one another or shrieking and giggling with paired boys in the soda fountain when she passed and went on along the serried[4] store fronts, in the doors of which the sitting and lounging men did not even follow her with their eyes any more.

III

The barber went swiftly up the street where the sparse lights, insect-swirled, glared in rigid and violent suspension in the lifeless air. The day had died in a pall of dust; above the darkened square, shrouded by the spent dust, the sky was as clear as the inside of a brass bell. Below the east was a rumor of the twice-waxed moon.

When he overtook them McLendon and three others were getting into a car parked in an alley. McLendon stooped his thick head, peering out beneath the

4 Close together.

top. "Changed your mind, did you?" he said. "Damn good thing; by God, tomorrow when this town hears about how you talked tonight—"

"Now, now," the other ex-soldier said. "Hawkshaw's all right. Come on, Hawk; jump in."

"Will Mayes never done it, boys," the barber said. "If anybody done it. Why, you all know well as I do there aint any town where they got better niggers than us. And you know how a lady will kind of think things about men when there aint any reason to, and Miss Minnie anyway—"

"Sure, sure," the soldier said. "We're just going to talk to him a little; that's all."

"Talk hell!" Butch said. "When we're through with the—"

"Shut up, for God's sake!" the soldier said. "Do you want everybody in town—"

"Tell them, by God!" McLendon said. "Tell every one of the sons that'll let a white woman—"

"Let's go; let's go: here's the other car." The second car slid squealing out of a cloud of dust at the alley mouth. McLendon started his car and took the lead. Dust lay like fog in the street. The street lights hung nimbused as in water. They drove on out of town.

A rutted lane turned at right angles. Dust hung above it too, and above all the land. The dark bulk of the ice plant, where the Negro Mayes was night watchman, rose against the sky. "Better stop here, hadn't we?" the soldier said. McLendon did not reply. He hurled the car up and slammed to a stop, the headlights glaring on the blank wall.

"Listen here, boys," the barber said; "if he's here, dont that prove he never done it? Dont it? If it was him, he would run. Dont you see he would?" The second car came up and stopped. McLendon got down; Butch sprang down beside him. "Listen, boys," the barber said.

"Cut the lights off!" McLendon said. The breathless dark rushed down. There was no sound in it save their lungs as they sought air in the parched dust in which for two months they had lived; then the diminishing crunch of McLendon's and Butch's feet, and a moment later McLendon's voice:

"Will! ... Will!"

Below the east the wan hemorrhage of the moon increased. It heaved above the ridge, silvering the air, the dust, so that they seemed to breathe, live, in a bowl of molten lead. There was no sound of nightbird nor insect, no sound save their breathing and a faint ticking of contracting metal about the cars. Where their bodies touched one another they seemed to sweat dryly, for no more moisture came. "Christ!" a voice said; "let's get out of here."

But they didn't move until vague noises began to grow out of the darkness ahead; then they got out and waited tensely in the breathless dark. There was another sound: a blow, a hissing expulsion of breath and McLendon cursing in undertone. They stood a moment longer, then they ran forward. They ran in a stumbling clump, as though they were fleeing something. "Kill him, kill the son," a voice whispered. McLendon flung them back.

"Not here," he said. "Get him into the car." "Kill him, kill the black son!" the voice murmured. They dragged the Negro to the car. The barber had waited beside the car. He could feel himself sweating and he knew he was going to be sick at the stomach.

"What is it, captains?" the Negro said. "I aint done nothing. 'Fore God, Mr John." Someone produced handcuffs. They worked busily about the Negro as though he were a post, quiet, intent, getting in one another's way. He submitted to the handcuffs, looking swiftly and constantly from dim face to dim face. "Who's here, captains?" he said, leaning to peer into the faces until they could feel his breath and smell his sweaty reek. He spoke a name or two. "What you all say I done, Mr John?"

McLendon jerked the car door open. "Get in!" he said.

The Negro did not move. "What you all going to do with me, Mr John? I aint done nothing. White folks, captains, I aint done nothing: I swear 'fore God." He called another name.

"Get in!" McLendon said. He struck the Negro. The others expelled their breath in a dry hissing and struck him with random blows and he whirled and cursed them, and swept his manacled hands across their faces and slashed the barber upon the mouth, and the barber struck him also. "Get him in there," McLendon said. They pushed at him. He ceased struggling and got in and sat quietly as the others took their places. He sat between the barber and the soldier, drawing his limbs in so as not to touch them, his eyes going swiftly and constantly from face to face. Butch clung to the running board. The car moved on. The barber nursed his mouth with his handkerchief.

"What's the matter, Hawk?" the soldier said.

"Nothing," the barber said. They regained the highroad and turned away from town. The second car dropped back out of the dust. They went on, gaining speed; the final fringe of houses dropped behind.

"Goddamn, he stinks!" the soldier said.

"We'll fix that," the drummer in front beside McLendon said. On the running board Butch cursed into the hot rush of air. The barber leaned suddenly forward and touched McLendon's arm.

"Let me out, John," he said.

"Jump out, niggerlover," McLendon said without turning his head. He drove swiftly. Behind them the sourceless lights of the second car glared in the dust. Presently McLendon turned into a narrow road. It was rutted with disuse. It led back to an abandoned brick kiln—a series of reddish mounds and weed- and vine-choked vats without bottom. It had been used for pasture once, until one day the owner missed one of his mules. Although he prodded carefully in the vats with a long pole, he could not even find the bottom of them.

"John," the barber said.

"Jump out, then," McLendon said, hurling the car along the ruts. Beside the barber the Negro spoke:

"Mr Henry."

The barber sat forward. The narrow tunnel of the road rushed up and past. Their motion was like an extinct furnace blast: cooler, but utterly dead. The car bounded from rut to rut.

"Mr Henry," the Negro said.

The barber began to tug furiously at the door. "Look out, there!" the soldier said, but the barber had already kicked the door open and swung onto the running board. The soldier leaned across the Negro and grasped at him, but he had already jumped. The car went on without checking speed.

The impetus hurled him crashing through dust-sheathed weeds, into the ditch. Dust puffed about him, and in a thin, vicious crackling of sapless stems he lay choking and retching until the second car passed and died away. Then he rose and limped on until he reached the highroad and turned toward town, brushing at his clothes with his hands. The moon was higher, riding high and clear of the dust at last, and after a while the town began to glare beneath the dust. He went on, limping. Presently he heard cars and the glow of them grew in the dust behind him and he left the road and crouched again in the weeds until they passed. McLendon's car came last now. There were four people in it and Butch was not on the running board.

They went on; the dust swallowed them; the glare and the sound died away. The dust of them hung for a while, but soon the eternal dust absorbed it again. The barber climbed back onto the road and limped on toward town.

IV

As she dressed for supper on that Saturday evening, her own flesh felt like fever. Her hands trembled among the hooks and eyes, and her eyes had a feverish look, and her hair swirled crisp and crackling under the comb. While she was still dressing the friends called for her and sat while she donned her sheerest underthings and stockings and a new voile dress. "Do you feel strong enough to go out?" they said, their eyes bright too, with a dark glitter. "When you have had time to get over the shock, you must tell us what happened. What he said and did; everything."

In the leafed darkness, as they walked toward the square, she began to breathe deeply, something like a swimmer preparing to dive, until she ceased trembling, the four of them walking slowly because of the terrible heat and out of solicitude for her. But as they neared the square she began to tremble again, walking with her head up, her hands clenched at her sides, their voices about her murmurous, also with that feverish, glittering quality of their eyes.

They entered the square, she in the center of the group, fragile in her fresh dress. She was trembling worse. She walked slower and slower, as children eat ice cream, her head up and her eyes bright in the haggard banner of her face, passing the hotel and the coatless drummers in chairs along the curb looking around at her: "That's the one: see? The one in pink in the middle." "Is that her? What did they do with the nigger? Did they—?" "Sure. He's all right." "All right, is he?" "Sure. He went on a little trip." Then the drug store, where even the young men lounging in the doorway tipped their hats and followed with their eyes the motion of her hips and legs when she passed.

They went on, passing the lifted hats of the gentlemen, the suddenly ceased voices, deferent, protective. "Do you see?" the friends said. Their voices sounded like long, hovering sighs of hissing exultation. "There's not a Negro on the square. Not one."

They reached the picture show. It was like a miniature fairyland with its lighted lobby and colored lithographs of life caught in its terrible and beautiful mutations. Her lips began to tingle. In the dark, when the picture began, it would be all right; she could hold back the laughing so it would not waste away so fast and so soon. So she hurried on before the turning faces, the undertones of low astonishment, and they took their accustomed places where she could see the aisle against the silver glare and the young men and girls coming in two and two against it.

The lights flicked away; the screen glowed silver, and soon life began to unfold, beautiful and passionate and sad, while still the young men and girls entered, scented and sibilant in the half dark, their paired backs in silhouette delicate and sleek, their slim, quick bodies awkward, divinely young, while beyond them the silver dream accumulated, inevitably on and on. She began to laugh. In trying to suppress it, it made more noise than ever; heads began to turn. Still laughing, her friends raised her and led her out, and she stood at the curb, laughing on a high, sustained note, until the taxi came up and they helped her in.

They removed the pink voile and the sheer underthings and the stockings, and put her to bed, and cracked ice for her temples, and sent for the doctor. He was hard to locate, so they ministered to her with hushed ejaculations, renewing the ice and fanning her. While the ice was fresh and cold she stopped laughing and lay still for a time, moaning only a little. But soon the laughing welled again and her voice rose screaming.

"Shhhhhhhhhhh! Shhhhhhhhhhhhhh!" they said, freshening the icepack, smoothing her hair, examining it for gray; "poor girl!" Then to one another: "Do you suppose anything really happened?" their eyes darkly aglitter, secret and passionate. "Shhhhhhhhhh! Poor girl! Poor Minnie!"

V

It was midnight when McLendon drove up to his neat new house. It was trim and fresh as a birdcage and almost as small, with its clean, green-and-white paint. He locked the car and mounted the porch and entered. His wife rose from a chair beside the reading lamp. McLendon stopped in the floor and stared at her until she looked down.

"Look at that clock," he said, lifting his arm, pointing. She stood before him, her face lowered, a magazine in her hands. Her face was pale, strained, and weary-looking. "Haven't I told you about sitting up like this, waiting to see when I come in?"

"John," she said. She laid the magazine down. Poised on the balls of his feet, he glared at her with his hot eyes, his sweating face.

"Didn't I tell you?" He went toward her. She looked up then. He caught her shoulder. She stood passive, looking at him.

"Dont, John. I couldn't sleep ... The heat; something. Please, John. You're hurting me."

"Didn't I tell you?" He released her and half struck, half flung her across the chair, and she lay there and watched him quietly as he left the room.

He went on through the house, ripping off his shirt, and on the dark, screened porch at the rear he stood and mopped his head and shoulders with the shirt and flung it away. He took the pistol from his hip and laid it on the table beside the bed, and sat on the bed and removed his shoes, and rose and slipped his trousers off. He was sweating again already, and he stooped and hunted furiously for the shirt. At last he found it and wiped his body again, and, with his body pressed against the dusty screen, he stood panting. There was no movement, no sound, not even an insect. The dark world seemed to lie stricken beneath the cold moon and the lidless stars.

—1931

ERNEST HEMINGWAY

Ernest Miller Hemingway lived such a varied and spectacular life that often his reputation as a Pulitzer- and Nobel Prize-winning author is overshadowed by the details of his biography. His work includes the novels *The Sun Also Rises* (1926), *A Farewell to Arms* (1929), and *The Old Man and the Sea* (1952); several collections of short stories; and non-fiction such as the memoir *A Moveable Feast* (1964). His writing style is noted for its extremely spare, journalistic qualities.

Born in 1899 in Oak Park, Illinois, Hemingway began honing his writing skills by writing for his high-school newspaper; he later worked for a short time as a cub reporter for the *Kansas City Star*. In 1918 he enlisted as an ambulance driver for the Red Cross and was sent to serve on the Italian front. At the very end of his first week at the front, Hemingway was hit by fragments of mortar shell, and while he was dragging a wounded soldier to shelter, machine-gun bullets hit him in the knee. He spent a year recuperating in a Red Cross hospital in Milan, where he had a love affair with a nurse, Agnes von Kurowski. This time during the war and his recuperation would serve as the raw material for *A Farewell to Arms*.

The rest of Hemingway's life was equally dramatic. He was married four times; lived in Paris, Spain, Cuba, and Florida; served as a war correspondent and reporter for newspapers such as the *Toronto Star*; fraternized with literary greats Gertrude Stein and Ezra Pound, among many others; and indulged in big game hunting, fishing, skiing, boxing, bull-fighting—all while producing a body of work that permanently altered the face of contemporary fiction written in English.

By the late 1950s Hemingway's reputation as a writer was sliding, as was his health; he suffered from recurring depression, hypertension, and a rare disease called hemochromatosis. He also sustained severe internal tissue damage and a serious concussion as a result of a plane crash during which he used his head to butt open the jammed door of the burning airplane. He died in 1961 of a self-inflicted shotgun wound.

During his lifetime, Hemingway wrote nine novels and more than fifty short stories. He wrote "Hills Like White Elephants" while he was based in Paris; he had just divorced his first wife, Hadley Richardson, and was preparing to marry Pauline Pfeiffer. The story is part of the 1927 short story collection *Men Without Women*. One review by Dorothy Parker in *The New Yorker* refers to the collection as "a truly magnificent work" and describes "Hills Like White Elephants" as "delicate and tragic." In spite of Parker's praise, Ernest Hemingway once complained to Max Perkins that "not one damn critic thought *anything* of [the story] when it came out." Hemingway's writing is at its most spare here. The story is largely taken up with dialogue between the American and his lover Jig, but for the reader what they say is not important; the narrative revolves around what they resolutely refuse to say.

Hills Like White Elephants

ERNEST HEMINGWAY

THE HILLS across the valley of the Ebro[1] were long and white. On this side there was no shade and no trees and the station was between two lines of rails in the sun. Close against the side of the station there was the warm shadow of the building and a curtain, made of strings of bamboo beads, hung across the open door into the bar, to keep out flies. The American and the girl with him sat at a table in the shade, outside the building. It was very hot and the express from Barcelona would come in forty minutes. It stopped at this junction for two minutes and went on to Madrid.

"What should we drink?" the girl asked. She had taken off her hat and put it on the table.

"It's pretty hot," the man said.

"Let's drink beer."

"Dos cervezas," the man said into the curtain.

"Big ones?" a woman asked from the doorway.

"Yes. Two big ones."

The woman brought two glasses of beer and two felt pads. She put the felt pads and the beer glasses on the table and looked at the man and the girl. The girl was looking off at the line of hills. They were white in the sun and the country was brown and dry.

---

1 The second largest river in Spain, rising in the Cantabrian Mountains and flowing to the Mediterranean Sea.

"They look like white elephants," she said.

"I've never seen one," the man drank his beer.

"No, you wouldn't have."

"I might have," the man said. "Just because you say I wouldn't have doesn't prove anything."

The girl looked at the bead curtain. "They've painted something on it," she said. "What does it say?"

"Anis del Toro. It's a drink."

"Could we try it?"

The man called "Listen" through the curtain. The woman came out from the bar.

"Four reales."

"We want two Anis del Toro."

"With water?"

"Do you want it with water?"

"I don't know," the girl said. "Is it good with water?"

"It's all right."

"You want them with water?" asked the woman.

"Yes, with water."

"It tastes like licorice," the girl said and put the glass down.

"That's the way with everything."

"Yes," said the girl. "Everything tastes of licorice. Especially all the things you've waited so long for, like absinthe."

"Oh, cut it out."

"You started it," the girl said. "I was being amused. I was having a fine time."

"Well, let's try and have a fine time."

"All right. I was trying. I said the mountains looked like white elephants. Wasn't that bright?"

"That was bright."

"I wanted to try this new drink. That's all we do, isn't it—look at things and try new drinks?"

"I guess so."

The girl looked across at the hills.

"They're lovely hills," she said. "They don't really look like white elephants. I just meant the coloring of their skin through the trees."

"Should we have another drink?"

"All right."

The warm wind blew the bead curtain against the table.

"The beer's nice and cool," the man said.

"It's lovely," the girl said.

"It's really an awfully simple operation, Jig," the man said. "It's not really an operation at all."

The girl looked at the ground the table legs rested on.

"I know you wouldn't mind it, Jig. It's really not anything. It's just to let the air in."

The girl did not say anything.

"I'll go with you and I'll stay with you all the time. They just let the air in and then it's all perfectly natural."

"Then what will we do afterward?"

"We'll be fine afterward. Just like we were before."

"What makes you think so?"

"That's the only thing that bothers us. It's the only thing that's made us unhappy."

The girl looked at the bead curtain, put her hand out and took hold of two of the strings of beads.

"And you think then we'll be all right and be happy."

"I know we will. You don't have to be afraid. I've known lots of people that have done it."

"So have I," said the girl. "And afterwards they were all so happy."

"Well," the man said, "if you don't want to you don't have to. I wouldn't have you do it if you didn't want to. But I know it's perfectly simple."

"And you really want to?"

"I think it's the best thing to do. But I don't want you to do it if you don't really want to."

"And if I do it you'll be happy and things will be like they were and you'll love me?"

"I love you now. You know I love you."

"I know. But if I do it, then it will be nice again if I say things are like white elephants, and you'll like it?"

"I'll love it. I love it now but I just can't think about it. You know how I get when I worry."

"If I do it you won't ever worry?"

"I won't worry about that because it's perfectly simple."

"Then I'll do it. Because I don't care about me."

"What do you mean?"

"I don't care about me."

"Well, I care about you."

"Oh, yes. But I don't care about me. And I'll do it and then everything will be fine."

"I don't want you to do it if you feel that way."

The girl stood up and walked to the end of the station. Across, on the other side, were fields of grain and trees along the banks of the Ebro. Far away, beyond the river, were mountains. The shadow of a cloud moved across the field of grain and she saw the river through the trees.

"And we could have all this," she said. "And we could have everything and every day we make it more impossible."

"What did you say?"

"I said we could have everything."

"We can have everything."

"No, we can't."

"We can have the whole world."

"No, we can't."

"We can go everywhere."

"No, we can't. It isn't ours any more."

"It's ours."

"No, it isn't. And once they take it away, you never get it back."

"But they haven't taken it away."

"We'll wait and see."

"Come on back in the shade," he said. "You mustn't feel that way."

"I don't feel any way," the girl said. "I just know things."

"I don't want you to do anything that you don't want to do—"

"Nor that isn't good for me," she said. "I know. Could we have another beer?"

"All right. But you've got to realize—"

"I realize," the girl said. "Can't we maybe stop talking?"

They sat down at the table and the girl looked across at the hills on the dry side of the valley and the man looked at her and at the table.

"You've got to realize," he said, "that I don't want you to do it if you don't want to. I'm perfectly willing to go through with it if it means anything to you."

"Doesn't it mean anything to you? We could get along."

"Of course it does. But I don't want anybody but you. I don't want any one else. And I know it's perfectly simple."

"Yes, you know it's perfectly simple."

"It's all right for you to say that, but I do know it."

"Would you do something for me now?"

"I'd do anything for you."

"Would you please please please please please please please stop talking?"

He did not say anything but looked at the bags against the wall of the station. There were labels on them from all the hotels where they had spent nights.

"But I don't want you to," he said, "I don't care anything about it."

"I'll scream," the girl said.

The woman came out through the curtains with two glasses of beer and put them down on the damp felt pads. "The train comes in five minutes," she said.

"What did she say?" asked the girl.

"That the train is coming in five minutes."

The girl smiled brightly at the woman, to thank her.

"I'd better take the bags over to the other side of the station," the man said. She smiled at him.

"All right. Then come back and we'll finish the beer."

He picked up the two heavy bags and carried them around the station to the other tracks. He looked up the tracks but could not see the train. Coming back, he walked through the barroom, where people waiting for the train were drinking. He drank an Anis at the bar and looked at the people. They were all waiting reasonably for the train. He went out through the bead curtain. She was sitting at the table and smiled at him.

"Do you feel better?" he asked.

"I feel fine," she said. "There's nothing wrong with me. I feel fine."

—1927

HISAYE YAMAMOTO

Hisaye Yamamoto's life as a second-generation Japanese American (or *nisei*) was unequivocally altered by the 1942 American Japanese Relocation Act that forced the relocation and detention of over 100,000 Japanese nationals and Americans of Japanese heritage who lived on the west coast of the United States. Along with her family, she was forced to move from Redondo Beach, California, where she was born in 1921, to live in internment camps in Poston, Arizona. Yamamoto had begun writing as a teenager, and, in spite of the hardship, she continued writing and submitting her work for publication. Her first publication in 1942, a mystery entitled "Death Rides the Rails to Poston," appeared in the internment camp newspaper, the *Poston Chronicle*.

After World War II ended and the camps were dissolved, Yamamoto moved to Los Angeles, where she worked from 1945 to 1948 as a columnist for the *Los Angeles Tribune*, an African American weekly newspaper and the only newspaper in Los Angeles that would hire Japanese people. In 1948, she sold her first story, "The High-Heeled Shoes," to *Partisan Review*; in 1950 she was awarded a John Hay Whitney Foundation Opportunity Fellowship. The fellowship allowed her to write for a year without worrying about money, and she turned to writing full-time. From 1953 to 1955 she volunteered at a Catholic Worker rehabilitation farm in Staten Island, New York.

In 1955, she married, returned to Los Angeles, and began having children; her life became so involved in raising her family that for a time she listed her profession as "housewife." She continued writing short stories, however, which were published in periodicals such as *Harper's Bazaar*, *Kenyon Review*, and *Arizona Quarterly*. Several of her stories were also included in anthologies; by 1980 her work had been included in at least 20 anthologies. As her stories accumulated, they received more and more critical attention, resulting in accolades such as an American Book Award for Lifetime Achievement from the Before Columbus Foundation in 1986. Her stories were eventually collected in *Seventeen Syllables: 5 Stories of Japanese American Life* (published in Japan in 1985), and *Seventeen Syllables and Other Stories*, published in 1988. Yamamoto died in 2011 at the age of 89, a year after receiving the 2010 Asian American Writers Workshop's Lifetime Achievement Award.

Written in 1949, "Seventeen Syllables" is one of Yamamoto's most well-known and frequently anthologized stories. A coming of age story about the teenaged protagonist Rosie, it explores the generational, cultural, and gender constraints that threaten to prevent Rosie from making her own choices as she approaches adulthood.

Seventeen Syllables

HISAYE YAMAMOTO

THE FIRST Rosie knew that her mother had taken to writing poems was one evening when she finished one and read it aloud for her daughter's approval. It was about cats, and Rosie pretended to understand it thoroughly and appreciate it no end, partly because she hesitated to disillusion her mother about the quantity and quality of Japanese she had learned in all the years now that she had been going to Japanese school every Saturday (and Wednesday, too, in the summer). Even so, her mother must have been skeptical about the depth of Rosie's understanding, because she explained afterwards about the kind of poem she was trying to write.

See, Rosie, she said, it was a *haiku*, a poem in which she must pack all her meaning into seventeen syllables only, which were divided into three lines of five, seven, and five syllables. In the one she had just read, she had tried to capture the charm of a kitten, as well as comment on the superstition that owning a cat of three colors meant good luck.

"Yes, yes, I understand. How utterly lovely," Rosie said, and her mother, either satisfied or seeing through the deception and resigned, went back to composing.

The truth was that Rosie was lazy; English lay ready on the tongue but Japanese had to be searched for and examined, and even then put forth tentatively (probably to meet with laughter). It was so much easier to say yes, yes, even when one meant no, no. Besides, this was what was in her mind to say: I was looking through one of your magazines from Japan last night, Mother, and towards the back I found some *haiku* in English that delighted me. There was one that made me giggle off and on until I fell asleep—

It is morning, and lo!
I lie awake, comme il faut,[1]
sighing for some dough.

---

1 French: As it should be; in keeping with social norms.

Now, how to reach her mother, how to communicate the melancholy song? Rosie knew formal Japanese by fits and starts, her mother had even less English, no French. It was much more possible to say yes, yes.

It developed that her mother was writing the *haiku* for a daily newspaper, the *Mainichi Shimbun*, that was published in San Francisco. Los Angeles, to be sure, was closer to the farming community in which the Hayashi family lived and several Japanese vernaculars were printed there, but Rosie's parents said they preferred the tone of the northern paper. Once a week, the *Mainichi* would have a section devoted to *haiku*, and her mother became an extravagant contributor, taking for herself the blossoming pen name, Ume Hanazono.

So Rosie and her father lived for awhile with two women, her mother and Ume Hanazono. Her mother (Tome Hayashi by name) kept house, cooked, washed, and along with her husband and the Carrascos, the Mexican family hired for the harvest, did her ample share of picking tomatoes out in the sweltering fields and boxing them in tidy strata in the cool packing shed. Ume Hanazono, who came to life after the dinner dishes were done, was an earnest, muttering stranger who often neglected speaking when spoken to and stayed busy at the parlor table as late as midnight scribbling with pencil on scratch paper or carefully copying characters on good paper with her fat, pale green Parker.

The new interest had some repercussions on the household routine. Before, Rosie had been accustomed to her parents and herself taking their hot baths early and going to bed almost immediately afterwards, unless her parents challenged each other to a game of flower cards or unless company dropped in. Now if her father wanted to play cards, he had to resort to solitaire (at which he always cheated fearlessly), and if a group of friends came over, it was bound to contain someone who was also writing *haiku*, and the small assemblage would be split in two, her father entertaining the nonliterary members and her mother comparing ecstatic notes with the visiting poet.

If they went out, it was more of the same thing. But Ume Hanazono's life span, even for a poet's, was very brief—perhaps three months at most.

One night they went over to see the Hayano family in the neighboring town to the west, an adventure both painful and attractive to Rosie. It was attractive because there were four Hayano girls, all lovely and each one named after a season of the year (Haru, Natsu, Aki, Fuyu), painful because something had been wrong with Mrs. Hayano ever since the birth of her first child. Rosie would sometimes watch Mrs. Hayano, reputed to have been the belle of her native village, making her way about a room, stooped, slowly shuffling, violently trembling (*always* trembling), and she would be reminded that this woman, in this same condition, had carried and given issue to three babies. She would look wonderingly at Mr. Hayano, handsome, tall, and strong, and she would look at her four pretty friends. But it was not a matter she could come to any decision about.

On this visit, however, Mrs. Hayano sat all evening in the rocker, as motionless and unobtrusive as it was possible for her to be, and Rosie found the greater part of the evening practically anesthetic. Too, Rosie spent most of it in the girls' room, because Haru, the garrulous one, said almost as soon as the bows and other greetings were over, "Oh, you must see my new coat!"

It was a pale plaid of gray, sand, and blue, with an enormous collar, and Rosie, seeing nothing special in it, said, "Gee, how nice."

"Nice?" said Haru, indignantly. "Is that all you can say about it? It's gorgeous! And so cheap, too. Only seventeen-ninety eight, because it was a sale. The saleslady said it was twenty-five dollars regular."

"Gee," said Rosie. Natsu, who never said much and when she said anything said it shyly, fingered the coat covetously and Haru pulled it away.

"Mine," she said, putting it on. She minced in the aisle between the two large beds and smiled happily. "Let's see how your mother likes it."

She broke into the front room and the adult conversation and went to stand in front of Rosie's mother, while the rest watched from the door. Rosie's mother was properly envious. "May I inherit it when you're through with it?"

Haru, pleased, giggled and said yes, she could, but Natsu reminded gravely from the door, "You promised me, Haru."

Everyone laughed but Natsu, who shamefacedly retreated into the bedroom. Haru came in laughing, taking off the coat. "We were only kidding, Natsu," she said. "Here, you try it on now."

After Natsu buttoned herself into the coat, inspected herself solemnly in the bureau mirror, and reluctantly shed it, Rosie, Aki, and Fuyu got their turns, and Fuyu, who was eight, drowned in it while her sisters and Rosie doubled up in amusement. They all went into the front room later, because Haru's mother quaveringly called to her to fix the tea and rice cakes and open a can of sliced peaches for everybody. Rosie noticed that her mother and Mr. Hayano were talking together at the little table—they were discussing a *haiku* that Mr. Hayano was planning to send to the *Mainichi*, while her father was sitting at one end of the sofa looking through a copy of *Life*, the new picture magazine. Occasionally, her father would comment on a photograph, holding it toward Mrs. Hayano and speaking to her as he always did—loudly, as though he thought someone such as she must surely be at least a trifle deaf also.

The five girls had their refreshments at the kitchen table, and it was while Rosie was showing the sisters her trick of swallowing peach slices without chewing (she chased each slippery crescent down with a swig of tea) that her father brought his empty teacup and untouched saucer to the sink and said, "Come on, Rosie, we're going home now."

"Already?" asked Rosie.

"Work tomorrow," he said.

He sounded irritated, and Rosie, puzzled, gulped one last yellow slice and stood up to go, while the sisters began protesting, as was their wont.

"We have to get up at five-thirty," he told them, going into the front room quickly, so that they did not have their usual chance to hang onto his hands and plead for an extension of time.

Rosie, following, saw that her mother and Mr. Hayano were sipping tea and still talking together, while Mrs. Hayano concentrated, quivering, on raising the handleless Japanese cup to her lips with both her hands and lowering it back to her lap. Her father, saying nothing, went out the door, onto the bright porch, and down the steps. Her mother looked up and asked, "Where is he going?"

"Where is he going?" Rosie said. "He said we were going home now."

"Going home?" Her mother looked with embarrassment at Mr. Hayano and his absorbed wife and then forced a smile. "He must be tired," she said.

Haru was not giving up yet. "May Rosie stay overnight?" she asked, and Natsu, Aki, and Fuyu came to reinforce their sister's plea by helping her make a circle around Rosie's mother. Rosie, for once having no desire to stay was relieved when her mother, apologizing to the perturbed Mr. and Mrs. Hayano for her father's abruptness at the same time, managed to shake her head no at the quartet, kindly but adamant, so that they broke their circle and let her go.

Rosie's father looked ahead into the windshield as the two joined him. "I'm sorry," her mother said. "You must be tired." Her father, stepping on the starter, said nothing. "You know how I get when it's *haiku*," she continued, "I forget what time it is." He only grunted.

As they rode homeward silently, Rosie, sitting between, felt a rush of hate for both—for her mother for begging, for her father for denying her mother. I wish this old Ford would crash, right now, she thought, then immediately, no, no, I wish my father would laugh, but it was too late: already the vision had passed through her mind of the green pick-up crumpled in the dark against one of the mighty eucalyptus trees they were just riding past, of the three contorted, bleeding bodies, one of them hers.

Rosie ran between two patches of tomatoes, her heart working more rambunctiously than she had ever known it to. How lucky it was that Aunt Taka and Uncle Gimpachi had come tonight, though, how very lucky. Otherwise she might not have really kept her half-promise to meet Jesus Carrasco. Jesus was going to be a senior in September at the same school she went to, and his parents were the ones helping with the tomatoes this year. She and Jesus, who hardly remembered seeing each other at Cleveland High where there were so many other people and two whole grades between them, had become great friends this summer—he always had a joke for her when he periodically drove the loaded pick-up up from the fields to the shed where she was usually sorting while her mother and father did the packing, and they laughed a great deal together over infinitesimal repartee during the afternoon break for chilled watermelon or ice cream in the shade of the shed.

What she enjoyed most was racing him to see who could finish picking a double row first. He, who could work faster, would tease her by slowing down until she thought she would surely pass him this time, then speeding up furiously to leave her several sprawling vines behind. Once he had made her screech hideously by crossing over, while her back was turned, to place atop the tomatoes in her green-stained bucket a truly monstrous, pale green worm (it had looked more like an infant snake). And it was when they had finished a contest this morning, after she had pantingly pointed a green finger at the immature tomatoes evident in the lugs at the end of his row and he had returned the accusation (with justice), that he had startlingly brought up the matter of their possibly meeting outside the range of both their parents' dubious eyes.

"What for?" she had asked.

"I've got a secret I want to tell you," he said.

"Tell me now," she demanded.

"It won't be ready till tonight," he said.

She laughed. "Tell me tomorrow then."

"It'll be gone tomorrow," he threatened.

"Well, for seven hakes, what is it?" she had asked, more than twice, and when he had suggested that the packing shed would be an appropriate place to find out, she had cautiously answered maybe. She had not been certain she was going to keep the appointment until the arrival of mother's sister and her husband. Their coming seemed a sort of signal of permission, of grace, and she had definitely made up her mind to lie and leave as she was bowing them welcome.

So as soon as everyone appeared settled back for the evening, she announced loudly that she was going to the privy outside, "I'm going to the *benjo*!"[2] and slipped out the door. And now that she was actually on her way, her heart pumped in such an undisciplined way that she could hear it with her ears. It's

2 Japanese: bathroom or toilet.

because I'm running, she told herself, slowing to a walk. The shed was up ahead, one more patch away, in the middle of the fields. Its bulk, looming in the dimness, took on a sinisterness that was funny when Rosie reminded herself that it was only a wooden frame with a canvas roof and three canvas walls that made a slapping noise on breezy days.

Jesus was sitting on the narrow plank that was the sorting platform and she went around to the other side and jumped backwards to seat herself on the rim of a packing stand. "Well, tell me," she said without greeting, thinking her voice sounded reassuringly familiar.

"I saw you coming out the door," Jesus said. "I heard you running part of the way, too."

"Uh-huh," Rosie said. "Now tell me the secret."

"I was afraid you wouldn't come," he said.

Rosie delved around the chicken-wire bottom of the stall for number two tomatoes, ripe, which she was sitting beside, and came up with a left-over that felt edible. She bit into it and began sucking out the pulp and seeds. "I'm here," she pointed out.

"Rosie, are you sorry you came?"

"Sorry? What for?" she said. "You said you were going to tell me something."

"I will, I will," Jesus said, but his voice contained disappointment, and Rosie fleetingly felt the older of the two, realizing a brand-new power which vanished without category under her recognition.

"I have to go back in a minute," she said. "My aunt and uncle are here from Wintersburg. I told them I was going to the privy."

Jesus laughed. "You funny thing," he said. "You slay me!"

"Just because you have a bathroom *inside*," Rosie said. "Come on, tell me."

Chuckling, Jesus came around to lean on the stand facing her. They still could not see each other very clearly, but Rosie noticed that Jesus became very sober again as he took the hollow tomato from her hand and dropped it back into the stall. When he took hold of her empty hand, she could find no words to protest; her vocabulary had become distressingly constricted and she thought desperately that all that remained intact now was yes and no and oh, and even these few sounds would not easily out. Thus, kissed by Jesus, Rosie fell for the first time entirely victim to a helplessness delectable beyond speech. But the terrible, beautiful sensation lasted no more than a second, and the reality of Jesus' lips and tongue and teeth and hands made her pull away with such strength that she nearly tumbled.

Rosie stopped running as she approached the lights from the windows of home. How long since she had left? She could not guess, but gasping yet, she went to the privy in back and locked herself in. Her own breathing deafened her in the dark, close space, and she sat and waited until she could hear at last the nightly calling of the frogs and crickets. Even then, all she could think to say was oh, my, and the pressure of Jesus' face against her face would not leave.

No one had missed her in the parlor, however, and Rosie walked in and through quickly, announcing that she was next going to take a bath. "Your father's in the bathhouse," her mother said, and Rosie, in her room, recalled that she had not seen him when she entered. There had been only Aunt Taka and Uncle Gimpachi with her mother at the table, drinking tea. She got her robe and straw sandals and crossed the parlor again to go outside. Her mother was telling them about the *haiku* competition in the *Mainichi* and the poem she had entered.

Rosie met her father coming out of the bathhouse. "Are you through, Father?" she asked. "I was going to ask you to scrub my back."

"Scrub your own back," he said shortly, going toward the main house.

"What have I done now?" she yelled after him. She suddenly felt like doing a lot of yelling. But he did not answer, and she went into the bathhouse. Turning on the dangling light, she removed her denims and T-shirt and threw them in the big carton for dirty clothes standing next to the washing machine. Her other things she took with her into the bath compartment to wash after her bath. After she had scooped a basin of hot water from the square wooden tub, she sat on the gray cement of the floor and soaped herself at exaggerated leisure, singing "Red Sails in the Sunset" at the top of her voice and using da-da-da where she suspected her words. Then, standing up, still singing, for she was possessed by the notion that any attempt now to analyze would result in spoilage and she believed that the larger her volume the less she would be able to hear herself think, she obtained more hot water and poured it on until she was free of lather. Only then did she allow herself to step into the steaming vat, one leg first, then the remainder of her body inch by inch until the water no longer stung and she could move around at will.

She took a long time soaking, afterwards remembering to go around outside to stoke the embers of the tin-lined fireplace beneath the tub and to throw on a few more sticks so that the water might keep its heat for her mother, and when she finally returned to the parlor, she found her mother still talking *haiku* with her aunt and uncle, the three of them on another round of tea. Her father was nowhere in sight.

At Japanese school the next day (Wednesday, it was), Rosie was grave and giddy by turns. Preoccupied at her desk in the row for students on Book Eight, she made up for it at recess by performing wild mimicry for the benefit of her friend

Chizuko. She held her nose and whined a witticism or two in what she considered was the manner of Fred Allen; she assumed intoxication and a British accent to go over the climax of the Rudy Vallee recording of the pub conversation about William Ewart Gladstone; she was the child Shirley Temple piping, "On the Good Ship Lollipop"; she was the gentleman soprano of the Four Inkspots trilling, "If I Didn't Care."[3] And she felt reasonably satisfied when Chizuko wept and gasped, "Oh, Rosie, you ought to be in the movies!"

Her father came after her at noon, bringing her sandwiches of minced ham and two nectarines to eat while she rode, so that she could pitch right into the sorting when they got home. The lugs were piling up, he said, and the ripe tomatoes in them would probably have to be taken to the cannery tomorrow if they were not ready for the produce haulers tonight. "This heat's not doing them any good. And we've got no time for a break today."

It *was* hot, probably the hottest day of the year, and Rosie's blouse stuck damply to her back even under the protection of the canvas. But she worked as efficiently as a flawless machine and kept the stalls heaped, with one part of her mind listening in to the parental murmuring about the heat and the tomatoes and with another part planning the exact words she would say to Jesus when he drove up with the first load of the afternoon. But when at last she saw that the pick-up was coming, her hands went berserk and the tomatoes started falling in the wrong stalls, and her father said, "Hey, hey! Rosie, watch what you're doing!"

"Well, I have to go to the *benjo*," she said, hiding panic.

"Go in the weeds over there," he said, only half-joking.

"Oh, Father!" she protested.

"Oh, go on home," her mother said. "We'll make out for awhile."

In the privy Rosie peered through a knothole toward the fields, watching as much as she could of Jesus. Happily she thought she saw him look in the direction of the house from time to time before he finished unloading and went back toward the patch where his mother and father worked. As she was heading for the shed, a very presentable black car purred up the dirt driveway to the house and its driver motioned to her. Was this the Hayashi home, he wanted to know. She nodded. Was she a Hayashi? Yes, she said, thinking that he was a good-looking man. He got out of the car with a huge, flat package and she saw that he warmly wore a business suit. "I have something here for your mother then," he said, in a more elegant Japanese than she was used to.

3 Fred Allen (1894–1956) was a popular radio comedian; Rudy Vallee (1901–86) was a popular singer in the 1920s; William E. Gladstone (1809–98) led the Liberal Party in Britain and was prime minister for many years; Shirley Temple (b. 1928) was a famous Hollywood child actor; The Ink Spots were a vocal quartet popular in the 1930s and 1940s.

She told him where her mother was and he came along with her, patting his face with an immaculate white handkerchief and saying something about the coolness of San Francisco. To her surprised mother and father, he bowed and introduced himself as, among other things, the *haiku* editor of the *Mainichi Shimbun*, saying that since he had been coming as far as Los Angeles anyway, he had decided to bring her the first prize she had won in the recent contest.

"First prize?" her mother echoed, believing and not believing, pleased and overwhelmed. Handed the package with a bow, she bobbed her head up and down numerous times to express her utter gratitude.

"It is nothing much," he added, "but I hope it will serve as a token of our great appreciation for your contributions and our great admiration of your considerable talent."

"I am not worthy," she said, falling easily into his style. "It is I who should make some sign of my humble thanks for being permitted to contribute."

"No, no, to the contrary," he said, bowing again.

But Rosie's mother insisted, and then saying that she knew she was being unorthodox, she asked if she might open the package because her curiosity was so great. Certainly she might. In fact, he would like her reaction to it, for personally, it was one of his favorite *Hiroshiges*.[4]

Rosie thought it was a pleasant picture, which looked to have been sketched with delicate quickness. There were pink clouds, containing some graceful calligraphy, and a sea that was a pale blue except at the edges, containing four sampans[5] with indications of people in them. Pines edged the water and on the far-off beach there was a cluster of thatched huts towered over by pine-dotted mountains of gray and blue. The frame was scalloped and gilt.

After Rosie's mother pronounced it without peer and somewhat prodded her father into nodding agreement, she said Mr. Kuroda must at least have a cup of tea after coming all this way, and although Mr. Kuroda did not want to impose, he soon agreed that a cup of tea would be refreshing and went along with her to the house, carrying the picture for her.

"Ha, your mother's crazy!" Rosie's father said, and Rosie laughed uneasily as she resumed judgment on the tomatoes. She had emptied six lugs when he broke into an imaginary conversation with Jesus to tell her to go and remind her mother of the tomatoes, and she went slowly.

---

4 Japanese artist Ando Hiroshige (1797–1858) is perhaps best known for his color woodblock prints of landscapes.

5 A type of small boat propelled by oars or a sail.

Mr. Kuroda was in his shirtsleeves expounding some *haiku* theory as he munched a rice cake, and her mother was rapt. Abashed in the great man's presence, Rosie stood next to her mother's chair until her mother looked up inquiringly, and then she started to whisper the message, but her mother pushed her gently away and reproached, "You are not being very polite to our guest."

"Father says the tomatoes ..." Rosie said aloud, smiling foolishly.

"Tell him I shall only be a minute," her mother said, speaking the language of Mr. Kuroda.

When Rosie carried the reply to her father, he did not seem to hear and she said again, "Mother says she'll be back in a minute."

"All right, all right," he nodded, and they worked again in silence. But suddenly, her father uttered an incredible noise, exactly like the cork of a bottle popping, and the next Rosie knew, he was stalking angrily toward the house, almost running in fact, and she chased after him crying, "Father! Father! What are you going to do?"

He stopped long enough to order her back to the shed. "Never mind!" he shouted. "Get on with the sorting!"

And from the place in the fields where she stood, frightened and vacillating, Rosie saw her father enter the house. Soon Mr. Kuroda came out alone, putting on his coat. Mr. Kuroda got into his car and backed out down the driveway onto the highway. Next her father emerged, also alone, something in his arms (it was the picture, she realized), and, going over to the bathhouse woodpile, he threw the picture on the ground and picked up the axe. Smashing the picture, glass and all (she heard the explosion faintly), he reached over for the kerosene that was used to encourage the bath fire and poured it over the wreckage. I am dreaming, Rosie said to herself, I am dreaming, but her father, having made sure that his act of cremation was irrevocable, was even then returning to the fields.

Rosie ran past him and toward the house. What had become of her mother? She burst into the parlor and found her mother at the back window watching the dying fire. They watched together until there remained only a feeble smoke under the blazing sun. Her mother was very calm.

"Do you know why I married your father?" she said without turning.

"No," said Rosie. It was the most frightening question she had ever been called upon to answer. Don't tell me now, she wanted to say, tell me tomorrow, tell me next week, don't tell me today. But she knew she would be told now, that the telling would combine with the other violence of the hot afternoon to level her life, her world to the very ground.

It was like a story out of the magazines illustrated in sepia, which she had consumed so greedily for a period until the information had somehow reached her that those wretchedly unhappy autobiographies, offered to her as the testimonials of living men and women, were largely inventions: Her mother, at nineteen, had come to America and married her father as an alternative to suicide.

At eighteen she had been in love with the first son of one of the well-to-do families in her village. The two had met whenever and wherever they could, secretly, because it would not have done for his family to see him favor her—her father had no money; he was a drunkard and a gambler besides. She had learned she was with child; an excellent match had already been arranged for her lover. Despised by her family, she had given premature birth to a stillborn son, who would be seventeen now. Her family did not turn her out, but she could no longer project herself in any direction without refreshing in them the memory of her indiscretion. She wrote to Aunt Taka, her favorite sister in America, threatening to kill herself if Aunt Taka would not send for her. Aunt Taka hastily arranged a marriage with a young man of whom she knew, but lately arrived from Japan, a young man of simple mind, it was said, but of kindly heart. The young man was never told why his unseen betrothed was so eager to hasten the day of meeting.

The story was told perfectly, with neither groping for words nor untoward passion. It was as though her mother had memorized it by heart, reciting it to herself so many times over that its nagging vileness had long since gone.

"I had a brother then?" Rosie asked, for this was what seemed to matter now; she would think about the other later, she assured herself, pushing back the illumination which threatened all that darkness that had hitherto been merely mysterious or even glamorous. "A half-brother?"

"Yes."

"I would have liked a brother," she said.

Suddenly, her mother knelt on the floor and took her by the wrists. "Rosie," she said urgently, "Promise me you will never marry!" Shocked more by the request than the revelation, Rosie stared at her mother's face. Jesus, Jesus, she called silently, not certain whether she was invoking the help of the son of Carrascos or of God, until there returned sweetly the memory of Jesus' hand, how it had touched her and where. Still her mother waited for an answer, holding her wrists so tightly that her hands were going numb. She tried to pull free. Promise, her mother whispered fiercely, promise. Yes, yes, I promise, Rosie said. But for an instant she turned away, and her mother, hearing the familiar glib agreement, released her. Oh, you, you, you, her eyes and twisted mouth said, you fool. Rosie, covering her face, began at last to cry, and the embrace and consoling hand came much later than she expected.

—1949

YASUNARI KAWABATA

Yasunari Kawabata was a critic, novelist, and short fiction writer who became the first Japanese writer to win the Nobel Prize for literature in 1968. His lyrical style and haunting images of ancient tradition and natural beauty in a changing world resonated with readers in his own country and around the world. He was a member of the Japan Art Academy, was chairman of the PEN Club of Japan, and he received the First Class Order of the Rising Sun after his death.

Kawabata was born in Osaka in 1899. He lost his father, a respected physician, at the age of two and then his mother at the age of three. His childhood would continue to be marked by bereavement as he experienced the deaths of his grandmother, sister, and grandfather by the time he was 15. In 1915, Kawabata went to live in a school dormitory and in 1920 he began attending Tokyo Imperial University.

With his sights set on becoming a writer, he earned a degree from the department of Japanese Literature in 1924. Along with writer Yokomitsu Riichi and several other fellow artists, Kawabata founded a journal, *Bungei Jidai* (*The Artistic Age*), through which they became known for a new literary movement: Shinkankaku, or Neo-Sensualism, which focused on beauty and language, turning away from the realistic writing dominant in Japan at the time. Within *Bungei Jidai*, Kawabata published his first successful novella, *Izu-no Odoriko* (*The Izu Dancer*), in 1927. He married in 1931 and lived and traveled in different Japanese cities during and after World War II.

Kawabata began writing one of his most celebrated novels, *Yukiguni* (*The Snow Country*), in 1935. He revised and rewrote it over many years; it was finally published in 1948. In 1954 he published *Yama-no Oto* (*The Sound of the Mountains*), a great critical success and winner of the Japanese Academy's literary prize. *Meijin* (*The Master of Go*), a fictionalized version of a 1938 match of Go (an ancient Chinese game), was published in 1972. In *Sembazuru* (*Thousand Cranes*), begun in 1949, Kawabata told an episodic story of waning tradition based on *Genji Monogatari* (*The Tale of Genji*), an eleventh-century Japanese novel that he had studied.

Later in his career, Kawabata traveled the United States giving lectures and helped campaign for Japanese conservative candidates at home. His writing shows a deep affinity for the complexities and beauty of the Japanese language, but in his speech at the Nobel banquet, he expressed hope for the possibilities of the written word to transcend cultural and language barriers and be enjoyed by a world audience. Kawabata committed suicide in 1972.

"Immortality" is one of Kawabata's "tanagokoro no shosetsu" or "Palm-of-the-hand" stories. The lovers, an old man at the end of a lonely life and a young woman, have a mournful feel to them (as do many of the characters in Kawabata's stories). Kawabata suggests a layering of past and present, memory and imagination, that ultimately leaves it up to readers to determine where and when the lovers' conversation takes place.

Immortality[1]

YASUNARI KAWABATA

AN OLD MAN and a young girl were walking together.

There were a number of curious things about them. They nestled close together like lovers, as if they did not feel the sixty years' difference in their ages. The old man was hard of hearing. He could not understand most of what the girl said. The girl wore maroon *hakama*[2] with a purple-and-white kimono in a fine arrow pattern. The sleeves were rather long. The old man was wearing clothes like those a girl would wear to pull weeds from a rice field, except that he wore no leggings. His tight sleeves and trousers gathered at the ankles looked like a woman's. His clothes hung loose at his thin waist.

They walked across a lawn. A tall wire net stood in front of them. The lovers did not seem to notice that they would run into it if they kept walking. They did not stop, but walked right through the net as a spring breeze might blow through it.

After they passed through, the girl noticed the net. "Oh." She looked at the man. "Shintarō, did you pass through the net, too?"

---

1 Translated by Lane Dunlop and J. Martin Holman.

2 Loose-fitting trousers, part of traditional Japanese dress. Although at one time predominantly worn by men, a maroon hakama worn over top of a kimono became a standard uniform for high school girls in the early part of the twentieth century.

The old man did not hear, but he grabbed the wire net. "You bastard. You bastard," he said as he shook it. He pulled too hard, and in a moment, the huge net moved away from him. The old man staggered and fell holding onto it.

"Watch out, Shintarō! What happened?" The girl put her arms around him and propped him up.

"Let go of the net ... Oh, you've lost so much weight," the girl said.

The old man finally stood up. He heaved as he spoke. "Thank you." He grasped the net again, but this time lightly, with only one hand. Then in the loud voice of a deaf person he said, "I used to have to pick up balls from behind a net day after day. For seventeen long years."

"Seventeen years is a long time? ... It's short."

"They just hit the balls as they pleased. They made an awful sound when they struck the wire net. Before I got used to it, I'd flinch. It's because of the sound of those balls that I became deaf."

It was a metal net to protect the ball boys at a golf driving range. There were wheels on the bottom so they could move forward and back and right and left. The driving range and golf course next to it were separated by some trees. Originally it had been a grove of all kinds of trees, but they had been cut until only an irregular row remained.

The two walked on, the net behind them.

"What pleasant memories it brings back to hear the sound of the ocean." Wanting the old man to hear these words, the girl put her mouth to his ear. "I can hear the sound of the ocean."

"What?" The old man closed his eyes. "Ah, Misako. It's your sweet breath. Just as it was long ago."

"Can't you hear the sound of the ocean? Doesn't it bring back fond memories?"

"The ocean ... Did you say the ocean? Fond memories? How could the ocean, where you drowned yourself, bring back fond memories?"

"Well, it does. This is the first time I've been back to my hometown in fifty-five years. And you've come back here, too. This brings back memories." The old man could not hear, but she went on. "I'm glad I drowned myself. That way I can think about you forever, just as I was doing at the moment I drowned myself. Besides, the only memories and reminiscences I have are those up to the time I was eighteen. You are eternally young to me. And it's the same for you. If I hadn't drowned myself and you came to the village now to see me, I'd be an old woman. How disgusting. I wouldn't want you to see me like that."

The old man spoke. It was a deaf man's monologue. "I went to Tokyo and failed. And now, decrepit with age, I've returned to the village. There was a girl who grieved that we were forced to part. She had drowned herself in the ocean, so I asked for a job at a driving range overlooking the ocean. I begged them to give me the job … if only out of pity."

"This area where we are walking is the woods that belonged to your family."

"I couldn't do anything but pick up balls. I hurt my back from bending over all the time … But there was a girl who had killed herself for me. The rock cliffs were right beside me, so I could jump even if I were tottering. That's what I thought."

"No. You must keep living. If you were to die, there wouldn't be anyone on earth who would remember me. I would die completely." The girl clung to him. The old man could not hear, but he embraced her.

"That's it. Let's die together. This time … You came for me, didn't you."

"Together? But you must live. Live for my sake, Shintarō." She gasped as she looked over his shoulder. "Oh, those big trees are still there. All three … just like long ago." The girl pointed, so the old man turned his eyes toward the trees.

"The golfers are afraid of those trees. They keep telling us to cut them down. When they hit a ball, they say it curves to the right as though sucked in by the magic of those trees."

"Those golfers will die in due time—long before those trees. Those trees are already hundreds of years old. Those golfers talk that way, but they don't understand the life span of a man," the girl said.

"Those are trees my ancestors have looked after for hundreds of years, so I had the buyer promise not to cut the trees when I sold the land to him."

"Let's go." The girl tugged at the old man's hand. They tottered toward the great trees.

The girl passed easily through the tree trunk. The old man did the same.

"What?" The girl stared at the old man and marveled. "Are you dead too, Shintarō? Are you? When did you die?"

He did not answer.

"You *have* died … Haven't you? How strange I didn't meet you in the world of the dead. Well, try walking through the tree trunk once more to test whether you're dead or alive. If you are dead we can go inside the tree and stay."

They disappeared inside the tree. Neither the old man nor the young girl appeared again.

The color of evening began to drift onto the small saplings behind the great trees. The sky beyond turned a faint red where the ocean sounded.

—1963

GRACE PALEY

Grace Paley, an American short story writer, poet, teacher, and social activist, was born in the Bronx in 1922. She is best known for her talkative, casual, and highly crafted stories, which focus on the mystery inherent in "ordinary, everyday life." She developed the short story genre into a lucid, flexible form for encapsulating women's experience, becoming an important influence on writers such as Alice Munro and Ann Beattie. Susan Sontag said of her that she had "a voice like no one else's: funny, sad, lean, modest, energetic, acute."

Paley's parents were Jewish socialists from the Ukraine, exiled by Tzar Nicholas II for political and religious reasons. They left for New York, where her father Isaac studied and became a doctor. Grace was their third child, growing up in a politically engaged family speaking three languages: Yiddish, Russian, and English. Her family life nurtured her passionate advocacy for social equality, anti-militarism, and the environment; she became a self-described "combative pacifist and cooperative anarchist." She developed a gift for communicating the vitality of voices, the masterful depiction of which became a defining characteristic of her art. She attended public schools in New York City and in the early 1940s studied with W.H. Auden at the New School for Social Research. Auden's politically engaged poetry, his irony, and his insistence that his students speak in their own voice were all influential on Paley. She married in 1942 and had two children; she later divorced and married fellow poet Robert Nichols in 1972.

Paley began writing stories when she was in her thirties, publishing her first collection, *The Little Disturbances of Man*, in 1959. At that time, she was active protesting nuclear proliferation and American militarization, as well as busy raising her young children. The volume's narrators, predominantly dynamic Jewish-American working-class women, reflect Paley's immediate community: women she met at the park playground. The stories are at once tough, ironic, and profoundly optimistic, touching on the varied joys and frustrations of daily life; they express, according to Philip Roth, "an understanding of loneliness, lust, selfishness, and fatigue that is splendidly comic and unladylike."

This first volume of stories was well received, and Paley was awarded a Guggenheim Fellowship for Fiction in 1961. Her second collection, *Enormous Changes at the Last Minute*, appeared in 1974; it is a darker, sparer, more overtly political volume. The stories are characteristically condensed, at times only two pages long, but conveying the texture of consciousness. A third volume, *Later the Same Day*, was published in 1985, and in 1994 *The Collected Stories* were published, for which she was nominated for the Pulitzer Prize and granted several awards, including the PEN/Malamud Award (1994).

Paley was a gifted and dedicated teacher as well as a writer and an activist. She taught creative writing at Sarah Lawrence College from 1966 to 1989, and at Columbia University, Syracuse University, and the City College of New York. She died in 2007.

"Wants" (1974) explores a woman's thoughts and memories as she runs into her ex-husband on the steps of the neighborhood library. It achieves in two pages a wry but tender meditation on character and its development under the pressure of time. With humor, pathos, and her inimitable narrative voice, Paley weighs the desires that shape our lives: financial, emotional, political, social—desires that cannot be fully attended to as time passes, as moral pressure alters and changes them, as decisions are made.

Wants

GRACE PALEY

I SAW MY ex-husband in the street. I was sitting on the steps of the new library.

Hello, my life, I said. We had once been married for twenty-seven years, so I felt justified.

He said, What? What life? No life of mine.

I said, O.K. I don't argue when there's real disagreement. I got up and went into the library to see how much I owed them.

The librarian said $32 even and you've owed it for eighteen years. I didn't deny anything. Because I don't understand how time passes. I have had those books. I have often thought of them. The library is only two blocks away.

My ex-husband followed me to the Books Returned desk. He interrupted the librarian, who had more to tell. In many ways, he said, as I look back, I attribute the dissolution of our marriage to the fact that you never invited the Bertrams to dinner.

That's possible, I said. But really, if you remember: first, my father was sick that Friday, then the children were born, then I had those Tuesday-night meetings, then the war began. Then we didn't seem to know them any more. But you're right. I should have had them to dinner.

I gave the librarian a check for $32. Immediately she trusted me, put my past behind her, wiped the record clean, which is just what most other municipal and/or state bureaucracies will not do.

I checked out the two Edith Wharton books I had just returned because I'd read them so long ago and they are more apropos now than ever. They were *The House of Mirth* and *The Children*, which is about how life in the United States in New York changed in twenty-seven years fifty years ago.

A nice thing I do remember is breakfast, my ex-husband said. I was surprised. All we ever had was coffee. Then I remembered there was a hole in the back of the kitchen closet which opened into the apartment next door. There, they always ate sugar-cured smoked bacon. It gave us a very grand feeling about breakfast, but we never got stuffed and sluggish.

That was when we were poor, I said.

When were we ever rich? he asked.

Oh, as time went on, as our responsibilities increased, we didn't go in need. You took adequate financial care, I reminded him. The children went to camp four weeks a year and in decent ponchos with sleeping bags and boots, just like everyone else. They looked very nice. Our place was warm in winter, and we had nice red pillows and things.

I wanted a sailboat, he said. But you didn't want anything.

Don't be bitter, I said. It's never too late.

No, he said with a great deal of bitterness. I may get a sailboat. As a matter of fact I have money down on an eighteen-foot two-rigger. I'm doing well this year and can look forward to better. But as for you, it's too late. You'll always want nothing.

He had had a habit throughout the twenty-seven years of making a narrow remark which, like a plumber's snake, could work its way through the ear down the throat, half-way to my heart. He would then disappear, leaving me choking with equipment. What I mean is, I sat down on the library steps and he went away.

I looked through *The House of Mirth*, but lost interest. I felt extremely accused. Now, it's true, I'm short of requests and absolute requirements. But I do want *something*. I want, for instance, to be a different person. I want to be the woman who brings these two books back in two weeks. I want to be the effective citizen who changes the school system and addresses the Board of Estimate[1] on the troubles of this dear urban center. I *had* promised my children to end the

1 A government body responsible for budget decisions in New York City until 1990.

war before they grew up. I wanted to have been married forever to one person, my ex-husband or my present one. Either has enough character for a whole life, which as it turns out is really not such a long time. You couldn't exhaust either man's qualities or get under the rock of his reasons in one short life.

Just this morning I looked out the window to watch the street for a while and saw that the little sycamores the city had dreamily planted a couple of years before the kids were born had come that day to the prime of their lives.

Well! I decided to bring those two books back to the library. Which proves that when a person or an event comes along to jolt or appraise me I *can* take some appropriate action, although I am better known for my hospitable remarks.

—1974

JAMES BALDWIN

James Baldwin had a varied, controversial career as a writer and as a prominent spokesperson for African Americans during the 1950s and 1960s American civil rights movement. Born in New York City in 1924, Baldwin was the eldest child in a family of nine children. Typical of most families in Harlem during the Depression, Baldwin's family suffered from severe poverty, and Baldwin took on a huge portion of the responsibility for the care of his siblings. From junior high school and on, Baldwin was writing, contributing to student publications, and fervently reading and re-reading Harriet Beecher Stowe's *Uncle Tom's Cabin* and works by Charles Dickens.

Upon graduating from high school, Baldwin moved to Greenwich Village in 1943, and for five years worked during the day and wrote at night. In 1948, he published his first short story, "Previous Condition," and, on the strength of his writing, won a Rosenwald Fellowship. In 1948, in the face of oppressive racism towards blacks in the United States and with a dawning awareness of his own homosexuality, Baldwin moved to Paris—with "holes in his socks and $40 in his pocket."

Baldwin never returned to live permanently in America again, but visited often—in his own words, as a "commuter"—for the rest of his life. Baldwin quickly fell in with Parisian culture and attitudes, and became part of the expatriate black Paris community known as "la Rive Noire." His first book, *Go Tell It on the Mountain* (1953), was a critical success but not a financial one, and he worked as a journalist in order to support himself. In 1957, he returned to the United States to report on the American South. His essays and journalistic pieces catapulted him to national prominence; he lectured and was present at major civil rights events, including the March on Washington and the drive to register voters in Selma, Alabama. He came in contact with major civil rights figures such as Martin Luther King, Jr., and later Malcolm X, Angela Davis, and Huey Newton, and for a time was regarded as one of the most important spokespersons for the civil rights movement.

Baldwin's political presence and literary career reached an all-time high in 1963 with the publication of his novel *The Fire Next Time*, which provided him with financial stability for the first time. His work continued to explore the uneasy complexities of racial oppression and the subject of homosexuality in a time of widespread intolerance. As the 1960s progressed, however, he fell out of favor, in part because of the perception that he had "sold out" to white America. Baldwin lived the remainder of his life primarily in Turkey and France, where in 1986 he received the French Legion of Honor. In 1987, in St. Paul de Vence, France, he died of cancer.

"Sonny's Blues" first appeared in 1957 in *Partisan Review*; it was reprinted in 1965 in the short story collection *Going to Meet the Man*. The story examines the complicated relationship between the narrator and his younger brother, Sonny. It is literally only through Sonny's "blues" that the brothers can approach a connection that explains their fraternal interaction; the narrator comes closest to Sonny through Sonny's music.

Sonny's Blues

JAMES BALDWIN

I READ about it in the paper, in the subway, on my way to work. I read it, and I couldn't believe it, and I read it again. Then perhaps I just stared at it, at the newsprint spelling out his name, spelling out the story. I stared at it in the swinging lights of the subway car, and in the faces and bodies of the people, and in my own face, trapped in the darkness which roared outside.

It was not to be believed and I kept telling myself that, as I walked from the subway station to the high school. And at the same time I couldn't doubt it. I was scared, scared for Sonny. He became real to me again. A great block of ice got settled in my belly and kept melting there slowly all day long, while I taught my classes algebra. It was a special kind of ice. It kept melting, sending trickles of ice water all up and down my veins, but it never got less. Sometimes it hardened and seemed to expand until I felt my guts were going to come spilling out or that I was going to choke or scream. This would always be at a moment when I was remembering some specific thing Sonny had once said or done.

When he was about as old as the boys in my classes his face had been bright and open, there was a lot of copper in it; and he'd had wonderfully direct brown eyes, and great gentleness and privacy. I wondered what he looked like now. He had been picked up, the evening before, in a raid on an apartment downtown, for peddling and using heroin.

I couldn't believe it but what I mean by that is that I couldn't find any room for it anywhere inside me, I had kept it outside me for a long time. I hadn't wanted to know. I had had suspicions, but I didn't name them. I kept putting them away. I told myself that Sonny was wild, but he wasn't crazy. And he'd always been a good boy, he hadn't ever turned hard or evil or disrespectful, the way kids can, so quick, so quick, especially in Harlem. I didn't want to believe that I'd ever see my brother going down, coming to nothing, all that light in his face gone out, in the condition I'd already seen so many others. Yet it had happened and here I was, talking about algebra to a lot of boys who might, every one of them for all I knew, be popping off needles every time they went to the head. Maybe it did more for them than algebra could.

I was sure that the first time Sonny had ever had horse, he couldn't have been much older than these boys were now. These boys, now, were living as we'd been living then, they were growing up with a rush and their heads bumped abruptly against the low ceiling of their actual possibilities. They were filled with rage. All they really knew were two darknesses, the darkness of their lives, which was now closing in on them, and the darkness of the movies, which had blinded them to that other darkness, and in which they now, vindictively, dreamed, at once more together than they were at any other time, and more alone.

When the last bell rang, the last class ended, I let out my breath. It seemed I'd been holding it for all that time. My clothes were wet—I may have looked as though I'd been sitting in a steam bath, all dressed up, all afternoon. I sat alone in the classroom a long time. I listened to the boys outside, downstairs, shouting and cursing and laughing. Their laughter struck me for perhaps the first time. It was not the joyous laughter which—God knows why—one associates with children. It was mocking and insular, its intent was to denigrate. It was disenchanted, and in this, also, lay the authority of their curses. Perhaps I was listening to them because I was thinking about my brother and in them I heard my brother. And myself.

One boy was whistling a tune, at once very complicated and very simple, it seemed to be pouring out of him as though he were a bird, and it sounded very cool and moving through all that harsh, bright air, only just holding its own through all those other sounds.

I stood up and walked over to the window and looked down into the courtyard. It was the beginning of the spring and the sap was rising in the boys. A teacher passed through them every now and again, quickly, as though he or she couldn't wait to get out of that courtyard, to get those boys out of their sight and off their minds. I started collecting my stuff. I thought I'd better get home and talk to Isabel.

The courtyard was almost deserted by the time I got downstairs. I saw this boy standing in the shadow of a doorway looking just like Sonny. I almost called his name. Then I saw that it wasn't Sonny, but somebody we used to know, a boy from around our block. He'd been Sonny's friend. He'd never been mine, having been too young for me, and, anyway, I'd never liked him. And now, even though he was a grown-up man, he still hung around that block, still spent hours on the street corners, was always high and raggy. I used to run into him from time to time and he'd often work around to asking me for a quarter or fifty cents. He always had some real good excuse, too, and I always gave it to him. I don't know why.

But now, abruptly, I hated him. I couldn't stand the way he looked at me, partly like a dog, partly like a cunning child. I wanted to ask him what the hell he was doing in the school courtyard.

He sort of shuffled over to me, and he said, "I see you got the papers. So you already know about it."

"You mean about Sonny? Yes, I already know about it. How come they didn't get you?"

He grinned. It made him repulsive and it also brought to mind what he'd looked like as a kid. "I wasn't there. I stay away from them people."

"Good for you." I offered him a cigarette and I watched him through the smoke. "You come all the way down here just to tell me about Sonny?"

"That's right." He was sort of shaking his head and his eyes looked strange, as though they were about to cross. The bright sun deadened his damp dark brown skin and it made his eyes look yellow and showed up the dirt in his kinked hair. He smelled funky. I moved a little away from him and I said, "Well, thanks. But I already know about it and I got to get home."

"I'll walk you a little ways," he said. We started walking. There were a couple of kids still loitering in the courtyard and one of them said goodnight to me and looked strangely at the boy beside me.

"What're you going to do?" he asked me. "I mean, about Sonny?"

"Look. I haven't seen Sonny for over a year, I'm not sure I'm going to do anything. Anyway, what the hell *can* I do?"

"That's right," he said quickly, "ain't nothing you can do. Can't much help old Sonny no more, I guess."

It was what I was thinking and so it seemed to me he had no right to say it.

"I'm surprised at Sonny, though," he went on—he had a funny way of talking, he looked straight ahead as though he were talking to himself—"I thought Sonny was a smart boy. I thought he was too smart to get hung."

"I guess he thought so too," I said sharply, "and that's how he got hung. And how about you? You're pretty goddamn smart, I bet."

Then he looked directly at me, just for a minute. "I ain't smart," he said. "If I was smart, I'd have reached for a pistol a long time ago."

"Look. Don't tell *me* your sad story, if it was up to me, I'd give you one." Then I felt guilty—guilty, probably, for never having supposed that the poor bastard *had* a story of his own, much less a sad one, and I asked, quickly, "What's going to happen to him now?"

He didn't answer this. He was off by himself some place.

"Funny thing," he said, and from his tone we might have been discussing the quickest way to get to Brooklyn, "when I saw the papers this morning, the first thing I asked myself was if I had anything to do with it. I felt sort of responsible."

I began to listen more carefully. The subway station was on the corner, just before us, and I stopped. He stopped, too. We were in front of a bar and he ducked slightly, peering in, but whoever he was looking for didn't seem to be there. The juke box was blasting away with something black and bouncy and I half watched the barmaid as she danced her way from the juke box to her place behind the bar. And I watched her face as she laughingly responded to something someone said to her, still keeping time to the music. When she smiled one saw the little girl, one sensed the doomed, still-struggling woman beneath the battered face of the semi-whore.

"I never *give* Sonny nothing," the boy said finally, "but a long time ago I come to school high and Sonny asked me how it felt." He paused, I couldn't bear to watch him, I watched the barmaid, and I listened to the music which seemed to be causing the pavement to shake. "I told him it felt great." The music stopped, the barmaid paused and watched the juke box until the music began again. "It did."

All this was carrying me some place I didn't want to go. I certainly didn't want to know how it felt. It filled everything, the people, the houses, the music, the dark quicksilver barmaid, with menace; and this menace was their reality.

"What's going to happen to him now?" I asked again.

"They'll send him away some place and they'll try to cure him." He shook his head. "Maybe he'll even think he's kicked the habit. Then they'll let him loose"—he gestured, throwing his cigarette into the gutter. "That's all."

"What do you mean, that's *all*?"

But I knew what he meant.

"I *mean*, that's *all*." He turned his head and looked at me, pulling down the corners of his mouth. "Don't you know what I mean?" he asked, softly.

"How the hell *would* I know what you mean?" I almost whispered it, I don't know why.

"That's right," he said to the air, "how would *he* know what I mean?" He turned toward me again, patient and calm, and yet I somehow felt him shaking, shaking as though he were going to fall apart. I felt that ice in my guts again, the dread I'd felt all afternoon; and again I watched the barmaid, moving about the bar, washing glasses, and singing. "Listen. They'll let him out and then it'll just start all over again. That's what I mean."

"You mean—they'll let him out. And then he'll just start working his way back in again. You mean he'll never kick the habit. Is that what you mean?"

"That's right," he said, cheerfully. "*You* see what I mean."

"Tell me," I said at last, "why does he want to die? He must want to die, he's killing himself, why does he want to die?"

He looked at me in surprise. He licked his lips. "He don't want to die. He wants to live. Don't nobody want to die, ever."

Then I wanted to ask him—too many things. He could not have answered, or if he had, I could not have borne the answers. I started walking. "Well, I guess it's none of my business."

"It's going to be rough on old Sonny," he said. We reached the subway station. "This is your station?" he asked. I nodded. I took one step down. "Damn!" he said, suddenly. I looked up at him. He grinned again. "Damn it if I didn't leave all my money home. You ain't got a dollar on you, have you? Just for a couple of days, is all."

All at once something inside gave and threatened to come pouring out of me. I didn't hate him any more. I felt that in another moment I'd start crying like a child.

"Sure," I said. "Don't sweat." I looked in my wallet and didn't have a dollar, I only had a five. "Here," I said. "That hold you?"

He didn't look at it—he didn't want to look at it. A terrible, closed look came over his face, as though he were keeping the number on the bill a secret from him and me. "Thanks," he said, and now he was dying to see me go. "Don't worry about Sonny. Maybe I'll write him or something."

"Sure," I said. "You do that. So long."

"Be seeing you," he said. I went on down the steps.

And I didn't write Sonny or send him anything for a long time. When I finally did, it was just after my little girl died, and he wrote me back a letter which made me feel like a bastard.

Here's what he said:

Dear brother,

You don't know how much I needed to hear from you. I wanted to write you many a time but I dug how much I must have hurt you and so I didn't write. But now I feel like a man who's been trying to climb up out of some deep, real deep and funky hole and just saw the sun up there, outside. I got to get outside.

I can't tell you much about how I got here. I mean I don't know how to tell you. I guess I was afraid of something or I was trying to escape from something and you know I have never been very strong in the head (smile). I'm glad Mama and Daddy are dead and can't see what's happened to their son and I swear if I'd known what I was doing I would never have hurt you so, you and a lot of other fine people who were nice to me and who believed in me.

I don't want you to think it had anything to do with me being a musician. It's more than that. Or maybe less than that. I can't get anything straight in my head down here and I try not to think about what's going to happen to me when I get outside again. Sometime I think I'm going to flip and *never* get outside and sometime I think I'll come straight back. I tell you one thing, though, I'd rather blow my brains out than go through this again. But that's what they all say, so they tell me. If I tell you when I'm coming to New York and if you could meet me, I sure would appreciate it. Give my love to Isabel and the kids and I was sure sorry to hear about little Gracie. I wish I could be like Mama and say the Lord's will be done, but I don't know it seems to me that trouble is the one thing that never does get stopped and I don't know what good it does to blame it on the Lord. But maybe it does some good if you believe it.

Your brother,
Sonny

Then I kept in constant touch with him and I sent him whatever I could and I went to meet him when he came back to New York. When I saw him many things I thought I had forgotten came flooding back to me. This was because I had begun, finally, to wonder about Sonny, about the life that Sonny lived inside. This life, whatever it was, had made him older and thinner and it had deepened the distant stillness in which he had always moved. He looked very unlike my baby brother. Yet, when he smiled, when we shook hands, the baby brother I'd never known looked out from the depths of his private life, like an animal waiting to be coaxed into the light.

"How you been keeping?" he asked me.

"All right. And you?"

"Just fine." He was smiling all over his face. "It's good to see you again."

"It's good to see you."

The seven years' difference in our ages lay between us like a chasm: I wondered if these years would ever operate between us as a bridge. I was remembering, and it made it hard to catch my breath, that I had been there when he was born; and I had heard the first words he had ever spoken. When he started to walk, he walked from our mother straight to me. I caught him just before he fell when he took the first steps he ever took in this world.

"How's Isabel?"

"Just fine. She's dying to see you."

"And the boys?"

"They're fine, too. They're anxious to see their uncle."

"Oh, come on. You know they don't remember me."

"Are you kidding? Of course they remember you."

He grinned again. We got into a taxi. We had a lot to say to each other, far too much to know how to begin.

As the taxi began to move, I asked, "You still want to go to India?"

He laughed. "You still remember that. Hell, no. This place is Indian enough for me."

"It used to belong to them," I said.

And he laughed again. "They damn sure knew what they were doing when they got rid of it."

Years ago, when he was around fourteen, he'd been all hipped on the idea of going to India. He read books about people sitting on rocks, naked, in all kinds of weather, but mostly bad, naturally, and walking barefoot through hot coals and arriving at wisdom. I used to say that it sounded to me as though they were getting away from wisdom as fast as they could. I think he sort of looked down on me for that.

"Do you mind," he asked, "if we have the driver drive alongside the park? On the west side—I haven't seen the city in so long."

"Of course not," I said. I was afraid that I might sound as though I were humoring him, but I hoped he wouldn't take it that way.

So we drove along, between the green of the park and the stony, lifeless elegance of hotels and apartment buildings, toward the vivid, killing streets of our childhood. These streets hadn't changed, though housing projects jutted up out of them now like rocks in the middle of a boiling sea. Most of the houses in which we had grown up had vanished, as had the stores from which we had stolen, the basements in which we had first tried sex, the rooftops from which we had hurled tin cans and bricks. But houses exactly like the houses of our past yet dominated the landscape, boys exactly like the boys we once had been found themselves smothering in these houses, came down into the streets for light and air and found themselves encircled by disaster. Some escaped the trap, most didn't. Those who got out always left something of themselves behind, as some animals amputate a leg and leave it in the trap. It might be said, perhaps, that I had escaped, after all, I was a school teacher; or that Sonny had, he hadn't lived in Harlem for years. Yet, as the cab moved uptown through streets which seemed, with a rush, to darken with dark people, and as I covertly studied Sonny's face, it came to me that what we both were seeking through our separate cab windows was that part of ourselves which had been left behind. It's always at the hour of trouble and confrontation that the missing member aches.

We hit 110th Street and started rolling up Lenox Avenue. And I'd known this avenue all my life, but it seemed to me again, as it had seemed on the day I'd first heard about Sonny's trouble, filled with a hidden menace which was its very breath of life.

"We almost there," said Sonny.

"Almost." We were both too nervous to say anything more.

We live in a housing project. It hasn't been up long. A few days after it was up it seemed uninhabitably new, now, of course, it's already rundown. It looks like a parody of the good, clean, faceless life—God knows the people who live in it do their best to make it a parody. The beat-looking grass lying around isn't enough to make their lives green, the hedges will never hold out the streets, and they know it. The big windows fool no one, they aren't big enough to make space out of no space. They don't bother with the windows, they watch the TV screen instead. The playground is most popular with the children who don't play at jacks, or skip rope, or roller skate, or swing, and they can be found in it after dark. We moved in partly because it's not too far from where I teach, and partly for the kids; but it's really just like the houses in which Sonny and I grew up. The same things happen, they'll have the same things to remember. The moment Sonny and I started into the house I had the feeling that I was simply bringing him back into the danger he had almost died trying to escape.

Sonny had never been talkative. So I don't know why I was sure he'd be dying to talk to me when supper was over the first night. Everything went fine, the oldest boy remembered him, and the youngest boy liked him, and Sonny had remembered to bring something for each of them; and Isabel, who is really much nicer than I am, more open and giving, had gone to a lot of trouble about dinner and was genuinely glad to see him. And she's always been able to tease Sonny in a way that I haven't. It was nice to see her face so vivid again and to hear her laugh and watch her make Sonny laugh. She wasn't, or, anyway, she didn't seem to be, at all uneasy or embarrassed. She chatted as though there were no subject which had to be avoided and she got Sonny past his first, faint stiffness. And thank God she was there, for I was filled with that icy dread again. Everything I did seemed awkward to me, and everything I said sounded freighted with hidden meaning. I was trying to remember everything I'd heard about dope addiction and I couldn't help watching Sonny for signs. I wasn't doing it out of malice. I was trying to find out something about my brother. I was dying to hear him tell me he was safe.

"Safe!" my father grunted, whenever Mama suggested trying to move to a neighborhood which might be safer for children. "Safe, hell! Ain't no place safe for kids, nor nobody."

He always went on like this, but he wasn't, ever, really as bad as he sounded, not even on weekends, when he got drunk. As a matter of fact, he was always on the lookout for "something a little better," but he died before he found it. He died suddenly during a drunken weekend in the middle of the war, when Sonny was fifteen. He and Sonny hadn't ever got on too well. And this was partly because Sonny was the apple of his father's eye. It was because he loved Sonny so much and was frightened for him, that he was always fighting with him. It doesn't do any good to fight with Sonny. Sonny just moves back, inside himself, where he can't be reached. But the principal reason that they never hit it off is that they were so much alike. Daddy was big and rough and loud-talking, just the opposite of Sonny, but they both had—that same privacy.

Mama tried to tell me something about this, just after Daddy died. I was home on leave from the army.

This was the last time I ever saw my mother alive. Just the same, this picture gets all mixed up in my mind with pictures I had of her when she was younger. The way I always see her is the way she used to be on a Sunday afternoon, say, when the old folks were talking after the big Sunday dinner. I always see her wearing pale blue. She'd be sitting on the sofa. And my father would be sitting in the easy chair, not far from her. And the living room would be full of church folks and relatives. There they sit, in chairs all around the living room, and the night is creeping up outside, but nobody knows it yet. You can see the darkness growing against the windowpanes and you hear the street noises every now and again, or maybe the jangling beat of a tambourine from one of the churches close by, but it's real quiet in the room. For a moment nobody's talking, but every face looks darkening, like the sky outside. And my mother rocks a little from the waist, and my father's eyes are closed. Everyone is looking at something a child can't see. For a minute they've forgotten the children. Maybe a kid is lying on the rug, half asleep. Maybe somebody's got a kid in his lap and is absent-mindedly stroking the kid's head. Maybe there's a kid, quiet and big-eyed, curled up in a big chair in the corner. The silence, the darkness coming, and the darkness in the faces frighten the child obscurely. He hopes that the hand which strokes his forehead will never stop—will never die. He hopes that there will never come a time when the old folks won't be sitting around the living room, talking about where they've come from, and what they've seen, and what's happened to them and their kinfolk.

But something deep and watchful in the child knows that this is bound to end, is already ending. In a moment someone will get up and turn on the light. Then the old folks will remember the children and they won't talk any more that day. And when light fills the room, the child is filled with darkness. He knows that every time this happens he's moved just a little closer to that darkness outside. The darkness outside is what the old folks have been talking about. It's what they've come from. It's what they endure. The child knows that they won't talk any more because if he knows too much about what's happened to *them*, he'll know too much too soon, about what's going to happen to *him*.

The last time I talked to my mother, I remember I was restless. I wanted to get out and see Isabel. We weren't married then and we had a lot to straighten out between us.

There Mama sat, in black, by the window. She was humming an old church song, *Lord, you brought me from a long ways off*. Sonny was out somewhere. Mama kept watching the streets.

"I don't know," she said, "if I'll ever see you again, after you go off from here. But I hope you'll remember the things I tried to teach you."

"Don't talk like that," I said, and smiled. "You'll be here a long time yet."

She smiled, too, but she said nothing. She was quiet for a long time. And I said, "Mama, don't you worry about nothing. I'll be writing all the time, and you be getting the checks ..."

"I want to talk to you about your brother," she said, suddenly. "If anything happens to me he ain't going to have nobody to look out for him."

"Mama," I said, "ain't nothing going to happen to you *or* Sonny. Sonny's all right. He's a good boy and he's got good sense."

"It ain't a question of his being a good boy," Mama said, "nor of his having good sense. It ain't only the bad ones, nor yet the dumb ones that gets sucked under." She stopped, looking at me. "Your Daddy once had a brother," she said, and she smiled in a way that made me feel she was in pain. "You didn't never know that, did you?"

"No," I said, "I never knew that," and I watched her face.

"Oh, yes," she said, "your Daddy had a brother." She looked out of the window again. "I know you never saw your Daddy cry. But *I* did—many a time, through all these years."

I asked her, "What happened to his brother? How come nobody's ever talked about him?"

This was the first time I ever saw my mother look old.

"His brother got killed," she said, "when he was just a little younger than you are now. I knew him. He was a fine boy. He was maybe a little full of the devil, but he didn't mean nobody no harm."

Then she stopped and the room was silent, exactly as it had sometimes been on those Sunday afternoons. Mama kept looking out into the streets.

"He used to have a job in the mill," she said, "and, like all young folks, he just liked to perform on Saturday nights. Saturday nights, him and your father would drift around to different places, go to dances and things like that, or just sit around with people they knew, and your father's brother would sing, he had a fine voice, and play along with himself on his guitar. Well, this particular Saturday night, him and your father was coming home from some place, and they were both a little drunk and there was a moon that night, it was bright like day. Your father's brother was feeling kind of good, and he was whistling to himself, and he had his guitar slung over his shoulder. They was coming down a hill and beneath them was a road that turned off from the highway. Well, your father's brother, being always kind of frisky, decided to run down this hill, and he did, with that guitar banging and clanging behind him, and he ran across the road, and he was making water behind a tree. And your father was sort of amused at him and he was still coming down the hill, kind of slow. Then he heard a car motor and that same minute his brother stepped from behind the tree, into the road, in the moonlight. And he started to cross the road. And your father started to run down the hill, he says he don't know why. This car was full of white men. They was all drunk, and when they seen your father's brother they let out a great whoop and holler and they aimed the car straight at him. They was having fun, they just wanted to scare him, the way they do sometimes, you know. But they was drunk. And I guess the boy being drunk, too, and scared, kind of lost his head. By the time he jumped it was too late. Your father says he heard his brother scream when the car rolled over him, and he heard the wood of that guitar when it give, and he heard them strings go flying, and he heard them white men shouting, and the car kept on a-going and it ain't stopped till this day. And, time your father got down the hill, his brother weren't nothing but blood and pulp."

Tears were gleaming on my mother's face. There wasn't anything I could say.

"He never mentioned it," she said, "because I never let him mention it before you children. Your Daddy was like a crazy man that night and for many a night thereafter. He says he never in his life seen anything as dark as that road after the lights of that car had gone away. Weren't nothing, weren't nobody on that road, just your Daddy and his brother and that busted guitar. Oh, yes. Your Daddy never did really get right again. Till the day he died he weren't sure but that every white man he saw was the man that killed his brother."

She stopped and took out her handkerchief and dried her eyes and looked at me.

"I ain't telling you all this," she said, "to make you scared or bitter or to make you hate nobody. I'm telling you this because you got a brother. And the world ain't changed."

I guess I didn't want to believe this. I guess she saw this in my face. She turned away from me, toward the window again, searching those streets.

"But I praise my Redeemer," she said at last, "that He called your Daddy home before me. I ain't saying it to throw no flowers at myself, but, I declare, it keeps me from feeling too cast down to know I helped your father get safely through this world. Your father always acted like he was the roughest, strongest man on earth. And everybody took him to be like that. But if he hadn't had me there—to see his tears!"

She was crying again. Still, I couldn't move. I said, "Lord, Lord, Mama, I didn't know it was like that."

"Oh, honey," she said, "there's a lot that you don't know. But you are going to find out." She stood up from the window and came over to me. "You got to hold on to your brother," she said, "and don't let him fall, no matter what it looks like is happening to him and no matter how evil you gets with him. You going to be evil with him many a time. But don't you forget what I told you, you hear?"

"I won't forget," I said. "Don't you worry, I won't forget. I won't let nothing happen to Sonny."

My mother smiled as though she was amused at something she saw in my face. Then, "You may not be able to stop nothing from happening. But you got to let him know you's *there*."

Two days later I was married, and then I was gone. And I had a lot of things on my mind and I pretty well forgot my promise to Mama until I got shipped home on a special furlough for her funeral.

And, after the funeral, with just Sonny and me alone in the empty kitchen, I tried to find out something about him.

"What do you want to do?" I asked him.

"I'm going to be a musician," he said.

For he had graduated, in the time I had been away, from dancing to the juke box to finding out who was playing what, and what they were doing with it, and he had bought himself a set of drums.

"You mean, you want to be a drummer?" I somehow had the feeling that being a drummer might be all right for other people but not for my brother Sonny.

"I don't think," he said, looking at me very gravely, "that I'll ever be a good drummer. But I think I can play a piano."

I frowned. I'd never played the role of the oldest brother quite so seriously before, had scarcely ever, in fact, *asked* Sonny a damn thing. I sensed myself in the presence of something I didn't really know how to handle, didn't understand. So I made my frown a little deeper as I asked: "What kind of musician do you want to be?"

He grinned. "How many kinds do you think there are?"

"Be *serious*," I said.

He laughed, throwing his head back, and then looked at me. "I *am* serious."

"Well, then, for Christ's sake, stop kidding around and answer a serious question. I mean, do you want to be a concert pianist, you want to play classical music and all that, or—or what?" Long before I finished he was laughing again. "For Christ's *sake*, Sonny!"

He sobered, but with difficulty. "I'm sorry. But you sound so—*scared*!" and he was off again.

"Well, you may think it's funny now, baby, but it's not going to be so funny when you have to make your living at it, let me tell you *that*." I was furious because I knew he was laughing at me and I didn't know why.

"No," he said, very sober now, and afraid, perhaps, that he'd hurt me, "I don't want to be a classical pianist. That isn't what interests me. I mean"—he paused, looking hard at me, as though his eyes would help me to understand, and then gestured helplessly, as though perhaps his hand would help—"I mean, I'll have a lot of studying to do, and I'll have to study *everything*, but, I mean, I want to play *with*—jazz musicians." He stopped. "I want to play jazz," he said.

Well, the word had never before sounded as heavy, as real, as it sounded that afternoon in Sonny's mouth. I just looked at him and I was probably frowning a real frown by this time. I simply couldn't see why on earth he'd want to spend his time hanging around nightclubs, clowning around on bandstands, while people pushed each other around a dance floor. It seemed—beneath him, somehow. I had never thought about it before, had never been forced to, but I suppose I had always put jazz musicians in a class with what Daddy called "good-time people."

"Are you *serious*?"

"Hell, *yes*, I'm serious."

He looked more helpless than ever, and annoyed, and deeply hurt.

I suggested, helpfully: "You mean—like Louis Armstrong?"

His face closed as though I'd struck him. "No. I'm not talking about none of that old-time, down home crap."

"Well, look, Sonny, I'm sorry, don't get mad. I just don't altogether get it, that's all. Name somebody—you know, a jazz musician you admire."

"Bird."

"Who?"

"Bird! Charlie Parker! Don't they teach you nothing in the goddamn army?"

I lit a cigarette. I was surprised and then a little amused to discover that I was trembling. "I've been out of touch," I said. "You'll have to be patient with me. Now. Who's this Parker character?"

"He's just one of the greatest jazz musicians alive," said Sonny, sullenly, his hands in his pockets, his back to me. "Maybe *the* greatest," he added, bitterly, "that's probably why *you* never heard of him."

"All right," I said. "I'm ignorant. I'm sorry. I'll go out and buy all the cat's records right away, all right?"

"It don't," said Sonny, with dignity, "make any difference to me. I don't care what you listen to. Don't do me no favors."

I was beginning to realize that I'd never seen him so upset before. With another part of my mind I was thinking that this would probably turn out to be one of those things kids go through and that I shouldn't make it seem important by pushing it too hard. Still, I didn't think it would do any harm to ask: "Doesn't all this take a lot of time? Can you make a living at it?"

He turned back to me and half leaned, half sat, on the kitchen table. "Everything takes time," he said, "and—well, yes, sure, I can make a living at it. But what I don't seem to be able to make you understand is that it's the only thing I want to do."

"Well, Sonny," I said gently, "you know people can't always do exactly what they *want* to do—"

"*No*, I don't know that," said Sonny, surprising me. "I think people *ought* to do what they want to do, what else are they alive for?"

"You getting to be a big boy," I said desperately, "it's time you started thinking about your future."

"I'm thinking about my future," said Sonny, grimly. "I think about it all the time."

I gave up. I decided, if he didn't change his mind, that we could always talk about it later. "In the meantime," I said, "you got to finish school." We had already decided that he'd have to move in with Isabel and her folks. I knew this wasn't the ideal arrangement because Isabel's folks are inclined to be dicty[1] and they hadn't especially wanted Isabel to marry me. But I didn't know what else to do. "And we have to get you fixed up at Isabel's."

There was a long silence. He moved from the kitchen table to the window. "That's a terrible idea. You know it yourself."

"Do you have a *better* idea?"

He just walked up and down the kitchen for a minute. He was as tall as I was. He had started to shave. I suddenly had the feeling that I didn't know him at all.

He stopped at the kitchen table and picked up my cigarettes. Looking at me with a kind of mocking, amused defiance, he put one between his lips. "You mind?"

"You smoking already?"

He lit the cigarette and nodded, watching me through the smoke. "I just wanted to see if I'd have the courage to smoke in front of you." He grinned and blew a great cloud of smoke to the ceiling. "It was easy." He looked at my face. "Come on, now. I bet you was smoking at my age, tell the truth."

---

1 Bossy or snobbish.

I didn't say anything but the truth was on my face, and he laughed. But now there was something very strained in his laugh. "Sure. And I bet that ain't all you was doing."

He was frightening me a little. "Cut the crap," I said. "We already decided that you was going to go and live at Isabel's. Now what's got into you all of a sudden?"

"*You* decided it," he pointed out. "*I* didn't decide nothing." He stopped in front of me, leaning against the stove, arms loosely folded. "Look, brother, I don't want to stay in Harlem no more, I really don't." He was very earnest. He looked at me, then over toward the kitchen window. There was something in his eyes I'd never seen before, some thoughtfulness, some worry all his own. He rubbed the muscle of one arm. "It's time I was getting out of here."

"Where do you want to *go*, Sonny?"

"I want to join the army. Or the navy, I don't care. If I say I'm old enough, they'll believe me."

Then I got mad. It was because I was so scared. "You must be crazy. You goddamn fool, what the hell do you want to go and join the *army* for?"

"I just told you. To get out of Harlem."

"Sonny, you haven't even finished *school*. And if you really want to be a musician, how do you expect to study if you're in the *army*?"

He looked at me, trapped, and in anguish. "There's ways. I might be able to work out some kind of deal. Anyway, I'll have the G.I. Bill when I come out."

"*If* you come out." We stared at each other. "Sonny, please. Be reasonable. I know the setup is far from perfect. But we got to do the best we can."

"I ain't learning nothing in school," he said. "Even when I go." He turned away from me and opened the window and threw his cigarette out into the narrow alley. I watched his back. "At least, I ain't learning nothing you'd want me to learn." He slammed the window so hard I thought the glass would fly out, and turned back to me. "And I'm sick of the stink of these garbage cans!"

"Sonny," I said, "I know how you feel. But if you don't finish school now, you're going to be sorry later that you didn't." I grabbed him by the shoulders. "And you only got another year. It ain't so bad. And I'll come back and I swear I'll help you do *whatever* you want to do. Just try to put up with it till I come back. Will you please do that? For me?"

He didn't answer and he wouldn't look at me.

"Sonny. You hear me?"

He pulled away. "I hear you. But you never hear anything *I* say."

I didn't know what to say to that. He looked out the window and then back at me. "OK," he said, and sighed. "I'll try."

Then I said, trying to cheer him up a little, "They got a piano at Isabel's. You can practice on it."

And as a matter of fact, it did cheer him up for a minute. "That's right," he said to himself. "I forgot that." His face relaxed a little. But the worry, the thoughtfulness, played on it still, the way shadows play on a face which is staring into the fire.

But I thought I'd never hear the end of that piano. At first, Isabel would write me, saying how nice it was that Sonny was so serious about his music and how, as soon as he came in from school, or wherever he had been when he was supposed to be at school, he went straight to that piano and stayed there until suppertime. And, after supper, he went back to that piano and stayed there until everybody went to bed. He was at the piano all day Saturday and all day Sunday. Then he bought a record player and started playing records. He'd play one record over and over again, all day long sometimes, and he'd improvise along with it on the piano. Or he'd play one section of the record, one chord, one change, one progression, then he'd do it on the piano. Then back to the record. Then back to the piano.

Well, I really don't know how they stood it. Isabel finally confessed that it wasn't like living with a person at all, it was like living with sound. And the sound didn't make any sense to her, didn't make any sense to any of them—naturally. They began, in a way, to be afflicted by this presence that was living in their home. It was as though Sonny were some sort of god, or monster. He moved in an atmosphere which wasn't like theirs at all. They fed him and he ate, he washed himself, he walked in and out of their door; he certainly wasn't nasty or unpleasant or rude. Sonny isn't any of those things; but it was as though he were all wrapped up in some cloud, some fire, some vision all his own; and there wasn't any way to reach him.

At the same time, he wasn't really a man yet, he was still a child, and they had to watch out for him in all kinds of ways. They certainly couldn't throw him out. Neither did they dare to make a great scene about that piano because even they dimly sensed, as I sensed, from so many thousands of miles away, that Sonny was at that piano playing for his life.

But he hadn't been going to school. One day a letter came from the school board and Isabel's mother got it—there had, apparently, been other letters but Sonny had torn them up. This day, when Sonny came in, Isabel's mother showed him the letter and asked where he'd been spending his time. And she finally got it out of him that he'd been down in Greenwich Village, with musicians and other characters, in a white girl's apartment. And this scared her and she started to scream at him and what came up, once she began—though she denies it to this day—was what sacrifices they were making to give Sonny a decent home and how little he appreciated it.

Sonny didn't play the piano that day. By evening, Isabel's mother had calmed down but then there was the old man to deal with, and Isabel herself. Isabel says she did her best to be calm but she broke down and started crying. She says she just watched Sonny's face. She could tell, by watching him, what was happening with him. And what was happening was that they penetrated his cloud, they had reached him. Even if their fingers had been a thousand times more gentle than human fingers ever are, he could hardly help feeling that they had stripped him naked and were spitting on that nakedness. For he also had to see that his presence, that music, which was life or death to him, had been torture for them and that they had endured it, not at all for his sake, but only for mine. And Sonny couldn't take that. He can take it a little better today than he could then but he's still not very good at it and, frankly, I don't know anybody who is.

The silence of the next few days must have been louder than the sound of all the music ever played since time began. One morning, before she went to work, Isabel was in his room for something and she suddenly realized that all of his records were gone. And she knew for certain that he was gone. And he was. He went as far as the navy would carry him. He finally sent me a postcard from some place in Greece and that was the first I knew that Sonny was still alive. I didn't see him any more until we were both back in New York and the war had long been over.

He was a man by then, of course, but I wasn't willing to see it. He came by the house from time to time, but we fought almost every time we met. I didn't like the way he carried himself, loose and dreamlike all the time, and I didn't like his friends, and his music seemed to be merely an excuse for the life he led. It sounded just that weird and disordered.

Then we had a fight, a pretty awful fight, and I didn't see him for months. By and by I looked him up, where he was living, in a furnished room in the Village, and I tried to make it up. But there were lots of other people in the room and Sonny just lay on his bed, and he wouldn't come downstairs with me, and he treated these other people as though they were his family and I weren't. So I got mad and then he got mad, and then I told him that he might just as well be dead as live the way he was living. Then he stood up and he told me not to worry about him any more in life, that he *was* dead as far as I was concerned. Then he pushed me to the door and the other people looked on as though nothing were happening, and he slammed the door behind me. I stood in the hallway, staring at the door. I heard somebody laugh in the room and then the tears came to my eyes. I started down the steps, whistling to keep from crying, I kept whistling to myself, *You going to need me, baby, one of these cold, rainy days.*

I read about Sonny's trouble in the spring. Little Grace died in the fall. She was a beautiful little girl. But she only lived a little over two years. She died of polio and she suffered. She had a slight fever for a couple of days, but it didn't seem like anything and we just kept her in bed. And we would certainly have called the doctor, but the fever dropped, she seemed to be all right. So we thought it had just been a cold. Then, one day she was up, playing, Isabel was in the kitchen fixing lunch for the two boys when they'd come in from school, and she heard Grace fall down in the living room. When you have a lot of children you don't always start running when one of them falls, unless they start screaming or something. And, this time, Gracie was quiet. Yet, Isabel says that when she heard that *thump* and then that silence, something happened to her to make her afraid. And she ran to the living room and there was little Grace on the floor, all twisted up, and the reason she hadn't screamed was that she couldn't get her breath. And when she did scream, it was the worst sound, Isabel says, that she'd ever heard in all her life, and she still hears it sometimes in her dreams. Isabel will sometimes wake me up with a low, moaning, strangling sound and I have to be quick to awaken her and hold her to me and where Isabel is weeping against me seems a mortal wound.

I think I may have written Sonny the very day that little Grace was buried. I was sitting in the living room in the dark, by myself, and I suddenly thought of Sonny. My trouble made his real.

One Saturday afternoon, when Sonny had been living with us, or anyway, been in our house, for nearly two weeks, I found myself wandering aimlessly about the living room, drinking from a can of beer, and trying to work up courage to search Sonny's room. He was out, he was usually out whenever I was home, and Isabel had taken the children to see their grandparents. Suddenly I was standing still in front of the living room window, watching Seventh Avenue. The idea of searching Sonny's room made me still. I scarcely dared to admit to myself what I'd be searching for. I didn't know what I'd do if I found it. Or if I didn't.

On the sidewalk across from me, near the entrance to a barbecue joint, some people were holding an old-fashioned revival meeting. The barbecue cook, wearing a dirty white apron, his conked hair reddish and metallic in the pale sun, and a cigarette between his lips, stood in the doorway, watching them. Kids and older people paused in their errands and stood there, along with some older men and a couple of very tough-looking women who watched everything that happened on the avenue, as though they owned it, or were maybe owned by it. Well, they were watching this, too. The revival was being carried on by three sisters in black, and a brother. All they had were their voices and their Bibles and a tambourine. The brother was testifying and while he testified two of the sisters stood together, seeming to say amen, and the third sister walked around with the tambourine outstretched and a couple of people dropped coins into it.

Then the brother's testimony ended and the sister who had been taking up the collection dumped the coins into her palm and transferred them to the pocket of her long black robe. Then she raised both hands, striking the tambourine against the air, and then against one hand, and she started to sing. And the two other sisters and the brother joined in.

It was strange, suddenly, to watch, though I had been seeing these meetings all my life. So, of course, had everybody else down there. Yet, they paused and watched and listened and I stood still at the window. "*'Tis the old ship of Zion,*" they sang, and the sister with the tambourine kept a steady, jangling beat, "*it has rescued many a thousand!*" Not a soul under the sound of their voices was hearing this song for the first time, not one of them had been rescued. Nor had they seen much in the way of rescue work being done around them. Neither did they especially believe in the holiness of the three sisters and the brother, they knew too much about them, knew where they lived, and how. The woman with the tambourine, whose voice dominated the air, whose face was bright with joy, was divided by very little from the woman who stood watching her, a cigarette between her heavy, chapped lips, her hair a cuckoo's nest, her face scarred and swollen from many beatings, and her black eyes glittering like coal. Perhaps they both knew this, which was why, when, as rarely, they addressed each other, they addressed each other as Sister. As the singing filled the air the watching, listening faces underwent a change; the eyes focusing on something within; the music seemed to soothe a poison out of them; and time seemed, nearly, to fall away from the sullen, belligerent, battered faces, as though they were fleeing back to their first condition, while dreaming of their last. The barbecue cook half shook his head and smiled, and dropped his cigarette and disappeared into his joint. A man fumbled in his pockets for change and stood holding it in his hand impatiently, as though he had just remembered a pressing appointment further up the avenue. He looked furious. Then I saw Sonny, standing on the edge of the crowd. He was carrying a wide, flat notebook, with a green cover, and it made him look, from where I was standing, almost like a schoolboy. The coppery sun brought out the copper in his skin, he was very faintly smiling, standing very still. Then the singing stopped, the tambourine turned into a collection plate again. The furious man dropped in his coins and vanished, so did a couple of the women, and Sonny dropped some change in the plate, looking directly at the woman with a little smile. He started across the avenue, toward the house. He has a slow, loping walk, something like the way Harlem hipsters walk, only he's imposed on this his own half-beat. I had never really noticed it before.

I stayed at the window, both relieved and apprehensive. As Sonny disappeared from my sight, they began singing again. And they were still singing when his key turned in the lock.

"Hey," he said.

"Hey, yourself. You want some beer?"

"No. Well maybe." But he came up to the window and stood beside me, looking out. "What a warm voice," he said.

They were singing *If I could only hear my mother pray again!*

"Yes," I said, "and she can sure beat that tambourine."

"But what a terrible song," he said, and laughed. He dropped his notebook on the sofa and disappeared into the kitchen. "Where's Isabel and the kids?"

"I think they went to see their grandparents. You hungry?"

"No." He came back into the living room with his can of beer. "You want to come some place with me tonight?"

I sensed, I don't know how, that I couldn't possibly say no. "Sure. Where?"

He sat down on the sofa and picked up his notebook and started leafing through it. "I'm going to sit in with some fellows in a joint in the Village."

"You mean, you're going to play, tonight?"

"That's right." He took a swallow of his beer and moved back to the window. He gave me a sidelong look. "If you can stand it."

"I'll try," I said.

He smiled to himself and we both watched as the meeting across the way broke up. The three sisters and the brother, heads bowed, were singing *God be with you till we meet again*. The faces around them were very quiet. Then the song ended. The small crowd dispersed. We watched the three women and the lone man walk slowly up the avenue.

"When she was singing before," said Sonny, abruptly, "her voice reminded me for a minute of what heroin feels like sometimes—when it's in your veins. It makes you feel sort of warm and cool at the same time. And distant. And—and sure." He sipped his beer, very deliberately not looking at me. I watched his face. "It makes you feel—in control. Sometimes you've got to have that feeling."

"Do you?" I sat down slowly in the easy chair.

"Sometimes." He went to the sofa and picked up his notebook again. "Some people do."

"In order," I asked, "to play?" And my voice was very ugly, full of contempt and anger.

"Well"—he looked at me with great, troubled eyes, as though, in fact, he hoped his eyes would tell me things he could never otherwise say—"they *think* so. And *if* they think so—!"

"And what do *you* think?" I asked.

He sat on the sofa and put his can of beer on the floor. "I don't know," he said, and I couldn't be sure if he were answering my question or pursuing his thoughts. His face didn't tell me. "It's not so much to *play*. It's to *stand* it, to be able to make it at all. On any level." He frowned and smiled: "In order to keep from shaking to pieces."

"But these friends of yours," I said, "they seem to shake themselves to pieces pretty goddamn fast."

"Maybe." He played with the notebook. And something told me that I should curb my tongue, that Sonny was doing his best to talk, that I should listen. "But of course you only know the ones that've gone to pieces. Some don't—or at least they haven't *yet* and that's just about all *any* of us can say." He paused. "And then there are some who just live, really, in hell, and they know it and they see what's happening and they go right on. I don't know." He sighed, dropped the notebook, folded his arms. "Some guys, you can tell from the way they play they on something *all* the time. And you can see that, well, it makes something real for them. But of course," he picked up his beer from the floor and sipped it and put the can down again, "they *want* to, too, you've got to see that. Even some of them that say they don't—*some*, not all."

"And what about you?" I asked—I couldn't help it. "What about you? Do *you* want to?"

He stood up and walked to the window and I remained silent for a long time. Then he sighed. "Me," he said. Then: "While I was downstairs before, on my way here, listening to that woman sing, it struck me all of a sudden how much suffering she must have had to go through—to sing like that. It's *repulsive* to think you have to suffer that much."

I said: "But there's no way not to suffer—is there, Sonny?"

"I believe not," he said and smiled, "but that's never stopped anyone from trying." He looked at me. "Has it?" I realized, with this mocking look, that there stood between us, forever, beyond the power of time or forgiveness, the fact that I had held silence—so long!—when he had needed human speech to help him. He turned back to the window. "No, there's no way not to suffer. But you try all kinds of ways to keep from drowning in it, to keep on top of it, and to make it seem—well, like *you*. Like you did something, all right, and now you're suffering for it. You know?" I said nothing. "Well, you know," he said, impatiently, "why *do* people suffer? Maybe it's better to do something to give it a reason, *any* reason."

"But we just agreed," I said, "that there's no way not to suffer. Isn't it better, then, just to—take it?"

"But nobody just takes it," Sonny cried, "that's what I'm telling you! *Everybody* tries not to. You're just hung up on the *way* some people try—it's not *your* way!"

The hair on my face began to itch, my face felt wet. "That's not true," I said, "that's not true. I don't give a damn what other people do, I don't even care how they suffer. I just care how *you* suffer." And he looked at me. "Please believe me," I said, "I don't want to see you—die—trying not to suffer."

"I won't," he said flatly, "die trying not to suffer. At least, not any faster than anybody else."

"But there's no need," I said, trying to laugh, "is there? in killing yourself."

I wanted to say more, but I couldn't. I wanted to talk about will power and how life could be—well, beautiful. I wanted to say that it was all within; but was it? or, rather, wasn't that exactly the trouble? And I wanted to promise that I would never fail him again. But it would all have sounded—empty words and lies.

So I made the promise to myself and prayed that I would keep it.

"It's terrible sometimes, inside," he said, "that's what's the trouble. You walk these streets, black and funky and cold, and there's not really a living ass to talk to, and there's nothing shaking, and there's no way of getting it out—that storm inside. You can't talk it and you can't make love with it, and when you finally try to get with it and play it, you realize *nobody's* listening. So *you've* got to listen. You got to find a way to listen."

And then he walked away from the window and sat on the sofa again, as though all the wind had suddenly been knocked out of him. "Sometimes you'll do *anything* to play, even cut your mother's throat." He laughed and looked at me. "Or your brother's." Then he sobered. "Or your own." Then: "Don't worry. I'm all right now and I think I'll *be* all right. But I can't forget—where I've been. I don't mean just the physical place I've been, I mean where I've *been*. And *what* I've been."

"What have you been, Sonny?" I asked.

He smiled—but sat sideways on the sofa, his elbow resting on the back, his fingers playing with his mouth and chin, not looking at me. "I've been something I didn't recognize, didn't know I could be. Didn't know anybody could be." He stopped, looking inward, looking helplessly young, looking old. "I'm not talking about it now because I feel *guilty* or anything like that—maybe it would be better if I did, I don't know. Anyway, I can't really talk about it. Not to you, not to anybody," and now he turned and faced me. "Sometimes, you know, and it was actually when I was most *out* of the world, I felt that I was in it, that I was *with* it, really, and I could play or I didn't really have to *play*, it just came out of me, it was there. And I don't know how I played, thinking about it now, but I know I did awful things, those times, sometimes to people. Or it wasn't that I *did* anything to them—it was that they weren't real." He picked up the beer can; it was empty; he rolled it between his palms: "And other times—well, I needed a fix, I needed to find a place to lean. I needed to clear a space to *listen*—and I couldn't find it, and I went *crazy*. I did terrible things to *me*, I was terrible *for* me." He began pressing the beer can between his hands, I watched the metal begin to give. It glittered, as he played with it like a knife, and I was afraid he would cut himself, but I said nothing. "Oh well. I can never tell you. I was all by myself at the bottom of something, stinking and sweating and crying and shaking, and I smelled it, you know? *my* stink, and I thought I'd die if I couldn't get away from it and yet, all the same, I knew that everything I was doing was just locking me in with it. And I didn't know," he paused, still flattening the beer can, "I didn't know, I still *don't* know, something kept telling me that maybe it was good to smell your own stink, but I didn't think that *that* was what I'd been trying to do—and—who can stand it?" and he abruptly dropped the ruined beer can, looking at me with a small, still smile, and then rose, walking to the window as though it were the lodestone rock. I watched his face, he watched the avenue. "I couldn't tell you when Mama died—but the reason I wanted to leave Harlem so bad was to get away from drugs. And then, when I ran away, that's what I was running from—really. When I came back, nothing had changed, *I* hadn't changed, I was just—older." And he stopped, drumming with his fingers on the windowpane. The sun had vanished, soon darkness would fall. I watched his face. "It can come again," he said, almost as though speaking to himself. Then he turned to me. "It can come again," he repeated. "I just want you to know that."

"All right," I said, at last. "So it can come again. All right."

He smiled, but the smile was sorrowful. "I had to try to tell you," he said.

"Yes," I said. "I understand that."

"You're my brother," he said, looking straight at me, and not smiling at all.

"Yes," I repeated, "yes, I understand that."

He turned back to the window, looking out. "All that hatred down there," he said, "all that hatred and misery and love. It's a wonder it doesn't blow the avenue apart."

We went to the only nightclub on a short, dark street, downtown. We squeezed through the narrow, chattering, jampacked bar to the entrance of the big room, where the bandstand was. And we stood there for a moment, for the lights were very dim in this room and we couldn't see. Then, "Hello, boy," said the voice and an enormous black man, much older than Sonny or myself, erupted out of all that atmospheric lighting and put an arm around Sonny's shoulder. "I been sitting right here," he said, "waiting for you."

He had a big voice, too, and heads in the darkness turned toward us.

Sonny grinned and pulled a little away, and said, "Creole, this is my brother. I told you about him."

Creole shook my hand. "I'm glad to meet you, son," he said, and it was clear that he was glad to meet me *there*, for Sonny's sake. And he smiled, "You got a real musician in *your* family," and he took his arm from Sonny's shoulder and slapped him, lightly, affectionately, with the back of his hand.

"Well. Now I've heard it all," said a voice behind us. This was another musician, and a friend of Sonny's, a coal-black, cheerful-looking man, built close to the ground. He immediately began confiding to me, at the top of his lungs, the most terrible things about Sonny his teeth gleaming like a lighthouse and his laugh coming up out of him like the beginning of an earthquake. And it turned out that everyone at the bar knew Sonny, or almost everyone, some were musicians, working there, or nearby, or not working, some were simply hangers-on, and some were there to hear Sonny play. I was introduced to all of them and they were all very polite to me. Yet, it was clear that, for them, I was only Sonny's brother. Here, I was in Sonny's world. Or, rather, his kingdom. Here, it was not even a question that his veins bore royal blood.

They were going to play soon and Creole installed me, by myself, at a table in a dark corner. Then I watched them, Creole, and the little black man, and Sonny, and the others, while they horsed around, standing just below the bandstand. The light from the bandstand spilled just a little short of them and, watching them laughing and gesturing and moving about, I had the feeling that they, nevertheless, were being most careful not to step into that circle of light too suddenly; that if they moved into the light too suddenly without thinking, they would perish in flame. Then, while I watched, one of them, the small black man, moved into the light and crossed the bandstand and started fooling around with his drums. Then—being funny and being, also, extremely ceremonious—Creole took Sonny by the arm and led him to the piano. A woman's voice called Sonny's name and a few hands started clapping. And Sonny, also being funny and being ceremonious, and so touched, I think, that he could have cried, but neither hiding it nor showing it, riding it like a man, grinned, and put both hands to his heart and bowed from the waist.

Creole then went to the bass fiddle and a lean, very bright-skinned brown man jumped up on the bandstand and picked up his horn. So there they were, and the atmosphere on the bandstand and in the room began to change and tighten. Someone stepped up to the microphone and announced them. Then there were all kinds of murmurs. Some people at the bar shushed others. The waitress ran around, frantically getting in the last orders, guys and chicks got closer to each other, and the lights on the bandstand, on the quartet, turned to a kind of indigo. Then they all looked different there. Creole looked about him for the last time, as though he were making certain that all his chickens were in the coop, and then he—jumped and struck the fiddle. And there they were.

All I know about music is that not many people ever really hear it. And even then, on the rare occasions when something opens within, and the music enters, what we mainly hear, or hear corroborated, are personal, private, vanishing evocations. But the man who creates the music is hearing something else, is dealing with the roar rising from the void and imposing order on it as it hits the air. What is evoked in him, then, is of another order, more terrible because it has no words, and triumphant, too, for that same reason. And his triumph, when he triumphs, is ours. I just watched Sonny's face. His face was troubled, he was working hard, but he wasn't with it. And I had the feeling that, in a way, everyone on the bandstand was waiting for him, both waiting for him and pushing him along. But as I began to watch Creole, I realized that it was Creole who held them all back. He had them on a short rein. Up there, keeping the beat with his whole body, waiting on the fiddle, with his eyes half closed, he was listening to everything, but he was listening to Sonny. He was having a dialogue with Sonny. He wanted Sonny to leave the shoreline and strike out for the deep water. He was Sonny's witness that deep water and drowning were not the same thing—he had been there, and he knew. And he wanted Sonny to know. He was waiting for Sonny to do the things on the keys which would let Creole know that Sonny was in the water.

And, while Creole listened, Sonny moved, deep within, exactly like someone in torment. I had never before thought of how awful the relationship must be between the musician and his instrument. He has to fill it, this instrument, with the breath of life, his own. He has to make it do what he wants it to do. And a piano is just a piano. It's made out of so much wood and wires and little hammers and big ones, and ivory. While there's only so much you can do with it, the only way to find this out is to try: to try and make it do everything.

And Sonny hadn't been near a piano for over a year. And he wasn't on much better terms with his life, not the life that stretched before him now. He and the piano stammered, started one way, got scared, stopped; started another way, panicked, marked time, started again; then seemed to have found a direction, panicked again, got stuck. And the face I saw on Sonny I'd never seen before. Everything had been burned out of it, and, at the same time, things usually hidden were being burned in, by the fire and fury of the battle which was occurring in him up there.

Yet, watching Creole's face as they neared the end of the first set, I had the feeling that something had happened, something I hadn't heard. Then they finished, there was scattered applause, and then, without an instant's warning, Creole started into something else, it was almost sardonic, it was *Am I Blue*. And, as though he commanded, Sonny began to play. Something began to happen. And Creole let out the reins. The dry, low, black man said something awful on the drums. Creole answered, and the drums talked back. Then the horn insisted, sweet and high, slightly detached perhaps, and Creole listened, commenting now and then, dry and driving, beautiful and calm and old. Then they all came together again, and Sonny was part of the family again. I could tell this from his face. He seemed to have found, right there beneath his fingers, a damn brand-new piano. It seemed that he couldn't get over it. Then, for a while, just being happy with Sonny, they seemed to be agreeing with him that brand-new pianos certainly were a gas.

Then Creole stepped forward to remind them that what they were playing was the blues. He hit something in all of them, he hit something in me, myself, and the music tightened and deepened, apprehension began to beat the air. Creole began to tell us what the blues were all about. They were not about anything very new. He and his boys up there were keeping it new, at the risk of ruin, destruction, madness, and death, in order to find new ways to make us listen. For, while the tale of how we suffer, and how we are delighted, and how we may triumph is never new, it always must be heard. There isn't any other tale to tell, it's the only light we've got in all this darkness.

And this tale, according to that face, that body, those strong hands on those strings, has another aspect in every country, and a new depth in every generation. Listen, Creole seemed to be saying, listen. Now these are Sonny's blues. He made the little black man on the drums know it, and the bright, brown man on the horn. Creole wasn't trying any longer to get Sonny in the water. He was wishing him Godspeed. Then he stepped back, very slowly, filling the air with the immense suggestion that Sonny speak for himself.

Then they all gathered around Sonny and Sonny played. Every now and again one of them seemed to say amen. Sonny's fingers filled the air with life, his life. But that life contained so many others. And Sonny went all the way back, he really began with the spare, flat statement of the opening phrase of the song. Then he began to make it his. It was very beautiful because it wasn't hurried and it was no longer a lament. I seemed to hear with what burning he had made it his, and what burning we had yet to make it ours, how we could cease lamenting. Freedom lurked around us and I understood, at last, that he could help us to be free if we would listen, that he would never be free until we did. Yet, there was no battle in his face now, I heard what he had gone through, and would continue to go through until he came to rest in earth. He had made it his: that long line, of which we knew only Mama and Daddy. And he was giving it back, as everything must be given back, so that, passing through death, it can live forever. I saw my mother's face again, and felt, for the first time, how the stones of the road she had walked on must have bruised her feet. I saw the moonlit road where my father's brother died. And it brought something else back to me, and carried me past it, I saw my little girl again and felt Isabel's tears again, and I felt my own tears begin to rise. And I was yet aware that this was only a moment, that the world waited outside, as hungry as a tiger, and that trouble stretched above us, longer than the sky.

Then it was over. Creole and Sonny let out their breath, both soaking wet, and grinning. There was a lot of applause and some of it was real. In the dark, the girl came by and I asked her to take drinks to the bandstand. There was a long pause, while they talked up there in the indigo light and after awhile I saw the girl put a Scotch and milk on top of the piano for Sonny. He didn't seem to notice it, but just before they started playing again, he sipped from it and looked toward me, and nodded. Then he put it back on top of the piano. For me, then, as they began to play again, it glowed and shook above my brother's head like the very cup of trembling.

—1957

FLANNERY O'CONNOR

Mary Flannery O'Connor was born in 1925 in Savannah, Georgia, the only child of Regina and Edward Francis O'Connor. Her father was afflicted with lupus for several years and in 1941 he succumbed to the disease that would later affect his daughter. After O'Connor graduated from high school, she attended Georgia State College for Women with the intention of completing an English degree; partway through she changed her major to Social Science, and received her Bachelor's degree in 1945.

A teacher at Georgia State submitted one of the stories O'Connor had published in the college literary quarterly to the prestigious Writers' Workshop at the State University of Iowa. O'Connor was awarded a Rinehart Fellowship from the university and embarked on a graduate degree in writing. O'Connor flourished at the Writers' Workshop, which she attended from 1945 to 1948. During that time, she sold "The Geranium," her first short story and one of the stories that would compose her MFA thesis, to *Accent* magazine. After receiving her MFA, O'Connor was invited to spend the winter of 1948 at Yaddo, the famous American writers' colony in Saratoga Springs, New York. Later, she moved to Connecticut and lived with writers Sally and Robert Fitzgerald while she worked on her novel, *Wise Blood.*

O'Connor probably would have stayed in the northern United States had she not been struck in 1950 by lupus. Weakened by the disease and the debilitating cortisone treatments, she went to live with her mother on her farm in Milledgeville, Georgia, where she continued to write for the remainder of her life.

Wise Blood was published in 1952, and in the following year O'Connor was awarded a *Kenyon Review* Fellowship. She published the short story collection *A Good Man Is Hard to Find* in 1955, and in 1957 received the O. Henry Prize for short fiction. She also traveled when her health permitted and gave lectures at various universities, colleges, and high schools. Using the financial support from a Ford Foundation grant, O'Connor completed her second novel, *The Violent Bear It Away* (1960), and finished the manuscript for her second short story collection, *Everything that Rises Must*

Converge (published posthumously in 1965). In 1963, O'Connor's health began to deteriorate seriously; she was diagnosed with acute anemia, and abdominal surgery to remove a benign tumour reactivated her lupus. She died in Milledgeville on August 3, 1964.

Flannery O'Connor's fiction is distinctive for its mingling of horror and humor, and for the ways in which it problematizes the "Southern grotesque" from the perspective of O'Connor's intensely deep Catholic faith. Indeed, she writes that "the meaning of life is centered in our Redemption by Christ and what I see in the world I see in its relation to that." These combinations result in provocative writing that is startling and enlightening. The short story "A Good Man Is Hard to Find" is the first story in the collection of the same name. The character of the Misfit is a prime example of the sort of "grotesque" that features in much of O'Connor's fiction. He is not so different from the "lady-like" grandmother, however, and his peculiar distortion of her values and beliefs is borne out in the story's shocking conclusion.

A Good Man Is Hard to Find

FLANNERY O'CONNOR

THE GRANDMOTHER didn't want to go to Florida. She wanted to visit some of her connections in east Tennessee and she was seizing at every chance to change Bailey's mind. Bailey was the son she lived with, her only boy. He was sitting on the edge of his chair at the table, bent over the orange sports section of the *Journal.* "Now look here, Bailey," she said, "see here, read this," and she stood with one hand on her thin hip and the other rattling the newspaper at his bald head. "Here this fellow that calls himself The Misfit is aloose from the Federal Pen and headed toward Florida and you read here what it says he did to these people. Just you read it. I wouldn't take my children in any direction with a criminal like that aloose in it. I couldn't answer to my conscience if I did."

Bailey didn't look up from his reading so she wheeled around then and faced the children's mother, a young woman in slacks, whose face was as broad and innocent as a cabbage and was tied around with a green head-kerchief that had two points on the top like rabbit's ears. She was sitting on the sofa, feeding the baby his apricots out of a jar. "The children have been to Florida before," the old lady said. "You all ought to take them somewhere else for a change so they would see different parts of the world and be broad. They never have been to east Tennessee."

The children's mother didn't seem to hear her but the eight-year-old boy, John Wesley, a stocky child with glasses, said, "If you don't want to go to Florida, why dontcha stay at home?" He and the little girl, June Star, were reading the funny papers on the floor.

"She wouldn't stay at home to be queen for a day," June Star said without raising her yellow head.

"Yes and what would you do if this fellow, The Misfit, caught you?" the grandmother asked.

"I'd smack his face," John Wesley said.

"She wouldn't stay at home for a million bucks," June Star said. "Afraid she'd miss something. She has to go everywhere we go."

"All right, Miss," the grandmother said. "Just remember that the next time you want me to curl your hair."

June Star said her hair was naturally curly.

The next morning the grandmother was the first one in the car, ready to go. She had her big black valise that looked like the head of a hippopotamus in one corner, and underneath it she was hiding a basket with Pitty Sing, the cat, in it. She didn't intend for the cat to be left alone in the house for three days because he would miss her too much and she was afraid he might brush against one of the gas burners and accidentally asphyxiate himself. Her son, Bailey, didn't like to arrive at a motel with a cat.

She sat in the middle of the back seat with John Wesley and June Star on either side of her. Bailey and the children's mother and the baby sat in front and they left Atlanta at eight forty-five with the mileage on the car at 55890. The grandmother wrote this down because she thought it would be interesting to say how many miles they had been when they got back. It took them twenty minutes to reach the outskirts of the city.

The old lady settled herself comfortably, removing her white cotton gloves and putting them up with her purse on the shelf in front of the back window. The children's mother still had on slacks and still had her head tied up in a green kerchief, but the grandmother had on a navy blue straw sailor hat with a bunch of white violets on the brim and a navy blue dress with a small white dot in the print. Her collars and cuffs were white organdy trimmed with lace and at her neckline she had pinned a purple spray of cloth violets containing a sachet. In case of an accident, anyone seeing her dead on the highway would know at once that she was a lady.

She said she thought it was going to be a good day for driving, neither too hot nor too cold, and she cautioned Bailey that the speed limit was fifty-five miles an hour and that the patrolmen hid themselves behind billboards and small clumps of trees and sped out after you before you had a chance to slow down. She pointed out interesting details of the scenery: Stone Mountain; the blue granite that in some places came up to both sides of the highway; the brilliant red clay banks slightly streaked with purple; and the various crops that made rows of green lace-work on the ground. The trees were full of silver-white sunlight and the meanest of them sparkled. The children were reading comic magazines and their mother had gone back to sleep.

"Let's go through Georgia fast so we won't have to look at it much," John Wesley said.

"If I were a little boy," said the grandmother, "I wouldn't talk about my native state that way. Tennessee has the mountains and Georgia has the hills."

"Tennessee is just a hillbilly dumping ground," John Wesley said, "and Georgia is a lousy state too."

"You said it," June Star said.

"In my time," said the grandmother, folding her thin veined fingers, "children were more respectful of their native states and their parents and everything else. People did right then. Oh look at the cute little pickaninny!"[1] she said and pointed to a Negro child standing in the door of a shack. "Wouldn't that make a picture, now?" she asked and they all turned and looked at the little Negro out of the back window. He waved.

"He didn't have any britches on," June Star said.

"He probably didn't have any," the grandmother explained. "Little niggers[2] in the country don't have things like we do. If I could paint, I'd paint that picture," she said.

The children exchanged comic books.

The grandmother offered to hold the baby and the children's mother passed him over the front seat to her. She set him on her knee and bounced him and told him about the things they were passing. She rolled her eyes and screwed up her mouth and stuck her leathery thin face into his smooth bland one. Occasionally he gave her a faraway smile. They passed a large cotton field with five or six graves fenced in the middle of it, like a small island. "Look at the graveyard!" the grandmother said, pointing it out. "That was the old family burying ground. That belonged to the plantation."

"Where's the plantation?" John Wesley asked.

"Gone With the Wind," said the grandmother. "Ha. Ha."

When the children finished all the comic books they had brought, they opened the lunch and ate it. The grandmother ate a peanut butter sandwich and

---

1 Derogatory term for an African American child.

2 This pejorative term remained in frequent use by many white Americans in the South until well into the 1960s.

an olive and would not let the children throw the box and the paper napkins out the window. When there was nothing else to do they played a game by choosing a cloud and making the other two guess what shape it suggested. John Wesley took one the shape of a cow and June Star guessed a cow and John Wesley said, no, an automobile, and June Star said he didn't play fair, and they began to slap each other over the grandmother.

The grandmother said she would tell them a story if they would keep quiet. When she told a story, she rolled her eyes and waved her head and was very dramatic. She said once when she was a maiden lady she had been courted by a Mr. Edgar Atkins Teagarden from Jasper, Georgia. She said he was a very good-looking man and a gentleman and that he brought her a watermelon every Saturday afternoon with his initials cut in it, E.A.T. Well, one Saturday, she said, Mr. Teagarden brought the watermelon and there was nobody at home and he left it on the front porch and returned in his buggy to Jasper, but she never got the watermelon, she said, because a nigger boy ate it when he saw the initials, E.A.T.! This story tickled John Wesley's funny bone and he giggled and giggled but June Star didn't think it was any good. She said she wouldn't marry a man that just brought her a watermelon on Saturday. The grandmother said she would have done well to marry Mr. Teagarden because he was a gentleman and had bought Coca-Cola stock when it first came out and that he had died only a few years ago, a very wealthy man.

They stopped at The Tower for barbecued sandwiches. The Tower was a part stucco and part wood filling station and dance hall set in a clearing outside of Timothy. A fat man named Red Sammy Butts ran it and there were signs stuck here and there on the building and for miles up and down the highway saying, TRY RED SAMMY'S FAMOUS BARBECUE. NONE LIKE FAMOUS RED SAMMY'S! RED SAM! THE FAT BOY WITH THE HAPPY LAUGH. A VETERAN! RED SAMMY'S YOUR MAN!

Red Sammy was lying on the bare ground outside The Tower with his head under a truck while a gray monkey about a foot high, chained to a small chinaberry tree, chattered nearby. The monkey sprang back into the tree and got on the highest limb as soon as he saw the children jump out of the car and run toward him.

Inside, The Tower was a long dark room with a counter at one end and tables at the other and dancing space in the middle. They all sat down at a board table next to the nickelodeon and Red Sam's wife, a tall burnt-brown woman with hair and eyes lighter than her skin, came and took their order. The children's mother put a dime in the machine and played "The Tennessee Waltz," and the grandmother said that tune always made her want to dance. She asked Bailey if he would like to dance but he only glared at her. He didn't have a naturally sunny disposition like she did and trips made him nervous. The grandmother's brown eyes were very bright. She swayed her head from side to side and pretended she was dancing in her chair. June Star said play something she could tap to so the children's mother put in another dime and played a fast number and June Star stepped out onto the dance floor and did her tap routine.

"Ain't she cute?" Red Sam's wife said, leaning over the counter. "Would you like to come be my little girl?"

"No I certainly wouldn't," June Star said. "I wouldn't live in a broken-down place like this for a million bucks!" and she ran back to the table.

"Ain't she cute?" the woman repeated, stretching her mouth politely.

"Ain't you ashamed?" hissed the grandmother.

Red Sam came in and told his wife to quit lounging on the counter and hurry up with these people's order. His khaki trousers reached just to his hip bones and his stomach hung over them like a sack of meal swaying under his shirt. He came over and sat down at a table nearby and let out a combination sigh and yodel. "You can't win," he said. "You can't win," and he wiped his sweating red face off with a gray handkerchief. "These days you don't know who to trust," he said. "Ain't that the truth?"

"People are certainly not nice like they used to be," said the grandmother.

"Two fellers come in here last week," Red Sammy said, "driving a Chrysler. It was a old beat-up car but it was a good one and these boys looked all right to me. Said they worked at the mill and you know I let them fellers charge the gas they bought? Now why did I do that?"

"Because you're a good man!" the grandmother said at once.

"Yes'm, I suppose so," Red Sam said as if he were struck with this answer.

His wife brought the orders, carrying the five plates all at once without a tray, two in each hand and one balanced on her arm. "It isn't a soul in this green world of God's that you can trust," she said. "And I don't count nobody out of that, not nobody," she repeated, looking at Red Sammy.

"Did you read about that criminal, The Misfit, that's escaped?" asked the grandmother.

"I wouldn't be a bit surprised if he didn't attact this place right here," said the woman. "If he hears about it being here, I wouldn't be none surprised to see him. If he hears it's two cent in the cash register, I wouldn't be a tall surprised if he ..."

"That'll do," Red Sam said. "Go bring these people their Co'-Colas," and the woman went off to get the rest of the order.

"A good man is hard to find," Red Sammy said. "Everything is getting terrible. I remember the day you could go off and leave your screen door unlatched. Not no more."

He and the grandmother discussed better times. The old lady said that in her opinion Europe was entirely to blame for the way things were now. She said the way Europe acted you would think we were made of money and Red Sam said it was no use talking about it, she was exactly right. The children ran outside into the white sunlight and looked at the monkey in the lacy chinaberry tree. He was busy catching fleas on himself and biting each one carefully between his teeth as if it were a delicacy.

They drove off again into the hot afternoon. The grandmother took cat naps and woke up every few minutes with her own snoring. Outside of Toombsboro she woke up and recalled an old plantation that she had visited in this neighborhood once when she was a young lady. She said the house had six white columns across the front and that there was an avenue of oaks leading up to it and two little wooden trellis arbors on either side in front where you sat down with your suitor after a stroll in the garden. She recalled exactly which road to turn off to get to it. She knew that Bailey would not be willing to lose any time looking at an old house, but the more she talked about it, the more she wanted to see it once again and find out if the little twin arbors were still standing. "There was a secret panel in this house," she said craftily, not telling the truth but wishing that she were, "and the story went that all the family silver was hidden in it when Sherman[3] came through but it was never found ..."

"Hey!" John Wesley said. "Let's go see it! We'll find it! We'll poke all the woodwork and find it! Who lives there? Where do you turn off at? Hey Pop, can't we turn off there?"

"We never have seen a house with a secret panel!" June Star shrieked. "Let's go to the house with the secret panel! Hey, Pop, can't we go see the house with the secret panel!"

"It's not far from here, I know," the grandmother said. "It wouldn't take over twenty minutes."

Bailey was looking straight ahead. His jaw was as rigid as a horseshoe. "No," he said.

The children began to yell and scream that they wanted to see the house with the secret panel. John Wesley kicked the back of the front seat and June Star hung over her mother's shoulder and whined desperately into her ear that they never had any fun even on their vacation, that they could never do what THEY wanted to do. The baby began to scream and John Wesley kicked the back of the seat so hard that his father could feel the blows in his kidney.

3 American Union commander William Tecumseh Sherman marched his troops through Georgia to Atlanta in 1864 during the American Civil War.

"All right!" he shouted and drew the car to a stop at the side of the road. "Will you all shut up? Will you all just shut up for one second? If you don't shut up, we won't go anywhere."

"It would be very educational for them," the grandmother murmured.

"All right," Bailey said, "but get this: this is the only time we're going to stop for anything like this. This is the one and only time."

"The dirt road that you have to turn down is about a mile back," the grandmother directed. "I marked it when we passed."

"A dirt road," Bailey groaned.

After they had turned around and were headed toward the dirt road, the grandmother recalled other points about the house, the beautiful glass over the front doorway and the candle-lamp in the hall. John Wesley said that the secret panel was probably in the fireplace.

"You can't go inside this house," Bailey said. "You don't know who lives there."

"While you all talk to the people in front, I'll run around behind and get in a window," John Wesley suggested.

"We'll all stay in the car," his mother said.

They turned onto the dirt road and the car raced roughly along in a swirl of pink dust. The grandmother recalled the times when there were no paved roads and thirty miles was a day's journey. The dirt road was hilly and there were sudden washes in it and sharp curves on dangerous embankments. All at once they would be on a hill, looking down over the blue tops of trees for miles around, then the next minute, they would be in a red depression with the dust-coated trees looking down on them.

"This place had better turn up in a minute," Bailey said, "or I'm going to turn around."

The road looked as if no one had traveled on it in months.

"It's not much farther," the grandmother said and just as she said it, a horrible thought came to her. The thought was so embarrassing that she turned red in the face and her eyes dilated and her feet jumped up, upsetting her valise in the corner. The instant the valise moved, the newspaper top she had over the basket under it rose with a snarl and Pitty Sing, the cat, sprang onto Bailey's shoulder.

The children were thrown to the floor and their mother, clutching the baby, was thrown out the door onto the ground; the old lady was thrown into the front seat. The car turned over once and landed right side-up in a gulch off the side of the road. Bailey remained in the driver's seat with the cat—gray-striped with a broad white face and an orange nose—clinging to his neck like a caterpillar.

As soon as the children saw they could move their arms and legs, they scrambled out of the car, shouting, "We've had an ACCIDENT!" The grandmother was curled up under the dashboard, hoping she was injured so that Bailey's wrath would not come down on her all at once. The horrible thought she had had before the accident was that the house she had remembered so vividly was not in Georgia but in Tennessee.

Bailey removed the cat from his neck with both hands and flung it out the window against the side of a pine tree. Then he got out of the car and started looking for the children's mother. She was sitting against the side of the red gutted ditch, holding the screaming baby, but she only had a cut down her face and a broken shoulder. "We've had an ACCIDENT!" the children screamed in a frenzy of delight.

"But nobody's killed," June Star said with disappointment as the grandmother limped out of the car, her hat still pinned to her head but the broken front brim standing up at a jaunty angle and the violet spray hanging off the side. They all sat down in the ditch, except the children, to recover from the shock. They were all shaking.

"Maybe a car will come along," said the children's mother hoarsely.

"I believe I have injured an organ," said the grandmother, pressing her side, but no one answered her. Bailey's teeth were clattering. He had on a yellow sport shirt with bright blue parrots designed in it and his face was as yellow as the shirt. The grandmother decided that she would not mention that the house was in Tennessee.

The road was about ten feet above and they could see only the tops of the trees on the other side of it. Behind the ditch they were sitting in there were more woods, tall and dark and deep. In a few minutes they saw a car some distance away on top of a hill, coming slowly as if the occupants were watching them. The grandmother stood up and waved both arms dramatically to attract their attention. The car continued to come on slowly, disappeared around a bend and appeared again, moving even slower, on top of the hill they had gone over. It was a big black battered hearse-like automobile. There were three men in it.

It came to a stop just over them and for some minutes, the driver looked down with a steady expressionless gaze to where they were sitting, and didn't speak. Then he turned his head and muttered something to the other two and they got out. One was a fat boy in black trousers and a red sweat shirt with a silver stallion embossed on the front of it. He moved around on the right side of them and stood staring, his mouth partly open in a kind of loose grin. The other had on khaki pants and a blue striped coat and a gray hat pulled down very low, hiding most of his face. He came around slowly on the left side. Neither spoke.

The driver got out of the car and stood by the side of it, looking down at them. He was an older man than the other two. His hair was just beginning to gray and he wore silver-rimmed spectacles that gave him a scholarly look. He had a long creased face and didn't have on any shirt or undershirt. He had on blue jeans that were too tight for him and was holding a black hat and a gun. The two boys also had guns.

"We've had an ACCIDENT!" the children screamed.

The grandmother had the peculiar feeling that the bespectacled man was someone she knew. His face was as familiar to her as if she had known him all her life but she could not recall who he was. He moved away from the car and began to come down the embankment, placing his feet carefully so that he wouldn't slip. He had on tan and white shoes and no socks, and his ankles were red and thin. "Good afternoon," he said. "I see you all had you a little spill."

"We turned over twice!" said the grandmother.

"Oncet," he corrected. "We seen it happen. Try their car and see will it run, Hiram," he said quietly to the boy with the gray hat.

"What you got that gun for?" John Wesley asked. "Whatcha gonna do with that gun?"

"Lady," the man said to the children's mother, "would you mind calling them children to sit down by you? Children make me nervous. I want all you all to sit down right together there where you're at."

"What are you telling US what to do for?" June Star asked.

Behind them the line of woods gaped like a dark open mouth. "Come here," said their mother.

"Look here now," Bailey began suddenly, "we're in a predicament! We're in ..."

The grandmother shrieked. She scrambled to her feet and stood staring. "You're The Misfit!" she said. "I recognized you at once!"

"Yes'm," the man said, smiling slightly as if he were pleased in spite of himself to be known, "but it would have been better for all of you, lady, if you hadn't of reckernized me."

Bailey turned his head sharply and said something to his mother that shocked even the children. The old lady began to cry and The Misfit reddened.

"Lady," he said, "don't you get upset. Sometimes a man says things he don't mean. I don't reckon he meant to talk to you thataway."

"You wouldn't shoot a lady, would you?" the grandmother said and removed a clean handkerchief from her cuff and began to slap at her eyes with it.

The Misfit pointed the toe of his shoe into the ground and made a little hole and then covered it up again. "I would hate to have to," he said.

"Listen," the grandmother almost screamed, "I know you're a good man. You don't look a bit like you have common blood. I know you must come from nice people!"

"Yes mam," he said, "finest people in the world." When he smiled he showed a row of strong white teeth. "God never made a finer woman than my mother and my daddy's heart was pure gold," he said. The boy with the red sweat shirt had come around behind them and was standing with his gun at his hip. The Misfit squatted down on the ground. "Watch them children, Bobby Lee," he said. "You know they make me nervous." He looked at the six of them huddled together in front of him and he seemed to be embarrassed as if he couldn't think of anything to say. "Ain't a cloud in the sky," he remarked, looking up at it. "Don't see no sun but don't see no cloud neither."

"Yes, it's a beautiful day," said the grandmother. "Listen," she said, "you shouldn't call yourself The Misfit because I know you're a good man at heart. I can just look at you and tell."

"Hush!" Bailey yelled. "Hush! Everybody shut up and let me handle this!" He was squatting in the position of a runner about to sprint forward but he didn't move.

"I pre-chate that, lady," The Misfit said and drew a little circle in the ground with the butt of his gun.

"It'll take a half a hour to fix this here car," Hiram called, looking over the raised hood of it.

"Well, first you and Bobby Lee get him and that little boy to step over yonder with you," The Misfit said, pointing to Bailey and John Wesley. "The boys want to ast you something," he said to Bailey. "Would you mind stepping back in them woods there with them?"

"Listen," Bailey began, "we're in a terrible predicament! Nobody realizes what this is," and his voice cracked. His eyes were as blue and intense as the parrots in his shirt and he remained perfectly still.

The grandmother reached up to adjust her hat brim as if she were going to the woods with him but it came off in her hand. She stood staring at it and after a second she let it fall on the ground. Hiram pulled Bailey up by the arm as if he were assisting an old man. John Wesley caught hold of his father's hand and Bobby Lee followed. They went off toward the woods and just as they reached the dark edge, Bailey turned and supporting himself against a gray naked pine trunk, he shouted, "I'll be back in a minute, Mamma, wait on me!"

"Come back this instant!" his mother shrilled but they all disappeared into the woods.

"Bailey Boy!" the grandmother called in a tragic voice but she found she was looking at The Misfit squatting on the ground in front of her. "I just know you're a good man," she said desperately. "You're not a bit common!"

"Nome, I ain't a good man," The Misfit said after a second as if he had considered her statement carefully, "but I ain't the worst in the world neither. My daddy said I was a different breed of dog from my brothers and sisters. 'You know,' Daddy said, 'it's some that can live their whole life out without asking about it and it's others has to know why it is, and this boy is one of the latters. He's going to be into everything!'" He put on his black hat and looked up suddenly and then away deep into the woods as if he were embarrassed again. "I'm sorry I don't have on a shirt before you ladies," he said, hunching his shoulders slightly. "We buried our clothes that we had on when we escaped and we're just making do until we can get better. We borrowed these from some folks we met," he explained.

"That's perfectly all right," the grandmother said. "Maybe Bailey has an extra shirt in his suitcase."

"I'll look and see terrectly," The Misfit said.

"Where are they taking him?" the children's mother screamed.

"Daddy was a card himself," The Misfit said. "You couldn't put anything over on him. He never got in trouble with the Authorities though. Just had the knack of handling them."

"You could be honest too if you'd only try," said the grandmother. "Think how wonderful it would be to settle down and live a comfortable life and not have to think about somebody chasing you all the time."

The Misfit kept scratching in the ground with the butt of his gun as if he were thinking about it. "Yes'm, somebody is always after you," he murmured.

The grandmother noticed how thin his shoulder blades were just behind his hat because she was standing up looking down on him. "Do you ever pray?" she asked.

He shook his head. All she saw was the black hat wiggle between his shoulder blades. "Nome," he said.

There was a pistol shot from the woods, followed closely by another. Then silence. The old lady's head jerked around. She could hear the wind move through the tree tops like a long satisfied insuck of breath. "Bailey Boy!" she called.

"I was a gospel singer for a while," The Misfit said. "I been most everything. Been in the arm service, both land and sea, at home and abroad, been twict married, been an undertaker, been with the railroads, plowed Mother Earth, been in a tornado, seen a man burnt alive oncet," and he looked up at the children's mother and the little girl who were sitting close together, their faces white and their eyes glassy; "I even seen a woman flogged," he said.

"Pray, pray," the grandmother began, "pray, pray ..."

"I never was a bad boy that I remember of," The Misfit said in an almost dreamy voice, "but somewheres along the line I done something wrong and got sent to the penitentiary. I was buried alive," and he looked up and held her attention to him by a steady stare.

"That's when you should have started to pray," she said. "What did you do to get sent to the penitentiary that first time?"

"Turn to the right, it was a wall," The Misfit said, looking up again at the cloudless sky. "Turn to the left, it was a wall. Look up it was a ceiling, look down it was a floor. I forget what I done, lady. I set there and set there, trying to remember what it was I done and I ain't recalled it to this day. Oncet in a while, I would think it was coming to me, but it never come."

"Maybe they put you in by mistake," the old lady said vaguely.

"Nome," he said. "It wasn't no mistake. They had the papers on me."

"You must have stolen something," she said.

The Misfit sneered slightly. "Nobody had nothing I wanted," he said. "It was a head-doctor at the penitentiary said what I had done was kill my daddy but I known that for a lie. My daddy died in nineteen ought nineteen of the epidemic flu and I never had a thing to do with it. He was buried in the Mount Hopewell Baptist churchyard and you can go there and see for yourself."

"If you would pray," the old lady said, "Jesus would help you."

"That's right," The Misfit said.

"Well then, why don't you pray?" she asked trembling with delight suddenly.

"I don't want no hep," he said. "I'm doing all right by myself."

Bobby Lee and Hiram came ambling back from the woods. Bobby Lee was dragging a yellow shirt with bright blue parrots in it.

"Thow me that shirt, Bobby Lee," The Misfit said. The shirt came flying at him and landed on his shoulder and he put it on. The grandmother couldn't name what the shirt reminded her of. "No, lady," The Misfit said while he was buttoning it up, "I found out the crime don't matter. You can do one thing or you can do another, kill a man or take a tire off his car, because sooner or later you're going to forget what it was you done and just be punished for it."

The children's mother had begun to make heaving noises as if she couldn't get her breath. "Lady," he asked, "would you and that little girl like to step off yonder with Bobby Lee and Hiram and join your husband?"

"Yes, thank you," the mother said faintly. Her left arm dangled helplessly and she was holding the baby, who had gone to sleep, in the other. "Hep that lady up, Hiram," The Misfit said as she struggled to climb out of the ditch, "and Bobby Lee, you hold onto that little girl's hand."

"I don't want to hold hands with him," June Star said. "He reminds me of a pig."

The fat boy blushed and laughed and caught her by the arm and pulled her into the woods after Hiram and her mother.

Alone with The Misfit, the grandmother found that she had lost her voice. There was not a cloud in the sky nor any sun. There was nothing around her but woods. She wanted to tell him that he must pray. She opened and closed her mouth several times before anything came out. Finally she found herself saying, "Jesus. Jesus," meaning, Jesus will help you, but the way she was saying it, it sounded as if she might be cursing.

"Yes'm," The Misfit said as if he agreed. "Jesus thown everything off balance. It was the same case with Him as with me except He hadn't committed any crime and they could prove I had committed one because they had the papers on me. Of course," he said, "they never shown me my papers. That's why I sign myself now. I said long ago, you get you a signature and sign everything you do and keep a copy of it. Then you'll know what you done and you can hold up the crime to the punishment and see do they match and in the end you'll have something to prove you ain't been treated right. I call myself The Misfit," he said, "because I can't make what all I done wrong fit what all I gone through in punishment."

There was a piercing scream from the woods, followed closely by a pistol report. "Does it seem right to you, lady, that one is punished a heap and another ain't punished at all?"

"Jesus!" the old lady cried. "You've got good blood! I know you wouldn't shoot a lady! I know you come from nice people! Pray! Jesus, you ought not to shoot a lady. I'll give you all the money I've got!"

"Lady," The Misfit said, looking beyond her far into the woods, "there never was a body that give the undertaker a tip."

There were two more pistol reports and the grandmother raised her head like a parched old turkey hen crying for water and called, "Bailey Boy, Bailey Boy!" as if her heart would break.

"Jesus was the only One that ever raised the dead," The Misfit continued, "and He shouldn't have done it. He thown everything off balance. If He did what He said, then it's nothing for you to do but thow away everything and follow Him, and if He didn't, then it's nothing for you to do but enjoy the few minutes you got left the best way you can—by killing somebody or burning down his house or doing some other meanness to him. No pleasure but meanness," he said and his voice had become almost a snarl.

"Maybe He didn't raise the dead," the old lady mumbled, not knowing what she was saying and feeling so dizzy that she sank down in the ditch with her legs twisted under her.

"I wasn't there so I can't say He didn't," The Misfit said. "I wisht I had of been there," he said, hitting the ground with his fist. "It ain't right I wasn't there because if I had of been there I would of known. Listen lady," he said in a high voice, "if I had of been there I would of known and I wouldn't be like I am now." His voice seemed about to crack and the grandmother's head cleared for an instant. She saw the man's face twisted close to her own as if he were going to cry and she murmured, "Why you're one of my babies. You're one of my own children!" She reached out and touched him on the shoulder. The Misfit sprang back as if a snake had bitten him and shot her three times through the chest. Then he put his gun down on the ground and took off his glasses and began to clean them.

Hiram and Bobby Lee returned from the woods and stood over the ditch, looking down at the grandmother who half sat and half lay in a puddle of blood with her legs crossed under her like a child's and her face smiling up at the cloudless sky.

Without his glasses, The Misfit's eyes were red-rimmed and pale and defenseless-looking. "Take her off and thow her where you thown the others," he said, picking up the cat that was rubbing itself against his leg.

"She was a talker, wasn't she?" Bobby Lee said, sliding down the ditch with a yodel.

"She would of been a good woman," The Misfit said, "if it had been somebody there to shoot her every minute of her life."

"Some fun!" Bobby Lee said.

"Shut up, Bobby Lee," The Misfit said. "It's no real pleasure in life."

—1953

URSULA K. LE GUIN

Ursula K. Le Guin was born in 1929 in Berkeley, California, to the cultural anthropologist Alfred Kroeber and the anthropologist and writer Theodora Kroeber. Le Guin studied at Radcliffe College and did graduate work at Columbia University. In addition to her twenty-two novels, she has published seven books of poetry, seven volumes of short stories, twelve books for children, and four works in translation, including a translation of Lao Tzu's *Tao Te Ching*.

Le Guin writes in many genres, but is best known for her pioneering work in science fiction and fantasy. Despite the lack of critical respect accorded these genres early in her career, she has achieved both popularity and acclaim; among her many honors are five Hugo Awards, five Nebula awards, and a National Book Award. Of her entry into science fiction, Le Guin has said: "Literature [had] been categorized as 'realism,' and if you weren't writing realism, you weren't respectable. I had to ignore that and say to myself that I could do things in science fiction that I could never do in realism."

Le Guin has created a number of vividly imagined fictional worlds in her speculative fiction. The most famous of these are the archipelago Earthsea, the setting of her six-part Books of Earthsea series, and the Hainish universe, a complex planetary system in which many of her works, beginning with *Rocannon's World* in 1966, are set. When "world-making," her focus is very largely on geography (she begins the creation of any new world by drawing a map) and on the details of everyday life.

Since the late 1960s, social justice and gender issues have been central concerns in Le Guin's writing. *The Left Hand of Darkness*, a 1969 novel, is set on a planet whose citizens are androgynous, and recent stories and novels in the Earthsea series have undermined the traditional science fiction model (often found in Le Guin's own early work, she admits) of the solitary male hero. Le Guin is also notable for deliberately writing protagonists that are people of color, but not emphasizing their race in the story; she has called this a "sneaky approach" to making readers empathize with characters of color.

"The Ones Who Walk Away from Omelas" was first published in *New Dimensions*, a science fiction anthology, in 1973. In her introduction to the story in her collection *The Wind's Twelve Quarters* (1975), Le Guin writes that she was inspired in part by a road sign ("Salem, Oregon" read backwards) and in part by a quotation from the philosopher William James, in which he writes of the "specifical and independent sort of emotion" that would make us resist perfect happiness for millions if it depended on the terrible suffering of one person.

The Ones Who Walk Away from Omelas

URSULA K. LE GUIN

WITH A clamor of bells that set the swallows soaring, the Festival of Summer came to the city. Omelas, bright-towered by the sea. The rigging of the boats in harbor sparkled with flags. In the streets between houses with red roofs and painted walls, between old moss-grown gardens and under avenues of trees, past great parks and public buildings, processions moved. Some were decorous: old people in long stiff robes of mauve and gray, grave master workmen, quiet, merry women carrying their babies and chatting as they walked. In other streets the music beat faster, a shimmering of gong and tambourine, and the people went dancing, the procession was a dance. Children dodged in and out, their high calls rising like the swallows' crossing flights over the music and the singing. All the processions wound towards the north side of the city, where on the great water-meadow called the Green Fields boys and girls, naked in the bright air, with mud-stained feet and ankles and long, lithe arms, exercised their restive horses before the race. The horses wore no gear at all but a halter without bit. Their manes were braided with streamers of silver, gold, and green. They flared their nostrils and pranced and boasted to one another; they were vastly excited, the horse being the only animal who has adopted our ceremonies as his own. Far off to the north and west the mountains stood up half encircling Omelas on her bay. The air of morning was so clear that the snow still crowning the Eighteen Peaks burned with white-gold fire across the miles of sunlit air, under the dark blue of the sky. There was just enough wind to make the banners that marked the racecourse snap and flutter now and then. In the silence of the broad green meadows one could hear the music winding through the city streets, farther and nearer and ever approaching, a cheerful faint sweetness of the air that from time to time trembled and gathered together and broke out into the great joyous clanging of the bells.

Joyous! How is one to tell about joy? How describe the citizens of Omelas?

They were not simple folk, you see, though they were happy. But we do not say the words of cheer much any more. All smiles have become archaic.[1] Given a description such as this one tends to make certain assumptions. Given a description such as this one tends to look next for the King, mounted on a splendid stallion and surrounded by his noble knights, or perhaps in a golden litter borne by great-muscled slaves. But there was no king. They did not use swords, or keep slaves. They were not barbarians. I do not know the rules and laws of their society, but I suspect that they were singularly few. As they did without monarchy and slavery, so they also got on without the stock exchange, the advertisement, the secret police, and the bomb. Yet I repeat that these were not simple folk, not dulcet shepherds, noble savages, bland utopians. They were not less complex than us. The trouble is that we have a bad habit, encouraged by pedants and sophisticates, of considering happiness as something rather stupid. Only pain is intellectual, only evil interesting. This is the treason of the artist: a refusal to admit the banality of evil and the terrible boredom of pain. If you can't lick 'em, join 'em. If it hurts, repeat it. But to praise despair is to condemn delight, to embrace violence is to lose hold of everything else. We have almost lost hold; we can no longer describe a happy man, nor make any celebration of joy. How can I tell you about the people of Omelas? They were not naive and happy children—though their children were, in fact, happy. They were mature, intelligent, passionate adults whose lives were not wretched. O miracle! but I wish I could describe it better. I wish I could convince you. Omelas sounds in my words like a city in a fairy tale, long ago and far away, once upon a time. Perhaps it would be best if you imagined it as your own fancy bids, assuming it will rise to the occasion, for certainly I cannot suit you all. For instance, how about technology? I think that there would be no cars or helicopters in and above the streets; this follows from the fact that the people of Omelas are happy people. Happiness is based on a just discrimination of what is necessary, what is neither necessary nor destructive, and what is destructive. In the middle category, however—that of the unnecessary but undestructive, that of comfort, luxury, exuberance, etc.—they could perfectly well have central heating, subway trains, washing machines, and all kinds of marvelous devices not yet invented here, floating light-sources, fuelless power, a cure for the common cold. Or they could have none of that: it doesn't matter. As you like it. I incline to think that people from towns up and down the coast have been coming in to Omelas during the last days before the Festival on very fast little trains and double-decked

1 A reference to the "archaic smile," an expression found on the faces of many sculpted figures from Ancient Greece.

trains and that the train station of Omelas is actually the handsomest building in town, though plainer than the magnificent Farmers' Market. But even granted trains, I fear that Omelas so far strikes some of you as goody-goody. Smiles, bells, parades, horses, blch. If so, please add an orgy. If an orgy would help, don't hesitate. Let us not, however, have temples from which issue beautiful nude priests and priestesses already half in ecstasy and ready to copulate with any man or woman, lover or stranger, who desires union with the deep godhead of the blood, although that was my first idea. But really it would be better not to have any temples in Omelas—at least, not manned temples. Religion yes, clergy no. Surely the beautiful nudes can just wander about, offering themselves like divine souffles to the hunger of the needy and the rapture of the flesh. Let them join the processions. Let tambourines be struck above the copulations, and the glory of desire be proclaimed upon the gongs, and (a not unimportant point) let the offspring of these delightful rituals be beloved and looked after by all. One thing I know there is none of in Omelas is guilt. But what else should there be? I thought at first there were no drugs, but that is puritanical. For those who like it, the faint insistent sweetness of *drooz* may perfume the ways of the city, *drooz* which first brings a great lightness and brilliance to the mind and limbs, and then after some hours a dreamy languor, and wonderful visions at last of the very arcana and inmost secrets of the Universe, as well as exciting the pleasure of sex beyond all belief; and it is not habit-forming. For more modest tastes I think there ought to be beer. What else, what else belongs in the joyous city? The sense of victory, surely, the celebration of courage. But as we did without clergy, let us do without soldiers. The joy built upon successful slaughter is not the right kind of joy; it will not do; it is fearful and it is trivial. A boundless and generous contentment, a magnanimous triumph felt not against some outer enemy but in communion with the finest and fairest in the souls of all men everywhere and the splendor of the world's summer: this is what swells the hearts of the people of Omelas, and the victory they celebrate is that of life. I really don't think many of them need to take *drooz*.

Most of the processions have reached the Green Fields by now. A marvelous smell of cooking goes forth from the red and blue tents of the provisioners. The faces of small children are amiably sticky; in the benign gray beard of a man a couple of crumbs of rich pastry are entangled. The youths and girls have mounted their horses and are beginning to group around the starting line of the course. An old woman, small, fat, and laughing, is passing out flowers from a basket, and tall young men wear her flowers in their shining hair. A child of nine or ten sits at the edge of the crowd, alone, playing on a wooden flute. People pause to listen, and they smile, but they do not speak to him, for he never ceases playing and never sees them, his dark eyes wholly rapt in the sweet, thin magic of the tune.

He finishes, and slowly lowers his hands holding the wooden flute.

As if that little private silence were the signal, all at once a trumpet sounds from the pavillion near the starting line: imperious, melancholy, piercing. The horses rear on their slender legs, and some of them neigh in answer. Sober-faced, the young riders stroke the horses' necks and soothe them, whispering, "Quiet, quiet, there my beauty, my hope...." They begin to form in rank along the starting line. The crowds along the racecourse are like a field of grass and flowers in the wind. The Festival of Summer has begun.

Do you believe? Do you accept the festival, the city, the joy? No? Then let me describe one more thing.

In a basement under one of the beautiful public buildings of Omelas, or perhaps in the cellar of one of its spacious private homes, there is a room. It has one locked door, and no window. A little light seeps in dustily between cracks in the boards, secondhand from a cobwebbed window somewhere across the cellar. In one corner of the little room a couple of mops, with stiff, clotted, foul-smelling heads, stand near a rusty bucket. The floor is dirt, a little damp to the touch, as cellar dirt usually is. The room is about three paces long and two wide: a mere broom closet or disused tool room. In the room a child is sitting. It could be a boy or a girl. It looks about six, but actually is nearly ten. It is feeble-minded. Perhaps it was born defective, or perhaps it has become imbecile through fear, malnutrition, and neglect. It picks its nose and occasionally fumbles vaguely with its toes or genitals, as it sits hunched in the corner farthest from the bucket and the two mops. It is afraid of the mops. It finds them horrible. It shuts its eyes, but it knows the mops are still standing there; and the door is locked; and nobody will come. The door is always locked; and nobody ever comes, except that sometimes—the child has no understanding of time or interval—sometimes the door rattles terribly and opens, and a person, or several people, are there. One of them may come in and kick the child to make it stand up. The others never come close, but peer in at it with frightened, disgusted eyes. The food bowl and the water jug are hastily filled, the door is locked, the eyes disappear. The people at the door never say anything, but the child, who has not always lived in the tool room, and can remember sunlight and its mother's voice, sometimes speaks. "I will be good," it says. "Please let me out. I will be good!" They never answer. The child used to scream for help at night, and cry a good deal, but now it only makes a kind of whining, "eh-haa, eh-haa," and it speaks less and less often. It is so thin there are no calves to its legs; its belly protrudes; it lives on a half-bowl of corn meal and grease a day. It is naked. Its buttocks and thighs are a mass of festered sores, as it sits in its own excrement continually.

They all know it is there, all the people of Omelas. Some of them have come to see it, others are content merely to know it is there. They all know that it has to be there. Some of them understand why, and some do not, but they all understand that their happiness, the beauty of their city, the tenderness of their friendships, the health of their children, the wisdom of their scholars, the skill of their makers, even the abundance of their harvest and the kindly weathers of their skies, depend wholly on this child's abominable misery.

This is usually explained to children when they are between eight and twelve, whenever they seem capable of understanding; and most of those who come to see the child are young people, though often enough an adult comes, or comes back, to see the child. No matter how well the matter has been explained to them, these young spectators are always shocked and sickened at the sight. They feel disgust, which they had thought themselves superior to. They feel anger, outrage, impotence, despite all the explanations. They would like to do something for the child. But there is nothing they can do. If the child were brought up into the sunlight out of that vile place, if it were cleaned and fed and comforted, that would be a good thing, indeed; but if it were done, in that day and hour all the prosperity and beauty and delight of Omelas would wither and be destroyed. Those are the terms. To exchange all the goodness and grace of every life in Omelas for that single, small improvement: to throw away the happiness of thousands for the chance of the happiness of one: that would be to let guilt within the walls indeed.

The terms are strict and absolute; there may not even be a kind word spoken to the child.

Often the young people go home in tears, or in a tearless rage, when they have seen the child and faced this terrible paradox. They may brood over it for weeks or years. But as time goes on they begin to realize that even if the child could be released, it would not get much good of its freedom: a little vague pleasure of warmth and food, no doubt, but little more. It is too degraded and imbecile to know any real joy. It has been afraid too long ever to be free of fear. Its habits are too uncouth for it to respond to humane treatment. Indeed, after so long it would probably be wretched without walls about it to protect it, and darkness for its eyes, and its own excrement to sit in. Their tears at the bitter injustice dry when they begin to perceive the terrible justice of reality and to accept it. Yet it is their tears and anger, the trying of their generosity and the acceptance of their helplessness, which are perhaps the true source of the splendor of their lives. Theirs is no vapid, irresponsible happiness. They know that they, like the child, are not free. They know compassion. It is the existence of the child, and their knowledge of its existence, that makes possible the nobility of their architecture, the poignancy of their music, the profundity of their science. It is because of the child that they are so gentle with children. They know that if the wretched one were not there sniveling in the dark, the other one, the flute-player, could make no joyful music as the young riders line up in their beauty for the race in the sunlight of the first morning of summer.

Now do you believe in them? Are they not more credible? But there is one more thing to tell, and this is quite incredible.

At times one of the adolescent girls or boys who go to see the child does not go home to weep or rage, does not, in fact, go home at all. Sometimes also a man or woman much older falls silent for a day or two, and then leaves home. These people go out into the street, and walk down the street alone. They keep walking, and walk straight out of the city of Omelas, through the beautiful gates. They keep walking across the farmlands of Omelas. Each one goes alone, youth or girl, man or woman. Night falls; the traveler must pass down village streets, between the houses with yellow-lit windows, and on out into the darkness of the fields. Each alone, they go west or north, towards the mountains. They go on. They leave Omelas, they walk ahead into the darkness, and they do not come back. The place they go towards is a place even less imaginable to most of us than the city of happiness. I cannot describe it at all. It is possible that it does not exist. But they seem to know where they are going, the ones who walk away from Omelas.

—1973

CHINUA ACHEBE

Albert Chinualumogu Achebe was born in 1930 in Ogidi, Igboland, in eastern Nigeria. Achebe's novels occupy a central place in the tradition of African literature; in content and form they trace African history from pre-colonialism through to decolonization and postcolonialism. He has been awarded numerous international literary prizes, including, in 2007, the Man Booker International Prize, which honors a living author for an entire body of work.

Achebe was born 30 years before Nigeria declared its independence from British colonial rule. As a boy he went to the Church Mission Society School, yet was simultaneously immersed in Igbo culture and tradition. In 1948 he began attending University College, Ibadan, initially to study medicine. He decided to quit medicine and take a degree in literature: "I was abandoning the realm of stories and they would not let me go."

Achebe's degree focused on the English canon, in which the only depiction of his own people was found in the narratives and language of colonizers—works such as Joyce Cary's *Mister Johnson* and Joseph Conrad's *Heart of Darkness*. Convinced of the power of stories to change history, Achebe became determined to re-tell the stories of Nigeria in order "to help my society regain belief in itself and put away the complexes of the years of denigration and self-abasement." *Things Fall Apart* (1958), Achebe's first novel, was followed by *No Longer At Ease* in 1960. Both are historical novels that begin in the precolonial period and trace the destructive legacy of colonialism through several generations. Though Achebe wrote in English, he forged a unique prose style that attempted to give voice to Nigerian experience in its own terms, weaving Igbo proverbs, terms, speech patterns, and images into the language of the colonizer.

In *Arrow of God* (1964) and *A Man of the People* (1966) Achebe continued to develop the themes of his earlier novels, but in these novels, set in the early years of Nigerian independence, he is also critical of the corruption and violence that were overtaking Nigerian politics. Achebe's work approaches experience and conflict from several perspectives, presenting them with intelligence and compassion: "Whatever you are is never enough; you must find a way to accept something however small from the other to make you whole."

In 1966 the Nigerian government was overthrown, and the country fell into chaos and civil war. Achebe joined the struggle to establish an independent Republic for the Igbo people, who were under threat of genocide. The Igbo Republic, Biafra, capitulated in 1970, after over a million civilians had starved to death as a result of an economic blockade. Achebe began writing poetry and short stories after this conflict; *Girls at War and Other Stories* was published in 1973.

A car accident in Nigeria in 1990 left Achebe paralyzed from the waist down; he moved to the United States for treatment, and has lived there since. "Dead Men's Path" is a story about Michael Obi, the young, idealistic headmaster of Ndume Central School. He and his wife intend to transform and beautify a school that had been considered behind the times. An ancestral path cuts across the school's organized garden, and the new headmaster refuses to allow the villagers to pass. The chaos and destruction that follow prompt many questions.

Dead Men's Path

CHINUA ACHEBE

MICHAEL OBI'S hopes were fulfilled much earlier than he had expected. He was appointed headmaster of Ndume Central School in January 1949. It had always been an unprogressive school, so the Mission authorities[1] decided to send a young and energetic man to run it. Obi accepted this responsibility with enthusiasm. He had many wonderful ideas and this was an opportunity to put them into practice. He had had sound secondary school education which designated him a "pivotal teacher" in the official records and set him apart from the other headmasters in the mission field. He was outspoken in his condemnation of the narrow views of these older and often less-educated ones.

"We shall make a good job of it, shan't we?" he asked his young wife when they first heard the joyful news of his promotion.

"We shall do our best," she replied. "We shall have such beautiful gardens and everything will be just *modern* and delightful...." In their two years of married life she had become completely infected by his passion for "modern methods" and his denigration of "these old and superannuated people in the teaching field

---

1 Many schools in African countries formerly colonized by the British were run by Christian missionary organizations.

who would be better employed as traders in the Onitsha[2] market." She began to see herself already as the admired wife of the young headmaster, the queen of the school.

The wives of the other teachers would envy her position. She would set the fashion in everything.... Then, suddenly, it occurred to her that there might not be other wives. Wavering between hope and fear, she asked her husband, looking anxiously at him.

"All our colleagues are young and unmarried," he said with enthusiasm which for once she did not share. "Which is a good thing," he continued.

"Why?"

"Why? They will give all their time and energy to the school."

Nancy was downcast. For a few minutes she became skeptical about the new school; but it was only for a few minutes. Her little personal misfortune could not blind her to her husband's happy prospects. She looked at him as he sat folded up in a chair. He was stoop-shouldered and looked frail. But he sometimes surprised people with sudden bursts of physical energy. In his present posture, however, all his bodily strength seemed to have retired behind his deep-set eyes, giving them an extraordinary power of penetration. He was only twenty-six, but looked thirty or more. On the whole, he was not unhandsome.

"A penny for your thoughts, Mike," said Nancy after a while, imitating the woman's magazine she read.

"I was thinking what a grand opportunity we've got at last to show these people how a school should be run."

Ndume School was backward in every sense of the word. Mr. Obi put his whole life into the work, and his wife hers too. He had two aims. A high standard of teaching was insisted upon, and the school compound was to be turned into a place of beauty. Nancy's dream-gardens came to life with the coming of the rains, and blossomed. Beautiful hibiscus and allamanda hedges in brilliant red and yellow marked out the carefully tended school compound from the rank neighborhood bushes.

One evening as Obi was admiring his work he was scandalized to see an old woman from the village hobble right across the compound, through a marigold flower-bed and the hedges. On going up there he found faint signs of an almost disused path from the village across the school compound to the bush on the other side.

---

2 A city in southeastern Nigeria.

"It amazes me," said Obi to one of his teachers who had been three years in the school, "that you people allowed the villagers to make use of this footpath. It is simply incredible." He shook his head.

"The path," said the teacher apologetically, "appears to be very important to them. Although it is hardly used, it connects the village shrine with their place of burial."

"And what has that got to do with the school?" asked the headmaster.

"Well, I don't know," replied the other with a shrug of the shoulders. "But I remember there was a big row some time ago when we attempted to close it."

"That was some time ago. But it will not be used now," said Obi as he walked away. "What will the Government Education Officer think of this when he comes to inspect the school next week? The villagers might, for all I know, decide to use the schoolroom for a pagan ritual during the inspection."

Heavy sticks were planted closely across the path at the two places where it entered and left the school premises. These were further strengthened with barbed wire.

Three days later the village priest of *Ani*[3] called on the headmaster. He was an old man and walked with a slight stoop. He carried a stout walking-stick which he usually tapped on the floor, by way of emphasis, each time he made a new point in his argument.

"I have heard," he said after the usual exchange of cordialities, "that our ancestral footpath has recently been closed…."

"Yes," replied Mr. Obi. "We cannot allow people to make a highway of our school compound."

"Look here, my son," said the priest bringing down his walking-stick, "this path was here before you were born and before your father was born. The whole life of this village depends on it. Our dead relatives depart by it and our ancestors visit us by it. But most important, it is the path of children coming in to be born…."

Mr. Obi listened with a satisfied smile on his face.

"The whole purpose of our school," he said finally, "is to eradicate just such beliefs as that. Dead men do not require footpaths. The whole idea is just fantastic. Our duty is to teach your children to laugh at such ideas."

"What you say may be true," replied the priest, "but we follow the practices of our fathers. If you reopen the path we shall have nothing to quarrel about. What I always say is: let the hawk perch and let the eagle perch." He rose to go.

---

3 The traditional belief system of the Igbo people of Nigeria, often called Odinani.

"I am sorry," said the young headmaster. "But the school compound cannot be a thoroughfare. It is against our regulations. I would suggest your constructing another path, skirting our premises. We can even get our boys to help in building it. I don't suppose the ancestors will find the little detour too burdensome."

"I have no more words to say," said the old priest, already outside.

Two days later a young woman in the village died in childbed. A diviner was immediately consulted and he prescribed heavy sacrifices to propitiate ancestors insulted by the fence.

Obi woke up next morning among the ruins of his work. The beautiful hedges were torn up not just near the path but right round the school, the flowers trampled to death and one of the school buildings pulled down … That day, the white Supervisor came to inspect the school and wrote a nasty report on the state of the premises but more seriously about the "tribal-war situation developing between the school and the village, arising in part from the misguided zeal of the new headmaster."

—1953

ALICE MUNRO

Jonathan Franzen has written in *The New York Times* that Alice Munro "has a strong claim to being the best fiction writer now working in North America." Her numerous short story collections have received a variety of awards, including three Governor General's Awards, two Giller Prizes, the Man Booker International Prize, and the Canada Council Molson Prize for her "outstanding lifetime contribution to the cultural and intellectual life of Canada." In 2010 she was honored as Knight of the Order of Arts and Letters for her literary contributions.

Munro was born in 1931 in Wingham, Huron County, Ontario. Her mother was an ex-elementary school teacher and her father a fox farmer who later turned to turkey farming. Munro left Wingham in 1949 to study journalism at the University of Western Ontario as a scholarship student. In her second year, she switched her major to English, and her first short stories appeared in the university publication *Folio*. In 1951, her scholarship money ran out; she dropped out of university and married James Munro. The Munros moved to the West Coast where she sold her first short story, "A Basket of Strawberries," to *Mayfair* in 1953, and continued to write while raising two daughters. Shortly after the birth of her third daughter in 1966, she published her first collection of short stories, *Dance of the Happy Shades* (1968), which won Canada's Governor General's Award for Fiction; this collection was followed by a collection of linked short stories entitled *Lives of Girls and Women*, which won the 1971 Canadian Bookseller's Award.

The demands of motherhood affected Munro's writing in significant ways. She put it this way in a 1973 interview with Graeme Gibson: "in twenty years I've never had a day when I didn't have to think about somebody else's needs. And this means the writing has to be fitted in around it.... I think it's a miracle that I've produced anything." In 1973, Alice and James Munro divorced and she moved back to Ontario. She remarried in 1976 and returned to Ontario's Huron County area. In recent years she has divided her time between Clinton, Ontario and Comox, British Columbia.

Her 2012 collection *Dear Life* was preceded by *Too Much Happiness* (2009), *The View from Castle Rock* (2006), and *Runaway* (2004).

Though Munro has set her stories in a wide variety of locations—from Scotland to Illinois to British Columbia—her use of Huron County as the setting for much of her fiction has led to the redefining of the area by national and international Munro readers and scholars as "Alice Munro country." Writing from the southern United States by authors such as Flannery O'Connor was influential for Munro, because, as she explains, she "felt there a country being depicted that was like my own … the part of the country I come from is absolutely Gothic." The "Ontario Gothic" in Munro's work touches on the complexity that underlies the domestic—what the main character Del Jordan in *Lives of Girls and Women* describes as "dull, simple, amazing and unfathomable—deep caves paved with kitchen linoleum." "Miles City, Montana" (from the 1986 collection *The Progress of Love*) explores the image of linoleum-lined "caves" and the Gothic nature of a small-town Ontario childhood—a daughter's temporary misadventure leads the female narrator to reflect on the porous boundary that separates the apparently innocent world of the child from the world of the adult.

Miles City, Montana

ALICE MUNRO

MY FATHER came across the field carrying the body of the boy who had been drowned. There were several men together, returning from the search, but he was the one carrying the body. The men were muddy and exhausted, and walked with their heads down, as if they were ashamed. Even the dogs were dispirited, dripping from the cold river. When they all set out, hours before, the dogs were nervy and yelping, the men tense and determined, and there was a constrained, unspeakable excitement about the whole scene. It was understood that they might find something horrible.

The boy's name was Steve Gauley. He was eight years old. His hair and clothes were mud-colored now and carried some bits of dead leaves, twigs, and grass. He was like a heap of refuse that had been left out all winter. His face was turned in to my father's chest, but I could see a nostril, an ear, plugged up with greenish mud.

I don't think so. I don't think I really saw all this. Perhaps I saw my father carrying him, and the other men following along, and the dogs, but I would not have been allowed to get close enough to see something like mud in his nostril. I must have heard someone talking about that and imagined that I saw it. I see his face unaltered except for the mud—Steve Gauley's familiar, sharp-honed, sneaky-looking face—and it wouldn't have been like that; it would have been bloated and changed and perhaps muddied all over after so many hours in the water.

To have to bring back such news, such evidence, to a waiting family, particularly a mother, would have made searchers move heavily, but what was happening here was worse. It seemed a worse shame (to hear people talk) that there was no mother, no woman at all—no grandmother or aunt, or even a sister—to receive Steve Gauley and give him his due of grief. His father was a hired man, a drinker but not a drunk, an erratic man without being entertaining, not friendly but not exactly a troublemaker. His fatherhood seemed accidental, and the fact that the child had been left with him when the mother went away, and that they continued living together, seemed accidental. They lived in a steep-roofed, gray-shingled hillbilly sort of house and that was just a bit better than a shack—the father fixed the roof and put supports under the porch, just enough and just in time—and their life was held together in a similar manner; that is, just well enough to keep the Children's Aid at bay. They didn't eat meals together or cook for each other, but there was food. Sometimes the father would give Steve money to buy food at the store, and Steve was seen to buy quite sensible things, such as pancake mix and macaroni dinner.

I had known Steve Gauley fairly well. I had not liked him more often than I had liked him. He was two years older than I was. He would hang around our place on Saturdays, scornful of whatever I was doing but unable to leave me alone. I couldn't be on the swing without him wanting to try it, and if I wouldn't give it up he came and pushed me so that I went crooked. He teased the dog. He got me into trouble—deliberately and maliciously, it seemed to me afterward—by daring me to do things I wouldn't have thought of on my own: digging up the potatoes to see how big they were when they were still only the size of marbles, and pushing over the stacked firewood to make a pile we could jump off. At school, we never spoke to each other. He was solitary, though not tormented. But on Saturday mornings, when I saw his thin, self-possessed figure sliding through the cedar hedge, I knew I was in for something and he would decide what. Sometimes it was all right. We pretended we were cowboys who had come to tame wild horses. We played in the pasture by the river, not far from the place where Steve drowned. We were horses and riders both, screaming and neighing and bucking and waving whips of tree branches beside a little nameless river that flows into the Saugeen in southern Ontario.

The funeral was held in our house. There was not enough room at Steve's father's place for the large crowd that was expected because of the circumstances.

I have a memory of the crowded room but no picture of Steve in his coffin, or of the minister, or of wreaths of flowers. I remember that I was holding one flower, a white narcissus, which must have come from a pot somebody forced indoors, because it was too early for even the forsythia bush or the trilliums and march marigolds in the woods. I stood in a row of children, each of us holding a narcissus. We sang a children's hymn, which somebody played on our piano: "When He Cometh, When He Cometh, to Make Up His Jewels." I was wearing white ribbed stockings, which were disgustingly itchy, and wrinkled at the knees and ankles. The feeling of these stockings on my legs is mixed up with another feeling in my memory. It is hard to describe. It had to do with my parents. Adults in general but my parents in particular. My father, who had carried Steve's body from the river, and my mother, who must have done most of the arranging of this funeral. My father in his dark-blue suit and my mother in her brown velvet dress with the creamy satin collar. They stood side by side opening and closing their mouths for the hymn, and I stood removed from them, in the row of children, watching. I felt a furious and sickening disgust. Children sometimes have an access of disgust concerning adults. The size, the lumpy shapes, the bloated power. The breath, the coarseness, the hairiness, the horrid secretions. But this was more. And the accompanying anger had nothing sharp and self-respecting about it. There was no release, as when I would finally bend and pick up a stone and throw it at Steve Gauley. It could not be understood or expressed, though it died down after a while into a heaviness, then just a taste, an occasional taste—a thin, familiar misgiving.

o o o

Twenty years or so later, in 1961, my husband, Andrew, and I got a brand-new car, our first—that is, our first brand-new. It was a Morris Oxford, oyster-colored (the dealer had some fancier name for the color)—a big small car, with plenty of room for us and our two children. Cynthia was six and Meg three and a half.

Andrew took a picture of me standing beside the ear. I was wearing white pants, a black turtleneck, and sunglasses. I lounged against the car door, canting my hips to make myself look slim.

"Wonderful," Andrew said. "Great. You look like Jackie Kennedy." All over this continent probably, dark-haired, reasonably slender young women were told, when they were stylishly dressed or getting their pictures taken, that they looked like Jackie Kennedy.

Andrew took a lot of pictures of me, and of the children, our house, our garden, our excursions and possessions. He got copies made, labeled them carefully, and sent them back to his mother and his aunt and uncle in Ontario. He got copies for me to send to my father, who also lived in Ontario, and I did so, but less regularly than he sent his. When he saw pictures he thought I had already sent lying around the house, Andrew was perplexed and annoyed. He liked to have this record go forth.

That summer, we were presenting ourselves, not pictures. We were driving back from Vancouver, where we lived, to Ontario, which we still called "home," in our new car. Five days to get there, ten days there, five days back. For the first time, Andrew had three weeks' holiday. He worked in the legal department at BC Hydro.

On a Saturday morning, we loaded suitcases, two thermos bottles—one filled with coffee and one with lemonade—some fruit and sandwiches, picture books and coloring books, crayons, drawing pads, insect repellent, sweaters (in case it got cold in the mountains), and our two children into the car. Andrew locked the house, and Cynthia said ceremoniously, "Goodbye, house."

Meg said, "Goodbye, house." Then she said, "Where will we live now?"

"It's not goodbye forever," said Cynthia. "We're coming back. Mother! Meg thought we weren't ever coming back!"

"I did not," said Meg, kicking the back of my seat.

Andrew and I put on our sunglasses, and we drove away, over the Lions Gate Bridge and through the main part of Vancouver. We shed our house, the neighborhood, the city, and—at the crossing point between Washington and British Columbia—our country. We were driving east across the United States, taking the most northerly route, and would cross into Canada again at Sarnia, Ontario. I don't know if we chose this route because the Trans-Canada Highway was not completely finished at the time or if we just wanted the feeling of driving through a foreign, a very slightly foreign, country—that extra bit of interest and adventure.

We were both in high spirits. Andrew congratulated the car several times. He said he felt so much better driving it than our old car, a 1951 Austin that slowed down dismally on the hills and had a fussy-old-lady image. So Andrew said now.

"What kind of image does this one have?" said Cynthia. She listened to us carefully and liked to try out new words such as "image." Usually she got them right.

"Lively," I said. "Slightly sporty. It's not show-off."

"It's sensible, but it has class," Andrew said. "Like my image."

Cynthia thought that over and said with cautious pride, "That means like you think you want to be, Daddy?"

As for me, I was happy because of the shedding. I loved taking off. In my own house, I seemed to be more often looking for a place to hide—sometimes from the children but more often from the jobs to be done and the phone ringing and the sociability of the neighborhood. I wanted to hide so that I could get busy at my real work, which was a sort of wooing of distant parts of myself. I lived in a state of siege, always losing just what I wanted to hold on to. But on trips there was no difficulty. I could be talking to Andrew, talking to the children and looking at whatever they wanted me to look at—a pig on a sign, a pony in a field, a Volkswagen on a revolving stand—and pouring lemonade into plastic cups, and all the time those bits and pieces would be flying together inside me. The essential composition would be achieved. This made me hopeful and lighthearted. It was being a watcher that did it. A watcher, not a keeper.

We turned east at Everett and climbed into the Cascades. I showed Cynthia our route on the map. First I showed her the map of the whole United States, which showed also the bottom part of Canada. Then I turned to the separate maps of each of the states we were going to pass through. Washington, Idaho, Montana, North Dakota, Minnesota, Wisconsin. I showed her the dotted line across Lake Michigan, which was the route of the ferry we would take. Then we would drive across Michigan to the bridge that linked the United States and Canada at Sarnia, Ontario. Home.

Meg wanted to see, too.

"You won't understand," said Cynthia. But she took the road atlas into the back seat.

"Sit back," she said to Meg. "Sit still. I'll show you."

I could hear her tracing the route for Meg, very accurately, just as I had done it for her. She looked up all the states' maps, knowing how to find them in alphabetical order.

"You know what that line is?" she said. "It's the road. That line is the road we're driving on. We're going right along this line."

Meg did not say anything.

"Mother, show me where we are right this minute," said Cynthia.

I took the atlas and pointed out the road through the mountains, and she took it back and showed it to Meg. "See where the road is all wiggly?" she said. "It's wiggly because there are so many turns in it. The wiggles are the turns." She flipped some pages and waited a moment. "Now," she said, "show me where we are." Then she called to me, "Mother, she understands! She pointed to it! Meg understands maps!"

It seems to me now that we invented characters for our children. We had them firmly set to play their parts. Cynthia was bright and diligent, sensitive, courteous, watchful. Sometimes we teased her for being too conscientious, too eager to be what we in fact depended on her to be. Any reproach or failure, any rebuff, went terribly deep with her. She was fair-haired, fair-skinned, easily showing the effects of the sun, raw winds, pride, or humiliation. Meg was more solidly built, more reticent—not rebellious but stubborn sometimes, mysterious. Her silences seemed to us to show her strength of character, and her negatives were taken as signs of imperturbable independence. Her hair was brown, and we cut it in straight bangs. Her eyes were a light hazel, clear and dazzling.

We were entirely pleased with these characters, enjoying the contradictions as well as the confirmations of them. We disliked the heavy, the uninventive, approach to being parents. I had a dread of turning into a certain kind of mother—the kind whose body sagged, who moved in woolly-smelling, milky-smelling fog, solemn with trivial burdens. I believed that all the attention these mothers paid, their need to be burdened, was the cause of colic, bed-wetting, asthma. I favored another approach—the mock desperation, the inflated irony of the professional mothers who wrote for magazines. In those magazine pieces, the children were splendidly self-willed, hard-edged, perverse, indomitable. So were the mothers, through their wit, indomitable. The real-life mothers I warmed to were the sort who would phone up and say, "Is my embryo Hitler by any chance over at your house?" They cackled clear above the milky fog.

We saw a dead deer strapped across the front of a pickup truck.

"Somebody shot it," Cynthia said. "Hunters shoot the deer."

"It's not hunting season yet," Andrew said. "They may have hit it on the road. See the sign for deer crossing?"

"I would cry if we hit one," Cynthia said sternly.

I had made peanut-butter-and-marmalade sandwiches for the children and salmon-and-mayonnaise for us. But I had not put any lettuce in, and Andrew was disappointed.

"I didn't have any," I said.

"Couldn't you have got some?"

"I'd have had to buy a whole head of lettuce just to get enough for the sandwiches, and I decided it wasn't worth it."

This was a lie. I had forgotten.

"They're a lot better with lettuce."

"I didn't think it made that much difference." After a silence, I said, "Don't be mad."

"I'm not mad. I like lettuce on sandwiches."

"I just didn't think it mattered that much."

"How would it be if I didn't bother to fill up the gas tank?"

"That's not the same thing."

"Sing a song," said Cynthia. She started to sing:

> Five little ducks went out one day,
> Over the hills and far away.

One little duck went
"Quack-quack-quack."
Four little ducks came swimming back.

Andrew squeezed my hand and said, "Let's not fight."

"You're right. I should have got lettuce."

"It doesn't matter that much."

I wish that I could get my feelings about Andrew to come together into a serviceable and dependable feeling. I had even tried writing two lists, one of things I liked about him, one of things I disliked—in the cauldron of intimate life, things I loved and things I hated—as if I hoped by this to prove something, to come to a conclusion one way or the other. But I gave it up when I saw that all it proved was what I already knew—that I had violent contradictions. Sometimes the very sound of his footsteps seemed to me tyrannical, the set of his mouth smug and mean, his hard, straight body a barrier interposed—quite consciously, even dutifully, and with a nasty pleasure in its masculine authority—between me and whatever joy or lightness I could get in life. Then, with not much warning, he became my good friend and most essential companion. I felt the sweetness of his light bones and serious ideas, the vulnerability of his love, which I imagined to be much purer and more straightforward than my own. I could be greatly moved by an inflexibility, a harsh propriety, that at other times I scorned. I would think how humble he was, really, taking on such a ready-made role of husband, father, breadwinner, and how I myself in comparison was really a secret monster of egotism. Not so secret, either—not from him.

At the bottom of our fights, we served up what we thought were the ugliest truths. "I know there is something basically selfish and basically untrustworthy about you," Andrew once said. "I've always known it. I also know that that is why I fell in love with you."

"Yes," I said, feeling sorrowful but complacent.

"I know that I'd be better off without you."

"Yes. You would."

"You'd be happier without me."

"Yes."

And finally—finally—racked and purged, we clasped hands and laughed, laughed at those two benighted people, ourselves. Their grudges, their grievances, their self-justification. We leap-frogged over them. We declared them liars. We would have wine with dinner, or decide to give a party.

I haven't seen Andrew for years, don't know if he is still thin, has gone completely gray, insists on lettuce, tells the truth, or is hearty and disappointed.

We stayed the night in Wenatchee, Washington, where it hadn't rained for weeks. We ate dinner in a restaurant built about a tree—not a sapling in a tub but a tall, sturdy cottonwood. In the early-morning light, we climbed out of the irrigated valley, up dry, rocky, very steep hillsides that would seem to lead to more hills, and there on the top was a wide plateau, cut by the great Spokane and Columbia rivers. Grainland and grassland, mile after mile. There were straight roads here, and little farming towns with grain elevators. In fact, there was a sign announcing that this county we were going through, Douglas County, had the second-highest wheat yield of any county in the United States. The towns had planted shade trees. At least, I thought they had been planted, because there were no such big trees in the countryside.

All this was marvellously welcome to me. "Why do I love it so much?" I said to Andrew. "Is it because it isn't scenery?"

"It reminds you of home," said Andrew. "A bout of severe nostalgia." But he said this kindly.

When we said "home" and meant Ontario, we had very different places in mind. My home was a turkey farm, where my father lived as a widower, and though it was the same house my mother had lived in, had papered, painted, cleaned, furnished, it showed the effects now of neglect and of some wild sociability. A life went on in it that my mother could not have predicted or condoned. There were parties for the turkey crew, the gutters and pluckers, and sometimes one or two of the young men would be living there temporarily, inviting their own friends and having their own impromptu parties. This life, I thought, was better for my father than being lonely, and I did not disapprove, had certainly no right to disapprove; Andrew did not like to go there, naturally enough, because he was not the sort who could sit around the kitchen table with the turkey crew, telling jokes. They were intimidated by him and contemptuous of him, and it seemed to me that my father, when they were around, had to be on their side. And it wasn't only Andrew who had trouble. I could manage those jokes, but it was an effort.

I wished for the days when I was little, before we had the turkeys. We had cows, and sold the milk to the cheese factory. A turkey farm is nothing like as pretty as a dairy farm or a sheep farm. You can see that the turkeys are on a straight path to becoming frozen carcasses and table meat. They don't have the pretence of a life of their own, a browsing idyll, that cattle have, or pigs in the dappled orchard. Turkey barns are long, efficient buildings—tin sheds. No beams or hay or warm stables. Even the smell of guano seems thinner and more offensive than the usual smell of stable manure. No hints there of hay coils and rail fences and songbirds and the flowering hawthorn. The turkeys were all let out into one long field, which they picked clean. They didn't look like great birds there but like fluttering laundry.

Once, shortly after my mother died, and after I was married—in fact, I was packing to join Andrew in Vancouver—I was at home alone for a couple of days with my father. There was a freakishly heavy rain all night. In the early light, we saw that the turkey field was flooded. At least, the low-lying parts of it were flooded—it was like a lake with many islands. The turkeys were huddled on these islands. Turkeys are very stupid. (My father would say, "You know a chicken? You know how stupid a chicken is? Well, a chicken is an Einstein compared with a turkey.") But they had managed to crowd to higher ground and avoid drowning. Now they might push each other off, suffocate each other, get cold and die. We couldn't wait for the water to go down. We went out in the old rowboat we had. I rowed and my father pulled the heavy, wet turkeys into the boat and we took them to the barn. It was still raining a little. The job was difficult and absurd and very uncomfortable. We were laughing. I was happy to be working with my father. I felt close to all hard, repetitive, appalling work, in which the body is finally worn out, the mind sunk (though sometimes the spirit can stay marvellously light), and I was homesick in advance for this life and this place. I thought that if Andrew could see me there in the rain, red-handed, muddy, trying to hold on to turkey legs and row the boat at the same time, he would only want to get me out of there and make me forget about it. The raw life angered him. My attachment to it angered him. I thought that I shouldn't have married him. But who else? One of the turkey crew?

And I didn't want to stay there. I might feel bad about leaving, but I would feel worse if somebody made me stay.

Andrew's mother lived in Toronto, in an apartment building looking out on Muir Park. When Andrew and his sister were both at home, his mother slept in the living room. Her husband, a doctor, had died when the children were still too young to go to school. She took a secretarial course and sold her house at Depression prices, moved to this apartment, managed to raise her children, with some help from relatives—her sister Caroline, her brother-in-law Roger. Andrew and his sister went to private schools and to camp in the summer.

"I suppose that was courtesy of the Fresh Air fund?" I said once, scornful of his claim that he had been poor. To my mind, Andrew's urban life had been sheltered and fussy. His mother came home with a headache from working all day in the noise, the harsh light of the department-store office, but it did not occur to me that hers was a hard or admirable life. I don't think she herself believed that she was admirable—only unlucky. She worried about her work in the office, her clothes, her cooking, her children. She worried most of all about what Roger and Caroline would think.

Caroline and Roger lived on the east side of the park, in a handsome stone house. Roger was a tall man with a bald, freckled head, a fat, firm stomach. Some operation on his throat had deprived him of his voice—he spoke in a rough whisper. But everybody paid attention. At dinner once in the stone house—where all the dining-room furniture was enormous, darkly glowing, palatial—I asked him a question. I think it had to do with Whittaker Chambers, whose story was then appearing in the *Saturday Evening Post*. The question was mild in tone, but he guessed its subversive intent and took to calling me Mrs. Gromyko, referring to what he alleged to be my "sympathies." Perhaps he really craved an adversary, and could not find one. At that dinner, I saw Andrew's hand tremble as he lit his mother's cigarette. His Uncle Roger had paid for Andrew's education, and was on the board of directors of several companies.

"He is just an opinionated old man," Andrew said to me later. "What is the point of arguing with him?"

Before we left Vancouver, Andrew's mother had written, "Roger seems quite intrigued by the idea of your buying a small car!" Her exclamation mark showed apprehension. At that time, particularly in Ontario, the choice of a small European car over a large American car could be seen as some sort of declaration—a declaration of tendencies Roger had been sniffing after all along.

"It isn't that small a car," said Andrew huffily.

"That's not the point," I said. "The point is, it isn't any of his business!"

We spent the second night in Missoula. We had been told in Spokane, at a gas station, that there was a lot of repair work going on along Highway 2, and that we were in for a very hot, dusty drive, with long waits, so we turned on to the interstate and drove through Coeur d'Alene and Kellogg into Montana. After Missoula, we turned south toward Butte, but detoured to see Helena, the state capital. In the car, we played Who Am I?

Cynthia was somebody dead, and an American, and a girl. Possibly a lady. She was not in a story. She had not been seen on television. Cynthia had not read about her in a book. She was not anybody who had come to the kindergarten, or a relative of any of Cynthia's friends.

"Is she human?" said Andrew, with a sudden shrewdness.

"No! That's what you forgot to ask!"

"An animal," I said reflectively.

"Is that a question? Sixteen questions!"

"No, it is not a question. I'm thinking. A dead animal."

"It's the deer," said Meg, who hadn't been playing.

"That's not fair!" said Cynthia. "She's not playing!"

"What deer?" said Andrew.

I said, "Yesterday."

"The day before," said Cynthia. "Meg wasn't playing. Nobody got it."

"The deer on the truck," said Andrew.

"It was a lady deer, because it didn't have antlers, and it was an American and it was dead," Cynthia said.

Andrew said, "I think it's kind of morbid, being a dead deer."

"I got it," said Meg.

Cynthia said, "I think I know what morbid is. It's depressing."

Helena, an old silver-mining town, looked forlorn to us even in the morning sunlight. Then Bozeman and Billings, not forlorn in the slightest—energetic, strung-out towns, with miles of blinding tinsel fluttering over used-car lots. We got too tired and hot even to play Who Am I? These busy, prosaic cities reminded me of similar places in Ontario, and I thought about what was really waiting there—the great tombstone furniture of Roger and Caroline's dining-room, the dinners for which I must iron the children's dresses and warn them about forks, and then the other table a hundred miles away, the jokes of my father's crew. The pleasures I had been thinking of—looking at the countryside or drinking a Coke in an old-fashioned drugstore with fans and a high, pressed-tin ceiling—would have to be snatched in between.

"Meg's asleep," Cynthia said. "She's so hot. She makes me hot in the same seat with her."

"I hope she isn't feverish," I said, not turning around.

What are we doing this for, I thought, and the answer came—to show off. To give Andrew's mother and my father the pleasure of seeing their grandchildren. That was our duty. But beyond that we wanted to show them something. What strenuous children we were, Andrew and I, what relentless seekers of approbation. It was as if at some point we had received an unforgettable, indigestible message—that we were far from satisfactory, and that the most commonplace success in life was probably beyond us. Roger dealt out such messages, of course—that was his style—but Andrew's mother, my own mother and father couldn't have meant to do so. All they meant to tell us was "Watch out. Get along." My father, when I was in high school, teased me that I was getting to think I was so smart I would never find a boyfriend. He would have forgotten that in a week. I never forgot it. Andrew and I didn't forget things. We took umbrage.

"I wish there was a beach," said Cynthia.

"There probably is one," Andrew said. "Right around the next curve."

"There isn't a curve," she said, sounding insulted.

"That's what I mean."

"I wish there was some more lemonade."

"I will just wave my magic wand and produce some," I said. "Okay, Cynthia? Would you rather have grape juice? Will I do a beach while I'm at it?"

She was silent, and soon I felt repentant. "Maybe in the next town there might be a pool," I said. I looked at the map. "In Miles City. Anyway, there'll be something cool to drink."

"How far is it?" Andrew said.

"Not so far," I said. "Thirty miles, about."

"In Miles City," said Cynthia, in the tones of an incantation, "there is a beautiful blue swimming pool for children, and a park with lovely trees."

Andrew said to me, "You could have started something."

But there was a pool. There was a park, too, though not quite the oasis of Cynthia's fantasy. Prairie trees with thin leaves—cottonwood and poplars—worn grass, and a high wire fence around the pool. Within this fence, a wall, not yet completed, of cement blocks. There were no shouts or splashes; over the entrance I saw a sign that said the pool was closed every day from noon until two o'clock. It was then twenty-five after twelve.

Nevertheless I called out, "Is anybody there?" I thought somebody must be around, because there was a small truck parked near the entrance. On the side of the truck were these words: "We have Brains, to fix your Drains. (We have Roto-Rooter too.)"

A girl came out, wearing a red lifeguard's shirt over her bathing suit. "Sorry, we're closed."

"We were just driving through," I said.

"We close every day from twelve until two. It's on the sign." She was eating a sandwich.

"I saw the sign," I said. "But this is the first water we've seen for so long, and the children are awfully hot, and I wondered if they could just dip in and out—just five minutes. We'd watch them."

A boy came into sight behind her. He was wearing jeans and a T-shirt with the words "Roto-Rooter" on it.

I was going to say that we were driving from British Columbia to Ontario, but I remembered that Canadian place names usually meant nothing to Americans. "We're driving right across the country," I said. "We haven't time to wait for the pool to open. We were just hoping the children could get cooled off."

Cynthia came running up barefoot behind me. "Mother, Mother, where is my bathing suit?" Then she stopped, sensing the serious adult negotiations. Meg was climbing out of the car—just wakened, and her top pulled up and her shorts pulled down, showing her pink stomach.

"Is it just those two?" the girl said.

"Just the two. We'll watch them."

"I can't let any adults in. If it's just the two, I guess I could watch them. I'm having my lunch." She said to Cynthia, "Do you want to come in the pool?"

"Yes, please," said Cynthia firmly.

Meg looked at the ground.

"Just a short time, because the pool is really closed," I said. "We appreciate this very much," I said to the girl.

"Well, I can eat my lunch out there, if it's just the two of them." She looked toward the car as if she thought I might try to spring some more children on her.

When I found Cynthia's bathing suit, she took it into the changing room. She would not permit anybody, even Meg, to see her naked. I changed Meg, who stood on the front seat of the car. She had a pink cotton bathing suit with straps that crossed and buttoned. There were ruffles across the bottom.

"She *is* hot," I said. "But I don't think she's feverish."

I loved helping Meg to dress or undress, because her body still had the solid unself-consciousness, the sweet indifference, something of the milky smell, of a baby's body. Cynthia's body had long ago been pared down, shaped and altered, into Cynthia. We all liked to hug Meg, press and nuzzle her. Sometimes she would scowl and beat us off, and this forthright independence, this ferocious bashfulness, simply made her more appealing, more apt to be tormented and tickled in the way of family love.

Andrew and I sat in the car with the windows open. I could hear a radio playing, and thought it must belong to the girl or her boyfriend. I was thirsty, and got out of the car to look for a concession stand, or perhaps a soft-drink machine, somewhere in the park. I was wearing shorts, and the backs of my legs were slick with sweat. I saw a drinking fountain at the other side of the park and was walking toward it in a roundabout way, keeping to the shade of the trees. No place became real till you got out of the car. Dazed with the heat, with the sun on the blistered houses, the pavement, the burned grass, I walked slowly. I paid attention to a squashed leaf, ground a Popsicle stick under the heel of my sandal, squinted at a trash can strapped to a tree. This is the way you look at the poorest details of the world resurfaced, after you've been driving for a long time—you feel their singleness and precise location and the forlorn coincidence of your being there to see them.

Where are the children?

I turned around and moved quickly, not quite running, to a part of the fence beyond which the cement wall was not completed. I could see some of the pool. I saw Cynthia, standing about waist-deep in the water, fluttering her hands on the surface and discreetly watching something at the end of the pool, which I could not see. I thought by her pose, her discretion, the look on her face, that she must be watching some byplay between the lifeguard and her boyfriend. I couldn't see Meg. But I thought she must be playing in the shallow water—both the shallow and deep ends of the pool were out of my sight.

"Cynthia!" I had to call twice before she knew where my voice was coming from. "Cynthia! Where's Meg?"

It always seems to me, when I recall this scene, that Cynthia turns very gracefully toward me, then turns all around in the water—making me think of a ballerina on point—and spreads her arms in a gesture of the stage. "Dis-ap-peared!"

Cynthia was naturally graceful, and she did take dancing lessons, so these movements may have been as I have described. She did say "Disappeared" after looking all around the pool, but the strangely artificial style of speech and gesture, the lack of urgency is more likely my invention. The fear I felt instantly when I couldn't see Meg—even while I was telling myself she must be in the shallower water—must have made Cynthia's movements seem unbearably slow and inappropriate to me, and the tone in which she could say "Disappeared" before the implications struck her (or was she covering, at once, some ever-ready guilt?) was heard by me as quite exquisitely, monstrously self-possessed.

I cried out for Andrew, and the lifeguard came into view. She was pointing toward the deep end of the pool, saying, "What's that?"

There, just within my view, a cluster of pink ruffles appeared, a bouquet, beneath the surface of the water. Why would a lifeguard stop and point, why would she ask what that was, why didn't she just dive into the water and swim to it? She didn't swim; she ran all the way around the edge of the pool. But by that time Andrew was over the fence. So many things seemed not quite plausible—Cynthia's behaviour, then the lifeguard's—and now I had the impression that Andrew jumped with one bound over this fence, which seemed about seven feet high. He must have climbed it very quickly, getting a grip on the wire.

I could not jump or climb it, so I ran to the entrance, where there was a sort of lattice gate, locked. It was not very high, and I did pull myself over it. I ran through the cement corridors, through the disinfectant pool for your feet, and came out on the edge of the pool.

The drama was over.

Andrew had got to Meg first, and had pulled her out of the water. He just had to reach over and grab her, because she was swimming somehow, with her head underwater—she was moving toward the edge of the pool. He was carrying her now, and the lifeguard was trotting along behind. Cynthia had climbed out of the water and was running to meet them. The only person aloof from the situation was the boyfriend, who had stayed on the bench at the shallow end, drinking a milkshake. He smiled at me, and I thought that unfeeling of him, even though the danger was past. He may have meant it kindly. I noticed that he had not turned the radio off, just down.

Meg had not swallowed any water. She hadn't even scared herself. Her hair was plastered to her head and her eyes were wide open, golden with amazement.

"I was getting the comb," she said. "I didn't know it was deep."

Andrew said, "She was swimming! She was swimming by herself. I saw her bathing suit in the water and then I saw her swimming."

"She nearly drowned," Cynthia said. "Didn't she? Meg nearly drowned."

"I don't know how it could have happened," said the lifeguard. "One moment she was there, and the next she wasn't."

What had happened was that Meg had climbed out of the water at the shallow end and run along the edge of the pool toward the deep end. She saw a comb that somebody had dropped lying on the bottom. She crouched down and reached in to pick it up, quite deceived about the depth of the water. She went over the edge and slipped into the pool, making such a light splash that nobody heard—not the lifeguard, who was kissing her boyfriend, or Cynthia, who was watching them. That must have been the moment under the trees when I thought, Where are the children? It must have been the same moment. At that moment, Meg was slipping, surprised, into the treacherously clear blue water.

"It's okay," I said to the lifeguard, who was nearly crying. "She can move pretty fast." (Though that wasn't what we usually said about Meg at all. We said she thought everything over and took her time.)

"You swam, Meg," said Cynthia, in a congratulatory way. (She told us about the kissing later.)

"I didn't know it was deep," Meg said. "I didn't drown."

○ ○ ○

We had lunch at a take-out place, eating hamburgers and fries at a picnic table not far from the highway. In my excitement, I forgot to get Meg a plain hamburger, and had to scrape off the relish and mustard with plastic spoons, then wipe the meat with a paper napkin, before she would eat it. I took advantage of the trash can there to clean out the car. Then we resumed driving east, with the car windows open in front. Cynthia and Meg fell asleep in the back seat.

Andrew and I talked quietly about what had happened. Suppose I hadn't had the impulse just at that moment to check on the children? Suppose we had gone uptown to get drinks, as we had thought of doing? How had Andrew got over the fence? Did he jump or climb? (He couldn't remember.) How had he reached Meg so quickly? And think of the lifeguard not watching. And Cynthia, taken up with the kissing. Not seeing anything else. Not seeing Meg drop over the edge.

Disappeared.

But she swam. She held her breath and came up swimming.

What a chain of lucky links.

That was all we spoke about—luck. But I was compelled to picture the opposite. At this moment, we could have been filling out forms. Meg removed from us, Meg's body being prepared for shipment. To Vancouver—where we had never noticed such a thing as a graveyard—or to Ontario? The scribbled drawings she had made this morning would still be in the back seat of the car. How could this be borne all at once, how did people bear it? The plump, sweet shoulders and hands and feet, the fine brown hair, the rather satisfied, secretive expression—all exactly the same as when she had been alive. The most ordinary tragedy. A child drowned in a swimming pool at noon on a sunny day. Things tidied up quickly. The pool opens as usual at two o'clock. The lifeguard is a bit shaken up and gets the afternoon off. She drives away with her boyfriend in the Roto-Rooter truck. The body sealed away in some kind of shipping coffin. Sedatives, phone calls, arrangements. Such a sudden vacancy, a blind sinking and shifting. Waking up groggy from the pills, thinking for a moment it wasn't true. Thinking if only we hadn't stopped, if only we hadn't taken this route, if only they hadn't let us use the pool. Probably no one would ever have known about the comb.

There's something trashy about this kind of imagining, isn't there? Something shameful. Laying your finger on the wire to get the safe shock, feeling a bit of what it's like, then pulling back. I believed that Andrew was more scrupulous than I about such things, and that at this moment he was really trying to think about something else.

When I stood apart from my parents at Steve Gauley's funeral and watched them, and had this new, unpleasant feeling about them, I thought that I was understanding something about them for the first time. It was a deadly serious thing. I was understanding that they were implicated. Their big, stiff, dressed-up bodies did not stand between me and sudden death, or any kind of death. They gave consent. So it seemed. They gave consent to the death of children and to my death not by anything they said or thought but by the very fact that they had made children—they had made me. They had made me, and for that reason my death—however grieved they were, however they carried on—would seem to them anything but impossible or unnatural. This was a fact, and even then I knew they were not to blame.

But I did blame them. I charged them with effrontery, hypocrisy. On Steve Gauley's behalf, and on behalf of all children, who knew that by rights they should have sprung up free, to live a new, superior kind of life, not to be caught in the snares of vanquished grown-ups, with their sex and funerals.

Steve Gauley drowned, people said, because he was next thing to an orphan and was let run free. If he had been warned enough and given chores to do and kept in check, he wouldn't have fallen from an untrustworthy tree branch into a spring pond, a full gravel pit near the river—he wouldn't have drowned. He was neglected, he was free, so he drowned. And his father took it as an accident, such as might happen to a dog. He didn't have a good suit for the funeral, and he didn't bow his head for the prayers. But he was the only grown-up that I let off the hook. He was the only one I didn't see giving consent. He couldn't prevent anything, but he wasn't implicated in anything, either—not like the others, saying the Lord's Prayer in their unnaturally weighted voices, oozing religion and dishonor.

At Glendive, not far from the North Dakota border, we had a choice—either to continue on the interstate or head north-east, toward Williston, taking Route 16, then some secondary roads that would get us back to Highway 2.

We agreed that the interstate would be faster, and that it was important to us not to spend too much time—that is, money—on the road. Nevertheless we decided to cut back to Highway 2.

"I just like the idea of it better," I said.

Andrew said, "That's because it's what we planned to do in the beginning."

"We missed seeing Kalispell and Havre. And Wolf Point. I like the name."

"We'll see them on the way back."

Andrew's saying "on the way back" was a surprising pleasure to me. Of course, I had believed that we would be coming back, with our car and our lives and our family intact, having covered all that distance, having dealt somehow with those loyalties and problems, held ourselves up for inspection in such a foolhardy way. But it was a relief to hear him say it.

"What I can't get over," said Andrew, "is how you got the signal. It's got to be some kind of extra sense that mothers have."

Partly I wanted to believe that, to bask in my extra sense. Partly I wanted to warn him—to warn everybody—never to count on it.

"What I can't understand," I said, "is how you got over the fence."

"Neither can I."

So we went on, with the two in the back seat trusting us, because of no choice, and we ourselves trusting to be forgiven, in time, for everything that had first to be seen and condemned by those children: whatever was flippant, arbitrary, careless, callous—all our natural, and particular, mistakes.

—1986

DONALD BARTHELME

Whether in tribute or accusation, the various epithets that have been applied to Donald Barthelme—absurdist, minimalist, metafictionist, surrealist, fabulist, antinovelist, and innovationist—reveal nothing so clearly as the difficulty of describing his work, much of which defies interpretation even as it cries out for it. Given his faith in fragments (which he called "the only form I trust"), Barthelme was most at ease with short fiction; but many of his stories, which routinely dispense with conventions of plot, character, dialogue, grammar, and any pretense to realism, can scarcely be called stories at all. In their unlikely juxtapositions, compelling incongruities, and irreducible strangeness, the finest of his "double-minded" imaginings are more like wonderments than stories, and the more to be wondered at for their characteristically deadpan presentation.

Barthelme was born in Philadelphia, where his father, then a studying architect, had met his mother, an English major, at the University of Pennsylvania. Shortly thereafter the family moved to Houston, where Barthelme's father established himself in a successful practice, eventually going on to teach at the University of Houston. Barthelme grew up in the company of the artists and academics who his parents frequently received as guests, and as a boy he spent long hours reading widely in the family library. His literary inclinations declared themselves at an early age, when he began writing and publishing precocious imitations of modernists such as Eliot and Joyce in his high-school newspaper, of which he also served as editor.

Before dropping out after his junior year at the University of Houston, Barthelme continued to nourish his fledgling interest in letters by contributing various pieces of fiction and nonfiction to the student paper. In the years that followed, he worked as a journalist at the *Houston Post,* then briefly with the army in Korea and Japan, before accepting a position in public relations with the University of Houston as an editor and speechwriter. His observation of incompetent military bureaucracy and the scholarly bombast and pretentious absurdities of academia provided him with much raw material, which he reworked into many of the adventurously experimental, seriocomic stories that he began publishing in *The New Yorker* in the 1960s.

Before he came to be regarded as the American heir of Kafka, Borges, and Beckett, Barthelme's stories were often met with puzzlement and even hostility. His reputation grew, however, with the appearance of collections such as *Come Back, Dr Caligari* (1964), *Unspeakable Practices, Unnatural Acts* (1968), *City Life* (1971), and *Sadness* (1972), which exemplify the postmodern aesthetic in their collages of advertising copy, newspaper headlines, book-jacket blurbs, jargon, nonsense, cliché—in short, the verbal detritus of modern mass culture that for Barthelme was like a sprawling trash heap, a chaotic, nearly incoherent "universe of discourse."

Barthelme's stories have lost none of their power to amuse, discompose, or move the reader unexpectedly. A laconic, melancholy wit is among the most distinctive features of his work, in which absurdity, alienation, loneliness, and despair are often leavened by an antic sense of the ludicrous. These qualities are evident in "The Palace at 4 A.M.," a story named for a surrealist Alberto Giacometti sculpture depicting the artist's pained sense of the fragility of an enchanting but lost love. Consisting of several fragmentary passages from the autobiography of a forlorn king who longs to be reunited with an estranged, supernatural lover, "The Palace" is a fantasy, comical and poignant by turns.

The Palace at 4 A.M.[1]

DONALD BARTHELME

My father's kingdom was and is, all authorities agree, large. To walk border to border east-west, the traveler must budget no less than seventeen days. Its name is Ho, the Confucian term for harmony. Confucianism was an interest of the first ruler (a strange taste in our part of the world), and when he'd cleared his expanse of field and forest of his enemies, two centuries ago, he indulged himself in an *hommage* to the great Chinese thinker, much to the merriment of some of our staider neighbors, whose domains were proper Luftlunds and Dolphinlunds. We have an economy based upon truffles, in which our forests are spectacularly rich, and electricity, which we were exporting when other countries still read by kerosene lamp. Our army

1 Name of a well-known surrealist sculpture by Alberto Giacometti (1901–66).

> is the best in the region, every man a colonel—the subtle secret of my father's rule, if the truth be known. In this land every priest is a bishop, every ambulance-chaser a robed justice, every peasant a corporation and every street-corner shouter Kant[2] himself. My father's genius was to promote his subjects, male and female, across the board, ceaselessly; the people of Ho warm themselves forever in the sun of Achievement. I was the only man in the kingdom who thought himself a donkey.
>
> —from the *Autobiography*

I AM writing to you, Hannahbella, from a distant country. I daresay you remember it well. The King encloses the opening pages of his autobiography. He is most curious as to what your response to them will be. He has labored mightily over their composition, working without food, without sleep, for many days and nights.

The King has not been, in these months, in the best of spirits. He has read your article and declares himself to be very much impressed by it. He begs you, prior to publication in this country, to do him the great favor of changing the phrase "two disinterested and impartial arbiters" on page thirty-one to "malign elements under the ideological sway of still more malign elements." Otherwise, he is delighted. He asks me to tell you that your touch is as adroit as ever.

Early in the autobiography (as you see) we encounter the words: "My mother the Queen made a mirror pie, a splendid thing the size of a poker table ..." The King wishes to know if poker tables are in use in faraway lands, and whether the reader in such places would comprehend the dimensions of the pie. He continues: "... in which reflections from the kitchen chandelier exploded when the crew rolled it from the oven. We were kneeling side-by-side, peering into the depths of a new-made mirror pie, when my mother said to me, or rather her celestial image said to my dark, heavy-haired one, 'Get out. I cannot bear to look upon your donkey face again.'"

The King wishes to know, Hannahbella, whether this passage seems to you tainted by self-pity, or is, rather, suitably dispassionate.

He walks up and down the small room next to his bedchamber, singing your praises. The decree having to do with your banishment will be rescinded, he says, the moment you agree to change the phrase "two disinterested and impartial arbiters" to "malign elements," etc. This I urge you to do with all speed.

The King has not been at his best. Peace, he says, is an unnatural condition. The country is prosperous, yes, and he understands that the people value peace,

---

2 Immanuel Kant (1724–1804), German philosopher.

that they prefer to spin out their destinies in placid, undisturbed fashion. But *his* destiny, he says, is to alter the map of the world. He is considering several new wars, small ones, he says, small but interesting, complex, dicey, even. He would very much like to consult with you about them. He asks you to change, on page forty-four of your article, the phrase "egregious usurpations" to "symbols of benign transformation." Please initial the change on the proofs, so that historians will not accuse us of bowdlerization.[3]

Your attention is called to the passage in the pages I send which runs as follows: "I walked out of the castle at dusk, not even the joy of a new sunrise to console me, my shaving kit with its dozen razors (although I shaved a dozen times a day, the head was still a donkey's) banging against the Walther .22 in my rucksack. After a time I was suddenly quite tired. I lay down under a hedge by the side of the road. One of the bushes above me had a shred of black cloth tied to it, a sign, in our country, that the place was haunted (but my head's enough to frighten any ghost)." Do you remember that shred of black cloth, Hannahbella? "I ate a slice of my mother's spinach pie and considered my situation. My princeliness would win me an evening, perhaps a fortnight, at this or that noble's castle in the vicinity, but my experience of visiting had taught me that neither royal blood nor novelty of aspect prevailed for long against a host's natural preference for folk with heads much like his own. Should I en-zoo myself? Volunteer for a traveling circus? Attempt the stage? The question was most vexing.

"I had not wiped the last crumbs of the spinach pie from my whiskers when something lay down beside me, under the hedge.

"'What's this?' I said.

"'Soft,' said the new arrival, 'don't be afraid, I am a bogle,[4] let me abide here for the night, your back is warm and that's a mercy.'

"'What's a bogle?' I asked, immediately fetched, for the creature was small, not at all frightening to look upon and clad in female flesh, something I do not hold in low esteem.

"'A bogle,' said the tiny one, with precision, 'is not a black dog.'

"Well, I thought, now I know.

"'A bogle,' she continued, 'is not a boggart.'

"'Delighted to hear it,' I said.

"'Don't you ever *shave*?' she asked. 'And why have you that huge hideous head on you, that could be mistaken for the head of an ass, could I see better so as to think better?'

---

3 Editing an original writing or historical account to remove material perceived as offensive; after Thomas Bowdler (1754–1825) for his expurgated edition of Shakespeare's works.

4 Ghost or goblin (term from Scottish and Northern English folklore).

"'You may lie elsewhere,' I said, 'if my face discountenances you.'

"'I am fatigued,' she said, 'go to sleep, we'll discuss it in the morning, move a bit so that your back fits better with my front, it will be cold, later, and this place is cursed, so they say, and I hear that the Prince has been driven from the palace, God knows what that's all about but it promises no good for us plain folk, police, probably, running all over the fens[5] with their identity checks and making you blow up their great balloons with your breath—'

"She was confusing, I thought, several issues, but my God! she was warm and shapely. Yet I deemed her a strange piece of goods, and made the mistake of saying so.

"'Sir,' she answered, 'I would not venture upon what's strange and what's not strange, if I were you,' and went on to say that if I did not abstain from further impertinence she would commit sewerpipe.[6] She dropped off to sleep then, and I lay back upon the ground. Not a child, I could tell, rather a tiny woman. A bogle."

The King wishes you to know, Hannahbella, that he finds this passage singularly moving and that he cannot read it without being forced to take snuff, violently. Similarly the next:

"What, precisely, is a donkey? As you may imagine, I have researched the question. My *Larousse*[7] was most delicate, as if the editors thought the matter blushful, but yielded two observations of interest: that donkeys came originally from Africa, and that they, or we, are 'the result of much crossing.' This urges that the parties to the birth must be ill-matched, and in the case of my royal parents, 'twas thunderously true. The din of their calamitous conversations reached every quarter of the palace, at every season of the year. My mother named me Duncan (var. of Dunkey, clearly) and went into spasms of shrinking whenever, youthfully, I'd offer a cheek for a kiss. My father, in contrast, could sometimes bring himself to scratch my head between the long, weedlike ears, but only, I suspect, by means of a mental shift, as if he were addressing one of his hunting dogs, the which, incidentally, remained firmly ambivalent about me even after long acquaintance.

"I explained a part of this to Hannahbella, for that was the bogle's name, suppressing chiefly the fact that I was a prince. She in turn gave the following account of herself. She was indeed a bogle, a semi-spirit generally thought to be of bad character. This was a libel, she said, as her own sterling qualities would quickly persuade me. She was, she said, of the utmost perfection in the female

5 Marshes.

6 I.e., commit suicide.

7 *La Petit Larousse*, a French-language encyclopedia.

line, and there was not a woman within the borders of the kingdom so beautiful as herself, she'd been told it a thousand times. It was true, she went on, that she was not of a standard size, could in fact be called small, if not minuscule, but those who objected to this were louts and fools and might usefully be stewed in lead, for the entertainment of the countryside. In the matter of rank and precedence, the meanest bogle outweighed the greatest king, although the kings of this earth, she conceded, would never acknowledge this but in their dotty solipsism[8] conducted themselves as if bogles did not even exist. And would I like to see her all unclothed so that I might glean some rude idea as to the true nature of the sublime?

"Well, I wouldn't have minded a bit. She was wonderfully crafted, that was evident, and held in addition the fascination surrounding any perfect miniature. But I said, 'No, thank you. Perhaps another day, it's a bit chill this morning.'

"'Just the breasts then,' she said, 'they're wondrous pretty,' and before I could protest further she'd whipped off her mannikin's tiny shirt. I buttoned her up again meanwhile bestowing buckets of extravagant praise. 'Yes,' she said in agreement, 'that's how I am all over, wonderful.'"

The King cannot reread this section, Hannahbella, without being reduced to tears. The world is a wilderness, he says, civilization a folly we entertain in concert with others. He himself, at his age, is beyond surprise, yet yearns for it. He longs for the conversations he formerly had with you, in the deepest hours of the night, he in his plain ermine robe, you simply dressed as always in a small scarlet cassock,[9] most becoming, a modest supper of chicken, fruit and wine on the sideboard, only the pair of you awake in the whole palace, at four o'clock in the morning. The tax evasion case against you has been dropped. It was, he says, a hasty and ill-considered undertaking, even spiteful. He is sorry.

The King wonders whether the following paragraphs from his autobiography accord with your own recollections: "She then began, as we walked down the road together (an owl pretending to be absent standing on a tree limb to our left, a little stream snapping and growling to our right), explaining to me that my father's administration of the realm left much to be desired, from the bogle point of view, particularly his mad insistence on filling the forests with heavy-footed truffle hounds. Standing, she came to just a hand above my waist; her hair was brown, with bits of gold in it; her quite womanly hips were encased in rust-colored trousers. 'Duncan,' she said, stabbing me in the calf with her sharp nails, 'do you know what that man has done? Nothing else but ruin,

8 Theory that one's own consciousness or mind is the only thing certain to exist.

9 Full-length robe worn by various church officials, usually during religious services and ceremonies.

absolutely ruin, the whole of the Gatter Fen with a great roaring electric plant that makes a thing that who in the world could have a use for I don't know. I think they're called volts. Two square miles of first-class fen paved over. We bogles are being squeezed to our knees.' I had a sudden urge to kiss her, she looked so angry, but did nothing, my history in this regard being, as I have said, infelicitous.

"'Duncan, *you're not listening!*' Hannahbella was naming the chief interesting things about bogles, which included the fact that in the main they had nothing to do with humans, or nonsemispirits; that although she might seem small to me she was tall, for a bogle, queenly, in fact; that there was a type of blood seas superior to royal blood, and that it was bogle blood; that bogles had no magical powers whatsoever, despite what was said of them; that bogles were the very best lovers in the whole world, no matter what class of thing, animal, vegetable, or insect, might be under discussion; that it was not true that bogles knocked bowls of mush from the tables of the deserving poor and caused farmers' cows to become pregnant with big fishes, out of pure mischief; that female bogles were the most satisfactory sexual partners of any kind of thing that could ever be imagined and were especially keen for large overgrown things with ass's ears, for example; and that there was a something in the road ahead of us to which it might, perhaps, be prudent to pay heed.

"She was right. One hundred yards ahead of us, planted squarely athwart the road, was an army."

The King, Hannahbella, regrets having said of you, in the journal *Vu*, that you have two brains and no heart. He had thought he was talking not-for-attribution, but as you know, all reporters are scoundrels and not to be trusted. He asks you to note that *Vu* has suspended publication and to recall that it was never read by anyone but serving maids and the most insignificant members of the minor clergy. He is prepared to give you a medal, if you return, any medal you like—you will remember that our medals are the most gorgeous going. On page seventy-five of your article, he requires you, most humbly, to change "monstrous over-reaching fueled by an insatiable if still childish ego" to any kinder construction of your choosing.

The King's autobiography, in chapters already written but which I do not enclose, goes on to recount how you and he together, by means of a clever stratagem of your devising, vanquished the army barring your path on that day long, long ago; how the two of you journeyed together for many weeks and found that your souls were, in essence, the same soul; the shrewd means you employed to place him in power, against the armed opposition of the Party of the Lily, on the death of his father; and the many subsequent campaigns which you endured together, mounted on a single horse, your armor banging against his armor. The

King's autobiography, Hannahbella, will run to many volumes, but he cannot bring himself to write the end of the story without you.

The King feels that your falling-out, over the matter of the refugees from Brise, was the result of a miscalculation on his part. He could not have known, he says, that they had bogle blood (although he admits that the fact of their small stature should have told him something). Exchanging the refugees from Brise for the twenty-three Bishops of Ho captured during the affair was, he says in hindsight, a serious error; more bishops can always be created. He makes the point that you did not tell him that the refugees from Brise had bogle blood but instead expected him to know it. Your outrage was, he thinks, a pretext. He at once forgives you and begs your forgiveness. The Chair of Military Philosophy at the university is yours, if you want it. You loved him, he says, he is convinced of it, he still cannot believe it, he exists in a condition of doubt. You are both old; you are both forty. The palace at four A.M. is silent. Come back, Hannahbella, and speak to him.

—1983

RAYMOND CARVER

The son of a hard-drinking, sawmill-worker father, Raymond Carver was born in Clatskanie, Oregon, in 1938, but grew up in Yakima, Washington, after his family moved there in 1941. After graduating from high school, Carver joined his father as a laborer at the sawmill, married Maryann Burk at the age of 19, and had two children in less than two years. Debt-ridden, Carver and his family moved in 1958 to California, where he enrolled part-time at Chico State College and received encouragement from writer John Gardner. To support himself and his family financially, Carver worked at what he called "crap jobs," including gas station attendant and hospital janitor, while his wife worked as a waitress and door-to-door salesperson. In 1960, he transferred to Humboldt State College, where he graduated with a BA in 1963; during this time he began to publish stories and poems in small periodicals. He also began to struggle with frequent moves, a lack of money, and alcoholism.

In 1970, Carver was fired from his editing job at Science Research Associates, but he won the National Endowment for the Arts Discovery Award for Poetry: this enabled him to complete his first short story collection, *Will You Please Be Quiet, Please* (published in 1976 and a National Book Award nominee), and the poetry book, *Winter Insomnia* (1970). His growing success as a writer was accompanied by growing alcoholism. In the early 1970s he worked in a number of teaching jobs, but his alcoholism made working difficult, and he and his wife separated in 1977.

Although he is best known as a short story writer, Carver's first two book-length publications were poetry collections. His work has appeared in many important anthologies, including *Best American Short Stories* and *Best Little Magazine Fiction*. Carver quit drinking in 1977 and the last decade of his life saw a variety of successes, including nominations for *Cathedral* for the Pulitzer Prize and the National Book Critics Circle Award. In 1983, he received the prestigious Mildred and Harold Strauss Living Award and was awarded a Doctorate of Letters from Hartford University. In 1988 he married long-time partner and poet Tess Gallagher and was elected to the

American Academy and Institute of Arts and Letters. He died of lung cancer in the same year.

Together with Alice Munro, Raymond Carver is often credited with rejuvenating the genre of the short story in the last quarter of the twentieth century. Some literary scholars have named him as second only to Ernest Hemingway in terms of his stylistic influence on the contemporary short story. Carver scholar Kirk Nesset has described the characters that populate his world:

> From the earliest story to the last, Carver's characters are unhappily estranged, out of work, disillusioned by meaningless jobs and meaningless marriages; they suffer in various degrees from alcoholism as well as bad luck and bad timing, battered by a world which typically leaves them inert and speechless in the wake of longings and fears they cannot begin to identify.

The main character in "Cathedral" (published in the collection *Cathedral*, in 1983) starts out very much in this mold. But in this case something positive begins to happen; the character Robert's physical blindness allows the insecure main character to "see" past his own prejudices.

Cathedral

RAYMOND CARVER

THIS BLIND man, an old friend of my wife's, he was on his way to spend the night. His wife had died. So he was visiting the dead wife's relatives in Connecticut. He called my wife from his in-laws'. Arrangements were made. He would come by train, a five-hour trip, and my wife would meet him at the station. She hadn't seen him since she worked for him one summer in Seattle ten years ago. But she and the blind man had kept in touch. They made tapes and mailed them back and forth. I wasn't enthusiastic about his visit. He was no one I knew. And his being blind bothered me. My idea of blindness came from the movies. In the movies, the blind moved slowly and never laughed. Sometimes they were led by seeing-eye dogs. A blind man in my house was not something I looked forward to.

That summer in Seattle she had needed a job. She didn't have any money. The man she was going to marry at the end of the summer was in officers' training school. He didn't have any money, either. But she was in love with the guy, and he was in love with her, etc. She'd seen something in the paper: HELP

WANTED—*Reading to Blind Man*, and a telephone number. She phoned and went over, was hired on the spot. She'd worked with this blind man all summer. She read stuff to him, case studies, reports, that sort of thing. She helped him organize his little office in the county social-service department. They'd become good friends, my wife and the blind man. How do I know these things? She told me. And she told me something else. On her last day in the office, the blind man asked if he could touch her face. She agreed to this. She told me he touched his fingers to every part of her face, her nose—even her neck! She never forgot it. She even tried to write a poem about it. She was always trying to write a poem. She wrote a poem or two every year, usually after something really important had happened to her.

When we first started going out together, she showed me the poem. In the poem, she recalled his fingers and the way they had moved around over her face. In the poem, she talked about what she had felt at the time, about what went through her mind when the blind man touched her nose and lips. I can remember I didn't think much of the poem. Of course, I didn't tell her that. Maybe I just don't understand poetry. I admit it's not the first thing I reach for when I pick up something to read.

Anyway, this man who'd first enjoyed her favors, the officer-to-be, he'd been her childhood sweetheart. So okay. I'm saying that at the end of the summer she let the blind man run his hands over her face, said goodbye to him, married her childhood etc., who was now a commissioned officer, and she moved away from Seattle. But they'd kept in touch, she and the blind man. She made the first contact after a year or so. She called him up one night from an Air Force base in Alabama. She wanted to talk. They talked. He asked her to send him a tape and tell him about her life. She did this. She sent the tape. On the tape, she told the blind man about her husband and about their life together in the military. She told the blind man she loved her husband but she didn't like it where they lived and she didn't like it that he was a part of the military-industrial thing. She told the blind man she'd written a poem about what it was like to be an Air Force officer's wife. The poem wasn't finished yet. She was still writing it. The blind man made a tape. He sent her the tape. She made a tape. This went on for years. My wife's officer was posted to one base and then another. She sent tapes from Moody AFB, McGuire, McConnell, and finally Travis, near Sacramento, where one night she got to feeling lonely and cut off from people she kept losing in that moving-around life. She got to feeling she couldn't go it another step. She went in and swallowed all the pills and capsules in the medicine chest and washed them down with a bottle of gin. Then she got into a hot bath and passed out.

But instead of dying, she got sick. She threw up. Her officer—why should he have a name? he was the childhood sweetheart, and what more does he want?—came home from somewhere, found her, and called the ambulance. In time, she put it all on a tape and sent the tape to the blind man. Over the years, she put all kinds of stuff on tapes and sent the tapes off lickety-split. Next to writing a poem every year, I think it was her chief means of recreation. On one tape, she told the blind man she'd decided to live away from her officer for a time. On another tape, she told him about her divorce. She and I began going out, and of course she told her blind man about it. She told him everything, or so it seemed to me. Once she asked me if I'd like to hear the latest tape from the blind man. This was a year ago. I was on the tape, she said. So I said okay, I'd listen to it. I got us drinks and we settled down in the living room. We made ready to listen. First she inserted the tape into the player and adjusted a couple of dials. Then she pushed a lever. The tape squeaked and someone began to talk in this loud voice. She lowered the volume. After a few minutes of harmless chitchat, I heard my own name in the mouth of this stranger, this blind man I didn't even know! And then this: "From all you've said about him, I can only conclude—" But we were interrupted, a knock at the door, something, and we didn't ever get back to the tape. Maybe it was just as well. I'd heard all I wanted to.

Now this same blind man was coming to sleep in my house.

"Maybe I could take him bowling," I said to my wife. She was at the draining board doing scalloped potatoes. She put down the knife she was using and turned around.

"If you love me," she said, "you can do this for me. If you don't love me, okay. But if you had a friend, any friend, and the friend came to visit, I'd make him feel comfortable." She wiped her hands with the dish towel.

"I don't have any blind friends," I said.

"You don't have *any* friends," she said. "Period. Besides," she said, "goddamn it, his wife's just died! Don't you understand that? The man's lost his wife!"

I didn't answer. She'd told me a little about the blind man's wife. Her name was Beulah. Beulah! That's a name for a colored woman.

"Was his wife a Negro?" I asked.

"Are you crazy?" my wife said. "Have you just flipped or something?" She picked up a potato. I saw it hit the floor, then roll under the stove. "What's wrong with you?" she said. "Are you drunk?"

"I'm just asking," I said.

Right then my wife filled me in with more detail than I cared to know. I made a drink and sat at the kitchen table to listen. Pieces of the story began to fall into place.

Beulah had gone to work for the blind man the summer after my wife had stopped working for him. Pretty soon Beulah and the blind man had themselves a church wedding. It was a little wedding—who'd want to go to such a wedding in the first place?—just the two of them, plus the minister and the minister's wife. But it was a church wedding just the same. It was what Beulah had wanted, he'd said. But even then Beulah must have been carrying the cancer in her glands. After they had been inseparable for eight years—my wife's word, *inseparable*—Beulah's health went into a rapid decline. She died in a Seattle hospital room, the blind man sitting beside the bed and holding on to her hand. They'd married, lived and worked together, slept together—had sex, sure—and then the blind man had to bury her. All this without his having ever seen what the goddamned woman looked like. It was beyond my understanding. Hearing this, I felt sorry for the blind man for a little bit. And then I found myself thinking what a pitiful life this woman must have led. Imagine a woman who could never see herself as she was seen in the eyes of her loved one. A woman who could go on day after day and never receive the smallest compliment from her beloved. A woman whose husband could never read the expression on her face, be it misery or something better. Someone who could wear makeup or not—what difference to him? She could, if she wanted, wear green eye-shadow around one eye, a straight pin in her nostril, yellow slacks and purple shoes, no matter. And then to slip off into death, the blind man's hand on her hand, his blind eyes streaming tears—I'm imagining now—her last thought maybe this: that he never even knew what she looked like, and she on an express to the grave. Robert was left with a small insurance policy and half of a twenty-peso Mexican coin. The other half of the coin went into the box with her. Pathetic.

So when the time rolled around, my wife went to the depot to pick him up. With nothing to do but wait—sure, I blamed him for that—I was having a drink and watching the TV when I heard the car pull into the drive. I got up from the sofa with my drink and went to the window to have a look.

I saw my wife laughing as she parked the car. I saw her get out of the car and shut the door. She was still wearing a smile. Just amazing. She went around to the other side to where the blind man was already starting to get out. This blind man, feature this, he was wearing a full beard! A beard on a blind man! Too much, I say. The blind man reached into the back seat and dragged out a suitcase. My wife took his arm, shut the car door, and, talking all the way, moved him down the drive and then up the steps to the front porch. I turned off the TV. I finished my drink, rinsed the glass, dried my hands. Then I went to the door.

My wife said, "I want you to meet Robert. Robert, this is my husband. I've told you all about him." She was beaming. She had this blind man by his coat sleeve.

The blind man let go of his suitcase and up came his hand.

I took it. He squeezed hard, held my hand, and then he let it go.

"I feel like we've already met," he boomed.

"Likewise," I said. I didn't know what else to say. Then I said, "Welcome. I've heard a lot about you." We began to move then, a little group, from the porch into the living room, my wife guiding him by the arm. The blind man was carrying his suitcase in his other hand. My wife said things like, "To your left here, Robert. That's right. Now watch it, there's a chair. That's it. Sit down right here. This is the sofa. We just bought this sofa two weeks ago."

I started to say something about the old sofa. I'd liked that old sofa. But I didn't say anything. Then I wanted to say something else, small-talk, about the scenic ride along the Hudson. How going *to* New York, you should sit on the right-hand side of the train, and coming *from* New York, the left-hand side.

"Did you have a good train ride?" I said. "Which side of the train did you sit on, by the way?"

"What a question, which side!" my wife said. "What's it matter which side?" she said.

"I just asked," I said.

"Right side," the blind man said. "I hadn't been on a train in nearly forty years. Not since I was a kid. With my folks. That's been a long time. I'd nearly forgotten the sensation. I have winter in my beard now," he said. "So I've been told, anyway. Do I look distinguished, my dear?" the blind man said to my wife.

"You look distinguished, Robert," she said. "Robert," she said. "Robert, it's just so good to see you."

My wife finally took her eyes off the blind man and looked at me. I had the feeling she didn't like what she saw. I shrugged.

I've never met, or personally known, anyone who was blind. This blind man was late forties, a heavy-set, balding man with stooped shoulders, as if he carried a great weight there. He wore brown slacks, brown shoes, a light-brown shirt, a tie, a sports coat. Spiffy. He also had this full beard. But he didn't use a cane and he didn't wear dark glasses. I'd always thought dark glasses were a must for the blind. Fact was, I wished he had a pair. At first glance, his eyes looked like anyone else's eyes. But if you looked close, there was something different about them. Too much white in the iris, for one thing, and the pupils seemed to move around in the sockets without his knowing it or being able to stop it. Creepy. As I stared at his face, I saw the left pupil turn in toward his nose while the other made an effort to keep in one place. But it was only an effort, for that eye was on the roam without his knowing it or wanting it to be.

I said, "Let me get you a drink. What's your pleasure? We have a little of everything. It's one of our pastimes."

"Bub, I'm a Scotch man myself," he said fast enough in this big voice.

"Right," I said. Bub! "Sure you are. I knew it."

He let his fingers touch his suitcase, which was sitting alongside the sofa. He was taking his bearings. I didn't blame him for that.

"I'll move that up to your room," my wife said.

"No, that's fine," the blind man said loudly. "It can go up when I go up."

"A little water with the Scotch?" I said.

"Very little," he said.

"I knew it," I said.

He said, "Just a tad. The Irish actor, Barry Fitzgerald? I'm like that fellow. When I drink water, Fitzgerald said, I drink water. When I drink whiskey, I drink whiskey." My wife laughed. The blind man brought his hand up under his beard. He lifted his beard slowly and let it drop.

I did the drinks, three big glasses of Scotch with a splash of water in each. Then we made ourselves comfortable and talked about Robert's travels. First the long flight from the West Coast to Connecticut, we covered that. Then from Connecticut up here by train. We had another drink concerning that leg of the trip.

I remembered having read somewhere that the blind didn't smoke because, as speculation had it, they couldn't see the smoke they exhaled. I thought I knew that much and that much only about blind people. But this blind man smoked his cigarette down to the nubbin and then lit another one. This blind man filled his ashtray and my wife emptied it.

When we sat down at the table for dinner, we had another drink. My wife heaped Robert's plate with cube steak, scalloped potatoes, green beans. I buttered him up two slices of bread. I said, "Here's bread and butter for you." I swallowed some of my drink. "Now let us pray," I said, and the blind man lowered his head. My wife looked at me, her mouth agape. "Pray the phone won't ring and the food doesn't get cold," I said.

We dug in. We ate everything there was to eat on the table. We ate like there was no tomorrow. We didn't talk. We ate. We scarfed. We grazed that table. We were into serious eating. The blind man had right away located his foods, he knew just where everything was on his plate. I watched with admiration as he used his knife and fork on the meat. He'd cut two pieces of meat, fork the meat into his mouth, and then go all out for the scalloped potatoes, the beans next, and then he'd tear off a hunk of buttered bread and eat that. He'd follow this up with a big drink of milk. It didn't seem to bother him to use his fingers once in a while, either.

We finished everything, including half a strawberry pie. For a few moments, we sat as if stunned. Sweat beaded on our faces. Finally, we got up from the table and left the dirty plates. We didn't look back. We took ourselves into the living room and sank into our places again. Robert and my wife sat on the sofa. I took the big chair. We had us two or three more drinks while they talked about the major things that had come to pass for them in the past ten years. For the most part, I just listened. Now and then I joined in. I didn't want him to think I'd left the room, and I didn't want her to think I was feeling left out. They talked of things that had happened to them—to them!—these past ten years. I waited in vain to hear my name on my wife's sweet lips: "And then my dear husband came into my life"—something like that. But I heard nothing of the sort. More talk of Robert. Robert had done a little of everything, it seemed, a regular blind jack-of-all-trades. But most recently he and his wife had had an Amway distributorship, from which, I gathered, they'd earned their living, such as it was. The blind man was also a ham radio operator. He talked in his loud voice about conversations he'd had with fellow operators in Guam, in the Philippines, in Alaska, and even in Tahiti. He said he'd have a lot of friends there if he ever wanted to go visit those places. From time to time, he'd turn his blind face toward me, put his hand under his beard, ask me something. How long had I been in my present position? (Three years.) Did I like my work? (I didn't.) Was I going to stay with it? (What were the options?) Finally, when I thought he was beginning to run down, I got up and turned on the TV.

My wife looked at me with irritation. She was heading toward a boil. Then she looked at the blind man and said, "Robert, do you have a TV?"

The blind man said, "My dear, I have two TVs. I have a color set and a black-and-white thing, an old relic. It's funny, but if I turn the TV on, and I'm always turning it on, I turn on the color set. It's funny, don't you think?"

I didn't know what to say to that. I had absolutely nothing to say to that. No opinion. So I watched the news program and tried to listen to what the announcer was saying.

"This is a color TV," the blind man said. "Don't ask me how, but I can tell."

"We traded up a while ago." I said.

The blind man had another taste of his drink. He lifted his beard, sniffed it, and let it fall. He leaned forward on the sofa. He positioned his ashtray on the coffee table, then put the lighter to his cigarette. He leaned back on the sofa and crossed his legs at the ankles.

My wife covered her mouth, and then she yawned. She stretched. She said, "I think I'll go upstairs and put on my robe. I think I'll change into something else. Robert, you make yourself comfortable," she said.

"I'm comfortable," the blind man said.

"I want you to feel comfortable in this house," she said.

"I am comfortable," the blind man said.

After she'd left the room, he and I listened to the weather report and then to the sports roundup. By that time, she'd been gone so long I didn't know if she was going to come back. I thought she might have gone to bed. I wished she'd come back downstairs. I didn't want to be left alone with a blind man. I asked him if he wanted to smoke some dope with me. I said I'd just rolled a number. I hadn't, but I planned to do so in about two shakes.

"I'll try some with you," he said.

"Damn right," I said. "That's the stuff."

I got our drinks and sat down on the sofa with him. Then I rolled us two fat numbers. I lit one and passed it. I brought it to his fingers. He took it and inhaled.

"Hold it as long as you can," I said. I could tell he didn't know the first thing.

My wife came back downstairs wearing her pink robe and her pink slippers.

"What do I smell?" she said.

"We thought we'd have us some cannabis," I said.

My wife gave me a savage look. Then she looked at the blind man and said, "Robert, I didn't know you smoked."

He said, "I do now, my dear. There's a first time for everything. But I don't feel anything yet."

"This stuff is pretty mellow," I said. "This stuff is mild. It's dope you can reason with," I said. "It doesn't mess you up."

"Not much it doesn't bub," he said, and laughed.

My wife sat on the sofa between the blind man and me. I passed her the number. She took it and toked and then passed it back to me. "Which way is this going?" she said. Then she said, "I shouldn't be smoking this. I can hardly keep my eyes open as it is. That dinner did me in. I shouldn't have eaten so much."

"It was the strawberry pie," the blind man said. "That's what did it," he said, and he laughed his big laugh. Then he shook his head.

"There's more strawberry pie," I said.

"Do you want some more, Robert?" my wife said.

"Maybe in a little while," he said.

We gave our attention to the TV. My wife yawned again. She said, "Your bed is made up when you feel like going to bed, Robert. I know you must have had a long day. When you're ready to go to bed, say so." She pulled his arm. "Robert?"

He came to and said, "I've had a real nice time. This beats tapes, doesn't it?"

I said, "Coming at you," and I put the number between his fingers. He inhaled, held the smoke, and then let it go. It was like he'd been doing it since he was nine years old.

"Thanks, bub," he said. "But I think this is all for me. I think I'm beginning to feel it," he said. He held the burning roach out for my wife.

"Same here," she said. "Ditto. Me, too." She took the roach and passed it to me. "I may just sit here for a while between you two guys with my eyes closed.

But don't let me bother you, okay? Either one of you. If it bothers you, say so. Otherwise, I may just sit here with my eyes closed until you're ready to go to bed," she said. "Your bed's made up, Robert, when you're ready. It's right next to our room at the top of the stairs. We'll show you up when you're ready. You wake me up now, you guys, if I fall asleep." She said that and then she closed her eyes and went to sleep.

The news program ended. I got up and changed the channel. I sat back down on the sofa. I wished my wife hadn't pooped out. Her head lay across the back of the sofa, her mouth open. She'd turned so that her robe had slipped away from her legs, exposing a juicy thigh. I reached to draw her robe back over her, and it was then that I glanced at the blind man. What the hell! I flipped the robe open again.

"You say when you want some strawberry pie," I said.

"I will," he said.

I said, "Are you tired? Do you want me to take you up to your bed? Are you ready to hit the hay?"

"Not yet," he said. "No, I'll stay up with you, bub. If that's all right. I'll stay up until you're ready to turn in. We haven't had a chance to talk. Know what I mean? I feel like me and her monopolized the evening." He lifted his beard and he let it fall. He picked up his cigarettes and lighter.

"That's all right," I said. Then I said, "I'm glad for the company."

And I guess I was. Every night I smoked dope and stayed up as long as I could before I fell asleep. My wife and I hardly ever went to bed at the same time. When I did go to sleep, I had these dreams. Sometimes I'd wake up from one of them, my heart going crazy.

Something about the church and the Middle Ages was on the TV. Not your run-of-the-mill TV fare. I wanted to watch something else. I turned to the other channels. But there was nothing on them, either. So I turned back to the first channel and apologized.

"Bub, it's all right," the blind man said. "It's fine with me. Whatever you want to watch is okay. I'm always learning something. Learning never ends. It won't hurt me to learn something tonight. I got ears," he said.

We didn't say anything for a time. He was leaning forward with his head turned at me, his right ear aimed in the direction of the set. Very disconcerting. Now and then his eyelids dropped and then they snapped open again. Now and then he put his fingers into his beard and tugged, like he was thinking about something he was hearing on the television.

On the screen, a group of men wearing cowls was being set upon and tormented by men dressed in skeleton costumes and men dressed as devils. The men dressed as devils wore devil masks, horns, and long tails. This pageant was part of a procession. The Englishman who was narrating the thing said it took place in Spain once a year. I tried to explain to the blind man what was happening.

"Skeletons," he said. "I know about skeletons," he said and he nodded.

The TV showed this one cathedral. Then there was a long, slow look at another one. Finally, the picture switched to the famous one in Paris, with its flying buttresses and its spires reaching up to the clouds. The camera pulled away to show the whole of the cathedral rising above the skyline.

There were times when the Englishman who was telling the thing would shut up, would simply let the camera move around over the cathedrals. Or else the camera would tour the countryside, men in fields walking behind oxen. I waited as long as I could. Then I felt I had to say something. I said, "They're showing the outside of this cathedral now. Gargoyles. Little statues carved to look like monsters. Now I guess they're in Italy. Yeah, they're in Italy. There's paintings on the walls of this one church."

"Are those fresco paintings, bub?" he asked, and he sipped from his drink.

I reached for my glass. But it was empty. I tried to remember what I could remember. "You're asking me are those frescoes?" I said. "That's a good question. I don't know."

The camera moved to a cathedral outside Lisbon. The differences in the Portuguese cathedral compared with the French and Italian were not that great. But they were there. Mostly the interior stuff. Then something occurred to me, and I said, "Something has occurred to me. Do you have any idea what a cathedral is? What they look like, that is? Do you follow me? If somebody says cathedral to you, do you have any notion what they're talking about? Do you know the difference between that and a Baptist church, say?"

He let the smoke dribble from his mouth. "I know they took hundreds of workers fifty or a hundred years to build," he said. "I just heard the man say that, of course. I know generations of the same families worked on a cathedral. I heard him say that, too. The men who began their life's work on them, they never lived to see the completion of their work. In that wise, bub, they're no different from the rest of us, right?" He laughed. Then his eyelids drooped again. His head nodded. He seemed to be snoozing. Maybe he was imagining himself in Portugal. The TV was showing another cathedral now. This one was in Germany. The Englishman's voice droned on. "Cathedrals," the blind man said. He sat up and rolled his head back and forth. "If you want the truth, bub, that's about all I know. What I just said. What I heard him say. But maybe you could describe one to me? I wish you'd do it. I'd like that. If you want to know, I really don't have a good idea."

I stared hard at the shot of the cathedral on the TV. How could I even begin to describe it? But say my life depended on it. Say my life was being threatened by an insane guy who said I had to do it or else.

I stared some more at the cathedral before the picture flipped off into the countryside. There was no use. I turned to the blind man and said, "To begin with, they're very tall." I was looking around the room for clues. "They reach way up. Up and up. Toward the sky. They're so big, some of them, they have to have these supports. To help hold them up, so to speak. These supports are called buttresses. They remind me of viaducts, for some reason. But maybe you don't know viaducts, either? Sometimes the cathedrals have devils and such carved into the front. Sometimes lords and ladies. Don't ask me why this is," I said.

He was nodding. The whole upper part of his body seemed to be moving back and forth.

"I'm not doing so good, am I?" I said.

He stopped nodding and leaned forward on the edge of the sofa. As he listened to me, he was running his fingers through his beard. I wasn't getting through to him, I could see that. But he waited for me to go on just the same. He nodded, like he was trying to encourage me. I tried to think what else to say. "They're really big," I said. "They're massive. They're built of stone. Marble, too, sometimes. In those olden days, when they built cathedrals, men wanted to be close to God. In those olden days, God was an important part of everyone's life. You could tell this from their cathedral-building. I'm sorry," I said, "but it looks like that's the best I can do for you. I'm just no good at it."

"That's all right, bub," the blind man said. "Hey, listen, I hope you don't mind my asking you. Can I ask you something? Let me ask you a simple question, yes or no. I'm just curious and there's no offense. You're my host. But let me ask if you are in any way religious? You don't mind my asking?"

I shook my head. He couldn't see that, though. A wink is the same as a nod to a blind man. "I guess I don't believe in it. In anything. Sometimes it's hard. You know what I'm saying?"

"Sure, I do," he said.

"Right," I said.

The Englishman was still holding forth. My wife sighed in her sleep. She drew a long breath and went on with her sleeping.

"You'll have to forgive me," I said. "But I can't tell you what a cathedral looks like. It just isn't in me to do it. I can't do any more than I've done."

The blind man sat very still, his head down, as he listened to me.

I said, "The truth is, cathedrals don't mean anything special to me. Nothing. Cathedrals. They're something to look at on late-night TV. That's all they are."

It was then that the blind man cleared his throat. He brought something up. He took a handkerchief from his back pocket. Then he said, "I get it, bub. It's okay. It happens. Don't worry about it," he said. "Hey, listen to me. Will you do me a favor? I got an idea. Why don't you find us some heavy paper? And a pen. We'll do something. We'll draw one together. Get us a pen and some heavy paper. Go on, bub, get the stuff," he said.

So I went upstairs. My legs felt like they didn't have any strength in them. They felt like they did after I'd done some running. In my wife's room, I looked around. I found some ballpoints in a little basket on her table. And then I tried to think where to look for the kind of paper he was talking about.

Downstairs, in the kitchen, I found a shopping bag with onion skins at the bottom of the bag. I emptied the bag and shook it. I brought it into the living room and sat down with it near his legs. I moved some things, smoothed the wrinkles from the bag, spread it out on the coffee table.

The blind man got down from the sofa and sat next to me on the carpet.

He ran his fingers over the paper. He went up and down the sides of the paper. The edges, even the edges. He fingered the corners.

"All right," he said. "All right, let's do her."

He found my hand, the hand with the pen. He closed his hand over my hand. "Go ahead, bub, draw," he said. "Draw. You'll see. I'll follow along with you. It'll be okay. Just begin now like I'm telling you. You'll see. Draw," the blind man said.

So I began. First I drew a box that looked like a house. It could have been the house I lived in. Then I put a roof on it. At either end of the roof, I drew spires. Crazy.

"Swell," he said. "Terrific. You're doing fine," he said. "Never thought anything like this could happen in your lifetime, did you, bub? Well, it's a strange life, we all know that. Go on now. Keep it up."

I put in windows with arches. I drew flying buttresses. I hung great doors. I couldn't stop. The TV station went off the air. I put down the pen and closed and opened my fingers. The blind man felt around over the paper. He moved the tips of his fingers over the paper, all over what I had drawn, and he nodded.

"Doing fine," the blind man said.

I took up the pen again, and he found my hand. I kept at it. I'm no artist. But I kept drawing just the same.

My wife opened up her eyes and gazed at us. She sat up on the sofa, her robe hanging open. She said, "What are you doing? Tell me, I want to know."

I didn't answer her.

The blind man said, "We're drawing a cathedral. Me and him are working on it. Press hard," he said to me. "That's right. That's good," he said. "Sure. You got it, bub. I can tell. You didn't think you could. But you can, can't you? You're cooking with gas now. You know what I'm saying? We're going to really have us something here in a minute. How's the old arm?" he said. "Put some people in there now. What's a cathedral without people?"

My wife said, "What's going on? Robert, what are you doing? What's going on?"

"It's all right," he said to her. "Close your eyes now," the blind man said to me.

I did it. I closed them just like he said.

"Are they closed?" he said. "Don't fudge."

"They're closed," I said.

"Keep them that way," he said. He said, "Don't stop now. Draw."

So we kept on with it. His fingers rode my fingers as my hand went over the paper. It was like nothing else in my life up to now.

Then he said, "I think that's it. I think you got it," he said. "Take a look. What do you think?"

But I had my eyes closed. I thought I'd keep them that way for a little longer. I thought it was something I ought to do.

"Well?" he said. "Are you looking?"

My eyes were still closed. I was in my house. I knew that. But I didn't feel like I was inside anything.

"It's really something," I said.

—1983

MARGARET ATWOOD

Canada's best-known writer, Margaret Atwood is the author of over 50 works, in genres as diverse as fiction, poetry, the critical essay, opera, and political comic strips. She is part of the literary generation that came of age in the explosion of Canadian nationalism in the 1960s and 1970s and that pushed Canadian writing and writers to the forefront of Canadian culture. She graduated from Victoria College, University of Toronto in 1961, and completed her MA in 1962 at Radcliffe College, where she studied Victorian literature and early American literature. She worked toward a PhD at Harvard, but returned to Canada in 1963. For a year she worked as a market researcher, an experience she later mined to write her first novel, *The Edible Woman* (1969). In 1966 she won the first of what would be several Governor General's Awards in her career for her first poetry collection, *The Circle Game* (1964).

Atwood has continued to publish acclaimed works of poetry, but she is best known for her fiction. Her major novels include works of speculative fiction such as *The Handmaid's Tale* (1986), *Oryx and Crake* (2003), and *The Year of the Flood* (2009); works of contemporary social satire such as *The Robber Bride* (1993); and historical novels such as *Alias Grace* (1996) and *The Blind Assassin* (winner of the prestigious Man Booker Prize in 2000).

Atwood intended her first book of literary criticism to be a general reader's guide and introduction to Canadian literature, but *Survival: A Thematic Guide to Canadian Literature* (1972) became a landmark in Canadian literary criticism, and sparked a charged debate about marginalized figures in Canadian writing. Atwood's career has also been notable for her literary and political activism; she is a co-founder and past president of the Writers' Union of Canada, and has been president of PEN International's Canadian English-speaking branch and vice-president of PEN International. Political issues are close to the surface in much of her fiction—as well as in *Payback: Debt and the Shadow Side of Wealth* (2008), which became a non-fiction bestseller.

Born in Ottawa in 1939, Atwood spent her childhood living with her family in Ottawa in the winters and spending the remaining parts of the year in Northern Quebec and Ontario while her entomologist father conducted his research on bees, spruce budworms, and tent caterpillars.

Living in Toronto with her partner, novelist Graeme Gibson, Atwood continues to be active in the Canadian arts and culture scene. Not long after her novel *The Year of the Flood* was published in 2009, she was commissioned to write her first chamber opera about author Pauline Johnson.

Atwood's short fiction ranges widely in style and genre, from realism to speculative fiction to the deliberately unclassifiable: the economical and grimly comic "Happy Endings," one of her best-known short stories. The work has often been described as a metafiction, but Atwood herself described it as a "mutant literary form," impossible to fit into any single category.

Happy Endings

MARGARET ATWOOD

John and Mary meet.
What happens next?
If you want a happy ending, try A.

A

JOHN AND Mary fall in love and get married. They both have worthwhile and remunerative jobs which they find stimulating and challenging. They buy a charming house. Real estate values go up. Eventually, when they can afford live-in help, they have two children, to whom they are devoted. The children turn out well. John and Mary have a stimulating and challenging sex life and worthwhile friends. They go on fun vacations together. They retire. They both have hobbies which they find stimulating and challenging. Eventually they die. This is the end of the story.

B

Mary falls in love with John but John doesn't fall in love with Mary. He merely uses her body for selfish pleasure and ego gratification of a tepid kind. He comes to her apartment twice a week and she cooks him dinner, you'll notice that he doesn't even consider her worth the price of a dinner out, and after he's eaten the dinner he fucks her and after that he falls asleep, while she does the dishes so he won't think she's untidy, having all those dirty dishes lying around, and puts on fresh lipstick so she'll look good when he wakes up, but when he wakes up he doesn't even notice, he puts on his socks and his shorts and his pants and his shirt and his tie and his shoes, the reverse order from the one in which he took them off. He doesn't take off Mary's clothes, she takes them off herself, she acts as if she's dying for it every time, not because she likes sex exactly, she doesn't, but she wants John to think she does because if they do it often enough surely he'll get used to her, he'll come to depend on her and they will get married, but John goes out the door with hardly so much as a goodnight and three days later he turns up at six o'clock and they do the whole thing over again.

Mary gets run-down. Crying is bad for your face, everyone knows that and so does Mary but she can't stop. People at work notice. Her friends tell her John is a rat, a pig, a dog, he isn't good enough for her, but she can't believe it. Inside John, she thinks, is another John, who is much nicer. This other John will emerge like a butterfly from a cocoon, a Jack from a box, a pit from a prune, if the first John is only squeezed enough.

One evening John complains about the food. He has never complained about the food before. Mary is hurt.

Her friends tell her they've seen him in a restaurant with another woman, whose name is Madge. It's not even Madge that finally gets to Mary: it's the restaurant. John has never taken Mary to a restaurant. Mary collects all the sleeping pills and aspirins she can find, and takes them and a half a bottle of sherry. You can see what kind of a woman she is by the fact that it's not even whiskey. She leaves a note for John. She hopes he'll discover her and get her to the hospital in time and repent and then they can get married, but this fails to happen and she dies.

John marries Madge and everything continues as in A.

C

John, who is an older man, falls in love with Mary, and Mary, who is only twenty-two, feels sorry for him because he's worried about his hair falling out. She sleeps with him even though she's not in love with him. She met him at work. She's in love with someone called James, who is twenty-two also and not yet ready to settle down.

John on the contrary settled down long ago: this is what is bothering him. John has a steady, respectable job and is getting ahead in his field, but Mary isn't impressed by him, she's impressed by James, who has a motorcycle and a fabulous record collection. But James is often away on his motorcycle, being free. Freedom isn't the same for girls, so in the meantime Mary spends Thursday evenings with John. Thursdays are the only days John can get away.

John is married to a woman called Madge and they have two children, a charming house which they bought just before the real estate values went up, and hobbies which they find stimulating and challenging, when they have the time. John tells Mary how important she is to him, but of course he can't leave his wife because a commitment is a commitment. He goes on about this more than is necessary and Mary finds it boring, but older men can keep it up longer so on the whole she has a fairly good time.

One day James breezes in on his motorcycle with some top-grade California hybrid and James and Mary get higher than you'd believe possible and they climb into bed. Everything becomes very underwater, but along comes John, who has a key to Mary's apartment. He finds them stoned and entwined. He's hardly in any position to be jealous, considering Madge, but nevertheless he's overcome with despair. Finally he's middle-aged, in two years he'll be bald as an egg and he can't stand it. He purchases a handgun, saying he needs it for target practice—this is the thin part of the plot, but it can be dealt with later—and shoots the two of them and himself.

Madge, after a suitable period of mourning, marries an understanding man called Fred and everything continues as in A, but under different names.

D

Fred and Madge have no problems. They get along exceptionally well and are good at working out any little difficulties that may arise. But their charming house is by the seashore and one day a giant tidal wave approaches. Real estate values go down. The rest of the story is about what caused the tidal wave and how they escape from it. They do, though thousands drown, but Fred and Madge are virtuous and lucky. Finally on high ground they clasp each other, wet and dripping and grateful, and continue as in A.

E

Yes, but Fred has a bad heart. The rest of the story is about how kind they both are until Fred dies. Then Madge devotes herself to charity work until the end of A. If you like, it can be "Madge," "cancer," "guilty and confused," and "bird watching."

F

If you think this is all too bourgeois, make John a revolutionary and Mary a counterespionage agent and see how far that gets you. Remember, this is Canada. You'll still end up with A, though in between you may get a lustful brawling saga of passionate involvement, a chronicle of our times, sort of.

You'll have to face it, the endings are the same however you slice it. Don't be deluded by any other endings, they're all fake, either deliberately fake, with malicious intent to deceive, or just motivated by excessive optimism if not by downright sentimentality.

The only authentic ending is the one provided here:

John and Mary die. John and Mary die. John and Mary die.

So much for endings. Beginnings are always more fun. True connoisseurs, however, are known to favor the stretch in between, since it's the hardest to do anything with.

That's about all that can be said for plots, which anyway are just one thing after another, a what and a what and a what.

Now try How and Why.

—1983

STEVEN MILLHAUSER

Steven Millhauser is an American writer whose novels, short stories, and novellas have been recognized as preeminent works of postmodern fiction. His debut work *Edwin Mullhouse* (1972) established his reputation, and *Martin Dressler: The Tale of an American Dreamer* (1996) was awarded the Pulitzer Prize, giving this elusive writer increased readership and critical attention.

Millhauser was born in New York City in 1943. His father was a professor of English at the University of Bridgeport in Fairfield, Connecticut. Millhauser thus grew up in Fairfield, a town and landscape that proved formative to his imagination. He moved back to New York City to attend Columbia, where he received his BA in 1965; he then pursued post-graduate work at Brown University from 1968 to 1970 and from 1976 to 1977. He was working toward a PhD in medieval and Renaissance literature but did not complete the dissertation, writing instead the manuscript of his first novel, *Edwin Mullhouse*, published in 1972. In 1984, Millhauser married, and he also took up a post as visiting associate professor of English at Williams College. In 1988 he began teaching at Skidmore College, where he became a full professor of English in 1992, and where he still teaches. He lives in Saratoga Springs, New York.

Millhauser's fictions mine the liminal spaces of the imagination, the fertile region where, as he himself says, "things cease to be themselves, when they begin to turn into something else, which has no name." Treading the mysterious borderlands of the concrete and the fantastic, Millhauser's stories invite the reader "into the woods, away from the main path." Once there, the stories offer renewed insight into the world of "reality," the world we think we know, transforming our perception of everyday life. Set in small-town Northeastern America, Millhauser's stories seek to reveal the hidden powers latent in all experience, hidden because we often don't pause to look carefully enough: "We walk through a world continually disappearing from view. One thing fiction does is restore the hidden and vanishing world." Millhauser's fictional worlds mirror our own in miniature, drawing on phenomena charged with imaginative potential: night, attics, subterranean spaces, childhood.

After the publication of his second novel, *Portrait of a Romantic* (1977), Millhauser began to focus increasingly on shorter forms: the novella and short story. His story collections *In the Penny Arcade* (1986), *The Barnum Museum* (1990), *The Knife Thrower and Other Stories* (1998), *Dangerous Laughter* (2008), and *We Others* (2011) have been widely praised, drawing comparisons to Hawthorne and Poe. Millhauser has written about the virtues of short fiction, lauding smallness as "the realm of elegance and grace." The short story, he says, "believes in transformation. It believes in hidden powers." Using postmodern manipulations of form and narrative voice, Millhauser focuses on the shifting border between reality and fantasy, waking life and dream, creating enticing tales that pair concrete, sensuous description with uncanny twists of the eerie and strange.

"A Visit" begins with an invitation and a vaguely drawn map that lead the narrator into unknown territory, into a "misguided adventure in the wilderness." In a shadowy house "well protected from view," he visits an old friend, whose surprising choice of wife destabilizes his preconceptions.

A Visit

STEVEN MILLHAUSER

ALTHOUGH I had not heard from my friend in nine years, I wasn't surprised, not really, to receive a short letter from him dashed off in pencil, announcing that he had "taken a wife," and summoning me to visit him in some remote upstate town I had never heard of. "Come see me on the 16th and 17th" was what he had actually written. "Be here for lunch." The off-hand peremptory tone was Albert all over. He had scribbled a map, with a little black circle marked "Village" and a little white square marked "My house." A wavy line connected the two. Under the line were the words "3½ miles, more or less." Over the line were the words "County Road 39." I knew those desolate little upstate villages, consisting of one Baptist church, three bars, and a gas station with a single pump, and I imagined Albert living at an ironic distance, with his books and his manias. What I couldn't imagine was his wife. Albert had never struck me as the marrying kind, though women had always liked him. I had plans for the weekend, but I canceled them and headed north.

I still considered Albert my friend, in a way my best friend, even though I hadn't heard from him in nine years. He had once been my best friend and it was hard to think of him in any other way. Even in the flourishing time of our friendship, in the last two years of college and the year after, when we saw each other daily, he had been difficult and exacting, scornful of convention, subject to sudden flare-ups and silences, earnest but with an edge of mockery, and cursed with an unfailing scent for the faintly fraudulent in a gesture or a phrase or a face. He was handsome in a sharp-featured New England way—his family, as he put it, had lived in Connecticut since the fall of the Roman Empire—but despite the inviting smiles of girls in his classes he confined himself to brisk affairs with leather-jacketed town girls with whom he had nothing in common. After graduating, we roomed together for a year in a little college town full of cafés and bookstores, sharing the rent and drifting from one part-time job to another, as I put off the inevitable suit-and-tie life that awaited me while he mocked my conventional fear of becoming conventional, defended business as America's only source of originality, and read his Plato and his "Modern Chess Openings" and tootled his flute. One day he left, just like that, to start what he called a new life. In the next year I received postcards from small towns all over America, showing pictures of Main Streets and quaint village railroad stations. They bore messages such as "Still looking" or "Have you seen my razor? I think I left it on the bathtub." Then there was nothing for six months, and then a sudden postcard from Eugene, Oregon, on which he described in minute detail a small unknown wooden object that he had found in the top drawer of the bureau in his rented bedroom, and then nine years of silence. During that time I settled into a job and almost married an old girlfriend. I had bought a house on a pleasant street lined with porches and maples, thought quite a bit about my old friend Albert, and wondered whether this was what I had looked forward to, this life I was now leading, in the old days, the days when I still looked forward to things.

The town was even worse than I had imagined. Slowly I passed its crumbling brick paper mill with boarded-up windows, its rows of faded and flaking two-family houses with sagging front porches where guys in black T-shirts sat drinking beer, its tattoo parlor, and its sluggish stream. County Road 39 wound between fields of Queen Anne's lace and yellow ragweed, with now and then a melancholy house or a patch of sun-scorched corn. Once I passed a rotting barn with a caved-in roof. At 3.2 miles on the odometer I came to a weathered house near the edge of the road. A bicycle lay in the high grass of the front yard, and an open garage was entirely filled with old furniture. Uncertainly I turned onto the unpaved drive, parked with the motor running, and walked up to the front door. There was no bell. I knocked on the wooden screen door, which banged loudly against the frame, and a tall, barefoot, and very pale woman with sleepy eyes came to the door, wearing a long rumpled black skirt and a lumberjack shirt over a T-shirt. When I asked for Albert she looked at me suspiciously, shook her head quickly back and forth, and slammed the inner door. As I walked back to the car I saw her pale face looking out at me past a pushed-aside pink curtain. It occurred to me that perhaps Albert had married this woman and that she was insane, and as I backed out of the drive I thought that I really should turn back now, right now, away from this misguided adventure in the wilderness. After all, I hadn't seen him for nine long years.

At 4.1 miles on the odometer I rounded a bend of rising road and saw a shadowy house set back in a cluster of dusty-looking trees. I turned in to the unknown dirt drive, deep-rutted and sprouting weeds, and as I stepped on the brake with a sharp sense of desolation and betrayal, for here I was, in the god-forsaken middle of nauseating nowhere, prowling around like a fool and a criminal, the front door opened and Albert came out, one hand in his pocket and one hand waving.

He looked the same, nearly the same, though browner and leatherier than I remembered, as if he had lived all those years in the sun, his face a little longer and leaner—a handsome man in jeans and a dark shirt. "I wondered if you'd show up," he said when he reached the car, and suddenly seemed to study me. "You look just the way you ought to," he then said.

I let the words settle in me. "It depends what I ought to look like," I answered, glancing at him sharply, but he only laughed.

"Isn't this a great place?" he said, throwing out one arm as he picked up my traveling bag to carry to the house. "Ten acres, and they were practically giving it away. First day after I bought the place I go walking around and—bingo! What do you think I found? Grapes. Billions of grapes. An old fallen-down grape arbor, grapes growing all over the ground. Italy in New York. Wait till you see the pond."

We stepped into the shade of the high trees, a little thicket of pines and maples that grew close to the house. Big bushes climbed halfway up the windows. It struck me that the house was well protected from view, a private place, a shadowy isle in a sea of fields. "And yet," I said, looking around for his wife, "I never thought of you as getting married, somehow."

"Not back then," he said. "Watch that rail."

We had climbed onto the steps of the long, deep-shaded front porch, and I had grasped a wobbly iron handrail that needed to be screwed into the wood. A coil of old garden hose hung over the porch rail. A few hornets buzzed about the ceiling light. On the porch stood a sunken chaise longue, an old three-speed bicycle, a metal garbage can containing a rusty snow shovel, and a porch swing on which sat an empty flowerpot.

He opened the wooden screen door and with a little flourish urged me in. "Humble," he said, "but mine own." He looked at me with a touch of excitement, an excitement I couldn't account for. The house was cool and almost dark. We entered the living room, where I noticed a rocking chair that leaned too far back and a couch with one pillow. Ancient wallpaper showed faded scenes of some kind repeating themselves all over the room. Albert, who seemed more and more excited, led me up the creaking worn-edged stairs to my room—a bed with a frilly pink spread, a lamp table on which lay a screwdriver with a transparent yellow handle—and quickly back down.

"You must be starving," he said, as he took me through an open doorway into a dining room that was almost dark. At a big round table there were three place settings, which glowed whitely in the gloom. One of the round-backed chairs appeared to be occupied. Only as I drew closer did I see that the occupant was a large frog, perhaps two feet high, which sat with its throat resting on the table edge. "My wife," Albert said, looking at me fiercely, as if he were about to spring at my face.

I felt I was being tested in some fiendish way. "Pleased to meet you," I said harshly, and sat down across from her. The table lay between us like a lake. I had thought she might be something else, maybe a stuffed toy of some sort, but even in the dark daylight I could see the large moist eyes looking here and there; could see her rapid breathing and smell her marshy odor. I thought that Albert must be making fun of me, trying to trick me into exposing what he took to be my hideous bourgeois soul, but whatever his game I wasn't going to give myself away.

"Help yourself," Albert said, pushing toward me a breadboard with a round loaf and a hunk of cheese on it. A big-bladed knife lay on the table, and I began cutting the bread. "And if you'd cut just a little piece of cheese for Alice." I immediately cut a little piece for Alice. Albert disappeared into the kitchen, and in the room's dusk I stared across the round table at Alice before looking away uncomfortably. Albert returned with a wax carton of orange juice and a small brown bottle of beer, both of which he set before me. "The choice," he said with a little bow, "is yours entirely." He picked up the piece of cheese I had cut for Alice, placed it on her plate, and broke it into smaller pieces. Alice looked at him—it seemed to me that she looked at him—with those moist and heavy-lidded eyes, and flicked up her cheese. Then she placed her throat on the table edge and sat very still.

Albert sat down and cut himself a piece of bread. "After lunch I want to show you the place. Take you down to the pond and so on." He looked at me, tilting his head in a way I suddenly remembered. "And you? It's been a while."

"Oh, still a roving bachelor," I said, and immediately disliked my fatuous tone. I had a sudden urge to talk seriously to Albert, as we'd done in the old days, watching the night turn slowly gray through our tall, arched windows. But I felt constrained. It had been too long a time. And though he had summoned me after all these years and though he had shown me his wife, it was all askew somehow, as if he hadn't shown me anything, as if he'd kept himself hidden away. "I see women," I continued, "but they're not the right ones. You know, I was always sure I'd be the one to get married, not you."

"It wasn't something I planned. But when the moment comes, you'll know." He looked at Alice with tenderness and suddenly leaned over and touched the side of her head lightly with his fingertips.

"How did you," I began, and stopped. I felt like bursting into screams of wild laughter, or of outrage, pure outrage, but I held myself down. "I mean, how did you meet? You two. If I may ask."

"So formal! If you may ask! Down by the pond—if I may answer. I saw her in the reeds one day. I'd never seen her before, but she was always there, after that. I'll show you the exact place after lunch."

His little mocking rebuke irritated me, and I recalled how he had always irritated me, and made me retreat deeply into myself, because of some little ironic look, and it seemed strange that someone who irritated me and made me retreat into myself was also the person who released me into a freer version of myself, superior to the constricted one that had always felt like my own hand on my throat. Who was Albert, after all, that he should have the power to release me or constrict me—this man I no longer knew, with his run-down house and his ludicrous frog-wife. Then I ate for a while in sullen silence, looking only at my food, and when I glanced up I saw him looking at me kindly, almost affectionately.

"It's all right," he said quietly, as if he understood, as if he knew how difficult it was for me, this journey, this wife, this life, and I was grateful, as I had always been, for we had been close, he and I, back then.

After lunch he insisted on showing me his land—his domain, as he called it. I had hoped that Alice might stay behind, so that I could speak with him alone, but it was clear that he wanted her to come with us. So as we made our way out the back door and into his domain she followed along, taking hops about two strides in length, always a little behind us or a little before. At the back of the house a patch of overgrown lawn led to a vegetable garden on both sides of a grassy path. There were vines of green peas and stringbeans climbing tall sticks, clusters of green peppers, rows of carrots and radishes identified by seed packets on short sticks, fat heads of lettuce and flashes of yellow squash—a rich and well-tended oasis, as if the living center of the house were here, on the outside, hidden in back. At the end of the garden grew a scattering of fruit trees, pear and cherry and plum. An old wire fence with a broken wooden gate separated the garden from the land beyond.

We walked along a vague footpath through fields of high grass, passed into thickets of oak and maple, crossed a stream. Alice kept up. Alice in sunlight, Alice in the open air no longer seemed a grotesque pet, a monstrous mistake of nature, a nightmare frog and freakish wife, but rather a companion of sorts—Albert's pal. And yet it was more than that. Once, when she emerged from tree shade into full sunlight, I sensed for a moment, with an inner start, Alice as she was, Alice in the sheer brightness and fullness of her being, as if the dark malachite sheen of her skin, the pale shimmer of her throat, the moist warmth of her eyes were as natural and mysterious as the flight of a bird. Then I rumbled back into myself and realized that I was walking with my old friend beside a monstrous lumbering frog who had somehow become his wife, and a howl of inward laughter and rage erupted in me.

The pond appeared suddenly, on the far side of a low rise. Reeds and cattails grew in thick clusters at the marshy edge. We sat down on flat-topped boulders and looked out at the green-brown water where a few brown ducks floated, out past fields to a line of low hills. There was a desolate beauty about the place, as if we had come to the edge of the world. "It was over there I first saw her," Albert said, pointing to a cluster of reeds. Alice sat off to one side, in a clump of grass at the water's edge. She was as still as a rock, except for her sides moving in and out as she breathed. I imagined her growing in the depths of the pond, under a mantle of lily pads and mottled scum, down below the rays of green sunlight, far down, at the silent bottom of the world.

Albert leaned back on both elbows, a pose I remembered well, and stared out at the water. For a long while we sat in a silence that struck me as uncomfortable, though he himself seemed at ease. It wasn't so much that I felt awkward in Alice's presence as that I didn't know what I had come all this way to say. Did I really want to speak at all? Then Albert said, "Tell me about your life." And I was grateful to him, for that was exactly what I wanted to talk about, my life. I told him about my almost-marriage; my friendships that lacked excitement; my girlfriends who lacked one thing or another; my good job that somehow wasn't exactly what I had been looking for, back then; and my feeling that things were all right but not as all right as they might be, that I was not unhappy but not really happy either, but caught in some intermediate place, looking both ways.

"It's hard," Albert then said, in the tone of someone who knew what I was talking about, and though I was soothed by his words, which were spoken gently, I was disappointed that he didn't say more, that he didn't show himself to me.

And I said, "Why did you write to me, after all this time?" which was only another way of saying, why didn't you write to me, in all this time.

"I waited," he said, "until I had something to show you." That was what he said: something to show me. And I thought that if all he had to show me after nine years was his run-down house and his marshy frog-wife, then I wasn't so badly off, in my own way, not really.

After that, we continued walking about his domain, with Alice always at our side. He showed me things, and I looked. He showed me the old grape arbor that he had put back up; unripe green grapes, hard as nuts, hung in bunches from the decaying slats. "Try one," he said, but it was bitter as a tiny lemon. He laughed at my grimace. "We like 'em this way," he said, plucking a few and tossing them into his mouth. He pulled off another handful and held them down to Alice, who devoured them swiftly: flick, flick, flick. He showed me a woodpecker's nest, and a slope of wild tiger lilies, and an old toolshed containing a rusty hoe and a rusty rake. Suddenly, from a nearby field, a big bird rose up with a loud beating of wings. "Did you see that!" cried Albert, seizing my arm. "A pheasant! Protecting her young. Over there." In the high grass, six furry little ducklike creatures walked in a line, their heads barely visible.

At dinner, Alice sat in her chair with her throat resting on the edge of the table while Albert walked briskly in and out of the kitchen. I was pleased to see a fat bottle of red wine, which he poured into two juice glasses. The glasses had pictures of Winnie-the-Pooh and Eeyore on them. "Guy gave them to me at a gas station," Albert said. He frowned suddenly, pressed his fingertips against his forehead, looked up with a radiant smile. "I've got it. The more it *snows* (Tiddely pom), the more it *goes* (Tiddely pom)."[1] He poured a little wine into a cereal bowl and placed it near Alice.

Dinner was a heated-up supermarket chicken, fresh squash from his garden, and big bowls of garden salad. Albert was in high spirits, humming snatches of songs, lighting a stub of candle in a green wine bottle, filling our wineglasses and Alice's bowl again and again, urging me to drink up, crunching lustily into his salad. The cheap wine burned my tongue but I kept drinking, taken by Albert's festive spirit, eager to carry myself into his mood. Even Alice kept finishing the wine he put in her cereal bowl. The candle flame seemed to grow brighter in the darkening room. A line of wax ran down the bottle and stopped. Albert brought in his breadboard, more salad, another loaf of bread. And as the meal continued, I had the sense that Alice, sitting there with her throat resting on the table edge, flicking up her wine, was looking at Albert with those large eyes of hers, moist and dark in the flamelight, trying to attract his attention. And Albert, leaning back in his chair, laughing, throwing his arm about as he talked, appeared to

1 From A.A. Milne's *The House at Pooh Corner* (1929).

be darting glances back at her. Yes, they were exchanging looks, there at the darkening dinner table, looks that struck me as amorous.

As I drank, I was filled with a warm, expansive feeling, which took in the room, the meal, the Winnie-the-Pooh glasses, the large moist eyes, the reflection of the candle flame in the window, the glances of Albert and his wife; for after all, she was the one he had chosen, up here in the wilderness, and who was I to say what was right in such matters.

Albert leaped up and returned with a bowl of pears and cherries from his fruit trees, and filled my glass again. I was settling back with my warm, expansive feeling, looking forward to a night of talk stretching lazily before me, when Albert announced that it was getting late, and that he and Alice would be retiring. I had the run of the house. Just be sure to blow out the candle. Nighty night. Through the roar of wine I was aware of my plunging disappointment. He pulled back Alice's chair and she hopped to the floor. Together they left the dining room and disappeared into the dark living room, where he turned on a lamp so dim that it was like lighting a candle. I heard him creaking up the stairs, and thought I heard a dull thumping sound, which must have been Alice lumbering her way up beside him.

I sat listening to the thumps and creaks of the upper hall, a sudden sharp rush of water in the bathroom sink, a squeak (what was that squeak?), a door shutting. In the abrupt silence, which seemed to spread outward from the table in widening ripples, I felt abandoned, there with the wine and the candle and the glimmering dishes. But it was bound to be this way. I had watched their amorous looks. Then I imagined Alice hopping onto the white sheets. And I tried to picture frog love, its possible pleasures, its oozy raptures, but I turned my mind violently away, for in the imagining I felt something petty and cruel, something in the nature of a violation.

I drank down the last of the wine and blew out the candle. From the dark room where I sat, I could see a ghostly corner of the refrigerator in the kitchen and a dim-lit reddish couch arm in the living room, like a moonlit dead flower. A car passed on the road. Then I became aware of the crickets, whole fields and meadows of them, the great hum that I had always heard rising from back yards and vacant lots in childhood summers, the long sound of summer's end. And yet it was only the middle of summer; just last week I had spent a day at the beach. So for a long time I sat at the dark table, in the middle of a decaying house, listening to the sound of summer's end. Then I picked up my empty glass, silently saluted Albert and his wife, and went up to bed.

But I could not sleep. Maybe it was the wine, or the mashed mattress, or the early hour, but I lay there twisting in my sheets, and as I turned restlessly, the day's adventures darkened in my mind and I saw only a crazed friend, a ruined house, an ugly and monstrous frog. And I saw myself, weak and absurd, wrenching my mind into grotesque shapes of sympathy and understanding.

I woke tense and exhausted in a sun-streaked room. It was nearly nine. I had three separate headaches: one behind my left eye, one in my right temple, and one at the back of my head. I washed and dressed quickly and made my way down the darkening stairs through a dusk that deepened as I drew toward the bottom. On the faded wallpaper I could make out two scenes repeating themselves in the distance: a faded boy in blue lying against a faded yellow haystack with a horn at his side, and a girl in white drawing water from a faded well.

The living room was empty. The whole house appeared to be deserted. On the round table in the twilight of the dining room the dishes still sat from dinner. All I wanted was a cup of coffee before leaving. In the kitchen I found an old jar of instant coffee and a chipped blue teapot decorated with a decal of an orange brontosaurus. I heard sharp sounds and through the leaves and branches in the kitchen window I saw Albert with his back to me, digging in the garden. Outside it was a bright, sunny day. Beside him, on the dirt, sat Alice.

I brought my cup of harsh-tasting, stale coffee into the dining room and drank it at the table while I listened to the sounds of Albert's shovel striking the soil. It was peaceful in the darkish room, at the round brown table. A thin slant of sun glittered in the open kitchen. There was the whistle of a bird, leaves in the window, the brown dusk, the sound of the shovel striking loam, tuning it over. It occurred to me that I could simply pack my things now and glide away without the awkwardness of a leave-taking.

I finished the dismal coffee and carried the cup into the kitchen, where the inner back door stood slightly open. There I paused, holding the empty cup in my hand. Obeying a sudden impulse, I opened the door a little more and slipped between it and the wooden screen door.

His sleeves were rolled up and his foot was pressing down on the blade of a shovel. He was digging up grassy dirt at the edge of the garden, turning it over, breaking up the soil, tossing away clumps of grass roots. Nearby sat Alice, watching him. From time to time, as he moved along the edge of the garden, he would look over at her. Their looks seemed to catch for a moment, before he returned to his garden. Standing in the warm shade of the half-open door, looking through the rippling screen at the garden quivering with sunlight, I sensed a mysterious rhythm between them, a lightness or buoyancy, a sunlit harmony. It was as if both of them had shed their skins and were mingling in air or dissolving into light, and as I felt that airy mingling, that tender dissolution, it came over me that what I lacked in my life was exactly that harmony. It was as if I were composed of some hard substance that could never dissolve in anything and Albert had discovered the secret of air. But my throat was beginning to hurt, the bright light burned my eyes, and setting down my cup on the counter, which sounded like the blow of a hammer, I pushed open the door and went out.

Albert turned around. "Sleep well?" he said, running the back of his hand slowly across his dripping forehead.

"Well enough. But you know, I've got to be getting back. A million things to do! You know how it is."

"Sure," Albert said. He rested both hands on the top of the long shovel handle and placed his chin on his hands. "I know how it is." His tone struck me as brilliantly poised between understanding and mockery.

He brought my bag down from my room and loaded it in the car. Alice had hopped through the dining room and living room and had come to rest in the deep shade of the front porch. It struck me that she kept carefully out of sight of the road. Albert bent over the driver's window and crossed his arms on the door. "If you're ever up this way," he said, "drop in."

"I'll do that," I said.

Albert stood up and stretched out an elbow, rubbed his shoulder. "Take care," he said, and gave a little wave and stepped away.

As I backed up the dirt driveway and began edging onto County Road 39, I had the sense that the house was withdrawing into its trees and shadows, fading into its island of shade. Albert had already vanished. From the road I could see only a stand of high trees clustered about a dark house. A few moments later, at the bend of the road, I glanced back again. I must have waited a second too long, because the road was already dipping, the house had sunk out of sight, and in the bright sunshine I saw only a scattering of roadside trees, a cloudless sky, fields of Queen Anne's lace stretching away.

—1997

TOBIAS WOLFF

Tobias Wolff is an American writer, born in Alabama in 1945. Best known for his short stories and memoirs, he has also written two novels. Wolff's stories belong to the tradition of Maupassant, Joyce, Hemingway, and Chekhov; they are highly crafted, realistic, and focused on the psychological dimensions of character.

In 1949, Wolff's parents separated, and he moved with his mother to Washington State, where they settled first in Seattle and then in the small town of Concrete. As a boy, he lived under the oppression of an abusive stepfather. Wolff's early life is chronicled in his memoir, *This Boy's Life* (1989), a book which received wide critical acclaim; many credited it with helping to revive the genre of memoir in America. *This Boy's Life* was made into a notable film in 1993, starring Robert De Niro and Leonardo DiCaprio.

One of Wolff's earliest creative endeavors was to escape his domestic situation by gaining a scholarship to a Pennsylvania prep school, The Hill School. He won the scholarship by means of forged documents attesting to his academic and athletic prowess. He spent two idyllic years there, before being expelled for his failures in mathematics. After a short period working at sea, he joined the American Army, serving for four years in Vietnam; his second memoir, *In Pharoah's Army* (1994), describes the horror and absurdity of his experiences during that time.

After the war, Wolff attended Oxford University; he graduated in 1975; that same year he published his first work of fiction, *Ugly Rumours*, a novel. His first short story collection, *In the Garden of the North American Martyrs*, (1981) was a critical success, and his novella *The Barracks Thief* (1984) won the PEN/Faulkner award. He has since published numerous short story collections, establishing himself as one of America's preeminent writers of short fiction. Wolff now teaches writing at Stanford University.

Wolff has been cited as a contributor to the "modern renaissance" of the American short story, which critics see as beginning in the 1970s and continuing until the present. Along with his friend Raymond Carver and Richard Ford, Wolff has also been associated with the "dirty realism" school of American writers who focus on working-class subjects, criminals, alcoholics, and domestic conflict. Wolff rejects such categorizations, saying that his association with Carver was social, not aesthetic, and that the idea of there having been a short story "renaissance" is inaccurate; he claims instead that there has been an unbroken line of great short stories in America, from Edgar Allan Poe onward. He says "the short story … is the perfect American form," capturing the nomadic, fragmented experience of modern American life.

"Bullet in the Brain," first published in *The New Yorker* in 1995, takes place over just a few minutes and in a single room. But a single powerful memory in the mind of its protagonist, a jaded book critic, conveys the elasticity of time—and the preciousness of life.

Bullet in the Brain

TOBIAS WOLFF

THE LINE was endless. Anders couldn't get to the bank until just before it closed and now he was stuck behind two women whose loud, stupid conversation put him in a murderous temper. He was never in the best of tempers anyway, Anders—a book critic known for the weary, elegant savagery with which he dispatched almost everything he reviewed.

With the line still doubled around the rope, one of the tellers stuck a Position Closed sign in her window and walked to the back of the bank, where she leaned against a desk and began to pass the time with a man shuffling papers. The women in front of Anders broke off their conversation and watched the teller with hatred. "Oh, that's nice," one of them said. She turned to Anders and added, confident of his accord, "One of those little human touches that keep us coming back."

Anders had conceived his own towering hatred of the teller, but he immediately turned it on the presumptuous crybaby in front of him. "Damned unfair," he said. "Tragic, really. If they're not chopping off the wrong leg, or bombing your ancestral village, they're closing their positions."

She stood her ground. "I didn't say it was tragic," she said. "I just think it's a pretty lousy way to treat your customers."

"Unforgivable," Anders said. "Heaven will take note."

She sucked in her checks but stared past him and said nothing. Anders saw that the other woman, her friend, was looking in the same direction. And then the tellers stopped what they were doing, and the customers slowly turned, and silence came over the bank. Two men wearing black ski masks and blue business suits were standing to the side of the door. One of them had a pistol pressed against the guard's neck. The guard's eyes were closed, and his lips were moving. The other man had a sawed-off shotgun. "Keep your big mouth shut!" the man with the pistol said, though no one had spoken a word. "One of you tellers hits the alarm, you're all dead meat. Got it?"

The tellers nodded.

"Oh, bravo," Anders said. "Dead meat." He turned to the woman in front of him. "Great script eh? The stern, brass-knuckled poetry of the dangerous classes."

She looked at him with drowning eyes.

The man with the shotgun pushed the guard to his knees. He handed the shotgun to his partner and yanked the guard's wrists up behind his back and locked them together with a pair of handcuffs. He then toppled him onto the floor with a kick between the shoulder blades. He took his shotgun back and went over to the security gate at the end of the counter. He was short and heavy and moved with peculiar slowness, even torpor. "Buzz him in," his partner said. The man with the shotgun sauntered along the line of tellers, handing each of them a Hefty bag. When he came to the empty position he looked over at the man with the pistol, who said, "Whose slot is that?"

Anders watched the teller. She put her hand to her throat and turned to the man she'd been talking to. He nodded. "Mine," she said.

"Then get your ugly ass in gear and fill that bag."

"There you go," Anders said to the woman in front of him. "Justice is done."

"Hey! Bright boy! Did I tell you to talk?"

"No," Anders said.

"Then shut your trap."

"Did you hear that?" Anders said. "'Bright boy.' Right out of 'The Killers.'"[1]

"Please be quiet," the woman said.

"Hey, you deaf or what?" The man with the pistol walked over to Anders. He poked the weapon into Anders' gut. "You think I'm playing games?"

"No," Anders said, but the barrel tickled like a stiff finger and he had to fight back the titters. He did this by making himself stare into the man's eyes, which were clearly visible behind the holes in the mask: pale-blue and rawly red-rimmed. The man's left eyelid kept twitching. He breathed out a piercing, ammoniac smell that shocked Anders more than anything that had happened, and he was beginning to develop a sense of unease when the man prodded him again with the pistol.

---

1 A 1946 American film noir based on a short story by Ernest Hemingway (1899-1961).

"You like me, bright boy?" he said. "You want to suck my dick?"

"No," Anders said.

"Then stop looking at me."

Anders fixed his gaze on the man's shiny wing-tip shoes.

"Not down there. Up there." He stuck the pistol under Anders' chin and pushed it upward until Anders was looking at the ceiling.

Anders had never paid much attention to that part of the bank, a pompous old building with marble floors and counters and pillars and gilt scrollwork over the tellers' cages. The domed ceiling had been decorated with mythological figures whose fleshy, toga-draped ugliness Anders had taken in at a glance many years earlier and afterward declined to notice. Now he had no choice but to scrutinize the painter's work. It was worse than he remembered, and all of it executed with the utmost gravity. The artist had a few tricks up his sleeve and used them again and again—a certain rosy blush on the underside of the clouds, a coy backward glance on the faces of the cupids and fauns. The ceiling was crowded with various dramas, but the one that caught Anders' eye was Zeus and Europa[2]—portrayed, in this rendition, as a bull ogling a cow from behind a haystack. To make the cow sexy, the painter had canted her hips suggestively and given her long, droopy eyelashes, through which she gazed back at the bull with sultry welcome. The bull wore a smirk and his eyebrows were arched. If there'd been a bubble coming out of his mouth, it would have said, "Hubba hubba."

"What's so funny, bright boy?"

"Nothing."

"You think I'm comical? You think I'm some kind of clown?"

"No."

"You think you can fuck with me?"

"No."

"Fuck with me again, you're history. *Capeesh*?"[3]

Anders burst out laughing. He covered his mouth with both hands and said, "I'm sorry, I'm sorry," then snorted helplessly through his fingers and said, "*Capeesh*, oh, God, *capeesh*," and at that the man with the pistol raised the pistol and shot Anders right in the head.

The bullet smashed Anders' skull and plowed through his brain and exited behind his right ear, scattering shards of bone into the cerebral cortex, the corpus callosum, back toward the basal ganglia, and down into the thalamus. But

---

2 In Greek mythology, Europa was abducted by Zeus while he was disguised as a white bull.

3 From the Italian *capisce*, or "Do you understand?"

before all this occurred, the first appearance of the bullet in the cerebrum set off a crackling chain of ion transports and neurotransmissions. Because of their peculiar origin, these traced a peculiar pattern, flukishly calling to life a summer afternoon some forty years past, and long since lost to memory. After striking the cranium, the bullet was moving at nine hundred feet per second, a pathetically sluggish, glacial pace compared with the synaptic lightning that flashed around it. Once in the brain, that is, the bullet came under the mediation of brain time, which gave Anders plenty of leisure to contemplate the scene that, in a phrase he would have abhorred, "passed before his eyes."

It is worth noting what Anders did not remember, given what he did remember. He did not remember his first lover, Sherry, or what he had most madly loved about her, before it came to irritate him—her unembarrassed carnality, and especially the cordial way she had with his unit, which she called Mr. Mole, as in "Uh-oh, looks like Mr. Mole wants to play," and "Let's hide Mr. Mole!" Anders did not remember his wife, whom he had also loved, before she exhausted him with her predictability, or his daughter, now a sullen professor of economics at Dartmouth. He did not remember standing just outside his daughter's door as she lectured her bear about his naughtiness and described the truly appalling punishments Paws would receive unless he changed his ways. He did not remember a single line of the hundreds of poems he had committed to memory in his youth so that he could give himself the shivers at will—not "Silent, upon a peak in Darien,"[4] or "My God I heard this day,"[5] or "All my pretty ones? Did you say all? O hell-kite! All?"[6] None of these did he remember, not one. Anders did not remember his dying mother saying of his father, "I should have stabbed him in his sleep."

He did not remember Professor Josephs telling his class how the Spartans had released Athenian prisoners from their mines if they could recite Aeschylus,[7] and then reciting Aeschylus himself, right there, in the Greek. Anders did not remember how his eyes had burned at those sounds. He did not remember the surprise of seeing a college classmate's name on the jacket of a novel not long after they graduated, or the respect he had felt after reading the book. He did not remember the pleasure of giving respect.

Nor did Anders remember seeing a woman leap to her death from the building opposite his own, just days after his daughter was born. He did not remember shouting, "Lord have mercy!" He did not remember deliberately crashing

4 From John Keats's "On First Looking into Chapman's Homer"(1816).

5 From George Herbert's "Man" (1633).

6 From Shakespeare's *Macbeth* 4.3.216–17.

7 Greek playwright, often called the father of tragedy (c. 525–456 BCE).

his father's car into a tree, or having his ribs kicked in by three policemen at an antiwar rally, or waking himself up with laughter. He did not remember when he began to regard the heap of books on his desk with boredom and dread, or when he grew angry at writers for writing them. He did not remember when everything began to remind him of something else.

This is what he remembered. Heat. A baseball field. Yellow grass, the whirr of insects, himself leaning against a tree as the boys of the neighborhood gather for a pickup game. The captains, precociously large boys named Burns and Darsch, argue the relative genius of Mantle and Mays.[8] They have been worrying this subject all summer, and it has become tedious to Anders; an oppression, like the heat.

Then the last two boys arrive, Coyle and a cousin of his from Mississippi. Anders has never met Coyle's cousin before and will never see him again. He says hi with the rest but takes no further notice of him until they've chosen sides and Darsch asks the cousin what position he wants to play. "Shortstop," the boy says. "Short's the best position they is." Anders turns and looks at him. He wants to hear Coyle's cousin repeat what he's just said, but he knows better than to ask. The others will think he's being a jerk, ragging the kid for his grammar. But that isn't it, not at all—it's that Anders is strangely roused, elated, by those final two words, their pure unexpectedness and their music. He takes the field in a trance, repeating them to himself.

The bullet is already in the brain; it won't be outrun forever, or charmed to a halt. In the end, it will do its work and leave the troubled skull behind, dragging its comet's tail of memory and hope and talent and love into the marble hall of commerce. That can't be helped. But for now Anders can still make time. Time for the shadows to lengthen on the grass, time for the tethered dog to bark at the flying ball, time for the boy in right field to smack his sweat-blackened mitt and softly chant, *They is, they is, they is.*

—1995

8 Mickey Mantle (1931–95) and Willie Mays (b. 1931), both professional American baseball players.

TIM O'BRIEN

One of the United States's most provocative writers, Tim O'Brien was born in 1946 in Austin, Minnesota, but lived the majority of his youth in Worthington, Minnesota, which he refers to as the "Turkey Capital of the World." Upon graduating with his BA in political science from Macalester College in 1968, he received his draft notice for the war in Vietnam. In a 1990 *New York Times* interview he spoke of the summer prior to his departing for Vietnam: "It was the most terrible summer of my life, worse than being in the war. My conscience kept telling me not to go, but my whole upbringing told me I had to. That horrible summer made me a writer." O'Brien resisted the impulse to either flee to Canada or go to jail (the other options available to men drafted for service at this time), and from February 1969 until March 1970, he served as an infantry foot soldier in Vietnam, an experience that informs much of his work.

On his return from the war, he studied American foreign policy at Harvard's School of Government, and, starting in 1972, interned at the *Washington Post*. He worked for the paper full-time as a national affairs reporter from 1974 to 1975. O'Brien's first book was a memoir entitled *If I Die in a Combat Zone, Box Me Up and Send Me Home* (1973). O'Brien's novels include the novel *Going After Cacciato* (1978), which won the National Book Award for Fiction in 1979, and *In the Lake of the Woods* (1994), winner of the James Fenimore Cooper Prize from the Society of American Historians and chosen best novel of the year by *Time* magazine. Among his other works are *Tomcat in Love* (1998) and *July, July* (2002). He lives in Texas with his sons and teaches at Texas State University.

His fifth book, *The Things They Carried* (1990), a collection of interrelated stories, won France's Prix du Meilleur Livre Etranger and was a finalist for the Pulitzer Prize and the National Book Critics Circle Award. The collection chronicles the experiences of an infantryman in Alpha Company during and after the war in Vietnam. The stories reveal O'Brien's interest in the complex nature of fiction. They feature a character named Tim O'Brien who O'Brien the author insists is not autobiographical. As well, the narratives are often interrupted by "true" stories that are made up, and by similar stories told from different points of view.

While "The Things They Carried" is primarily about the American experience of war in Vietnam, it is also about the nature of story-telling, and the ways in which story-telling can be a means of coping with the unknown.

The Things They Carried

TIM O'BRIEN

FIRST Lieutenant Jimmy Cross carried letters from a girl named Martha, a junior at Mount Sebastian College in New Jersey. They were not love letters, but Lieutenant Cross was hoping, so he kept them folded in plastic at the bottom of his rucksack. In the late afternoon, after a day's march, he would dig his foxhole, wash his hands under a canteen, unwrap the letters, hold them with the tips of his fingers, and spend the last hour of light pretending. He would imagine romantic camping trips into the White Mountains in New Hampshire. He would sometimes taste the envelope flaps, knowing her tongue had been there. More than anything, he wanted Martha to love him as he loved her, but the letters were mostly chatty, elusive on the matter of love. She was a virgin, he was almost sure. She was an English major at Mount Sebastian, and she wrote beautifully about her professors and roommates and midterm exams, about her respect for Chaucer and her great affection for Virginia Woolf. She often quoted lines of poetry; she never mentioned the war, except to say, Jimmy, take care of yourself. The letters weighed 10 ounces. They were signed Love, Martha, but Lieutenant Cross understood that Love was only a way of signing and did not mean what he sometimes pretended it meant. At dusk, he would carefully return the letters to his rucksack. Slowly, a bit distracted, he would get up and move among his men, checking the perimeter, then at full dark he would return to his hole and watch the night and wonder if Martha was a virgin.

The things they carried were largely determined by necessity. Among the necessities or near-necessities were P-38 can openers, pocket knives, heat tabs, wristwatches, dog tags, mosquito repellent, chewing gum, candy, cigarettes, salt tablets, packets of Kool-Aid, lighters, matches, sewing kits, Military Payment Certificates, C rations, and two or three canteens of water. Together, these items weighed between 15 and 20 pounds, depending upon a man's habits or rate of metabolism. Henry Dobbins, who was a big man, carried extra rations; he was especially fond of canned peaches in heavy syrup over pound cake. Dave Jensen, who practiced field hygiene, carried a toothbrush, dental floss, and several hotel-sized bars of soap he'd stolen on R&R in Sydney, Australia. Ted Lavender, who was scared, carried tranquilizers until he was shot in the head outside the village of Than Khe in mid-April. By necessity, and because it was SOP,[1] they all carried steel helmets that weighed 5 pounds including the liner and camouflage cover. They carried the standard fatigue jackets and trousers. Very few carried underwear. On their feet they carried jungle boots—2.1 pounds—and Dave Jensen carried three pairs of socks and a can of Dr. Scholl's foot powder as a precaution against trench foot. Until he was shot, Ted Lavender carried six or seven ounces of premium dope, which for him was a necessity. Mitchell Sanders, the RTO,[2] carried condoms. Norman Bowker carried a diary. Rat Kiley carried comic books. Kiowa, a devout Baptist, carried an illustrated New Testament that had been presented to him by his father, who taught Sunday school in Oklahoma City, Oklahoma. As a hedge against bad times, however, Kiowa also carried his grandmother's distrust of the white man, his grandfather's old hunting hatchet. Necessity dictated. Because the land was mined and booby-trapped, it was SOP for each man to carry a steel-centered, nylon-covered flak jacket, which weighed 6.7 pounds, but which on hot days seemed much heavier. Because you could die so quickly, each man carried at least one large compress bandage, usually in the helmet band for easy access. Because the nights were cold, and because the monsoons were wet, each carried a green plastic poncho that could be used as a raincoat or groundsheet or makeshift tent. With its quilted liner, the poncho weighed almost two pounds, but it was worth every ounce. In April, for instance, when Ted Lavender was shot, they used his poncho to wrap him up, then to carry him across the paddy, then to lift him into the chopper that took him away.

They were called legs or grunts.

To carry something was to hump it, as when Lieutenant Jimmy Cross humped his love for Martha up the hills and through the swamps. In its intransitive form, to hump meant to walk, or to march, but it implied burdens far beyond the intransitive.

Almost everyone humped photographs. In his wallet, Lieutenant Cross carried two photographs of Martha. The first was a Kodacolor snapshot signed Love, though he knew better. She stood against a brick wall. Her eyes were gray and neutral, her lips slightly open as she stared straight-on at the camera. At night, sometimes, Lieutenant Cross wondered who had taken the picture, because he

1 Standard operating procedure.

2 Radio telephone operator.

knew she had boyfriends, because he loved her so much, and because he could see the shadow of the picture-taker spreading out against the brick wall. The second photograph had been clipped from the 1968 Mount Sebastian yearbook. It was an action shot—women's volleyball—and Martha was bent horizontal to the floor, reaching, the palms of her hands in sharp focus, the tongue taut, the expression frank and competitive. There was no visible sweat. She wore white gym shorts. Her legs, he thought, were almost certainly the legs of a virgin, dry and without hair, the left knee cocked and carrying her entire weight, which was just over one hundred pounds. Lieutenant Cross remembered touching that left knee. A dark theater, he remembered, and the movie was *Bonnie and Clyde*, and Martha wore a tweed suit, and during the final scene, when he touched her knee, she turned and looked at him in a sad, sober way that made him pull his hand back, but he would always remember the feel of the tweed skirt and the knee beneath it and the sound of the gunfire that killed Bonnie and Clyde, how embarrassing it was, how slow and oppressive. He remembered kissing her good night at the dorm door. Right then, he thought, he should've done something brave. He should've carried her up the stairs to her room and tied her to the bed and touched that left knee all night long. He should've risked it. Whenever he looked at the photographs, he thought of new things he should've done.

What they carried was partly a function of rank, partly of field specialty.

As a first lieutenant and platoon leader, Jimmy Cross carried a compass, maps, code books, binoculars, and a .45-caliber pistol that weighed 2.9 pounds fully loaded. He carried a strobe light and the responsibility for the lives of his men.

As an RTO, Mitchell Sanders carried the PRC-25 radio, a killer, 26 pounds with its battery.

As a medic, Rat Kiley carried a canvas satchel filled with morphine and plasma and malaria tablets and surgical tape and comic books and all the things a medic must carry, including M&M's for especially bad wounds, for a total weight of nearly 20 pounds.

As a big man, therefore a machine gunner, Henry Dobbins carried the M-60, which weighed 23 pounds unloaded, but which was almost always loaded. In addition, Dobbins carried between 10 and 15 pounds of ammunition draped in belts across his chest and shoulders.

As PFCs[3] or Spec 4s, most of them were common grunts and carried the standard M-16 gas-operated assault rifle. The weapon weighted 7.5 pounds unloaded, 8.2 pounds with its full 20-round magazine. Depending on numerous

3 Privates first class.

factors, such as topography and psychology, the riflemen carried anywhere from 12 to 20 magazines, usually in cloth bandoliers, adding on another 8.4 pounds at minimum, 14 pounds at maximum. When it was available, they also carried M-16 maintenance gear—rods and steel brushes and swabs and tubes of LSA oil—all of which weighed about a pound. Among the grunts, some carried the M-79 grenade launcher, 5.9 pounds unloaded, a reasonably light weapon except for the ammunition, which was heavy. A single round weighed 10 ounces. The typical load was 25 rounds. But Ted Lavender, who was scared, carried 34 rounds when he was shot and killed outside Than Khe, and he went down under an exceptional burden, more than 20 pounds of ammunition, plus the flak jacket and helmet and rations and water and toilet paper and tranquilizers and all the rest, plus the unweighed fear. He was dead weight. There was no twitching or flopping. Kiowa, who saw it happen, said it was like watching a rock fall, or a big sandbag or something—just boom, then down—not like the movies where the dead guy rolls around and does fancy spins and goes ass over teakettle—not like that, Kiowa said, the poor bastard just flat-fuck fell. Boom. Down. Nothing else. It was a bright morning in mid-April. Lieutenant Cross felt the pain. He blamed himself. They stripped off Lavender's canteens and ammo, all the heavy things, and Rat Kiley said the obvious, the guy's dead, and Mitchell Sanders used his radio to report one U.S. KIA[4] and to request a chopper. Then they wrapped Lavender in his poncho. They carried him out to a dry paddy, established security, and sat smoking the dead man's dope until the chopper came. Lieutenant Cross kept to himself. He pictured Martha's smooth young face, thinking he loved her more than anything, more than his men, and now Ted Lavender was dead because he loved her so much and could not stop thinking about her. When the dustoff arrived, they carried Lavender aboard. Afterward they burned Than Khe. They marched until dusk, then dug their holes, and that night Kiowa kept explaining how you had to be there, how fast it was, how the poor guy just dropped like so much concrete. Boom-down, he said. Like cement.

In addition to the three standard weapons—the M-60, M-16, and M-79—they carried whatever presented itself, or whatever seemed appropriate as a means of killing or staying alive. They carried catch-as-catch-can. At various times, in various situations, they carried M-14s and CAR-15s and Swedish Ks and grease guns and captured AK-47s and Chi-Coms and RPGs and Simonov carbines and black market Uzis and .38-caliber Smith & Wesson handguns and 66 mm LAWs[5] and shotguns and silencers and blackjacks and bayonets and C-4

---

4 Killed in action.

5 A kind of shoulder-fired rocket.

plastic explosives. Lee Strunk carried a slingshot; a weapon of last resort, he called it. Mitchell Sanders carried brass knuckles. Kiowa carried his grandfather's feathered hatchet. Every third or fourth man carried a Claymore antipersonnel mine—3.5 pounds with its firing device. They all carried fragmentation grenades—14 ounces each. They all carried at least one M-18 colored smoke grenade—24 ounces. Some carried CS[6] or tear gas grenades. Some carried white phosphorus grenades. They carried all they could bear, and then some, including a silent awe for the terrible power of the things they carried.

In the first week of April, before Lavender died, Lieutenant Jimmy Cross received a good-luck charm from Martha. It was a simple pebble, an ounce at most. Smooth to the touch, it was a milky white color with flecks of orange and violet, oval-shaped, like a miniature egg. In the accompanying letter, Martha wrote that she had found the pebble on the Jersey shoreline, precisely where the land touched water at high tide, where things came together but also separated. It was this separate-but-together quality, she wrote, that had inspired her to pick up the pebble and to carry it in her breast pocket for several days, where it seemed weightless, and then to send it through the mail, by air, as a token of her truest feelings for him. Lieutenant Cross found this romantic. But he wondered what her truest feelings were, exactly, and what she meant by separate-but-together. He wondered how the tides and waves had come into play on that afternoon along the Jersey shoreline when Martha saw the pebble and bent down to rescue it from geology. He imagined bare feet. Martha was a poet, with the poet's sensibilities, and her feet would be brown and bare, the toenails unpainted, the eyes chilly and somber like the ocean in March, and though it was painful, he wondered who had been with her that afternoon. He imagined a pair of shadows moving along the strip of sand where things came together but also separated. It was phantom jealousy, he knew, but he couldn't help himself. He loved her so much. On the march, through the hot days of early April, he carried the pebble in his mouth, turning it with his tongue, tasting sea salt and moisture. His mind wandered. He had difficulty keeping his attention on the war. On occasion he would yell at his men to spread out the column, to keep their eyes open, but then he would slip away into daydreams, just pretending, walking barefoot along the Jersey shore, with Martha, carrying nothing. He would feel himself rising. Sun and waves and gentle winds, all love and lightness.

What they carried varied by mission.

When a mission took them to the mountains, they carried mosquito netting, machetes, canvas tarps, and extra bug juice.

---

6 Riot-control gas.

If a mission seemed especially hazardous, or if it involved a place they knew to be bad, they carried everything they could. In certain heavily mined AOs,[7] where the land was dense with Toe Poppers and Bouncing Betties, they took turns humping a 28-pound mine detector. With its headphones and big sensing plate, the equipment was a stress on the lower back and shoulders, awkward to handle, often useless because of the shrapnel in the earth, but they carried it anyway, partly for safety, partly for the illusion of safety.

On ambush, or other night missions, they carried peculiar little odds and ends, Kiowa always took along his New Testament and a pair of moccasins for silence. Dave Jensen carried night-sight vitamins high in carotene. Lee Strunk carried his slingshot; ammo, he claimed, would never be a problem. Rat Kiley carried brandy and M&M's candy. Until he was shot, Ted Lavender carried the starlight scope, which weighed 6.3 pounds with its aluminum carrying case. Henry Dobbins carried his girlfriend's pantyhose wrapped around his neck as a comforter. They all carried ghosts. When dark came, they would move out single file across the meadows and paddies to their ambush coordinates, where they would quietly set up the Claymores and lie down and spend the night waiting.

Other missions were more complicated and required special equipment. In mid-April, it was their mission to search out and destroy the elaborate tunnel complexes in the Than Khe area south of Chu Lai. To blow the tunnels, they carried one-pound blocks of pentrite high explosives, four blocks to a man, 68 pounds in all. They carried wiring, detonators, and battery-powered clackers. Dave Jensen carried earplugs. Most often, before blowing the tunnels, they were ordered by higher command to search them, which was considered bad news, but by and large they just shrugged and carried out orders. Because he was a big man, Henry Dobbins was excused from tunnel duty. The others would draw numbers. Before Lavender died there were 17 men in the platoon, and whoever drew the number 17 would strip off his gear and crawl in headfirst with a flashlight and Lieutenant Cross's .45-caliber pistol. The rest of them would fan out as security. They would sit down or kneel, not facing the hole, listening to the ground beneath them, imagining cobwebs and ghosts, whatever was down there—the tunnel walls squeezing in—how the flashlight seemed impossibly heavy in the hand and how it was tunnel vision in the very strictest sense, compression in all ways, even time, and how you had to wiggle in—ass and elbows—a swallowed-up feeling—and how you found yourself worrying about odd things: Will your flashlight go dead? Do rats carry rabies? If you screamed, how far would the sound carry?

7 Area of operations.

Would your buddies hear it? Would they have the courage to drag you out? In some respects, though not many, the waiting was worse than the tunnel itself. Imagination was a killer.

On April 16, when Lee Strunk drew the number 17, he laughed and muttered something and went down quickly. The morning was hot and very still. Not good, Kiowa said. He looked at the tunnel opening, then out across a dry paddy toward the village of Than Khe. Nothing moved. No clouds or birds or people. As they waited, the men smoked and drank Kool-Aid, not talking much, feeling sympathy for Lee Strunk but also feeling the luck of the draw. You win some, you lose some, said Mitchell Sanders, and sometimes you settle for a rain check. It was a tired line and no one laughed.

Henry Dobbins ate a tropical chocolate bar. Ted Lavender popped a tranquilizer and went off to pee.

After five minutes, Lieutenant Jimmy Cross moved to the tunnel, leaned down, and examined the darkness. Trouble, he thought—a cave-in maybe. And then suddenly, without willing it, he was thinking about Martha. The stresses and fractures, the quick collapse, the two of them buried alive under all that weight. Dense, crushing love. Kneeling, watching the hole, he tried to concentrate on Lee Strunk and the war, all the dangers, but his love was too much for him, he felt paralyzed, he wanted to sleep inside her lungs and breathe her blood and be smothered. He wanted her to be a virgin and not a virgin, all at once. He wanted to know her. Intimate secrets: Why poetry? Why so sad? Why that grayness in her eyes? Why so alone? Not lonely, just alone—riding her bike across campus or sitting off by herself in the cafeteria—even dancing, she danced alone—and it was the aloneness that filled him with love. He remembered telling her that one evening. How she nodded and looked away. And how, later, when he kissed her, she received the kiss without returning it, her eyes wide open, not afraid, not a virgin's eyes, just flat and uninvolved.

Lieutenant Cross gazed at the tunnel. But he was not there. He was buried with Martha under the white sand at the Jersey shore. They were pressed together, and the pebble in his mouth was her tongue. He was smiling. Vaguely, he was aware of how quiet the day was, the sullen paddies, yet he could not bring himself to worry about matters of security. He was beyond that. He was just a kid at war, in love. He was twenty-four years old. He couldn't help it.

A few moments later Lee Strunk crawled out of the tunnel. He came up grinning, filthy but alive. Lieutenant Cross nodded and closed his eyes while the others clapped Strunk on the back and made jokes about rising from the dead.

Worms, Rat Kiley said. Right out of the grave. Fuckin' zombie.

The men laughed. They all felt great relief.

Spook city, said Mitchell Sanders.

Lee Strunk made a funny ghost sound, a kind of moaning, yet very happy, and right then, when Strunk made that high happy moaning sound, when he went *Ahhooooo*, right then Ted Lavender was shot in the head on his way back from peeing. He lay with his mouth open. The teeth were broken. There was a swollen black bruise under his left eye. The cheekbone was gone. Oh shit, Rat Kiley said, the guy's dead. The guy's dead, he kept saying, which seemed profound—the guy's dead. I mean really.

The things they carried were determined to some extent by superstition. Lieutenant Cross carried his good-luck pebble. Dave Jensen carried a rabbit's foot. Norman Bowker, otherwise a very gentle person, carried a thumb that had been presented to him as a gift by Mitchell Sanders. The thumb was dark brown, rubbery to the touch, and weighted four ounces at most. It had been cut from a VC[8] corpse, a boy of fifteen or sixteen. They'd found him at the bottom of an irrigation ditch, badly burned, flies in his mouth and eyes. The boy wore black shorts and sandals. At the time of his death he had been carrying a pouch of rice, a rifle, and three magazines of ammunition.

You want my opinion, Mitchell Sanders said, there's a definite moral here.

He put his hand on the dead boy's wrist. He was quiet for a time, as if counting a pulse, then he patted the stomach, almost affectionately, and used Kiowa's hunting hatchet to remove the thumb.

Henry Dobbins asked what the moral was.

Moral?

You know. *Moral.*

Sanders wrapped the thumb in toilet paper and handed it across to Norman Bowker. There was no blood. Smiling, he kicked the boy's head, watched the flies scatter, and said, It's like with that old TV show—Paladin. Have gun, will travel.[9]

Henry Dobbins thought about it.

Yeah, well, he finally said. I don't see no moral.

There it *is*, man.

Fuck off.

They carried USO stationery and pencils and pens. They carried Sterno, safety pins, trip flares, signal flares, spools of wire, razor blades, chewing tobacco, liberated joss sticks and statuettes of the smiling Buddha, candles, grease pencils, *The Stars and Stripes*, fingernail clippers, Psy Ops leaflets, bush hats, bolos, and much

8 Viet Cong.

9 *Have Gun, Will Travel* was a television show set in the wild American West. The show's protagonist, a gun-for-hire, was named Paladin.

more. Twice a week, when the resupply choppers came in, they carried hot chow in green mermite cans and large canvas bags filled with iced beer and soda pop. They carried plastic water containers, each with a two-gallon capacity. Mitchell Sanders carried a set of starched tiger fatigues for special occasions. Henry Dobbins carried Black Flag insecticide. Dave Jensen carried empty sandbags that could be filled at night for added protection. Lee Strunk carried tanning lotion. Some things they carried in common. Taking turns, they carried the big PRC-77 scrambler radio, which weighed 30 pounds with its battery. They shared the weight of memory. They took up what others could no longer bear. Often, they carried each other, the wounded or weak. They carried infections. They carried chess sets, basketballs, Vietnamese-English dictionaries, insignia of rank, Bronze Stars and Purple Hearts, plastic cards imprinted with the Code of Conduct. They carried diseases, among them malaria and dysentery. They carried lice and ringworm and leeches and paddy algae and various rots and molds. They carried the land itself—Vietnam, the place, the soil—a powdery orange-red dust that covered their boots and fatigues and faces. They carried the sky. The whole atmosphere, they carried it, the humidity, the monsoons, the stink of fungus and decay, all of it, they carried gravity. They moved like mules. By daylight they took sniper fire, at night they were mortared, but it was not battle, it was just the endless march, village to village, without purpose, nothing won or lost. They marched for the sake of the march. They plodded along slowly, dumbly, leaning forward against the heat, unthinking, all blood and bone, simple grunts, soldiering with their legs, toiling up the hills and down into the paddies and across the rivers and up again and down, just humping, one step and then the next and then another, but no volition, no will, because it was automatic, it was anatomy, and the war was entirely a matter of posture and carriage, the hump was everything, a kind of inertia, a kind of emptiness, a dullness of desire and intellect and conscience and hope and human sensibility. Their principles were in their feet. Their calculations were biological. They had no sense of strategy or mission. They searched the villages without knowing what to look for, not caring, kicking over jars of rice, frisking children and old men, blowing tunnels, sometimes setting fires and sometimes not, then forming up and moving on to the next village, then other villages, where it would always be the same. They carried their own lives. The pressures were enormous. In the heat of early afternoon, they would remove their helmets and flak jackets, walking bare, which was dangerous but which helped ease the strain. They would often discard things along the route of march. Purely for comfort, they would throw away rations, blow their Claymores and grenades, no matter, because by nightfall the resupply choppers would arrive with more of the same, then a day or two later still more, fresh watermelons and crates of ammunition and sunglasses and woolen sweaters—the resources were stunning—sparklers for the Fourth of

July, colored eggs for Easter—it was the great American war chest—the fruits of science, the smokestacks, the canneries, the arsenals at Hartford, the Minnesota forests, the machine shops, the vast fields of corn and wheat—they carried like freight trains; they carried it on their backs and shoulders—and for all the ambiguities of Vietnam, all the mysteries and unknowns, there was at least the single abiding certainty that they would never be at a loss for things to carry.

After the chopper took Lavender away, Lieutenant Jimmy Cross led his men into the village of Than Khe. They burned everything. They shot chickens and dogs, they trashed the village well, they called in artillery and watched the wreckage, then they marched for several hours through the hot afternoon, and then at dusk, while Kiowa explained how Lavender died, Lieutenant Cross found himself trembling.

He tried not to cry. With his entrenching tool, which weighed five pounds, he began digging a hole in the earth.

He felt shame. He hated himself. He had loved Martha more than his men, and as a consequence Lavender was now dead, and this was something he would have to carry like a stone in his stomach for the rest of the war.

All he could do was dig. He used his entrenching tool like an ax, slashing, feeling both love and hate, and then later, when it was full dark, he sat at the bottom of his foxhole and wept. It went on for a long while. In part, he was grieving for Ted Lavender, but mostly it was for Martha, and for himself, because she belonged to another world, which was not quite real, and because she was a junior at Mount Sebastian College in New Jersey, a poet and a virgin and uninvolved, and because he realized she did not love him and never would.

Like cement, Kiowa whispered in the dark. I swear to God—boom, down. Not a word.

I've heard this, said Norman Bowker.

A pisser, you know? Still zipping himself up. Zapped while zipping.

All right, fine. That's enough.

Yeah, but you had to see it, the guy just—

I *heard*, man. Cement. So why not shut the fuck *up*?

Kiowa shook his head sadly and glanced over at the hole where Lieutenant Jimmy Cross sat watching the night. The air was thick and wet. A warm dense fog had settled over the paddies and there was the stillness that precedes rain.

After a time Kiowa sighed.

One thing for sure, he said. The lieutenant's in some deep hurt. I mean that crying jag—the way he was carrying on—it wasn't fake or anything, it was real heavy-duty hurt. The man cares.

Sure, Norman Bowker said.

Say what you want, the man does care.

We all got problems.

Not Lavender.

No, I guess not, Bowker said. Do me a favor, though.

Shut up?

That's a smart Indian. Shut up.

Shrugging, Kiowa pulled off his boots. He wanted to say more, just to lighten up his sleep, but instead he opened his New Testament and arranged it beneath his head as a pillow. The fog made things seem hollow and unattached. He tried not to think about Ted Lavender, but then he was thinking how fast it was, no drama, down and dead, and how it was hard to feel anything except surprise. It seemed unchristian. He wished he could find some great sadness, or even anger, but the emotion wasn't there and he couldn't make it happen. Mostly he felt pleased to be alive. He liked the smell of the New Testament under his cheek, the leather and ink and paper and glue, whatever the chemicals were. He liked hearing the sounds of night. Even his fatigue, it felt fine, the stiff muscles and the prickly awareness of his own body, a floating feeling. He enjoyed not being dead. Lying there, Kiowa admired Lieutenant Jimmy Cross's capacity for grief. He wanted to share the man's pain, he wanted to care as Jimmy Cross cared. And yet when he closed his eyes, all he could think, was Boom-down, and all he could feel was the pleasure of having his boots off and the fog curling in around him and the damp soil and the Bible smells and the plush comfort of night.

After a moment Norman Bowker sat up in the dark.

What the hell, he said. You want to talk, *talk*. Tell it to me.

Forget it.

No, man, go on. One thing I hate, it's a silent Indian.

For the most part they carried themselves with poise, a kind of dignity. Now and then, however, there were times of panic, when they squealed or wanted to squeal but couldn't, when they twitched and made moaning sounds and covered their heads and said Dear Jesus and flopped around on the earth and fired their weapons blindly and cringed and sobbed and begged for the noise to stop and went wild and made stupid promises to themselves and to God and to their mothers and fathers, hoping not to die. In different ways, it happened to all of them. Afterward, when the firing ended, they would blink and peek up. They would touch their bodies, feeling shame, then quickly hiding it. They would force themselves to stand. As if in slow motion, frame by frame, the world would take on the old logic—absolute silence, then the wind, then sunlight, then voices. It was the burden of being alive. Awkwardly, the men would reassemble themselves, first in private, then in groups, becoming soldiers again. They would repair the leaks in their eyes. They would check for casualties, call in dustoffs, light cigarettes, try to smile, clear their throats and spit and begin cleaning their weapons. After a time someone would shake his head and say, No lie, I almost shit my pants, and someone else would laugh, which meant it was bad, yes, but the guy had obviously not shit his pants, it wasn't that bad, and in any case nobody would ever do such a thing and then go ahead and talk about it. They would squint into the dense, oppressive sunlight. For a few moments, perhaps, they would fall silent, lighting a joint and tracking its passage from man to man, inhaling, holding in the humiliation. Scary stuff, one of them might say. But then someone else would grin or flick his eyebrows and say, Roger-dodger, almost cut me a new asshole, *almost*.

There were numerous such poses. Some carried themselves with a sort of wistful resignation, others with pride or stiff soldierly discipline or good humor or macho zeal. They were afraid of dying but they were even more afraid to show it.

They found jokes to tell.

They used a hard vocabulary to contain the terrible softness. *Greased* they'd say. *Offed, lit up, zapped while zipping.* It wasn't cruelty, just stage presence. They were actors. When someone died, it wasn't quite dying, because in a curious way it seemed scripted, and because they had their lines mostly memorized, irony mixed with tragedy, and because they called it by other names, as if to encyst and destroy the reality of death itself. They kicked corpses. They cut off thumbs. They talked grunt lingo. They told stories about Ted Lavender's supply of tranquilizers, how the poor guy didn't feel a thing, how incredibly tranquil he was.

There's a moral here, said Mitchell Sanders.

They were waiting for Lavender's chopper, smoking the dead man's dope.

The moral's pretty obvious, Sanders said, and winked. Stay away from drugs. No joke, they'll ruin your day every time.

Cute, said Henry Dobbins.

Mind blower, get it? Talk about wiggy. Nothing left, just blood and brains.

They made themselves laugh.

There it is, they'd say. Over and over—there it is, my friend, there it is—as if the repetition itself were an act of poise, a balance between crazy and almost crazy, knowing without going, there it is, which meant be cool, let it ride, because Oh yeah, man, you can't change what can't be changed, there it is, there it absolutely and positively and fucking well *is*.

They were tough.

They carried all the emotional baggage of men who might die. Grief, terror, love, longing—these were intangibles, but the intangibles had their own mass and specific gravity, they had tangible weight. They carried shameful memories. They carried the common secret of cowardice barely restrained, the instinct to run or freeze or hide, and in many respects this was the heaviest burden of all, for it could never be put down, it required perfect balance and perfect posture. They carried their reputations. They carried the soldier's greatest fear, which was the fear of blushing. Men killed, and died, because they were embarrassed not to. It was what had brought them to the war in the first place, nothing positive, no dreams of glory or honor, just to avoid the blush of dishonor. They died so as not to die of embarrassment. They crawled into tunnels and walked point and advanced under fire. Each morning, despite the unknowns, they made their legs move. They endured. They kept humping. They did not submit to the obvious alternative, which was simply to close the eyes and fall. So easy, really. Go limp and tumble to the ground and let the muscles unwind and not speak and not budge until your buddies picked you up and lifted you into the chopper that would roar and dip its nose and carry you off to the world. A mere matter of falling, yet no one ever fell. It was not courage, exactly; the object was not valor. Rather, they were too frightened to be cowards.

By and large they carried these things inside, maintaining the masks of composure. They sneered at sick call. They spoke bitterly about guys who had found release by shooting off their own toes or fingers. Pussies, they'd say. Candyasses. It was fierce, mocking talk, with only a trace of envy or awe, but even so the image played itself out behind their eyes.

They imagined the muzzle against flesh. So easy: squeeze the trigger and blow away a toe. They imagined it. They imagined the quick, sweet pain, then the evacuation to Japan, then a hospital with warm beds and cute geisha nurses.

And they dreamed of freedom birds.

At night, on guard, staring into the dark, they were carried away by jumbo jets. They felt the rush of takeoff. *Gone!* they yelled. And then velocity—wings and engines—a smiling stewardess—but it was more than a plane, it was a real bird, a big sleek silver bird with feathers and talons and high screeching. They were flying. The weights fell off; there was nothing to bear. They laughed and held on tight, feeling the cold slap of wind and altitude, soaring, thinking *It's over, I'm gone!*—they were naked, they were light and free—it was all lightness, bright and fast and buoyant, light as light, a helium buzz in the brain, a giddy bubbling in the lungs as they were taken up over the clouds and the war, beyond duty, beyond gravity and mortification and global entanglements—*Sin loi!*[10] they yelled. *I'm sorry, motherfuckers, but I'm out of it, I'm goofed, I'm on a space cruise, I'm gone!*—and it was a restful, unencumbered sensation, just riding the

10 Vietnamese: pardon me.

light waves, sailing that big silver freedom bird over the mountains and oceans, over America, over the farms and great sleeping cities and cemeteries and highways and the golden arches of McDonald's, it was flight, a kind of fleeing, a kind of falling, falling higher and higher, spinning off the edge of the earth and beyond the sun and through the vast, silent vacuum where there were no burdens and where everything weighed exactly nothing—*Gone!* they screamed. *I'm sorry but I'm gone!*—and so at night, not quite dreaming, they gave themselves over to lightness, thcy were carried, they were purely borne.

On the morning after Ted Lavender died, First Lieutenant Jimmy Cross crouched at the bottom of his foxhole and burned Martha's letters. Then he burned the two photographs. There was a steady rain falling, which made it difficult, but he used heat tabs and Sterno to build a small fire, screening it with his body, holding the photographs over the tight blue flame with the tips of his fingers.

He realized it was only a gesture. Stupid, he thought. Sentimental, too, but mostly just stupid.

Lavender was dead. You couldn't burn the blame.

Besides, the letters were in his head. And even now, without photographs, Lieutenant Cross could see Martha playing volleyball in her white gym shorts and yellow T-shirt. He could see her moving in the rain.

When the fire died out, Lieutenant Cross pulled his poncho over his shoulders and ate breakfast from a can.

There was no great mystery, he decided.

In those burned letters Martha had never mentioned the war, except to say, Jimmy, take care of yourself. She wasn't involved. She signed the letters Love, but it wasn't love, and all the fine lines and technicalities did not matter. Virginity was no longer an issue. He hated her. Yes, he did. He hated her. Love, too, but it was a hard, hating kind of love.

The morning came up wet and blurry. Everything seemed part of everything else, the fog and Martha and the deepening rain.

He was a soldier, after all.

Half smiling, Lieutenant Jimmy Cross took out his maps. He shook his head hard, as if to clear it, then bent forward and began planning the day's march. In ten minutes, or maybe twenty, he would rouse the men and they would pack up and head west, where the maps showed the country to be green and inviting. They would do what they had always done. The rain might add some weight, but otherwise it would be one more day layered upon all the other days.

He was realistic about it. There was that new hardness in his stomach. He loved her but he hated her.

No more fantasies, he told himself.

Henceforth, when he thought about Martha, it would be only to think that she belonged elsewhere. He would shut down the daydreams. This was not Mount Sebastian, it was another world, where there were no pretty poems or mid-term exams, a place where men died because of carelessness and gross stupidity. Kiowa was right. Boom-down, and you were dead, never partly dead.

Briefly, in the rain, Lieutenant Cross saw Martha's gray eyes gazing back at him.

He understood.

It was very sad, he thought. The things men carried inside. The things men did or felt they had to do.

He almost nodded at her, but didn't.

Instead he went back to his maps. He was now determined to perform his duties firmly and without negligence. It wouldn't help Lavender, he knew that, but from this point on he would comport himself as an officer. He would dispose of his good-luck pebble. Swallow it, maybe, or use Lee Strunk's slingshot, or just drop it along the trail. On the march he would impose strict field discipline. He would be careful to send out flank security, to prevent straggling or bunching up, to keep his troops moving at the proper pace and at the proper interval. He would insist on clean weapons. He would confiscate the remainder of Lavender's dope. Later in the day, perhaps, he would call the men together and speak to them plainly. He would accept the blame for what had happened to Ted Lavender. He would be a man about it. He would look them in the eyes, keeping his chin level, and he would issue the new SOPs in a calm, impersonal tone of voice, a lieutenant's voice, leaving no room for argument or discussion. Commencing immediately, he'd tell them, they would no longer abandon equipment along the route of march. They would police up their acts. They would get their shit together, and keep it together, and maintain it neatly and in good working order.

He would not tolerate laxity. He would show strength, distancing himself.

Among the men there would be grumbling, of course, and maybe worse, because their days would seem longer and their loads heavier, but Lieutenant Jimmy Cross reminded himself that his obligation was not to be loved but to lead. He would dispense with love; it was not now a factor. And if anyone quarreled or complained, he would simply tighten his lips and arrange his shoulders in the correct command posture. He might give a curt little nod. Or he might not. He might just shrug and say, Carry on, then they would saddle up and form into a column and move out toward the villages west of Than Khe.

—1990

JAMAICA KINCAID

Jamaica Kincaid is the pen name of Elaine Potter Richardson, the daughter of Annie Richardson and Kincaid's stepfather, David Drew (she did not meet her biological father, Roderick Potter, until she was an adult). She was born in 1949 in St. Johns, Antigua, and, until the birth of her three brothers in rapid succession (starting when she was nine years old), she maintained an extremely close relationship with her mother. With the birth of her brothers, however, her parents' attention turned away from Kincaid. Their plans focused on her brothers' future university educations; Kincaid was sent to apprentice with a seamstress. When Kincaid was 13, her mother withdrew her from her schooling so that Kincaid could help take care of her brothers and her ailing stepfather. When she was 17, Kincaid's parents sent her to the United States to work as an *au pair* in order to help out the family financially. Kincaid would not return to Antigua or see her mother again until almost 20 years later.

In the United States, Kincaid went to work for an Upper East Side New York couple—Kincaid would later draw from this experience for her novel *Lucy*. As Kincaid once stated in an interview, the relationship between her life and what she writes is a complicated mesh. "I write about myself for the most part, and about things that have happened to me. Everything I say is true, and everything I say is not true." After several false starts at other jobs and pursuing courses at various post-secondary institutions, Kincaid eventually began freelance writing for magazines such as *Ms*, *Ingenue*, and *The New Yorker*. In 1973, with her first publication, she changed her name to Jamaica Kincaid: "Part of the reason I changed my name was so that they wouldn't know I was writing. I was afraid I would be laughed at, though it would not have stopped me. Nothing has made me not do what I wanted to do." Many of the stories that appear in *At the Bottom of the River* developed from Kincaid's columns in the "Talk of the Town" section of *The New Yorker*. Kincaid has said that writing for "Talk of the Town" "did two things":

> It showed me how to write, and it allowed me to write in my own voice.... I wrote many very weird "Talk" stories that appeared in *The New Yorker*, very experimental "Talk" stories, and it was from them that I learned how to do the stories in *At the Bottom of the River*.

At the Bottom of the River was published in 1983, went on to win the Morton Dauwen Zabel Award of the American Academy and Institute of Arts and Letters, and was nominated for the PEN/Faulkner Award. Kincaid has published several works since then, including the novels *Annie John* and *Lucy*, and the memoirs *A Small Place* and *My Brother*. She worked at *The New Yorker* as a staff writer from 1976 until 1995; in 1994 she started teaching literature and creative writing part-time at Harvard's African American Studies department.

"Girl" is the first story in the short story collection *At the Bottom of the River*. Kincaid wrote the one-sentence story in 1978 and has said that it was inspired by Elizabeth Bishop's poem "In the Waiting Room." Kincaid writes in the voice of a mother giving a list of impossible instructions to her daughter; as she does so we come to see a fractious relationship between mother and daughter—a motif ubiquitous in Kincaid's work.

Girl

JAMAICA KINCAID

WASH the white clothes on Monday and put them on the stone heap; wash the color clothes on Tuesday and put them on the clothesline to dry; don't walk barehead in the hot sun; cook pumpkin fritters in very hot sweet oil; soak your little cloths right after you take them off; when buying cotton to make yourself a nice blouse, be sure that it doesn't have gum on it, because that way it won't hold up well after a wash; soak salt fish overnight before you cook it; is it true that you sing benna[1] in Sunday school?; always eat your food in such a way that it won't turn someone else's stomach; on Sundays try to walk like a lady and not like the slut you are so bent on becoming; don't sing benna in Sunday school; you mustn't speak to wharf-rat boys, not even to give directions; don't eat fruits on the street—flies will follow you; *but I don't sing benna on Sundays at all and never in Sunday school*; this is how to sew on a button; this is how to make a button-hole for the button you have just sewed on; this is how to hem a dress when you see the hem coming down and so to prevent yourself from

1 A type of Calypso music.

looking like the slut I know you are so bent on becoming; this is how you iron your father's khaki shirt so that it doesn't have a crease; this is how you iron your father's khaki pants so that they don't have a crease; this is how you grow okra—far from the house, because okra tree harbors red ants; when you are growing dasheen,[2] make sure it gets plenty of water or else it makes your throat itch when you are eating it; this is how you sweep a corner; this is how you sweep a whole house; this is how you sweep a yard; this is how you smile to someone you don't like too much; this is how you smile to someone you don't like at all; this is how you smile to someone you like completely; this is how you set a table for tea; this is how you set a table for dinner; this is how you set a table for dinner with an important guest; this is how you set a table for lunch; this is how you set a table for breakfast; this is how to behave in the presence of men who don't know you very well, and this way they won't recognize immediately the slut I have warned you against becoming; be sure to wash every day even if it is with your own spit; don't squat down to play marbles—you are not a boy, you know; don't pick people's flowers—you might catch something; don't throw stones at blackbirds, because it might not be a blackbird at all; this is how to make a bread pudding; this is how to make doukona;[3] this is how to make pepper pot;[4] this is how to make a good medicine for a cold; this is how to make a good medicine to throw away a child before it even becomes a child; this is how to catch a fish; this is how to throw back a fish you don't like, and that way something bad won't fall on you; this is how to bully a man; this is how a man bullies you; this is how to love a man, and if this doesn't work there are other ways, and if they don't work don't feel too bad about giving up; this is how to spit up in the air if you feel like it, and this is how to move quick so that it doesn't fall on you; this is how to make ends meet; always squeeze bread to make sure it's fresh; *but what if the baker won't let me feel the bread?*; you mean to say that after all you are really going to be the kind of woman who the baker won't let near the bread?

—1983

2 Another name for taro, a type of edible root plant cultivated in the tropics.

3 Pudding made from plantains, a banana-like fruit.

4 Meat stew.

DENIS JOHNSON

Denis Johnson is an American poet, writer, journalist, and playwright. His work is known for its themes of addiction and drug use, its strange yet authentic depictions of life in the American Midwest, and its colloquial, blue-collar narrators. Johnson's 2011 novel, the reworked *Train Dreams*, was a Pulitzer Prize finalist and he won a National Book Award for *Tree of Smoke* in 2007. A self-described "criminal hedonist turned citizen of life," Johnson identifies as an unconventional Christian.

Denis Johnson was born on July 1st, 1949 in Munich, Germany, to Vera and Alfred Johnson. His father worked for the United States Information Agency; Johnson spent his childhood in Tokyo and his adolescence in Manila. He finished high school in Alexandria, Virginia, in 1967 and did his BA at the University of Iowa. During his undergraduate work, Johnson published his first book of poetry, *The Man Among the Seals*, which was widely praised. Johnson took his MFA in the well-known Writers' Workshop program at the University of Iowa, studying under Marvin Bell.

After completing his MFA, Johnson taught at Lake Forest College in Chicago, before resigning and moving to Washington, where he worked at odd jobs in the Seattle area. After publishing his second book of poetry, *Inner Weather*, in 1976, Johnson sought treatment for alcohol and heroin addiction, taking a two-year hiatus from writing. He then taught at Arizona State Prison in Florence, AZ.

In 1981, upon winning a fellowship from the Fine Arts Work Center in Provincetown, MA, Johnson relocated to Cape Cod and wrote his next three books: *The Incognito Lounge* (1982), a book of poetry that won the National Poetry Series Award; *Angels* (1983), a novel that won the Sue Kaufman Award from the American Institute of Arts and Letters, *Fiskadoro* (1985), and *The Stars at Noon* (1986), also novels. With these works, Johnson cemented his reputation as a "chronicler of the unusual aspects of American culture," a writer with a visionary voice and an eye for the striking and surprising.

"Emergency" is a short story that first appeared in *The New Yorker* in 1991 and was later included in Johnson's best-known book, *Jesus' Son* (1992), a collection of short stories. Set in 1973, the story follows the narrator, an orderly, and his friend, Georgie, through a day of their lives. The writer Tobias Wolff said of this story, "Stories like this become a part of your own memory, as if it happened to you." According to Johnson, the stories in *Jesus' Son* were originally anecdotes or bar stories that he wrote down, not necessarily perceiving his constructions as literature; however, the book has become a touchstone of American fiction from this period.

Emergency

DENIS JOHNSON

I'D BEEN working in the emergency room for about three weeks, I guess. This was in 1973, before the summer ended. With nothing to do on the overnight shift but batch the insurance reports from the daytime shifts, I just started wandering around, over to the coronary-care unit, down to the cafeteria, et cetera, looking for Georgie, the orderly, a pretty good friend of mine. He often stole pills from the cabinets.

He was running over the tiled floor of the operating room with a mop. "Are you still doing that?" I said.

"Jesus, there's a lot of blood here," he complained.

"Where?" The floor looked clean enough to me.

"What the hell were they doing in here?" he asked me.

"They were performing surgery, Georgie," I told him.

"There's so much goop inside of us, man," he said, "and it all wants to get out." He leaned his mop against a cabinet.

"What are you crying for?" I didn't understand.

He stood still, raised both arms slowly behind his head, and tightened his ponytail. Then he grabbed the mop and started making broad random arcs with it, trembling and weeping and moving all around the place really fast. "What am I *crying* for?" he said. "Jesus. Wow, oh boy, perfect."

I was hanging out in the E.R. with fat, quivering Nurse. One of the Family Service doctors that nobody liked came in looking for Georgie to wipe up after him. "Where's Georgie?" this guy asked.

"Georgie's in O.R.," Nurse said.

"Again?"

"No," Nurse said. "Still."

"Still? Doing what?"

"Cleaning the floor."

"Again?"

"No," Nurse said again. "Still."

Back in O.R., Georgie dropped his mop and bent over in the posture of a child soiling its diapers. He stared down with his mouth open in terror.

He said, "What am I going to do about these fucking *shoes*, man?"

"Whatever you stole," I said, "I guess you already ate it all, right?"

"Listen to how they squish," he said, walking around carefully on his heels.

"Let me check your pockets, man."

He stood still a minute, and I found his stash. I left him two of each, whatever they were. "Shift is about half over," I told him.

"Good. Because I really, really, really need a drink," he said. "Will you please help me get this blood mopped *up*?"

Around 3:30 A.M. a guy with a knife in his eye came in, led by Georgie.

"I hope *you* didn't do that to him," Nurse said.

"Me?" Georgie said. "No. He was like this."

"My wife did it," the man said. The blade was buried to the hilt in the outside corner of his left eye. It was a hunting knife kind of thing.

"Who brought you in?" Nurse said.

"Nobody. I just walked down. It's only three blocks," the man said.

Nurse peered at him. "We'd better get you lying down."

"O.K., I'm certainly ready for something like that," the man said.

She peered a bit longer into his face. "Is your other eye," she said, "a glass eye?"

"It's plastic, or something artificial like that," he said.

"And you can see out of *this* eye?" she asked, meaning the wounded one.

"I can see. But I can't make a fist out of my left hand because this knife is doing something to my brain."

"My God," Nurse said.

"I guess I'd better get the doctor," I said.

"There you go," Nurse agreed.

They got him lying down, and Georgie says to the patient, "Name?"

"Terrence Weber."

"Your face is dark. I can't see what you're saying."

"Georgie," I said.

"What are you saying, man? I can't see."

Nurse came over, and Georgie said to her, "His face is dark."

She leaned over the patient. "How long ago did this happen, Terry?" she shouted down into his face.

"Just a while ago. My wife did it. I was asleep," the patient said.

"Do you want the police?"

He thought about it and finally said, "Not unless I die."

Nurse went to the wall intercom and buzzed the doctor on duty, the Family Service person. "Got a surprise for you," she said over the intercom. He took his time getting down the hall to her, because he knew she hated Family Service and her happy tone of voice could only mean something beyond his competence and potentially humiliating.

He peeked into the trauma room and saw the situation: the clerk—that is, me—standing next to the orderly, Georgie, both of us on drugs, looking down at a patient with a knife sticking up out of his face.

"What seems to be the trouble?" he said.

The doctor gathered the three of us around him in the office and said, "Here's the situation. We've got to get a team here, an entire team. I want a good eye man. A great eye man. The best eye man. I want a brain surgeon. And I want a really good gas man, get me a genius. I'm not touching that head. I'm just going to watch this one. I know my limits. We'll just get him prepped and sit tight. Orderly!"

"Do you mean me?" Georgie said. "Should I get him prepped?"

"Is this a hospital?" the doctor asked. "Is this the emergency room? Is that a patient? Are you the orderly?"

I dialed the hospital operator and told her to get me the eye man and the brain man and the gas man.

Georgie could be heard across the hall, washing his hands and singing a Neil Young song that went "Hello cowgirl in the sand. Is this place at your command?"[1]

"That person is not right, not at all, not one bit," the doctor said.

"As long as my instructions are audible to him it doesn't concern me," Nurse insisted, spooning stuff up out of a little Dixie cup. "I've got my own life and the protection of my family to think of."

"Well, O.K., O.K. Don't chew my head off," the doctor said.

The eye man was on vacation or something. While the hospital's operator called around to find someone else just as good, the other specialists were hurrying through the night to join us. I stood around looking at charts and chewing up

---

1 "Cowgirl in the Sand," from Neil Young's 1969 album *Everybody Knows This is Nowhere.*

more of Georgie's pills. Some of them tasted the way urine smells, some of them burned, some of them tasted like chalk. Various nurses, and two physicians who'd been tending somebody in I.C.U., were hanging out down here with us now.

Everybody had a different idea about exactly how to approach the problem of removing the knife from Terrence Weber's brain. But when Georgie came in from prepping the patient—from shaving the patient's eyebrow and disinfecting the area around the wound, and so on—he seemed to be holding the hunting knife in his left hand.

The talk just dropped off a cliff.

"Where," the doctor asked finally, "did you get that?"

Nobody said one thing more, not for quite a long time.

After a while, one of the I.C.U. nurses said, "Your shoelace is untied." Georgie laid the knife on a chart and bent down to fix his shoe.

There were twenty more minutes left to get through.

"How's the guy doing?" I asked.

"Who?" Georgie said.

It turned out that Terrence Weber still had excellent vision in the one good eye, and acceptable motor and reflex, despite his earlier motor complaint. "His vitals are normal," Nurse said. "There's nothing wrong with the guy. It's one of those things."

After a while you forget it's summer. You don't remember what the morning is. I'd worked two doubles[2] with eight hours off in between, which I'd spent sleeping on a gurney in the nurses' station. Georgie's pills were making me feel like a giant helium-filled balloon, but I was wide awake. Georgie and I went out to the lot, to his orange pickup.

We lay down on a stretch of dusty plywood in the back of the truck with the daylight knocking against our eyelids and the fragrance of alfalfa thickening on our tongues.

"I want to go to church," Georgie said.

"Let's go to the county fair."

"I'd like to worship. I would."

"They have these injured hawks and eagles there. From the Humane Society," I said.

"I need a quiet chapel about now."

---

2 Double shifts.

Georgie and I had a terrific time driving around. For a while the day was clear and peaceful. It was one of the moments you stay in, to hell with all the troubles of before and after. The sky is blue, and the dead are coming back. Later in the afternoon, with sad resignation, the county fair bares its breasts. A champion of the drug LSD, a very famous guru of the love generation, is being interviewed amid a TV crew off to the left of the poultry cages. His eyeballs look like he bought them in a joke shop. It doesn't occur to me, as I pity this extraterrestrial, that in my life I've taken as much acid as he has.

After that, we got lost. We drove for hours, literally hours, but we couldn't find the road back to town.

Georgie started to complain. "That was the worst fair I've been to. Where were the rides?"

"They had rides," I said.

"I didn't see one ride."

A jackrabbit scurried out in front of us, and we hit it.

"There was a merry-go-round, a Ferris wheel, and a thing called the Hammer that people were bent over vomiting from after they got off," I said. "Are you completely blind?"

"What was that?"

"A rabbit."

"Something thumped."

"You hit him. *He* thumped."

Georgie stood on the brake pedal. "Rabbit stew."

He threw the truck in reverse and zigzagged back toward the rabbit. "Where's my hunting knife?" He almost ran over the poor animal a second time.

"We'll camp in the wilderness," he said. "In the morning we'll breakfast on its haunches." He was waving Terrence Weber's hunting knife around in what I was sure was a dangerous way.

In a minute he was standing at the edge of the fields, cutting the scrawny little thing up, tossing away its organs. "I should have been a doctor," he cried.

A family in a big Dodge, the only car we'd seen for a long time, slowed down and gawked out the windows as they passed by. The father said, "What is it, a snake?"

"No, it's not a snake," Georgie said. "It's a rabbit with babies inside it."

"Babies!" the mother said, and the father sped the car forward, over the protests of several little kids in the back.

Georgie came back to my side of the truck with his shirtfront stretched out in front of him as if he were carrying apples in it, or some such, but they were, in fact, slimy miniature bunnies. "No way I'm eating those things," I told him.

"Take them, take them. I gotta drive, take them," he said, dumping them in my lap and getting in on his side of the truck. He started driving along faster and faster, with a look of glory on his face. "We killed the mother and saved the children," he said.

"It's getting late," I said. "Let's get back to town."

"You bet." Sixty, seventy, eighty-five, just topping ninety.

"These rabbits better be kept warm." One at a time I slid the little things in between my shirt buttons and nestled them against my belly. "They're hardly moving," I told Georgie.

"We'll get some milk and sugar and all that, and we'll raise them up ourselves. They'll get as big as gorillas."

The road we were lost on cut straight through the middle of the world. It was still daytime, but the sun had no more power than an ornament or a sponge. In this light the truck's hood, which had been bright orange, had turned a deep blue.

Georgie let us drift to the shoulder of the road, slowly, slowly, as if he'd fallen asleep or given up trying to find his way.

"What is it?"

"We can't go on. I don't have any headlights," Georgie said.

We parked under a strange sky with a faint image of a quarter-moon superimposed on it.

There was a little woods beside us. This day had been dry and hot, the buck pines and what all simmering patiently, but as we sat there smoking cigarettes it started to get very cold.

"The summer's over," I said.

That was the year when arctic clouds moved down over the Midwest, and we had two weeks of winter in September.

"Do you realize it's going to snow?" Georgie asked me.

He was right, a gun-blue storm was shaping up. We got out and walked around idiotically. The beautiful chill! That sudden crispness, and the tang of evergreen stabbing us!

The gusts of snow twisted themselves around our heads while the night fell. I couldn't find the truck. We just kept getting more and more lost. I kept calling, "Georgie, can you see?" and he kept saying, "See what? See what?"

The only light visible was a streak of sunset flickering below the hem of the clouds. We headed that way.

We bumped softly down a hill toward an open field that seemed to be a military graveyard, filled with rows and rows of austere, identical markers over soldiers' graves. I'd never before come across this cemetery. On the farther side of the field, just beyond the curtains of snow, the sky was torn away and the angels were descending out of a brilliant blue summer, their huge faces streaked with light and full of pity. The sight of them cut through my heart and down the knuckles of my spine, and if there'd been anything in my bowels I would have messed my pants from fear.

Georgie opened his arms and cried out, "It's the drive-in, man!"

"The drive-in ..." I wasn't sure what these words meant.

"They're showing movies in a fucking blizzard!" Georgie screamed.

"I see. I thought it was something else," I said.

We walked carefully down there and climbed through the busted fence and stood in the very back. The speakers, which I'd mistaken for grave markers, muttered in unison. Then there was tinkly music, of which I could very nearly make out the tune. Famous movie stars rode bicycles beside a river, laughing out of their gigantic lovely mouths. If anybody had come to see this show, they'd left when the weather started. Not one car remained, not even a broken-down one from last week, or one left here because it was out of gas. In a couple of minutes, in the middle of a whirling square dance, the screen turned black, the cinematic summer ended, the snow went dark, there was nothing but my breath.

"I'm starting to get my eyes back," Georgie said in another minute.

A general grayness was giving birth to various shapes, it was true. "But which ones are close and which ones are far off?" I begged him to tell me.

By trial and error, with a lot of walking back and forth in wet shoes, we found the truck and sat inside it, shivering.

"Let's get out of here," I said.

"We can't go anywhere without headlights."

"We've gotta get back. We're a long way from home."

"No, we're not."

"We must have come three hundred miles."

"We're right outside town, Fuckhead. We've just been driving around and around."

"This is no place to camp. I hear the interstate over there."

"We'll just stay here till it gets late. We can drive home late. We'll be invisible."

We listened to the big rigs going from San Francisco to Pennsylvania along the interstate, like shudders down a long hacksaw blade, while the snow buried us.

Eventually Georgie said, "We better get some milk for those bunnies."

"We don't have *milk*," I said.

"We'll mix sugar up with it."

"Will you forget about this milk all of a sudden?"

"They're mammals, man."

"Forget about those rabbits."

"Where are they, anyway?"

"You're not listening to me. I said. 'Forget the rabbits.'"

"Where are they?"

The truth was I'd forgotten all about them, and they were dead.

"They slid around behind me and got squashed," I said tearfully.

"They slid around *behind*?"

He watched while I pried them out from behind my back.

I picked them out one at a time and held them in my hands and we looked at them. There were eight. They weren't any bigger than my fingers, but everything was there.

Little feet! Eyelids! Even whiskers! "Deceased," I said.

Georgie asked, "Does everything you touch turn to shit? Does this happen to you every time?"

"No wonder they call me Fuckhead."

"It's a name that's going to stick."

"I realize that."

"'Fuckhead' is gonna ride you to your grave."

"I just said so. I agreed with you in advance," I said.

Or maybe that wasn't the time it snowed. Maybe it was the time we slept in the truck and I rolled over on the bunnies and flattened them. It doesn't matter. What's important for me to remember now is that early the next morning the snow was melted off the windshield and the daylight woke me up. A mist covered everything and, with the sunshine, was beginning to grow sharp and strange. The bunnies weren't a problem yet, or they'd already been a problem and were already forgotten, and there was nothing on my mind. I felt the beauty of the morning. I could understand how a drowning man might suddenly feel a deep thirst being quenched. Or how the slave might become a friend to his master. Georgie slept with his face right on the steering wheel.

I saw bits of snow resembling an abundance of blossoms on the stems of the drive-in speakers—no, revealing the blossoms that were always there. A bull elk stood still in the pasture beyond the fence giving off an air of authority and stupidity. And a coyote jogged across the pasture and faded away among the saplings.

That afternoon we got back to work in time to resume everything as if it had never stopped happening and we'd never been anywhere else.

"The Lord," the intercom said, "is my shepherd." It did that each evening because this was a Catholic hospital. "Our Father, who art in Heaven," and so on.

"Yeah, yeah," Nurse said.

The man with the knife in his head, Terrence Weber, was released around suppertime. They'd kept him overnight and given him an eyepatch—all for no reason, really.

He stopped off at E.R. to say goodbye. "Well, those pills they gave me make everything taste terrible," he said.

"It could have been worse," Nurse said.

"Even my tongue."

"It's just a miracle you didn't end up sightless or at least dead," she reminded him.

The patient recognized me. He acknowledged me with a smile. "I was peeping on the lady next door while she was out there sunbathing," he said. "My wife decided to blind me."

He shook Georgie's hand. Georgie didn't know him. "Who are you supposed to be?" he asked Terrence Weber.

Some hours before that, Georgie had said something that had suddenly and completely explained the difference between us. We'd been driving back toward town, along the Old Highway, through the flatness. We picked up a hitchhiker, a boy I knew. We stopped the truck and the boy climbed slowly up out of the fields as out of the mouth of a volcano. His name was Hardee. He looked even worse than we probably did.

"We got messed up and slept in the truck all night," I told Hardee.

"I had a feeling," Hardee said. "Either that or, you know, driving a thousand miles."

"That, too," I said.

"Or you're sick or diseased or something."

"Who's this guy?" Georgie asked.

"This is Hardee. He lived with me last summer. I found him on the doorstep. What happened to your dog?" I asked Hardee.

"He's still down there."

"Yeah, I heard you went to Texas."

"I was working on a bee farm," Hardee said.

"Wow. Do those things sting you?"

"Not like you'd think," Hardee said. "You're part of their daily drill. It's all part of a harmony."

Outside the same identical stretch of ground repeatedly rolled past our faces. The day was cloudless, blinding. But Georgie said, "Look at that," pointing straight ahead of us.

One star was so hot it showed, bright and blue, in the empty sky.

"I recognized you right away," I told Hardee. "But what happened to your hair? Who chopped it off?"

"I hate to say."

"Don't tell me."

"They drafted me."

"Oh no."

"Oh yeah. I'm AWOL. I'm bad AWOL. I got to get to Canada."

"Oh, that's terrible," I said to Hardee.

"Don't worry," Georgie said. "We'll get you there."

"How?"

"Somehow. I think I know some people. Don't worry. You're on your way to Canada."

That world! These days it's all been erased and they've rolled it up like a scroll and put it away somewhere. Yes, I can touch it with my fingers. But where is it?

After a while Hardee asked Georgie, "What do you do for a job?," and Georgie said, "I save lives."

—1991

EDWARD P. JONES

Edward P. Jones is an American short story writer and novelist based in Washington, DC. His work has brought him international recognition and many awards, including the Pulitzer Prize, the PEN/Hemingway award, and a MacArthur "Genius Grant." Most recently he was awarded the PEN/Malamud Award for excellence in the art of the short story. Dave Eggers wrote of his novel *The Known World* (2002) that "it's difficult to think of a contemporary novel that rivals its sweep, its humanity, the unvarnished perfection of its prose and its ultimately crushing power."

Jones was born in Washington, DC. His mother, Jeanette, brought up Jones and his two siblings by herself, his father having left when Jones was three. Jeanette had moved to Washington from her home in the South, along with the many descendants of slaves who migrated to northern cities in the early years of the twentieth century. Jones grew up in this community of migrants in Washington, and it is they and their descendants who people his fiction. Jeanette, who never learned to read and write, worked as a dish-washer and maid, making barely enough money to keep her and the children afloat. They moved 18 times in 18 years, "each place worse than the place before." Jones's mother is the central influence on his life and work; her kindness, hard work, and sacrifice define his vision as a writer, and all three of his books are dedicated to her memory.

The family's nomadic life helped confirm Jones's solitary tendencies. He withdrew from the company of other children into the world of reading. He was granted a scholarship to Holy Cross College, where he took a degree in English in 1972. He then returned to Washington and began working odd jobs and caring for his ailing mother, who died in 1975. Four years later he enrolled at the University of Virginia, where he completed an MFA in Creative Writing in 1981. He then took a position with Tax Analysts, where he worked for 18 years as a proofreader and writer, summarizing tax stories from the news. Jones has always lived alone and lived simply, and to this day he has an apartment with almost no furniture; he sleeps on a pallet on the floor, and his books are in boxes lined up along the walls. "I'm not afraid of my own company," he says, "I was made to be at home."

During the years at Tax Analysts, Jones was composing short stories, often working them out in his head long before writing them down. After reading James Joyce's *Dubliners*, he was inspired to "do the same thing" for Washington, to give a sense of the city no one knew: the other Washington, the African American neighborhoods in which he had grown up. *Lost in the City* came out in 1992, each story tracing, in simple prose, the full and complex lives of the forgotten and willfully overlooked. Jones spent the next decade thinking about his novel, *The Known World* (2003), which he wrote in three months after the loss of his daytime job. This novel won the Pulitzer and many other awards, allowing Jones to live on the proceeds of his creative work. His second short story collection, *All Aunt Hagar's Children* (2007), is a collection that parallels the first, picking up the characters and developing the themes of an earlier story in *Lost in the City*. In 2010, Jones began teaching creative writing at George Washington University.

"Young Lions" tells the story of Caesar Matthews, a troubled and violent twenty-four-year-old who has taken up a life of crime. Caesar seems unredeemable, cold, and cruel-hearted, but Jones, in his determination to show Caesar's full character, makes his motives and perceptions vividly present, if not entirely understandable: "Some people are lost and they eventually find their way a bit, and other people are lost and they can't ever return."

Young Lions

EDWARD P. JONES

I

HE STOOD naked before the open refrigerator in the darkened kitchen, downing the last of the milk in a half-gallon carton. Carol, once again, had taped a note to the carton. Caesar Matthews did not have to read it to know that it told him she loved him with all her heart, or that she would miss him all that day. She used to pin such notes to her pillow before she went off in the morning, leaving him still asleep. But in the night, when she brushed her hair as she prepared for bed, she would find the notes still pinned to the pillow, undisturbed and so perhaps unread. So now she taped them to milk cartons, for he could not begin his day without drinking milk, or she taped them to his gold key ring, or pinned them to the zippers of the expensive pants she knew he would wear that day. In more than two years, the wording on the notes had not changed very much.

Sometimes, when he thought of it, he would fold the paper with the words and place it on the kitchen table between the salt and pepper shakers, to let her know he had come upon it before he ventured out.

This morning, after he had finished the last of the milk, without reading the words, he tossed the carton in a high arc across the room into the trash can. He pulled up the window shade and let in the morning light. He was anxious to be out in the streets; there was nothing like an empty apartment to bring down the soul.

The night before, for the fourth time in a week, he had dreamed about the retarded woman. Sherman would have told him such dreams were a good sign. Caesar was left now with only fragments of the dreams, the splintered memory that he had been roaming about in some foreign land, and the retarded woman had been standing among tall trees in that land. She never seemed to be hiding, as she should have been, but appeared to wave to him. He could not remember anything after she waved. He did remember with certainty that in all the dreams the woman was known to him not as being retarded but as being feeble-minded, which was the phrase his father had always used.

He was still naked when the telephone rang, standing at the bathroom door wondering if he wanted a shower. "These are the times," Carol would have joked, "when we miss our mothers most."

Manny, on the telephone, asked if he wanted to tend bar that evening and make some change. "I was about to hop over your place," Caesar said. He never liked Manny Soto calling his apartment, for Manny always whispered on the phone and made each word he spoke sound obscene. "He talk that way cause he's a fence and every other bad thing in the world," Sherman had said once. "He think people are listenin to everything he says, and maybe by whisperin, they'll hear a little less."

"Coincidences. Coincidences. Heh, heh," Manny said. "Good minds think a lot,[1] they say. I was just checking to be sure, heh, heh, to see if you might be available, heh, heh." The inappropriate laughing was also why he didn't like Manny calling.

"But listen: You heard what Sherman is doing now, heh, heh, heh?" Manny said. This time he obviously felt the whole thing was funny, and he asked Caesar again.

Caesar told him no, that he had last seen Sherman in Howard Hospital.[2] "Two, three months ago," he said.

---

1 Misquotation of the expression, "Great minds think alike."

2 Primary teaching hospital of Howard University College of Medicine.

"Well, since you last saw him, he's gone up in the world. Or gone down, whichever the case may be, heh, heh." He hung up without another word.

While dressing, Caesar found another note pinned to the collar of his shirt. He read it, crumbled it for effect, and propped it against a picture they had had taken together at a Southeast club. He would remind Carol of all the notes when he told her about the retarded woman. "Dancing with me don't end that way," were the first words she had ever spoken to him. "Try me and see." He had gone to Manny's place with Sherman Wheeler and Sherman's old lady, Sandra Wallington, and, after a good bit of coaxing by Sandra, he had asked a woman sitting alone two tables away to dance. He and the woman had slow-dragged through one record, then another, and as the woman ground her body into his, she would bite and tug at his earlobe with her lips. When the second record ended, she unwound herself and went back without a word to her table. There was now a man at her table, and the man stood and pulled the woman's chair away from the table for her. The man and the woman sat down. The woman's back was to Caesar, who stood dumbly looking at the back of her neck and at the man. The man stood again, and he looked at Caesar with the patience of someone who had nothing better to do. "No one," the man said finally, "gets more than two dances free." He sat again and Caesar, after a few moments, found his way back to Sherman and Sandra.

"Dancing with me don't end that way." He had been about to sit when Carol tugged at his shirt sleeve. He allowed her to lead him away to the dance floor. "Try me and see."

He decided that morning on the desert-brown leather jacket, a present from Carol for his twenty-second birthday two years ago. It was October, and in that month and in November before the days turned colder heading into December, he enjoyed wearing the jacket, enjoyed the opulent sound of leather with each move he made. He checked the jacket's pockets to make certain he had his address book. There was not much in the book—a few names and telephone numbers of people he knew from Manny's. But there were also the addresses and phone numbers of the three women—their names coded to read like male friends in case Carol saw them—he would go to when he and Carol argued, or when he simply wanted to spend the night with a woman whose body, whose responses, he could not easily anticipate.

He put the Beretta in one of the jacket's pockets. The moment he touched it the memory of the times he had used it came back to him. He liked remembering. The last time had been eight months ago when they crossed into Maryland and he shot the 7-Eleven clerk in the face. A few miles from the store, back in DC, Caesar was still laughing about how the man's face had drained of blood as the gun came toward his face. A month before that he had placed the pistol beside the head of a man he and Sherman had caught far up New Hampshire Avenue near the Silver Spring line. The man had looked insulted to be robbed, and Caesar, dangling the man's watch before his eyes, had pulled the trigger to scare him into the proper frame of mind. "I wasn't gonna take this cheap-ass thing," Caesar said about the watch, "but you just ain't got the proper attitude." The bullet had nicked the man's ear, and so it didn't count the way a blast in the face counted. The nice thing about the retarded woman was that he wouldn't even have to take the pistol out of his pocket.

Sherman Wheeler had rarely carried a gun. "My daddy got his toe shot off tryin to quick-draw one a those things," he said once. "Sides, my mind is the only gun I need." Then he had made his hand into a gun, placed it against his temple, and pretended to pull a trigger. He hadn't liked Caesar carrying a gun, and in their first months together he pulled rank and told him to leave the guns at home when they weren't needed, but Caesar would sneak them out anyway. From the beginning, with the first cheap piece he had stolen during a burglary at a home in Arlington,[3] Caesar had liked carrying a gun. And now, having to work alone without Sherman, he would not step outside the apartment without one.

II

In the vestibule of Manny's Haven at Georgia Avenue and Ingraham Street, there was an impressive collection of Polaroid pictures displayed behind a locked glass case. In most of the dozens of photographs, Manny, always wearing a Hawaiian shirt, stood in the center, his arms around Washington politicians, two-bit celebrities, customers for whom he had a special affection, or wild-eyed, out-of-town relatives. At the very bottom of the display, in two and a half rows, there were also photographs of men who had, as Manny put it, "made irredeemable fools of themselves in my house," as he called his bar. Most of these men, usually too drunk even to remember where they were, had refused to leave the bar when told, and Manny had had the bouncers toss them out. But throwing them out was never enough, and he would also have the bouncers beat them on the sidewalk. "Take his picture! Take his goddamn picture!" became his euphemism to the bouncers for throwing a man out and putting a hurting on him. The majority of the men were photographed leaning against the front of the bar just below the neon sign that blinked Manny's Haven. They were alone in their pictures with their bloodied faces, except, now and again, for the hand of some unseen bouncer that kept the fellow from falling over.

3 Arlington County, Virginia.

Manny was reading the *Post* aloud at a table near the bar when Caesar arrived that morning. Manny was alone, which didn't make Caesar happy. The whole place was dark, except for the tiny lamp on the table. Manny did not look up at first when Caesar sat down across from him and said, "Mornin."

Manny finished the page and put the newspaper aside, took off his glasses and rubbed his closed eyes with his knuckles. "Young Blood," he said, squinting. "Ain't seen you in a month of Sundays. Thought you mighta gone away on vacation." Manny dressed the way a very small child would without the help of an adult. "I always expect to look under the table and find him with his shoes on the wrong feet," Sherman had said once, "with knots and shit in the shoelaces, insteada little bows." Manny had hundreds of Hawaiian shirts, including some very expensive ones dating back to the 1920s and 1930s. He wore one every day of the year. This morning he had on a particularly loud silk and rayon thing with palm trees that looked not like trees but tiny green explosions. He was quite a thin man, and all his shirts hung loosely on him, the way they would hang on wire hangers.

"I'll need you for tonight and two three more nights this week," Manny said. "You got time for that?"

Caesar nodded. Bartending would tide him over until things were finished with the retarded woman. He could hear the rumblings of the men in the basement, sorting and cataloging the stolen stuff Manny had bought from thieves. Manny would send all of it on to an apartment on Florida Avenue where people came shopping to buy it for a little more than what Manny paid for it.

"What's this about you not hearing about Sherman?" Manny said. "Thought you two was closer than dick and his two nuts."

"We was once," Caesar said. Manny blinked, waiting for more. He undoubtedly knew everything already, but Caesar knew that having to tell him was the price of doing business with him. Besides, there was nothing to betray. He told Manny what little Sherman had told him in the hospital the last time he saw him: Sherman had ODed[4] at the home of a woman who catered to a small group of people with "functional habits," people who could work and carry on their lives without the rest of the world knowing they needed special recreation in their off hours. A person could go to one of Regina's houses on M Street and relax in one of her small rooms, and after a few hours of traveling, get up and go home.

"I know this woman," Manny said. "Regina Carstairs. Oh, such a fine house in the Gold Coast. I went to her place for a function once, raising money for the mayor. The house where no junkie is allowed. But I didn't enjoy myself because

4 Overdosed.

she had somebody watch me all the time like I was going to steal something." Manny indicated with his fingers that he wanted more.

There's not much more, Caesar said. Sherman had traveled out on a far limb one night with just a one-way ticket. Regina thought he was dead or near-dead and had people dump him in a tree box on a street blocks and blocks from her house. ("Another satisfied customer," Manny interjected. "One million and counting.") Caesar did not tell Manny that in the hospital he and Sandra, Sherman's woman, had argued, with Sandra accusing him of dumping Sherman at death's door. He had looked to Sherman for support, but in the end Sherman had raised the arm without the IV and begged Caesar to go. "I'll call you," Sherman had said.

"I got some pictures here you might be interested in, heh, heh," Manny said. "Got some nice pictures. Oh, do I got the nice pictures. Bet a million you didn't know he was on that heroin shit, did you?"

Caesar said no.

"Well, I did. It's hard to tell with some fools, but I knew." He was leaning back in his chair, his arms crossed. He was thin enough for Caesar to see the edges of the chair on either side of him. "That's the thing with that heroin shit. You see, with your average crackhead, they're climbing the walls and everything. You ask them the time and they're ready to kill you cause you ain't got your own watch. But with heroin, you ask them the time, and they're ready to give you the watch. And Sherman was the mellowest man I knew." He leaned forward. "You wanna see my pictures, heh, heh? The proof from our man Polaroid that our man from Sixteenth Street has come up in the world."

Caesar was curious, but he did not want to see. It was as if someone had asked if he wanted to see pictures of his naked father. "We can take him," Caesar had said once about Manny. "We can take him. Come in wearin masks and shit. We can clean his ass out and live like kings." "And then where we gonna live?" Sherman had said. "Even if we got a million dollars from him, where in the fuckin world would we live? Stop bein such a hothead all the time, man. Manny still payin people back for some small thing they probably did to him when he was five years old."

"Come on," Manny said. "Peek on the wild side." In fall and winter, Manny's Hawaiian shirts had two pockets, and he took a set of photographs out of the left pocket.

The pictures were of a security guard standing with folded arms between two paintings in what was clearly a museum. The man seemed to stand with an air of importance and authority, but the more Caesar studied the first pictures the more he saw that the man would never be anything more than a guard whose job was simply to stand between two paintings. The man's expression changed but slightly in the series of photographs, but in the last one, as if he was finally aware that he was the photographer's real subject, he was turning his head away and the camera caught only a blur. The guard, in a dark blue uniform, wore a dark blue hat with a shiny shield in the front, and though the hat was pulled down low over his forehead, Caesar could see that the mouth and chin were Sherman's. "My father gave me my eyes and nose, but I got my mouth and chin from my old lady." Sherman had been on his own since he was ten, but he always spoke of his parents as if he had had a full life with them.

"They were taken in the Smithsonian," Manny was saying. "Not the one with that big elephant—that's my favorite—but the art museum, the one with the paintings. When I heard he was working there, I just had to see it. So I had this guy and his whore that owed me a favor: Act like tourists and go down there and pretend they were Bamas[5] in town to see the pictures, heh, heh." Manny tapped his forehead. "Smart. Real smart."

Caesar got up. "I gotta be movin. Be back at seven, okay?"

"Seven's fine," Manny said, kissing the pictures and putting them back in his pocket. "Any later and you'll be late."

III

He felt suddenly exhausted and afraid and considered returning to the apartment, but Carol was not there and an empty place brought down the soul. Then he thought of the retarded woman and things brightened a bit. He took a bus downtown to see the woman for what would be the last time before Friday.

He had been following her for all of two months, since a week or so after he saw Sherman in the hospital. He had first come upon her waiting for the bus with three of her housemates. They were all adults, all at least thirty years old, but they talked as if they were new to the world and excited about being in it. The two men talked very loudly, as if they were not afraid to share whatever they were saying. Caesar figured from the beginning that the larger of the two women was the weakest, would be the easiest to pick off.

He had stood a few feet from them, pretending he too was waiting for the bus. Days later he learned that the retarded woman lived only two blocks from the bus stop in a house with perhaps six other retarded people of various ages and with a woman in her fifties. He figured the older woman was there to look after the seven. Except for the older woman, he learned, all of them worked, or at least did something that took them out of the house each morning. The

5 Slang word originally used in the DC metropolitan area to refer to people who do not dress well.

retarded woman he was interested in worked in a French restaurant on Connecticut Avenue near Lafayette Park.[6]

And so for two months he had secretly placed himself in her life, doing all the scoping out, the drudgery that had once been left up to Sherman. "You'd fuck it up," Sherman had said once. "I know you." "Have some faith in me," Caesar would laugh. "Have a little faith." "I know you, mothafucka."

Week after week, Caesar had followed the retarded woman as she made her way to work, sitting in the back of the bus so he could see when she got off. At K Street, she always walked the block and a half to the restaurant. He hung around near the restaurant, sometimes for the entire day, learning her schedule. He often saw her sweeping up the alley in the back where the employees entered and where deliveries were made. About two thirty or so most afternoons, after they had probably eaten lunch, the retarded woman and a much older woman would walk to Lafayette Park and stay for up to thirty minutes. After they went back to work, he would not see the girl again until about five, when she left work and took the bus home.

On Saturdays, she came to work at noon and stayed until eight or nine in the evening. But it was only the Fridays that concerned him now. For on Fridays, each Friday evening, she left work and walked up Connecticut Avenue to Dupont Circle,[7] where she deposited her paycheck at American Security. He would stand beside her on most Fridays over those months as she took forever to fill out the deposit slip, making first one mistake, then another, then dropping the crossed-out slips into the wastebasket beside the table. After she got on line, he would pick up every slip she had dropped. Then he would stand behind her until she had completed things with the teller.

It was a little before two when he got to the restaurant. The retarded woman and her friend soon came out to Connecticut, heading for Lafayette Park. Not quite two thirty, but close enough to the times of other days not to worry. As the women often did, they walked holding hands. They wore green uniforms and though they seemed to polish their white shoes every day, he had noticed that they were scuffed plenty by midday. He knew their first and last names, he knew where the old woman lived, having followed her home one evening, he knew the retarded woman's favorite candy, he even knew the station the old woman had her radio tuned to.

"I can see me sometime holdin my own little baby," the retarded woman said after they sat down on a bench facing the White House, "rockin her and feedin

6 Historic public park located north of the White House.

7 Historic neighborhood and park in Washington, DC.

her and doin such." The sun was warm, and Caesar sat on the grass Indian-style a few feet behind the women. He opened a newspaper he had taken from a trash can, but he watched the tourists taking photographs and the government people eating their lunches.

"Thought everything would work with Fred and me," the retarded woman said. "He like the job they got him. Me and him would sit on the stoop, makin plans bout our future."

Caesar knew about her Fred, but he had never learned if he was one of those loud talkers he had seen in the first weeks at the bus stop.

"People call us the lovebirds," the retarded woman said. "'Look at em. Look at them lovebirds.'"

The old woman was eating orange pieces from a small plastic bag, and now and again, when the breeze shifted, the smell of oranges came to Caesar. He watched a black family come up to a very old white man at the Lafayette statue. The father gave his camera to the white man and then stood in front of the statue beside his wife and behind his three children. The oldest boy closed his eyes and would not open them again until it was all done. The old man took the family's picture, and when the mother raised one finger, the old man advanced the film and snapped again.

"Then he commence to change. He talk back to Miss Prentiss," the retarded woman was saying. "His job call Miss Prentiss and said he all the time late. Wouldn't do what they told him."

"Anna, he musta told you what was the matter," the old woman said.

"No, ma'am, Miss Elsie," the retarded woman said. "He never did. Yesday I got home, a car came with two men and they took him back to Laurel."[8] Caesar watched as the father read what was on the side of the statue and then the father looked up at the man on the horse, shading his eyes. His little girl did the same.

The black family crossed Pennsylvania Avenue, and the father gave the oldest boy the camera so he could take pictures of the White House. Then they went down to the corner and joined the line going in.

Caesar was only half listening; there was no more that would help on Friday. The problem would be Carol. He put the newspaper aside and lay down, closing his eyes. He would not follow them back to work. On another day not long ago, he had waited for the retarded woman across the street in front of the copier business until she got off from work. He had followed her to the bus stop. She was overweight, and he saw that walking was not easy for her in the heat. For the first time since he had been following her, she was not wearing her uniform. She had on a blue skirt and a pink blouse, which she wore outside the skirt. She

8 Laurel, Maryland.

had on tiny, gold-plated earrings a person might not notice until he was within a foot or so of her, and that was how close he was when he walked past her. She smelled of garlic and, beneath that, of a soap that reminded him of the halls in the hospital where his mother had died.

It was a crime, Sherman had said, to fall asleep anywhere but in a safe place, and so he was up and off a few minutes after the women left. He felt he wanted to see Sherman and left the park at the corner of Pennsylvania and 16th, heading in the direction where he thought the museum was. In both his lives, he had never come down to the world below Constitution Avenue, except for those times when relatives came from out of town. His mother and father would bring everyone down to see the Washington they put on postcards and in the pages of expensive coffee-table books. He knew that his father worked in one of the government buildings, but he didn't know which one. His father was the kind of man who, if he looked out his office window and saw his son, would come down the stairs three at a time and hold him until someone called the police. "Call the law! I have a thief who robbed me! Call the law!"

At 15th and Constitution, among the tourists and office workers, he gave up the idea of seeing Sherman. It would be better to start working on Carol. He could see no problems with Anna, the retarded woman, but retarded or not, she was still a woman and there was a danger of her being skittish. He called Carol at work.

He told her that he loved her, then he told her that he missed her. In his mind, he read the words written on her notes.

"I'm glad you told me," she said. "I was beginning to wonder. You made my day."

He promised to fix her dinner before he went to Manny's and he told her once again that he loved her.

"I wish I could record that," she said, "and play it back any time I wanted."

IV

When people found out that Angelo Billings, Caesar's cousin, had in fact stolen the flowers from an I Street florist and taken them to the funeral home, they said he would never again have good luck. Never mind, they said, that he loved Caesar's mother as much as he loved anyone and that stealing the flowers was his way of showing that love. There were some things God would not tolerate, and stealing flowers for the dead was one of them.

Caesar, though, was moved, and they grew closer after his mother's funeral. Angelo introduced him to Sherman. Angelo, before Caesar gave up on school, would wait for him outside Cardozo High, and they would go to Sherman's two-bedroom apartment on 16th Street, a few blocks up from Malcolm X Park.[9] What fascinated Caesar most about the apartment was the dominance of sound, of noise, as if Sherman were afraid of silence. In every room, there was something playing each second of the day, whether a radio or television or cassette player. In the bathroom, hanging from the shower curtain rod, there was a transistor radio that played around the clock. Sherman lived alone in the apartment, but he had two children by Sandra, who lived elsewhere in the building with the children. Most of the time when Caesar and Angelo visited, they would find Sherman wrapped in his bathrobe sitting on the couch, listening to one of dozens of cassette tapes that Sandra had recorded of the children talking and playing with each other. There were four speakers in the living room that stood three feet high, and he enjoyed playing those cassettes so loud that the noise of the children made it sound like a playground with a hundred children. Now and again, one child would hit the other or say something mean and there would be a fit of crying on the tape. Sherman would jump up and speed the tape past the crying to a place where the talking and playing resumed.

The apartment, despite the noise, became another home for Caesar and he began going there without Angelo after school. Before long, he was leaving home at least two or three days a week and going not to school but straight to Sherman's place, where he'd drop his books at the door beside the two-foot-high porcelain bulldog and make a place for himself in front of the television. In the beginning, he was able to get back home in the evening before his father arrived from work. But as the months wore away to winter, to spring, he was getting home later and later.

One night in April, Sherman dropped him off about three in the morning, and Caesar stood on the sidewalk for a long while looking up at his house. For the first time, all the lights in the house were off. When he opened the front door, his father was standing before him in the darkened hall.

"I'm just slaving away my life to raise up another Angelo," his father hissed, turning on the hall light. "A goddamn no-account." As soon as his hand was off the light switch, he slapped Caesar, knocking him back against the front door. Before Caesar could recover, his father had grabbed him by the shirt with one hand, opened the door with the other, and threw him out on the sidewalk.

"I gave you more chances than you deserved," his father said and closed the inner and outer doors to the house. Caesar, still sprawled on the ground, saw the hall light go out. Seconds later, he saw the light in the upstairs front bedroom, his father's room, go on, and a moment later, that light went out.

---

9 Meridian Hill Park, unofficially known as Malcolm X Park after the African American human rights activist.

He got to his feet and looked up and down French Street. The new leaves rattled as if something were shaking the trees, and the sound unnerved him. He brushed off his clothes, not because of dirt or debris, but because right then he did not know what else to do. Under the street lamp, he looked at the watch Sherman had given him the week before, and it occurred to him that he had never before been awake at that hour in the morning. A cool wind sauntered up the street and chilled him, unnerving him even more, and he suppressed the urge to cry.

He considered pounding on the door, calling his father as loudly as he could and then running away. But he stood quiet. For all of his life, he had been Lemuel Matthews's son, and even now, standing in the dark outside the walls of his father's house, he was still his son and he knew he could not be a bad boy at such a place at such a time in the morning.

He saw the brighter lights at the half smoke joint at the 9th Street corner and he went toward those lights. The place was closed, but he used the outdoor telephone to call Sherman. Sandra answered, and after he had told her what happened, she told him to stay put, that Sherman would be back down to pick him up. While he waited, he called his father's house several times, stepping out of the telephone booth with the receiver as he listened to the ringing. He looked up tree-lined French Street, but there was not enough light to distinguish his house from all the others.

It was true what people said about Angelo's bad luck. He robbed the Riggs Bank on 15th Street in early May, using a gun he had rented for twenty-five dollars a day and a Safeway shopping bag. He was so curious about how much he had gotten away with that as he ran down M Street, he looked in the shopping bag, and at that moment the money, booby-trapped with a red dye packet, exploded in his face. He dropped the bag, cursing the bank teller, but he continued running, trying for the next several blocks to wipe the dye from his face and hands with the shirt he had taken off.

Sherman had thought that Angelo, eager, cocksure, had potential as a partner, but soon after the government people put Angelo away, he began to consider Caesar, who was now staying with him. Caesar knew Sherman didn't have a real job, but he didn't learn until he had been with him two months what he did for a living. He was not particularly surprised or disappointed. Caesar was seventeen, and for the first time in his life, he was living his days without the cocoon of family, and beyond that cocoon, he was learning, anything was possible.

"The first thing we do," Sherman said one day, "is get all your shit from your daddy's place. You gotta have an identity. Get you out in the world so you can stop all that mopin."

The next morning they drove down to the house on French Street and waited in the car until Caesar was certain his father had left for work and his brother and sister had gone to school. Caesar opened the front door with his key. He was surprised his father had not changed the lock, but Sherman was not surprised. "What's there to be afraid of from his own little boy?" Sherman said. Caesar stepped into the hall. Had his father suddenly appeared before him, it would have seemed the most natural thing. Indeed, he expected him, and when he stepped into the living room, he expected his father to be there as well. Sherman, silent, followed as Caesar went through the rooms on the first floor. Caesar touched nearly everything along the way—a lace piece made by his grandmother that was on the back of the easy chair in the living room; a drawing of the house signed and dated by his sister taped to the refrigerator; the kitchen curtains he had helped his mother put up. In a corner of the kitchen counter he found wrapped in a rubber band the letters he had been sending to his father; only the first one had been opened.

"Let's get your stuff," Sherman said after a bit. "Enough of this."

They went upstairs, and in the closet of his father's bedroom, Sherman found a small metal box, broke its tiny lock with his hand, and leisurely went through the papers in the box, putting aside Caesar's birth certificate and the Social Security card he had gotten the year before in hopes of finding an after-school job. Caesar watched.

"You want your mom's death certificate?" Sherman said, reaching the end of the papers in the box.

"No." He turned away and went to his sister's room, where he touched the heads of the three stuffed animals sitting on the pillows of her bed. In the room he had shared with his brother, he took as many of his clothes as he could carry, his hands shaking each time he picked up an item.

In the hall, Sherman was waiting at the head of the stairs. He took some of the clothes from Caesar. "He had a little money in the box, some cash and some gold pieces," Sherman said. "And I found a stack of pictures in a drawer. I got a few of em, mostly some with you in em. Must be your mother, too. I got a lot of em. You might want em later on when you start to forget."

Caesar nodded. In a few minutes they were on 11th Street, heading back uptown. He knew what his father would look like when he realized he had been robbed: the fist pounding the air, that pulsating vein at the left side of his head. For months and months after that, he could conjure up the image whenever he wanted and replay it. That night, they went to Manny's and Carol said what she said about dancing with her not ending that way, about trying her and seeing. She took him home that night, and when he woke up the next morning, she was lying on her side watching him. She leaned over and kissed his forehead. "It's all right," she said, "I already went and brushed my teeth." Aside from the ones in Sherman's magazines, she was the first naked woman he had ever seen. She kissed his ear. "There's a toothbrush in there with your name on it," she said. "And I bet I spelled your name right."

Two weeks after Caesar and Sherman went into Caesar's father's house, Sherman took him out for the first time, to burglarize a home in Chevy Chase.[10] Sherman peed on the sofa in the recreation room, having taken a quick dislike to a large painting behind the sofa of a man in a tennis outfit whom he took to be the owner. The next night, in a light rain, they followed a light-skinned, well-dressed fellow from a bar on Capitol Hill to his car parked a block away. The man had tottered the whole distance, not bothering to open the umbrella he was carrying. "Not a sound," Caesar said, placing the pistol at the man's head just as he stuck his key in the car door. "Not a sound. No words. Not one word." Sherman went through the man's pockets, took his wallet and then his watch. "Please, please," the man kept saying, his arms extended high into the air. The man was balding and the hair he had left was combed perfectly to either side of a bald path that went back to the middle of his head. With the light of the street lamps, the robbers could see the beads of rain on the bald path and on his eyeglasses. "Next time," Caesar said as they stepped away from the man, "buy your shit in a liquor store and take it home to drink."

V

On the way home from following Anna that last time, Caesar bought white carnations for Carol and the ingredients for a shrimp creole dinner. He had dinner prepared when she came home, and after they had eaten, with her head swirling just a bit from the wine, he made love to her because he did not know what kind of mood he would be in when he returned from Manny's that night.

Later, as he told her about the retarded woman, he rested his hand on her bare stomach. He could feel her tensing up with each word. He massaged her stomach, then he took her belly button between two fingers and rubbed it gently.

"Don't ask me to do any of that," she said. "Don't bring me into any of that." As long as she believed it did not involve another woman, she had never wanted to know what he and Sherman did. But now she felt all of the not-wanting-to-know had come due and she pulled the sheet up to her neck against the cold.

"There's nothin to it," Caesar said. "In an out. Before you know it, we'll be back home, Carol. I promise."

10 Chevy Chase, Maryland.

"Stop. I'm not like you. I don't want to hurt anybody."

"It's just the money," he said, getting up. He began to dress.

"Don't go just yet," she said. She was naked and she got out of bed and put her arms around him. The cold came in the window and she shivered.

"I don't ask a whole fuckin lot of you," he said, "and when I do, you act like this." He left the room and she called to him as she put on her robe. He was out of the apartment before she got in the living room. He took the stairs two at a time, and she continued calling him as she leaned over the banister.

That was Monday. He did not go back home all that week. Manny told him on Friday that he was tired of Carol calling the bar. "Talk to her," Manny said. "Do something to shut that pussy up."

"Come home," Carol said when he finally called her Saturday afternoon. "Come home."

"You forgot what I asked you to do?" he said.

"No, I didn't forget," she said. "Come home."

"Then what do you have ta say bout what I asked?"

She said, "Yes. Yes. C, I can't hurt anybody. I just can't."

"Who said anything about somebody gettin hurt? Nobody'll get hurt. I already told you."

"Come home," she said.

The final days of that October were pleasant, but as the sun set, it grew cooler. There had been rain a few evenings, and when there was no rain, a wind came up that chilled as much as the rain. Caesar wore the tan Burberry[11] Carol had bought for him. And as he sat in Dupont Circle Park watching Carol standing before American Security, there was still enough sunlight left for him to see Anna, a block or so away, make her way with the crowd up Connecticut Avenue.

Carol did not look over at him, and as she paced, she would occasionally pull from her purse the picture of a boy about three years old, study it as if trying to memorize the boy's features, and then return the picture to her purse. Caesar had taken it from Manny's wall of Polaroids, but no one at the bar, not even Manny, could remember who the child was. Carol, however, believed that Caesar knew the boy, and when Caesar laughed, she had flung the picture at him. It had taken him most of the rest of Thursday evening to calm her, convince her that, as his father would have said, he didn't know the boy from Adam.

Still, he could tell from the way she looked at the photograph that everything he had said and done that Thursday was wearing off. Carol finally looked over

---

11 Designer trench coat made by Burberry.

at him. When Anna was but several yards from her, Caesar pointed at Anna and Carol walked to her. She took Anna by the arm and gently pulled her from the flow of the crowd. "Always say nice, soothin things," he had told Carol. "Talk to her like you were longtime sisters or somethin."

The lights in the park and along the streets came on. Anna's back was to him, but he could see Carol's face. She appeared calm and this surprised him. "The makins of a pro," Sherman would have said. The boy in the picture, dressed in green swimming trunks with his back to some ocean, could well be a grown man by now, or he could be in his grave, Caesar thought, but today, on that street, his mother was saying he needed five thousand dollars for an operation or he would die as sure as anything. "Always make it seem like the choice is hers—whether he lives or whether he dies." Anna took the picture and she looked at it, holding it but a few inches from her face.

Just the way Anna was standing told him that of the million things in the world she could do, she would do the one thing he wanted. And knowing this made up for not being with Sherman. It made up for that old woman who had cut his hand two weeks before when he ran by and tried to grab her money from her coat pocket.

Anna gave back the picture. Satisfied, he took his eyes from the women and watched the passersby heading home. Somewhere, Sherman was about to do the same. He could see Sherman closing a giant museum door so people could not see his roomful of paintings. "No more. No more for the day." It did not hurt as much to think of him now. He looked back at the women in time to see them enter the bank.

When they came out, they crossed the street, and Caesar thought it a nice touch that Carol took Anna by the arm as they crossed. Anna sat on a bench across from Peoples,[12] and for a minute or so more, Carol talked to her. Anna nodded. Everything now should be the closeout, he thought, and he felt she was taking too long. He waited until Carol walked by him and crossed the street, heading down Massachusetts Avenue. When he caught up with her, he took her by the elbow and she pulled away.

"You did good," he said, putting his arm around her. "You did real good. How much did you get?"

"Can't you wait?" she said. "Can't you even wait!" They crossed 18th Street. "Do we have to go into all this out here like this?"

---

12 Peoples Drug Store (1904-94), a chain of popular drugstores based in the Washington, DC area.

"It's all right, Carol," he said. "She back there. Nothin can happen now." Midway down the block, he reached for her purse, but again she pulled away from him.

"Stop! Jesus!" She quickened her pace.

He stopped momentarily. "What's wrong with you?"

At Massachusetts and 17th, he managed to lead her into the tiny park. The place was empty except for a bum who was sleeping on a bench several yards away from them. "What the fuck's wrong with you?" He took the purse.

"Don't!" she said, taking it back. "For God sakes, don't!"

He slapped her and grabbed for the bag with the other hand. It opened and everything inside fell out. Seeing the money fall to the ground, he slapped her again, and she began to cry. Her nose bled, and her bottom lip was split in two places, and it bled as well. The bum had awakened, and seeing the woman get slapped, he asked, "What is it there with you two peoples?"

Caesar dropped the purse, and Carol knelt down and began putting things back in it. He pulled her to her feet. "What the hell's wrong with you?"

"Leave me alone. Just leave me alone."

She knelt and he pulled her up again. "I said leave me alone." He slapped her. He could now see the distance between them growing, and seeing that distance and knowing he no longer had the power to close it, he slapped her once more. The blow sent her back a few feet. She said ohh several times, but everything sounded to him like no. She put her hand to her face and trembled.

"Hey there, fella," the bum said. "We gentlemens don't—"

"You want me to come over there and kick your ass?"

The bum was silent. He knew these young lions. He eased himself off the bench and rolled under it. Better to face the rats and the filth than face a young lion in his wrath.

"Carol, get the stuff and let's go home."

She watched him. Stepping up to her, he took out the Beretta and held it to her cheek. "Did you hear what I said?" There was no surprise in her face, and there was no fear. He realized that if he beat her with the pistol, that, too, would not surprise her. And had he shot her, in the face or through the heart, she would not have been surprised at that either. He pocketed the gun and stepped back.

She walked around him and was crying softly as she gathered up the money and her belongings. It had begun to rain and she shook each thing before putting it in the bag. When she was done, she stood and looked at him. Then, as if there was all the time in the world, she walked slowly out of the park, heading down Massachusetts. He watched her until she disappeared among the lights of Dupont Circle, and then he turned away.

There was something in the air, but he could not make out what it was. He walked out of the park. He kept looking behind him, expecting something or someone, but he was alone on the street and he saw nothing but the swirling of dead leaves. He continued looking behind him as he made his way up 17th Street. He took out the address book, but found he could not read the names or the numbers under the feeble street lights. He hurried, hoping for a telephone booth where the light would be brighter. He began to run, and as he ran, he kept trying to read the names and numbers, but the rain was now turning them to blurs. He did not know what was in the air. He only knew that tonight would not be a night to be without shelter.

—1992

SANDRA CISNEROS

Born in 1954 as the only daughter in a family of seven children living in the Puerto Rican district of Chicago, Sandra Cisneros readily admits in interviews that her background, gender, and cultural heritage have had a major impact on her writing. Cisneros is part of an important wave of Chicana writers in the United States—Gloria Anzaldúa, Ana Castillo, Denise Chavez, and Cisneros—who first attracted attention in the 1980s by exploring in their work the complexities of race and gender from a specifically Chicana perspective. Cisneros has written one novel, three books of poetry, two short story collections, and a children's book entitled *Hairs/Pelitos*. Her first book of interconnected short stories, *The House on Mango Street* (1984), won the Before Columbus Foundation's Book Award. Her work has received a Lannan Foundation Literary Award, an American Book Award, and fellowships from the National Endowment for the Arts and the MacArthur Foundation.

Cisneros graduated with a BA from Loyola University (Chicago) in 1976, and an MFA in Creative Writing from the Iowa Writers Workshop in 1978. She has described her Iowa experience as particularly important:

> My consciousness of growing up, the consciousness of myself, the subjects that I write about, the voice that I write in—I suppose all of that began in Iowa in a seminar class.... I ceased to be ashamed because I realized that I knew something that they [the other students] could never learn at universities. It was all of a sudden that I realized something that I know that I was the authority on.

She began while in Iowa to write the pieces that would make up *The House on Mango Street.* Following her graduate work, she worked at a variety of jobs, including teacher to high-school dropouts, poet-in-the-schools, college recruiter, and arts administrator. She has taught creative writing at the University of California at Berkeley, the University of California at Irvine, and at the University of Michigan in Ann Arbor. She makes her home in the Southwestern United States.

Having grown up with a Spanish-speaking, Mexican father and English-speaking, Mexican-American mother, Cisneros developed an intimate knowledge of the complexities of Chicano culture in the United States and in Mexico. She has described how she feels when she visits Mexico: "like this woman caught in mid-air with my own identity." She regularly includes untranslated Spanish words in her English writing, because "incorporating the Spanish ... allows me to create new expressions in English—to say things in English that have never been said before."

"My Lucy Friend Who Smells Like Corn" is the first story in Cisneros's collection of short stories, *Woman Hollering Creek* (1991). The story is in a section of the book that revolves around the experiences of a group of children and reflects Cisneros's continuing interest in how the inter-mixing of individuals from different cultures and/or backgrounds creates new meanings on the level both of language and of interpersonal relationships.

My Lucy Friend Who Smells Like Corn

SANDRA CISNEROS

LUCY Anguiano, Texas girl who smells like corn, like Frito Bandito chips, like tortillas, something like that warm smell of *nixtamal* or bread the way her head smells when she's leaning close to you over a paper cut-out doll or on the porch when we are squatting over marbles trading this pretty crystal that leaves a blue star on your hand for that giant cat-eye with a grasshopper green spiral in the center like the juice of bugs on the windshield when you drive to the border, like the yellow blood of butterflies.

Have you ever eaten dog food? I have. After crunching like ice, she opens her big mouth to prove it, only a pink tongue rolling around in there like a blind worm, and Janey looking in because she said Show me. But me I like that Lucy corn smell hair and aqua flipflops just like mine that we bought at the Kmart for only 79 cents same time.

I'm going to sit in the sun, don't care if it's a million trillion degrees outside, so my skin can get so dark it's blue where it bends like Lucy's. Her whole family like that. Eyes like knife slits. Lucy and her sisters. Norma, Margarita, Ofelia, Herminia, Nancy, Olivia, Cheli, *y la* Amber Sue.

Screen door with no screen. *Bang!* Little black dog biting his fur. Fat couch on the porch. Some of the windows painted blue, some pink, because her daddy got tired that day or forgot. Mama in the kitchen feeding clothes into the wringer washer and clothes rolling out all stiff and twisted and flat like paper. Lucy got her arm stuck once and had to yell Maaa! and her mama had to put the machine in reverse and then her hand rolled back, the finger black and later, her nail fell off. *But did your arm get flat like the clothes? What happened to your arm? Did they have to pump it with air?* No, only the finger, and she didn't cry neither.

Lean across the porch rail and pin the pink sock of the baby Amber Sue on top of Cheli's flowered T-shirt, and the blue jeans of *la* Ofelia over the inside seam of Olivia's blouse, over the flannel nightgown of Margarita so it don't stretch out, and then you take the work shirts of their daddy and hang them upside down like this, and this way all the clothes don't get so wrinkled and take up less space and you don't waste pins. The girls all wear each other's clothes, except Olivia, who is stingy. There ain't no boys here. Only girls and one father who is never home hardly and one mother who says *Ay! I'm real tired* and so many sisters there's no time to count them.

I'm sitting in the sun even though it's the hottest part of the day, the part that makes the streets dizzy, when the heat makes a little hat on the top of your head and bakes the dust and weed grass and sweat up good, all steamy and smelling like sweet corn.

I want to rub heads and sleep in a bed with little sisters, some at the top and some at the feets. I think it would be fun to sleep with sisters you could yell at one at a time or all together, instead of alone on the fold-out chair in the living room.

When I get home Abuelita[1] will say *Didn't I tell you?* and I'll get it because I was supposed to wear this dress again tomorrow. But first I'm going to jump off an old pissy mattress in the Anguiano yard. I'm going to scratch your mosquito bites, Lucy, so they'll itch you, then put Mercurochrome smiley faces on them. We're going to trade shoes and wear them on our hands. We're going to walk over to Janey Ortiz's house and say *We're never ever going to be your friend again forever!* We're going to run home backwards and we're going to run home frontwards, look twice under the house where the rats hide and I'll stick one foot in there because you dared me, sky so blue and heaven inside those white clouds. I'm going to peel a scab from my knee and eat it, sneeze on the cat, give you three M & M's I've been saving for you since yesterday, comb your hair with my fingers and braid it into teeny-tiny braids real pretty. We're going to wave to a lady we don't know on the bus. Hello! I'm going to somersault on the rail of the front porch even though my *chones* show. And cut paper dolls we draw ourselves, and color in their clothes with crayons, my arm around your neck.

And when we look at each other, our arms gummy from an orange Popsicle we split, we could be sisters, right? We could be, you and me waiting for our teeths to fall and money. You laughing something into my ear that tickles, and me going Ha Ha Ha Ha. Her and me, my Lucy friend who smells like corn.

—1991

---

1 A Spanish endearment for grandmother; literally, "little grandmother."

GISH JEN

Gish Jen is an American short story writer and novelist known primarily for her portrayal of individuals and families who grapple with cultural hybridity and identity. Her work places immigrants and the children of immigrants at the center of the American experience instead of the margins. She has been praised as "one of the leading chroniclers of the Chinese-American experience."

Jen's Chinese parents immigrated to the United States in the 1940s; she was born in 1955, and raised in Yonkers and then in Scarsdale, New York. Born Lillian C. Jen, she picked up the nickname "Gish" (a reference to the early twentieth-century screen star Lillian Gish) while at school. Jen has said that as the child of immigrants, she never considered the possibility of a writing career until she was encouraged to pursue it as a craft by one of her college professors. She earned her undergraduate degree from Harvard, and then attended the Stanford Graduate School of Business. She left Stanford without finishing the program, however; a few years later she graduated with her MFA from the Iowa Writers' Workshop. While at Iowa she published her first short stories, "Bellying-Up" (1981) and "The Small Concerns of Sparrows" (1982).

Jen's first novel, *Typical American* (1991), was nominated for a National Book Critics Circle Award. Five years later, she published *Mona in the Promised Land*, a novel often read as a sequel to her previous book. In it, she continues to follow members of the Chang family, Chinese immigrants and their American born progeny, as they pursue their own versions of the "American Dream." In 1999, Jen published the short story collection *Who's Irish?* Her most recent novel, *World and Town* (2011), won the Massachusetts Book Award for Fiction. In recognition of her contributions to American literature, Jen was elected to the Academy of Arts and Sciences in 1999; she has received fellowships from the National Endowment of the Arts and the Guggenheim Foundation.

"The Third Dumpster" chronicles the attempt by two brothers, Goodwin and Morehouse Lee, to build their elderly parents a new house. The two struggle to reconcile their filial duty to their Chinese parents with their own American values. Focusing on family dynamics, the story also raises issues of labor, ethics, and language.

The Third Dumpster

GISH JEN

GOODWIN Lee and his brother Morehouse had bought it at auction, for nothing. Even the local housing shark had looked down at his list and frowned and pinched or maybe itched his nose, but then waved his hand to clarify: no bid. The house was a dog. However, it had a bedroom on the first floor and was located in the same town as Goodwin and Morehouse.

They were therefore fixing it up for their parents. Goodwin and Morehouse were good with fixer-uppers, after all; they were, in fact, when they were working, contractors. And their parents were *Chinese, end of story*, as Morehouse liked to say. Meaning that though they had been Americans for fifty years and could no longer belay themselves hand over hand up their apartment stair rail to get to their bedroom, they nonetheless could not go into assisted living because of the food. Western food every day? *Cannot eat*, they said.

Goodwin had brought them to a top-notch facility anyway, just to visit. He had pointed out the smooth smooth paths, so wonderful for walking. He had pointed out the wide wide doorways, so open and inviting. And the elevators! Didn't they make you want to go up? He had pointed out the mah-jong. The karaoke. The six-handed pinochle. The senior tai qi. The lobby was full of plants, fake and alive. Always something in bloom! he said, hopefully.

But, distracted as they could be, his parents had frowned undistractedly and replied, *Lamb chops! Salad!* And that was that. His brother, Morehouse, of course, did not entirely comprehend their refusal to eat salad, believing as he did in raw foods. He began every day with a green shake whirled in a blender with an engine like a lawnmower's; the drink looked like a blended lawn, perfect for cows. But never mind. Morehouse accepted, as Goodwin did not quite, that their parents were fundamentally different; their Chineseness was inalienable. Morehouse and Goodwin, on the other hand, would never be *American, end of story*, which was why their parents had never been at a loss for words in their prime. *You are finally learn how to act! You are finally learn how to talk! You are finally learn how to think!* they had said in their kinder moods. Now, though, setting their children straight had at last given way to keeping their medications straight. They also had their sodium levels to think of. One might not think the maintenance of a low-salt diet could be a contribution to inter-generational peace, but, in truth, Goodwin found it made his parents easier to love—more like the diffuse-focus old people of fairy tales, and less like people who had above all held steadfast against the irresponsible fanning of their children's self-regard.

The house, however, was a challenge. See these walls? Morehouse had said. And he was right. They were like the walls of a refrigerator box that had been left out in the rain. The bathroom was veined a deep penicillin green; its formerly mauve ceiling was purpurating.[1] Which was why Goodwin was out scouting for dumpsters. Because this was what the recession meant in their neck of the woods: old people moving into purpurating ranch homes unless their unemployed children could do something about it. He did not, of course, like the idea of illicit trash disposal; he would have preferred to do this, as all things, in an above-board manner. But Morehouse had pushed up his sun visor, flashing a Taoist ba gua[2] tattoo, and then held this position as if in a yoga class.

Tell me, he said patiently. Tell me—what choice do we have? Tell me.

The gist of his patience being: Sure it was illegal to use other people's dumpsters, but it was going to save him and Goodwin eight hundred dollars! Eight hundred dollars they didn't have between them, four hundred they didn't have each. It was about dignity for their parents, said Morehouse. It was about doing what they were able to do. It was about doing what sons were bound to do, which was not to pussyfoot around. Morehouse said he would do the actual dumping. Goodwin just had to figure out where other people were having work done, and whether their dumpsters were night-time accessible. As for why Goodwin should do the scouting, that was because Morehouse was good with a sledgehammer and could get the demo started. Goodwin was dangerous with a sledgehammer, especially to himself.

Now he scouted carefully, in his old Corolla wagon, eating Oreos. One dumpster was maybe too close, he thought. Might not its change of fill level be linked with their dumpsterless job right around the corner? Another possibility was farther away. That was a small dumpster, though—too small for the job, really. Someone was being cheap. Also, it was close to a number of houses. People might wake up and hear them.

The third dumpster was a little farther away yet. No houses nearby; that was because it was for the repurposing of a bowling-alley. Who knew what the alley

1 Turning purple.

2 Series of eight Taoist trigrams arranged in an octagon around the Yin-Yang symbol.

was being repurposed for, but an enormous bowling-pin-shaped sign lay on the ground, leaning horizontally against the cinder-block building. It looked as if the pin had been knocked down for eternity and would never be reset. The dumpster in front of it, in contrast, was fresh and empty, apparently brand new. Bright mailbox-blue, it looked so much more like the Platonic ideal[3] of a dumpster than the real-world item itself that Goodwin found it strangely heartening. Not that he would ever have said so to Morehouse, of course. And, in fact, its pristine state posed a kind of problem, as dumping things into an empty dumpster made noise; the truly ideal dumpster was at least one-quarter full. Goodwin had faith, though, that this one would soon attain that condition. The bowling alley was closed; a construction company had put its sign up by the street. There would be trash. It was true that there were street lights nearby, one of them in working order. That meant Goodwin and Morehouse would not have the cover of darkness. On the other hand, they themselves would be able to see. That was a plus.

At the house, Goodwin found Morehouse out back, receiving black plastic bags full of debris from some workers. The workers lifted them up to him like offerings; he heaved them, in turn, into a truck. Of course, the workers were illegal, as Goodwin well knew. He knew too that Morehouse knew Goodwin to be against the use of illegals, and that Morehouse knew Goodwin knew Morehouse knew that. There was probably no point in even taking him aside. Still, Goodwin took him aside.

Did you really expect me to demo this place all by my friggin' self? asked Morehouse. Anyway, they need the work.

The workers were Guatemalan—open-miened men who nonetheless looked at each other before they said or did anything. Their names were Jose and Ovidio. They shared a water bottle. As Morehouse did not speak Spanish, and the Guatemalans did not speak English, they called him Señor Morehouse and saved their swearing for each other. Goodwin remembered enough from his Vista teaching days to pick up *¡serote!* and *¡hijo de la gran puta!* and *¡que vaina!*[4] Still the demo was apparently going fine. Goodwin watched as they delivered another half-dozen bags of debris to Morehouse.

And that's not even the end of the asbestos, said Morehouse.

Asbestos? cried Goodwin.

---

3 Refers to the philosopher Plato's idea that objects are imperfect versions of perfect, nonmaterial forms.

4 *serote* Spanish: piece of shit; *hijo ... puta* Spanish: son of a bitch; *que vaina* Spanish: what the hell.

You can't be surprised there's asbestos, said Morehouse.

And indeed, Goodwin was not surprised, when he thought about it. How, though, could Morehouse have asked Jose and Ovidio to remove it? Their lungs! Goodwin objected.

They want to do it, Morehouse shrugged. We paid them extra. They've got it half in the bags already.

But it's illegal!

We have no choice, said Morehouse. And: They have a choice. They don't have to say yes. They can say no.

Are you saying that they are better off than we are? That they have choices where we have none? That is a gross distortion of the situation! argued Goodwin.

Morehouse looked at his watch: time for his seitan[5] burger.

Dumping asbestos is like putting melamine in milk, Goodwin went on. It's like rinsing off IV needles and selling them back to hospitals. It bespeaks the sort of total disregard for public safety that makes one thankful for lawsuits, as Jeannie used to say.

Jeannie was Goodwin's prosecutor ex-wife—a woman of such standards that she'd been through some two or three marriages since theirs. Morehouse smirked with extra zest at the sound of her name.

You seem to think we have no choice, but we absolutely do have a choice, declared Goodwin then. We could, for example, take Mom and Dad in to live with one of us.

For this was the hot truth; it seared him to say it.

Morehouse, though, gave him the look of a man whose wife brought home the bacon now. It was the look of a man who knew what would fly in his house, *end of story*. He lowered his dust mask.

Did you or did you not find a friggin' dumpster? he asked. His mask was not clean, but neither was it caked with dust, like the masks of Jose and Ovidio. What you could see of their faces looked dull and crackled, like ancient earthworks that had started off as mud.

In the end, Goodwin looked the other way as more bags were filled. And though Morehouse had promised to do the dumping, it was Goodwin, finally, who drove the bags to the mailbox-blue dumpster. At least there was, as he predicted, some trash in it now. He did not make much noise as he threw his bags in deep, where they were less likely to be seen by the bowling-alley crew in the morning. The bags were heavy and shifted as if with some low-valence life force. Still, he hurled them as best he could, glad for the working street light but a little

5 Wheat gluten (often used as a meat substitute).

paranoid that someone would drive by and see him. No one did. He did think he saw, though, a bit of white smoke rise from the dumpster as he drove away. That was not really possible. The asbestos was in bags, after all; the bags were tied up. He was probably seeing some distortion in the lamplight. And didn't other things send up dust besides asbestos? Sheetrock, for example. Sheetrock sent up dust. Still, he thought he saw asbestos rising up on that dump, and on another dump he made before switching to yet another dumpster he had found, behind a Masonic temple. He didn't think there was asbestos in any of the new bags of trash, but who knew? He didn't ask, and Morehouse didn't say.

In a further effort to save money, Goodwin and Morehouse roughed out the walls themselves; and though they didn't have an electrician's licence, they took care of the wiring too. They even set a new used cast-iron tub, or tried to. In fact, they got it three inches too high and had to turn once again to Jose and Ovidio for help getting the thing back out. Of course, Jose and Ovidio shook their heads and laughed when they saw what had happened. *¡Que jodida!*[6] they said. Then they spent an entire day grimacing and straining, their faces almost as purple as the ceiling. When the tub finally rested back on a pallet in the hall, Ovidio stared at it a long moment. *¡Tu madre!* he muttered, to which Jose swore back *¡La tuya!*,[7] his arms jerking up and down, his neck twitching with anger. He pulled up his pants, maybe because they were too big; Goodwin made a mental note to bring him a belt, though what Jose and Ovidio probably needed was more food. Would Goodwin have been right to insist, as he wanted to, on finishing the job without them? After they'd already helped with the dirtiest and most grueling parts? He decided to let Morehouse have his way, and had to admit that Jose, at least, looked happy to have the work. Goodwin gave him a belt, which he seemed to appreciate; he slipped both men an extra twenty too. Take it, Goodwin told them. *Por favor.*

Was this why the work went quickly and well? And yet, still, Morehouse and Goodwin kept their parents from the site for as long as possible, knowing that something about the project was bound to spark their disapproval. *House cost nothing, but look how much you spend on renovation*, their mother might say. Or, *How come even you have no job, you hire other people to work?* Morehouse, naturally, was well stocked with rebuttals, starting with, *Don't worry, we barely pay those workers anything*. What difference these could make, though, was unclear.

---

6 Spanish: that's screwed up.

7 *Tu madre* Spanish: your mom; *La tuya* Spanish: yours (i.e., *your* mom).

Finally, though, it couldn't be helped; their parents came for a visit. They looked around stupefied. The house was not much bigger than their apartment, but it was big enough to make them seem smaller; and all new as it was, it made them look older.

Very nice, said their mother finally. She clutched her leather-trim pocketbook as if to ward off attackers; she showed real excitement about the window in the bathroom and the heating ducts. *No radiators!* she exclaimed. Their father looked as much at Jose and Ovidio as at the house. *Spanish guys*, he said. Jose and Ovidio laughed and kept working. Goodwin tried to explain what they were doing. What the house used to look like. What it was going to look like. And how much they, his parents, were going to like it. It was like trying to sell them on the assisted-living place. Everything on one floor! Close to their sons! Right in the same town! His pitch was so good that Morehouse stopped and listened—suddenly touched himself, it seemed, by what they had wrought. He beamed as if to say, Behold what we've done for you! He leaned toward their shuffling father, as if expecting to hear, What great sons you boys are!

Instead their father tripped over a toolbox and fell as if hit by a sledgehammer. Dad? Dad? He was conscious but open-mouthed and breathing hard; there was some blood, but only, Goodwin was relieved to see, a little. *I fine*, he insisted, flapping a shaking hand in the vicinity of his hip. Your hip? asked Goodwin. Their father nodded a little, grimacing—his brown age spots growing prominent as his real self, it seemed, paled. Don't move, it's OK, said Goodwin. It's OK. And, to Morehouse: Do you have an ice pack in your lunch box?

Morehouse called an ambulance. People said the ambulance service was quick around here, or could be; that was reassuring. As he and his family waited, though, Goodwin stared at his father lying on the floor, and was shocked at how like a house that could not be fixed up he seemed. He stared into the air with his milky eyes as if he did not want any of them to be there and, oddly, covered his mouth with his still-trembling hand. It was a thing he did now at funny times, as if he knew how yellow his teeth were; or maybe it was something else. Goodwin's father had always been a mystery. Now he was more manifestly obscured than ever. The few things he said were like ever darkening peepholes into fathomless depths. *You don't know what old is*, he said sometimes. *Everything take long time. Long, long time.* And once, simply: *No fun.*

His more demonstrative mother cried the whole way to the hospital, saying that his father fell because he didn't want to move into this house, and that she didn't either. It was her way of making herself clear. She didn't care whether or not it was the sort of house a person could live in by herself one day, she said. Chinese people, she said, did not live by themselves.

They were passing the turn-off for Goodwin's house when she said that. Goodwin was glad they were in an ambulance. He smiled reassuringly at his father though his eyes were closed tight; he had an oxygen mask on.

Right now we need to focus on Dad, Goodwin said.

His mother would not take her pocketbook off her lap.

Morehouse, following them in his car so that they would have a car at the hospital, called Goodwin on his cellphone.

If they ask whether Dad needs a translator tell them to fuck off, he said.

Does he need a translator? asked the admitting nurse.

He's lived here for fifty years, answered Goodwin politely.

The nurse was at least a grown-up. The doctor looked like a paper boy.

Does he need a translator? he asked.

Fuck off, said Morehouse, walking in.

How Goodwin wished he had said that! And how much he wished he had ended up like Morehouse instead of like Morehouse turned inside out. For maybe if he had, he would not have sat in the waiting room later, endlessly hearing what his mother wanted him to say—*You guys can come live with me*—much less what she would say if he said it: *You are finally learn how to take care of people. Who knows, maybe next time your wife get divorced, she come back, marry you again.*

Instead his mother was probably going to say, *You know why your wife dump you? She is completely American, that's why. Even she marry you again, she just dump you again. You wait and see.*

Fuck off, he would want to say then, like Morehouse. Fuck off!

But, of course, not even Morehouse would say that to their mother any more. Now, in deference to her advanced and ever-advancing age, even Morehouse would probably nod and agree. Their mother would say, *That's what American people are. Dump people like garbage. That's what they are.*

And Morehouse would answer, *That's what they are, all right, the fuckers.*

Nodding and nodding, even as he went on building.

—2012

LORRIE MOORE

The author of two novels and three short story collections, Marie Lorena Moore (her parents nicknamed her Lorrie) was born in 1957 in Glens Falls, New York, to an insurance executive and an ex-nurse turned housewife. She attended St. Lawrence University, and, while doing her undergraduate work, won the short story contest in *Seventeen* magazine at the age of 19. Upon graduation, Moore worked as a paralegal for two years. In 1980 she enrolled in Cornell's MFA program and while there had her short fiction published in a number of magazines, including *Ms*, *Fiction International*, and *StoryQuarterly*. Her first collection of short stories, *Self-Help*, was published in 1985; it is primarily made up of the funny, caustic stories she wrote for her MFA thesis at Cornell. Moore's brand of humor is apparent in the opening line of the story "How to Become a Writer": "First, try to be something, anything, else."

From 1982 to 1984 she worked as a lecturer at Cornell, and in 1984 she began teaching at the University of Wisconsin, where she is currently a full professor and teaches creative writing. Her work has appeared in many periodicals, including *The New Yorker*, *Harper's*, *Granta*, *The Paris Review*, and *Rolling Stone*. Her first novel, *Anagrams*, was published in 1986 and was followed by the short story collection, *Like Life* (1990), the novel *Who Will Run the Frog Hospital?* (1994), and another short story collection, *Birds of America* (1998), which was named by *The New York Times* as one of the Best Books of 1998 and nominated for the National Book Critics Circle Award. *The Collected Stories* (2008) compilation brought into print three previously unpublished stories, and Moore's 2009 novel, *A Gate at the Stairs,* was a finalist for the PEN/Faulkner Award for Fiction. She has written juvenile fiction (*The Forgotten Helper*, 1987), and edited the anthology *I Know Some Things: Stories about Childhood by Contemporary Writers* (1992). She is the recipient of a John Simon Guggenheim Memorial Foundation Fellowship and a National Endowment for the Arts Fellowship (1989). In 2006, she was welcomed into the prestigious American Society of Arts and Letters.

"You're Ugly, Too" was originally published in *The New Yorker* and is one of the eight stories that comprise *Like Life*. In this story, Moore's characteristic wit while dealing with serious subject matter comes to the fore. Rather than undermining the seriousness of the story, however, the humor highlights the quiet dilemma that the main character Zoë Hendricks faces as she realizes she has reached an impasse in her life.

You're Ugly, Too

LORRIE MOORE

YOU HAD to get out of them occasionally, those Illinois towns with the funny names: Paris, Oblong, Normal. Once, when the Dow Jones dipped two hundred points, a local paper boasted the banner headline "NORMAL MAN MARRIES OBLONG WOMAN." They knew what was important. They did! But you had to get out once in a while, even if it was just across the border to Terre Haute for a movie.

Outside of Paris, in the middle of a large field, was a scatter of brick buildings, a small liberal-arts college by the improbable name of Hilldale-Versailles. Zoë Hendricks had been teaching American history there for three years. She taught "The Revolution and Beyond" to freshmen and sophomores, and every third semester she had the senior seminar for majors, and although her student evaluations had been slipping in the last year and a half—*Professor Hendricks is often late for class and usually arrives with a cup of hot chocolate, which she offers the class sips of*—generally the department of nine men was pleased to have her. They felt she added some needed feminine touch to the corridors—that faint trace of Obsession and sweat, the light, fast clicking of heels. Plus they had had a sex-discrimination suit, and the dean had said, well, it was time.

The situation was not easy for her, they knew. Once, at the start of last semester, she had skipped into her lecture hall singing "Getting to Know You"—all of it. At the request of the dean, the chairman had called her into his office, but did not ask her for an explanation, not really. He asked her how she was and then smiled in an avuncular way. She said, "Fine," and he studied the way she said it, her front teeth catching on the inside of her lower lip. She was almost pretty, but her face showed the strain and ambition of always having been close but not quite. There was too much effort with the eyeliner, and her earrings, worn, no doubt, for the drama her features lacked, were a little frightening, jutting out the sides of her head like antennae.

"I'm going out of my mind," said Zoë to her younger sister, Evan, in Manhattan. *Professor Hendricks seems to know the entire soundtrack to "The King and I." Is this history?* Zoë phoned her every Tuesday.

"You always say that," said Evan, "but then you go on your trips and vacations and then you settle back into things and then you're quiet for a while and then you say you're fine, you're busy, and then after a while you say you're going crazy again, and you start all over." Evan was a part-time food designer for photo shoots. She cooked vegetables in green dye. She propped up beef stew with a bed of marbles and shopped for new kinds of silicone sprays and plastic ice cubes. She thought her life was O.K. She was living with her boyfriend of many years, who was independently wealthy and had an amusing little job in book publishing. They were five years out of college, and they lived in a luxury midtown high rise with a balcony and access to a pool. "It's not the same as having your own pool," Evan was always sighing, as if to let Zoë know that, as with Zoë, there were still things she, Evan, had to do without.

"Illinois. It makes me sarcastic to be here," said Zoë on the phone. She used to insist it was irony, something gently layered and sophisticated, something alien to the Midwest, but her students kept calling it sarcasm, something they felt qualified to recognize, and now she had to agree. It wasn't irony. "What is your perfume?" a student once asked her. "Room freshener," she said. She smiled, but he looked at her, unnerved.

Her students were by and large good midwesterners, spacey with estrogen from large quantities of meat and eggs. They shared their parents' suburban values; their parents had given them things, things, things. They were complacent. They had been purchased. They were armed with a healthy vagueness about anything historical or geographic. They seemed actually to know very little about anything, but they were good-natured about it. "All those states in the East are so tiny and jagged and bunched up," complained one of her undergraduates the week she was lecturing on "The Turning Point of Independence: The Battle at Saratoga." "Professor Hendricks, you're from Delaware originally, right?" the student asked her.

"Maryland," corrected Zoë.

"Aw," he said, waving his hand dismissively. "New England."

Her articles—chapters toward a book called *Hearing the One About: Uses of Humor in the American Presidency*—were generally well received, though they came slowly for her. She liked her pieces to have something from every time of day in them—she didn't trust things written in the morning only—so she reread and rewrote painstakingly. No part of a day—its moods, its light—was allowed to dominate. She hung on to a piece for a year sometimes, revising at all hours, until the entirety of a day had registered there.

The job she'd had before the one at Hilldale-Versailles had been at a small college in New Geneva, Minnesota, Land of the Dying Shopping Mall. Everyone was so blond there that brunettes were often presumed to be from foreign countries. *Just because Professor Hendricks is from Spain doesn't give her the right to be so negative about our country.* There was a general emphasis on cheerfulness. In New Geneva you weren't supposed to be critical or complain. You weren't supposed to notice that the town had overextended and that its shopping malls were raggedy and going under. You were never to say you weren't "fine, thank you—and yourself?" You were supposed to be Heidi. You were supposed to lug goat milk up the hills and not think twice. Heidi did not complain. Heidi did not do things like stand in front of the new IBM photocopier saying, "If this fucking Xerox machine breaks on me one more time, I'm going to slit my wrists."

But now in her second job, in her fourth year of teaching in the Midwest, Zoë was discovering something she never suspected she had: a crusty edge, brittle and pointed. Once she had pampered her students, singing them songs, letting them call her at home even, and ask personal questions, but now she was losing sympathy. They were beginning to seem different. They were beginning to seem demanding and spoiled.

"You act," said one of her senior-seminar students at a scheduled conference, "like your opinion is worth more than everyone else's in the class."

Zoë's eyes widened. "I *am* the teacher," she said. "I do get paid to act like that." She narrowed her gaze at the student, who was wearing a big leather bow in her hair like a cowgirl in a TV ranch show. "I mean, otherwise *everybody* in the class would have little offices and office hours." *Sometimes Professor Hendricks will take up the class's time just talking about movies she's seen.* She stared at the student some more, then added, "I bet you'd like that."

"Maybe I sound whiny to you," said the girl, "but I simply want my history major to mean something."

"Well, there's your problem," said Zoë, and, with a smile, she showed the student to the door. "I like your bow," she said.

Zoë lived for the mail, for the postman—that handsome blue jay—and when she got a real letter with a real full-price stamp from someplace else, she took it to bed with her and read it over and over. She also watched television until all hours and had her set in the bedroom—a bad sign. *Professor Hendricks has said critical things about Fawn Hall, the Catholic religion, and the whole state of Illinois. It is unbelievable.* At Christmastime she gave twenty-dollar tips to the mailman and to Jerry, the only cabbie in town, whom she had gotten to know from all her rides to and from the Terre Haute airport, and who, since he realized such rides were an extravagance, often gave her cut rates.

"I'm flying in to visit you this weekend," announced Zoë.

"I was hoping you would," said Evan. "Charlie and I are having a party for Halloween. It'll be fun."

"I have a costume already. It's a bonehead. It's this thing that looks like a giant bone going through your head."

"Great," said Evan.

"It is, it's great."

"All I have is my moon mask from last year and the year before. I'll probably end up getting married in it."

"Are you and Charlie getting *married*?" Zoë felt slightly alarmed.

"Hmmmmmmnnno, not immediately."

"Don't get married."

"Why?"

"Just not yet. You're too young."

"You're only saying that because you're five years older than I am and *you're* not married."

"*I'm* not married? Oh, my God," said Zoë, "I forgot to get married."

Zoë had been out with three men since she'd come to Hilldale-Versailles. One of them was a man in the municipal bureaucracy who had fixed a parking ticket she'd brought in to protest and then asked her out for coffee. At first, she thought he was amazing—at last, someone who did not want Heidi! But soon she came to realize that all men, deep down, wanted Heidi. Heidi with cleavage. Heidi with outfits. The parking-ticket bureaucrat soon became tired and intermittent. One cool fall day, in his snazzy, impractical convertible, when she asked him what was wrong he said, "You would not be ill served by new clothes, you know." She wore a lot of gray-green corduroy. She had been under the impression that it brought out her eyes, those shy stars. She flicked an ant from her sleeve.

"Did you have to brush that off in the car?" he said, driving. He glanced down at his own pectorals, giving first the left, then the right, a quick survey. He was wearing a tight shirt.

"Excuse me?"

He slowed down at an amber light and frowned. "Couldn't you have picked it up and thrown it outside?"

"The ant? It might have bitten me. I mean, what difference does it make?"

"It might have bitten you! Ha! How ridiculous! Now it's going to lay eggs in my car!"

The second guy was sweeter, lunkier, though not insensitive to certain paintings and songs, but too often, too, things he'd do or say would startle her. Once, in a restaurant, he stole the garnishes off her dinner plate and waited for her to notice. When she didn't, he finally thrust his fist across the table and said, "Look," and when he opened it, there was her parsley sprig and her orange slice crumpled to a wad. Another time, he described to her his recent trip to the Louvre. "And there I was in front of Delacroix's *The Barque of Dante*, and everyone else had wandered off, so I had my own private audience with it, all those agonized shades splayed in every direction, and there's this motion in that painting that starts at the bottom, swirling and building up into the red fabric of Dante's hood, swirling out into the distance, where you see these orange flames—" He was breathless in the telling. She found this touching, and smiled in encouragement. "A painting like that," he said, shaking his head. "It just makes you shit."

"I have to ask you something," said Evan. "I know every woman complains about not meeting men, but really, on my shoots I meet a lot of men. And they're not at all gay, either." She paused. "Not anymore."

"What are you asking?"

The third guy was a political-science professor named Murray Peterson, who liked to go out on double dates with colleagues whose wives he was attracted to. Usually, the wives would consent to flirt with him. Under the table sometimes there was footsie, and once there was even kneesie. Zoë and the husband would be left to their food, staring into their water glasses, chewing like goats. "Oh, Murray," said one wife, who had never finished her master's in physical therapy and wore great clothes. "You know, I know everything about you: your birthday, your license-plate number. I have everything memorized. But then that's the kind of mind I have. Once, at a dinner party, I amazed the host by getting up and saying goodbye to every single person there, first *and* last names."

"I knew a dog who could do that," said Zoë with her mouth full. Murray and the wife looked at her with vexed and rebuking expressions, but the husband seemed suddenly twinkling and amused. Zoë swallowed. "It was a talking Lab, and after about ten minutes of listening to the dinner conversation this dog knew everyone's name. You could say, 'Take this knife to Murray Peterson,' and it would."

"Really," said the wife, frowning, and Murray Peterson never called again.

"Are you seeing anyone?" said Evan. "I'm asking for a particular reason. I'm not just being like Mom."

"I'm seeing my house. I'm tending to it when it wets, when it cries, when it throws up." Zoë had bought a mint-green ranch house near campus, though now she was thinking that maybe she shouldn't have. It was hard to live in a house. She kept wandering in and out of the rooms, wondering where she had put things. She went downstairs into the basement for no reason at all except that it amused her to own a basement. It also amused her to own a tree.

Her parents, in Maryland, had been very pleased that one of their children had at last been able to afford real estate, and when she closed on the house they sent her flowers with a congratulations card. Her mother had even UPS'd a box of old decorating magazines saved over the years—photographs of beautiful rooms her mother used to moon over, since there never had been any money to redecorate. It was like getting her mother's pornography, that box, inheriting her drooled-upon fantasies, the endless wish and tease that had been her life. But to her mother it was a rite of passage that pleased her. "Maybe you will get some ideas from these," she had written. And when Zoë looked at the photographs, at the bold and beautiful living rooms, she was filled with longing. Ideas and ideas of longing.

Right now Zoë's house was rather empty. The previous owner had wallpapered around the furniture, leaving strange gaps and silhouettes on the walls, and Zoë hadn't done much about that yet. She had bought furniture, then taken it back, furnishing and unfurnishing, preparing and shedding, like a womb. She had bought several plain pine chests to use as love seats or boot boxes, but they came to look to her more and more like children's coffins, so she returned them. And she had recently bought an Oriental rug for the living room, with Chinese symbols on it she didn't understand. The salesgirl had kept saying she was sure they meant "Peace" and "Eternal Life," but when Zoë got the rug home she worried. What if they didn't mean "Peace" and "Eternal Life"? What if they meant, say, "Bruce Springsteen"? And the more she thought about it, the more she became convinced she had a rug that said "Bruce Springsteen," and so she returned that, too.

She had also bought a little baroque mirror for the front entryway, which, she had been told by Murray Peterson, would keep away evil spirits. The mirror, however, tended to frighten *her*, startling her with an image of a woman she never recognized. Sometimes she looked puffier and plainer than she remembered. Sometimes shifty and dark. Most times she just looked vague. "You look like someone I know," she had been told twice in the last year by strangers in restaurants in Terre Haute. In fact, sometimes she seemed not to have a look of her own, or any look whatsoever, and it began to amuse her that her students and colleagues were able to recognize her at all. How did they know? When she walked into a room, how did she look so that they knew it was she? Like this? Did she look like this? And so she returned the mirror.

"The reason I'm asking is that I know a man I think you should meet," said Evan. "He's fun. He's straight. He's single. That's all I'm going to say."

"I think I'm too old for fun," said Zoë. She had a dark bristly hair in her chin, and she could feel it now with her finger. Perhaps when you had been without the opposite sex for too long, you began to resemble them. In an act of desperate invention, you began to grow your own. "I just want to come, wear my bonehead, visit with Charlie's tropical fish, ask you about your food shoots."

She thought about all the papers on "Our Constitution: How It Affects Us" she was going to have to correct. She thought about how she was going in for ultrasound tests on Friday because, according to her doctor and her doctor's assistant, she had a large, mysterious growth in her abdomen. Gallbladder, they kept saying. Or ovaries or colon. "You guys practice medicine?" asked Zoë, aloud, after they had left the room. Once, as a girl, she brought her dog to a vet, who had told her, "Well, either your dog has worms or cancer or else it was hit by a car."

She was looking forward to New York.

"Well, whatever. We'll just play it cool. I can't wait to see you, hon. Don't forget your bonehead," said Evan.

"A bonehead you don't forget," said Zoë.

"I suppose," said Evan.

The ultrasound Zoë was keeping a secret, even from Evan. "I feel like I'm dying," Zoë had hinted just once on the phone.

"You're not dying," said Evan, "you're just annoyed."

"Ultrasound," Zoë now said jokingly to the technician who put the cold jelly on her bare stomach. "Does that sound like a really great stereo system or what?"

She had not had anyone make this much fuss over her bare stomach since her boyfriend in graduate school, who had hovered over her whenever she felt ill, waved his arms, pressed his hands upon her navel, and drawled evangelically, "Heal! Heal for thy Baby Jesus' sake!" Zoë would laugh and they would make love, both secretly hoping she would get pregnant. Later they would worry together, and he would sink a cheek to her belly and ask whether she was late, was she late, was she sure, she might be late, and when after two years she had not gotten pregnant they took to quarreling and drifted apart.

"O.K.," said the technician absently.

The monitor was in place, and Zoë's insides came on the screen in all their gray and ribbony hollowness. They were marbled in the finest gradations of black and white, like stone in an old church or a picture of the moon. "Do you suppose," she babbled at the technician, "that the rise in infertility among so many couples in this country is due to completely different species trying to reproduce?" The technician moved the scanner around and took more pictures. On one view in particular, on Zoë's right side, the technician became suddenly alert, the machine he was operating clicking away.

Zoë stared at the screen. "That must be the growth you found there," suggested Zoë.

"I can't tell you anything," said the technician rigidly. "Your doctor will get the radiologist's report this afternoon and will phone you then."

"I'll be out of town," said Zoë.

"I'm sorry," said the technician.

Driving home, Zoë looked in the rearview mirror and decided she looked—well, how would one describe it? A little wan. She thought of the joke about the guy who visits his doctor and the doctor says, "Well, I'm sorry to say you've got six weeks to live."

"I want a second opinion," says the guy. *You act like your opinion is worth more than everyone else's in the class.*

"You want a second opinion? O.K.," says the doctor. "You're ugly, too." She liked that joke. She thought it was terribly, terribly funny.

She took a cab to the airport. Jerry the cabbie was happy to see her.

"Have fun in New York," he said, getting her bag out of the trunk. He liked her, or at least he always acted as if he did. She called him Jare.

"Thanks, Jare."

"You know, I'll tell you a secret: I've never been to New York. I'll tell you two secrets: I've never been on a plane." And he waved at her sadly as she pushed her way in through the terminal door. "Or an escalator!" he shouted.

The trick to flying safely, Zoë always said, was to never buy a discount ticket and to tell yourself you had nothing to live for anyway, so that when the plane crashed it was no big deal. Then, when it didn't crash, when you succeeded in keeping it aloft with your own worthlessness, all you had to do was stagger off, locate your luggage, and, by the time a cab arrived, come up with a persuasive reason to go on living.

"You're here!" shrieked Evan over the doorbell, before she even opened the door. Then she opened it wide. Zoë set her bags on the hall floor and hugged Evan hard. When she was little, Evan had always been affectionate and devoted. Zoë had always taken care of her—advising, reassuring—until recently, when it seemed Evan had started advising and reassuring *her*. It startled Zoë. She suspected it had something to do with her being alone. It made people uncomfortable.

"How *are* you?"

"I threw up on the plane. Besides that, I'm O.K."

"Can I get you something? Here, let me take your suitcase. Sick on the plane. *Eeeyew.*"

"It was into one of those sickness bags," said Zoë, just in case Evan thought she'd lost it in the aisle. "I was very quiet."

The apartment was spacious and bright, with a view all the way downtown along the East Side. There was a balcony and sliding glass doors. "I keep forgetting how nice this apartment is. Twenty-first floor, doorman ..." Zoë could work her whole life and never have an apartment like this. So could Evan. It was Charlie's apartment. He and Evan lived in it like two kids in a dorm, beer cans and clothes strewn around. Evan put Zoë's bag away from the mess, over the fish tanks. "I'm so glad you're here," she said. "Now what can I get you?"

Evan made them lunch—soup from a can and saltines.

"I don't know about Charlie," she said after they had finished. "I feel like we've gone all sexless and middle-aged already."

"Hmmmm," said Zoë. She leaned back into Evan's sofa and stared out the window at the dark tops of the buildings. It seemed a little unnatural to live up in the sky like this, like birds that out of some wrong-headed derring-do had nested too high. She nodded toward the lighted fish tanks and giggled. "I feel like a bird," she said, "with my own personal supply of fish."

Evan sighed. "He comes home and just sacks out on the sofa, watching fuzzy football. He's wearing the psychic cold cream and curlers, if you know what I mean."

Zoë sat up, readjusted the sofa cushions. "What's fuzzy football?"

"We haven't gotten cable yet. Everything comes in fuzzy. Charlie just watches it that way."

"Hmm, yeah, that's a little depressing," Zoë said. She looked at her hands. "Especially the part about not having cable."

"This is how he gets into bed at night." Evan stood up to demonstrate. "He whips all his clothes off, and when he gets to his underwear he lets it drop to one ankle. Then he kicks up his leg and flips the underwear in the air and catches it. I, of course, watch from the bed. There's nothing else. There's just that."

"Maybe you should just get it over with and get married."

"Really?"

"Yeah. I mean, you guys probably think living together like this is the best of both worlds, but—" Zoë tried to sound like an older sister; an older sister was supposed to be the parent you could never have, the hip, cool mom. "But I've always found that as soon as you think you've got the best of both worlds"—she thought now of herself, alone in her house, of the toad-faced cicadas that flew around like little men at night and landed on her screens, staring; of the size-fourteen shoes she placed at the doorstep, to scare off intruders; of the ridiculous, inflatable blowup doll someone had told her to keep propped up at the breakfast table—"it can suddenly twist and become the worst of both worlds."

"Really?" Evan was beaming. "Oh, Zoë. I have something to tell you. Charlie and I *are* getting married."

"Really." Zoë felt confused.

"I didn't know how to tell you."

"Yeah, I guess the part about fuzzy football misled me a little."

"I was hoping you'd be my maid of honor," said Evan, waiting. "Aren't you happy for me?"

"Yes," said Zoë, and she began to tell Evan a story about an award-winning violinist at Hilldale-Versailles—how the violinist had come home from a competition in Europe and taken up with a local man who made her go to all his summer softball games, made her cheer for him from the stands, with the wives, until she later killed herself. But when Zoë got halfway through, to the part about cheering at the softball games, she stopped.

"What?" said Evan. "So what happened?"

"Actually, nothing," said Zoë lightly. "She just really got into softball. You should have seen her."

Zoë decided to go to a late afternoon movie, leaving Evan to chores she needed to do before the party—"I have to do them alone, really," she'd said, a little tense after the violinist story. Zoë thought about going to an art museum, but women alone in art museums had to look good. They always did. Chic and serious, moving languidly, with a great handbag. Instead, she walked down through Kips Bay, past an earring boutique called Stick It in Your Ear, past a hair salon called Dorian Gray. That was the funny thing about "beauty," thought Zoë. Look it up in the yellow pages and you found a hundred entries, hostile with wit, cutesy with warning. But look up "truth"—Ha! There was nothing at all.

Zoë thought about Evan getting married. Would Evan turn into Peter Pumpkin Eater's wife? Mrs. Eater? At the wedding, would she make Zoë wear some flouncy lavender dress, identical with the other maids'? Zoë hated uniforms, had even in the first grade refused to join Elf Girls because she didn't want to wear the same dress as everyone else. Now she might have to. But maybe she could distinguish it. Hitch it up on one side with a clothespin. Wear surgical gauze at the waist. Clip to her bodice one of those pins that say in loud letters "Shit Happens."

At the movie—*Death by Number*—she bought strands of red licorice to tug and chew. She took a seat off to one side in the theater. She felt strangely self-conscious sitting alone, and hoped for the place to darken fast. When it did, and the coming attractions came on, she reached inside her purse for her glasses. They were in a Baggie. Her Kleenex was also in a Baggie. So were her pen and her aspirin and her mints. Everything was in Baggies. This was what she'd become: *a woman alone at the movies with everything in a Baggie.*

At the Halloween party, there were about two dozen people. There were people with ape heads and large hairy hands. There was someone dressed as a leprechaun. There was someone dressed as a frozen dinner. Some man had brought his two small daughters: a ballerina and a ballerina's sister, also dressed as a ballerina. There was a gaggle of sexy witches—women dressed entirely in black, beautifully made up and jeweled. "I hate those sexy witches. It's not in the spirit of Halloween," said Evan. Evan had abandoned the moon mask and dolled herself up as hausfrau, in curlers and an apron, a decision she now regretted. Charlie, because he liked fish, because he owned fish and collected fish, had decided to go as a fish. He had fins, and eyes on the sides of his head. "Zoë! How are you! I'm sorry I wasn't here when you first arrived!" He spent the rest of his time chatting up the sexy witches.

"Isn't there something I can help you with here?" Zoë asked her sister. "You've been running yourself ragged." She rubbed her sister's arm, gently, as if she wished they were alone.

"Oh, God, not at all," said Evan, arranging stuffed mushrooms on a plate. The timer went off, and she pulled another sheetful out of the oven. "Actually, you know what you can do?"

"What?" Zoë put on her bonehead.

"Meet Earl. He's the guy I had in mind for you. When he gets here, just talk to him a little. He's nice. He's fun. He's going through a divorce."

"I'll try," Zoë groaned. "O.K.? I'll try." She looked at her watch.

When Earl arrived, he was dressed as a naked woman, steel wool glued strategically to a body stocking, and large rubber breasts protruding like hams.

"Zoë, this is Earl," said Evan.

"Good to meet you," said Earl, circling Evan to shake Zoë's hand. He stared at the top of Zoë's head. "Great bone."

Zoë nodded. "Great tits," she said. She looked past him, out the window at the city thrown glittering up against the sky; people were saying the usual things: how it looked like jewels, like bracelets and necklaces unstrung. You could see the clock of the Con Ed building, the orange-and-gold-capped Empire State, the Chrysler like a rocket ship dreamed up in a depression. Far west you could glimpse Astor Plaza, with its flying white roof like a nun's habit. "There's beer out on the balcony, Earl. Can I get you one?" Zoë asked.

"Sure, uh, I'll come along. Hey, Charlie, how's it going?"

Charlie grinned and whistled. People turned to look. "Hey, Earl," someone called from across the room. "Va-va-va-voom."

They squeezed their way past the other guests, past the apes and the sexy witches. The suction of the sliding door gave way in a whoosh, and Zoë and Earl stepped out onto the balcony, a bonehead and a naked woman, the night air roaring and smoky cool. Another couple were out there, too, murmuring privately. They were not wearing costumes. They smiled at Zoë and Earl. "Hi," said Zoë. She found the plastic-foam cooler, dug in and retrieved two beers.

"Thanks," said Earl. His rubber breasts folded inward, dimpled and dented, as he twisted open the bottle.

"Well," sighed Zoë anxiously. She had to learn not to be afraid of a man, the way, in your childhood, you learned not to be afraid of an earthworm or a bug. Often, when she spoke to men at parties, she rushed things in her mind. As the man politely blathered on, she would fall in love, marry, then find herself in a bitter custody battle with him for the kids and hoping for a reconciliation, so that despite all his betrayals she might no longer despise him, and, in the few minutes remaining, learn, perhaps, what his last name was and what he did for a living, though probably there was already too much history between them. She would nod, blush, turn away.

"Evan tells me you're a history professor. Where do you teach?"

"Just over the Indiana border into Illinois."

He looked a little shocked. "I guess Evan didn't tell me that part."

"She didn't?"

"No."

"Well, that's Evan for you. When we were kids we both had speech impediments."

"That can be tough," said Earl. One of his breasts was hidden behind his drinking arm, but the other shone low and pink, full as a strawberry moon.

"Yes, well, it wasn't a total loss. We used to go to what we called peach pearapy. For about ten years of my life, I had to map out every sentence in my mind, way ahead, before I said it. That was the only way I could get a coherent sentence out."

Earl drank from his beer. "How did you do that? I mean, how did you get through?"

"I told a lot of jokes. Jokes you know the lines to already. You can just say them. I love jokes. Jokes and songs."

Earl smiled. He had on lipstick, a deep shade of red, but it was wearing off from the beer. "What's your favorite joke?"

"Uh, my favorite joke is probably—O.K., all right. This guy goes into a doctor's office, and—"

"I think I know this one," interrupted Earl eagerly. He wanted to tell it himself. "A guy goes into a doctor's office, and the doctor tells him he's got some good news and some bad news—that one, right?"

"I'm not sure," said Zoë. "This might be a different version."

"So the guy says, 'Give me the bad news first,' and the doctor says, 'O.K. You've got three weeks to live.' And the guy cries, 'Three weeks to live! Doctor, what is the good news?' And the doctor says, 'Did you see that secretary out front? I finally fucked her.'"

Zoë frowned.

"That's not the one you were thinking of?"

"No." There was accusation in her voice. "Mine was different."

"Oh," said Earl. He looked away and then back again. "What kind of history do you teach?"

"I teach American, mostly—eighteenth- and nineteenth-century." In graduate school, at bars the pickup line was always, "So what's your century?"

"Occasionally, I teach a special theme course," she added. "Say, 'Humor and Personality in the White House.' That's what my book's on." She thought of something someone once told her about bowerbirds, how they build elaborate structures before mating.

"Your book's on *humor*?"

"Yeah, and, well, when I teach a theme course like that I do all the centuries." *So what's your century?*

"All three of them."

"Pardon?" The breeze glistened her eyes. Traffic revved beneath them. She felt high and puny, like someone lifted into heaven by mistake and then spurned.

"Three. There's only three."

"Well, four, really." She was thinking of Jamestown, and of the Pilgrims coming here with buckles and witch hats to say their prayers.

"I'm a photographer," said Earl. His face was starting to gleam, his rouge smearing in a sunset beneath his eyes.

"Do you like that?"

"Well, actually, I'm starting to feel it's a little dangerous."

"Really?"

"Spending all your time is a dark room with that red light and all those chemicals. There's links with Parkinson's, you know."

"No, I didn't."

"I suppose I should wear rubber gloves, but I don't like to. Unless I'm touching it directly, I don't think of it as real."

"Hmmm," said Zoë. Alarm buzzed mildly through her.

"Sometimes, when I have a cut or something, I feel the sting and think, *Shit.* I wash constantly and just hope. I don't like rubber over the skin like that."

"Really."

"I mean, the physical contact. That's what you want, or why bother?"

"I guess," said Zoë. She wished she could think of a joke, something slow and deliberate with the end in sight. She thought of gorillas, how when they had been kept too long alone in cages they would smack each other in the head instead of mating.

"Are you—in a relationship?" Earl suddenly blurted.

"Now? As we speak?"

"Well, I mean, I'm sure you have a relationship to your *work*." A smile, a little one, nestled in his mouth like an egg. She thought of zoos in parks, how when cities were under siege, during world wars, people ate the animals. "But I mean, with a *man*."

"No, I'm not in a relationship with a *man*." She rubbed her chin with her hand and could feel the one bristly hair there. "But my last relationship was with a very sweet man," she said. She made something up. "From Switzerland. He was a botanist—a weed expert. His name was Jerry. I called him Jare. He was so funny. You'd go to the movies with him and all he would notice was the plants. He would never pay attention to the plot. Once, in a jungle movie, he started rattling off all these Latin names, out loud. It was very exciting for him." She paused, caught her breath. "Eventually, he went back to Europe to, uh, study the edelweiss." She looked at Earl. "Are you involved in a relationship? With a *woman*?"

Earl shifted his weight and the creases in his body stocking changed, splintering outward like something broken. His pubic hair slid over to one hip, like a corsage on a saloon girl. "No," he said, clearing his throat. The steel wool in his underarms was inching down toward his biceps. "I've just gotten out of a marriage that was full of bad dialogue like 'You want more *space*? I'll give you more space!' *Clonk*. Your basic Three Stooges."

Zoë looked at him sympathetically. "I suppose it's hard for love to recover after that."

His eyes lit up. He wanted to talk about love. "But I keep thinking love should be like a tree. You look at trees and they've got bumps and scars from tumors, infestations, what have you, but they're still growing. Despite the bumps and bruises, they're—straight."

"Yeah, well," said Zoë, "where I'm from they're all married or gay. Did you see that movie *Death by Number*?"

Earl looked at her, a little lost. She was getting away from him. "No," he said.

One of his breasts had slipped under his arm, tucked there like a baguette. She kept thinking of trees, of parks, of people in wartime eating the zebras. She felt a stabbing pain in her abdomen.

"Want some hors d'oeuvres?" Evan came pushing through the sliding door. She was smiling, though her curlers were coming out, hanging bedraggled at the ends of her hair like Christmas decorations, like food put out for the birds. She thrust forward a plate of stuffed mushrooms.

"Are you asking for donations or giving them away?" said Earl wittily. He liked Evan, and he put his arm around her.

"You know, I'll be right back," said Zoë.

"Oh," said Evan, looking concerned.

"Right back. I promise."

Zoë hurried inside, across the living room into the bedroom, to the adjoining bath. It was empty; most of the guests were using the half-bath near the kitchen.

She flicked on the light and closed the door. The pain had stopped, and she didn't really have to go to the bathroom, but she stayed there anyway, resting. In the mirror above the sink, she looked haggard beneath her bonehead, violet-grays showing under the skin like a plucked and pocky bird's. She leaned closer, raising her chin a little to find the bristly hair. It was there, at the end of the jaw, sharp and dark as a wire. She opened the medicine cabinet, pawed through it until she found some tweezers. She lifted her head again and poked at her face with the metal tips, grasping and pinching and missing. Outside the door, she could hear two people talking low. They had come into the bedroom and were discussing something. They were sitting on the bed. One of them giggled in a false way. Zoë stabbed again at her chin, and it started to bleed a little. She pulled the skin tight along the jawbone, gripped the tweezers hard around what she hoped was the hair, and tugged. A tiny square of skin came away but the hair remained, blood bright at the root of it. Zoë clenched her teeth. "Come on," she whispered. The couple outside in the bedroom were now telling stories, softly and laughing. There was a bounce and squeak of mattress, and the sound of a chair being moved out of the way. Zoë aimed the tweezers carefully, pinched, then pulled gently, and this time the hair came, too, with a slight twinge of pain, and then a great flood of relief. "Yeah!" breathed Zoë. She grabbed some toilet paper and dabbed at her chin. It came away spotted with blood, and so she tore off some more and pressed hard until it stopped. Then she turned off the light, opened the door, and rejoined the party. "Excuse me," she said to the couple in the bedroom. They were the couple from the balcony, and they looked at her, a bit surprised. They had their arms around each other, and they were eating candy bars.

Earl was still out on the balcony, alone, and Zoë rejoined him there. "Hi," she said.

He turned around and smiled. He had straightened his costume out a bit, though all the secondary sex characteristics seemed slightly doomed, destined to shift and flip and zip around again any moment. "Are you O.K.?" he asked. He had opened another beer and was chugging.

"Oh, yeah. I just had to go to the bathroom." She paused. "Actually, I have been going to a lot of doctors recently."

"What's wrong?" asked Earl.

"Oh, probably nothing. But they're putting me through tests." She sighed. "I've had sonograms. I've had mammograms. Next week I'm going in for a candygram." He looked at her, concerned. "I've had too many gram words," she said.

"Here, I saved you these." He held out a napkin with two stuffed mushroom caps. They were cold and leaving oil marks on the napkin.

"Thanks," said Zoë, and pushed them both in her mouth. "Watch," she said with her mouth full. "With my luck it'll be a gallbladder operation."

Earl made a face. "So your sister's getting married," he said, changing the subject. "Tell me, really, what you think about love."

"*Love*?" Hadn't they done this already? "I don't know." She chewed thoughtfully and swallowed. "All right. I'll tell you what I think about love. Here is a love story. This friend of mine—"

"You've got something on your chin," said Earl, and he reached over to touch it.

"What?" said Zoë, stepping back. She turned her face away and grabbed at her chin. A piece of toilet paper peeled off it, like tape. "It's nothing," she said. "It's just—it's nothing."

Earl stared at her.

"At any rate," she continued, "this friend of mine was this award-winning violinist. She traveled all over Europe and won competitions; she made records, she gave concerts, she got famous. But she had no social life. So one day she threw herself at the feet of this conductor she had a terrible crush on. He picked her up, scolded her gently, and sent her back to her hotel room. After that, she came home from Europe. She went back to her old hometown, stopped playing the violin, and took up with a local boy. This was in Illinois. He took her to some Big Ten bar every night to drink with his buddies from the team. He used to say things like 'Katrina here likes to play the violin,' and then he'd pinch her cheek. When she once suggested that they go home, he said, 'What, you think you're too famous for a place like this? Well, let me tell you something. You may think you're famous, but you're not *famous* famous.' Two famouses. 'No one here's ever heard of you.' Then he went up and bought a round of drinks for everyone but her. She got her coat, went home, and shot a bullet through her head."

Earl was silent.

"That's the end of my love story," said Zoë.

"You're not at all like your sister," said Earl.

"Oh, really," said Zoë. The air had gotten colder, the wind singing minor and thick as a dirge.

"No." He didn't want to talk about love anymore. "You know, you should wear a lot of blue—blue and white—around your face. It would bring out your coloring." He reached an arm out to show her how the blue bracelet he was wearing might look against her skin, but she swatted it away.

"Tell me, Earl. Does the word 'fag' mean anything to you?"

He stepped back, away from her. He shook his head in disbelief. "You know, I just shouldn't try to go out with career women. You're all stricken. A guy can really tell what life has done to you. I do better with women who have part-time jobs."

"Oh, yes?" said Zoë. She had once read an article entitled "Professional Women and the Demographics of Grief." Or, no, it was a poem. *If there were a lake, the moonlight would dance across it in conniptions.* She remembered that line. But perhaps the title was "The Empty House: Aesthetics of Barrenness." Or maybe "Space Gypsies: Girls in Academe." She had forgotten.

Earl turned and leaned on the railing of the balcony. It was getting late. Inside, the party guests were beginning to leave. The sexy witches were already gone. "Live and learn," Earl murmured.

"Live and get dumb," replied Zoë. Beneath them on Lexington there were no cars, just the gold rush of an occasional cab. He leaned hard on his elbows, brooding.

"Look at those few people down there," he said. "They look like bugs. You know how bugs are kept under control? They're sprayed with bug hormones—female bug hormones. The male bugs get so crazy in the presence of this hormone they're screwing everything in sight—trees, rocks, everything but female bugs. Population control. That's what's happening in this country," he said drunkenly. "Hormones sprayed around, and now men are screwing rocks. Rocks!"

In the back, the Magic Marker line on his buttocks spread wide, a sketchy black on pink, like a funnies page. Zoë came up, slow, from behind, and gave him a shove. His arms slipped forward, off the railing, out over the street. Beer spilled out of his bottle, raining twenty stories down to the street.

"Hey, what are you doing!" he said, whipping around. He stood straight and readied, and moved away from the railing, sidestepping Zoë. "What the *hell* are you doing?"

"Just kidding," she said. "I was just kidding." But he gazed at her, appalled and frightened, his Magic Marker buttocks turned away now toward all of downtown, a naked pseudo-woman with a blue bracelet at the wrist, trapped out on a balcony with—with *what*? "Really, I was just kidding!" Zoë shouted. The wind lifted the hair up off her head, skyward in spines behind the bone. If there were a lake, the moonlight would dance across it in conniptions. She smiled at him and wondered how she looked.

—1989

GEORGE SAUNDERS

George Saunders is an American writer of short fiction, essays, and novellas. His stories, suffused with ironic satire and beleaguered idealism, have earned him a place among the forefront of contemporary American writers. His work is published regularly in *The New Yorker*, *Harper's*, *McSweeney's*, and *GQ*, and his short story collections have brought him numerous awards, including several National Magazine Awards and O. Henry Awards, a MacArthur "Genius Grant," and a Guggenheim Fellowship.

Saunders grew up on the South Side of Chicago, enjoying what he describes as a "very happy" childhood: "I had a ton of freedom, just did whatever I wanted, whenever I wanted." After high school, he was accepted to the Colorado School of Mines, where he earned a BSc in geophysical engineering in 1981. He also became influenced by the philosophy of Ayn Rand; he says that at that time he wanted "to be one of the earth movers, the scientific people who power the world ... not one of these lisping liberal artsy leeches." During and after 15 months of work in Sumatra as an oil-field engineer, Saunders began to read more widely, rejecting Rand's philosophy and beginning to think about writing stories. He was influenced by George Orwell, Ernest Hemingway, Jack Kerouac, Kurt Vonnegut, and Monty Python's *Flying Circus*, among others. Reading more contemporary writers, particularly Vonnegut, was key to his discovery of his own values as a writer: "The tools of art do not need to be—in fact cannot be—any but the ones ready at hand. That everyday language of yours? Use it. That messy pop-culture bag of referents? We collectively made that for a reason—reach into it."

In 1988 Saunders completed an MA in creative writing at Syracuse University. He had married the year previously, and his two daughters were born in 1988 and 1990. To support his family, Saunders worked from 1989 to 1996 as a technical writer and environmental engineer at a firm in Rochester, New York, but he continued to write stories. His first publication, "A Lack of Order in the Floating Object Room," came out in the *Northwest Review* in 1986, and several others appeared throughout the early 1990s in *The New Yorker* and *Harper's*. Saunders's first collection, *CivilWarLand in Bad Decline*, was published in 1996. The volume was very well received, and in 1997 he left his engineering job and became a faculty member at Syracuse, teaching creative writing. His second collection of stories, *Pastoralia*, was published in 2000, followed by *In Persuasion Nation* in 2006. He also wrote a novella, *The Brief and Frightening Reign of Phil* (2005) and a children's book, *The Very Persistent Gappers of Frip* (2000).

Saunders tends to set his stories in "bloated, exaggerated" circumstances that foster his particular kind of satire, one that exposes a dehumanizing world of modern distraction and futility. Most often set in the first person, his stories reveal troubled, sometimes dysfunctional narrators trapped by terrible and bizarre situations. Saunders manages to provoke laughter at the sick absurdity of modern culture while at the same time eliciting our compassion for those lost in it. He exposes "the human heart as it actually is, the tragic way time passes, the way actual cowardice and inadequacy looks and feels."

Sea Oak is a place, we are told in the story, where there is neither sea nor oak, but "a hundred subsidized apartments and a rear view of FedEx." In this bleak, dystopic landscape, the characters struggle to carry out a circumscribed version of the American dream: "You start out in a dangerous craphole and work hard so you can someday move up to a somewhat less dangerous craphole." Saunders characteristically elicits a madhouse combination of laughter and despair, giving "the full measure of Tragedy (and fear, and horror, and death) by understating it."

Sea Oak

GEORGE SAUNDERS

AT TEN Mr. Frendt comes on the P.A. and shouts, "Welcome to Joysticks!" Then he announces Shirts Off. We take off our flight jackets and fold them up. We take off our shirts and fold them up. Our scarves we leave on. Thomas Kirster's our beautiful boy. He's got long muscles and bright-blue eyes. The minute his shirt comes off two fat ladies hustle up the aisle and stick some money in his pants and ask will he be their Pilot. He says sure. He brings their salads. He brings their soup. My phone rings and the caller tells me to come see her in the Spitfire mockup. Does she want me to be her Pilot? I'm hoping. Inside the Spitfire is Margie, who says she's been diagnosed with Chronic Shyness Syndrome, then hands me an Instamatic and offers me ten bucks for a closeup of Thomas's tush.

Do I do it? Yes I do.

It could be worse. It is worse for Lloyd Betts. Lately he's put on weight and his hair's gone thin. He doesn't get a call all shift and waits zero tables and winds up sitting on the P-51 wing, playing solitaire in a hunched-over position that gives him big gut rolls.

I Pilot six tables and make thirty dollars in tips plus five an hour in salary.

After closing we sit on the floor for Debriefing. "There are times," Mr. Frendt says, "when one must move gracefully to the next station in life, like for example certain women in Africa or Brazil, I forget which, who either color their faces or don some kind of distinctive headdress upon achieving menopause. Are you with me? One of our ranks must now leave us. No one is an island in terms of being thought cute forever, and so today we must say goodbye to our friend Lloyd. Lloyd, stand up so we can say goodbye to you. I'm sorry. We are all so very sorry."

"Oh God," says Lloyd. "Let this not be true."

But it's true. Lloyd's finished. We give him a round of applause, and Mr. Frendt gives him a Farewell Pen and the contents of his locker in a trash bag and out he goes. Poor Lloyd. He's got a wife and two kids and a sad little duplex on Self-Storage Parkway.

"It's been a pleasure!" he shouts desperately from the doorway, trying not to burn any bridges.

What a stressful workplace. The minute your Cute Rating drops you're a goner. Guests rank us as Knockout, Honeypie, Adequate, or Stinker. Not that I'm complaining. At least I'm working. At least I'm not a Stinker like Lloyd.

I'm a solid Honeypie/Adequate, heading home with forty bucks cash.

At Sea Oak there's no sea and no oak, just a hundred subsidized apartments and a rear view of FedEx. Min and Jade are feeding their babies while watching "How My Child Died Violently." Min's my sister. Jade's our cousin. "How My Child Died Violently" is hosted by Matt Merton, a six-foot-five blond who's always giving the parents shoulder rubs and telling them they've been sainted by pain. Today's show features a ten-year-old who killed a five-year-old for refusing to join his gang. The ten-year-old strangled the five-year-old with a jump rope, filled his mouth with baseball cards, then locked himself in the bathroom and wouldn't come out until his parents agreed to take him to FunTimeZone. The audience is shrieking threats at the parents of the killer while the parents of the victim urge restraint and forgiveness to such an extent that finally the audience starts shrieking threats at them, too. Then it's a commercial. Min and Jade put down the babies and light cigarettes and pace the room while quizzing each other for their G.E.D.s. It doesn't look good. Jade says "regicide" is a virus. Min locates Biafra one planet from Saturn. I offer to help and they start yelling at me for condescending.

"You're lucky, man!" my sister says. "You did high school. You got your frigging diploma. We don't. That's why we have to do this G.E.D. shit. If we had our diplomas we could just watch TV and not be all distracted."

"Really," says Jade. "Now shut it, chick! We got to study. Show's almost on."

They debate how many sides a triangle has. They agree that Churchill was in opera. Matt Merton comes back and explains that last week's show on suicide, in which the parents watched a reenactment of their son's suicide, was a healing process for the parents, then shows a video of the parents admitting it was a healing process.

My sister's baby is Troy. Jade's baby is Mac. They crawl off into the kitchen and Troy gets his finger caught in the heat vent. Min rushes over and starts pulling.

"Jesus freaking Christ!" screams Jade. "Watch it! Stop yanking on him and get the freaking Vaseline. You're going to give him a really long arm, man!"

Troy starts crying. Mac starts crying. I go over and free Troy no problem. Meanwhile Jade and Min get in a slap fight and nearly knock over the TV.

"Yo, chick!" Min shouts at the top of her lungs. "I'm sure you're slapping me? And then you knock over the freaking TV? Don't you care?"

"I care!" Jade shouts back. "You're the slut who nearly pulled off her own kid's finger for no freaking reason, man!"

Just then Aunt Bernie comes in from DrugTown in her DrugTown cap and hobbles over and picks up Troy and everything calms way down.

"No need to fuss, little man," she says. "Everything's fine. Everything's just hunky-dory."

"Hunky-dory," says Min, and gives Jade one last pinch.

Aunt Bernie's a peacemaker. She doesn't like trouble. Once this guy backed over her foot at FoodKing and she walked home with ten broken bones. She never got married, because Grandpa needed her to keep house after Grandma died. Then he died and left all his money to a woman none of us had ever heard of, and Aunt Bernie started in at DrugTown. But she's not bitter. Sometimes she's so non-bitter it gets on my nerves. When I say Sea Oak's a pit she says she's just glad to have a roof over her head. When I say I'm tired of being broke she says Grandpa once gave her pencils for Christmas and she was so thrilled she sat around sketching horses all day on the backs of used envelopes. Once I asked was she sorry she never had kids and she said no, not at all, and besides, weren't we her kids?

And I said yes we were.

But of course we're not.

For dinner it's beanie-wienies. For dessert it's ice cream with freezer burn.

"What a nice day we've had," Aunt Bernie says once we've got the babies in bed.

"Man, what an optometrist," says Jade.

Next day is Thursday, which means a visit from Ed Anders, from the Board of Health. He's in charge of insuring that our penises never show. Also that we don't kiss anyone. None of us ever kisses anyone or shows his penis except Sonny Vance, who does both, because he's saving up to buy a FaxIt franchise. As for our Penile Simulators, yes, we can show them, we can let them stick out the top of our pants, we can even periodically dampen our tight pants with spray bottles so our Simulators really contour, but our real penises, no, those have to stay inside our hot uncomfortable oversized Simulators.

"Sorry fellas, hi fellas," Anders says as he comes wearily in. "Please know that I don't like this any better than you do. I went to school to learn how to inspect meat, but this certainly wasn't what I had in mind. Ha ha!"

He orders a Lindbergh Enchilada and eats it cautiously, as if it's alive and he's afraid of waking it. Sunny Vance is serving soup to a table of hair stylists on a bender when, for a twenty, he shoots them a quick look at his unit.

Just then Anders glances up from his Lindbergh.

"Oh for crying out loud," he says, and writes up a Shutdown and we all get sent home early. Which is bad. Every cent counts. Lately I've been sneaking toilet paper home in my briefcase. I can fit three rolls in. By the time I get home they're usually flat and don't work so great on the roller but still it saves a few bucks.

I clock out and cut through the strip of forest behind FedEx. Very pretty. A raccoon scurries over a fallen oak and starts nibbling at a rusty bike. As I come out of the woods I hear a shot. At least I think it's a shot. It could be a backfire. But no, it's a shot, because then there's another one, and some kids sprint across the courtyard yelling that Big Scary Dawgz rule.

I run home. Min and Jade and Aunt Bernie and the babies are huddled behind the couch. Apparently they had the babies outside when the shooting started. Troy's walker got hit. Luckily, he wasn't in it. It's supposed to look like a duck but now the beak's missing.

"Man, fuck this shit!" Min shouts.

"Freak this crap, you mean," says Jade. "You want the babies growing up with shit-mouths like us? Crap-mouths I mean?"

"I just want them growing up, period," says Min.

"Boo-hoo, Miss Dramatic," says Jade.

"Fuck off, Miss Ho," shouts Min.

"I mean it, jagoff, I'm not kidding," shouts Jade and punches Min in the arm.

"Girls, for crying out loud!" says Aunt Bernie. "We should be thankful. At least we got a home. And at least none of them bullets actually hit nobody."

"No offense, Bernie?" says Min. "But you call this a freaking home?"

Sea Oak's not safe. There's an ad-hoc crackhouse in the laundry room and last week Min found some brass knuckles in the kiddie pool. If I had my way I'd move everybody up to Canada. It's nice there. Very polite. We went for a weekend last fall and got a flat tire and these two farmers with bright-red faces insisted on fixing it, then springing for dinner, then starting a college fund for the babies. They sent us the stock certificates a week later, along with a photo of all of us eating cobbler at a diner. But moving to Canada takes bucks. Dad's dead and left us nada and Ma now lives with Freddie, who doesn't like us, plus he's not exactly rich himself. He does phone polls. This month he's asking divorced women how often they backslide and sleep with their exes. He gets ten bucks for every completed poll.

So not lucrative, and Canada's a moot point.

I find the beak of Troy's duck and fix it with Elmer's.

"Actually, you know what?" says Aunt Bernie. "I think that looks even more like a real duck now. Because sometimes their beaks are cracked? I seen one like that downtown."

"Oh my God," says Min. "The kid's duck gets shot in the face and she says we're lucky."

"Well, we are lucky," says Bernie.

"Somebody's beak is cracked," says Jade.

"You know what I do if something bad happens?" Bernie says. "I don't think about it. Don't take it so serious. It ain't the end of the world. That's what I do. That's what I always done. That's how I got where I am."

My feeling is, Bernie, I love you, but where are you? You work at DrugTown for minimum. You're sixty and own nothing. You were basically a slave to your father and never had a date in your life.

"I mean, complain if you want," she says. "But I think we're doing pretty darn good for ourselves."

"Oh, we're doing great," says Min, and pulls Troy out from behind the couch and brushes some duck shards off his sleeper.

Joysticks reopens on Friday. It's a madhouse. They've got the fog on. A bridge club offers me fifteen bucks to oil-wrestle Mel Turner. So I oil-wrestle Mel Turner. They offer me twenty bucks to feed them chicken wings from my hand. So I feed them chicken wings from my hand. The afternoon flies by. Then the evening. At nine the bridge club leaves and I get a sorority. They sing intelligent nasty songs and grope my Simulator and say they'll never be able to look their boyfriends' meager genitalia in the eye again. Then Mr. Frendt comes over and says phone. It's Min. She sounds crazy. Four times in a row she shrieks get home.

When I tell her calm down, she hangs up. I call back and no one answers. No biggie. Min's prone to panic. Probably one of the babies is puky. Luckily I'm on FlexTime.

"I'll be back," I say to Mr. Frendt.

"I look forward to it," he says.

I jog across the marsh and through FedEx. Up on the hill there's a light from the last remaining farm. Sometimes we take the boys to the adjacent car wash to look at the cow. Tonight, however, the cow is elsewhere.

At home Min and Jade are hopping up and down in front of Aunt Bernie, who's sitting very very still at one end of the couch.

"Keep the babies out!" shrieks Min. "I don't want them seeing something dead!"

"Shut up, man!" shrieks Jade. "Don't call her something dead!"

She squats down and pinches Aunt Bernie's cheek.

"Aunt Bernie?" she shrieks. "Fuck!"

"We already tried that like twice, chick!" shrieks Min. "Why are you doing that shit again? Touch her neck and see if you can feel that beating thing!"

"Shit, shit, shit!" shrieks Jade.

I call 911 and the paramedics come out and work hard for twenty minutes, then give up and say they're sorry and it looks like she's been dead most of the afternoon. The apartment's a mess. Her money drawer's empty and her family photos are in the bathtub.

"Not a mark on her," says one cop.

"I suspect she died of fright," says another. "Fright of the intruder?"

"My guess is yes," says a paramedic.

"Oh God," says Jade. "God, God, God."

I sit down beside Aunt Bernie. I think: I am so sorry. I'm sorry I wasn't here when it happened and sorry you never had any fun in your life and sorry I wasn't rich enough to move you somewhere safe. I remember when she was young and wore pink stretch pants and made us paper chains out of DrugTown receipts while singing "Froggie Went A-Courting." All her life she worked hard. She never hurt anybody. And now this.

Scared to death in a crappy apartment.

Min puts the babies in the kitchen but they keep crawling out. Aunt Bernie's in a shroud on this sort of dolly and on the couch are a bunch of forms to sign.

We call Ma and Freddie. We get their machine.

"Ma, pick up!" says Min. "Something bad happened! Ma, please freaking pick up!"

But nobody picks up.

So we leave a message.

Lobton's Funeral Parlor is just a regular house on a regular street. Inside there's a rack of brochure's with titles like "Why Does My Loved One Appear Somewhat Larger?" Lobton looks healthy. Maybe too healthy. He's wearing a yellow golf shirt and his biceps keep involuntarily flexing. Every now and then he touches his delts as if to confirm they're still big as softballs.

"Such a sad thing," he says.

"How much?" asks Jade. "I mean, like for basic. Not super-fancy."

"But not crappy either," says Min. "Our aunt was the best."

"What price range were you considering?" says Lobton, cracking his knuckles. We tell him and his eyebrows go up and he leads us to something that looks like a moving box.

"Prior to usage we'll moisture-proof this with a spray lacquer," he says. "Makes it look quite woodlike."

"That's all we can get?" says Jade. "Cardboard?"

"I'm actually offering you a slight break already," he says, and does a kind of pushup against the wall. "On account of the tragic circumstances. This is Sierra Sunset. Not exactly cardboard. More of a fiberboard."

"I don't know," says Min. "Seems pretty gyppy."

"Can we think about it?" says Ma.

"Absolutely," says Lobton. "Last time I checked this was still America."

I step over and take a closer look. There are staples where Aunt Bernie's spine would be. Down at the foot there's some writing about folding Tab A into Slot B.

"No freaking way," says Jade. "Work your whole life and end up in a Mayflower box? I doubt it."

We've got zip in savings. We sit at a desk and Lobton does what he calls a Credit Calc. If we pay it out monthly for seven years we can afford the AmberMist, which includes a double-thick balsa box and two coats of lacquer and a one-hour wake.

"But seven years, jeez," says Jade.

"We got to get her the good one," says Min. "She never had anything nice in her life."

So AmberMist it is.

We bury her at St. Leo's, on the hill up near BastCo. Her part of the graveyard's pretty plain. No angels, no little rock houses, no flowers, just a bunch of flat stones like parking bumpers and here and there a Styrofoam cup. Father Brian says a prayer and then one of us is supposed to talk. But what's there to say? She never had a life. Never married, no kids, work, work, work. Did she ever go on a cruise? All her life it was buses. Buses, buses, buses. Once she went with Ma on a bus to Quigley, Kansas, to gamble and shop at an outlet mall. Someone broke into her room and stole her clothes and took a dump in her suitcase while they were at the Roy Clark[1] show. That was it. That was the extent of her tourism. After that it was DrugTown, night and day. After fifteen years as Cashier she got demoted to Greeter. People would ask where the Cold Remedies were and she'd point to some big letters on the wall that said Cold Remedies.

Freddie, Ma's boyfriend, steps up and says he didn't know her very long but she was an awful nice lady and left behind a lot of love, etc., etc., blah blah blah. While it's true she didn't do much in her life, still she was very dear to those of us who knew her and never made a stink about anything but was always content with whatever happened to her, etc., etc., blah blah blah.

Then it's over and we're supposed to go away.

"We gotta come out here like every week," says Jade.

"I know I will," says Min.

"What, like I won't?" says Jade. "She was so freaking nice."

"I'm sure you swear at a grave," says Min.

"Since when is freak a swear, chick?" says Jade.

"Girls," says Ma.

"I hope I did O.K. in what I said about her," says Freddie in his full-of-crap way, smelling bad of English Navy. "Actually I sort of surprised myself."

"Bye-bye, Aunt Bernie," says Min.

"Bye-bye, Bern," says Jade.

"Oh my dear sister," says Ma.

I scrunch my eyes tight and try to picture her happy, laughing, poking me in the ribs. But all I can see is her terrified on the couch. It's awful. Out there, somewhere, is whoever did it. Someone came in our house, scared her to death, watched her die, went through our stuff, stole her money. Someone who's still living, someone who right now might be having a piece of pie or running an errand or scratching his ass, someone who, if he wanted to, could drive west for three days or whatever and sit in the sun by the ocean.

We stand a few minutes with heads down and hands folded.

Afterward Freddie takes us to Trabanti's for lunch. Last year Trabanti died and three Vietnamese families went in together and bought the place, and it still serves pasta and pizza and the big oil of Trabanti is still on the wall but now from the kitchen comes this very pretty Vietnamese music and the food is somehow better.

---

1 American country singer and television personality, known for hosting the variety show *Hee Haw* (1969–92).

Freddie proposes a toast. Min says remember how Bernie always called lunch dinner and dinner supper? Jade says remember how when her jaw clicked she'd say she needed oil?

"She was a excellent lady," says Freddie.

"I already miss her so bad," says Ma.

"I'd like to kill that fuck that killed her," says Min.

"How about let's don't say fuck at lunch," says Ma.

"It's just a word, Ma, right?" says Min. "Like pluck is just a word? You don't mind if I say pluck? Pluck, pluck, pluck?"

"Well, shit's just a word, too," says Freddie. "But we don't say it at lunch."

"Same with puke," says Ma.

"Shit puke, shit puke," says Min.

The waiter clears his throat. Ma glares at Min.

"I love you girls' manners," Ma says.

"Especially at a funeral," says Freddie.

"This ain't a funeral," says Min.

"The question in my mind is what you kids are gonna do now," says Freddie. "Because I consider this whole thing a wakeup call, meaning it's time for you to pull yourselfs up by the bootstraps like I done and get out of that dangerous craphole you're living at."

"Mister Phone Poll speaks," says Min.

"Anyways it ain't that dangerous," says Jade.

"A woman gets killed and it ain't that dangerous?" says Freddie.

"All's we need is a dead bolt and a eyehole," says Min.

"What's a bootstrap?" says Jade.

"It's like a strap on a boot, you doof," says Min.

"Plus where we gonna go?" says Min. "Can we move in with you guys?"

"I personally would love that, and you know that," says Freddie. "But who would not love that is our landlord."

"I think what Freddie's saying is it's time for you girls to get jobs," says Ma.

"Yeah right, Ma," says Min. "After what happened last time?"

When I first moved in, Jade and Min were working the info booth at HardwareNiche. Then one day we picked the babies up at day care and found Troy sitting naked on top of the washer and Mac in the yard being nipped by a Pekingese and the day-care lady sloshed and playing KillerBirds on Nintendo.

So that was that. No more HardwareNiche.

"Maybe one could work, one could babysit?" says Ma.

"I don't see why I should have to work so she can stay home with her baby," says Min.

"And I don't see why I should have to work so she can stay home with her baby," says Jade.

"It's like a freaking veece versa," says Ma.

"Let me tell you something," says Freddie. "Something about this country. Anybody can do anything. But first they gotta try. And you guys ain't. Two don't work and one strips naked? I don't consider that trying. You kids make squat. And therefore you live in a dangerous craphole. And what happens in a dangerous craphole? Bad tragic shit. It's the freaking American way—you start out in a dangerous craphole and work hard so you can someday move up to a somewhat less dangerous craphole. And finally maybe you get a mansion. But at this rate you ain't even gonna make it to the somewhat less dangerous craphole."

"Like you live in a mansion," says Jade.

"I do not claim to live in no mansion," says Freddie. "But then again I do not live in no slum. The other thing I also do not do is strip naked."

"Thank God for small favors," says Min.

"Anyways he's never actually naked," says Jade.

Which is true. I always have on at least a T-back.

"No wonder we never take these kids out to a nice lunch," says Freddie.

"I do not even consider this a nice lunch," says Min.

For dinner Jade microwaves some Stars-n-Flags. They're addictive. They put sugar in the sauce and sugar in the meat nuggets. I think also caffeine. Someone told me the brown streaks in the Flags are caffeine. We have like five bowls each.

After dinner the babies get fussy and Min puts a mush of ice cream and Hershey's syrup in their bottles and we watch "The Worst That Could Happen," a half hour of computer simulations of tragedies that have never actually occurred but theoretically could. A kid gets hit by a train and flies into a zoo, where he's eaten by wolves. A man cuts his hand off chopping wood and while wandering around screaming for help is picked up by a tornado and dropped on a preschool during recess and lands on a pregnant teacher.

"I miss Bernie so bad," says Min.

"Me too," says Jade sadly.

The babies start howling for more ice cream.

"That is so cute," says Jade. "They're like, *Give it the fuck up!*"

"We'll give it the fuck up, sweeties, don't worry," says Min. "We didn't forget about you."

Then the phone rings. It's Father Brian. He sounds weird. He says he's sorry to bother us so late. But something strange has happened. Something bad. Something sort of, you know, unspeakable. Am I sitting? I'm not, but I say I am.

Apparently someone has defaced Bernie's grave.

My first thought is there's no stone. It's just grass. How do you deface grass? What did they do, pee on the grass on the grave? But Father's nearly in tears.

So I call Ma and Freddie and tell them to meet us, and we get the babies up and load them into the K-car.

"Deface," says Jade on the way over. "What does that mean, deface?"

"It means like fucked it up," says Min.

"But how?" says Jade. "I mean, like what did they do?"

"We don't know, dumbass," says Min. "That's why we're going there."

"And why?" says Jade. "Why would someone do that?"

"Check out Miss Sherlock Holmes," says Min. "Someone done that because someone is a asshole."

"Someone is a big-time asshole," says Jade.

Father Brian meets us at the gate with a flashlight and a golf cart.

"When I saw this," he says, "I literally sat down in astonishment. Nothing like this has ever happened here. I am so sorry. You seem like nice people."

We're too heavy and the wheels spin as we climb the hills, so I get out and jog alongside.

"O.K., folks, brace yourselves," Father says, and shuts off the engine.

Where the grave used to be is just a hole. Inside the hole is the AmberMist, with the top missing. Inside the AmberMist is nothing. No Aunt Bernie.

"What the hell," says Jade. "Where's Bernie?"

"Somebody stole Bernie?" says Min.

"At least you folks have retained your feet," says Father Brian. "I'm telling you I literally sat right down. I sat right down on that pile of dirt. I dropped as if shot. See that mark? That's where I sat."

On the pile of grave dirt is a butt-shaped mark.

The cops show up and one climbs down in the hole with a tape measure and a camera. After three or four flashes he climbs out and hands Ma a pair of blue pumps.

"Her little shoes," says Ma. "Oh my God."

"Are those them?" says Jade.

"Those are them," says Min.

"I am freaking out," says Jade.

"I am totally freaking out," says Min.

"I'm gonna sit," says Ma, and drops into the golf cart.

"What I don't get is who'd want her?" says Min.

"She was just this lady," says Jade.

"Typically it's teens?" the cop says. "Typically we find the loved one nearby? Once we found the loved one nearby with, you know, a cigarette between its lips, wearing a sombrero? These kids today got a lot more nerve than we ever did.

I never would've dreamed of digging up a dead corpse when I was a teen. You might tip over a stone, sure, you might spray-paint something on a crypt, you might, you know, give a wino a hotfoot."

"But this, jeez," says Freddie. "This is a entirely different ballgame."

"Boy howdy," says the cop, and we all look down at the shoes in Ma's hands.

Next day I go back to work. I don't feel like it, but we need the money. The grass is wet and it's hard getting across the ravine in my dress shoes. The soles are slick. Plus they're too tight. Several times I fall forward on my briefcase. Inside the briefcase are my T-backs and a thing of mousse.

Right off the bat I get a call from a tableful of MediBen women seated under a banner that says "Best of Luck, Beatrice, No Hard Feelings." I take off my shirt and serve their salads. I take off my flight pants and serve their soup. One drops a dollar on the floor and tells me feel free to pick it up.

I pick it up.

"Not like that, not like that," she says. "Face the other way, so when you bend we can see your crack."

I've done this about a million times, but somehow I can't do it now.

I look at her. She looks at me.

"What?" she says. "I'm not allowed to say that? I thought that was the whole point."

"That is the whole point, Phyllis," says another lady. "You stand your ground."

"Look," Phyllis says. "Either bend how I say or give back the dollar. I think that's fair."

"You go, girl," says her friend.

I give back the dollar. I return to the Locker Area and sit awhile. For the first time ever, I'm voted Stinker. There are thirteen women at the MediBen table and they all vote me Stinker. Do the MediBen women know my situation? Would they vote me Stinker if they did? But what am I supposed to do, go out and say, please, ladies, my aunt just died, plus her body's missing?

Mr. Frendt pulls me aside.

"Perhaps you need to go home," he says. "I'm sorry for your loss. But I'd like to encourage you not to behave like one of those Comanche ladies who bite off their index fingers when a loved one dies. Grief is good, grief is fine, but too much grief, as we all know, is excessive. If your aunt's death has filled your mouth with too many bitten-off fingers, for crying out loud, take a week off, only don't take it out on our guests, they didn't kill your dang aunt."

But I can't afford to take a week off. I can't even afford to take a few days off.

"We really need the money," I say.

"Is that my problem?" he says. "Am I supposed to let you dance without vigor just because you need the money? Why don't I put an ad in the paper for all sad people who need money? All the town's sad could come here and strip. Goodbye. Come back when you feel halfway normal."

From the pay phone I call home to see if they need anything from the FoodSoQuik.

"Just come home," Min says stiffly. "Just come straight home."

"What is it?" I say.

"Come home," she says.

Maybe someone's found the body. I imagine Bernie naked, Bernie chopped in two, Bernie posed on a bus bench. I hope and pray that something only mildly bad's been done to her, something we can live with.

At home the door's wide open. Min and Jade are sitting very still on the couch, babies in their laps, staring at the rocking chair, and in the rocking chair is Bernie. Bernie's body.

Same perm, same glasses, same blue dress we buried her in.

What's it doing here? Who could be so cruel? And what are we supposed to do with it?

Then she turns her head and looks at me.

"Sit the fuck down," she says.

In life she never swore.

I sit. Min squeezes and releases my hand, squeezes and releases, squeezes and releases.

"You, mister," Bernie says to me, "are going to start showing your cock. You'll show it and show it. You go up to a lady, if she wants to see it, if she'll pay to see it, I'll make a thumbprint on the forehead. You see the thumbprint, you ask. I'll try to get you five a day, at twenty bucks a pop. So a hundred bucks a day. Seven hundred a week. And that's cash, so no taxes. No withholding. See? That's the beauty of it."

She's got dirt in her hair and dirt in her teeth and her hair is a mess and her tongue when it darts out to lick her lips is black.

"You, Jade," she says. "Tomorrow you start work. Andersen Labels, Fifth and Rivera. Dress up when you go. Wear something nice. Show a little leg. And don't chomp your gum. Ask for Len. At the end of the month, we take the money you made and the cock money and get a new place. Somewhere safe. That's part one of Phase One. You, Min. You babysit. Plus you quit smoking. Plus you learn how to cook. No more food out of cans. We gotta eat right to look our best. Because I am getting me so many lovers. Maybe you kids don't know this but I died a freaking virgin. No babies, no lovers. Nothing went in, nothing came out. Ha ha! Dry as a bone, completely wasted, this pretty little thing God gave me between my legs. Well, I am going to have lovers now, you fucks! Like in the movies, big shoulders and all, and a summer house, and nice trips, and in the morning in my room a big vase of flowers, and I'm going to get my nipples hard standing in the breeze from the ocean, eating shrimp from a cup, you sons of bitches, while my lover watches me from the veranda, his big shoulders shining, all hard for me, that's one damn thing I will guarantee you kids! Ha ha! You think I'm joking? I ain't freaking joking. I never got nothing! My life was shit! I was never even up in a freaking plane. But that was that life and this is this life. My new life. Cover me up now! With a blanket. I need my beauty rest. Tell anyone I'm here, you all die. Plus they die. Whoever you tell, they die. I kill them with my mind. I can do that. I am very freaking strong now. I got powers! So no visitors. I don't exactly look my best. You got it? You all got it?"

We nod. I go for a blanket. Her hands and feet are shaking and she's grinding her teeth and one falls out.

"Put it over me, you fuck, all the way over!" she screams, and I put it over her.

We sneak off and whisper in the kitchen.

"It looks like her," says Min.

"It is her," I say.

"It is and it ain't," says Jade.

"We better do what she says," Min says.

"No shit," Jade says.

All night she sits in the rocker under the blanket, shaking and swearing.

All night we sit in Min's bed, fully dressed, holding hands.

"See how strong I am!" she shouts around midnight, and there's a cracking sound, and when I go out the door's been torn off the microwave but she's still sitting in the chair.

In the morning she's still there, shaking and swearing.

"Take the blanket off!" she screams. "It's time to get this show on the road."

I take the blanket off. The smell is not good. One ear is now in her lap. She keeps absent-mindedly sticking it back on her head.

"You, Jade!" she shouts. "Get dressed. Go get that job. When you meet Len, bend forward a little. Let him see down your top. Give him some hope. He's a sicko, but we need him. You, Min! Make breakfast. Something homemade. Like biscuits."

"Why don't you make it with your powers?" says Min.

"Don't be a smartass!" screams Bernie. "You see what I did to that microwave?"

"I don't know how to make freaking biscuits," Min wails.

"You know how to read, right?" Bernie shouts. "You ever heard of a recipe? You ever been in the grave? It sucks so bad! You regret all the things you never did. You little bitches are gonna have a very bad time in the grave unless you get on the stick, believe me! Turn down the thermostat! Make it cold. I like cold. Something's off with my body. I don't feel right."

I turn down the thermostat. She looks at me.

"Go show your cock!" she shouts. "That is the first part of Phase One. After we get the new place, then that's the end of the first part of Phase Two. You'll still show your cock, but only three days a week. Because you'll start community college. Pre-law. Pre-law is best. You'll be a whiz. You ain't dumb. And Jade'll work weekends to make up for the decrease in cock money. See? See how that works? Now get out of here. What are you gonna do?"

"Show my cock?" I say.

"Show your cock, that's right," she says, and brushes back her hair with her hand, and a huge wad comes out leaving her almost bald on one side.

"Oh God," says Min. "You know what? No way me and the babies are staying here alone."

"You ain't alone," says Bernie. "I'm here."

"Please don't go," Min says to me.

"Oh, stop it," Bernie says, and the door flies open and I feel a sort of invisible fist punching me in the back.

Outside it's sunny. A regular day. A guy's changing his oil. The clouds are regular clouds and the sun's the regular sun and the only non-regular thing is that my clothes smell like Bernie, a combo of wet cellar and rotten bacon.

Work goes well. I manage to keep smiling and hide my shaking hands, and my mid-shift rating is Honeypie. After lunch this older woman comes up and says I look so much like a real Pilot she can hardly stand it.

On her forehead is a thumbprint. Like Ash Wednesday, only sort of glowing.

I don't know what to do, Do I just come out and ask if she wants to see my cock? What if she says no? What if I get caught? What if I show her and she doesn't think it's worth twenty bucks?

Then she asks if I'll surprise her friend with a birthday table dance. She points out her friend. A pretty girl, no thumbprint. Looks somehow familiar.

We start over and at about twenty feet I realize it's Angela.

Angela Silveri.

We dated senior year. Then Dad died and Ma had to take a job at Patty Melt Depot. From all the grease Ma got a bad rash and could barely wear a blouse. Plus Min was running wild. So Angela would come over and there'd be Min getting high under a tarp on the carport and Ma sitting in her bra on a kitchen stool with a fan pointed at her gut. Angela had dreams. She had plans. In her notebook she'd pasted a picture of an office from the J.C. Penney catalogue and under it wrote, "My (someday?) office." Once we saw this black Porsche and she said very nice but make hers red. The last straw was Ed Edwards, a big drunk, one of Dad's cousins. Things got so bad Ma rented him the utility room. One night Angela and I were making out on the couch late when Ed came in soused and started peeing in the dishwasher.

What could I say? He's only barely related to me? He hardly ever does that?

Angela's eyes were like these little pies.

I walked her home, got no kiss, came back, cleaned up the dishwasher as best I could. A few days later I got my class ring in the mail and a copy of "The Prophet."

"You will always be my first love," she'd written inside. "But now my path converges to a higher ground. Be well always. Walk in joy. Please don't think me cruel, it's just that I want so much in terms of accomplishment, plus I couldn't believe that guy peed right on your dishes."

No way am I table-dancing for Angela Silveri. No way am I asking Angela Silveri's friend if she wants to see my cock. No way am I hanging around here so Angela can see me in my flight jacket and T-backs and wonder to herself how I went so wrong, etc., etc.

I hide in the kitchen until my shift is done, then walk home very, very slowly because I'm afraid of what Bernie's going to do to me when I get there.

Min meets me at the door. She's got flour all over her blouse and it looks like she's been crying.

"I can't take any more of this," she says. "She's like falling apart. I mean shit's falling off her. Plus she made me bake a freaking pie."

On the table is a very lumpy pie. One of Bernie's arms is now disconnected and lying across her lap.

"What are you thinking of?" she shouts. "You didn't show your cock even once? You think it's easy making those thumbprints? You try it, smartass! Do you or do you not know the plan? You gotta get us out of here! And to get us out, you gotta use what you got. And you ain't got much. A nice face. And a decent unit. Not huge, but shaped nice."

"Bernie, God," says Min.

"What, Miss Priss?" shouts Bernie, and slams the severed arm down hard on her lap and her other ear falls off.

"I'm sorry, but this is too fucking sickening," says Min. "I'm going out."

"What's sickening?" says Bernie. "Are you saying I'm sickening? Well, I think you're sickening. So many wonderful things in life and where is your mind? You think with your lazy ass. Whatever life hands you, you take. You're not going anywhere. You're staying home and studying."

"I'm what?" says Min. "Studying what? I ain't studying. Chick comes into my house and starts ordering me so study? I freaking doubt it."

"You don't know nothing!" Bernie says. "What fun is life when you don't know nothing? You can't find your own town on the map. You can't name a single President. When we go to Rome you won't know nothing about the history. You're going to study the World Book. Do we still have those World Books?"

"Yeah right," says Min. "We're going to Rome."

"We'll go to Rome when he's a lawyer," says Bernie.

"Dream on, chick," says Min. "And we'll go to Mars when I'm a stock-breaker."

"Don't you dare make fun of me!" Bernie shouts, and our only vase goes flying across the room and nearly nails Min in the head.

"She's been like this all day," says Min.

"Like what?" shouts Bernie. "We had a perfectly nice day."

"She made me help her try on my bras," says Min.

"I never had a nice sexy bra," says Bernie.

"And now mine are all ruined," says Min. "They got this sort of goo on them."

"You ungrateful shit!" shouts Bernie. "Do you know what I'm doing for you? I'm saving your boy. And you got the nerve to say I made goo on your bras! Troy's gonna get caught in a crossfire in the courtyard. In September. September 18th. He's gonna get thrown right off his little trike. With one leg twisted under him and blood pouring out of his ear. It's a freaking prophecy. You know that word? It means prediction. You know that word? You think I'm bullshitting? Well, I ain't bullshitting. I got the power. Watch this: All day Jade sat licking labels at a desk by a window. Her boss bought everybody subs for lunch. She's bringing some home in a green bag."

"That ain't true about Troy, is it?" says Min. "Is it? I don't believe it."

"Turn on the TV!" Bernie shouts. "Give me the changer."

I turn on the TV. I give her the changer. She puts on "Nathan's Body Shop." Nathan says washboard abs drive the women wild. Then there's a closeup of his washboard abs.

"Oh yes," says Bernie. "Them are for me. I'd like to give those a lick. A lick and a pinch. I'd like to sort of straddle those things."

Just then Jade comes through the door with a big green bag.

"Oh God," says Min.

"Told you so!" says Bernie, and pokes Min in the ribs. "Ha h-ha! I really got the power!"

"I don't get it," Min says, all desperate. "What happens? Please. What happens to him? You better freaking tell me."

"I already told you," Bernie says. "He'll fly about fifteen feet and live about three minutes."

"Bernie, God," Min says, and starts to cry. "You used to be so nice."

"I'm still so nice," says Bernie, and bites into a sub and takes off the tip of her finger and starts chewing it up.

Just after dawn she shouts out my name.

"Take the blanket off," she says. "I ain't feeling so good."

I take the blanket off. She's basically just this pile of parts: both arms in her lap, head on the arms, heel of one foot touching the heel of the other, all of it sort of wrapped up in her dress.

"Get me a washcloth," she says. "Do I got a fever? I feel like I got a fever. Oh, I knew it was too good to be true. But O.K. New plan. New plan. I'm changing the first part of Phase One. If you see two thumbprints, that means the lady'll screw you for cash. We're in a fix here. We gotta speed this up. There ain't gonna be nothing left of me. Who's gonna be my lover now?"

The doorbell rings.

"Son of a bitch," Bernie snarls.

It's Father Brian with a box of doughnuts. I step out quick and close the door behind me. He says he's just checking in. Perhaps we'd like to talk? Perhaps we're feeling some residual anger about Bernie's situation? Which would of course be completely understandable. Once when he was a young priest someone broke in and drew a mustache on the Virgin Mary with a permanent marker, and for weeks he was tortured by visions of bending back the finger of the vandal until he or she broke into tears of apology.

"I knew that wasn't appropriate," he says. "I knew that by indulging in that fantasy I was honoring violence. And yet it gave me pleasure. I also thought of catching them in the act and boinking them in the head with a rock. I also thought of jumping up and down on their backs until something in their spinal column cracked. Actually I had about a million ideas. But you know what I did instead? I scrubbed and scrubbed our Holy Mother, and soon she was as good as new. Her statue, I mean. She herself of course is always good as new."

From inside comes the sound of breaking glass. Breaking glass and then something heavy falling, and Jade yelling and Min yelling and the babies crying.

"Oops, I guess?" he says. "I've come at a bad time? Look, all I'm trying to do is urge you, if at all possible, to forgive the perpetrators, as I forgave the perpetrators that drew on the Virgin Mary. The thing lost, after all, is only your aunt's body, and what is essential, I assure you, is elsewhere, being well taken care of."

I nod. I smile. I say thanks for stopping by. I take the doughnuts and go back inside.

The TV's broke and the refrigerator's tipped over and Bernie's parts are strewn across the living room like she's been shot out of a cannon.

"She tried to get up," says Jade.

"I don't know where the hell she thought she was going," says Min.

"Come here," the head says to me, and I squat down. "That's it for me. I'm fucked. As per usual. Always the bridesmaid, never the bride. Although come to think of it I was never even the freaking bridesmaid. Look, show your cock. It's the shortest line between two points. The world ain't giving away nice lives. You got a trust fund? You a genius? Show your cock. It's what you got. And remember: Troy in September. On his trike. One leg twisted. Don't forget. And also. Don't remember me like this. Remember me like how I was that night we all went to Red Lobster and I had that new perm. Ah Christ. As least buy me a stone."

I rub her shoulder, which is next to her foot.

"We loved you," I say.

"Why do some people get everything and I got nothing?" she says. "Why? Why was that?"

"I don't know," I say.

"Show your cock," she says, and dies again.

We stand there looking down at the pile of parts. Mac crawls toward it and Min moves him back with her foot.

"This is too freaking much," says Jade, and starts crying.

"What do we do now?" says Min.

"Call the cops," Jade says.

"And say what?" says Min.

We think about this awhile.

I get a Hefty bag. I get my winter gloves.

"I ain't watching," says Jade.

"I ain't watching either," says Min, and they take the babies into the bedroom.

I close my eyes and wrap Bernie up in the Hefty bag and twistie-tie the bag shut and lug it out to the trunk of the K-car. I throw in a shovel. I drive up to St. Leo's. I lower the bag into the hole using a bungee cord, then fill the hole back in.

Down in the city are the nice houses and the so-so houses and the lovers making out in dark yards and the babies crying for their moms and I wonder if, other than Jesus, this has ever happened before. Maybe it happens all the time. Maybe there's angry dead all over, hiding in rooms, covered with blankets, bossing around their scared embarrassed relatives. Because how would we know?

I for sure don't plan on broadcasting this.

I smooth over the dirt and say a little prayer: If it was wrong for her to come back, forgive her, she never got beans in this life, plus she was trying to help us.

At the car I think of an additional prayer: But please don't let her come back again.

When I get home the babies are asleep and Jade and Min are watching a phone-sex infomercial, three girls in leather jumpsuits eating bananas in slo-mo while across the screen runs a constant disclaimer: "Not Necessarily the Girls Who Man the Phones! Not Necessarily the Girls Who Man the Phones!"

"Them chicks seem to really be enjoying those bananas," says Min in a thin little voice.

"I like them jumpsuits, though," says Jade.

"Yeah, them jumpsuits look decent," says Min.

Then they look up at me. I've never seen them so sad and beat and sick.

"It's done," I say.

Then we hug and cry and promise never to forget Bernie the way she really was, and before bed I use some Resolve on the rug and they do a little reading in their World Books.

Next day I go in early. I don't see a single thumbprint. But it doesn't matter. I get with Sonny Vance and he tells me how to do it. First you ask the woman would she like a private tour. Then you show her the fake P-40, the Gallery of Historical Aces, the shower stall where we get oiled up, etc., etc., and then in the hall near the rest room you ask if there's anything else she'd like to see. It's sleazy. It's gross. But when I do it I think of September. September and Troy in the crossfire, his little leg bent under him, etc., etc.

Most say no but quite a few say yes.

I've got a place picked out at a complex called Swan's Glen. They've never had a shooting or a knifing and the public school is great and every Saturday they have a nature walk for kids behind the clubhouse.

For every hundred bucks I make, I set aside five for Bernie's stone.

What do you write on something like that? LIFE PASSED HER BY? DIED DISAPPOINTED? CAME BACK TO LIFE BUT FELL APART? All true, but too sad, and no way I'm writing any of those.

BERNIE KOWALSKI, it's going to say. BELOVED AUNT.

Sometimes she comes to me in dreams. She never looks good. Sometimes she's wearing a dirty smock. Once she had on handcuffs. Once she was naked and dirty and this mean cat was clawing its way up her front. But every time it's the same thing.

"Some people get everything and I got nothing," she says. "Why? Why did that happen?"

Every time I say I don't know.

And I don't.

—1998

HELEN SIMPSON

Helen Simpson is a London-based short story author and librettist. Known for her caustic wit, experimentation with form, and clear-eyed yet sympathetic portrayals of human nature, she is often compared with writers such as Flannery O'Connor, Alice Munro, and Katherine Mansfield. A Fellow of the Royal Society of Literature, Simpson is a recipient of the E.M. Forster Award (2002) and the Somerset Maugham Award (1991), and was named one of *Granta* magazine's "Best Young British Novelists" in 1993.

Born in Bristol, Simpson spent much of her childhood in Willesden, north London, and her university years at Oxford, where she wrote a doctoral thesis on Restoration comedy. While still in graduate school, she applied for a work experience placement at *Vogue*, for which she was required to compose a brief autobiography. Her submission—a completely invented life story full of "savagery and drama"—garnered her the placement at *Vogue*, where she would remain as a staff writer for the next five years. Encouraged by her editor, who published her first short story in the magazine, Simpson embarked on a career as a writer of short fiction. Her first collection, *Four Bare Legs in a Bed* (1990), received great critical acclaim, including the *Sunday Times* Young Writer of the Year Award.

Since 1990, Simpson has published a book every five years, each volume dominated by a theme that takes a central place in some, but not all, of the stories. Many of the stories in *Four Bare Legs in a Bed*, for instance, focus on sexuality and relationships, while *Dear George and Other Stories* (1994) and *Hey Yeah Right Get a Life* (2000) concentrate increasingly on the realities of childbearing and motherhood. These two collections are perhaps her best-known work, celebrated for unsentimentally examining the lives of women with children at a time when such writing was still relatively rare; *Hey Yeah Right Get a Life* was awarded the Hawthornden Prize. *Constitutional* (2005) confronts the experience of middle age, while a third of the stories in *In-Flight Entertainment* (2010) address the theme of climate change. Generally, Simpson is interested in probing the cultural unease surrounding "uncomfortable subjects," from the implication "that motherhood isn't all bliss" to the suggestion that "it's a good idea to cut back on air travel for the sake of the future."

Simpson's fiction is remarkable, critics suggest, for its "ability to pinpoint and draw out the common experience" at the center of an imagined storyline. She believes that such personal resonance is achieved in her work through the elimination of extraneous elements; her ideal short story is as compact as "a geologic core sample," encompassing "everything you need to know about the history and geography and inhabitants and social conditions of the area, in wonderfully concise form."

"Bed and Breakfast" begins with a pair of young lovers on the verge of adulthood traveling to the countryside in search of a perfect rendezvous. The story appeared in *Dear George and Other Stories*, a book that prompted a reviewer in *The Times* to claim that "of all contemporary writers, Simpson has the most honest, the most authentic voice."

Bed and Breakfast

HELEN SIMPSON

THEY SAT side by side not holding hands. Back on the platform and in the ticket office, people had turned to stare at them. It was visible, the intensity of their candle power, joined, no matter how they tried to bank it down and look everydayish.

Proud and shy out in the public air, they avoided the larky or lovey-dovey behavior common to their age group. It was enough to allow themselves to glance at each other now and then, glances arrowing beams of sheepish delight.

With a swish of doors and a sigh the train slid away. Light poured in through the smeary windows. Nicola lowered her eyelids and broke into a half-smile, the edges of her teeth showing in the sunny flood like a fringe of daisy petals. She was very fair. Simon looked sideways at her face, the snowy printless forehead, and then she, turning, opened her eyes straight into his and he blushed, gasped, burrowed in his sports bag and brought out a mathematically arranged cheese sandwich. This he placed furtively in her lap.

"To keep your strength up," he muttered, frowning at the couple opposite, fending off ridicule. The man was older than them, in his early twenties, stout, strong, sulky, his thumbs sunk angrily into the waistband of his jeans, muscular legs in a V-sign hogging more than their share of space. He was staring glumly out of the window as they sped past vegetable allotments and chimney stacks, his glare on autopilot. Beside him his girlfriend sat poring over a magazine article headed "What Makes a Girl a Good Lay?"

These two ignored each other till the next station, when they slouched off the train like a couple of Alsatians. Nicola watched them snapping and snarling on the platform as the train pulled out.

"That's what we're *not* like," she whispered, her lips like feathers against Paul's glowing ear-rim. "We're not like that."

"No!" he murmured, in frantic agreement.

All the talk of who fancied whom, who'd got off with whom, and words like shagging, she was above all that, he thought, it needed a quite different vocabulary to describe what was between them.

"Slag," she'd said, for instance. "If you ever use that word about anyone I'll never speak to you again. Or scrubber.[1] Or dog." He agreed with her, he was in no position not to. Half the time preoccupied, the *princesse lointaine*,[2] miles away, and then the center of attraction without even trying, you could feel the physical force of that phrase pulling power, she had it; though he should find a better way to put this, of course.

She had come into power certainly, but was, sweetly priggish, concerned not to abuse it. Daily she examined her emotions for signs of corruption.

Only last weekend she had told him about the two German students who had followed her round Boots,[3] who'd kept asking her out, quite politely, and when finally she had said, no, really no, they had left meekly, one of them pausing first to say, "Thank God indeed that he has made such beautiful faces for us to look at."

"Bastard," Simon had said before he could help it. Then, after a gratified smirk, she had looked embarrassed and even apologized.

The three other passengers in their carriage were all disembarking. Nicola and Simon looked at each other and waited, taut, until the doors sighed unevenly and they were quite out of the station, then collected themselves into each other's arms with a mutual groan. Their eyes flickered shut, their lips pressed open each to the other's, she curved her hand round his bare neck while he twisted his fingers in her hair during the unstoppered kisses. His hand moved to cover her breast, she smudged her heated face into his hot neck with a sigh, and his body pressed trembling, heavy and graceful against hers.

This was nothing to do with anybody else, and was certainly light years from those distant shameful sessions in the Bio Lab with the video and the Tupperware lunchbox full of contraceptives. There had been a pungent smell coming from the earthworms slit lengthwise in half and staked out with dressmaking

---

1 Both British slang words meaning promiscuous woman.

2 French: distant princess; used to describe a perfect but unattainable woman.

3 Drugstore chain in Britain.

pins half an hour earlier by the first year. *À propos* of nothing they had been plonked in front of the mooing woman, so hefty, so gross compared with the wildflower girls whom the documentary had devastated in front of the boys. Then the stirruped splay and bloody debouchment, to which the pious voiceover had instructed them to respond with wonder, with awe, had made even the snickering boys go green.

"They weren't being educational there, that was just propaganda," she'd fumed. "That was meant as a deterrent. How dare they." Therefore she had rejected the whole lot, the official sentimental education on offer, part and parcel, and was determined to reinvent the business of love for herself. Her attitude was the determined opposite of pragmatic. It took some nerve. She was the Lydia Languish[4] of her set.

At the next station a flurry of new people piled in. This time the two of them sat opposite each other, looking out of the windows, turning occasionally for another secretive dazzled exchange of eyes. They rested their heads against carriage seats upholstered in shabby prickling green stuff which lit up under the sun like moss. They had never been properly alone together before, they were too young, they were both still living at home. They could not bear the thought of any of their various parents or step-parents or siblings knowing, so they had met in parks or walked by railway tracks, but it was the end of summer now and it was driving them mad.

They wanted something but weren't quite sure what they wanted. It was to do with something vital, though, it was there at the center of their nascent sense of selfhood, and it was this which had caused to spring up the fierce protective hedge of silence and pride around the one area of their lives where they perceived their elders had no business, nor anybody else either.

"It's got to be *right*," Nicola insisted.

"What will make it right?" asked Simon.

"We'll just know," she said, confident, Rousseauesque.[5]

It was difficult to convince her it was right when they could never be alone in a room together. Simon shared a room with two brothers, Nicola shared with her sister, their homes were packed to the gills and the fastidious simply did not thrive.

"I don't feel I belong to myself properly yet," she had told him a while back. "Dad's always on about how much I'm costing. I don't feel I'm my own property,

4 Character in Richard Brinsley Sheridan's play "The Rivals" (1775); Lydia is a romantic who dreams of eloping with her lover.

5 Jean-Jacques Rousseau (1712–78), French philosopher who thought that humankind's understanding of right and wrong is instinctive and innate.

not my body anyway. He does it sometimes to the plate of food in front of me, tots up how much the chips cost, the pie, the beans."

That was why they were on this journey. Simon had found a guide in the library and chosen a place for the sake of its rural name, Meadowsweet, and, though he had not mentioned this, because it was the cheapest; although even so it was not cheap by the standards of what they could afford, in fact quite the opposite.

She leaned over and touched his arm. It was their station. All at once, there they were, deep in the country, standing on a tiny platform in the startlingly clean sweet air. Once the train had gone it was very quiet. They both jumped at a scuttering noise, but it was only a dry leaf bowling along the tarmac. Then they embraced, swaying, until they were light-headed, giddy, drawing away from each other with enormous smiles, almost shyly.

Simon got his map out.

"I think it might be quite a way," he said, starting to look worried. "There don't seem to be any buses either. Or taxis."

"Oh, taxis," said Nicola, as if she were sick to death of taxis. "You don't go to the country for taxis. You *walk* in the country."

They examined the map together, and it could have meant anything since it was the first time either of them had tried to use one.

"Let's see where that leads," he said, pointing to a green lane edged with hawthorn bushes, for no other reason than that he liked the look of it.

The first five miles or so were in daylight, or at least, dusk. They followed the single track road past flat tilting fields and hedgerows with little brown birds jumping in and out of them. A mistiness and moistness of rain in the air pressed coolness to their faces and blurred their hair with droplets. As they walked, they discussed life, death, and later on, when it became relevant, the weather.

Their voices piped away into the evening.

"Truth," said Nicola.

"Not using other people," they agreed solemnly.

"Love," said Simon. "Who you love."

They stopped to hug each other. He squeezed her so hard that her breath came puffing out, her ribs creaked and her feet left the ground.

"I feel incredibly strong," he marveled. "I feel I could lift you to the top of that tree with one hand."

They compared notes on how, in each other's company, they felt full of power, flickering like flames, capable of tremendous effortless speed; and how this fading light was lovely and mysterious, seemingly criss-crossed with satiny threads of excitement. They made each other feel so alive, they agreed; all those other people on the train, they'd been dozy, half conscious in comparison.

She picked a blade of grass, stretched it between her thumbs and pursed her lips to blow. Kid's stuff, he pronounced this, copying her, and soon their piercing whistles split the air for half a mile around.

Time passed. It grew dark. The sky was a black meadow of silvered *petits moutons*; a gibbous moon[6] backlit the scalloped border of each cloudlet. Some five or six fields away they could see a pub, a far-off gaudy box of rhythmic noise.

"We could ask there," said Nicola.

"Too far," said Simon. He peered at the map. "Soon we hit a B-road, then we're laughing."

"Can I have a look?" said Nicola. "Ah. Mmm. I think we're here, look, that last Church was marked. And, I see, that's where we're going. Yes. Quite a bit further."

It started to rain.

By the time they reached the Meadowsweet Guest House it was nearly ten o'clock. They were drenched. Simon pressed the doorbell, and flashed her a desperate grin, like a plague victim. She returned a distant smile.

"We've got those chimes at home," she said pensively. "I didn't think they'd have them in the country."

The door opened a crack and a suspicious bespectacled face peered at them over the guard-chain. Simon stepped forward.

"We booked," he said. "Simon Morrison."

"It's ten o'clock," said the face.

"It was a bit of a way from the station," said Simon.

"You *walked*?" said the face disbelievingly. There was the scrabble and clink of various security measures being unfettered, then they were in, wiping their feet like a couple of children in the narrow hall.

"And you are Mr Morrison?" said their host, staring at Simon, who was looking his most half-baked.

"Thass right," murmured Simon.

Their host's wife came to stare.

"I don't know," she said at last. "Come on, leave your wet shoes on the mat, then I'll bring you both a hot drink in the lounge." She shook her head and bustled off, tutting, to the kitchen.

---

6 *petits moutons* French: little sheep; *gibbous moon* When the moon is either between full and the first quarter (waxing) or full and the last quarter (waning).

In the lounge, the leaping screen of the television was just one brightness among many. The room was small and savagely lit by a 150-watt bulb refracted through a complex chandelier which tinkled madly as Simon's head brushed it.

"Derek and Janet, I'd like you to meet our two strangers in the night," said their host, who had decided to revert to jollity. "Simon and, er."

"Nicola," said Nicola grimly. She and Simon stood awkwardly, sodden, in their socks. She glanced at him. He looked as though he wanted to hide behind the curtains. He looked, she thought, like a big child.

Derek and Janet gaped up at them from the settee.

"Raining, is it?" said Derek at last, gazing at Nicola's dripping elf-locks and rats-tails.

"Just a bit," laughed their host, rubbing his hands. "She looks like a little mermaid, doesn't she." He put his arm matily round her shoulders. "Sit ye down, Nicola, sit ye down."

"Hot chocolate," said his wife coldly from the door.

Up in their room at last, Nicola fell like a stone onto one of the twin beds.

"At least it's warm," volunteered Simon. "Clean. We can push the beds together."

"No we can't," snapped Nicola. "I'd rather be under a haystack. This isn't the country. It's just like back at home."

"It's the country outside, though," said Simon, trying to draw her to him.

She shrugged him off.

"Nylon sheets," she said bitterly. "Horrible butterflies all over the duvet covers. Horrible little ornaments, rabbits in crinolines, mice on penny farthings."[7]

"But that sort of thing," he said, amazed, "it doesn't matter. I hadn't even noticed."

"No, well," she said. "I thought, I thought at least there would be cotton sheets."

"But that doesn't *matter*," he persisted, earnest and gawky beneath another searchlight. "Not at all. That's nothing."

"Oh is it," she sniffed.

"It sounded OK in the guide," he said. "'Cosy and welcoming.' We couldn't afford the ones with stars."

"Don't," she said, turning away from his boy's face. The caparisoned fairy tale personage had reverted to plain lizard.

"You'd like me more if I was five years older. Ten. And my skin puts you off," he said. "Be honest."

---

7 Early bicycles with large front wheels and small back wheels.

"Shut up," she said, and started to cry. He sat down beside her and tried to draw her into his shoulder. She resisted. He swore. She cried harder.

"Please Nicola," he said, pacing the room. "It can't be just the duvet covers."

"It's not!" she said wildly. "It's life!"

"How do you mean?" he said. "Life."

"Look," she snarled, "can't you see it ahead? We're going to end up like them."

"Never," he soothed.

"Boring. Dead!"

She was restlessly beating her foot. A violent cyclonic mood would arrive like this sometimes, inexplicable, devastating, tearing through one or the other of them like a runaway freight train leaving maximum damage in its wake. She shuddered.

"Can't you see?" she said, trying to be calm. "We'd struggle along for a bit but we'd never get beyond this. It's all mapped out."

He held his arms out to her, trying to hug her, but she cackled like a witch and shrank away.

"All those feelings of flame," she continued, "speed, being strong, they're rubbish, you know. They're just like the adverts, rubbish to keep us quiet for a bit."

"Not what I feel for you," he said stubbornly. "That's real."

"No," she said. She was hurtling downwards now, nothing could stop her. "Like my dad says, it's shaft or be shafted." She thumped the bouncy foam pillows. "Like he says, what makes me think *I'm* so special?"

"You are," he said.

"Not long before I'm screaming at some man in front of the children, just like Mum. *If* he's still there."

"I'd never leave you," he said sadly.

"You say that now," she scoffed.

And so they continued under the comfortless white glare, for several hours, until they fell asleep at last athwart the winsome bed linen, fully dressed, clasped in each other's arms, as dawn broke over the fields outside their bedroom window.

Summoned to breakfast by a peremptory knock at the door and a brusque Wakeywakey! from their host, they shuffled downstairs white-faced and red-eyed. The morning sun winked on stainless steel toast racks and tea in tin pots, it put a shine on the varnished sausages, and cruelly exposed the pallor of bacon fat, the bluish jelly on fried eggs.

Nicola sat glowering at the pink-jacketed hunting melée on her table mat, ignoring everything and everybody around her. Even so, Simon was not cowed.

An hour ago he had had an amazing dream, a tremendous panoply of sensualism, intensely gratifying, shudderingly happy, easy. It had unfurled a prospect of utmost melting pleasure, and she was in it all right, right at the heart of it. He felt full of optimism. He wanted to tell her, she looked so gloomy, but decided it could wait.

The room was cramped, and the two other couples at neighboring tables were whispering like embarrassed children, although they were in late middle age. The clatter of cutlery was deafening in this tense demi-silence.

"Soft-boiled I think you said, Peter," sang their host, reentering the room with the air of a man under extreme pressure. "And fried for you, Marjorie. Now have I got that right."

"You're not from these parts originally?" chirruped Marjorie, cocking her head up at him, brave in the hushed room.

"No, no," smiled their host. "Does it show? We've only recently moved from Berkshire.[8] Hence the tablemats. And you?"

"We're from Norfolk,"[9] said Marjorie. "Originally."

"Ah, from Norfolk are you. The land of the lazy wind—it doesn't go round you, it goes through you."

"That's right!" said Marjorie gaily, as though this were a fresh thought to her, a surprise.

"Now, can I tempt you to another sausage, Marjorie?" said their host, courtly in his offer, "There's one going begging here."

"No really, I couldn't," protested Marjorie. "I've had sufficient."

"Oh come now," said their host roguishly. "Haven't you got a little crack? A leetle leetle crack? I think you have!"

Simon was grabbed by a terrible rude desire to laugh. He frowned and coughed, but low down inside him it was taking over. He glanced at Nicola's stony face and away again quickly.

"Just one weeny sausage!" wheedled their host. "Go on, Marjorie. I'm going to be very upset if you can't fit it in, very disappointed."

With an imploring pout he waved his offering temptingly beneath her nose.

"Just for me!" he leered.

Simon's eyes started to stream. His face disintegrated and rapidly he took cover behind his napkin. He began to whimper softly, trying to disguise it with coughing. Now Nicola too unwillingly succumbed. Shoulders heaving, she looked at him, alarmed, her breath starting to come in uneven shudders. Hastily, they stumbled up from their table, appalled, jostling each other like cattle in

8 County in southern England.

9 County in eastern England.

their hurry to get through the doorway, then clattered up the stairs, almost out of control.

The door of their room closed safe behind them, they fell onto their beds, sobbed into the pillows, they hooted until their ribs hurt and they had to hold their sides. Whenever either of them showed signs of calming down, the other caught their eye and they were off again.

"Oh don't," they groaned. "No more."

The gloomy shreds of the hateful night they had passed in that room flapped off into the hinterland on leathery broken wings. They paid and left as soon as they were able.

Outside it was a morning of hot sun with a cool surfy breeze, the air like clear liquid with bubbles rising, and they gulped great effervescent draughts as though newly escaped from prison.

Everything around them looked beautiful or interesting, freshly oxygenated as they were to the point of euphoria. Weeds, long and lush but on their last legs, fringed the lane, and they saw that the greenish-white flowers of the stinging nettles were giving way to tassels of seeds. Blackberries in the hedge were still pale pink or purplish, underjuiced, too sour to eat yet. They spat out sample mouthfuls.

Simon dethorned a branch of early rosehips, light orange, large and impeccably lacquered, broke off the top three inches, heavily fruited, and stuck it behind his ear. Considering what a disaster last night had been, he felt surprisingly jubilant, almost as though they had triumphed over circumstance after all. That was because he felt sure that nothing important was stopping them from doing so. In fact, he realized, he was quite certain that it would be all right now. His dream warmed him, a smug heap of gold in some inward chamber of his mind. He smiled fatly, scooped Nicola up and swung her round in the air, ululating.[10]

Having missed their breakfast earlier, they bought bread and cheese at the next village, silent while the elderly woman who was serving them chatted on to her crony about somebody else's unacceptable behavior, cuddling the cordless phone between her chin and shoulder as she sliced the half-pound of cheddar.

Most of the cottages they passed had gardens visible from the road, all given over to vegetables. They paused to stare at a row of tall green teepees stuck with scarlet flowers.

"They're for cucumbers, aren't they?" said Simon uncertainly.

"I don't know," said Nicola. "But those over there are cabbages. Definitely. And that's rhubarb! I could grow rhubarb if I lived in the country."

---

10 Loud, wordless shouting or wailing to express a particularly strong emotion.

"Rhubarb?" said Simon, startled.

"Not *just* rhubarb," she said, embarrassed. "But, think, if you were vegetarian round here you'd need hardly any money."

A few steps on by the side of the road was a carrier bag full of apples, in front of it a handwritten sign saying HELP YOURSELF.

"Look at that!" said Simon, amazed. He walked all round the bag as though some trick must be involved.

"You see?" said Nicola, choosing a couple of unbruised apples. "You wouldn't need much money living out here. You could keep hens too. Bees, even."

"I don't know about bees," frowned Simon. "You have to know about these things."

As they walked on, they marveled at how nobody in the country seemed much under sixty, and doubted they would ever be able to afford somewhere to live. They touched on the captiousness of their parents, the advantages of tents and caravans, and wondered whether or not common land really was common these days. They talked about who owned what, and how, and why, and contemplated the traveler's life, the blessed freedom, the openness to weather, even bad weather, and the fate of travelers who fell ill or grew old. Nicola put forward the view that it would have been preferable to live in the old days, at least you could put up a fight then, they'd got everybody taped now; Simon disagreed, pointing out that she would have been blackleading the grates up at the big house until carried off by TB or the umpteenth baby, they were better off now, more able to live free even if it seemed otherwise sometimes, and he had faith, things would change.

On they walked, past fields just harvested, the stubble in burnished zigzags against the earth, bales of hay stacked like great slabs of golden cake.

"This is what I wanted," said Nicola, pausing at a gate and flinging out her arms towards the fields, the cool bright air, golds and ochers turning miles away to bluish grays and greens, and on, rising up to the sky, a fierce tender blue, and cohorts of cumulus clouds, banked and ranked as far as the eye could see, luminous, their top curves taking the sun.

They climbed over the gate and threw down their jackets under a tree in the corner of this field with a view. Here they spread their picnic and hungrily made up for their earlier frustrated breakfast.

"Last night," she said as they finished eating, and she flushed a sudden miserable red. "I didn't. I mean, I wasn't. I felt so, you know. I thought I could *kill* myself."

"Don't," he said. "It's gone. But this morning ... That business with the ... 'There's one going begging!'"

He started to gasp again, looking at her in momentary surprise.

"'Go on, Marjorie,'" she remembered, joining him. "Oh her face!"

The irresistible joke had come to life again, helium-filled. They fell on their backs and abandoned themselves to it, it was like some drug, the laughing, leaving a wake of foamy euphoria.

When they calmed down at last they were lying side by side, quite private, looking at the leafy canopy above them from whose shelter issued the thoughtful soothings of wood-pigeons. They turned and lay in a sideways hug, staring into each other's eyes, smiling occasionally.

"Last night," murmured Simon after a while. "Last night wasn't so bad after all."

He nuzzled up under her chin and blew softly into her hair, into her neck, to foment his nerve. Then, although no one else was anywhere in sight, let alone hearing distance, he began to whisper his dream into her ear.

—1995

SHERMAN ALEXIE

Sherman Alexie is a Native American writer born in 1966. In 1999 he was named one of *The New Yorker*'s "20 under 40," a list of young writers who "are or will be key to their generation." He grew up on the Spokane Indian reservation in Wellpinit, Washington. At birth, Alexie suffered from hydrocephalus, and he underwent successful surgery at six months of age. This condition left him with a disfigured skull and led to bullying at school. His father, an alcoholic, often left the family for many weeks at a time, and his mother raised her six children, supporting them by the making and selling of quilts.

Alexie survived these early challenges, and his social isolation encouraged an avid interest in reading. He left the reservation and attended high school in Reardon, a town 30 miles away. There he excelled in academics and athletics, particularly basketball, a sport he continues to follow attentively. He won a scholarship to Gonzaga University and began to study medicine, but his studies were interrupted by his own struggles with alcoholism. In 1987 he gave up alcohol and returned to school, this time to Washington State University. He took a poetry class with Alex Kuo, and the experience was transformative. He began to write, and after graduation published two volumes of poems, *I Would Steal Horses* (1992) and *The Business of Fancydancing* (1992). His first volume of short stories, *The Lone Ranger and Tonto Fistfight in Heaven*, was published in 1993 and won the PEN/Hemingway Award for Best First Book of Fiction.

In 1995, Alexie published his first novel, *Reservation Blues*. This was followed by *Indian Killer* in 1996. Both novels are about contemporary Native American experience, exploring themes of despair, helplessness, anger, and redemption. The at-times harsh realism of his stories is tempered by a rebellious, comic voice, and by an ironic humor that contrasts the actuality of Native life with common stereotypes. He says that he avoids writing about Native spirituality, focusing instead on everyday experience: "There are Indian writers who write about things they aren't supposed to. They know. They'll pay for it … I wouldn't go near that kind of writing. I'd be afraid of the repercussions. I write about a drunk in a bar, or a guy who plays basketball."

Joyce Carol Oates writes that Alexie is "the bad boy among [Native writers], mocking, self-mocking, unpredictable, unassimilable." Alexie continues to write poetry and stories; in recent years he has also written screenplays and performed stand-up comedy.

"Do You Know Where I Am" is a coming-of-age story that was published in the volume *Ten Little Indians* (2003). It is an archetypal tale about the loss of innocence, but, as with all of Alexie's work, he refuses to mythologize, and the story remains realistic and concrete.

Do You Know Where I Am?

SHERMAN ALEXIE

SHARON AND I were college sweethearts at St. Jerome the Second University in Seattle, or, as it is affectionately known, St. Junior's. We met at the first mixer dance of our freshman year and soon discovered we were the only confirmed Native American Roman Catholics within a three-mile radius of campus, so we slept together that inaugural night, in open defiance of Pope Whomever, and kept sleeping together for the next three years. It was primary love: red girl and red boy on white sheets.

Sharon was Apache, and I was Spokane, but we practiced our tribal religions like we practiced Catholicism: We loved all of the ceremonies but thought they were pitiful cries to a disinterested god.

My white mother, Mary, bless her soul, raised me all by herself in Seattle because my Indian daddy, Marvin, died of stomach cancer when I was a baby. I never knew him, but I spent half of every summer on the Spokane Reservation with his mother and father, my grandparents. My mother wanted me to keep in touch with my tribal heritage, but mostly, I read spy novels to my grandfather and shopped garage sales and secondhand stores with my grandmother. I suppose, for many Indians, garage sales and trashy novels are highly traditional and sacred. We all make up our ceremonies as we go along, right? I thought the reservation was ordinary and magical, like a sedate version of Disneyland. All told, I loved to visit but loved my home much more. In Seattle, my mother was a corporate lawyer for old-money companies and sent me to Lakeside Upper School, where I was a schoolmate of Bill Gates and Paul Allen,[1] who have become the new-money kings of the world.

1 Co-founders of Microsoft.

Sharon went to St. Therese's School for Girls. Her parents, Wilson and Pauline, were both architects; they helped build three of the tallest skyscrapers in downtown Seattle. If Zeus[2] ate a few million pounds of glass, steel, and concrete, his offal would look something like those buildings. However fecal, those monstrosities won awards and made Wilson and Pauline very popular and wealthy. They lived in a self-designed home on Lake Washington that was lovely and tasteful in all ways except for its ridiculously turquoise exterior. I don't know whether they painted the house turquoise to honor the sacred stone of the Southwest or if they were being ironic: *Ha! We're Apache Indians from the desert, and this is our big blue house on the water! Deal with it!*

Sharon and I were Native American royalty, the aboriginal prince and princess of western Washington. Sure, we'd been thoroughly defeated by white culture, but dang it, we were conquered and assimilated National Merit Scholars in St. Junior's English honors department.

Sharon and I were in love and happy and young and skinny and beautiful and hyperliterate. We recited Shakespeare monologues as foreplay: *To be or not to be, take off your panties, oh, Horatio, I knew him well, a fellow of infinite jest, I'm going to wear your panties now.* All over campus, we were known as Sharon-and-David-the-Bohemian-Indians. We were inseparable. We ate our meals together and fed each other. Risking expulsion for moral violations, we sneaked into each other's dorm rooms at night and made love while our respective roommates covered their heads with pillows. Sharon and I always tried to take the same classes and mourned the other's absence whenever we couldn't. We read the same books and discussed them while we were naked and intertwined. Oh Lord, we were twins conjoined at the brain, heart, and crotch.

I proposed to Sharon on the first day of our senior year, and she accepted, and we planned to secretly elope on the day after our graduation.

In June, the day before graduation, Sharon and I were taking one last walk along the path beside the anonymous creek that ran through the middle of campus. We were saying good-bye to a good place. Overgrown with fern and blackberry thickets, the creek had been left wild and wet.

"'Whose woods these are I think I know,'" I said.

"Robert Frost wrote the poem," said Sharon. We were playing Name the Poet, a game of our own invention.

"'Know' and 'poem,'" I said. "A clumsy rhyme, don't you think?"

"You stink," she said and laughed too loudly. Her joy was always rowdy, rude, and pervasive. I laughed with her and pulled her close to me and pressed my

2 Greek mythology: the god of thunder and ruler of gods.

face into her hair and breathed in her scent. After the first time we'd made love, she'd said, *Now I know what you smell like, and no matter what else happens to us, I'm always going to know what you smell like.*

"Hey," I said as we walked the creek. "How about we climb into the bushes and I get you a little wild and wet?"

We kissed and kissed until she pulled away.

"Do you hear that?" she said.

"What?"

"I think it's a cat. Can you hear it meowing?"

I listened and heard nothing.

"You're imagining things," I said.

"No, it's a cat. I can hear it. It sounds pitiful."

"There must be a hundred cats around here. City cats. They're tough."

"No, it sounds hurt. Listen."

I listened and finally heard the faint feline cry.

"It's down there in the creek somewhere," she said.

We peered over the edge and could barely see the water through the thick and thorny overgrowth.

"I'm sure it's hunting rats or something," I said. "It's okay."

"No, listen to it. It's crying. I think it's stuck."

"What do you want me to do? It's just a dumb-ass cat."

"Can you go find it?"

I looked again at the jungle between that cat and me.

"I'd need a machete to get through there," I said.

"Please," said Sharon.

"I'm going to get all cut up."

"'All in green went my love riding,'" she whispered in that special way, "'on a great horse of gold into the silver dawn.'"

"Cummings wrote the poem, and I'm in love and gone," I said and made my slow way down the creek side. I didn't want to save the cat; I wanted to preserve Sharon's high opinion of me. If she hadn't been there to push me down the slope, I never would have gone after that cat. As it was, I cursed the world as I tripped over ferns and pushed blackberry branches out of the way. I was cut and scraped and threatened by spiders and wasps, all for a dumb cat.

"It's like *Wild Kingdom* down here," I said.

"Do you see him?" she said, more worried about the cat. I could hear the love in her voice. I was jealous of that damn cat!

I stopped and listened. I heard the cry from somewhere close.

"He's right around here," I said.

"Find him," she said, her voice choking with fierce tears.

I leaned over, pushed aside one last fern, and saw him, a black cat trapped in blackberry branches. He was starved, too skinny to be alive, I thought, but his eyes were bright with fear and pain.

"Man," I said. "I think he's been caught in here for a long time."

"Save him, save him."

I reached in, expecting the cat to bite or claw me, but he remained gratefully passive as I tore away the branches and freed him. I lifted and carried him back up the bank. He was dirty and smelly, and I wanted all of this to be over.

"Oh my God," said Sharon as she took him from me. "Oh, he's so sad, so sad." She hugged him, and he accepted it without protest.

"What are we going to do with him?" I asked.

"I don't know."

"We can't keep him," I said. "Let's let him go here. He's free now. He'll be okay."

"What if he gets stuck again?"

"Then it'll be natural selection. Come on, he doesn't have a tag or anything. He's just a stray cat."

"No, he's tame, he's got a home somewhere." She stared the cat in the eyes as if he could tell us his phone number and address.

"Oh, wait, wait," she said. "I remember, in the newspaper, last week or something, there was a lost-cat ad. It said he was black with white heart-shaped fur on his belly."

Sharon had a supernatural memory; she could meet a few dozen new people at a party and rattle off their names two days later. During an English-department party our sophomore year, she recited by memory seventy-three Shakespeare sonnets in a row. It was the most voluminous display of erudition any of us had ever witnessed. Tenured English professors wept. But I was the one who enjoyed the honor and privilege of taking her home that night and making her grunt in repetitive monosyllables.

Beside the creek, Sharon gently turned the cat over, and we both saw the white heart. Without another word, Sharon ran back to her dorm room, and I followed her. She searched for the newspaper in her desk but couldn't find it, and none of her floormates had a copy of the old paper, either, so she ran into the basement and climbed into the Dumpster. I held the cat while she burrowed into the fetid pile of garbage.

"Come on," I said. "You're never going to find it. Maybe you imagined the whole thing. Let's take him to the shelter. They can take care of him."

She ignored me and kept searching. I felt like throwing the cat into the wall.

"This is it," she said and pulled a greasy newspaper out of the mess. She flipped to the classifieds, found the lost-cat ad, and shouted out the phone number. She jumped out of the Dumpster, grabbed the cat, ran back to her room, and quickly dialed.

"Hello," said Sharon over the telephone. "We have your cat. Yes, yes, yes. We found him by the creek. At St. Junior's. We'll bring him right over. What's your address? Oh God, that's really close."

Sharon ran out of the dorm; I ran after her.

"Slow down," I called after her, but she ignored me. Maybe Sharon wasn't a good Apache or Catholic, but she was religious when she found the proper mission.

We sprinted through a residential neighborhood, which may or may not have been a good idea for two brown kids, no matter how high our grade-point averages. But it felt good to run fast, and I dreamed about being a superhero. Fifteen minutes later and out of breath, Sharon knocked on the front door of a small house. An old couple opened the door.

"Lester," shouted the old man and took the cat from Sharon. The old woman hugged the man and the cat. All three cried to one another.

"How'd you find him?" asked the old man, weeping hard now, barely able to talk, but unashamed of his tears. "He's been gone for a month."

"I heard him crying," I said (I lied) and stepped into the doorway. Sharon stood behind me and peered over my shoulder.

"Oh, thank you, bless you," said the old woman.

"I pulled him out of some blackberry thorns," I said. "And then I remembered your ad in the newspaper, and I found the paper in the garbage, and I called you, and here I am."

The old man and woman hugged me, holding the cat between us, all of us celebrating the reunion, while Sharon stood silently by. I think I lied because I wanted to be briefly adored by strangers, to be remembered as a handsome and kind man, a better man, more complete, even saintly. But it was Orwell who wrote that "saints should be always judged guilty until they are proved innocent."[3]

All during this time, Sharon never spoke. I can only guess at her emotions, but I imagine she was shocked and hurt by my disloyalty. Standing in the presence of such obvious commitment between two people and their damn cat, she must have lost faith in me and, more importantly, in herself.

"How can we ever repay you?" asked the old woman.

"Nothing," I said. "We need nothing."

"Here, here," said the old man as he opened his wallet and offered me a twenty.

3 The opening words of George Orwell's essay "Reflections on Gandhi" (1949).

"No, no," I said. "I don't need that. I just wanted to be good, you know?"

He forced the money into my hand; I accepted it.

"You're a good man," said the old woman.

I shook my head, took Sharon's hand, and walked away, leaving those grateful strangers to their beloved pet.

"Why did you do that?" Sharon asked as we walked.

"I needed to," I said. That was the best answer I could give her. It wasn't enough.

"You lied to me, you lied to them, and you took their money," she said. "How could you do that?"

"I don't know," I said.

Sharon broke away from me and ran.

I didn't see her that night as I got ready for graduation, and I didn't see her the next morning.

"Where's Sharon?" asked my mother as she adjusted my cap and gown.

"She's with her parents," I said, which was a true statement, I suppose, but hardly close to the truth.

I went through the ceremony alone; Sharon went through the ceremony alone; we sat ten chairs apart.

The day after graduation, Sharon was still missing. I didn't know where she was. When my mother asked me about her absence, I said she was on a spiritual retreat.

"One month of silence," I said, lying to my mother, to another woman who loved me. "After a big event, like a graduation or birth, the Apaches leave for a month. It's an Apache thing."

"I wish I could do that," she said. "I think everybody should do that. Make it a law. Once a year, everybody has to be silent for a month. We'd all rotate, you know? You have to be quiet during your birth month."

"It's a good idea, Mom, I'm sure it would go over well."

"Sarcasm is a sin, honey."

After another day of unceremonial silence, I assumed Sharon had left me forever, and I finally confessed my fears to my mother.

"Mom," I said. "I love Sharon and I destroyed her."

Was I overreacting to Sharon's overreaction? I'd told such a small lie, had taken credit and reward for such a small act of heroism. But then I wondered if Sharon had always had her doubts about my character, and perhaps had always considered me an undependable braggart. What if she'd been gathering evidence against me all along, and I'd finally committed the last unpardonable crime?

"You have to go find her," my mother said.

"I can't," I said, and it was true and cowardly.

My mother turned away from me and cried while she fixed dinner. Later that night, while she washed dishes and I dried, my mother told me how much she still missed my father.

"He's been gone twenty-two years," she said. "But I can still feel him right here in the room with us. I can still smell him, his hair, his skin."

My mother didn't call my father by name because she wanted the dead to stay dead; I wanted to learn magic and open a twenty-four-hour supermarket that sold resurrection and redemption.

The next morning, Sharon came to see me. I was so grateful for her presence that I leaned against the wall to keep from falling down. My mother hugged Sharon until they both cried. Then Sharon asked my mother to give us some privacy. After my mother left, Sharon took my face in her hands.

"You're a liar," Sharon said. "I'm going to marry a liar."

I didn't want to ask her why she came back. We were so fragile, I worried that one wrong word could completely break us.

For the next twenty-nine years, we lived as wife and husband, as the mother and father of four kids (Sarah, Rachael, Francis, and Joshua) who suddenly grew into adults and became wives and husbands and mothers and fathers. During our long marriage, Sharon and I buried her mother and father and my mother, all of our grandparents, and many of our aunts, uncles, and cousins. I covered high school sports and reviewed movies for the local alternative weekly; an odd pair of beats, I suppose, but I enjoyed the appearance of being odd while living a sedate life. Sharon ran her own coffee shop and wrote lyric odes she never published. We paid our taxes, owned a modest home, and made love an average of three times a week. We didn't have nearly as much money as our parents, and that could be viewed as our failure, but we felt successful. We weren't triumphant, by any means, but we lived a good and simple life, and I often wondered if I deserved it.

All during those years, at every house party, group dinner, family gathering, and company picnic, Sharon told the story of the lost cat.

"My husband, the liar," she always called me. At first, she told the story to hurt me, then she told it out of habit, and then she told it because she'd turned it into a wildly funny and exaggerated adventure: *And then he fell in the creek!* She loved to make people laugh, and so they laughed at my small sins. I wanted the laughter to absolve me, but I'm not sure if that was its purpose. I never asked to be forgiven, and Sharon never offered her forgiveness. We never talked about the lost cat in private; it was our most public secret.

But there were other secrets, of course. Sharon kept most of hers, and I kept most of mine. Those kept secrets were small and ordinary, having to do with broken diets and hidden pornography, and they were of little consequence, but one evening, a decade into our marriage, Sharon confessed to an extramarital affair.

"I don't love him," she said. "It's over now. I only slept with him three times. To be fair, you can ask me three questions about it, and I'll answer them as honestly as possible, and then I don't ever want to talk about it again."

I was hurt by the frankness of her words, by her deal-making, but she cried, and her voice trembled as she spoke, and she'd never been one to feign emotion or cry for dramatic purposes, so I was lost in her contradictions.

"How could you do that to me?" I asked.

"Is that a real question?" she asked. "Or is it rhetorical?"

I panicked. I didn't want to waste my three questions. I wanted to know details, the facts and figures, and not emotional states. But which particular details did I want to know? And which questions would elicit the most information? I needed to be a brutally efficient interrogator. I couldn't believe I was participating in this horrible transaction.

"Listen," I said, "this is ridiculous. Let's talk this out like normal people."

"That's the problem," she said. "Everything is so normal. You didn't used to be normal. I didn't marry normal."

She was a thirty-two-year-old woman with four young kids, and she owned and managed a small business. So she was one of those notorious superwomen. I knew she was always exhausted, but what could I do to help her? I could never tell her she worked too hard, and I certainly couldn't tell her she should spend more time with the kids. I couldn't ask her to choose between her work life and her home life. As a man, I would never be asked to make a similar choice. I spent most Friday and Saturday nights watching other people's children play football, basketball, and volleyball. What kind of father was I? I could best be described as cordially absent on weekends and lovingly distracted on weekdays. What kind of husband was I? Apparently, I was the kind of husband whose wife needed to sleep with at least one other man and an untold number of others who might be waiting in line. There are millions of those clueless husbands, aren't there? Wasn't I yet another cuckolded husband, slightly distinguished by knowing how to self-define with an Old English word? I was eight hundred years old. I was historic, predictable, and planned. I was normal.

"Who is he?" I asked.

"His name is Michael Joyce," she said. "He's a regular at the shop. I've asked him to never come back. He agreed. He's a good man."

I was surprised to discover I wanted to hit my wife. I wanted to punch her in the stomach and make her fall to the floor. I wanted to see her gasping with physical pain. I would never hurt her that way—I hadn't struck another human being since the third grade—but the violent impulse was there, and I was frightened and exhilarated by it. My wife had no idea how dangerous I could be. I felt better knowing I could hurt her far more than she'd hurt me. And then I was revolted. How could I love a person and want to hurt her so much? How could I look at my wife, the mother of my children, and feel only the need for revenge? I paced around the room, ran my fingers roughly through my hair, because I needed to move. I needed to find another space in which to exist. I studied the details of the living room: the antique lamps purchased for full price and the end tables rescued from garage sales and refurbished; the brown leather couch and black leather recliner; the Monet and Kahlo[4] prints on the walls; the bookshelves stuffed with novels and sports histories; and the coffee tables adorned with art books. All of it was tasteful and beautiful and appropriate and hard-earned and useless.

Sharon wore a red blouse and blue jeans. Her feet were bare and needed a pedicure. Once a month, her feet were scrubbed clean and polished by a Vietnamese woman whose name and exact place of business I would never know. Sharon wore a fake pearl necklace her mother had given her for some birthday, and real pearl earrings I'd given her on our fifth anniversary. The fake pearls were prettier than the real ones. I don't know why I noticed her physical details, but it seemed important to take note of all I could. I felt the insistent need to be exact. Since it was laundry day, I knew she'd be wearing her oldest brassiere, and would never initiate lovemaking while wearing it, but would gladly receive my advances after first dashing into the bathroom to quickly remove the tattered bra. How many times had she emerged topless from the bathroom and run laughing toward me? Who keeps accurate count of such wonderful moments? Wouldn't a better husband know that number by heart?

"I'm a bad husband," I said. Why was I apologizing?

She turned away and sat on the couch as far away from me as possible. I kept pacing around the room.

"He's white," she said, volunteering the information, and I was strangely relieved. My emotions were changing and shifting randomly. If I'd been an actor in a musical, I would have broken into song for no apparent reason. I would have tap-danced to the primal 4/4 beat of betrayal. I would have leaped over the couch where she was sitting and rewon her heart with my grace and strength. What a dream life I have, and how instantly I can immerse myself in it! Can you believe I was happy to hear she'd slept with only a white man? I would have been

4 Claude Monet (1840–1926), a French Impressionist painter, and Frida Kahlo (1907–54), a Mexican painter.

tortured to hear she'd slept with another Indian man. Considering her beauty, ambition, and intelligence, I could conceive of an amazing white man or black man who might love her and be loved in return, but I doubted another Indian man of my particular talents existed out there in the world. Call it a potent mix of arrogance and self-hatred, but I was certain I was the one Indian man who was good enough for my Indian wife.

I believed I was being rational, but who can be rational in such a painful situation? Wouldn't my wife and I hold entirely different standards for what made a man good or great? What if she'd slept with a plumber or a construction worker? What if she'd slept with a supermarket graveyard-shift worker or a high school dropout? I couldn't stand the thought of my wife sleeping with a blue-collar man who'd read fewer books than I had. I wanted to believe my wife slept with another man because she needed to be loved in a new way, a more educated and intellectual way, and not because she wanted to hurt me. I didn't understand what I was feeling, and I didn't know what to do, and I couldn't ask her to help me, because that might qualify as my second question and would leave me with only one.

"Don't look at me that way," she said.

"What way?" I asked.

"Like this is inconceivable. Like I'm the Loch Ness Monster."

"I don't know what I'm thinking, feeling, or seeing."

"That's the problem. You've been blind for years."

I sat on the couch beside her. I tried to take her hand, but she pulled it away.

"No," she said. "You don't get to comfort me. And I don't get to comfort you. You have two questions. Ask them."

I was struck with the terrible fear that she'd had sex with Michael Joyce in our house, in our bed.

"Where did it happen?" I asked.

"The first time was in a hotel," she said. "The Westin downtown. A suite. Early. Eight in the morning. I got the kids off to school, opened up the shop. Jody ran the register and Rick made the coffee and Christy waited tables. I told them I had a dentist appointment."

"You told me you had a dentist appointment," I said.

"Yes," she said. "I lied to you directly. I never wanted to do that. I knew I was lying to you indirectly, but I hated to look you in the eyes and lie to you. I hated it."

"The Westin is a decent hotel," I said. Jesus, I sounded like a travel agent.

"The second time was in his car. We parked down on Lake Washington. You were down in Tacoma, covering the football championships."

"I called home that night," I said. "Sara was watching the kids. She said you had an emergency at the shop. The espresso maker was overheating."

"She didn't know I was lying. She thought I was at the shop."

Once or twice a month, I ran the path alongside Lake Washington. I knew I would never run it again. How can I survive this? I thought. How many more of my routines will I have to change? Again I tried to take my wife's hand. This time she let me. We interlaced our fingers. A small moment of intimacy, but enough to keep me from running out of the room and house and fleeing down the street.

"The third time was in his apartment," she said. "In his bed. Lunchtime. I fell asleep with him. I hated that. That's why I ended it. Falling asleep with him felt like the worst thing I could do. I never felt evil until I fell asleep with him."

She leaned over and kissed my forehead. I felt her heat. I didn't want to feel her heat. I didn't want to smell her scent. I didn't want to taste her. And it felt like time squared and cubed and then exploded exponentially. Days and months and years passed before I would find enough stupid courage to ask my third question.

"What did you do with him?"

"What do you mean?" she asked.

"I mean, into which parts of you did he put it?"

She flinched so painfully that I might as well have punched her in her chest. I was briefly happy about that.

"Do you really want to know that?" she asked.

"Yes."

She stood and walked away from me. I assume she was afraid I might really punch her.

"We," she said. "He—I mean, we—did everything."

"Say it exactly."

"I don't want to."

"You have to. It's part of the deal."

"I can't. It hurts too much."

"You don't get to feel as much pain as me. Now say it. Tell me exactly."

She closed her eyes and moaned like some tortured animal, like she was the first animal feeling the first pain. I heard that sound again when she buried her mother and, thirteen months later, her father.

"Tell me," I said. "Exactly."

She couldn't speak. Instead, she pointed at her mouth, her vagina, and her ass. She looked like a pornographic mime. I started laughing. I lay down on the couch and laughed. I couldn't stop laughing. She stared at me like I was crazy. Then she started laughing with me. Softly at first, but soon she had to sit down laughing on the floor so she wouldn't fall down laughing on the floor. She crawled across the floor and climbed onto the couch with me. We held each other and laughed. Then, as suddenly as it started, it stopped. We held each other in the silence.

"If you still love me," she said, "please, please, build me a time machine."

She sounded like a little girl talking to her father. I didn't know what to say. But we lay there together for hours until the kids came home from school and surprised us.

"Mommy and Daddy were doing it!" the four of them chanted and danced around the living room. "Mommy and Daddy were doing it!"

Sharon and I danced with our children. We danced the family dance, three quick spins, two hops, and a scream at the ceiling, and then Sharon and I made dinner, and we ate with our kids and gossiped about their school days and played *Chutes and Ladders* and watched *The Lion King* and made them brush their teeth and wash their faces and forced them into their pajamas and pushed them down the hallways into their beds and read them *Curious George* and *Go, Dog, Go!* and turned off the lights and told them good night and gave them our love, and we sat in the kitchen across from each other and drank coffee and added up our wins and our losses and decided to stay married.

It was Emily Dickinson[5] who wrote, "After great pain, a formal feeling comes." So Sharon and I formally rebuilt our marriage. And it was blue-collar work, exhausting and painful. We didn't argue more often than before, but we did live with longer and greater silences. There were times when both of us wanted to quit, but we always found the strength to get up in the morning and go back to the job. And then, one winter night two years after her confession, after eating a lovely dinner at a waterfront restaurant and slow-dancing in the parking lot while a small group of tourists cheered for us, she read a book in bed while I stood at our bedroom window and stared out into the dark. We were comfortable in the silence. A day or week or month or year before, I would have felt the need to end such a wonderful evening by making love to her, by proving I could share our bed and her body with ghosts. But I felt no such need that night, and I realized we'd completed the rebuilding project, we'd constructed a brand-new marriage, a new home, that sat next to the old marriage and its dusty and shuttered house. Standing at the window, I could almost see our old house out there in the dark, and I missed it. I often thought of it as we continued with our lives.

Suddenly, Sharon and I were forty. For my birthday that year, she and the kids all pitched in together and gave me a T-shirt that read LOST CAT on the front and DO YOU KNOW WHERE I AM? on the back.

I laughed and wore that shirt as pajamas. For two years, Sharon fell asleep next to me wearing that shirt.

---

5 Emily Dickinson (1830–86), an American poet.

"Oh, Lord," I said to Sharon on the day I finally tossed the ragged T-shirt into the trash. "With every new day comes a new monument to our love and pain."

"Who wrote that?" she asked.

"I did."

"It's free verse," she said. "I hate free verse."

We laughed and kissed and made love and read books in bed. We read through years of books, decades of books. There were never enough books for us. Read, partially read, and unread, our books filled the house, stacked on shelves and counters, piled into corners and closets. Our marriage became an eccentric and disorganized library. Whitman in the pantry! The Brontë sisters in the television room! Hardy on the front porch! Dickinson in the laundry room! We kept a battered copy of *Native Son* in the downstairs bathroom so our guests would have something valuable to read![6]

How do you measure a marriage? Three of our children still lived in Seattle and taught high school English, history, and Spanish respectively, while the fourth managed a homeless shelter in Portland, Oregon. Maybe Sharon and I had never loved each other well enough, but our kids were smart and talented and sober. They made less money than we did, as we made less than our parents did. We were going the wrong way on the social-class map! How glorious!

Every Sunday night, we all gathered for dinner (Joshua drove up from Portland with his partner, Aaron, and their son) and told one another the best stories of our weeks. We needed those small ceremonies. Our contentment was always running only slightly ahead of our dissatisfaction.

Was it enough? I don't know. But we knew enough not to ask ourselves too often. We knew to ask ourselves such questions during daylight hours. We fought hard for our happiness, and sometimes we won. Over the years, we won often enough to develop a strong taste for winning.

And then suddenly and mortally, Sharon and I were sixty-six years old.

On her birthday that year, surrounded by her husband, daughters, sons, and six grandkids, Sharon blew out the candles on her cake, closed her eyes, and made some secret wish.

One year later, after chemotherapy, radiation, organic food, acupuncture, and tribal shaman, Sharon lay on her deathbed in Sacred Hope Hospital. Our children had left their children to gather around Sharon, and it was good-bye Rachael! Good-bye Sarah! Good-bye Francis! Good-bye Joshua! She asked our children to give us some privacy. They cried and hugged her and left us alone.

---

6 Walt Whitman (1818–92), an American poet; Charlotte, Emily, and Anne Brontë, nineteenth-century English novelists and poets; Thomas Hardy (1840–1928), an English novelist and poet; *Native Son*, a 1940 novel by African American novelist Richard Wright.

"I'm going to die soon," Sharon said.

"I know," I said.

"I'm okay with it."

"I'm not. Because I love you so much," I said, "I would fistfight Time to win back your youth."

"You're a liar," she said and smiled, too tired to laugh.

"I lied to you once," I said. "But I haven't lied to you since."

"Is that the truth?"

"Yes," I said.

—2003

ZZ PACKER

In 2010, American writer ZZ Packer was named one of *The New Yorker*'s top "20 under 40" authors on the strength of her only published book, the short story collection *Drinking Coffee Elsewhere* (2003). Her award-winning stories have been praised for capturing a diverse range of voices—from black teenage girls in the American South to unemployed immigrants in Tokyo—and for their penetrative insight and originality.

Zuwena Packer was born in Chicago in 1973 to a mother employed by the Social Security Administration and a father who owned a bar; five years later, they moved to Atlanta. At 12, Packer moved with her mother and sister to Louisville, Kentucky, following her parents' divorce. Growing up, she attended her mother's strict evangelical church, and in high school she was enrolled in a program for gifted minority teens that encouraged her to apply to Ivy League universities. When she began as a scholarship student at Yale, she was planning on a career in engineering, not believing "that writing was something that you could actually do."

After she graduated from Yale with a BA, having resolved to be a writer, Packer earned a series of prestigious graduate degrees, grants, and fellowships in what she describes as an attempt "to patch together funding from year to year." She achieved an MA from Johns Hopkins and an MFA from the Iowa Writers' Workshop. While continuing to write, she briefly supplemented her income with work as a high school teacher, then as a copywriter for commercial websites. In the early 2000s her stories began to appear in magazines such as *Harper's* and *The New Yorker*, and these successes led to the publication of *Drinking Coffee Elsewhere*.

Packer is often praised for her "fresh view of the African American experience." While she acknowledges the importance of racial dynamics in many of her stories—"you don't have the luxury of being able to decide whether or not to pay attention to race, because if you don't, someone else will"—she also refuses to let race eclipse the individuality or humanity of her characters. "In the context of just being human and falling in love and all of the things that human beings do, I don't necessarily think [race] should erupt," she says. "I am really concentrating on the characters and what are their circumstances and motivations and what do they want." Referring to Packer's characteristic blend of satirical social observation and nuanced understanding of individual character, *O* magazine has compared her to Jane Austen.

Packer lives in Pacifica, California, with her husband and two children. She has spent the past several years working on a historical novel about the "Buffalo Soldiers," African American military regiments that played a major role in the settlement of the American West (and the suppression of Native American rebellion) immediately after the Civil War. *Granta* magazine printed an excerpt from this work in progress in 2007, and included Packer on its list of "Best Young American Novelists."

"Brownies" appeared in *The Best American Short Stories* (2000) as well as *Drinking Coffee Elsewhere*. In this story of racial tension, the protagonist's all-black Brownie troop attend the same camp as an all-white troop; the events that follow expose the complex relationship between prejudice, anger, and cruelty in a world corrupted by discrimination of all kinds.

Brownies

ZZ PACKER

By our second day at Camp Crescendo, the girls in my Brownie troop had decided to kick the asses of each and every girl in Brownie Troop 909. Troop 909 was doomed from the first day of camp; they were white girls, their complexions a blend of ice cream: strawberry, vanilla. They turtled out from their bus in pairs, their rolled-up sleeping bags chromatized with Disney characters: Sleeping Beauty, Snow White, Mickey Mouse; or the generic ones cheap parents bought: washed-out rainbows, unicorns, curly-eyelashed frogs. Some clutched Igloo coolers and still others held on to stuffed toys like pacifiers, looking all around them like tourists determined to be dazzled.

Our troop was wending its way past their bus, past the ranger station, past the colorful trail guide drawn like a treasure map, locked behind glass.

"Man, did you smell them?" Arnetta said, giving the girls a slow once-over, "They smell like Chihuahuas. *Wet* Chihuahuas." Their troop was still at the entrance, and though we had passed them by yards, Arnetta raised her nose in the air and grimaced.

Arnetta said this from the very rear of the line, far away from Mrs. Margolin, who always strung our troop behind her like a brood of obedient ducklings. Mrs. Margolin even looked like a mother duck—she had hair cropped close to a small ball of a head, almost no neck, and huge, miraculous breasts. She wore enormous belts that looked like the kind that weightlifters wear, except hers would be cheap metallic gold or rabbit fur or covered with gigantic fake sunflowers, and often these belts would become nature lessons in and of themselves. "See," Mrs. Margolin once said to us, pointing to her belt, "this one's made entirely from the feathers of baby pigeons."

The belt layered with feathers was uncanny enough, but I was more disturbed by the realization that I had never actually *seen* a baby pigeon. I searched weeks for one, in vain—scampering after pigeons whenever I was downtown with my father.

But nature lessons were not Mrs. Margolin's top priority. She saw the position of troop leader as an evangelical post. Back at the A.M.E. church[1] where our Brownie meetings were held, Mrs. Margolin was especially fond of imparting religious aphorisms by means of acrostics—"Satan" was the "Serpent Always Tempting and Noisome"; she'd refer to the "Bible" as "Basic Instructions Before Leaving Earth." Whenever she quizzed us on these, expecting to hear the acrostics parroted back to her, only Arnetta's correct replies soared over our vague mumblings. "Jesus?" Mrs. Margolin might ask expectantly, and Arnetta alone would dutifully answer, "Jehovah's Example, Saving Us Sinners."

Arnetta always made a point of listening to Mrs. Margolin's religious talk and giving her what she wanted to hear. Because of this, Arnetta could have blared through a megaphone that the white girls of Troop 909 were "wet Chihuahuas" without so much as a blink from Mrs. Margolin. Once, Arnetta killed the troop goldfish by feeding it a french fry covered in ketchup, and when Mrs. Margolin demanded that she explain what had happened, claimed the goldfish had been eyeing her meal for *hours*, then the fish—giving in to temptation—had leapt up and snatched a whole golden fry from her fingertips.

"*Serious* Chihuahua," Octavia added, and though neither Arnetta nor Octavia could *spell* "Chihuahua," had ever *seen* a Chihuahua, trisyllabic words had gained a sort of exoticism within our fourth-grade set at Woodrow Wilson Elementary. Arnetta and Octavia would flip through the dictionary, determined to work the vulgar-sounding ones like "Djibouti" and "asinine" into conversation.

"*Caucasian* Chihuahuas," Arnetta said.

That did it. The girls in my troop turned elastic: Drema and Elise doubled up on one another like inextricably entwined kites; Octavia slapped her belly; Janice jumped straight up in the air, then did it again, as if to slam-dunk her own head. They could not stop laughing. No one had laughed so hard since a boy

---

1 African Methodist Episcopal Church, a primarily African American Methodist religious denomination.

named Martez had stuck a pencil in the electric socket and spent the whole day with a strange grin on his face.

"Girls, girls," said our parent helper, Mrs. Hedy. Mrs. Hedy was Octavia's mother, and she wagged her index finger perfunctorily, like a windshield wiper. "Stop it, now. Be good." She said this loud enough to be heard, but lazily, bereft of any feeling or indication that she meant to be obeyed, as though she could say these words again at the exact same pitch if a button somewhere on her were pressed.

But the rest of the girls didn't stop; they only laughed louder. It was the word "Caucasian" that got them all going. One day at school, about a month before the Brownie camping trip, Arnetta turned to a boy wearing impossibly high-ankled floodwater jeans and said, "What are you? *Caucasian?*" The word took off from there, and soon everything was Caucasian. If you ate too fast you ate like a Caucasian, if you ate too slow you ate like a Caucasian. The biggest feat anyone at Woodrow Wilson could do was to jump off the swing in midair, at the highest point in its arc, and if you fell (as I had, more than once) instead of landing on your feet, knees bent Olympic gymnast–style, Arnetta and Octavia were prepared to comment. They'd look at each other with the silence of passengers who'd narrowly escaped an accident, then nod their heads, whispering with solemn horror, "*Caucasian.*"

Even the only white kid in our school, Dennis, got in on the Caucasian act. That time when Martez stuck a pencil in the socket, Dennis had pointed and yelled, "That was *so* Caucasian!"

When you lived in the south suburbs of Atlanta, it was easy to forget about whites. Whites were like those baby pigeons: real and existing, but rarely seen or thought about. Everyone had been to Rich's to go clothes shopping, everyone had seen white girls and their mothers coo-cooing over dresses; everyone had gone to the downtown library and seen white businessmen swish by importantly, wrists flexed in front of them to check the time as though they would change from Clark Kent into Superman at any second. But those images were as fleeting as cards shuffled in a deck, whereas the ten white girls behind us—*invaders*, Arnetta would later call them—were instantly real and memorable, with their long, shampoo-commercial hair, straight as spaghetti from the box. This alone was reason for envy and hatred. The only black girl most of us had ever seen with hair that long was Octavia, whose hair hung past her butt like a Hawaiian hula dancer's. The sight of Octavia's mane prompted other girls to listen to her reverentially, as though whatever she had to say would somehow activate their own follicles. For example, when, on the first day of camp, Octavia made as if to speak, and everyone fell silent. "Nobody," Octavia said, "calls us niggers."

At the end of that first day, when half of our troop made their way back to the cabin after tag-team restroom visits, Arnetta said she'd heard one of the Troop 909 girls call Daphne a nigger. The other half of the girls and I were helping Mrs. Margolin clean up the pots and pans from the campfire ravioli dinner. When we made our way to the restrooms to wash up and brush our teeth, we met up with Arnetta midway.

"Man, I completely heard the girl," Arnetta reported. "Right, Daphne?"

Daphne hardly ever spoke, but when she did, her voice was petite and tinkly, the voice one might expect from a shiny new earring. She'd written a poem once, for Langston Hughes[2] Day, a poem brimming with all the teacher-winning ingredients—trees and oceans, sunsets and moons—but what cinched the poem for the grown-ups, snatching the win from Octavia's musical ode to Grandmaster Flash and the Furious Five, were Daphne's last lines:

> You are my father, the veteran
> When you cry in the dark
> It rains and rains and rains in my heart

She'd always worn clean, though faded, jumpers and dresses when Chic jeans were the fashion, but when she went up to the dais to receive her prize journal, pages trimmed in gold, she wore a new dress with a velveteen bodice and a taffeta skirt as wide as an umbrella. All the kids clapped, though none of them understood the poem. I'd read encyclopedias the way others read comics, and I didn't get it. But those last lines pricked me, they were so eerie, and as my father and I ate cereal, I'd whisper over my Froot Loops, like a mantra, "*You are my father, the veteran. You are my father, the veteran, the veteran, the veteran,*" until my father, who acted in plays as Caliban and Othello[3] and was not a veteran, marched me up to my teacher one morning and said, "Can you tell me what's wrong with this kid?"

I thought Daphne and I might become friends, but I think she grew spooked by me whispering those lines to her, begging her to tell me what they meant, and I soon understood that two quiet people like us were better off quiet alone.

"Daphne? Didn't you hear them call you a nigger?" Arnetta asked, giving Daphne a nudge.

The sun was setting behind the trees, and their leafy tops formed a canopy of black lace for the flame of the sun to pass through. Daphne shrugged her

---

2 African American poet (1902-67).

3 Characters in the plays *The Tempest* and *Othello*, by William Shakespeare.

shoulders at first, then slowly nodded her head when Arnetta gave her a hard look.

Twenty minutes later, when my restroom group returned to the cabin, Arnetta was still talking about Troop 909. My restroom group had passed by some of the 909 girls. For the most part, they deferred to us, waving us into the restrooms, letting us go even though they'd gotten there first.

We'd seen them, but from afar, never within their orbit enough to see whether their faces were the way all white girls appeared on TV—ponytailed and full of energy, bubbling over with love and money. All I could see was that some of them rapidly fanned their faces with their hands, though the heat of the day had long passed. A few seemed to be lolling their heads in slow circles, half purposefully, as if exercising the muscles of their necks, half ecstatically, like Stevie Wonder.

"We can't let them get away with that," Arnetta said, dropping her voice to a laryngitic whisper. "We can't let them get away with calling us niggers. I say we teach them a lesson." She sat down cross-legged on a sleeping bag, an embittered Buddha, eyes glimmering acrylic-black. "We can't go telling Mrs. Margolin, either. Mrs. Margolin'll say something about doing unto others and the path of righteousness and all. Forget that shit." She let her eyes flutter irreverently till they half closed, as though ignoring an insult not worth returning. We could all hear Mrs. Margolin outside, gathering the last of the metal campware.

Nobody said anything for a while. Usually people were quiet after Arnetta spoke. Her tone had an upholstered confidence that was somehow both regal and vulgar at once. It demanded a few moments of silence in its wake, like the ringing of a church bell or the playing of taps. Sometimes Octavia would ditto or dissent to whatever Arnetta had said, and this was the signal that others could speak. But this time Octavia just swirled a long cord of hair into pretzel shapes.

"*Well?*" Arnetta said. She looked as if she had discerned the hidden severity of the situation and was waiting for the rest of us to catch up. Everyone looked from Arnetta to Daphne. It was, after all, Daphne who had supposedly been called the name, but Daphne sat on the bare cabin floor, flipping through the pages of the Girl Scout handbook, eyebrows arched in mock wonder, as if the handbook were a catalogue full of bright and startling foreign costumes. Janice broke the silence. She clapped her hands to broach her idea of a plan.

"They gone be sleeping," she whispered conspiratorially, "then we gone sneak into they cabin, then we'll put daddy longlegs in they sleeping bags. Then they'll wake up. Then we gone beat 'em up till they're as flat as frying pans!" She jammed her fist into the palm of her hand, then made a sizzling sound.

Janice's country accent was laughable, her looks homely, her jumpy acrobatics embarrassing to behold. Arnetta and Octavia volleyed amused, arrogant smiles whenever Janice opened her mouth, but Janice never caught the hint, spoke whenever she wanted, fluttered around Arnetta and Octavia futilely offering her opinions to their departing backs. Whenever Arnetta and Octavia shooed her away, Janice loitered until the two would finally sigh and ask, "What *is* it, Miss Caucausoid? What do you *want*?"

"Shut up, Janice," Octavia said, letting a fingered loop of hair fall to her waist as though just the sound of Janice's voice had ruined the fun of her hair twisting.

Janice obeyed, her mouth hung open in a loose grin, unflappable, unhurt.

"All right," Arnetta said, standing up. "We're going to have a secret meeting and talk about what we're going to do."

Everyone gravely nodded her head. The word "secret" had a built-in importance, the modifier form of the word carried more clout than the noun. A secret meant nothing; it was like gossip: just a bit of unpleasant knowledge about someone who happened to be someone other than yourself. A secret *meeting*, or a secret *club* was entirely different.

That was when Arnetta turned to me as though she knew that doing so was both a compliment and a charity.

"Snot, you're not going to be a bitch and tell Mrs. Margolin, are you?"

I had been called "Snot" ever since first grade, when I'd sneezed in class and two long ropes of mucus had splattered a nearby girl.

"Hey," I said. "Maybe you didn't hear them right—I mean—"

"Are you gonna tell on us or not?" was all Arnetta wanted to know, and by the time the question was asked, the rest of our Brownie troop looked at me as though they'd already decided their course of action, me being the only impediment.

Camp Crescendo used to double as a high-school-band and field hockey camp until an arcing field hockey ball landed on the clasp of a girl's metal barrette, knifing a skull nerve and paralyzing the right side of her body. The camp closed down for a few years and the girl's teammates built a memorial, filling the spot on which the girl fell with hockey balls, on which they had painted—all in nail polish—get-well tidings, flowers, and hearts. The balls were still stacked there, like a shrine of ostrich eggs embedded in the ground.

On the second day of camp, Troop 909 was dancing around the mound of hockey balls, their limbs jangling awkwardly, their cries like the constant summer squeal of an amusement park. There was a stream that bordered the field hockey lawn, and the girls from my troop settled next to it, scarfing down the last of lunch: sandwiches made from salami and slices of tomato that had gotten waterlogged from the melting ice in the cooler. From the stream bank, Arnetta eyed the Troop 909 girls, scrutinizing their movements to glean inspiration for battle.

"Man," Arnetta said, "we could bumrush them right now if that damn lady would *leave*."

The 909 troop leader was a white woman with the severe pageboy hairdo of an ancient Egyptian. She lay on a picnic blanket, sphinx-like, eating a banana, sometimes holding it out in front of her like a microphone. Beside her sat a girl slowly flapping one hand like a bird with a broken wing. Occasionally, the leader would call out the names of girls who'd attempted leapfrogs and flips, or of girls who yelled too loudly or strayed far from the circle.

"I'm just glad Big Fat Mama's not following us here," Octavia said. "At least we don't have to worry about her." Mrs. Margolin, Octavia assured us, was having her Afternoon Devotional, shrouded in mosquito netting, in a clearing she'd found. Mrs. Hedy was cleaning mud from her espadrilles in the cabin.

"I handled them." Arnetta sucked on her teeth and proudly grinned. "I told her we was going to gather leaves."

"Gather leaves," Octavia said, nodding respectfully. "That's a good one. Especially since they're so mad-crazy about this camping thing." She looked from ground to sky, sky to ground. Her hair hung down her back in two braids like a squaw's. "I mean, I really don't know why it's even called *camping*—all we ever do with Nature is find some twigs and say something like, 'Wow, this fell from a tree.'" She then studied her sandwich. With two disdainful fingers, she picked out a slice of dripping tomato, the sections congealed with red slime. She pitched it into the stream embrowned with dead leaves and the murky effigies of other dead things, but in the opaque water, a group of small silver-brown fish appeared. They surrounded the tomato and nibbled.

"Look!" Janice cried. "Fishes! Fishes!" As she scrambled to the edge of the stream to watch, a covey of insects threw up tantrums from the wheatgrass and nettle, a throng of tiny electric machines, all going at once. Octavia sneaked up behind Janice as if to push her in. Daphne and I exchanged terrified looks. It seemed as though only we knew that Octavia was close enough—and bold enough—to actually push Janice into the stream. Janice turned around quickly, but Octavia was already staring serenely into the still water as though she was gathering some sort of courage from it. "What's so funny?" Janice said, eyeing them all suspiciously.

Elise began humming the tune to "Karma Chameleon," all the girls joining in, their hums light and facile. Janice also began to hum, against everyone else, the high-octane opening chords of "Beat It."

"I love me some Michael Jackson," Janice said when she'd finished humming, smacking her lips as though Michael Jackson were a favorite meal. "I *will* marry Michael Jackson."

Before anyone had a chance to impress upon Janice the impossibility of this, Arnetta suddenly rose, made a sun visor of her hand, and watched Troop 909 leave the field hockey lawn.

"Dammit!" she said. "We've got to get them *alone*."

"They won't ever be alone," I said. All the rest of the girls looked at me, for I usually kept quiet. If I spoke even a word, I could count on someone calling me Snot. Everyone seemed to think that we could beat up these girls; no one entertained the thought that they might fight *back*. "The only time they'll be unsupervised is in the bathroom."

"Oh shut up, Snot," Octavia said.

But Arnetta slowly nodded her head. "The bathroom," she said. "The bathroom," she said, again and again. "The bathroom! The bathroom!"

According to Octavia's watch, it took us five minutes to hike to the restrooms, which were midway between our cabin and Troop 909's. Inside, the mirrors above the sinks returned only the vaguest of reflections, as though someone had taken a scouring pad to their surfaces to obscure the shine. Pine needles, leaves, and dirty, flattened wads of chewing gum covered the floor like a mosaic. Webs of hair matted the drain in the middle of the floor. Above the sinks and below the mirrors, stacks of folded white paper towels lay on a long metal counter. Shaggy white balls of paper towels sat on the sinktops in a line like corsages on display. A thread of floss snaked from a wad of tissues dotted with the faint red-pink of blood. One of those white girls, I thought, had just lost a tooth.

Though the restroom looked almost the same as it had the night before, it somehow seemed stranger now. We hadn't noticed the wooden rafters coming together in great V's. We were, it seemed, inside a whale, viewing the ribs of the roof of its mouth.

"Wow. It's a mess," Elise said.

"You can say that again."

Arnetta leaned against the doorjamb of a restroom stall. "This is where they'll be again," she said. Just seeing the place, just having a plan seemed to satisfy her. "We'll go in and talk to them. You know, 'How you doing? How long'll you be here?' That sort of thing. Then Octavia and I are gonna tell them what happens when they call any one of us a nigger."

"I'm going to say something, too," Janice said.

Arnetta considered this. "Sure," she said. "Of course. Whatever you want."

Janice pointed her finger like a gun at Octavia and rehearsed the line she'd thought up, "'We're gonna teach you a *lesson*!' That's what I'm going to say." She narrowed her eyes like a TV mobster. "'We're gonna teach you little girls a lesson!'"

With the back of her hand, Octavia brushed Janice's finger away. "You couldn't teach me to shit in a toilet."

"But," I said, "what if they say, 'We didn't say that? We didn't call anyone an N-I-G-G-E-R.'"

"Snot," Arnetta said, and then sighed. "Don't think. Just fight. If you even know how."

Everyone laughed except Daphne. Arnetta gently laid her hand on Daphne's shoulder. "Daphne. You don't have to fight. We're doing this for you."

Daphne walked to the counter, took a clean paper towel, and carefully unfolded it like a map. With it, she began to pick up the trash all around. Everyone watched.

"C'mon," Arnetta said to everyone. "Let's beat it." We all ambled toward the doorway, where the sunshine made one large white rectangle of light. We were immediately blinded, and we shielded our eyes with our hands and our forearms.

"Daphne?" Arnetta asked. "Are you coming?"

We all looked back at the bending girl, the thin of her back hunched like the back of a custodian sweeping a stage, caught in limelight. Stray strands of her hair were lit near-transparent, thin fiber-optic threads. She did not nod yes to the question, nor did she shake her head no. She abided, bent. Then she began again, picking up leaves, wads of paper, the cotton fluff innards from a torn stuffed toy. She did it so methodically, so exquisitely, so humbly, she must have been trained. I thought of those dresses she wore, faded and old, yet so pressed and clean. I then saw the poverty in them; I then could imagine her mother, cleaning the houses of others, returning home, weary.

"I guess she's not coming."

We left her and headed back to our cabin, over pine needles and leaves, taking the path full of shade.

"What about our secret meeting?" Elise asked.

Arnetta enunciated her words in a way that defied contradiction: "We just had it."

It was nearing our bedtime, but the sun had not yet set.

"Hey, your mama's coming," Arnetta said to Octavia when she saw Mrs. Hedy walk toward the cabin, sniffling. When Octavia's mother wasn't giving bored, parochial orders, she sniffled continuously, mourning an imminent divorce from her husband. She might begin a sentence, "I don't know what Robert will do when Octavia and I are gone. Who'll buy him cigarettes?" and Octavia would hotly whisper, "*Mama*," in a way that meant: Please don't talk about our problems in front of everyone. Please shut up.

But when Mrs. Hedy began talking about her husband, thinking about her husband, seeing clouds shaped like the head of her husband, she couldn't be quiet, and no one could dislodge her from the comfort of her own woe. Only one thing could perk her up—Brownie songs. If the girls were quiet, and Mrs. Hedy was in her dopey, sorrowful mood, she would say, "Y'all know I like those songs, girls. Why don't you sing one?" Everyone would groan, except me and Daphne. I, for one, liked some of the songs.

"C'mon, everybody," Octavia said drearily. "She likes the Brownie song best."

We sang, loud enough to reach Mrs. Hedy:

"I've got something in my pocket;
It belongs across my face.
And I keep it very close at hand
 in a most convenient place.
I'm sure you couldn't guess it
If you guessed a long, long while.
So I'll take it out and put it on—
It's a great big Brownie smile!"

The Brownie song was supposed to be sung cheerfully, as though we were elves in a workshop, singing as we merrily cobbled shoes, but everyone except me hated the song so much that they sang it like a maudlin record, played on the most sluggish of rpms.

"That was good," Mrs. Hedy said, closing the cabin door behind her. "Wasn't that nice, Linda?"

"Praise God," Mrs. Margolin answered without raising her head from the chore of counting out Popsicle sticks for the next day's craft session.

"Sing another one," Mrs. Hedy said. She said it with a sort of joyful aggression, like a drunk I'd once seen who'd refused to leave a Korean grocery.

"God, Mama, get over it," Octavia whispered in a voice meant only for Arnetta, but Mrs. Hedy heard it and started to leave the cabin.

"Don't go," Arnetta said. She ran after Mrs. Hedy and held her by the arm. "We haven't finished singing." She nudged us with a single look. "Let's sing the 'Friends Song.' For Mrs. Hedy."

Although I liked some of the songs, I hated this one:

Make new friends
But keep the o-old,
One is silver
And the other gold.

If most of the girls in the troop could be any type of metal, they'd be bunched-up wads of tinfoil, maybe, or rusty iron nails you had to get tetanus shots for.

"No, no, no," Mrs. Margolin said before anyone could start in on the "Friends Song." "An uplifting song. Something to lift her up and take her mind off all these earthly burdens."

Arnetta and Octavia rolled their eyes. Everyone knew what song Mrs. Margolin was talking about, and no one, no one, wanted to sing it.

"Please, no," a voice called out. "Not 'The Doughnut Song.'"

"Please not 'The Doughnut Song,'" Octavia pleaded.

"I'll brush my teeth two times if I don't have to sing 'The Doughnut—'"

"Sing!" Mrs. Margolin demanded.

We sang:

> "Life without Jesus is like a do-ough-nut!
> Like a do-ooough-nut!
> Like a do-ooough-nut!
> Life without Jesus is like a do-ough-nut!
> There's a hole in the middle of my soul!"

There were other verses, involving other pastries, but we stopped after the first one and cast glances toward Mrs. Margolin to see if we could gain a reprieve. Mrs. Margolin's eyes fluttered blissfully. She was half asleep.

"Awww," Mrs. Hedy said, as though giant Mrs. Margolin were a cute baby, "Mrs. Margolin's had a long day."

"Yes indeed," Mrs. Margolin answered. "If you don't mind, I might just go to the lodge where the beds are. I haven't been the same since the operation."

I had not heard of this operation, or when it had occurred, since Mrs. Margolin had never missed the once-a-week Brownie meetings, but I could see from Daphne's face that she was concerned, and I could see that the other girls had decided that Mrs. Margolin's operation must have happened long ago in some remote time unconnected to our own. Nevertheless, they put on sad faces. We had all been taught that adulthood was full of sorrow and pain, taxes and bills, dreaded work and dealings with whites, sickness and death. I tried to do what the others did. I tried to look silent.

"Go right ahead, Linda," Mrs. Hedy said. "I'll watch the girls." Mrs. Hedy seemed to forget about divorce for a moment; she looked at us with dewy eyes, as if we were mysterious, furry creatures. Meanwhile, Mrs. Margolin walked through the maze of sleeping bags until she found her own. She gathered a neat stack of clothes and pajamas slowly, as though doing so was almost painful. She took her toothbrush, her toothpaste, her pillow. "All right!" Mrs. Margolin said, addressing us all from the threshold of the cabin. "Be in bed by nine." She said it with a twinkle in her voice, letting us know she was allowing us to be naughty and stay up till nine-fifteen.

"C'mon everybody," Arnetta said after Mrs. Margolin left. "Time for us to wash up."

Everyone watched Mrs. Hedy closely, wondering whether she would insist on coming with us since it was night, making a fight with Troop 909 nearly impossible. Troop 909 would soon be in the bathroom, washing their faces, brushing their teeth—completely unsuspecting of our ambush.

"We won't be long," Arnetta said. "We're old enough to go to the restrooms by ourselves."

Mrs. Hedy pursed her lips at this dilemma. "Well, I guess you Brownies are almost Girl Scouts, right?"

"Right!"

"Just one more badge," Drema said.

"And about," Octavia droned, "a million more cookies to sell." Octavia looked at all of us, *Now's our chance*, her face seemed to say, but our chance to do *what*, I didn't exactly know.

Finally, Mrs. Hedy walked to the doorway where Octavia stood dutifully waiting to say goodbye but looking bored doing it. Mrs. Hedy held Octavia's chin. "You'll be good?"

"Yes, Mama."

"And remember to pray for me and your father? If I'm asleep when you get back?"

"Yes, Mama."

When the other girls had finished getting their toothbrushes and washcloths and flashlights for the group restroom trip, I was drawing pictures of tiny birds with too many feathers. Daphne was sitting on her sleeping bag, reading.

"You're not going to come?" Octavia asked.

Daphne shook her head.

"I'm gonna stay, too," I said. "I'll go to the restroom when Daphne and Mrs. Hedy go."

Arnetta leaned down toward me and whispered so that Mrs. Hedy, who'd taken over Mrs. Margolin's task of counting Popsicle sticks, couldn't hear. "No, Snot. If we get in trouble, you're going to get in trouble with the rest of us."

We made our way through the darkness by flashlight. The tree branches that had shaded us just hours earlier, along the same path, now looked like arms sprouting menacing hands. The stars sprinkled the sky like spilled salt. They seemed fastened to the darkness, high up and holy, their places fixed and definite as we stirred beneath them.

Some, like me, were quiet because we were afraid of the dark; others were talking like crazy for the same reason.

"Wow!" Drema said, looking up. "Why are all the stars out here? I never see stars back on Oneida Street."

"It's a camping trip, that's why," Octavia said. "You're supposed to see stars on camping trips."

Janice said, "This place smells like my mother's air freshener."

"These woods are *pine*," Elise said. "Your mother probably uses *pine* air freshener."

Janice mouthed an exaggerated "Oh," nodding her head as though she just then understood one of the world's great secrets.

No one talked about fighting. Everyone was afraid enough just walking through the infinite deep of the woods. Even though I didn't fight to fight, was afraid of fighting, I felt I was part of the rest of the troop; like I was defending something. We trudged against the slight incline of the path, Arnetta leading the way.

"You know," I said, "their leader will be there. Or they won't even be there. It's dark already. Last night the sun was still in the sky. I'm sure they're already finished."

Arnetta acted as if she hadn't heard me. I followed her gaze with my flashlight, and that's when I saw the squares of light in the darkness. The bathroom was just ahead.

But the girls were there. We could hear them before we could see them.

"Octavia and I will go in first so they'll think there's just two of us, then wait till I say, 'We're gonna teach you a lesson,'" Arnetta said. "Then, bust in. That'll surprise them."

"That's what I was supposed to say," Janice said.

Arnetta went inside, Octavia next to her. Janice followed, and the rest of us waited outside.

They were in there for what seemed like whole minutes, but something was wrong. Arnetta hadn't given the signal yet. I was with the girls outside when I heard one of the Troop 909 girls say, "NO. That did NOT happen!"

That was to be expected, that they'd deny the whole thing. What I hadn't expected was *the voice* in which the denial was said. The girl sounded as though her tongue were caught in her mouth. "That's a BAD word!" the girl continued. "We don't say BAD words!"

"Let's go in," Elise said.

"No," Drema said, "I don't want to. What if we get beat up?"

"Snot?" Elise turned to me, her flashlight blinding. It was the first time anyone had asked my opinion, though I knew they were just asking because they were afraid.

"I say we go inside, just to see what's going on."

"But Arnetta didn't give us the signal," Drema said. "She's supposed to say, 'We're gonna teach you a lesson,' and I didn't hear her say it."

"C'mon," I said. "Let's just go in."

We went inside. There we found the white girls—about five girls huddled up next to one big girl. I instantly knew she was the owner of the voice we'd heard. Arnetta and Octavia inched toward us as soon as we entered.

"Where's Janice?" Elise asked, then we heard a flush. "Oh."

"I think," Octavia said, whispering to Elise, "they're retarded."

"We ARE NOT retarded!" the big girl said, though it was obvious that she was. That they all were. The girls around her began to whimper.

"They're just pretending," Arnetta said, trying to convince herself. "I know they are."

Octavia turned to Arnetta. "Arnetta. Let's just leave."

Janice came out of a stall, happy and relieved, then she suddenly remembered her line, pointed to the big girl, and said, "We're gonna teach you a lesson."

"Shut up, Janice," Octavia said, but her heart was not in it. Arnetta's face was set in a lost, deep scowl. Octavia turned to the big girl and said loudly, slowly, as if they were all deaf, "We're going to leave. It was nice meeting you, O.K.? You don't have to tell anyone that we were here. O.K.?"

"Why not?" said the big girl, like a taunt. When she spoke, her lips did not meet, her mouth did not close. Her tongue grazed the roof of her mouth, like a little pink fish. "You'll get in trouble. I know. *I* know."

Arnetta got back her old cunning. "If you said anything, then you'd be a tattletale."

The girl looked sad for a moment, then perked up quickly. A flash of genius crossed her face. "I *like* tattletale."

"It's all right, girls. It's gonna be all right!" the 909 troop leader said. All of Troop 909 burst into tears. It was as though someone had instructed them all to cry at once. The troop leader had girls under her arm, and all the rest of the girls crowded about her. It reminded me of a hog I'd seen on a field trip, where all the little hogs gathered about the mother at feeding time, latching onto her teats. The 909 troop leader had come into the bathroom, shortly after the big girl had threatened to tell. Then the ranger came, then, once the ranger had radioed the station, Mrs. Margolin arrived with Daphne in tow.

The ranger had left the restroom area, but everyone else was huddled just outside, swatting mosquitoes.

"Oh. They *will* apologize," Mrs. Margolin said to the 909 troop leader, but she said this so angrily, I knew she was speaking more to us than to the other troop leader. "When their parents find out, every one a them will be on punishment."

"It's all right, it's all right," the 909 troop leader reassured Mrs. Margolin. Her voice lilted in the same way it had when addressing the girls. She smiled the whole time she talked. She was like one of those TV-cooking-show women who talk and dice onions and smile all at the same time.

"See. It could have happened. I'm not calling your girls fibbers or anything." She shook her head ferociously from side to side, her Egyptian-style pageboy flapping against her cheeks like heavy drapes. "It *could* have happened. See. Our girls are *not* retarded. They are *delayed* learners." She said this in a syrupy instructional voice, as though our troop might be delayed learners as well. "We're from the Decatur Children's Academy. Many of them just have special needs."

"Now we won't be able to walk to the bathroom by ourselves!" the big girl said.

"Yes you will," the troop leader said, "but maybe we'll wait till we get back to Decatur—"

"I don't want to wait!" the girl said. "I want my Independence badge!"

The girls in my troop were entirely speechless. Arnetta looked stoic, as though she were soon to be tortured but was determined not to appear weak. Mrs. Margolin pursed her lips solemnly and said, "Bless them, Lord. Bless them."

In contrast, the Troop 909 leader was full of words and energy. "Some of our girls are echolalic—" She smiled and happily presented one of the girls hanging onto her, but the girl widened her eyes in horror, and violently withdrew herself from the center of attention, sensing she was being sacrificed for the village sins. "Echolalic," the troop leader continued. "That means they will say whatever they hear, like an echo—that's where the word comes from. It comes from 'echo.'" She ducked her head apologetically, "I mean, not all of them have the most *progressive* of parents, so if they heard a bad word, they might have repeated it. But I guarantee it would not have been *intentional*."

Arnetta spoke. "I saw her say the word. I heard her." She pointed to a small girl, smaller than any of us, wearing an oversized T-shirt that read: "Eat Bertha's Mussels."

The troop leader shook her head and smiled, "That's impossible. She doesn't speak. She can, but she doesn't."

Arnetta furrowed her brow. "No. It wasn't her. That's right. It was *her*."

The girl Arnetta pointed to grinned as though she'd been paid a compliment. She was the only one from either troop actually wearing a full uniform: the mocha-colored A-line shift, the orange ascot, the sash covered with badges, though all the same one—the Try-It patch. She took a few steps toward Arnetta and made a grand sweeping gesture toward the sash. "See," she said, full of self-importance, "I'm a Brownie." I had a hard time imagining this girl calling anyone a "nigger"; the girl looked perpetually delighted, as though she would have cuddled up with a grizzly if someone had let her.

On the fourth morning, we boarded the bus to go home.

The previous day had been spent building miniature churches from Popsicle sticks. We hardly left the cabin. Mrs. Margolin and Mrs. Hedy guarded us so closely, almost no one talked for the entire day.

Even on the day of departure from Camp Crescendo, all was serious and silent. The bus ride began quietly enough. Arnetta had to sit beside Mrs. Margolin; Octavia had to sit beside her mother. I sat beside Daphne, who gave me her prize journal without a word of explanation.

"You don't want it?"

She shook her head no. It was empty.

Then Mrs. Hedy began to weep. "Octavia," Mrs. Hedy said to her daughter without looking at her, "I'm going to sit with Mrs. Margolin. All right?"

Arnetta exchanged seats with Mrs. Hedy. With the two women up front, Elise felt it safe to speak. "Hey," she said, then she set her face into a placid, vacant stare, trying to imitate that of a Troop 909 girl. Emboldened, Arnetta made a gesture of mock pride toward an imaginary sash, the way the girl in full uniform had done. Then they all made a game of it, trying to do the most exaggerated imitations of the Troop 909 girls, all without speaking, all without laughing loud enough to catch the women's attention.

Daphne looked down at her shoes, white with sneaker polish. I opened the journal she'd given me. I looked out the window, trying to decide what to write, searching for lines, but nothing could compare with what Daphne had written, "*My father, the veteran*," my favorite line of all time. It replayed itself in my head, and I gave up trying to write.

By then, it seemed that the rest of the troop had given up making fun of the girls in Troop 909. They were now quietly gossiping about who had passed notes to whom in school. For a moment the gossiping fell off, and all I heard was the hum of the bus as we sped down the road and the muffled sounds of Mrs. Hedy and Mrs. Margolin talking about serious things.

"You know," Octavia whispered, "why did *we* have to be stuck at a camp with retarded girls? You know?"

"*You* know why," Arnetta answered. She narrowed her eyes like a cat. "My mama and I were in the mall in Buckhead,[4] and this white lady just kept looking at us. I mean, like we were foreign or something. Like we were from China."

"What did the woman say?" Elise asked.

"Nothing," Arnetta said. "She didn't say nothing."

A few girls quietly nodded their heads.

"There was this time," I said, "when my father and I were in the mall and—"

"Oh shut up, Snot," Octavia said.

I stared at Octavia, then rolled my eyes from her to the window. As I watched the trees blur, I wanted nothing more than to be through with it all: the bus ride, the troop, school—all of it. But we were going home. I'd see the same girls in school the next day. We were on a bus, and there was nowhere else to go.

"Go on, Laurel," Daphne said to me. It seemed like the first time she'd spoken the whole trip, and she'd said my name. I turned to her and smiled weakly so as not to cry, hoping she'd remember when I'd tried to be her friend, thinking maybe that her gift of the journal was an invitation of friendship. But she didn't smile back. All she said was, "What happened?"

I studied the girls, waiting for Octavia to tell me to shut up again before I even had a chance to utter another word, but everyone was amazed that Daphne had spoken. The bus was silent. I gathered my voice. "Well," I said. "My father and I were in this mall, but *I* was the one doing the staring." I stopped and glanced from face to face. I continued. "There were these white people dressed like Puritans or something, but they weren't Puritans. They were Mennonites.[5] They're these people who, if you ask them to do a favor, like paint your porch or something, they have to do it. It's in their rules."

"That sucks," someone said.

"C'mon," Arnetta said. "You're lying."

"I am not."

"How do you know that's not just some story someone made up?" Elise asked, her head cocked full of daring. "I mean, who's gonna do whatever you ask?"

"It's not made up. I know because when I was looking at them, my father said, 'See those people? If you ask them to do something, they'll do it. Anything you want.'"

No one would call anyone's father a liar—then they'd have to fight the person. But Drema parsed her words carefully. "How does your *father* know that's not just some story? Huh?"

---

4 Business and shopping district in Atlanta, Georgia.

5 Members of a Protestant religious group; some members wear "plain dress," or modest and old-fashioned clothing.

"Because," I said, "he went up to the man and asked him would he paint our porch, and the man said yes. It's their religion."

"Man, I'm glad I'm a Baptist," Elise said, shaking her head in sympathy for the Mennonites.

"So did the guy do it?" Drema asked, scooting closer to hear if the story got juicy.

"Yeah," I said. "His whole family was with him. My dad drove them to our house. They all painted our porch. The woman and girl were in bonnets and long, long skirts with buttons up to their necks. The guy wore this weird hat and these huge suspenders."

"Why," Arnetta asked archly, as though she didn't believe a word, "would someone pick a *porch*? If they'll do anything, why not make them paint the whole *house*? Why not ask for a hundred bucks?"

I thought about it, and then remembered the words my father had said about them painting our porch, though I had never seemed to think about his words after he'd said them.

"He said," I began, only then understanding the words as they uncoiled from my mouth, "it was the only time he'd have a white man on his knees doing something for a black man for free."

I now understood what he meant, and why he did it, though I didn't like it. When you've been made to feel bad for so long, you jump at the chance to do it to others. I remembered the Mennonites bending the way Daphne had bent when she was cleaning the restroom. I remembered the dark blue of their bonnets, the black of their shoes. They painted the porch as though scrubbing a floor. I was already trembling before Daphne asked quietly, "Did he thank them?"

I looked out the window. I could not tell which were the thoughts and which were the trees. "No," I said, and suddenly knew there was something mean in the world that I could not stop.

Arnetta laughed. "If I asked them to take off their long skirts and bonnets and put on some jeans, would they do it?"

And Daphne's voice, quiet, steady: "Maybe they would. Just to be nice."

—2003

SHAUN TAN

Shaun Tan is a freelance artist, writer, and director living in Melbourne, Australia. His award-winning picture books use words and illustration to transform the usual narrative landscape; his surreal imagery and dream-like sequences of drawings bring depth and psychological intensity to his spare narratives, which hover on the edges of experience and consciousness.

Born in 1974, Tan grew up in the northern suburbs of Perth, Western Australia, and his drawings still retain qualities of that environment: vast cloudscapes and vistas of land, wasted, hot, and empty, scribbled over with repetitive urban sprawl underneath a sunlit sky. As children he and his brother would take walks to the beach, collecting shells and objects which Tan would then draw. His father, an architect, instilled in him the habits of working with precision and care; he also gave him his first paid job at the age of seven—20 cents for adding a tree to an architectural sketch.

Tan attended a special high school art program, where he had the advantage of being taught by practicing artists. He then went to the University of Western Australia and took a degree in English Literature and Fine Arts. He began to draw for money, creating illustrations for magazines, book covers, music posters, flyers, and newsletters. Tan says that his work for science fiction magazines directed his drawings toward certain subjects: time, space, death, history, art, sexuality, and horror, "usually set in some other world (past, future or inter-planetary) than our own."

As Tan began making his own books, he became interested in the interplay between text and image, creating picture books that elude categorization. Books such as *The Rabbits* (1998), *The Red Tree* (2001), *Tales from Outer Suburbia* (2008), and the wordless novel *The Arrival* (2006) are enjoyed by readers of all ages, though Tan is often cited as a writer for children. His mysterious narratives create fables from minimal text interwoven with silent, full-page drawings; the stories are layered and deepened by this technique. Detailed, surreal drawings take the reader into subconscious worlds that contrast with and yet connect to the suburban landscapes where many of these stories begin.

Tan's books have received great critical acclaim, and he has won numerous awards, most recently the prestigious Astrid Lindgren Memorial Award for Children's Literature. In 2011, he won an Oscar as director of *The Lost Thing,* a short animated film based on his 1999 picture book.

"Grandpa's Story," from *Tales from Outer Suburbia*, is a fable about relationship and commitment. The narrator's grandparents embark on an adventure that takes them to otherworldly lands, where, to prepare themselves for marriage, they must complete a series of ritual trials. The lands they visit are "beyond the edge of outer suburbia, past the very last railway line, a treacherous place without logic and comfort." The story shows a way back to a clear, safe, brightly lit world—but a world that can never be looked upon with the same eyes once they return.

Grandpa's Story

SHAUN TAN

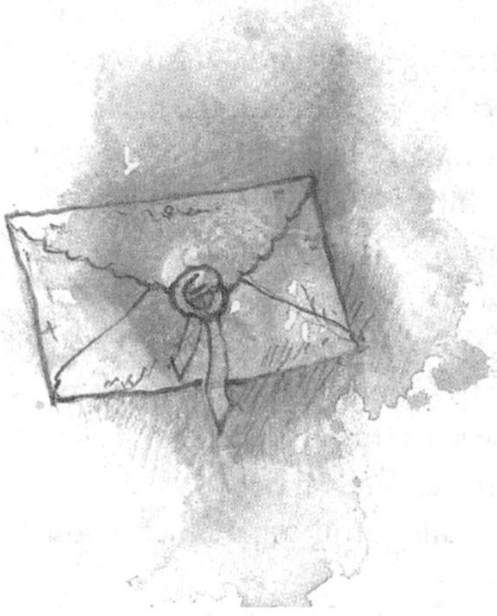

"YOU KNOW that big hill you can see from your bedroom window?" says Grandpa, pointing. "Well, your grandma and I got married on the other side of it, long before you lot came along. Of course, weddings were more complicated in those days, not the short 'n' sweet kind you see today.

"For a start, the bride and groom were sent away before the ceremony, and they were only allowed to have one photo taken upon leaving, and no more until they came back, which might be a long time later. That's why there are so many blank pages in our wedding album—the dark pages we call them. Lucky for us that first picture came out good. Look at the family, all dressed up on the driveway. Look at your grandma there, as though she's just stepped out of a movie. Talk about stylish.

"After the photographer left, we were given a sealed envelope, a compass, and traditional wedding boots—hardy things they were, with steel caps. Each guest told us a special riddle, like a cryptic crossword clue.

We had to listen hard and remember them all, strange instructions that would supposedly make sense later on. We were mad keen to get started and figure it all out, so we didn't hang around. We were off!"

Grandpa is a bit vague at this stage in his story, so it's not clear where they actually went. Somewhere "past the factories and landfills" and "beyond all the signs and roads." When we ask him to show us on a map, he simply shakes his head in an amused way, as if to say "one day you'll know."

He waves aside our further questions and continues: "We weren't allowed to open the envelope until we arrived. Inside was a list of objects we had to find before the end of the day, each corresponding to a clue. This was the Scavenger Hunt, always the most troublesome and feared part of any wedding. Well, we expected to be back home and dressed for the well-rehearsed vows in no time at all—we were young and full of confidence, always in a hurry too. Of course, it was not too long before we ran into trouble, a whole lot of trouble...."

Frustratingly, Grandpa goes off to make a cup of tea at this point. We follow him to the kitchen and press for details. Grandpa just shrugs. "It's hard to explain the terrible things that happened out there. In fact, the more I tell you, the less you will actually understand. Some things in life are like that. You have to find out for yourself....

"They were perilous times. But every setback only made us more determined. Scared? Sure, sometimes, but we had each other. That must be what it's all about, we thought: As long as we stick together, nothing can stop us!

"And true enough, one by one we found those objects on the list. It was hard work, and we had trouble remembering some of the clues. But there was a lot of happiness discovering so many small things in unexpected places. We tied everything to the rear bumper with wedding string in the customary way.

"The sound of that rattling from the back of the car was very satisfying at first, but really started to get on our nerves after hours and hours of driving around. It was late by then, and we had a big problem. A really big problem. You see, the last two objects on our list seemed impossible to find, and I think both of us were beginning to wonder if they even existed. Yet we couldn't return unless we found them. We searched and searched, wracked our brains and did everything we were supposed to. Still nothing.

NADA
FORGET IT
NO
CLOSED
NO
NO VACANCY
NO VACANCY
NO VAC
NO VACANCY
NO
NO VACANCY

"We became anxious, desperate, obsessed, driving farther and faster, not thinking about where we were going. Eventually we found ourselves lost in a vast magnetic desert, unable to get a reliable compass bearing. My own old grandpa once spoke of a place all lovers are doomed to visit at least once—maybe this was what he was talking about, I thought. It was terrible!

"The sun was creeping below the horizon. We would never make it back in time for the vows. We'd missed our big moment. Our smiles vanished. We stopped holding hands. And then—*BANG!*—the back tire burst on a pointy rock! Well that was it! Your grandma leapt out, slammed the door furiously, and started blaming me for everything. I leapt out, slammed the door furiously, and started blaming her for everything. We shouted and yelled and carried on, and said a few things we've since lived to regret … well, you know what it's like when your grandma and I have one of our events.

"Then there was a long and terrible silence, of a kind we had never known before. We refused to even look at each other. It was like all the stones in that desert went down our throats and into our hearts. We wanted to just sink into the ground and stay there forever.

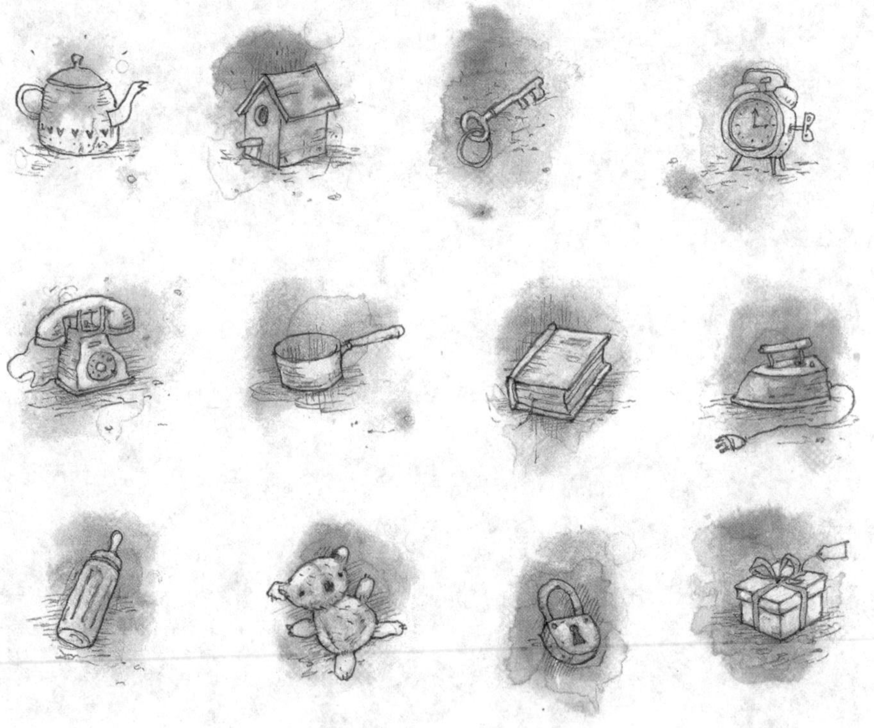

"Of course, as the light faded and the temperature dropped, we soon realized that we would have to do something quick-smart if we were to have any hope of returning to civilization. And we'd have to do it together.

"The spare tire—which we'd never needed before—was somehow rusted into the back of the car; it required the leverage of our combined weight on a crowbar to budge it. With one almighty heave it finally popped free. Our sense of relief was overwhelming. We almost didn't notice something twinkling in the hollow muddy pan of the car's boot. Twinkling just like stars. Well, we rinsed off the mud with the last of the drinking water and still couldn't believe our eyes—two of the most perfect rings you ever saw! If you don't believe me, have a look at this!" Grandpa holds up his hand with a ring on it.

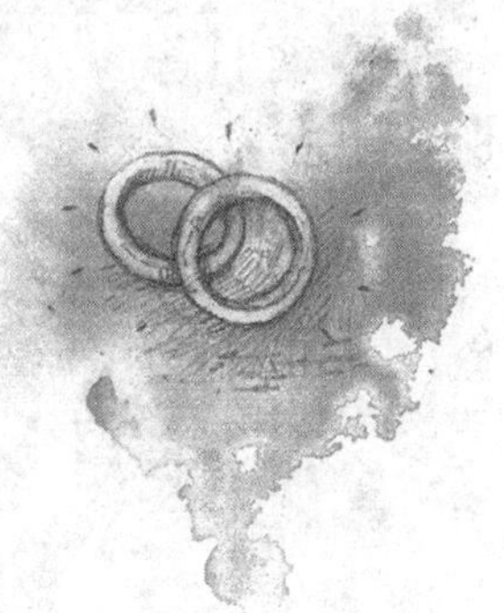

"From that moment on, we picked a random direction and took off at top speed, with a determination that could make any destination turn up on the far side of a bug-plastered windscreen. And sure enough, as we crested that last big hill, we could see all the lights of the outer suburbs unfold before us, streets like old friends, welcoming us home.

"By the time we pulled into the driveway, there was just enough time to shower, dress, exchange our vows, and do all that ceremonial stuff we had rehearsed. It was as if we had been away for only a couple of hours, and everything was normal, with everyone saying congratulations over and over. Your grandma and I kept looking at each other, as though we had just returned from another planet.

"Anyway, that's pretty much it, the story of how we got married, beyond that big hill you can see from the window. Long before you lot came along."

Grandpa shuffles off to the toilet, and then to check on his fruit trees. Admittedly, we are skeptical about everything we've heard, particularly as Grandpa can have a very lively imagination. There is only one thing to do—ask Grandma.

"Well, you know I rarely agree with your grandpa's account of *anything*," she tells us. "But in this case I'll make a rare exception." And she shows us the other ring they found under the spare tire, out in the desert.

—2008

JUST
MARRIED

ACKNOWLEDGEMENTS

We would like to thank the writers and editors who prepared material for this edition and/or assisted with editorial research: Nora Ruddock, Laura Buzzard, Tara Bodie, Kaitlyn Till, Paul Johnson Byrne, Victoria Duncan, Emily Farrell, and Amber LaPiana.

We would also like to thank the academics who provided helpful comments and suggestions for this edition, among them Anne Bartlett, Teague Bohlen, Caryn Chaden, David Ebenbach, William Flesch, David Thoreen, and Robin Werner.

Finally, we would like to acknowledge Julia Gaunce and Suzette Mayr, whose fine work on the first edition of *The Broadview Anthology of Short Fiction* provided a model for later editions.

SOURCES

Achebe, Chinua. "Dead Men's Path," from *Girls at War and Other Stories* by Chinua Achebe. Copyright © 1972, 1973 by Chinua Achebe. Used by permission of Doubleday, a division of Random House, Inc. Any third party use of this material, outside of this publication, is prohibited. Interested parties must apply directly to Random House, Inc. for permission.

Alexie, Sherman. "Do You Know Where I Am?" from *Ten Little Indians*, copyright © 2003 by Sherman Alexie. Used by permission of Grove/Atlantic, Inc. Any third party use of this material, outside of this publication, is prohibited.

Anderson, Emily. "Love, the Frontier," originally published in *McSweeney's* 25, 2007. Reprinted with the permission of the author.

Atwood, Margaret. "Happy Endings," from *Good Bones and Simple Murders* by Margaret Atwood, copyright © 1983, 1992, 1994, by O.W. Toad Ltd. A Nan A. Talese Book. Used by permission of Doubleday, a division of Random House, Inc. Any third party use of this material, outside of this publication, is prohibited. Interested parties must apply directly to Random House, Inc. for permission.

Baldwin, James. "Sonny's Blues," copyright © 1957 by James Baldwin, was originally published in *Partisan Review*. Copyright renewed. Collected in *Going to Meet the Man*, Vintage Books. Reprinted by arrangement with the James Baldwin Estate.

Barthelme, Donald. "The Palace at 4 a.m." Currently collected in *Forty Stories* by Donald Barthelme. Copyright © 1987 by Donald Barthelme, used by permission of The Wylie Agency LLC.

Carver, Raymond. "Cathedral," from *Cathedral* by Raymond Carver, copyright © 1981, 1982, 1983 by Raymond Carver. Used by permission of Alfred A. Knopf, a division of Random House, Inc. Any third party use of this material, outside of this publication, is prohibited. Interested parties must apply directly to Random House, Inc. for permission.

Chopin, Kate. "The Storm," from *The Complete Works of Kate Chopin*; copyright © 1969 Louisiana State UP. Reprinted with the permission of Louisiana State UP.

Cisneros, Sandra. "My Lucy Friend Who Smells Like Corn," from *Woman Hollering Creek*. Copyright © 1991 by Sandra Cisneros. Published by Vintage Books, a division of Random House, Inc. and originally in hard cover by Random House, Inc. Reprinted by permission of Susan Bergholz Literary Services, New York, NY, and Lamy, NM. All rights reserved.

Faulkner, William. "Dry September," from *Collected Stories of William Faulkner* by William Faulkner, copyright © 1930 & renewed 1958 by William Faulkner. Used by permission of Random House, Inc. Any third party use of this material, outside of this publication, is prohibited. Interested parties must apply directly to Random House, Inc. for permission.

Hemingway, Ernest. "Hills Like White Elephants," from *The Short Stories of Ernest Hemingway* by Ernest Hemingway. Copyright © 1927 by Charles Scribner's Sons. Copyright renewed 1955 by Ernest Hemingway. Reprinted with the permission of Scribner, an imprint of Simon & Schuster, Inc. All rights reserved.

Jen, Gish. "The Third Dumpster," originally published in *Granta 120: Medicine*. Copyright © 2012 by Gish Jen. Reprinted with permission by Melanie Jackson Agency, LLC.

Johnson, Denis. "Emergency," from *Jesus' Son* by Denis Johnson. Copyright © 1992 by Denis Johnson. Reprinted by permission of Farrar, Straus and Giroux, LLC.

Jones, Edward P. "Young Lions," from *Lost in the City* by Edward P. Jones. Copyright © 1992 by Edward P. Jones. Reprinted by permission of HarperCollins Publishers.

Kawabata, Yasunari. "Immortality," from *Palm of the Hand Stories*. North Point Press, 1988. Copyright © 1988 by Yasunari Kawabata. Reprinted by permission of Farrar, Straus and Giroux, LLC.

Kincaid, Jamaica. "Girl," from *At the Bottom of the River* by Jamaica Kincaid. Copyright © 1983 by Jamaica Kincaid. Reprinted by permission of Farrar, Straus and Giroux, LLC.

Le Guin, Ursula K. "Those Who Walk Away From Omelas," from *The Wind's Twelve Quarters*. First published in *New Dimensions* 3. Copyright © 1973, 2001 by Ursula K. Le Guin. Reprinted by permission of the author and the author's agent, the Virginia Kidd Agency, Inc.

Lindsey, O.A. "Hers," first published in *Forty Stories: New Writing from Harper Perennial*. Harper Perennial, 2012. Reprinted with the permission of the author. http://files.harpercollins.com/Mktg/ItBooks/FortyStories.pdf

GLOSSARY

allegory A story with both a literal meaning and a second, less obvious meaning. This secondary narrative runs parallel to the action of the first (working as an extended **metaphor**) and presents a moral (religious or political) lesson. Characters often represent abstract concepts such as evil, justice, or faith. "The Minister's Black Veil" is an allegorical story about faith, sin, and human nature. See **fable** and **parable**.

allusion A direct or indirect reference in a literary work to a person, place, object, event, or artistic work. This reference is not elaborated upon in the work; rather, its effect depends upon the reader's understanding of the reference. See **intertextuality**, **parody**, and **satire**.

ambiguity An "opening" of language created by the writer that allows for multiple meanings or differing interpretations. In literature, ambiguity may be deliberately employed to enrich meaning; this differs from any unintentional, unwanted ambiguity in non-literary prose.

analepsis See **flashback**.

archetype A **theme**, character, **symbol**, or event that recurs throughout literatures of different ages, cultures, and languages, and is therefore considered to reflect a conventional truth (or, sometimes, a stereotype) or a common human experience. The protagonist's walk along the dangerous path also suggests an archetypical theme (the descent to the underworld).

atmosphere See **tone**.

bathos In literature, an anticlimactic effect brought about by descending from elevated subject matter to the trivial or ordinary.

canon In literature, a collective term for those works that are commonly accepted as possessing authority or importance. In practice, "canonical" texts or authors are those that are discussed most frequently by scholars and taught most frequently in university courses.

characterization The means by which an author develops and presents a character's personality qualities, and distinguishing traits. A character may be established in the story by descriptive commentary or may be developed less directly—for example, through his or her words, actions, thoughts, and interactions with other characters.

chronology The way a story is organized in terms of time. Linear narratives run continuously from one point in time to a later point, while non-linear narratives are non-continuous and may jump forward and backward in time. A flashback, in which a story jumps to a scene previous in time, is an example of non-linearity.

closure The sense of completion evoked at the end of a story when all or most aspects of the major conflicts have been resolved. An example of the resolution of an internal conflict in "The Yellow Wallpaper" is the narrator's "merging" with the woman behind the paper. Not every story has a strong sense of closure.

comedy As a literary term, used originally to denote that class of ancient Greek drama in which the action ends happily. More broadly, the term has been used to describe a wide variety of literary forms of a more-or-less light-hearted character. See also **tragedy**.

conflict Struggles between characters and opposing forces. Conflict can be internal (psychological) or external (conflict with another character, for instance, or with society or nature). The narrator in "The Yellow Wallpaper" experiences an extreme internal conflict. An important element in "The Open Boat" is the (external) conflict between humans and nature.

connotation The implied, often unspoken meaning(s) of a given word or phrase, as distinct from its denotation, or literal meaning.

denotation See **connotation**.

denouement That portion of a narrative that follows a dramatic crisis, in which conflicts are resolved and the narrative is brought to a close. Traditional accounts of narrative structure often posit a triangle or arc, with rising action followed by a crisis and then by a denouement. (Such accounts bear little relation, however, to the ways in which most actual narratives are structured—particularly most twentieth- and twenty-first-century literary fictions.)

dialogue The words spoken by characters in a story.

diction The author's choice of words. Different types of diction (for example, formal or informal, simple or elaborate, concrete or abstract) produce different effects, and an author may vary diction according to the character, context, or intended purpose of the work. The diction in "My Lucy Friend Who Smells Like Corn" is distinguished by colloquial language (slang, conversational usage) and helps establish the story's intimate **tone**. The story's seamless incorporation of Spanish words also evokes a particular cultural context.

embedded narrative A story contained within another story.

epiphany In literature, a moment at which matters of significance are suddenly illuminated for a literary character (or for the reader), typically triggered by something small and seemingly of little importance. The term first came into wide currency in connection with the fiction of James Joyce.

exposition In fiction, material that functions to provide information—to fill in background for the reader, to summarize parts of the story that have happened "off-stage," and/or to provide commentary on characters or situations.

fable A short **allegorical** tale that conveys an explicit moral lesson. The characters are often animals or objects with human speech and mannerisms. See **parable.**

fantasy In fiction, a sub-genre characterized by the presence of magical or miraculous elements—usually acknowledged as such by the characters and the narrative voice. In **magic realism**, by contrast, miraculous occurrences tend to be treated by the characters and/or the narrative voice as if they were entirely ordinary. In fantasy (also in contrast to magic realism), the fictional world generally has an internal consistency to it that precludes any sense of absurdity on the part of the reader; and the plot tends to build a strong sense of expectation in the reader.

fiction Imagined or invented narrative. In literature, the term is usually used to refer to prose narratives (such as novels and short stories).

first person narrative Narrative recounted using *I* and *me*. See also **narrative perspective**.

flashback In fiction, the inclusion in the primary thread of a story's narrative of a scene (or scenes) from an earlier point in time. Flashbacks may be used to revisit from a different viewpoint events that have already been recounted in the main thread of narrative; to present material that had been left out in the initial recounting; or to present relevant material from a time before the beginning of the main thread of narrative. The use of flashbacks in fiction is sometimes referred to as **analepsis**.

flashforward The inclusion in the primary thread of a story's narrative of a scene (or scenes) from a later point in time. See also **prolepsis**.

foreshadowing The inclusion of elements in a story that hint at some later development(s) in the same story. For example, in "A Good Man Is Hard to Find," the old family burying ground that the family sees on their drive foreshadows the violence that follows.

form Generally, form refers to the shape and structure of a work, which can be described by referring to (for example) its **genre**, and to the organization of its various components (such as **plot**, **diction**, **characters**, and **style**).

free indirect discourse In prose fiction, commentary in which a seemingly objective and omniscient narrative voice assumes the point of view of one or more characters. When we hear through the third person narrative voice of Jane Austen's *Pride and Prejudice*, for example, that Mr. Darcy "was the proudest, most disagreeable man in the world, and everybody hoped that he would never come there again," the narrative voice has assumed the point of view of "everybody in the community"; we as readers are not meant to take it that Mr. Darcy is indeed the most disagreeable man in the world. Similarly, in the following passage from James Joyce's "The Dead," we are meant to take it as being the view of the character Gabriel that Miss Ivors "had no right to call him a West Briton" and had "tried to make him ridiculous," not to take it as an objective statement of truth on the part of the novel's third person narrative voice:

> Gabriel tried to banish from his mind all memory of the unpleasant incident with Miss Ivors. Of course the girl or woman, or whatever she was, was an enthusiast but there was a time for all things. Perhaps he ought not to have answered her like that. But she had no right to call him a West Briton before people, even in joke. She had tried to make him ridiculous before people, heckling him and staring at him with her rabbit's eyes.

The inclusion here of phrases such as "he thought that" ("But he thought that she had no right to …") would have the effect of making the narrative perspective more plain to the reader—but it would also make the prose less immediate in its tone, and more wordy.

The term "free indirect discourse" is also sometimes applied to situations in which it may not be entirely clear if the thoughts expressed emanate from the character, the narrator, or some combination of the two.

genre Class or type of literary work. The concept of genre may be used with different levels of generality. At the most general, poetry, drama, and prose fiction are distinguished as separate genres. At a lower level of generality various sub-genres are frequently distinguished, such as (within the genre of prose fiction) the novel, the novella, and the short story; and, at a still lower level of generality, the mystery novel, the detective novel, the novel of manners, and so on.

Gothic In architecture and the visual arts, a term used to describe styles prevalent from the twelfth to the fourteenth centuries, but in literature a term used to describe work with a sinister or grotesque tone that seeks to evoke a sense of terror on the part of the reader or audience. Gothic literature originated as a genre in the eighteenth century with works such as Horace Walpole's *The Castle of Otranto*. To some extent the notion of the medieval itself then carried with it associations of the dark and the grotesque, but from the beginning an element of intentional exaggeration (sometimes verging on self-parody) attached itself to the genre. The Gothic trend of youth culture that began in the late twentieth century is less clearly associated with the medieval, but shares with the various varieties of Gothic literature (from Walpole in the eighteenth century, to Bram Stoker in the early twentieth, to Stephen King and Anne Rice in the late twentieth) a fondness for the sensational and the grotesque, as well as a propensity to self-parody.

"The Cask of Amontillado" is one story in this anthology that incorporates many elements of the Gothic.

grotesque Literature of the grotesque is characterized by a focus on extreme or distorted aspects of human characteristics. (The term can also refer particularly to a character who is odd or disturbing.) This focus can serve to comment on and challenge societal norms. The story "A Good Man Is Hard to Find" employs elements of the grotesque.

imagery Words or phrases about something within the physical world (an action, sight, sound, smell, taste, or touch) that illustrate something about a story's characters, settings, or situations.

implied author See **narrator**.

intertextuality The relationships between one literary work and other literary works. **Allusion**, imitation, **parody**, and **satire** are examples of intertextuality.

irony A discrepancy between an apparent reality or statement and its meaning. Three types of irony are verbal irony (in which there is an apparent discrepancy between what is said and what is meant), situational irony (when an event turns out very differently than expected), and dramatic irony (when the reader and sometimes other characters know something that one character does not know). In "Cathedral," the narrator's confession (that he "didn't think much" of his wife's poem, because, he says, "I just don't understand poetry") is a verbal irony. In "The Yellow Wallpaper," the narrator's obsession with the woman behind the paper is a dramatic irony. See also **parody** and **satire**.

magic realism A style of fiction in which miraculous or bizarre things often happen but are treated in a matter-of-fact fashion by the characters and/or the narrative voice. There is often an element of the absurd to magic realist narratives, and they tend not to have any strong plot structure generating expectations in the reader's mind. See also **fantasy**.

melodrama Originally a term used to describe nineteenth-century plays featuring sensational story lines and a crude separation of characters into moral categories, with the pure and virtuous pitted against evil villains. Early melodramas employed background music throughout the action of the play as a means of heightening the emotional response of the audience. By extension, certain sorts of prose fictions or poems are often described as having melodramatic elements.

metafiction Fiction that calls attention to itself as fiction, in an effort to explore the relationships between fiction and reality. Examples of metafictional situations occur when the writing refers to the act of reading or writing, or an author seems to insert him or herself into the story as a character, or an author seems to address the reader directly or interrupt the narrative. In "The Yellow Wallpaper," the fictional situation of the narrator's relationship to her writing has implications for the significance of the story itself, because this suggests the possibility of certain relationships between "The Yellow Wallpaper," its author, and its reader.

metaphor A *figure of speech* (in this case, a **trope**) in which a comparison is made or identity is asserted between two unrelated things or actions without the use of "like" or "as." The primary subject is known as the *tenor*; to illuminate its nature, the writer links it to wholly different images, ideas, or actions (referred to as the *vehicle*). Unlike a **simile**, which is a direct comparison of two things, a metaphor "fuses" the separate qualities of two things, creating a new idea. For example, in "The Open Boat" the captain speaks to the other men in the boat, "soothing his children." The metaphor likens the relationship between captain and men (the tenor) to that between parent and children (the vehicle). The same idea expressed in a simile would be less concise; in place of "soothing his children" one might write "speaking to his men as if they were his children."

modernism In the history of literature, music, and the visual arts, a movement that began in the early twentieth century, characterized by a thoroughgoing rejection of the then-dominant conventions of literary plotting and characterization, of melody and harmony, and of perspective and other naturalistic forms of visual representation. In literature (as in music and the visual arts), Modernists endeavored to represent the complexity of what seemed to them to be an increasingly fragmented world by adopting techniques of presenting story material, illuminating character, and employing imagery that emphasized (in the words of Virginia Woolf) "the spasmodic, the obscure, the fragmentary."

motif An idea, image, action, or plot element that recurs throughout a literary work, creating new levels of meaning and strengthening structural coherence. The term is taken from music, where it describes recurring melodies or themes. The recurring focus on blindness in "Cathedral" is suggestive of the narrator's isolation and lack of emotional bearings or direction.

motivation The forces that seem to cause characters to act, or why characters do what they do.

narration The process of storytelling.

narrative perspective In fiction, the point of view from which the story is narrated. A first person narrative is recounted using *I* and *me*, whereas a third person narrative is recounted using *he*, *she*, *they*, and so on. (Second person narratives, in which the story is recounted using *you*, are extremely rare.) When a narrative is written in the third person and the narrative voice evidently "knows" all that is being done and thought, the story is typically described as being recounted by an "omniscient narrator." Third person narratives may also present limited perspectives, however; whether writing in the third person or the first person, authors will sometimes intentionally present narrative perspectives that the reader will have grounds to interpret as unreliable. (See also **free indirect discourse**, **stream of consciousness**.)

narrator The voice (or voices) telling the story. The narrator is distinct from both the author (a real, historical person) and the implied author (whom the reader imagines the author to be). Narrators can be distinguished according to the degree to which they share the reality of the other characters in the story and the extent to which they participate in the action; according to how much information they are privy to (and how much of that information they are willing to share with the reader); and according to whether or not they are perceived by the reader as reliable or unreliable sources of information. See also **narrative perspective**.

omniscient narrator See **narrative perspective**.

parable A brief allegorical story that illustrates a moral or lesson. The term is religious in origin, referring to the stories told by Jesus in the New Testament. Unlike the characters in **fables**, the characters in parables are usually human.

parody Parody (a type of **satire**) is the imitation of another literary work or style in order to ridicule a target. Parody is recognizable by the extent to which the imitation differs from its original model in a ludicrous way; this difference is achieved by exaggerating or debasing (or otherwise making ridiculous) some aspect of the original. See **intertextuality**, **allusion**, and **satire**.

pathos An appeal to (or the technique of appealing to) the emotions of the reader or listener. In ancient Greece pathos was defined as one of the three methods through which persuasion might be accomplished (the others being *logos*—persuasion through words offering reasoned argument; and *ethos*—persuasion through the presentation of heroic or otherwise ethically admirable characters). In discussing literature the term pathos is most often applied to works (or scenes within works) that arouse feelings of pity or sorrow in the reader or audience through the presentation of narrative material concerning pain, suffering, or loss.

persona The assumed identity or "speaking voice" that a writer projects in a discourse. The term "persona" literally means "mask."

personification A figure of speech in which objects, ideas, or non-human animals are referred to as if they were human (or in which a human figure is created to represent abstract entities such as Wisdom or Peace). An example of personification occurs in "The Open Boat" when the shore is described as "lonely."

plot The organization of story materials within a literary work. The order in which story material is presented; the inclusion of elements that allow or encourage the reader or audience to form expectations as to what is likely to happen; the decision to present story material directly to the reader as part of the narrative or to have it recounted in summary form through exposition—all these are matters of plotting.

point of view See **narrative perspective**.

postmodernism In literature and the visual arts, a movement influential in the late twentieth and early twenty-first centuries. In some ways postmodernism represents a reaction to modernism, in others an extension of it. With roots in the work of French philosophers such as Jacques Derrida and Michel Foucault, it is deeply colored by theory; indeed, it may be said to have begun at the "meta" level of theorizing rather than at the level of practice. It is notoriously resistant to definition—indeed, resistance to fixed definitions is itself a characteristic of postmodernism. Like modernism, postmodernism embraces difficulty and distrusts the simple and straightforward. More broadly, postmodernism is characterized by a rejection of absolute truth or value, of closed systems, of grand unified narratives.

Postmodernist fiction is characterized by a frequently ironic or playful tone in dealing with reality and illusion; by a willingness to combine different styles or forms in a single work (just as in architecture the postmodernist spirit embodies a willingness to borrow from seemingly disparate styles in designing a single structure); and by a highly attuned awareness of the problematized state of the writer, artist, or theorist as observer.

prolepsis Originally a rhetorical term used to refer to the anticipation of possible objections by someone advancing an argument, prolepsis is used in discussions of fiction to refer to elements in a narrative that anticipate the future of the story. The **flashforward** technique of storytelling is often described as a form of prolepsis; the inclusion in a narrative of material that foreshadows future developments is also sometimes treated as a form of prolepsis.

protagonist The central character in a literary work.

realism An approach to literature that endeavors to represent the world in ways that are true to real life. Just as notions of what constitutes "real life" may vary widely, so too has "realism" taken on a variety of meanings. The term "realism" (and later, the term naturalism) originated in the nineteenth century to denote literature that eschewed romance and that did not shy away from presenting the grim, unpleasant, and ugly aspects of the real. In the twentieth century social realism became a term used to convey very similar notions, while also suggesting that the most important defining conditions of reality are broad social conditions that are susceptible to political forces—and that can be changed by political activism. The term psychological realism, on the other hand, refers to fiction that endeavors to portray persuasively the perceptions of one or more individuals. (When the term "realistic" is used to refer to fiction that features plausible and consistent characters, settings, and situations, it is psychological realism that is being drawn attention to the reader's attention.) See also **magic realism**.

satire A literary work designed to make fun of (and, often, seriously criticize) human failings, social evils, and corrupt institutions. See also **parody**.

setting The time, place, and cultural environment in which a story takes place.

simile The comparison of one thing with another, using the words "as" or "like." The story "A Good Man Is Hard to Find," for example, includes the simile "the line of woods gaped like a dark open mouth." See also **metaphor**.

story Narrative material, independent of the manner in which it may be presented or the ways in which the narrative material may be organized. Story is thus distinct from **plot** (see above).

stream of consciousness A narrative technique that conveys the inner workings of a character's mind, in which a character's thoughts, feelings, memories, and impressions are related in an unbroken flow, without concern for **chronology** or coherence. The technique was perhaps most famously employed by James Joyce in *Ulysses* (1922); that novel concludes with a 44-page monologue from the point of view of the character Molly Bloom, which opens in this way:

> yes because he never did a thing like that before as ask to get his breakfast in bed with a couple of eggs since the *City Arms* hotel when he used to be pretending to be laid up with a sick voice doing his highness to make himself interesting to that old faggot Mrs Riordan that he thought he had a great leg of and she never left us a farthing all for masses for herself and her soul greatest miser ever was actually afraid to lay out 4d for her methylated spirit tell-

> ing me all her ailments she had too much old chat in her about politics and earthquakes and the end of the world let us have a bit of fun first …

Some critics apply the term "stream of consciousness" only to passages such as this one, which are written entirely in the first person. The term is also often used more loosely, though, to refer to any one of (or combination of) a range of techniques that attempt to convey in prose fiction a sense of the progression of thoughts and sensations occurring within a character's mind; extended passages of prose fiction written in **free indirect discourse**, for example, are often described as employing a stream of consciousness technique.

style A distinctive or specific use of language and form.

subtext Implicit or unstated meaning. There is a strong sense of subtext in "Hills Like White Elephants," where much of the story's meaning is suggested by the characters' silence.

symbol Something that represents another thing (an idea, quality, or another object, for example) beyond or in addition to itself.

theme A central idea, unifying principle, or underlying message of a story. A single work may have a number of themes. A predominant theme in "The Open Boat," for example, is nature's indifference to human suffering.

third person narrative A narrative in which there is no *I* or *me* in the story; all the characters are seen "from the outside" as *he*, *she*, or *they*. See also **narrative perspective**.

tone The overall or most dominant impression produced by a work; its atmosphere or mood. For example, stories may be bleak, humorous, hopeful, romantic, alienating, wry, or suspenseful in tone.

tragedy In the traditional definition originating from discussions of ancient Greek drama, a serious narrative recounting the downfall of the protagonist. More loosely, the term has been applied to a wide variety of literary forms in which the tone is predominantly a dark one and the narrative does not end happily.

trope Any figure of speech that plays on our understanding of words to extend, alter, or transform "literal" meaning. Common tropes include **metaphor**, **simile**, **personification**, hyperbole, metonymy, oxymoron, and **irony**.

unreliable narrator See **narrative perspective**.

CHRONOLOGY

Publication dates indicate first publication in book form, with exceptions noted.* Please see introductions for more information.

Nathaniel Hawthorne (1804–64)
THE MINISTER'S BLACK VEIL (1836)*

Edgar Allan Poe (1809–49)
THE BLACK CAT (1843)*
THE TELL-TALE HEART (1843)*

Nathaniel Hawthorne
YOUNG GOODMAN BROWN (1846)

Edgar Allan Poe
THE CASK OF AMONTILLADO (1846)*

Herman Melville (1819–91)
BARTLEBY, THE SCRIVENER (1856)

Anton Chekhov (1860–1904)
AN UPHEAVAL (1886)

Charlotte Perkins Gilman (1860–1935)
THE YELLOW WALLPAPER (1892)*

Thomas Hardy (1840–1928)
THE SON'S VETO (1894)

Kate Chopin (1851–1904)
THE STORM (1898)

Stephen Crane (1871–1900)
THE OPEN BOAT (1898)

* *periodical publication*

James Joyce (1882–1941)
ARABY (1914)
EVELINE (1914)
THE DEAD (1914)

Katherine Mansfield (1888–1923)
THE DOLL'S HOUSE (1922)*
THE GARDEN PARTY (1922)*

Ernest Hemingway (1899–1961)
HILLS LIKE WHITE ELEPHANTS (1927)

Katherine Anne Porter (1890–1980)
THE JILTING OF GRANNY WEATHERALL (1930)

William Faulkner (1897–1962)
DRY SEPTEMBER (1931)*

Hisaye Yamamoto (1921–2011)
SEVENTEEN SYLLABLES (1949)*

Chinua Achebe (b. 1930)
DEAD MEN'S PATH (1953)

Flannery O'Connor (1925–64)
A GOOD MAN IS HARD TO FIND (1953)

James Baldwin (1924–87)
SONNY'S BLUES (1957)*

Yasunari Kawabata (1899–1972)
IMMORTALITY (1963)

Ursula K. Le Guin (b. 1929)
THE ONES WHO WALK AWAY FROM OMELAS (1973)*

Grace Paley (1922–2007)
WANTS (1973)

Raymond Carver (1938–88)
CATHEDRAL (1983)

Jamaica Kincaid (b. 1949)
GIRL (1983)

Donald Barthelme (1931–89)
THE PALACE AT 4 A.M. (1983)*

Margaret Atwood (b. 1939)
HAPPY ENDINGS (1983)

Alice Munro (b. 1931)
MILES CITY, MONTANA (1986)

Lorrie Moore (b. 1957)
YOU'RE UGLY, TOO (1989)*

Tim O'Brien (b. 1946)
THE THINGS THEY CARRIED (1990)

Sandra Cisneros (b. 1954)
MY LUCY FRIEND WHO SMELLS LIKE CORN (1991)

Denis Johnson (b. 1949)
EMERGENCY (1991)*

Edward P. Jones (b. 1951)
YOUNG LIONS (1992)

Tobias Wolff (b. 1945)
BULLET IN THE BRAIN (1995)*

Helen Simpson (b. 1959)
BED AND BREAKFAST (1995)

Steven Millhauser (b. 1943)
A VISIT (1997)*

George Saunders (b. 1958)
SEA OAK (1998)*

Gloria Sawai (b. 1932)
MOTHER'S DAY (2001)

Sherman Alexie (b. 1966)
DO YOU KNOW WHERE I AM? (2002)*

ZZ Packer (b. 1973)
BROWNIES (2003)

Shaun Tan (b. 1974)
GRANDPA'S STORY (2008)

Gish Jen (b. 1955)
THE THIRD DUMPSTER (2012)*